Cezar Giosan

The American

D1570552

Photo credit last page: The Statue of Liberty-Ellis Island Foundation, Inc.

Photo front cover: Mitu Popescu, cca 1913. © Cezar Giosan

ISBN-13: 978-1481851688

ISBN-10: 1481851683

THE AMERICAN

Cezar Giosan

In memory of Dumitru (Mitu) Popescu Sr.,
whose life made this book possible

Inspired from true events

PROLOGUE

Micu Popescu had only been in America for a week visiting his daughter when he learned he was a millionaire—and had been one for a few decades without ever having a clue.

Even the weather seemed harmoniously attuned to and somehow foreseeing of the unexpected happiness that was about to follow in a few hours. The warming rays of the sun cast a shiny and playful transparency over the Big Apple. It was one of those remarkable autumn days that can be experienced only in New York—a day so clear and enticing, when the mere idea of working for a living carries negative connotations, and one suddenly realizes that the purpose of living couldn't possibly be the mundane ritual of waking up each morning and heading to the office for the survival paycheck at the end of each month, but an open invitation to an unending roving through the luring *City that Never Sleeps*.

Coco had awoken early in the morning and kept fussing to her father while getting ready for the trip they had planned.

"Daddy, today we're going to visit the Statue of Liberty and Ellis Island! Maybe we'll find records of Grandpa!" she said cheerfully to him, checking her cheek in the mirror to make sure it wasn't too red from her blush.

Micu watched her lovingly. His daughter was so beautiful. He couldn't figure out exactly whom she resembled in the family. With her dark hair, black eyes, smooth alabaster skin, distinct elegance and joyful disposition, she could have easily been mistaken for an actress, he often thought. Maybe she took after his side of the family after all; her grandfather had been quite good-looking, driving women crazy in his days.

He brushed a speck of dust off his sleeve and then smoothed the folds of his coat, which hid a protruding belly that he always carried with ease. His appearance was impeccable as always: black suit, blue shirt, and a chestnut-hued tie—the kind that couldn't easily be found on the streets of New York City.

"Well, Coco, didn't you say last night we were going to find out whether your grandpa's stockholder certificates were worth anything or not?"

"Yes, but first we're going to Ellis Island since they close early, and then we'll go to the evaluation office. It's nearby, on Broadway. They're expecting us. I spoke to them on the phone last week and gave them the names of the companies on the documents, so they'd have the time to look into them."

"You know best, my dear, of course..." he tried to spring up from the white leather couch where he had spent the night, but his weight impeded his youthful impulse.

Coco had decided they were going to take the 7 subway train, which in Queens runs not underground, but on the surface, spewing sparks and grunting like a giant fire dragon. This was an opportunity to show her father a few glimpses of New York's beauty as the trip taken above ground would present a richer sightseeing opportunity than one through the earth's entrails.

They got off the subway at Queensboro Plaza and got on a bus so they would be able to see the stupefying skyline of Manhattan in the distance. They crossed the East River, arriving at the lower end of Upper East Side, where, she explained, lived men so influential that even those who worked for them were makers of history in their own right. They changed buses right under the railway going to Roosevelt Island and started towards the south of Manhattan Island, going through Midtown, passing the Chrysler and the Empire State Building, then through East Village and the Lower East Side—where, a century before, immigrants gathered looking for work—then through the incredible swarm of Chinatown, to eventually stop, more than an hour later, in Battery Park, right there on the shore where the Statue of Liberty could be seen in its mystical emergence from the water.

They embarked on the ferryboat going to the Statue, but only spent a few minutes there; the wait to enter was longer than two hours, and that was more than they could bear. They got on the small boat heading for Ellis Island.

Micu went to sit at the boat's bow, ignoring the wind fluttering his grizzled hair. He was gazing at the southern part of Manhattan's skyline as it appeared from the water, an intricate agglomeration of majestic old buildings and ultra-modern, steel and glass structures—a splendid vision that you have to see first to imagine later.

"I never thought a country could reach this level of development without a socialistic system!" joked Micu, but then he became solemn. "God, Coco, it'd be a shame to die without ever seeing New York... take a picture of me with the Manhattan skyline in the background. I wonder if Dad came through here, and if this was what he saw for the first time..."

"We'll look for that the moment we arrive on Ellis Island, daddy. I've read that half of the immigrants arriving in New York at the beginning of the century came through here, and they still keep the archives. If we're lucky, we'll find something." Coco took her father's arm. "Aren't you chilly? Let's go in," she suggested warily, pulling him gently inside to the warmth.

They were rapidly approaching the island. The young woman showed her father a long building resembling a royal palace, with red brick walls, tall, elegant windows and stately doors. It was the Main Building—the place in which, for half a century, countless waves of immigrants had arrived to the Promised Land in the pursuit of happiness.

"Maybe Grandpa came through here!"

Micu wiped a tear with the back of his hand, embarrassed by his vulnerability. He hadn't fully realized the idea that he was following in his father's footsteps nearly a hundred years later. That was his first trip abroad, and he had come not just anywhere, but to America—the very protagonist of the stories told by his father in his childhood. With the exception of the years spent in college in Cluj, he had lived his whole life in Cernădia, then Novaci, teaching history and Romanian to generations of children, many of whom had gone to foreign lands, while he had only learned of such places through books and other people's stories.

The line to visit the Ellis Island Immigration Museum was nowhere near the size of the one for the Statue of Liberty. They entered the Great Hall in a few minutes. It was an immense room where the immigrants arriving from Europe at the beginning of the past century would undergo medical checkups.

They walked around for about an hour, looking at the paintings and reading the inscriptions on exhibits in glass cases. How many tragedies those walls had witnessed! Many souls and their winding destinies, fortunate or not, had entered the doors, anxiously trembling to receive the stamp making them, in a blink of an eye, residents of the most sought-after country in the world. How envious were those they had left behind, who read their letters received back home with sick curiosity.

"Daddy, when did Grandpa come here? When was he born?" Coco asked as she sat in front of a computer especially placed there for visitors trying to find an ancestor.

"I don't know, dear...but since he went to war as an American soldier, that means before it, right? Somewhere between 1900 and 1920. And, if he was seventeen when he got here, he must have been born at the end of the nineteenth century. Don't know the year exactly. Why, you found him?" Micu asked incredulously, doubting there could be information in a New York museum on his father—a shepherd from Cernădia.

She didn't answer, but continued to watch the monitor intensely, typing something unintelligible to him, moving quickly from one page to the next.

"What name did he use through customs?" she asked, skimming the names of the immigrants on the fine print lists of those who arrived to New York aboard ships.

"What do you mean 'what name,' Coco? His name, Dumitru Popescu...they used to call him Mitu..."

Coco was moving her eyes mechanically from the screen to the keys and back, when she suddenly froze up. Her big, round eyes were glinting with emotion.

"I think this is it...it's here, Dad, it's here! I found him! It's his name! Dumitru Popescu from Cernădia, 1913! Look at what it says: Cernădia!" she burst with laughter at the thought of the little village being mentioned in an official American document. Her eyes welled up, "We found Grandpa, Daddy! Can you believe it?"

Micu came closer to the screen, reading glasses perched on his nose:

"Where?" he asked doubtfully, amazed at the possibility of finding such information without fumbling through tons of archived paperwork.

Coco pointed to a name on the screen:

"Look here, this is a picture of the passenger list! It's called a 'manifest,' and here is his name! It says Cernădia! It says Cernădia, Dad! He came with twenty dollars in his pocket! He only had twenty dollars on him!"

"Well, Coco, I'll be...it's him! It's really him! It's Dad!" Micu mumbled, full of emotion. "Tell me, what else does it say?"

She quickly translated the name of the boat and the address in America given by her grandfather in 1913, how much money he'd had on him, from where he had sailed, with whom he'd traveled, and the date of his arrival to New York; then she clicked the mouse a few more times and printed an image.

"This is the boat he arrived on here at Ellis Island. It was called 'La Savoie.' It sailed from France. We can get a picture and frame it. It's twenty bucks..." she said, disappointed at the rather steep price of something that was in essence a glorified copy of a picture.

"Buy three, can you? One for me, one for you, and one for your brother. I'll take it to him when I go to California next week. Oh Lord, Coco...poor Dad...I wonder what was on his mind while on this giant of a boat! What thoughts ran through his head when he set foot in New York? He was just a kid, only seventeen years old..."

They read the information on the screen once more, as though they wanted to learn everything by heart and then spent half an hour in a café waiting for the boat to take them back to Manhattan. Watching the throngs of visitors clamoring to take pictures, Mitu began reminiscing on his childhood—poor, but happy: the stool he climbed on to reach the dinner table, his father's tales about America, the box holding the things brought from over the ocean, in which he would surreptitiously rummage from time to time.

"Well, Coco, it took my coming here for you to find out about Dad!" he suddenly awoke from his daydreaming. "You couldn't have done this before? You have an excuse because you only moved here a few years ago, but Cristi, your brother?! He's been here for the last ten years; what did he wait for? I'll give him a piece of my mind when I talk to him today on the phone!"

"But Grandpa never told you to go to America?" Coco asked rhetorically.

"Well, he never told us to flee because he was afraid. Trying to cross the border during communism was suicide. They'd shoot you on the spot or you'd drown in the Danube. And he loved us too much to tell us to leave knowing that could happen if we did. But I have seen him crying for America many times! He really regretted it—a lot. What can I say? He never made peace with his going back to Romania. And how could he? During communism, when life was so hard, when the only joy in his life was the violin, with nothing else to do, how could he not regret it? And then the Gherla Prison..."

"Poor grandpa..."

Micu smiled and sighed.

"Life's not so short on irony...it took the sacrifice of a generation—ours—so that you could leave and make it on your own. But it's not the same; yours and Cristi's gumption to leave Romania doesn't compare to what Dad did...Dad had it tough; he put his life in danger. You came here on scholarships to a comfy life; neither you nor your brother could stomach a trip over the ocean like they had to back then. I don't think you'd make it...he was resilient. He had great strength. He could have been somebody if..."

"Pity the alcohol destroyed him..."

"Pity, yes, great pity he liked to drink. Poor Ma, how she suffered because of it!"

"Yes, Dad, but we had it good! During that time, we had a better life than everyone else in Novaci, right? Where would we have had dollars from during Ceaușescu's time, if not him?

"Well, the dollars came after the old man died, not while he was alive. That money was from Mama Maria's pension—God rest her soul—after he died. As the wife of an American veteran, she had the right to a five hundred dollars a month pension, which was a lot of money during the '60s and '70s. But the communists only gave us a quarter of the pension in dollars and the rest in lei."

"So, that was still something, wasn't it? Who in Romania received pension money in dollars during Ceaușescu's time? Because of Grandpa, we were able to go to shops0F* and buy whatever our hearts desired. I remember even now how everybody envied me for the jeans I wore. I had Levi Strauss, Tic-Tacs, and Pepsi! And who had the first color TV set in Novaci with all the neighbors coming to watch documentaries at our house? And who drove the first car in Novaci, the little red Skoda?"

"Yes, Coco, I'm not saying...but he could have done so much more—a lot more. Maybe you'll accomplish his unfulfilled dream of becoming rich, though it's hard to imagine, with you being a chemist and your brother a mathematician, neither of you with much business sense. And you're not scoundrels either, like those who rob our country blind. Well...what time is it? Aren't we going to be late for those certificates?"

The boat took them back from Ellis Island to Manhattan. Micu turned his head once more to look at the museum, which he thought he might never see again, imprinting its image into his mind forever. "This is where my Dad came..." he repeated to himself, still amazed at having found traces of his father there.

They came ashore in Battery Park and walked towards Broadway, entering from the south, then continued up to Wall Street. There, Coco found her way through some winding, picturesque streets, bustling with people and peppered with little shops full of knickknacks. After circling around a few times searching for the address they entered a large stone building, in which

---

* 'Shops' – during communist Romania, 'shops' were stores that sold imported goods from Western countries. Only foreigners (or very few Romanians who legally owned foreign currency), could buy from them. The merchandise (e.g., Pepsi cans, Tic-Tacs, jeans, imported soaps or deodorant), was very much sought after by the Romanian people. It was a status enhancer and was also used in bribes.

Coco had learned of an office executing evaluations of old documents. She had been looking for such an office since her father's arrival, and now that she found it, she had made an appointment for that afternoon with the pile of stockholder certificates that had once belonged to her grandfather, and which Micu had brought from Romania, in her hand.

"How would it be to find out today that we're millionaires?" Micu murmured as they pressed the button on the interphone with his trademark tongue-in-cheek smile.

The girl looked at him amused, remembering briefly the commercial for the New York Lottery—*You cannot live the dream if you don't play the game*—which made her buy a ticket every time.

The clerk—a boisterous young man, ruddy faced and freckled with a belly bigger than Micu's—was waiting for them, or at least pretending to do so.

"Great to meet you guys, let's see. What's your story? What have you got?"

Coco placed the documents on his desk.

"This is the stuff I told you about when we spoke on the phone, sir."

The clerk grabbed a magnifying glass and inspected the papers carefully, without haste, passing slowly from one to the other and then replacing them piously on the table as though they were holy relics. Every now and then he would throw Coco and her father a look expressing his obvious disdain for these people who, being in the possession of historical documents—whether of true value or not—kept them rumpled and thrown God-knows-where.

"Let's see," he cleared his throat, retaking the first sheet and typing something onto the computer. "This company went bankrupt during the Great Depression. This certificate is worthless. It's interesting just as a historical piece. You could put it on eBay and get a few hundred dollars for it, maybe."

Although she hadn't gotten her hopes up, Coco turned to her father and translated for him:

"He said it's just a worthless piece of paper...a few hundred dollars."

"Maybe they're all like that, dear," Micu answered. "I brought them because you insisted, but there can't ever be money without work, you know that! We'll take these to frame and hang them on the wall in your grandfather's memory."

The clerk had already taken the next document and was studying it carefully.

"Same story here, guys. Sorry..."

"Well, at least we tried, Dad. We had to find out sooner or later..."

"Yes, but let's not waste any more time around here. I still want to visit—what did you call it? Empire State—that building you said it's the tallest after the Twin Towers collapsed, and it's already late."

"But we have..."

"Folks, this is another story," the clerk interrupted them suddenly, having moved on to another certificate. "If I am not mistaken, this was Penn Mills

Corporation. This is a different ballgame! Seventy shares in 1928 were worth three hundred dollars. Mills was bought out by Mama Steel in 1950, and then again by J&L Inc. in 1997. Let's see. The value at yesterday's market price would be exactly 536,034 dollars."

Micu looked inquisitively at Coco. He didn't understand English, but he had noticed the man's excitement and his articulation of a few big numbers.

"How much?" she asked surprised and unconvinced she had heard him correctly.

The clerk repeated the approximate sum.

"Half a million, folks."

"Dollars?"

"Yes, Ma'am, dollars."

"Half a million" she mumbled. "Dad, half a million!" she almost screamed.

"Get outta here...how could it be half a million? Of what? Dollars? Pffft, it can't be true, God bless us! Did you understand well what this man said? Maybe he said cents, not dollars!"

"That's what I understood. It's what he said, what more do you want?" she answered excitedly.

Meanwhile, the clerk had inspected two more certificates, which he had placed in the valueless pile.

"Nothing here. Just historical documents. A few hundred dollars, maybe," he said and moved on to the next document, a green piece of paper with a torn corner, put aside during the first perusal. He analyzed it methodically with the loupe and then typed something on the computer, staring at the screen. A few minutes later, he went back to analyzing the paper again. He checked its verso, touching it gingerly, and then placed it back on the table under the stronger light of a lamp for an even closer look.

"When you told me you about this on the phone, I didn't believe you had stock in this firm. We might be onto something big here, folks. Really big. Wait for me for a minute. I'll be right back," he said and disappeared with the paper behind a door.

Coco's heart started pounding.

"What did he say, dear?" Micu asked.

"I don't know—that it might be worth a lot of money. Let's wait and see."

"How much could it be? Maybe he wants to steal it from us! Where did this guy go?"

"How can he steal it from us, Dad? This isn't Romania..."

The clerk came back in a few minutes accompanied by a bearded man with gold-rimmed glasses and the allure of a professor, who smiled courteously at them and shook their hands. Since he had been in the business, he had made it a custom to greet those entering his office poor and coming out wealthy just a few minutes later.

"Folks, this is my boss. I had to run it by him, just to make sure. I looked into this certificate when you called last week and told me the name of the company. Now it's called Doox, Inc.—it's an international mining company. I have some fantastic news for you! If this piece is not a fake, it is worth, at the yesterday's closing bell, more than twenty-six million dollars. Whoever bought this did it during the Great Depression, when the company was almost bankrupt and the stock was next to nothing. Phenomenal foresight, this unknown Warren Buffett of yours! Congratulations, guys! You struck it rich today!" he told them giddy, as this meant a fat commission for him as well.

Coco attempted to say something, but she slipped softly on the chair instead.

"Dad...twenty-six million dollars..." she mumbled vaguely.

"How much, dear?" Micu came closer. He'd had some hearing trouble for a few years, but he refused to wear the hearing aid sent by his children from America.

"Twenty-six million, Dad. We're rich..." she said weakly, but then, suddenly invigorated, she jumped from the chair and hugged her father. "Twenty-six and a half million dollars!"

THE BEGINNING

Chapter 1

The year was 1906. A cold, white, December morning was dawning on Berceşti, hamlet of Cernădia Village, a small rural community lying shabby and forlorn at the foot of the Parâng Mountain, north of Oltenia, Romania. The frozen sky was glaring intensely on the pastures seemingly covered by steel-blue snow banks from time immemorial. A silent and merciless wind burned the faces of the few men gathered to clean up the country lane to make way for carriages. The rusty gnashing of the metal shovels and mattocks could be heard from afar through the glossy stillness, perturbed only by a few odd crows gliding ominously over the cross on the church's steeple.

"Hey, Mitu, fetch me that wine flask," called out Dumitru, one of the men drudging away, to a ten-year-old boy aiming snowballs at the highest branches of a time-forsaken evergreen tree.

The boy dashed to a satchel and grabbed a bottle from inside of it.

"Here it is, Dad. Can I get some?"

The man handed him the bottle and the boy gulped heartily from it.

"It's good for my throat, Dad—it's still hot."

"I'll show you throat in a sec, you scamp—you wanna become a drunkard? Get to work, or I'll take the rod and give you somethin'...you won't remember your name! That head of yours is full of shenanigans!"

The child hunched forward, ran to replace the bottle, and began pushing a firewood-filled wheelbarrow down the road. He stopped a few times to breathe into his numbed hands, then stuffed his fists deep down into the shredded pockets of his sheepskin waistcoat, huffing and grunting as he went. "To hell with this work and this winter!" he said under his breath, wiggling his toes to see if he could still feel them.

"Lil' Mitu, you love child, your father's working you hard!" a twelve-year-old boy yelled as he waylaid Mitu from behind, hitting him square in the back of the head with a snowball.

Mitu flinched at the coldness of the snow seeping into his wool sweater and sprang towards the boy to take him down. They fought grimly for a few minutes, and Mitu's face contorted into a grimace evocative of frontline soldiers facing their deadly foes.

"I'm gonna kill you, Nistor!" he howled into the boy's ear as Nistor nailed him to the ground.

"Yeah? You gonna'...kill me?" Mitu roared, slapping him and pinning his hands with his knees. "Why? Because you ain't your old man's son, and your mama was a whore, and the whole village knows it! You know who you are? You're the squire's whore's son, that's who! You're Poppa's sonny!"

Mitu tensed up as he tried to free himself, but his assailant's weight was too much for his scrawny arms.

"Look at me," he said, ceasing to writhe for a moment. When Nistor turned to face him, he spat between his eyes, only to receive a hard blow to the jaw that almost made him faint.

His cry of pain made it all the way to Dumitru, who rushed towards them.

"Fuckin' bunch of outlaws, you lost your minds? Nistor, you fool, I'll beat the daylights outta you if you don't leave my Mitu alone!" he yelled, pretending to run after him.

The boy vanished quickly into somebody's front yard, watching and snickering at them from behind the fence.

"Let's go, kid," Dumitru turned to Mitu, "that's how people are—now stop your crying and act like a man. What the hell!" he lifted him up from the snow as the boy was trying to hold back his tears.

"But why do they all say that you ain't my father? You are my father, ain't you? Why do they say it? They all mock me and say I'm Squire Poppa's son, not yours," the boy whispered, nestling into his father's chest.

Dumitru took his face into his palms and was about to say something, but stopped and wiped his forehead with the back of his sleeve. Beads of sweat trickled down onto his frost-chapped lips.

"Whose could you be, child, if not mine?" he eventually uttered, placing his hands on the boy's shoulders and setting out slowly towards their home. "Listen to me, son, don't mind other people because they're evil, and spiteful, and full of lies, and they only want to hurt you. No one loves you more than I do, my lil' Mitu," he whispered through the muffled cadence of their steps.

It took them half an hour to make it home, tramping over the knee-high snow banks. Mitu's cheeks had already regained their ruddiness after the scrap with Nistor, and now he was scampering left and right, trying to find the best pathway home. Dumitru was following behind, his gaze lingering on the boy every now and then. "The Lord gave me good children—I hope to have many grandchildren and playful great grandchildren when the time comes..."

As they were getting close to their house's front gate, Mitu rushed forward.

"Mama," he yelled, "it's so beautiful down in the village. The pine trees in Nastasia's front yard look like they're from the fairytales you used to tell me when I was little. Can I go play with Maria's son, Ion? C'mon, let me!"

"Not now, little Mitu, come and eat. I saw you coming from afar and got somethin' on the table for you."

"Lenuța, lemme loosen them boots—some cold I endured today," Dumitru sighed while slowly taking his coat off at the entrance. "Mitu, go on 'n get those animals some water. Quick, stop lazying around!" he turned to the boy.

The child looked defiantly at him.

"But why can't you send my brother? Why, doesn't he put his pants on one leg at a time like the rest of us?"

"Listen boy, God damn it, I say who does what in this household. I tell Ghiță the work he has to do, I tell your sister, Gheorghița, and I tell you what to do! I done told you to do this, and you'll do it if you don't wanna get beaten half to death!"

Mitu went to the well, filled the pail with water, and dragged it awkwardly towards the stable, cursing through his teeth. "I'll run away from home one day all the way to the end of the world, and that'll show them—when I'm not around anymore."

"Drink, damn you!" he struck the mare, whose threatening neigh made him leap backwards. He started shoveling the floor, spitting in disgust a few times while making a small pile of straw, mud, and manure right next to the stable's door. He then loaded everything into a rusted wheelbarrow. "Who the fuck am I to clean animal shit?" he sulked, straining to push the barrow towards the garden.

"Mitu, you comin' to eat or not?" he heard Dumitru's gruffly voice calling out from the window.

"Be right there, just wait a tick to dump the barrow—I can't split myself in two! Why don't you tell Ghiţă to haul the dung?"

"Lazybones, takes you half an hour to clean a damn stable! I'll teach you to stop sleepin' on the job!" his father snorted angrily.

"Get your ass over here, you fuckin' imp! Who do you think you're talkin' to? Filthy mongrel! Get over here, now!" he yelled as the boy approached penitently, dusting the snow off himself.

Mitu knew what was to come. He had experienced it quite often before, and many times he had tried to change the end result, but to no avail. Each time after being punished, he'd promised himself never to talk back to his father, but his mouth always got the best of him.

"Father, I won't do it again, I swear to you, I'll never say nothin' again. Just don't beat me up—please, don't hit me!" he begged, while the terror of what was to come unfolded on his face.

Dumitru gave him a cross look.

"Bend over the table, mongrel, and get what you deserve!" he growled, slowly unbuckling his thick leather belt.

"For Heaven's sake Dumitru, leave him alone—don't you see how pitiful and shivery he is?" Lenuţa timorously intervened.

"Woman, you don't tell me what to do with my own brat, or you'll have your share at once!" he shoved her aside and then slapped the boy with force.

Mitu shrieked under the bite of the first strike, which never hurt too much, but was more of a trial.

"How many is it gonna be this time? Last time it was thirteen," he thought while clenching his jaw and fists, bracing for the next strike.

The hits came regularly, followed just as regularly by a pant and a short cry of repentance, "I won't do it again! I won't do it again!"

"Now go 'n eat, you wretched scoundrel!" Dumitru concluded at long last, slipping the belt back through the loops of his pants. "And enough with the whining, unless you want some more!"

"Dad, why must you pound so hard? If you only knew how it hurts!" Mitu complained in tears.

"It hurts—my ass! You're so good at whining, better than anyone else I know! Next time I'll give you a whipping you won't forget! Listen here boy, I want to make a man outta you, teach you how to take care of a household and how to make a living, because nobody'll give it to you for free when I'm not around anymore. Look at Frizzy, how he helps around the house—he takes the cows grazing in the morning and comes back with them late at night, he mends fences and the roof of the house. When we need to bring firewood from the mountains, he's the first one up at four in the morning, ahead of me. But when it comes to you...you're slower than molasses gettin' outta bed! Why can't you be more like him—don't you wanna amount to somethin' in this life?"

Mitu cast down his eyes, swallowing hard the pork rinds from the clay bowl. *"If only I could get away from here! Oh Lord, if only I could! When I grow up, I'll run away from this place like a bat outta hell!"*

Before going to bed that night, he cuddled up closely to his mother.

"Forget about it, my lil' Mitu, don't be so upset. You know your father has a short temper, but he is good-hearted and loves you more than anything in this world," Lenuța said, trying to soothe him.

"But Ma, I can't bear this no more! I fear to look him in the eye. I fear he'll beat me up. I'm always afraid of him! Listen, I got into a fight with Nistor again today!"

"Why can't you let him be; you know he's a good-for-nothin'."

"But what d'you mean—he's right? I ain't dad's child? Why does father love Frizzy more than me? I'm so much worse than him? If I was his son, he wouldn't hit me so hard. D'you know how hard he beat me today? Do you?"

"Go to sleep now, Mitu, and get this nonsense outta your head," his mother sighed, tucking him in with a heavy wool blanket worn out by time.

Chapter 2

The house inhabited by the Popescu Family was a modest wood dwelling. In the kitchen, an oversized bed spanned from the heating stove to the opposing wall in which the children slept in order of height: Gheorghiţa— also known as Curly, the only daughter—was the closest to the stove; then Mitu, and next to the window, Lenuţa, the mother. The kitchen communicated with the other room used by Dumitru, the father, and the eldest son Ghiţă, nicknamed Frizzy. The children had received those monikers because, unlike Mitu, they were their father's splitting image: the same curly hair, the same eyes, the same lips, and even the same yielding obedience to tradition.

Behind the house, the narrow brook—Boţota—streamed among the plum, apple, and cherry trees, finally flowing into a small pond farther down. In the springtime, the purling of the water and the vibrant green of the grass gave the impression that God had mistakenly dropped a crumb of paradise in a world otherwise too wretched and consumed by poverty to appreciate any beauty.

To the right of the house, the stable sheltered a mare and two cows, which the Popescus worked very hard to keep.

"The animals and nothin' else. Nothin' else," Dumitru would often say when he was striving to teach his children life lessons. "The cattle will keep you alive. You oughta take better care of them than you do of yourselves!"

The cold and snowy days of winter passed slowly, making room for the warmer rays of sun. In waiting for the spring to come, Mitu spent almost all of his time either by the heating stove or in the front yard, horsing around with his siblings, bringing firewood from the shed, or begrudgingly helping his father with household chores.

"Maybe I'll live to see this brat of mine married and with a family," Dumitru would say to himself while watching his son work with such reluctance. "Maybe I'll make it to that day..."

One Sunday morning he took Mitu to Novaci to buy some twine and a new pair of boots from the market. He had made plans with a Transylvanian shepherd, Ivan from the Novacii Streini Village1F[*] over the Gilort River, to herd a few hundred sheep up in the mountains near Rânca, and he was in need of those things.

After browsing through the market for about an hour and spending another hour at the local tavern, they set out homeward. Mitu had gotten a new belt and a pheasant feather adorned hat, and the excitement over his new

---

[*] Novacii Streini ("The Foreign Novaci") represents the area on the left side of the Gilort River, inhabited by the "ungureni," who came from Transylvania and began arriving there from the sixteenth century due to oppression after the peasantry's revolts. Their main occupation was sheepherding in the Parâng and Lotru Mountains during summertime, and in Danube and Banat Fields in the winter.

possessions took away the weariness of walking back home the few miles between Novaci and Cernădia.

They had reached the point where the main road split into a narrow track climbing up to Rânca and another heading over the Gilort River back to their village.

"Dad, who's that over there?" the boy asked, pointing to a horse-drawn carriage.

"Well, Son, those would be kulaks from the Sabin Family. Compared to them, our Squire Poppa is quite poor. These people own mountains and grazing fields. I heard they have tens of servants and they even went to foreign lands once—far away, in America—and they saw an automobile."

"What you mean, an automobile?" Mitu's eyes widened in wonder.

"I mean it's some kinda carriage with an engine but no horses that runs on oil or gas, somethin' like that...I don't know. Enough with the questions—you're driving me nuts!"

"What about us? Can we buy ourselves one?"

"Eh, only the rich can afford things like that, not us," Dumitru answered sullenly.

Mitu arched his back with curiosity and made it straight to the carriage.

"Get back here, rascal, where you going?"

"I wanna see them closer, Daddy. Can I?"

"What do you wanna see closer, lil' devil?"

"I want to see what they look like! I'm going there for just a bit..." the boy answered as he approached the carriage. When he reached it, he couldn't help himself and quickly peeked inside the window. An elderly woman appeared from behind the curtain and scolded him harshly.

"What do you want little pauper, what are you looking at?"

Mitu lowered his eyes and a deep red color flooded his cheeks.

"God damn it, child! Get over here. Get over here, I said!" Dumitru howled fiercely, running towards him and grabbing him by the ear. "Who taught you to mind other people's business—who? Is that what I taught you, wretched boy?"

"But what did I do? I didn't do nothing!"

"Hey, you over there, come here for a moment!" demanded the woman in the carriage.

"Go on, go! What are you waitin' for? A second invitation?" Dumitru hissed.

Mitu approached the carriage timidly, wiping his tears with the back of his sleeve.

"Here you go, take this candy!" the woman said, handing him a piece of chocolate.

As the boy reached for the treat and was about to take it, the woman threw it deliberately to the ground.

"Take it from there!" she ordered sharply watching him bend down to pick up the candy from the dirt.

"Thank you, Ma'am. God bless you for it" he said as he picked it up. Then, he threw the chocolate in her face and dashed off over the footbridge.

"You swine, you filthy little peasant, you dirtied my carriage, and I'll have you sent to jail!" the woman shrilled behind him. "I'll catch you and skin you alive!"

Dumitru set foot after the boy and grabbed his arm, dragging him behind.

"Is that what I taught you, fiend? See what's waiting for you at home! I'm gonna kill you! With a wet switch! I made ya, I'll kill ya, wretched mongrel!" he seethed, making the boy cringe.

The whipping Mitu received that time was like no other he'd had before. Dumitru used a thin piece of wood designed specifically for the occasion. Mitu collapsed to the floor, curling up in pain, tears streaming down his cheeks. After lying down for half an hour, he started walking his fingers up and down his back and bottom, trying to figure out where it hurt the worst.

"I swear on my life that I'll gather so much money, I'll buy all this land and mountains, and I'll be the richest man around. And everybody will be coming to me asking for help. I swear, swear that's what I'm gonna do!" he avowed to himself angrily, getting up with a grunt and going to a small metal box that held all his possessions. He pulled out some coins and after counting them, a dreadful feeling of helplessness flooded his heart.

"These pennies aren't even enough for a few loaves of bread..."

When his mother entered the room, he burst into tears again.

"It's alright, my lil' Mitu, don't be so upset. Let me mend you a bit," she said as she soothed him, undressing him to look for the traces of the hits. She soaked a rag to clean the blood coming through the cracked skin.

Mitu shuddered under his mother's touch, then turned to her.

"Ma, don't you see how bad he beats me? Why don't you say something to him? Why?" he mumbled.

"What started it this time?"

"I looked inside a carriage to see who was in it, and then he started beating me."

"What carriage?"

"Don't know, someone from the Sabin Family, Dad said."

His mother winced:

"Who was in it?"

"A woman who threw a chocolate at me on the ground."

"My dear Mitu, always keep your head down in front of the rich. Please listen to your mama's advice. One sign from them and you're done for."

"But why? Aren't they people like the rest of us?"

"Our good Lord knows everyone's good and bad deeds. If you are a good person and do no harm to nobody, He will see it. Come on now, go to bed."

When they woke up the next day at four in the morning, Mitu's body still ached from Dumitru's beating. The boy was slouching on the bed, eyeballing his brother Ghiță who was already outside, prepared and ready to go. They had a long hike to Rânca; it was time to transmigrate the sheep flocks up into the mountains until the beginning of October, when they would be brought back down and divided accordingly among their owners.

Lenuța gave them something quick to eat and put some grub in their burlap satchels, wishing them a good trip and sprinkling some salt in their wake.

"May God watch over you and bring you back in good health," she whispered as they left.

At the periphery of the village, they met Ivan and two other herders who were waiting for them with a few hundred sheep.

As soon as they set out on the road towards Păpușa Mountain, Mitu, fully back to his senses after the insufferable early morning he'd had, forgot all about the lashing received the day before and started singing airily, ignoring everyone around him.

His crystal-clear voice reverberated in the quiet morning disturbed only by the cautionary bark of a watchdog or the bells hanging on the rams' necks. He was belting out songs without minding the people around, whom he didn't know all that well.

"Listen, man, d'you hear the voice on that kid?" Ivan came close to Dumitru.

"He's singing, what else to do...better than cryin'!"

"But listen to what a nice voice he's got, Dumitru! He could do music this kid of yours. Why don't you send him to Corcoveanu in Baia to learn how to play the accordion?"

"You crazy, Ivan! What's Mitu gonna do with music? Go from door to door looking to sing at weddings and expect other people's money? Beg for a few pennies? I wanna make a real man outta him, not the village's fiddler!"

"But look at him, can't you see? Mitu's frail, not made for hard work! Ghiță, your oldest, is hardworking, strong, and quick—you can tell he's gonna have a household like no other when he comes into his own. But Mitu, if he doesn't like taking care of animals, you have to find somethin' else for him; send him to school or something."

"But where should I get the goddamn money for school? What, did I go to school? And I have a wife, and kids, and a home...what does he need school for?"

"Hey, man, I didn't mean no trouble, I just wanted to give you some advice..." Ivan defended himself, but then went on, "if he was my son, I'd send him to Corcoveanu to learn music."

Dumitru slowed down a little and started contemplating.

"Why do others tell me what to do? What? I tell them how to raise their brats?" he furrowed his brow. Anger distorted his face the way it did each time he prepared to give Mitu a whipping, and wrinkles deepened on his forehead. "Look what I've become, to be told by some Transylvanian squatter what to do, like I don't have a mind of my own. Pffft, these fuckin' people!"

Chapter 3

Mitu sang without interruption the whole way to Rânca. He hummed a little something each time they stopped to grab a bite.

"Hey, lad, some nice voice you got there! Do you know this song? What about this other one?" the shepherds gathered around him. With their trolling off various melodies, the boy was eventually able to sing their requests.

During the two days of the trip, he learned five new songs that he rehearsed tirelessly, adding variations and nuances with his young, meandering voice. Before then, his singing had been limited to humming while playing, especially when he knew no one could hear him. But as the games became more engaging, his singing would dwindle away.

They spent the last night together and chugged some bottles of *ţuică*, a kind of crystal-clear, not-too-strong plum brandy. They also took to lamenting a few mournful songs until streams of tears poured out of their eyes.

Lucky am I to know croonin'
My heart's ache to stop from bloomin'
If you want to end your sadness
Sing 'n' dance an' you'll feel gladness

Early in the morning, with a bad hangover from the previous night, they all went their separate ways. Dumitru and the boys went back to Cernădia while the shepherds continued their trip with the flocks through the mountain ranges, climbing the Urdele Pass and over Păpuşa, going towards Gâlcescu Lake, all the way to the slopes where they would remain for months upon months.

Dumitru started thinking again about Ivan's words on the way back home.

"What's gonna become of Mitu?" he wondered gloomily.

The child had no idea of his father's inner turmoil; his face beamed each time he found a wild berry. He pestered his brother, or roughhoused with the dog. Once in a while, he sat down next to a tree to breathe a little, closed his eyes, and began singing one of the yodeling songs he learned from Ivan.

Sing one for the shepherd,
'Nother for the donkey herdsman,
One more for the lamb guardsman,
And one for the ram watchman,
For the watchdogs, sing one more,
And the guardsmen you crooned for,
Chant another if you can,
Have enough for all of them!

"Maybe these people are right," Dumitru said to himself, "maybe he could sing in church...That, yes, would be a good thing."

Closer to Cernădia, he called out to his son.

"Lil' Mitu, come here, boy. Where did you go?

Mitu, who'd forgotten about his dad and had gained some distance between them while playing with the dog, rushed back.

"Yes, Daddy."

"Listen, boy," Dumitru started, "I see your heart's not set on looking after animals and working the land. I thought it over and over; I'm gonna send you to Baia de Fier to the fiddler to teach you the trade. Maybe something will come out of it because you chirp like you have the devil in you."

Ghiţă sulked. His father had never sent him to learn anything but always made and expected him to work hard. Why? Was his little brother special or something? he glowered.

"Really, Daddy? Do you really wanna send me to Corcoveanu?" Mitu cried out overwhelmed with delight, and started skipping left and right, instantly making up a few rhymes and a fragment of a melody.

> *Corcoveanu, here I come!*
> *A great fiddler to become,*
> *Money'n pocket makes me hum,*
> *From fieldwork I always run.*
> *If my luck should be galore,*
> *Fire'll burn in my heart core,*
> *I will dance an' dance some more,*
> *Good for 'naught but for folklore.*

"Listen to you, little devil!" Dumitru reprimanded him jokingly. "You put a smile on my face with your song. How did you think it up so fast?" A bright grin was lighting his face—a rare thing for him since his children's coltish antics were never a reason for happiness.

"And how am I gonna go there? How will I get to Baia?"

"It's about two and a half miles from our home to Baia. If you wanna learn music, you'll have to walk. You don't expect me to haul you back and forth with the carriage like a little prince, do you?"

Mitu jumped with joy.

"I can't wait, Dad, I can't wait! You're the best father in the world!" he hugged him affectionately.

Dumitru sulked. His plans for his youngest son—to make him a self-sufficient provider with his own home just like his father—were now gone with the wind.

"Ghiţă, my oldest, is so hardworking and trustworthy! And this lil' one...I don't even know who he's like! He acts like he's nobility! If he's not good at music, he'll have to learn some other trade, or else he'll end up the village bum, and I'm not taking him back home."

Once in the village, Dumitru made his way towards Cercescu's home, who was Nistor's father.

"Why do we have to pass by their house?" Mitu pouted.

"He borrowed a hatchet from me a while ago to make a wooden cart for little Nistor, and now I need it back."

"I don't wanna go there..."

"What's the matter, rascal? You're not scared, are you? What, with the two of us here with you..."

Mitu followed them moping. When they arrived, he was relieved not to see Nistor anywhere. Dumitru opened the gate and stepped into the front yard, but then stopped suddenly:

"Ah, motherfucker!" he cried, lifting his leg and checking carefully the sole of his boots. He had stepped in a rain puddle and had been stung by something.

"What is it, Dad? What did I do?" Mitu asked frightened. Any burst of anger from Dumitru stunned him with fear.

"I got something in my foot. You didn't do nothing, boy."

Mitu raked through the puddle and found a piece of wood with a few thick nails sticking out from it.

"One of these got you? Does it hurt much?"

Dumitru shrugged and knocked on Cercescu's door. He finished his business quickly, took back his hatchet, and then they set off towards home. Mitu was no longer skipping ahead but walking along his brother, taking pleasure in the fact that Nistor hadn't been around.

Lenuţa was glad to see them home.

"Welcome back! I'll get you something to eat right away. I've been waiting for you for a while now. What kept you?"

"Let me be now, Lenuţa, because I'm very tired. I'm going to bed. My whole body aches from walking so much," answered Dumitru, removing his boots.

"What happened to your foot?" the woman asked, seeing his wool sock reddened by blood.

"Well, I stepped on a nail. I almost forgot about it," he answered faintly, throwing himself onto the bed and waving his hand indifferently. "This life's hard...so much work and sweat, for nothin'..." he mumbled and fell asleep instantly, exhausted by the trip.

When he removed his socks the next day, he noticed the hot swelling had widened around the puncture. He washed the wound with warm water and homemade soap and bandaged it with some cotton, stepping gingerly on his foot to avoid the stinging pain.

Dumitru developed a slight fever with bouts of dizziness over the next few days, but he recovered somewhat under Lenuţa's tender care. She kept bringing him hot soups and teas. Two weeks later, though, he took to bed burning like a stove. He was hallucinating and rolling his eyes aimlessly—telltale signs that God was testing him hard.

"Listen woman, if anything happens to me," he told Lenuța in a lucid moment, "I have to tell you something—if I die, send Mitu to Corcoveanu in Baia to learn music. Swear to me you'll do it!"

"What nonsense are you saying here? How can you say you'll die?" Lenuța replied.

A short while later, his state worsened so much that his wife thought to call the priest for last rites. He could barely swallow anymore, and tremors seized his body. His jaws clenched up and his face froze up in short and repeated grimaces. His fever wasn't letting up anymore, and his sleep became increasingly deeper and longer.

"Lord, please don't take him from me! My God Almighty, what have I done to deserve this? What am I gonna do alone? I'm gonna die also!" Lenuța broke down one morning while trying to wake him up.

Dumitru didn't answer. He wasn't moving. His eyelids weren't pulsating any longer. Only the deep, raspy breathing was proof that he was still alive.

He died a day later, at daybreak. When Lenuța gave the news to the children, a deafening silence engulfed the house for a few moments. Death was something they hadn't experienced firsthand before. They had seen it in other families, especially at funerals, where the kids went hoping to score a few pennies. But they had never felt it so close. At last, Ghiță and Gheorghița burst into tears. Mitu remained frozen and mute. After a minute, he went outside and sat down by the brook behind the house, as he always did when upset. Odd thoughts ran through his mind and his gaze kept falling over inane things unnoticeable until that very moment, as though his being were trying to protect itself in a hard shell, allowing only frivolities in. "Look at that ugly yellow bug in the cherry tree!"

Suddenly, he felt guilty.

"Why can't I cry? How come I don't feel like crying?" He tried to force himself to shed a tear, but couldn't—as though his heart were hollow. "I gotta help Mama!" he thought, and went back in the house.

The funeral was simple. Dumitru was laid to rest in a coffin fashioned from slabs of wood from their shed and taken to the cemetery in a carriage draped in a few rugs from inside their house. Following him was Lenuța, sobbing and holding onto Ghiță for support. Then came the relatives and the rest of the village.

Mitu went to the cemetery as though the funeral wasn't his father's. He was checking out people's clothes, looking for stains on their trousers and creases on their shirts. A strange disgust invaded him each time his eyes fell unwillingly on the coffin, and on Dumitru's ashen face.

"Lil' Mitu, try to behave and take care of your mama because she's alone now and she needs you more than anything in this world," a few people advised him at the end, after the alms were given and funeral repast. "If you need anything—anything at all—come over; you're like our own child."

While preparing to go back home, Mitu noticed Nistor trailing behind. He tried to avoid him, but the boy reached him quickly.

"God sees everything and always does justice," he sneered and darted away.

Mitu tried to stop his tears, but couldn't. For the first time in three days he burst into a gut-wrenching howl. He crouched down by a fence and bawled.

"Daddy, Daddy, please forgive me for not being how you wanted me to be. I didn't mean to, I didn't mean to. Where have you gone and left me all alone?"

A peculiar feeling came over him when he saw the black cloth hanging in their fence from afar. The front yard, the shed, the house—everything seemed different. The place in which he lived until then appeared strange and empty, enshrouded by an odd quietness despite the continuous noises made by the cattle and his mother's sobs.

"When I grow up, I'm gonna kill Nistor. Dad died because of him! Because of that damned cart of his!" he vowed to himself as he walked inside the house and saw Dumitru's bed empty. "I will kill him!"

THE BOW

Chapter 4

A few months after Dumitru's funeral, Mitu began forgetting. A man's life follows a natural course, with good and bad events bringing happiness or sadness for shorter intervals of time than one would think, and Mitu was no exception.

His visits to Corcoveanu, demanded by his father on his deathbed, had turned into somewhat of a zealotry. Initially done twice a month, they had multiplied to a few days each week as the years passed. He walked all the way from Bercești to Baia de Fier—summer or winter, rain or shine—following steadfast all his lessons. Of all the instruments played by his teacher, the most renowned musician of the region, Mitu preferred the violin and not the accordion as everyone had thought. The moment he had laid his eyes on the varnished wooden box capable of giving off such a vast array scarlet, sun-kissed, transparent tones, he knew that it was an instrument after his own heart.

"Hey kid, your fingertips will be hurting! Slow down a bit! Don't get carried away and overdo it!" Corcoveanu would say to him, worried that the boy might destroy his instruments with fervor.

The first time he played for an audience was right before he turned sixteen. When telling him about the weekend *hora*2F* at Țapa in Novaci, Corcoveanu asked Mitu whether he felt up to making his big debut.

"Really, Uncle Corcoveanu? Well, surely I can do it!" he answered, elated since that meant he was officially a musician in his own right.

In the few days that followed, the thought that he was going to play in front of many people—not only from Cernădia, but from many other villages—kept him up well past midnight. As the day of his first public performance drew closer, his stage fright worsened. The fear that he might forget a verse or mangle the melody was so great that his thoughts were incessant.

"I'm scared Ma..." he'd tell Lenuța. "What if they laugh at me?"

"How are they gonna laugh? You're nuts?" she'd encourage him. "Well, don't you think they already know how you play? The word of the mouth in the village is that there ain't nobody better than you with a fiddlestick!"

"That's exactly it. If I mess up, what do I do? I'm gonna die of shame and I won't be able to face nobody again!"

"Well, I didn't know you for a fraidy cat! Like a little girl you are! You think after a bottle of *țuică* anyone'll notice if you mess up a bit here'n'there?"

When the big Saturday finally arrived, Mitu donned his best garb, combed his hair meticulously and incessantly whisked inconspicuous specks

---

* *Hora* is a traditional Romanian folk dance that gathers everyone into a big closed circle. The dancers hold each other's hands and the circle usually spins clockwise as each participant follows a sequence of three steps forward and one step backward.

of lint off his pants. He had prepared his clothes the night before, starching and ironing the collar of his shirt, and painstakingly shining his shoes.

He started walking to Novaci at about noon—leisurely, to delay the moment of facing his audience, rehearsing the songs in his mind. He made it to Ţapa shivering with dread as though he were about to face his Maker on Judgment Day. Corcoveanu scolded him for being late, then pushed him on the small, improvised stage, handing him a violin. His eyes darted over the crowd, but no one was paying attention to him. He froze up for a few minutes, waiting for incentives to start when somebody cheered him on.

"Let's hear it, Mitu! Up an' at them! Stop wastin' time thinkin' of them young girls!"

His fear disappeared as though removed by an invisible hand.

"Don't worry about it because here it comes, Ion, my friend. You just worry about keepin' up with the music!" he answered with an up-bow on the cords, readily accompanied by the rest of the *taraf*, his gypsy bandmates.

Right away, everybody came together and interlaced their hands in a *hora*. After a while, the music changed to a specific dance for pairs and continued on for some time until beads of sweat started to trickle down the dancers' temples.

When they all finally stopped dancing and took a break to eat and drink a little something, Mitu's eyes were glistening. He couldn't believe he hadn't made an ass of himself! He sat down, pleased with his performance, and grabbed a bottle of wine. He now had a moment to look around and see if he knew anyone. Next to him, a man seemed familiar, but he couldn't figure from where he knew him. The man stared at him for a while, then came closer.

"Whose are you, troubadour?"

"I'm Lenuţa Popescu's son, the widow of Dumitru Popescu from Berceşti. Mitu. I think I know you, but I can't reckon where from."

"You don't say! It's really you, lil' Mitu? *Pffft*, I didn't recognize you! You've grown so much. You're a young lad now! How old are you?"

"I'll be sixteen in two months."

"God, how time flies! Today young, tomorrow old," the man sighed philosophically, taking a long swig from a bottle of wine. "Just yesterday, you were holding on to your mother's skirts and now you're ready to be married. You don't recognize me, do you? Know who I am?"

Mitu shrugged uncaringly.

"Forgettin' lies upon us, yes. Just as..." the man stuttered.

Mitu chuckled to himself, "this one's drunk outta his mind," but then asked where they had met.

"Well boy, now you're starting to upset me. Look at me careful! I'm Vasile, Pistol's uncle, don't you remember me? Well, I did leave the village a long time ago, and out of sight, out of mind...I have some things to look after here, and I thought I'd stop by the village dance. I haven't been here for many years. I live in Petroşani."

"Pistol's uncle? Now you're talkin! Now I remember you! Why didn't Pistol come?"

The man stepped even closer, leaning in as if he were going to divulge a great secret.

"He would've, the poor lad, but he needs to make money. So he stayed to get some work."

"Yeah, but miss dancing for that? On a Saturday? What kind of work can he do on a Saturday afternoon anyway?"

Vasile whispered in his ear.

"He wants to gather a whole lot of money to leave this place. But swear you won't tell no one."

"Leave? Where to?"

"He wants to go to America on a ship. Shhh!" Vasile placed a finger on his lips.

Mitu stood agape.

"America?! You're serious?! Pistol wants to do this? And he didn't say a word to me..."

"Don't tell nobody—swear to me!"

Suddenly, Mitu remembered the old woman in the carriage yelling at him through the curtained window, and the thought depressed him. "Oh, how lucky, those going away to make money..."

"Now tell me, have you set your eyes on one of them young girls?" Vasile brought him back from his thoughts.

"How could I when I didn't even have time to eat!" he said glancing over the crowd. "Who's that in the corner, at the table on the left?"

"Well, I don't know, since I left long ago, but maybe Iosif knows." Vasile turned to a man grappling with a bottle. "Hey, Iosif, who's that girl?"

The man seemed to struggle understanding what was being asked of him. Then, as though a glimpse of clarity defogged his mind, he answered.

"Well, she's from Transylvania. Mioara, the daughter of Anton Munteanu from Novacii Streini. Mitu, I'll introduce you to her. She's eighteen and she's looking to get married."

Vasile furrowed his brow.

"Kid, she's two years older than you..."

Mitu shrugged, "So what? Can't he see how rosy and beautiful she is?"

Mitu and the girl spent the rest of the evening together whenever allowed by the intermissions between songs. They made a great pair. She laughed at his jokes, blushed at his compliments, and threw allusive gazes his way.

When the dance ended late in the evening, they left together, not towards the center of the village but through Gilort River's valley. They walked for a while, silent and shy. It was Mitu's first time being so close to a girl. He had thought about it many times, made plans, and spoken with his pals about it, but none of that seemed relevant now. He said a few senseless words and asked a few odd questions, then an uncomfortable silence encompassed them.

"Mitu, all the girls were eyeing you tonight," Mioara grabbed his hand all of a sudden. "Did you know?"

"Oh, yeah? Well, good for them! Because I only had eyes for you," he replied, surprised at the quickness and wittiness of his own answer.

The girl blushed and kissed him softly on the cheek.

"Ain't shy, are you, crooner boy. Let's take a shortcut..."

They walked through the pinewoods and then stopped in a shadowy thicket. He looked at her full of desire, clasped his arms around her waist and kissed her, uncertain of what he was doing. The girl smiled at his awkwardness, returned a passionate kiss, and invited him to sit on the grass.

An hour later, they got up and walked back to the village, hand-in-hand. One persisting thought was stirring Mitu's mind.

"I never thought there could be something even more beautiful than music. What have I been doing all these years?!"

Chapter 5

That Saturday marked the sixth anniversary of Dumitru's death. Through all the passing years, the naughty, playful, and pouty kid that Mitu once was had become a handsome and strong young lad, with proud and defined features, all of which were but feeble remainders of his yonder years.

The success he had experienced at that first *hora* had not only sparked, but fueled his love for the violin. If up until that point he had been handling the bow for his own pleasure, the others' appreciation of his talents was now giving him an even sweeter satisfaction. Wedding after wedding, baptism after baptism, celebration after celebration, he played with Corcoveanu's orchestra until his fingers swelled up and reddened from plucking the strings.

His voice had changed as well—no longer childlike crystalline and high pitched, it was now strong, slightly hoarse, more mature and confident, with raspy inflections on higher pitches, prompting the audience to listen admiringly to his soulful songs.

"Go on and sing some more, Mitu, because you're so right. This life ain't nothin' but sorrow," they'd say, inviting him to a drink.

He would down the first glass and then keep going until his legs staggered, unable to carry him any longer, but the power of his music would give him the strength to go on. The quality of his sounds seemed to improve. There were no discordant tones, his fingers were more precise than ever. It was as though music absolved him of his inebriated state, automatically guiding his moves and nullifying the alcohol's effects.

After playing at weddings for a few months, Corcoveanu appointed him the head of the orchestra; the young apprentice had now surpassed the master and was ready to bestow his gift onto others. And this brought him, within the first year of his debut, local fame among the musical brethren.

After a short while, to distinguish him from many other Dumitrus or Mitus of the region, people started calling him "Mitu the Fiddler."

It was his first nickname.

Along with that bit of fame came money—not a lot, but certainly more than before. For the first time in his life, what he made from tips exceeded the bare necessities; the box that had been empty throughout his childhood was now bursting at the seams.

"My child, who would've thought you'd make such a pretty penny outta this! Your father, may God rest his soul, knew what he was talkin' about on his deathbed!" his mother would say each time he gave her a little something for household expenses. "But, Mitu dear, please listen to your mother. Stop drinking, my sonny because you'll destroy yourself if you go down this path, and now that you're all grown up, you know what's right and wrong!"

"Forget about it, Ma, a bottle of wine won't be the end of me! Stop worrying so much. A real man's gotta drink, ain't that right?" he'd laugh, dismissing her advice.

As is the case with any chain reaction in this world, where a gain leads to many others, Mitu's musical success made him increasingly desirable in the eyes of young women from the neighboring villages. With Mioara, his first amorous conquest, he had spent countless passionate nights full of eternal love promises. Eventually, their encounters rarefied until they stopped completely, only to be replaced with visits to a new lover, who'd soon lose her newness as well, and then another, and another.

Mitu had entered life tumultuously, his music giving him a formidable advantage over many young men his age who fought hard for the heart of fiery young women from the area. He had become very popular, with all those invitations to Sunday dances, weddings, and Christenings parties, wool and hemp-spinning bees, corn shucking and pumpkin seed cleaning corvees, where people came not only to work, but also to dance all the night through until the break of dawn.

He was content with the good things coming his way, yet one thought kept recurring: Vasile's drunken confession that his nephew was planning to go to America. Since then, he could barely help not asking Pistol about it, and seeing that his friend never mentioned anything when they got together, he became even more irritated.

"Some good chum he is, keeping such secrets from me..."

The first time Pistol admitted that he was indeed planning on leaving the country was at a wedding. They got together during one of Mitu's intermissions and began chatting. Pistol was accompanied by Boncu, a thirty-year old neighbor of his, who had left the village and was now working in the town of Târgu-Jiu.

"Some nice music you're playing there, Fiddler," they said when Mitu joined their table for a drink.

"Well, I manage the best I can. How about you? How you doin'?"

"What can we do—looking for women, because that's why we're here. You don't expect we came for you!"

"Why are you looking for them? They should be looking for you!" Mitu laughed.

"Well, can't do that because we want to go to America, me and Boncu," Pistol answered, "and we wanna take some women with us. When they'll find out we wanna leave, they'll all be looking for us!"

Mitu feigned surprise.

"You wanna go to America? The two of you? Why didn't you tell me nothin'?"

"I'm telling you now. But you can't come anyway, because you gotta be eighteen."

Mitu nodded without saying anything.

"Hey listen, crooner boy, now that we're talking about women, who do you think is the best looking woman in Cernădia nowadays?" Boncu asked him. Having left the village for some time, he didn't know which of the girls had meanwhile bloomed into young women, and he was dying to find out.

"In Cernădia? Well, the most beautiful is Moraru's daughter, Angelica, but I didn't see her here tonight," Mitu livened up all of a sudden.

"Angelica? I think the most beautiful is Ana, Nistor's wife," Pistol added.

Mitu curled his brow.

"Nistor? Nistor Cercescu?"

"That's the one. Lil' Nistor."

"Lil' Nistor..." he frowned.

"Yes, I remember Ana, she's really good-looking!" Boncu agreed, daydreaming away.

"Yeah? I've never noticed that woman," Mitu mused. "You remember the trouble I used to have with Nistor when we were kids. He'd beat me up each time he saw me. The shit I put up with because of him, may he burn in hell! I haven't spoken to him in years. And I'm never gonna," he mumbled grumpily.

"What you mean you're never gonna?" Pistol smirked." Why not? What's the point of holding the grudge? You were little then, but now he's jealous of you for sure with your music success and all..."

Mitu nodded. "Let him be jealous..." he chugged the rest of his drink and went back to his leading place on the stage. The discussion with Pistol and Boncu had dampened his spirits. He placed the violin under his chin, and in the rhythmic accompaniment of the others players, he made some long, sinister, air-chilling sounds, and began singing in a low, trembling, mournful voice, punctuating the end of each verse with a shrill from his violin.

> *Open my tomb, gravedigger, and let me go outside*
> *The home that I grew up in, once more to go inside*
> *My parents and my siblings I want to see again*
> *My brokenhearted young bride, who now laments in vain*
> *His heart full of compassion, the sexton let me out*
> *My skeleton was covered in dark and heavy shroud*
> *Weepin' an' sighin' deeply, I dragged my blanched, bare bones*
> *Leavin' my tomb behind, amid the other stones*

A few peasants raised their eyes to him, then sighed deeply and fixed their eyes onto the ground, refilling their glasses. They knew what was coming next:

My home when I arrived to, oh, dear Lord, the view
Of my wife dressed in black, in bed with someone new
In his arms she forgot the weddin' vows she made
And that when life was over, we both would share a grave
My good friends who forgot me, enjoy a glass of wine
My siblings care no longer, I left before my time
I saw my poor mama, her heart wretched for me
Together with my father—the saddest man was he
The graveyard sees 'em daily, these so-called grievin' wives
But none cries for her husband, no tears in her eyes
Their husbands lie forever in cold and lonely beds
While the survivin' women can't wait again to wed

"That's how it is, these goddamn women...well said, fiddler boy!" some people agreed, touched by the song's lyrics.

After two more fast paced dances, which left the performers panting and drenched in sweat, Mitu took another break and slowly made his way to Nistor's table. Once there, he stopped, surprised as though he hadn't seen him there from the beginning,

"Hey, Nistor, where you been? I haven't seen you in a long time. Trudgin' at the sawmill, aintcha?

"Well, I been around, Fiddler," Nistor answered, confounded since they hadn't spoken since Dumitru's funeral and had always passed each other as if they were two strangers.

An awkward silence lay between them. Nistor looked away trying to make Mitu understand he should mind his own business.

Mitu continued unperturbed.

"So, what else you doing?"

"Well, I work..." Nistor answered ambiguously, avoiding his gaze. "You?"

"Well, I play...hey, Ana," he turned to Nistor's wife, "Did my players manage to cheer you up a bit and bring some sunshine into your heart?"

The woman flinched and smiled awkwardly. They used to play together and scour the lands as children, but Mitu hadn't paid any attention to her since she had gotten married to Nistor, avoiding her whenever their paths crossed. Her thoughts had wondered to him on occasion, especially since he had turned into such a handsome young man. And to her amazement, she always felt the pings of jealousy when learning of his amorous endeavors with the many women for whom he composed songs and bought gifts and things—something Nistor had never done for her.

"Well, Mitu, you know your way around a fiddle," she nodded, feigning indifference.

They continued to make idle chat for a while. Nistor was watching him warily, afflicted by the suspicion that his childhood nemesis was up to no good.

He waited for Mitu to leave, but Mitu didn't budge, asking about this and that with no apparent intention to leave. At last, Nistor could no longer hold in the glasses of alcohol he had already ingested and got up.

"I'm going outside to take a whiz and grab a smoke..."

Mitu followed him with his eyes, and after the door closed behind Nistor, he turned to Ana.

"Sweetheart, you look like a princess from fairytales, so beautiful you are! Lissome like a willow! That husband of yours is very lucky. I saw you from afar and couldn't take my eyes off of you! What are you doing to me, Ana? Now I'm not gonna be able to play when I get on stage because of you!

The woman flinched and flushed intensely at his words and proceeded to fix her head kerchief. Even while wooing her, her husband had never paid her such compliments. On the contrary, she suspected he had married her only for the land making up her dowry.

She was about to say something, but Mitu was ahead of her.

"I want to see you again, Ana. I've been avoiding you lately, but that's because I lose my head when I'm around you. But I want to see you...in secret, not like this in public, because I really can't resist your beauty..."

She winced again. She had dreamed about this, but she couldn't believe nor admit it to herself.

"Oh, my goodness, I am a married woman, what's gotten into you?" she riposted. "If anyone should hear you and tell my husband, you're in big trouble!" she said affectedly.

Mitu was relentless.

"Ana, the day after tomorrow, when your man goes to the mountains, I'll come by at noon. If I find the front gate open, I'll come in. If it's closed, I'll turn around and never talk about this again. The day after tomorrow, at noon—don't forget!"

The woman gave him an astonished look. "Did anyone figure out what we're talking about?" she wondered uneasily. And Mitu, without waiting for her answer, turned right around and went back on stage for another performance, which Ana took to be meant solely for her.

Mitu glanced meaningfully at her at the end, then climbed in the carriage with Boncu and Pistol, prodding the horse on.

"Hey, that Ana's got her eye on me," he gloated. "I'll be going to her on Tuesday at noon, when Nistor's not at home. She's gonna leave the front gate open..."

Pistol raised his brows incredulously. He knew his pal was a philanderer, but that was too much.

"Wait a tick, lemme get this straight...you mean, on Tuesday at twelve, you're gonna go there and enter the gate without callin' or knockin', you do what you need to do with her and then leave and mind your own business? She agreed to something like this?" he scoffed.

"Ha! You're jealous! But I know what I know. I know when a woman has her needs! Do you wanna make a bet? How about you, Boncu?" Mitu said excitedly. "You wanna bet a bottle of *țuică*? If I win, you owe me a bottle each."

"All that drinking wasn't enough for you? You still want more? And two bottles at once? Now that it comes to it, I ain't never heard of any housewife cheating on her husband in Cernădia. You realize what a big deal that'd be? Somebody might get killed over something like that!" Pistol predicted. "You'll have to run if this ever gets out. You'll need to get far away from here—to America..."

Boncu intervened quickly.

"Ana seems a respectable woman. I don't know her all that well, but that's what I think..."

"Yes, yes!" Mitu retorted. "Well, you think a married woman has eyes for her husband only? The needs of the flesh are strong, my friends, and vows mean nothing. You'll see in two days who gets the last laugh..."

On Tuesday, when Mitu saw Ana's front gate wide open, he rejoiced, but not because he had won the bet with Boncu and Pistol, but because, although the two men were older than him, he could weigh and judge things more correctly than they could. With the first words exchanged with Ana, he had known he could have her, and the thought that he would sleep with his enemy's wife aroused him and gave him a feeling of superiority, making him all the more eager to hold her in his arms.

What attracted him to her wasn't a burning desire, as he had had for other women, but an ambition smoldering inside him for many years—the ambition to prove to himself that he was more powerful than Nistor. "A man's worth is measured in the number of women he sleeps with, not the riches he has," he'd say often, especially since his recent success with women and the envy of other young men. Moreover, he thought, a man's triumph over another man was not measured in the weight of fists, the debasing power of words, the wealth amassed, the dodging of conflict, but in the conquest of his woman.

The time spent with Ana during their first encounter was passionate. The woman, he realized, deserved all the compliments paid to her by Boncu and Pistol.

"My husband never had me the way you did! Now I have no energy to do my evening chores," she whispered at the end exhausted, watching him in the doorway getting ready to leave. She conspiratorially showed him a bruising on the neck and a few scratches on the arms.

"I'll come back again," he said. "I will, just so you know..."

She lowered her eyes. It was the first time she was cheating on her husband and she was considering telling Mitu never to come back, but something stopped her, and the words came out as if spoken by someone else.

"I'll be waiting...whenever you can...the gate will be open for you..."

"Lord, please make her pregnant with my child without that foul Nistor ever finding out," Mitu chuckled walking away.

Chapter 6

Mitu's weekly escapades with Ana continued for months on end, interrupted only by the occasional weekends Nistor spent home. They usually met over her place in the afternoon while the whole village was working in the field, or at dusk. They never spent too much time together; after about half an hour, Mitu would leave surreptitiously, content with himself and making plans for their next encounter.

"Mitu, what will become of us?" she'd ask him, afraid to hear what he had to say. "What?"

He never gave her a straight answer. In fact, what he really wanted was for Nistor to find out what was going on, as retribution for all that had happened between them in their childhood. After all, what kind of a vengeance is it when its target knows nothing of it? And, as he realized that things were now following a somewhat natural course—his encounters with Ana went on unnoticed—he would imagine more and more his enemy's face stupidly bewildered when learning of his wife's countless amorous jaunts with him.

Ana lived in constant fear, wondering how much longer their reprieve would last before Nistor would find out about the affair. She had noticed that Mitu no longer cared about her reputation; he seemed to try less and less to hide his visits to her, and she had considered ending it. But something pushed her back into his arms each time. She longed for him. She missed his gasps for breath during their love-making, the way he grabbed her hair while having her right there on the ottoman in the guest room. And her dread, thinking what would come to pass when caught, would increase all the more especially since she had been the one to let it all happen by leaving the gate unlocked for Mitu.

For a while, Mitu curbed his enthusiasm of bragging to Pistol, who only knew of his first episode with Ana. But too much time had elapsed, and his desire to share his victory with others was burning him. So, after telling Pistol he also told Boncu, who, in turn, told others, and so on, until the whole village was aware of the affair, except, of course, for Nistor.

Nistor continued his drudgery at the sawmill in the mountains, oblivious that he was the gossip of the village, being known by everybody as the fool breaking his back to support his two timing wife.

He eventually found out, but not from his neighbors, nor his friends, nor the people from the village, but from Mitu himself.

That day he had come down from Galbenu and had stopped off at a corvee, leaving Ana home busy with her chores. Mitu had finished playing and was about to chug yet another glass of plum *țuică*—maybe his tenth—when he saw him from afar, smiling in a rather particular way, which reminded him of the empty feeling of despondence and powerlessness he had felt while kneeling by the church after Dumitru's funeral. He got up and made his way to him with a peevish demeanor.

"Hey, lil' Nistor, whatcha doin'? Thought you should come down from the mountains to our neck of the woods? Where's Ana?"

Nistor gave him a confused look.

"Why's that your business? She's at home with her chores. What, I'm s'pposed to take her everywhere I go?"

"Yeah, you left her to have fun all by herself..." Mitu sneered. "Out of lack of somethin' better..."

"Why dontcha mind your own business, you hear! Don't make me come over there, or you'll be sorry you were born!" Nistor snapped, watching him menacingly.

"Hey, fool, cuckold," Mitu aped his face, "d'you know how that Ana of yours plays you when you ain't home? Like you wouldn't believe!"

Nistor looked at him confounded and couldn't believe his ears, but after the initial shock wore off, his face became pale.

"What...what...? What are you talking about? What?" he croaked, inching towards him. "I'm gonna kill you, I'll split you in two! Leave my woman alone, and I'll leave your mother alone. Your mother, the village whore!"

Mitu waited for him to get closer and then laughed in his face.

"You can't do to my Ma what I done to your wife!" he said loudly so that everyone could hear, staggering unsteadily on his feet. "You should see how she screams when I do her from behind: 'ah, ah, ah, ah, ohhhhhhh!'" he mocked Ana, turning to some of the people who were watching befuddled. "And listen, you shithead, that beauty mark on her right thigh is in the perfect spot!" he grinned, glaring at him. He knew, even under the heavy and mind-fogging influence of booze, that his last words had been a stab right through Nistor's heart.

Nistor threw himself at Mitu and grabbed him by the collar.

"Tell me it ain't true or I'll kill you! Tell me!" he roared, snarling like a rabid dog. He hit Mitu in the neck and aimed at him with an empty bottle but missed. He attacked, pouncing on him incessantly with his fists until Mitu collapsed wheezing on the floor.

Luckily, this time they weren't alone as in the past, and the people nearby intervened. Pistol lifted Mitu by the shoulders while the others stood in Nistor's way, keeping them apart. At last, Mitu found enough strength for one last shout.

"Use your member right, because your wife says you don't! Or maybe you're a woman too! Check your pants, maybe you're missin' it! Ana's having my child, because you can't even get that right!" he hissed with all his might.

Nistor was cursing and straining to escape the men's constraint, but they held him until Mitu was carried out by Pistol, who took him home.

Mitu awoke the next morning with a terrible hangover and a sharp pain through his head, quite unable to figure out how he had gotten the cuts on his face and the bruises on his ribs. He rose to his feet exhausted and went to the brook to wash his face and clear his thoughts but couldn't put together any of the events from the previous night, except for some odd images involving him and Pistol.

When he went back inside the house, he asked his mother, fearful of what she might tell him.

"Mama, what happened to me last night?"

She looked at him with a blend of pity, reprimand, and worry.

"Well, Pistol brought you home because you were too drunk to walk on your own, and you were hurt and bloody. When I asked you what happened, you mentioned Nistor's name, but I didn't understand."

He made it for Pistol's house. By the way Pistol received and looked at him, it seemed he had been waiting for his arrival. He took him quickly aside and told him what he had done the night before.

"Pistol, I'm scared for Ana. I'm scared for her life. That fiend will kill her." Mitu said, chilled to the bone by what he had heard.

"If I was you, I wouldn't worry about Ana—I'd worry about myself. Think Nistor'll just sit idle by and do nothing? He knows that bunch of hooligans from Bengeşti, and for a few rams in his flock, he can have one of them kill you."

"Yeah, right! Don't you think I'd find that out from my gypsies?"

"Don't know what to say. You're my best friend and I love you like a brother, so I have to tell you this: you don't do something about it, drinking will be the end of you. What came over you to tell Nistor all those things last night?"

"Don't know. You think I wanted to do that? Well, so what? Fuck him! Good he found out! Got my vengeance! Until now he was a thorn in my side, but from now on, I don't give a shit about him. I got him!"

"You may not give a shit about him, but he does about you! The whole village will know about it!" Pistol reprimanded him. "You have to run away, or he'll find you and kill you. But that's not what I meant; I was talking about your drinking."

"You find me a sober man in Cernădia, and I'll hang myself..."

"Drinking aside, but to get a man's wife and disrespect her, and then tell the husband right to his face—what were you thinking? It's a wonder he hasn't killed you yet. If it was me, I would've come to you in the middle of the night and slit your throat."

Mitu left Pistol's house in deep thought, trying to convince himself that what he had done the night before wasn't the big deal his pal was making it out to be.

Halfway through, he stopped and turned towards Ana's home.

He saw her bustling about in the yard but stayed hidden watching her. After a while, he went closer staring at her until the woman, feeling she was being watched, turned her head. She ran inside the house when she saw him but then peered from behind the door, her face white with fear.

"Go away from here before somebody gets killed!"

"Ana, wait a bit to tell you something. I swear on my life that I didn't wanna cause you no trouble," Mitu's face blanched with anger when he noticed her bruised eyes and busted lip. "The bastard, I'm gonna kill him if he touches you again!"

"Mitu, you got your life and I got mine. I chose to do what I did, and it ain't your fault that my husband hit me. Did you think he wasn't gonna find out about us? If he did to me what I did to him, I'd punch him in the face too. You be careful because he's coming after you to kill you. I heard him talking to people, and he has some friends who, for a bottle of booze, would kill their own mother. I beg you for your life, just do something and leave this place because it won't be long before he gets his hands on you. He will catch you and split your head open with a hatchet. It's the only thing he's mumblin' about and he's not afraid to go to jail for killing you!"

Mitu stared at her. What had he been thinking to confront the bastard? Deep inside, he knew Ana was right to tell him to run away. But how could he flee like a sissy? Wouldn't that mean Nistor had won? On the other hand, how could he remain there, when everybody knew? How could he play in front of people when he was the gossip of the village? How could he look them in the eyes anymore?

"Ana, I don't know what you're saying here, but I'm not running like a coward."

He left in a hurry towards Pistol's house. On the short trip there, he remembered that Pistol had also advised him to get away, and now the idea didn't seem so far-fetched after all. But if he left, where would he go?

By the time he entered Pistol's yard, he knew exactly what he was going to do. Like many times from that moment on, making drastic decisions on a whim, without much consideration, he spoke to Pistol.

"I just left Ana's and she also told me to run. Pistol, I'm in a really tight spot now, yes, I am. I wanna go with you to America. I oughta leave here as quick as I can. Can you take me with you?"

"I'd take you, but it's not up to me; I told you—you gotta be eighteen, otherwise you can't cross the border. You can only go if you're eighteen."

Mitu became pensive.

"So? When are you and Boncu leaving?"

"As soon as we can. In a few months, by the end of the year."

Pistol brought a parchment of paper; he didn't know how to read, but others had read it to him. It was a letter he had received a few months before from a friend of his who had gone to America. Mitu read it with bated breath and his face brightened up.

"Look what this Marinică of yours writes here, that he's making lots of money! He says he's got horses and a few thousand sheep in his care. Well, if he came back to Novaci with this kind of money, he'd be a kulak. Pistol, I must come with you! This is what I've always wanted: to become somebody, go somewhere far away, come back here and buy lands and properties. And now, because of the thing I got with that vile Nistor, I have to leave! With the money I make from playing, I'll never get rich! What am I gonna do twenty years from now? Wonder from village to village with the fiddle under my arm? Look what it says here—the streets, the houses they have. What documents do I need to go?'

"Well, you need the birth certificate to prove you're eighteen and money for traveling. You don't need no passport, but it'd be good to have one."

Mitu leaned against the wall and wiped his forehead with the back of his sleeve. "Big deal, a piece of paper!" he thought.

"And when you leavin' again? In a few months?

"Yeah, by the end of December—beginnin' of January."

"And you'll take me with you if I get my papers in order?"

Pistol looked at him without understanding.

"Well, yeah, but what are you gettin' at?"

Mitu smiled waggishly with a twinkle in his eye.

"My business!"

Chapter 7

The following morning at five, Mitu woke up in a hurry, saddled up his favorite white mare, and set out to Pociovaliştea Village at a hurried trot. His destination was Iosif Albu, an ex-con who had done time for theft and fraud. The man had been on the wrong side of the law for many years, breaking it many more times than what he had paid his dues for. His house was one of the fanciest ones in the area, and although he didn't work a day in his life, he somehow never ran out of money, as though he had treasures buried in his basement. The local gendarmerie had paid him many visits suspecting foul play, but couldn't pin down any of his crimes.

"Sooner or later we'll get you, Albu, and we'll put you back behind bars," the officers would always say, irritated by his haughty smile while he showed them to the door.

Mitu used a pebble to knock on a window and waited patiently until Iosif peered sullenly from behind the curtains.

"Hey fiddler, what's bringing you to my door at the break of day? If you came to serenade me, you got the wrong house, because I have something hanging between my legs, and my name ain't Ana!"

"Hey, man, I didn't come to chat with you! Can you help me with something a bit shady?"

Iosif turned serious, took him inside, and carefully locked the door and the windows.

"What do you need? A few fellers to put Nistor six feet under when he comes to split you in half with his scythe?"

"Just as I thought, the whole country knows the deed I done...Oh, Lord," Mitu sighed.

"No, man, if I wanted that, I would've gotten one of my gypsies from the tribe, because you know they have my back. Listen, I need a fake birth certificate to show that I am a year older."

Iosif scratched his chin and nodded pensively, an imperceptible smile curling the corners of his mouth.

"What you need that for? You wanna cross the ocean? That's what you'd need it for to show you're older. Y'know, if I were younger, I'd go to America to start fresh and wipe the slate clean too."

"Well, you can't erase the past, you can only change your future, and that's why I wanna go. Tell me if you can help me," Mitu insisted.

"But what's your hurry? What you scared of? Can't you wait a bit—a year or two?"

"I ain't scared, Iosif, but I wanna leave here soon."

"What you're asking could put me in jail for many years if they catch me." He scratched his head.

"No one's gonna catch you, because I won't say a word, I swear!"

"Yeah?" Iosif exclaimed incredulously, "And, when the gendarmes break your fingers with pliers to confess, will you remember your promise?

Oaths have value as long as one don't need to break them, I know that all too
well. You're a child and still got things to learn. Why you think I went to jail?
because of my own doing? No—because someone sold my skin! My best
friend, so he could save his own ass!"

"I swear to you on my life that I'm gonna be deaf and dumb about it, just
help me..."

Iosif took a moment to think.

"It'll cost you two hundred lei. Half now, half after," he said flatly.

Mitu felt the ground slipping from under him.

"What? Did you say two hundred? You lost your mind, Iosif? That's a
teacher's salary! Where would I get that kind of money from with the fifty I
barely make a month?

"Well then, maybe you don't really wanna leave, kid! I don't know what
you heard about me, but I don't haggle and I don't deal with nobody who
tries to lower my price. If you had to break into the town hall and steal a blank
birth certificate, how much would you charge for it? It's worth in cheap
cheese?"

"No man, but that's too steep. Who's got that kinda money? I'm poor as
dirt as it is."

"Then make the certificate yourself."

"C'mon Iosif, lower your price a bit. What the hell! What do I take with
me if I give you all the money I got?"

"If you really wanna leave, you'll leave. And if you keep on bargaining
with me, I'll throw you outta my home and never let you back in! Get that
through your thick skull before openin' your mouth again, y'hear?"

Mitu left overwhelmed by thoughts. Everything he had managed to save
until then amounted to less than a hundred, a sum that he now had to give
Iosif as earnest. How was he going to go to America without this money?
And where was he going to get another hundred lei? What about the money
necessary for the trip itself? He would need another four hundred lei.

When Lenuța saw him entering the yard with such a glum expression,
she thought he had gotten himself into some mess yet again.

"Where did you go so early in the morning? Don't get any ideas with
that Nistor! Things will get back to normal, but you have to stop looking for
trouble. I'm scared he's got it in his head to harm you!"

He fastened his eyes onto hers.

"Ma, I decided to sell the horse. I need some money."

She looked surprised at him, especially since he was the one bringing
home the most money.

"What do you need it for? Think about it because it's hard getting back
what you give away. If you sell the horse and then waste the money, you'll
get nothin' in the end. What do you do then? What about Ghiță? What's he
gonna do because he makes use of the horse too? Ghiță, come over here. Your
brother's selling the mare!" she called out to her eldest, who was mending a
fence.

"I need every penny I can get, Mama, because I decided I'm going to America next winter with Boncu and Pistol."

Lenuţa took a step back, looking at him in disbelief for a few moments, not comprehending his words.

"Get outta here," she almost yelled at him, "you can't be serious! You're too green behind the ears to get yourself into something like that!"

Ghiţă, who had come closer, gave him an incredulous look.

"Well, many things I heard coming from your mouth, kid, but this one takes the cake! Barely done being a babe in your mama's arms and you're talking about leavin?! No worries, I'll guard you from Nistor, if that's what got your trousers in a knot!"

"I don't need you to defend me. Mind your own and stop meddling, y'hear?" Mitu brushed him off.

"All right, but you'll be the one coming to me when you're in a pickle, just so you know."

Mitu turned to Lenuţa.

"If I don't leave now with them, I'll never leave. I'm all grown up, can't you see? I've gathered some money, but I don't wanna stay here in these mountains while others go away to get rich to come back and pay me to play at their weddings. I wanna pay others to play at my table, and I think you're just as sick of bein' poor as I am! I'll come back from America with lots of cash! Lots of it!"

"Ghiţă's right. It's because of Nistor you're leaving, ain't you? That's why." she murmured faintly. "The whole village's talking. He wants to kill you..."

"That also, I admit, but not only, I swear to you! I wanna find something better in life, Ma. I spoke with everyone and got everything I need."

Lenuţa looked woefully at him, not because she didn't believe his words, but because after Dumitru's death, her youngest son had been a great help to her. And, since he had begun playing his music, the money he brought home amounted to more than what the other two children and she made together, making her wonder whether Dumitru had been wrong all along in thinking that a decent life can only be obtained through hard work. Her son had managed to make her life a lot easier than her husband had done while alive.

"Ghiţă," Mitu said suddenly, "why don't you come with me! If the four of us go, there's nothin' we can't do. It's better when there's more people!"

His brother waved his hand dismissively and looked at him as though he were a child talking nonsense.

"I'll never leave Cernădia, even if I die of hunger. This is where I belong. Go where? Be a squatter in the world? I don't know no one, I don't speak their tongue, where am I gonna go? What's wrong with this place? Why don't you ask your sister to go with you?"

"She's a woman; where is she gonna go with three men?! You'll regret not going. You will, wait'n'see. By the way, where is my sis'?"

"She went to Novaci, to get something from the market," Lenuţa answered, holding back her tears. "There's still some time till the winter, maybe you'll change your mind. But if you have to go, then that's how the One Up Above wants it. There's nothing I can do. I've been saving a little money for some time, a penny a day; I'll give it to you because you'll sure need it. It's not much, about fifty lei, something like that."

Mitu was surprised. Since he had started making money with his music, he never thought he'd need help from his mother ever again.

"Ma, I can't take your money! I'll only borrow it, and I swear I'll give it back to you doubled!" he said full of emotion and gratefulness.

Lenuţa grabbed his hand, squeezed it in hers, then disappeared into the house. Her eyes were brimming with tears, but she didn't want her children to see how weak she was. She was still hoping that Mitu's words were idle talk and he wasn't serious, although she was afraid, having seen him so resolute and with such well thought-out plans.

"Ghiţă, come with me!" Mitu tried once more, but his brother gave him the same gesture of indifference as before.

"Well then...maybe it's better that way, because it'd be hard for Ma to be left only with Gheorghiţa."

In a few hours, he rushed back to Pociovaliştea to give Albu the down payment. This time around, Albu gave him a friendly reception—the way he welcomed all his paying customers—and promised the certificate within a few days upon receiving the other half of the money.

"You can count on me, Fiddler... And good luck with your plans..."

When he left Albu's house, Mitu was full of apprehension. "Everything I've made so far gone with wind!" he thought, then the fear of not being able to come up with the balance flooded his heart. "What if I can't get the rest in the next few months? What if something happens and Albu can't get the certificate? What if he takes my money and then lies about it? What if he robs me blind, the crook?" he worried the whole way home.

Chapter 8

Mitu grappled with remorse for the next few days. The thought that he was going to leave his mother overpowered him. "How's she gonna manage without my help? Ghiţă barely brings any money home," he kept thinking, trying afterward to ease his thoughts, saying to himself that his worries were in vain, and that helping his mother from America would be much easier than what he could do for her in Cernădia.

He went through such tribulations for a while, wavering between the idea of leaving and the idea of giving up. He maintained his daily routine of doing this and that around the house during the day and playing with his *taraf* at night and during weekends, until one night, when he realized he was not yet off the hook. He was coming back from a *hora*, alone and tipsy, when three shadows jumped him from some bushes and knocked him down. It all lasted but a few moments. His luck was that a neighbor, Ion Todea, who lived two houses down and happened to be outside at that hour, opened his front gate and asked loudly "What's goin' on? Who's there?" The three ran, leaving him on the ground with his good violin shattered to smithereens.

The incident removed the last shred of doubt he had about leaving. He started working day and night to gather the rest of the money he owed Iosif Albu. He was convinced the three hit men had been sent by Nistor. Their timing had been too good to think otherwise.

The upcoming days and weeks proved grueling. He awoke every morning at five to pick up the milk from each household to deliver it to the cheese makers; then he returned to the village for any type of day labor he could find; fixing a roof, helping with a construction, splitting fire logs—whatever came his way. Sometimes he went to Rânca up in the mountains for firewood, taking careful measures to avoid Nistor, who sometimes worked up there. He also went to the market in Târgu-Jiu to sell apples. In the evening, when he still felt up to it, he played with his *taraf* here and there, coming back home well after midnight and collapsing exhausted onto his bed.

After a whole month of continuous work, when he finally counted all of his earnings, he realized dejectedly that he was nowhere near the sum he still owed Iosif. At his pace, it would take years to amass all the money he still needed. The day of the departure was drawing near. Pistol and Boncu had decided to leave during the last days of December, and Mitu felt stuck, as though he were treading water without any hope for progress.

He had to do something and get a move on. He could no longer stay in the village. He had found out from people that Nistor kept beating Ana senselessly, but that Ana didn't want to leave him and move back with her folks, saying that she deserved the punishment as fair retribution for her sin. He worried about her, but he was also worried about his sister, Gheorghiţa, fearing that the foul Nistor, in his insanity, might try to defile her out of vengeance. He had to leave right away and let time mend things.

He finally decided he was going to borrow the money he still needed. He had thought about it earlier, but considered it to be his last resort, afraid that people were going to deride his destitute condition.

However, he no longer had a choice; he went to all his friends, promising he would double everything he owed them.

The day he had the last penny, he ran to Pociovaliştea to pay Iosif Albu.

"When can you give me the certificate?" he asked apprehensively. He was afraid Iosif had changed his mind in the interim.

"Pfft, kid, you came through!" Iosif seemed surprised. "I was thinking you wasn't gonna return! I could've bet you was gonna ask for the money back."

"Well, what made you think that? A promise is a promise! What do you take me for? You gonna help me or not?"

Iosif scratched his chin and pursed his lips. Mitu watched him suspiciously. "What if he made a deal with Nistor to kill me and keep my money?" the thought flashed through his head.

"All right then, come by the day after tomorrow at dusk. Alone. Be very careful and don't say nothin' to nobody and tell those two lunatics you leaving with to keep their mouths shut, hear? I know Pistol can keep a secret, but that Boncu is a chatterbox. Don't get me in trouble, or I'll take you down with me, because it's you using fake documents, not me!"

"Don't worry, I'll never give you trouble," Mitu answered wondering why the man cautioned him to be so secretive and to come back alone. "Maybe he wants to kill me in his yard and bury me in the shed..."

When they met two days later, Mitu would not step foot into Iosif's yard under any circumstance. Iosif gave him the certificate and shook his hand.

"Good luck with it... and come back again if you ever need my help with things like that..."

The blank certificate brought tears to his eyes. He could now be rid of Nistor! This yellow piece of parchment was his ticket to happiness! He could go to America without any worries. He was forever done with any fieldwork and the unfortunate Ana affair. He could start anew!

For the first time in his life he felt hopeful about the future. Penniless and full of debt, he wasn't concerned in the least. The important thing was that he could get away scot-free. The important thing was that he no longer had to worry about Nistor, about Ana, about Nistor's folks, about Ana's folks, or about anyone else for that matter! The important thing was that, upon his return from America, he could repay his debt to all who had helped him. "When I get there, I'll send gifts to all of them!" he thought, imagining his first steps onto the New World.

He said goodbye to Albu, who gave him a brotherly pat on the shoulder as though he were sorry to have charged him so much money after all.

"Listen Fiddler, I don't meddle in people's lives, but I can't help not saying this to you. It's good you're leaving. Nistor came to me a few weeks ago to ask me to be his witness. He's fixin' to find you somewhere and kill you, and he wanted me to say in court that you attacked him first. Be wary, because I don't know what he's planning to do. I told him I can't do what he's asking cause I'm a God-fearin' man."

Mitu furrowed his brow. He had never thought Nistor was capable of masterminding such plans.

"Iosif, all the more reason I need to go. And the sooner the better, because that bastard's gonna stay hidden for a while, but after things settle down a bit and people forget, he'll strike back thinking no one will believe it's him, right? It's a good thing I'm leaving in a few months, a good thing," he said walking away.

The following days passed by quickly. Mitu sold the horse and gathered all kinds of things from around the house that he bartered for items he thought might be useful on his trip. He organized everything in a big wooden trunk which now held light clothes, a few wool sweaters, a black suit, shaving blades, homemade soap, a pair of leather shoes and a pair of rubber boots, a mirror, a couple of pans, spoons and knives, socks and a money pouch, a leather hat, two books, a pencil and some paper, and a few other trinkets stuffed in the corners. He visited Pistol and Boncu every day, excitedly planning and replanning their trip. He read letters sent to relatives by people who had left to America until he learned them by heart and visited all of those who had someone abroad to inquire about their lives.

The big moment arrived at last. On a very cold winter day, after saying a tearful goodbye to his mother and siblings, Mitu left together with Boncu and Pistol and a few donkeys carrying their measly belongings. They headed out on the road climbing up to La Cazărmi, planning on avoiding the northern border checkpoint and thusly sneak into the Austro-Hungarian Empire.

THE DEPARTURE

Chapter 9

"When will I see these places again?" Mitu wondered as he mounted the donkey and set out with Pistol and Boncu on the steep road climbing up to Rânca.

It was a glassy night, forever forgotten by God in an icy state. The sky flickered frozen and lifeless in the full moon's light, whose rays reigned over the extensive torpor. The snow crunched under the hooves, impeding their already difficult climb.

Everything was still. The trees' silhouettes expanded to monstrous sizes, casting shapeless black shadows on the snow. The creaking of their rhythmic steps tore the thick air like a bow scratching the hoarse chords of a discordant violin. The ground was tough as flint, so solidly petrified it was hard to believe it would thaw out in the spring and become green with vegetation again. Boncu urged his donkey in front of the pack, trying to peer ahead and figure out how much longer it was to the top.

"If we don't croak here, we'll never die," he said, blowing his nose loudly and scratching his eye with a finger. Rings of warm breath escaped from his mouth and separated into deformed vapors, at last becoming one with the air.

"Yeah well, we just left and you're already whining like a woman! Don't you see you're not makin' no sense?" Pistol retorted, grunting from the effort of bridling his donkey on the abrupt road. The frost on the collar of his sheepskin waistcoat sparkled in the moon's light with each move he made. Because he was the one who had organized the trip, he considered himself the leader of their group, and Boncu's self-promotion to commander irritated him.

Mitu was walking behind them, deep in thought, not looking around, moving automatically as if pulled by a rope. "What's gonna happen to Ana after all?" he wondered a few times, then dismissed such thoughts.

"What do we do if they catch us crossing the border? They'll throw us in jail" he said. Crossing the border with fake documents terrified him.

Pistol shrugged.

"Whatever the good Lord wants with us. There's just so much we can do."

"If they catch one of us and the others get away, we won't betray one another, right? That's what we said; that's what we'll do," Boncu reminded them, afraid that Mitu, the youngest of them, might crack under pressure and turn them all in if questioned by the gendarmes.

They passed the Lake, Omul de Piatră and Colți. Then Runcul, in order to reach Țapi, Jaroștea Mare and Jaroștea Mică. By the Măgura lui Urs, they climbed along the Gilorțel, reached Bâgzele and arrived near Cazărmi, close to the border. They zigzagged through the pinewoods at Florile Albe, and went by the Urdele Pass, taking a roundabout way towards Obârșia Lotrului.

After another hour-long hike, they stopped for a short repose, hidden deeply in the heart of the woods. They tethered the donkeys carefully and then pulled some *ţuică*, bacon and onions, and rock-hard bread from their satchels. Only their tired breath filled the frozen air with a wisp of warmth.

"God, how I wish I had my violin with me," Mitu whispered vaguely, his fingers drumming on his knees the rhythm of a *hora*, which reminded him of his father and their trips on those very paths right about the time he had first enjoyed the taste of singing.

"Right, that's what you need right now, the fiddle," Pistol said sarcastically, not understanding how someone could think about entertainment on such a difficult journey.

A deafening silence lay upon them, giving the impression they were in a ruinous, forgotten world. Everything stood still as though a blanket of heavy ice covered the land. Their munching of the food and the donkeys' grunts were the only noises bringing a smidgen a life into the bareness surrounding them.

"Could you believe how easy we had it, with no one bothering us so far. I can't wait to get there! I wonder how it is," Boncu said cheerfully when they finished eating, blowing in his palms to warm them. He rubbed his teary and reddened eyes with the back of his hand. "These damn eyes, they keep burnin'," he said under his breath, getting up and replacing the bottle in his satchel. "Time to go now, before we freeze to death on them here places!"

Pistol mumbled something under his breath and got up reluctantly to show that he only did so because that was what he considered was the right thing to do, and not because Boncu had told them.

"We freeze, my ass," he said. "It's not even all that cold... By my calculations, we've already crossed onto the other side. We left Corneşu long behind."

"We gotta get movin'. Come on, crooner, get up. Don't just lay there like a woman!" said Boncu.

Mitu jumped to his feet, beside himself with glee. He had shaken in his boots until then, afraid they might get caught crossing the border.

They started walking again, climbing up hills and down valleys, with short and frequent stops. The air glimmered with steely-blue reflections from the snow, and the sun with its bright but lifeless rays mesmerized them with its alluring, cold image. The Făgăraşi Mountains rose majestically in the horizon, borrowing their white countenance from the fleecy clouds in the sky.

Along with the hills left behind, Mitu was also shedding all of his memories. As he was getting farther away from Berceşti, his village became smaller with each step he made; its people and things gradually vanishing from his mind only to be replaced by new concerns. "What will become of me? Will I be able to manage? What if I can't find work and I come back to the village as poor as before?"

They arrived in Obârşia in the afternoon. They hadn't slept since the previous day, stopping only for a quick bite and riding their donkeys to exhaustion. Tired beyond belief, they pulled out some heavy wool blankets and spent the night huddling up together, covering themselves well above their heads in the attempt to keep the heat from spilling out into the air, thirstily absorbing any shred of live energy.

In the morning, they set out for Sebeş, making their way along the Lotru River.

"Look, something even more beautiful than the valley of Gilort!" Mitu thought, getting farther and farther from Romania with each hoof beat. They took in the sights with sharpened curiosity as if they were traveling in foreign lands, even though everything in their way—the mountains, the valleys, the air, and even the people who spoke the Romanian tongue—looked exactly the same as those left behind.

"Lord, what nonsense! The Romanian people cut into two. We're a laughingstock I tell you," said Boncu, surreptitiously wiping a tear as he passed a man perched on a donkey who wished him a good day.

Mitu nodded. His thoughts exactly; he noticed that the Empire didn't differ in the least from Cernădia.

"What's the matter Boncu, now you're weepin' because you found Romanian fellers on this side of the mountain? I'd say you should become a minister if you're so touched by the situation, and unite these two halves so that my kids' kids will learn of you in history classes!" Pistol found yet another occasion to take a stab at his friend.

"Why you gotta attack me all the time? What did I do to you that you won't leave me alone?" Boncu scowled. "Where did you see I was cryin'? My eyes are teary from the cold! Mind your own, shithead, and leave me the fuck alone!"

"What's with you two? You're completely nuts," intervened Mitu, who was too happy to have gotten so far away to get into stupid fights. "Better let's talk about what we're gonna do when we get to New York."

"We'll have enough time for that when we're on the boat. There's gonna be lotsa people there for us to learn from," Boncu said.

"How will we learn? In 'eengleesh?'" Pistol derided him. "Maybe you can teach us some, if you know it so good. When did you study it, last night in Obârşia?"

"Well Pistol, I may not know English, but at least I know how to read and write, unlike others," Mitu answered wryly.

Pistol scowled, but had no reply. "Smug asshole!" he cursed him in his head and pulled the reins to fall back behind the group.

"If anyone heard you, they'd think *you* were young and stupid, not me," Mitu added, irritated by their bickering. "What the hell's wrong with you to quarrel like this? Haven't even gotten all that far. Why are you at each other's throats?"

"Don't you see how he's always on my case?" Boncu answered surly, talking about Pistol as if he weren't there. "Makin' fun of me for cryin'."

"I don't know. I'm just saying. It's not my business; you can kill each other if you want," Mitu answered indifferently, returning to his thoughts. "How will we manage in France?"

They still had a few hours before reaching Sebeş and spent the rest of the trip without saying much, except for a few short questions followed by "yes" and "no." No one dared to break the ice. The tension was thick and they were ready to snap at each other at the smallest comment.

Mitu was caught between a rock and a hard place; he was Pistol's pal, but was on Boncu's side in the matter. He said nothing else until they reached the town. They spent the night in an Inn on the outskirts of Sebeş, sharing a single bed in a room without heat. Early next morning, they went to the market to sell their donkeys.

The bitter cold was worse than what they had experienced in the mountains. The market was almost empty with the exception of a few peasants, frozen to the bone, trying to sell whatever to whomever.

They sold their animals for a derisory sum to the first person who was interested, without bargaining at all, then they paid someone to take them in a carriage to the train station.

Only when they got onboard the train did they truly feel that they were going to America for the first time, leaving behind the life they knew up to then. In Budapest, they got on The Orient Express, which was to take them across the continent all the way to Paris. The rest of the trip, and the most difficult part of it—the hundred and fifty miles through Normandy to the Le Havre Port—they had to manage somehow, perhaps taking a local train or the like.

Chapter 10

Dead tired, they reached Le Havre on a cold morning in January and took a room at the "Emigrants' Hotel" on the outskirts of the city.3F* The Inn was an imposing stone building with long rooms hosting twenty beds each, heated only by the warmth of those sleeping there. When the outside temperature went below zero degrees Celsius, and not even the steamy breath of the travelers could defrost the air, then some of them would get a bit of heat by placing metal recipients filled with smoldering ashes from the kitchen under the straw mattresses.

Mitu couldn't last in the room more than five minutes; an unbridled curiosity led him outside, and without much planning, he started scouring the streets of the city. It was his first visit somewhere far away from his home, in a foreign land of which he had heard only in stories, and not even the dreadful fatigue amassed during the train ride could stop him.

He gaited around for a while. He admired the Bishop's Cathedral then stopped in front of the Saint Joseph Church, where he crossed himself three times, after which he strolled aimlessly around the city, bewildered by the impressive buildings inhabited by people just like him.

An immeasurable happiness invaded him when he saw the Seine River separating Le Havre from Honfleur, flowing into the English Channel. He walked along the shore trying to catch a glimpse of the city on the other side, wondering how its name was properly pronounced. After a while, he arrived in the port, fascinated by the endlessness of water before his eyes. It was his first time seeing the ocean.

He sat on the beach for an hour, breathing in the salty aroma of the frozen breeze and picking up shells, which he stuffed into his pockets to keep as mementos.

After another hour of rambling about, he returned to the Inn. Exhausted but joyful, he awoke Boncu and Pistol, still sound asleep.

"I saw the ships! C'mon, get up! What, you came to France to sleep?"

"What are you doin', Mitu? Leave me alone. I'm tired!" Pistol mumbled. "What's with you, you walked through the city? How are the ships? Can they take us to New York?"

Mitu chortled.

"What do you think? They'll take us, of course. What we've heard about the so-called 'floating coffins' where people going to America dying by the thousands and being thrown to the sharks are just stories. Stories! These ships are huge! I never imagined something like that could be made by human

---

* That type of hotel was becoming popular in all European ports from which ships sailed to America at the beginning of the twentieth century, given the unpredictability of the ships' and trains' schedules, and the long processing of traveling documents that could delay the passengers' departure for weeks or even months.

hands! They can haul hundreds or thousands of people. The whole of Cernădia could fit into a corner!"

"Yeah sure, I believe it," Boncu commented incredulously. "The Titanic was huge too, and it sank last year in April. Fifteen hundred people died because they didn't have enough lifeboats."

After half an hour, they all left for the port to find out about boat tickets, taking the roundabout way through the center of the city for more sightseeing. The difference between the place they came from and Le Havre was unbelievable, Mitu thought. The type of two-room houses from Bercești was nowhere to be found in this city; the people riding everywhere in horse-drawn carriages were well-groomed; the men wore black fedoras and bow ties; the women were beautiful and coquettish in long, elegant winter coats. As hard as he tried, he couldn't find anyone wearing pig hide shoes as the people in his village did.

Hundreds of people gathered in groups in the port waiting for ships. They looked for a long time for someone who could help them, and after many trials, they eventually found a big poster from which they understood only the first sentence: *Steamship La Savoie, Le Havre-New York, forty dollars, third class, January 18.*

"So, what does it say? 'Steam-ship' is 'boat,' I know that from the letters. This must be it. It leaves in a week. This is the one we need to take. Expensive! Forty dollars!" Boncu said flustered.

"Forty...?!" Mitu cringed. "Wasn't it thirty? Now what do I do?" The Orient Express had cost more than expected and now he only had fifty dollars left. He had to show he had at least twenty dollars in his pocket upon entering New York.

"The good Lord will take care of me like He did till now!" he tried to comfort himself, and then followed Boncu and Pistol who were looking for information left and right. He envied them. They each had sixty dollars, as though they knew beforehand the exact sum they needed.

At last, they went to a kiosk for some paperwork. The clerk, whose plumped figure betrayed too much good food and wine, was checking people's documents with great care and scribbled something in a folder.

When it was Mitu's turn, the clerk measured him with his eyes from head to toe and verified his papers twice. He then asked him something in French but didn't receive an answer. He motioned him to wait there, then he took all his papers and disappeared behind a closed door.

A cold shiver went down Mitu's spine. At last, his fake documents had caught up with him! He went in a corner, trying to stop the shuddering of his teeth. He rubbed his hands and stuffed them in his pockets, then crouched down and looked around. The indifferent crowd, dressed in black and shabby clothes, coming and going to different kiosks, seemed completely oblivious to his terror. They all minded their own lonely and difficult life journey, unable to realize when others might need a shoulder to cry on.

After an agonizingly long time, the clerk returned and summoned him to approach. He got up from his corner petrified he might get arrested. When his eyes met those of the clerk, he lost control over his body: an unnatural wet warmth slithered down his pants to his knees and then his ankles.

The clerk handed him back his papers, watching curiously the liquid trail behind him:

"*Que s'est il passe, monsieur? Bon voyage!*" he smiled.

Mitu grabbed timidly his certificate, exited quickly and stopped overwhelmed by embarrassment in front of Boncu and Pistol, who were waiting outside.

"I have to go back to the Inn because I just made an ass of myself. I pissed myself afraid they were gonna arrest me and throw me in jail because of the birth certificate. Oh my God, I could drop dead right here, I'm so ashamed!"

The two burst out laughing.

"Ha, never thought we'd see this. Look at that, the lover of all women in Cernădia pissed himself because of a man who puts stamps on documents!"

"Gimme a break, you two, you have no idea what I just went through!"

They came back to the port early next morning, this time lugging their bags behind them, and set in line to buy their tickets.

Hundreds of people were cramming to the front, kicking with their elbows to move ahead, and curses in all types of languages could be heard everywhere. Right next to them, a young woman holding a baby in her arms was watching absentmindedly the ocean of people, while her husband had his arms clasped protectively around her. Farther ahead, two young men were tenaciously inching ahead in an effort to bypass everyone.

After waiting in the bitter cold for two hours, they finally got their turn. They each paid the forty dollars for the third class tickets, then were directed to a tall stone building. There, a doctor signaled them to undress. Stark naked for a few minutes, they were inspected in passing from behind thick eyeglasses, after which the nurse took them in a long hall emanating a choking smell of disinfectant. They took a bath, and a barber gave them a prison-like haircut, then they were brought back. Another nurse gave each one of them three stinging shots in the shoulder, marking something—the names of vaccines, they found out later on—next to their names on a list.

Cheerful and freshly groomed—as though ready for a party—they looked for their luggage only to realize to their dismay it was nowhere to be found. No bags, no trunks, no satchels, not theirs nor anyone else's!

They ran up and down the hallways looking agitated for their bags, when the nurse who had previously administered their shots noticed their problem.

"*Les bagages sont en train d'être décontaminés....*" she said, pointing out the window.

Indeed, right outside, a few porters were unloading bags and satchels from carriages, organizing them in rows. After some frantic searching, they were able to recuperate their measly belongings. Mitu opened his trunk to see whether something was missing and couldn't believe his eyes: his things had undergone a steam-bath for disinfection, and all of his clothes, papers, and soap were now destroyed.

With a blank stare he struggled to understand his situation, and at last he broke down.

"How can I go on a trip with nothing? I ain't got no clothes, nothing but the knives, spoons, and iron pans! Fuckin' idiots! They messed up everything we had! Now where am I gonna get the money for what I need?"

"It's alright, we're together, and the three of us we'll manage somehow. This won't be the end of us," Pistol tried to encourage him.

"That's what you think? Wait'n'see when we get to New York—that's if we don't croak and they throw us overboard beforehand! You know they can send us back if they don't like our mugs, right? They can put us back on the boat and send our asses right where we came from, with no explanation! You think we're off the hook yet?"

Pistol mumbled weakly.

"We've climbed the Carpathians on donkeys in the dead of winter and then crossed the whole of Europe and still made it. I reckon we'll cross the ocean too."

"Mitu, whatcha gonna do about the money?" Boncu asked. "You only have ten dollars left, and you need to show you got twenty when we get there."

He shrugged.

"I should be able to find someone on the boat to borrow from just to show I got the money," he said uncertainly.

Chapter 11

They spent the next few days before the departure quarantined in a tall building. Mitu devoted countless hours to memorizing new English expressions, repeating over and over words he heard here and there, and paid special attention to learning the right answers for the immigration officers in New York.

The big moment arrived on January 18, 1913. That particularly cold morning, a clerk checked their papers and tickets and asked them a series of questions, which they did not understand but to which they answered "no." They had learned from others in quarantine that they would be questioned on whether they were polygamists or anarchists, and even if they answered "yes" because they didn't understand the language, they would be forbidden from embarking. The clerk asked their occupation and wrote "laborer" next to their names, then gave them a piece of paper with a few words written in Romanian and asked them to read. Pistol shook his head, and the man wrote "does not know how to read" under his name.

They waited in an interminable line to board the boat. A long, slithering worm of hundreds of people bustled to take the big step into the unknown. The crowd was swarming to reach the narrow metal footbridge uniting the two worlds—the shore and the deck—yelling and gesticulating, hauling trunks, carrying pieces of luggage and young children, and turning to wave goodbye to those left on land hoping to make that same trip one day as well.

"*Bon voyage! Non dimenticare di scrivere! Revenez bientôt!* God bless you there!" they would shout, wiping their eyes and trying to hide their sadness.

Having passed the ticket check with great anxiety after his episode of incontinence suffered a few days before, Mitu breathed a deep sigh of relief and clenched his fists with excitement. As he stepped on the boat, he almost choked with joy.

"I made it! I'm on my way! May God keep helping me from now on!"

He walked on the deck looking around and only then was he taken aback by the size of the boat. La Savoie was a transatlantic liner eleven thousand tons heavy and could reach a speed of twenty knots. Built in 1900 for the Compagnie Générale Transatlantique, a French shipping company whose main undertaking was taking immigrants to America or Canada, it transported hundreds of people who displayed their social status by the price paid on the tickets; the first class, in big, luxurious rooms, decorated with silk curtains and sumptuous furnishings; the second class, in clean and cozy, albeit smaller rooms; and the third class—the poor—buried deep into the belly of the ship, right over the massive machinery thrusting the boat forward.

The three men descended down the steep stairs to the giant compartmented hall where they were to spend a whole week. A man who had been throwing curious looks their way accosted them full of excitement.

"Look at that, I finally hear someone speaking Romanian, God bless! How great! I found some fellow countrymen!"

He was a man of about thirty, with an emaciated body and yellowish but piercing eyes, whose articulated and measured speech seemed to cover up his true feelings for the world. Boncu started with the inquiries right away: who he was, where he came from, where was he going, for how long, what he did for a living...

"My name is Miu Pavelescu, I'm from Câmpina, folks. I'm a teacher. I mean, I was a teacher. I told them here that I was a carpenter to show them I had a useful kind of job. I heard you speaking and I thought I'd talk to you, since it's so much better traveling with companions. Where are you going?"

"Well, to America, man. Where else?" Pistol mocked him, winking at Mitu.

"Well, that I know, but where exactly in America?" he inquired with a slight Transylvanian accent, not smiling nor acknowledging Pistol's sarcastic remark.

"New York first, then we'll see..."

"New York! My God, what luck! You're actually stopping in New York? I will also. I have to tell you again, I'm so happy I met you! If you don't mind, let's travel together, because any trip is shorter when shared by many."

They chose their beds next to one another, stuffed their baggage in the tight space between them, and lay down exhausted but happy. By each bed, they found heavy blankets and life vests, which could also be used as pillows.

Farther down in a corner, Mitu saw some kind of a giant kettle atop a blistering fire. He sniffed the tantalizing aroma of bean stew and realized just how hungry he was.

"Look how fast these people set out to cook!" he commented, nostrils dilated.

"It's three meals a day. And they're pretty good," said Pavelescu. "They make it in this big kettle here, and they serve it morning, noon, and evening. A few years ago one in ten passengers died during a transatlantic trip. But now it's better; we have drinkable water, not salty like back then, and the food's not so bad..."

"How do you know? Been on one before?"

He avoided the answer:

"Well, I'm off to bed now; I'm really tired after such a long day," he said, pulling the covers. A deep cough shook him. He fell asleep a little later, snoring loudly.

Mitu tried to doze off, but after tossing and turning for an hour, he made some idle chat with Boncu and Pistol while waiting for the tardy meal. After another hour, he began walking around the big cargo hall to familiarize himself with essential spots such as sinks and toilets, then he rearranged and organized his things, folding them carefully to take less space. Later, he stood in the food line and heartily ate the hot bean stew. An unexpected acrid smell flowed through the air, and Mitu discovered a surprising, tiny mound of

animal manure under a wooden bench. He pointed it to the cook who said
something in French, but realizing that Mitu hadn't understood a word, he
pulled a piece of paper and drew a boat carrying people to America, and
another one transporting cattle when returning to Europe.

*"Sur le chemin du retour on transporte du bétail. Personne ne va en
Europe depuis l'Amerique, monsieur!"*

He nodded, although he was still confused, and sat down at the narrow
table where another ten people just like him, were wolfing down their food.
He wanted to talk to them but realized he wouldn't have made himself
understood, so he decided to go out on the top deck. He climbed the narrow
stairs to the upper story, throwing sly peeks to the doors behind which he
guessed lay first class lavishness, and finally made it all the way up to the
deck, shrinking under the terrible cold. The wind stung his face and made his
eyes tear. He went by the rail to get a better look at the ocean.

Right at that moment, he heard a furious cry behind him.

"Steerage! Steerage!"

He turned his head and saw an officer flailing his arms angrily at him to
return to the cargo hall.

Slightly peeved, he went back down the stairs. It was almost nighttime
when he finally laid down on his bed, feeling the sweet torpor of slumber
invading his body. He squinted around. To his right, somebody was sleeping
with their head on a table. "Maybe he's drunk," he thought. Not far off, a man
of fifty was watching him with a blank expression. He was wearing a brown
hat, an unbuttoned long wool coat, white shirt, and thin, greenish pants. Mitu
wondered if the man was cold. He turned his gaze to the left, where two young
men about his age lolled on the floor while sharing a flask of alcohol,
gesticulating and talking in a language that sounded like it might be Russian.
At the sight of booze, he began salivating; he got up and went straight to
them, signaling them to give him a swig.

"Davay buhnem, bratan!" they smiled kindly.

He took a hearty gulp and closed his eyes, relishing the hotness of the
alcohol slipping like a fiery smoke down his throat.

"Oh, how good! I wish I had a bottle with me!"

He thanked them a few times and went back to his bed. On his left, Miu,
their new companion, was snoring away, and on the right Boncu and Pistol
were sleeping soundly as well. He made a note of each bed's number: 143,
144, 145, 146. "I'll have to remember them all my life; maybe one day they'll
bring me luck..." he thought as he fell asleep. He dreamed of big steamships,
horses pulling carriages at a fierce gallop, and the clerk from Le Havre
binding him in chains and throwing him in jail because of the fake documents.

He woke up drenched in sweat not knowing where he was, and
eventually slipped back into a state of watchful sleep. A terrifying cry cutting
the silent night like a sharp knife woke him up shortly after. He got up trying
to figure out what was happening. He felt an agitated breathing on his neck

and he turned to distinguish Miu's shadow perched on the bed, panting frantically.

He got a little closer to see him better; Miu's eyes were bulging out and his body was shaking with convulsions. His hands were clenched on the metal headboard of the bed, and his breathing was shallow and fast. Sweat soaked his temples.

"What's the matter, man, you're not well? What happened to you? Pistol, get up. Miu's not well. Get up! Boncu, get up!"

The two scrambled to their feet and looked around confused.

"What is it? What's goin' on?"

"Miu's not well. He's shaking and his eyes are bulging!"

Pistol rubbed his eyes and cursed through his teeth.

"Pavelescu, what happened, brother?" he asked, then went to fetch a glass of water.

"I'll be alright. Get back to your beds, come on, just let me be," he choked.

"But what happened? You had a bad dream?"

Miu sighed. His eyes reflected some unspeakable terror. He tried to answer, but stopped. Mitu came closer and insisted.

"You can tell me; I'm your friend! What happened to you?"

The man gave him an intense look then began talking as if he were delivering a monologue.

"For nine years now, I can only sleep a few hours. Each night I wake up to a sea of cadavers floating before my eyes. Screams and cries of terror swallowed by water haunt my dreams. Have you heard of the 'Norge'?"

"'Norge?' Who's that?" asked Boncu.

"I was on it nine years ago when it sank," Miu continued. "We were heading to New York from Copenhagen. I was twenty years old and wanted to try my luck in America. At about seven in the morning, I awoke to a screeching sound of metal grinding onto something hard. It was the 'Norge'. It had hit a massive cliff. I remember it as it if was yesterday: the 28th of June, 1904. I remember the captain's voice. 'On the deck immediately or you'll drown!' he said. I got out quickly, I was among the first who reached the top since my bed was by the door. The captain ordered the lifeboats be dropped to the water. The people were crowding, but they did not show any fear yet. If they only knew what was coming next! We climbed into a lifeboat and moved away. Through the mist, we clearly saw how the boat was filling with water and sinking bow-first. That's when the people still on desk began their desperate swarm to the lifeboats, fighting for a spot. They were pushing ahead with their fists, kicking and screaming. The men howled and cursed. One of them kicked a pregnant woman to the ground and stepped on her, ignoring her screams. A few women and their children got into one of the lifeboats, but the ropes tore and the boat fell into the water. The poor women grabbed onto the edge of the ship with one hand and had the other clenched onto their children—all in vain! A wave smashed them against the ship, instantly killing a few and drowning the others a moment later. Only a few lifeboats made it through: most of them shattered against the ship or capsized. Some of those still on deck were desperately trying to put on their life vests but couldn't; the straps were too old and ripped or couldn't be tied. Others had given up and were on their knees in prayer. I can still see their terrified eyes and outstretched arms, begging us to take them along."

Mitu was listening, dumbfounded. Miu wiped a few tears but could no longer contain himself and choked in fits of crying. He spat some blood into a handkerchief, his face hidden in his palms, then went on:

"Hundreds of people were in the water, screaming and begging. At one point—twenty minutes after it all began—the boat filled with water and sank quickly, taking with it everybody still on deck. We could see their fists lifted up to the sky and heard their curses against God as they were swallowed by the waves. When the boat disappeared completely under, a huge whirlpool formed in its wake, pulling down those who had jumped ship a few minutes before. The people who, by the grace of God, had managed to escape, swam desperately towards our lifeboats. Some made it to ours, but since there were too many of us in it already, we hit them with the oars. I killed some—mercy me—I pushed them with my foot, or I broke their fingers as they grabbed onto the edge. I wake up at night haunted by the unforgiving eyes of a man who had resigned himself to fate and was peacefully awaiting his end. Each night he watches me reproachfully, and I can't take my eyes off of his."

Pistol, Boncu, and Mitu had forgotten to breathe, utterly engrossed in his story.

"At last, there was silence. The screams stopped as though taken by the wind. You could still hear a grunt, a piercing howl, or a child's cry, but after that...nothing. Hundreds of bodies floated smacking against one another."

"And who found you?" Pistol asked quietly.

"We drifted for six days, eating a cookie or two. We only had water for a day and we all shared a drop. No one had thought about provisions in that quagmire. As we were beginning to lose any hope, a Scottish boat spotted us and brought us to Aberdeen. It was the 4th of July—I remember it well. There, I was given some money and I went back to Romania. During the first years I was terrified to even come close to a river. I wanted to kill myself a few times, but then I thought I'd be buried without a cross on the fringe of the cemetery. I've had nightmares almost every night since, and sometimes, even during the day I forget where I am, and jarring images from that night flash before my eyes. Slowly, I started thinking about leaving again. Here I am, though I don't think I'll make it now either. I started coughing a few months ago; I hope to slip past the medical checkup on Ellis Island."

Mitu had read about it in the letters; when entering America, if you showed the smallest sign of disease, you were deported without any explanation. Miu was pale and had deep circles around his eyes, barely recovered from interminable bouts of coughing, and he kept spitting blood into his handkerchief.

"Pal, he said, you need to be seen by a doctor..."

There were plenty of doctors. For each person whose entry to America was denied, the ship was fined over a hundred dollars, so the maritime companies employed medical personnel to check the passengers, treat them to the best of their abilities, and keep detailed notes throughout the trip on personal logs, which were to be shown to the New York authorities upon arrival.

Miu nodded in agreement, and Mitu left to look into it. He came back with a doctor, who checked Miu carefully, listening to his heart and lungs with the stethoscope, taking his temperature, and feeling his abdomen. He gave him some medicine and recommended that he stay mostly in bed.

"*Restez au chaud, mangez chaud, monsieur, et je reviendrai demain matin.*"

They all fell asleep in a few minutes, but were awaken by Miu's noisy and interminable cough. Mitu came close to Pistol and whispered to him.

"I don't like how he looks; I think he's got consumption or something. Do you hear the wheezing in his chest?"

"He'll be all right before we get there, we only have a few days left, and it's nice'n'warm in here. When he sees New York, he'll be as happy as a newborn baby at his mother's bosom."

"I don't know..." Mitu insisted. "And I ain't got medicine with me, I haven't brought any, and I even thought about it before leaving!"

They finally fell asleep and woke up late in the day, upset that they had missed their breakfast. Pistol and Boncu started a game of cards. Mitu pulled out a piece of paper and began writing English words to memorize later, and seeing that Miu had a Webster's English Dictionary with many translations scribbled on the margins, he grabbed it quickly and spent many hours spelling and repeating: "*man*" and "*woman*" and "*town*" and "*job*" and "*money.*"

The day passed quickly; they walked on the deck on the sly, since they were from third class and were not allowed up there. Mitu kept close to Miu, asking him how to pronounce various words from the dictionary and rehearsing the expressions Miu said to him.

"I want work."

"My name is Popescu."

"I am from Romania."

"I am eighteen years old."

Miu's cough worsened the following night, shaking him hard and keeping him up until dawn. Mitu called the doctor again, but after checking him up, he shrugged helplessly.

"*Je ne sais pas quoi lui faire d'autre, mes amis...*"

Three days later, Miu's fever spiked, and not even the heavy blankets piled on could ease his frissons.

Seeing him shivering and spitting blood, Mitu had a somber feeling.

"He's not gonna make it to the Statue of Liberty..."

He didn't need doctors to figure it out. When Miu gave him the dictionary as a souvenir and asked him to take his money and send it back to his family in Câmpina, Mitu began sobbing as if all those years of hardship from Bercești had made him not stronger, but even more susceptible to pain.

Miu Pavelescu died under the helpless eyes of those around him, who managed to light a candle for his soul right before his last breath. He missed arriving in America by two days. A few sailors grabbed him from the underarms and feet and placed him on a wooden gurney. Tens of people gathered for the ceremony, in one of the few occasions when parallel worlds invisibly but significantly distanced—the haves and the have-nots—face together an event equal to all: the end.

Mitu crouched down between Pistol and Boncu as if he were afraid to be seen by others, and looked at the pale cadaver, devoid of feeling, wondering senselessly why people don their best attire at funerals.

In a dreamlike state, he could hear the voice of the pastor, who, so accustomed to people dying at sea, repeated the same words without much emotion:

The Lord is my shepherd, I shall not want. He makes me lie down in green pastures; He leads me beside still waters; He restores my soul. He leads me in paths of righteousness for His name's sake. Though I walk through the valley of the shadow of death, I fear no evil; for you are with me; your rod and your staff—they comfort me. You prepare a table before me in the presence of my enemies; you anoint my head with oil; my cup overflows. Surely goodness and mercy shall follow me all the days of my life, and I shall dwell in the house of the Lord forever.

At last, Miu was shrouded in a white cloth tightly cinched at both ends by the two sailors. On top, they placed an American flag carefully tied with some rope, then lifted the gurney up to the rail and tilted it. The body fell into the water as the people around crossed themselves and crowded to the edge to watch with morbid curiosity. On some of their faces one could read a tacit satisfaction that they had made it through God's mysterious game of fate.

At night, when Mitu turned to the right and saw the empty bed next to him, he couldn't help but wonder whether there was any point to all of that and whether a quiet living in Cernădia wouldn't have been better than a life among strangers.

NEW YORK

Chapter 12

La Savoie reached New York on the twenty fifth of January, 1913. The captain had announced they were getting close to the port, and every soul on the ship, young and old, mother and child, man or woman gathered up on the deck.

The first thing they saw was Staten Island, the big island framing Manhattan on the south, now on the port side of the ship. Then, right in front of them and a bit to the left, the Statue of Liberty appeared enshrouded in fog. The crowd swarmed to the bow, madly enthusiastic.

"Statue of Liberty! *Die Freiheitsstatue! Estatua de la Libertad! Statue de la Liberté!*"

As they were passing it, the men removed their hats and shook them saluting. The people hugged one another teary-eyed, marveling at the sights.

"Fiddler boy, we made it! God saw us through! Look at what's around here! I never thought I'd live to see something like this!" Pistol grabbed Mitu's arm, gawking, amazed at the south side of Manhattan where a few buildings taller than anything he had imagined in his life could be seen in the cold sky.

"Yes, we made it. We were lucky—very lucky! Let's see from now on!" Mitu said, unable to take his eyes off the Brooklyn Bridge, the longest suspended bridge at the time, stretching like a metal arch over the East River.

The ship anchored somewhere on the Hudson River—an immense gathering of many streams and smaller rivers coming from the north somewhere, dividing the island of Manhattan from New Jersey and flowing into the ocean.

"All those stories we've heard of America weren't just stories. They're true! This water is bigger than the Danube River! Everything is gigantic here! A small stream like Gilort isn't even on the map."

At the captain's signal they all went into the cargo to get their luggage. When they came back to the deck, Mitu noticed that the first and second class passengers were already preparing to debark and watched them enviously.

"Damn money—it gets you anywhere!"

Indeed, a few minutes after disembarking, the well-off travelers, after being inspected summarily by some very friendly clerks, descended the small footbridge uniting the ship with the shore and set towards the customs kiosks waiting for them right there; a moment later, they stepped onto the New World.

Mitu continued to watch, disheartened by their contented faces, thinking of the many hoops he might have to jump through to obtain the right to enter America. For more than a week now, he slept whenever he could, ate whatever he found, and was kept with hundreds of others in a sort of prison, breathing in the stench of stale air. His companions from third class looked pitiful; some had been seasick the whole time, the children were fussy, and the majority couldn't even rejoice that they had finally reached the end of the journey.

He thought they were going to leave the ship by nightfall, but instead they stayed onboard for another night. Then another. And another. After three days, they were finally led to a ferryboat connecting the port to Ellis Island. The January cold was bitter and the passengers huddled together for a hint of heat.

There wasn't any kind of shelter on the ferryboat, not even for the children; they all had to stay under the clear sky, weathering the cold air, rocking from one foot to the other and rubbing their hands to get the blood flowing.

"God, what bedlam over here!" Mitu sighed, raising the collar of his coat over his ears.

"These people are from all the boats that arrived here in the last few days!" Boncu observed, wiping away a stray tear.

"What's the matter Boncu? Cryin' like a baby, are ya?" Mitu asked amused, trying to shake the cold penetrating his bones.

"Leave me alone, hear, and better remember you pissed yourself in France!" Boncu laughed. "These damn eyes are burning so bad! I think it's from this cold wind..."

Right next to them, a woman with a four-year-old child—his face and hands covered by red spots—was trying to stay warm by shifting her body from one foot to the other, and kept watching her son and covering him with a heavy shawl.

Mitu stepped back, trying to give her some room but also to avoid coming in contact with the child, following the primeval instinct of standing clear of anyone afflicted by a disease. The child began coughing and mumbling something unintelligible. The woman put her hand on his forehead and feeling his hot breath, called out weakly.

"Help, help, my child is dying, help!"

"What did she say?" Pistol asked.

"I didn't understand nothin', but I think her child is dying...only death around us. It's like a curse."

They called for a doctor, but no one answered, so Mitu ran to the control bridge of the ferryboat and knocked on the window.

"Doctor, doctor!"

The captain watched him amiably, but his expression showed this wasn't the first time he saw it happening, and pointed to the island, gesturing that they would find a doctor there.

When he returned, he found the woman kneeling down, weeping softly and clutching the dead child to her chest. The boy had died in the few minutes Mitu had been looking for a doctor. People had made a circle around her. He squeezed through them and patted her softly on the shoulder, but she shunned him and continued to rock her baby, refusing to accept what was happening.

After a while, everyone left, and the woman remained, sitting by a thick metal pillar, shivering with a vacant stare in her eyes.

The ferryboat started moving slowly an hour later, blowing its horn. In a few minutes, it anchored down with a muffled thud. Mitu's heart skipped a beat as he set foot on land.

"Lord, am I gonna make it through customs?" If until then, his devil-may-care attitude had served him well, now the uncertainty of the future overpowered him—especially seeing that so many others were holding on to the same mirage of the Promise Land by the skin of their teeth. He burst into a wail that shook him to the core.

"What's the matter? Why you cryin' like a woman? You're sick?" Boncu asked.

"Yeah, what's with you? You're not well?" Pistol intervened.

"Why can't you just let me be!" Mitu thought, withdrawing to a rail.

"La Savoie passengers, come on up!" a powerful voice called out.

They got up from sitting on their luggage and went up a long, steep set of stairs leading to the Great Hall. A few doctors were carefully observing the passengers hauling their belongings. Their trained eyes could identify various diseases at a glance; they monitored the freshly arrived immigrants climbing the stairs for any evidence of abnormal fatigue, cough, paleness, or any other signs of illness. Those who looked suspicious were marked with chalk on the back of their clothes: H for heart, L for lameness or handicaps, X for mental illness, and so on.

Mitu's eyes were still red from crying as he passed one of them, and the doctor called him closer and wrote something on the back of his coat, then waved him on.

"Boncu, what did he write on my back" he asked anxiously.

"I don't know. He wrote two letters— 'SI'4F*—what could it be?"

"I don't know, but whatever they write on you can't be good. Pistol, come a little closer. You too, Boncu, stand in front of me, so they can't see me. I'm gonna turn my coat inside out."

"Mitu, you're crazy? If they catch you, they throw you in jail and us too!"

"Just do what I told you, ain't no one goin' to jail. Come on, come close to me quick!"

Hidden from everyone's eyes, he took his coat off, turned it inside out, put it back on, and continued walking. He was lucky; nobody had seen him, and his wool coat could be worn inside out without looking suspicious.

When they reached the Great Hall, some doctors organized them in and then proceeded to examine them. The papers signed by the ship doctor were checked again, and some nurses listened to their chests with stethoscopes,

* "SI" stood for "special inquiry," meaning the person would have to undergo a detailed inspection—either a more thorough medical checkup or a careful investigation of the documentation.

had them stick their tongues out, and made them undress. At last, they rolled back their eyelids with some kind of a button hook. Boncu grunted in pain when they lifted his lids, so a doctor came to him, looked carefully at his eyes, and then wrote "CT" with chalk on his coat.

Mitu and Pistol were invited to wait while the rest of their papers were being verified, and Boncu was sent through a different door, for a more detailed checkup.

"We'll wait for you outside if we come out first, yeah? Don't be late, because we can't wait too long for your lazy ass!"

"Yes, alright...If I don't get out fast, you'll come back tomorrow, right?"

"We will, we will, don't worry. We won't leave you alone here, no worries..."

By the time he faced the last officer checking his documents, Mitu knew the battle was almost won. With Pavelescu's money he now had forty dollars—much more than what he needed to be allowed to enter America, and he knew by heart all the right answers to the twenty-nine questions he was about to be asked. Realizing Mitu spoke no English, the officer called a translator who knew a few words of Romanian:

"What is final destination?" he asked.

"Helena, Montana. I have a friend there who's waiting for me and my pal," Mitu lied nonchalantly.

"There a job waiting for you?

"No, sir..."

Many had trouble with that question, because of the vicious cycle of options it opened up; if they lacked sufficient funds, they could be deported because they would become a burden on the American government. If they didn't have enough money, but said they had a job waiting for them, they could also be deported, because the practice of paying for the tickets of some emigrants brought over to work for paltry wages—practice overused by some companies—had been outlawed since the nineteenth century. Those who were to be deported from Ellis Island for medical or financial reasons often committed suicide before climbing aboard Europe-bound ships.

"How much money?" the clerk went on.

"I have twenty dollars..." he pulled a few bills from his pocket.

"Your passage, who pays?

"I did, sir, with the money I made working in the field in Romania..."

He made it through the whole interview without a glitch and when the clerk handed back his papers at the end, he asked what 'CT' meant.

"'CT' is trachoma. Back to Europe if he have mark on back!" the answer came.

Mitu lowered his eyes. He wanted to say something else but knew it wasn't going to make a difference.

"We all have our own fate..." he thought sullenly. They had just arrived in New York, and there were only two left. "Oh, brother, what's waitin' for us from now on? Poor Boncu—how much he wanted to come to America..."

On the way out, he saw three sets of stairs leading in three different directions; "the stairs of separation", as they were known. He looked at the ones straight ahead, those going to detention and hospitalization, and ultimately, deportation; the ones on the right, going to the train stations making the connection to the rest of America. He climbed down the stairs on the left leading to the ferry-boats going to the city. He thanked Miu Pavelescu in his head and said a prayer for him, thinking that if it weren't for him, he might have been with Boncu on the way back to Europe.

"We did it, Pistol!" he said at last, unable to take his eyes off the imposing buildings on the south side of the island.

"Yes, we did. We did it! Poor Boncu..."

Chapter 13

Mitu and Pistol found shelter in one of the numerous buildings called "tenements"—a type of rundown, substandard apartment building for unskilled laborers—mushrooming all over the south of Manhattan since the middle of the nineteenth century. While on the ship, they had heard only horror stories about these places; that they hosted the immense numbers of immigrants arriving to New York for price-gouging rent and terrible conditions. That they were cold, scarce and sinister, oozed of disease, and didn't have running water. And that they were dangerous.

For them, however, it was the only choice. As steep as they were for their pockets, the tenements still represented the cheapest alternative, not to mention that the buildings were on the Lower East Side—where they wanted to live, having learned that it was the area with jobs for unqualified laborers.

After trying to find housing for a while, they had to give up on official tenements since they were too expensive; they found something else: a clandestine building, old and decrepit, hidden from view. Under the front of a messenger business, it illegally housed immigrants in miserable accommodations for little money.

Their first step onto the Promise Land seemed a huge leap into an abyss. They had landed straight onto the underbelly of American society; the dark and narrow hallways stank of indescribable smells and filth, and an infernal noise made it through from the outside all night long. The entrance door had no windows, and the tenants had to manage their way through the dark hallways the best they could with dim candlelight. They had an outhouse in the backyard, with newspapers as toilet paper, which the tenants had to bring on their own. They could wash themselves in a public bathroom across the street. The room Mitu and Boncu shared with five other people had no windows, their only light coming from two gas lamps. The fireplace, burning mostly wood and newspapers, choked them with stinging smoke.

Large families with members of all ages, poor as church mice, all lived together. The narrow rooms and hallways, bitterly cold in the winter and suffocating with heat in the summer, were witnesses to the worst kind of human decay: alcoholics, cripples, mentally alienated, inhabited the dark corners of the building for a few cents a week. Their clothing smelled, not having been laundered in months, and long johns and nightgowns barely rinsed in cold water hung on rusty hooks all around the windows.

At night, the young people went to steal, and the elderly went scouring the garbage. Most of them were immigrants who had left their homes in search of a dream that was unattainable to the majority—a dream exaggerated in letters.

The tenement was overcrowded, so they could not find a bed. They had to sleep on the floor in a corner on a few heavy blankets, waking up in the morning with stiff, numb backs.

As soon as he left his somber dwelling and reached the hustle and bustle of the city, Mitu came alive. He whiled away the first few days, captivated by the unbelievable novelty surrounding him, which surpassed his imagination. Le Havre had impressed him as well, but New York was unbelievable: charming, entrancing, and thrilling—like a Babel Tower that could only be truly appreciated by first-hand experience. His original representation of the city had been truncated, made of whatever images he had been able to conjure up from letters and postcards, just as a blind person tries to imagine the rainbow by knowing the wavelengths of the colors in its spectrum. One could feel the uniqueness and plenitude of New York's splendor only by living there and mixing in with the crowd, becoming an integral, albeit small, part of the great city.

He wandered around for days on end, mostly by himself, amazed by any baffling little thing he found in his way. He drank in the air, trying to exchange a few words with vendors on the street, window-shopping for fine suits and luxurious garments ostentatiously displayed in vitrines. Every now and then, he would spare a penny on a cookie in coquettish pastry shops in Little Italy, or would taste enticing samples from beautiful Italian women.

If he ever passed an elegant woman walking her dog, he took off his hat to salute her, only to hunch over a second later embarrassed by his shabby appearance and thinking of the social gorge between them, remembering his place: the humility and servitude level. Lavishly dressed, sophisticated and delicate, those women appeared to be untouchable goddesses. It was then that he realized even more acutely his meager status of "poor immigrant"—a squatter arrived there from the remotest boondocks, thinking that only a miracle of God could push him up a rung or two on the social ladder.

The buildings weren't the most impressive sights to him; yes, he had been amazed by incredible architectural wonders, such as the Manhattan Life Building, the Flatiron Building, or the Woolworth Building. But as extraordinary as they were, they lacked soul. The pulsating life around him awed him the most: the streets and alleys, horse-drawn carriages, noisy automobiles spewing thick, black fumes—all of them trying to find their way through the mayhem. Traffic rules, in effect for three years only, were not very effective yet.

The novelty of rambling about aimlessly wore off soon. In about a week, he started fretting about the future again.

"How will we make a living?" he kept mumbling to Pistol. "Just the two us, with poor Boncu God-knows-where. We can't speak, we don't know nothing 'cept takin' care of sheep, and no one here listens to the kind of music I play..."

"Don't worry, Mitu, I ain't heard of a starving Romanian yet! We'll manage..."

"Whatever kind of work I can get. I ain't ashamed of doing anything, even if I have to shine shoes. I'd be happy just to have enough for a loaf of bread and to put somethin' aside. I have to pay my debts and I don't wanna spend Pavelescu' s money, God rest his soul. I have to send it as soon as I can to his family in Câmpina. I don't even know how to write them he's dead..."

One day, Pistol brought him the classifieds section of a newspaper. With the Webster's dictionary from Miu and a sharpened pencil in his hand, Mitu started translating advertisements from the Help Wanted section.

"Experienced worker for construction needed. Paying one dollar/day..."

"Looking for carriage drivers, six dollars/week..."

"Landscaper needed, two days/week, a dollar fifty..."

"Paper delivery, twenty-five cents/day, two hours/mornings..."

He circled all the ads he considered interesting enough, ranking them according to the pay, the time he needed to show up, and the proximity of address.

The first ad he chose was the one for carriage drivers. For six dollars a week, he could drive through the city all day and meet people who might give him tips, he thought. Early next morning, he put on his best suit and went to the meeting place much earlier than when he was supposed to. He circled the place for a while, anxiously trying to figure out the questions he needed to answer. After some time, three or four more people arrived. When the owner showed up two hours later, he asked who had been the first, and Mitu lifted timidly his hand.

"Okay, get in and take me to Broom Street," he said without any other introduction.

Mitu looked inquiringly at him, not understanding a word in English.

"Okay, I got it; you're no good for this. Next please!" he waved his hand annoyed.

Mitu watched him even more confused, and the man started yelling angrily at him.

"I said get out, leave now; don't waste my time, you imbecile!"

Mitu left scared. When he told Pistol his incident, he was on the verge of tears.

"Come on, don't be a baby. You'll find more boors like this one and you hafta be prepared," Pistol tried to hearten him up rather uncertainly, having gone through a similar experience that morning.

"I have no luck in this life! It's clear as daylight I made a mistake comin' here! What was I thinking?! I'll never learn English and I won't have no job because of that! I'll starve to death and I'm never goin' back home because I won't have the money to pay my debts!"

"Keep yourself together, man. You expect dollars raining down from the sky? That's how the beginning is, don't you remember from the letters how everybody said the first months are tough as hell? We'll take it easy, and we'll make it! God will be with us, like till now."

"What do you mean like till now? That He hasn't killed us yet?"

They asked for employment left and right during the following days. And they had plenty of places and people to ask; there were many shops on the

Lower East Side, and hundreds of merchants pushed their carts back and forth, bustling about until late at night and bargaining with their clients to the last penny.

Garment industry posters were found everywhere in their neighborhood, stuck to the windows of bars and stores, and even their own tenement. The textile industry was flourishing. Thousands of small shops hidden from view were strewn everywhere, many of them in the very rooms inhabited by the owners—generally large families crammed into a two-bedroom apartment. The type of unskilled work required almost no communication, so even those with no experience and no English could find employment. When Mitu figured it all out, he familiarized himself quickly with the trade lingo and began his search.

"I'll find my place around here. I'll find a job somewhere to make a living after all," he'd say to himself, breathing a little easier and going once more over the ads of the hiring places closer in the area, thinking he should try his luck there first.

Chapter 14

After knocking on many doors with "garment laborers wanted" signs posted on them, Mitu was hired with a miserable salary in a tailor workshop across the street—one of the many shops strewn all over the Lower East Side that paid starvation wages. Pistol was able to find a job at a similar place on a neighboring street.

Mitu started working immediately. He was to iron fabrics for evening gowns, and he worked alongside six more adults—all Russians—and an eleven-year old boy. Many tailor shop owners purposefully hired laborers who spoke the same language, many times coming from the same place in Europe, to prevent them from learning English; as a consequence, they weren't able to figure out that they were being exploited.

He put in ten hours each day, seven days a week, handling a heavy iron heated on a hot stove. The business was headquartered in a one-bedroom apartment of a tenement on Delancey Street, after the name of the man who, two centuries before, had owned half of the area and currently belonged to two German Jews, Jan and Stella Herzowig, who also lived there along with their four children. During the day, the children stayed in the back room, a tight bedroom with just a bed and a closet. But, weather permitting, they sometimes played out in the street or on the roof of the building with other children.

The workshop itself was in the living room—the only one with a window—and was nothing more than a massive sewing machine surrounded by long tables for laying out the fabric. Each morning, the eleven-year old boy brought the pieces of fabric cut out and ready to be sewn, and four women and two men worked tirelessly on them until evening, breathing in the stuffy air full of cigarette smoke and lint.

Mitu thought that, in a way, he was lucky. He ironed in the kitchen, and with the exception of the times when Stella, the owner's pregnant wife, cooked for the workers (in exchange for money, of course), he was all by himself. Being so close to the hot stove was great in February, although the continuous cries of the youngest child left there on a cot irritated him. However, during the infernal heat of summer, he would later learn, the kitchen was the worst place to be, since it boiled like a witch's cauldron.

The first hours on the job didn't seem hard; he had to smooth out the creases on already-made evening gowns or other tailored pieces. The iron weighed a few good pounds, but he didn't mind it and was handling it pretty well for someone doing so for the first time.

By lunch, however, he realized there was no way he could make his quota. He was being paid by the piece, and seeing that he wasn't progressing as he wanted, he ironed all day without a break, and when he finally put the iron down, he felt heavy with fatigue.

"How was it today, Mitu? What did they have you do?" Pistol asked him at night when they came home after their first day of work in America.

"They hired me to iron, and I was up on my feet all day! My knees are killin' me! And I didn't even eat nothin', because I didn't wanna waste any time when I could have made a few extra pennies. How about you? Did they hire you to iron, too?"

"No, they have me help out with everythin'—carryin' things, washin' floors, doin' this'n that! They pay me five dollars a week and I don't work Sundays," Pistol answered, uncertain whether his day off was a good thing or a bad thing.

"Well, I think I make a dollar or two more than you, because they pay me by the piece. This is tough, real tough, and I have to work Sundays too. But look at the money we make now. It would've taken us months and months in Romania to get paid the salaries we get here in a week or two!" he said, content that, only a few weeks after their arrival, he had solved the thorniest problem for any immigrant who spoke no English: finding a job.

"Good for you! You're gonna be a millionaire!" Pistol mocked him, slightly resentful that someone who was fifteen years his junior could earn more than him from the start.

The next months introduced Mitu to the grim reality untold in letters, but common to all immigrants coming to the Promised Land hoping for a better life. Drudging away all day, living in unimaginable filth, stepping on rat droppings in his tenement, getting calluses on his hands for a measly dollar a day with no time to breathe, eating only bread and chain smoking all day, he was now one of the cogs turning the economic machine of a country which, in a little over two decades, had become the biggest industrial power in the world.

The novelty that had kept him afloat in the beginning was slowly vanishing. During the time spent on the Lower East Side, he had become accustomed to the new world, which now seemed ordinary and uninteresting.

He missed his home; the stream of Boțota, the shed and the cattle, Ghiță and Gheorghița, his mother, the village dances and corvees, his _taraf_—oh, how much he missed them and the music they played together! —the tavern, where all the villagers, with whom he had brotherly relationships, came together; fishing trout in the wonderful valley of Gilort, the Novaci market, as poor as it was when compared to the ones here; the beautiful women for whom he longed tremendously.

With the money he made, he realized dejectedly that he couldn't save more than four or five dollars a month. The Lower East Side was expensive. The ice cream parlors—something he'd never seen before—were too tempting. The meat sold from street carts melted in his mouth. The shoes and clothes cost a pretty penny. His money disappeared on all kinds of things: shaving blades, cigarettes, food, cookies...

When he sat down to count his savings and saw how little it was and how much more he needed to pay back his debt, he could only drown his sorrow in a bottle of whiskey bought for a few cents from the liquor store across the street.

"Nothing has changed—just the place. My life used to be just as good back in the village..."

A mouthful of Jack Daniels would make the bitterness, anguish, and somber thoughts magically disappear. In a chatty mood and with the bottle of booze stuffed in his pocket, he'd drag Pistol along on his wanderings, talking and gesturing as if the whole world were his own.

"Oh brother, the things here...I never thought I'd make it to the center of the world! You know what I'd like to have with me? My violin. What was I thinking leaving it at home? What an idiot! I'd give anything to strum the strings of an instrument, but I ain't got the money to buy one."

"It's alright, Mitu, we'll make good money someday. Everything in its good time. You don't expect to sleep all day and get paid for it, do you!"

"The day will come for me when I'll get paid while doing nothing—just livin' the good life! You'll see..."

His excitement never lasted long. As the bottle emptied, his eyes welled up at thoughts of his village. "What am I doing here? What?"

"Oh, if I could only find a better paying job", he kept telling Pistol, "because I just wanna die when I see how much I work and how little I get paid. Why did we leave, if we work ourselves to the bone for nothing? Don't you see we're servants to kulaks?"

Even as he was complaining, he knew he was exaggerating. In reality, he wasn't sure what to think of his situation, as things were both good and bad. Since he had been employed by Herzowig, he'd gotten used to the workshop and become much more productive. He filled his quota before the end of the day and now he did overtime each night, ironing dress after dress and fabric after fabric. On payday, he was quite content that his compensation was greater than the previous time—sometimes by twenty cents, sometimes by a whole dollar—and that was enough to make him happy for a while. That was when he'd become hopeful and started making plans for the future; to save enough and buy an automobile, and later on to rent a place on Orchard Street to open his own store and stop working for others. "I'll make something of myself one day and stop barely scraping by, if not for my sake at least for my Dad's, God rest his soul!"

Actually, without knowing how, Mitu had grown quite gutsy in his new world. Although he had complained to Pistol countless times that Herzowig had hired only Russians in his shop, and because of it he couldn't speak to anyone all day, the new circumstances had been very favorable. His only interlocutors were the owner and his family, so he had to speak the little English he knew—an impossible language, he thought! Word by word, month after month, he now knew enough to put sentences together and even write them, much to Pistol's vexation, who, at thirty-three, was still struggling with the letters of the alphabet.

Mitu realized one day that he understood more than half of what the vendors on the street said, and so boastful and confident he felt, he began considering looking for a better job.

"That's it. I've spent enough time working for this dummy. I need to move on." He mulled over it carefully for a few weeks, but couldn't find a solution in case his plan didn't work out. By quitting, he could be without a job for a while and even be thrown out on the street after depleting his savings. By remaining at Herzowig, who worked him all day except for the few minutes for lunch, he didn't even have a chance to find something better.

At last, his desire to change became greater than his fear. He calculated that his savings could last him for at least three months—a period of time in which it would have been impossible not to find a better job—and he decided to tell his boss he was leaving.

It was a warm day at the end of June when Mitu arrived at the workshop earlier than usual, thinking to take Herzowig aside and have the discussion with him, then wander the streets for the rest of the day. When he entered the shop and glanced at the sewing machine to which his boss seemed nailed most of the time, he didn't see him there. One of the Russian seamstresses smiled and put her finger on her lips.

"*Posmotri v spalne...*" she whispered.

He knocked, then opened the door to the bedroom. Herzowig and an unknown woman soaking some rags in a wash bin were tending to his wife as she lay in bed, and an unknown woman. He watched them confused, but then realized, "she's about to give birth..."

He closed the door behind him and went back to his spot in the kitchen. His plans of leaving the shop that day had gone to hell. How was he going to tell Herzowig he was leaving when the man was about to have a kid?

He grabbed the iron and started working on his quota, stacking fabrics and listening to the groans coming from the bedroom, and suddenly his heart filled with pity.

"This cheat boss of mine can't be that cheap to have his wife give birth at home without a doctor." Then he thought that taking her to a hospital must have been so costly, that not even Herzowig, a business owner, could afford it. "After all we're not so different, me and him."

They heard the cry of the newborn baby in a few hours, and all of them clapped and shouted congratulations.

"*Dolgoy zhizni tvoyemu malishu! Pust budet schastliv! Hrani yego Gospodi! Să vă trăiască!*"

Herzowig came out a few minutes later and gave them a tired look.

"Thank you! Thank you very much! It's a boy. I wanted to have a boy so much, God heard my prayers this time as well!" he said agitated, rocking from one foot to the other. Then he stopped talking, as though remembering something unpleasant, sat down at his machine and started sewing, engrossed in his work in an evident attempt to make up for the few hours he hadn't produced anything.

Mitu waited until the end of the day to tell him what he wanted to say in the morning. After everyone left in the evening, he mustered up his courage and told him he wanted to find a better job. Herzowig seemed dismissive for a few seconds, pretending he didn't understand anything, but quickly analyzed the situation in his head. Workers on the Lower East Side seldom quit because, although numerous, the jobs were the same everywhere. Mitu, this young and handsome Romanian whom he'd hired at first because he had been in a hurry and had no other choices, had proven to be one of the hardest working employees he had ever had. The idea of losing him so unexpectedly, especially now that he had another mouth to feed, was unacceptable.

"Well lad, you can't be serious! You can't leave now, don't you see my situation? Where am I gonna find another employee like you? I'd need to teach 'em the trade, and I don't have the time right now," he said unctuously, hoping to change his mind, as if the power had miraculously shifted to Mitu's side.

Mitu squirmed, not knowing how to answer, but then continued.

"Sir, no food money. Can't make saving. Want leave visit family this year. And pay debt. Please. Need find better money!"

Herzowig pretended to be stunned for a second, though this had happened countless times. Then he put on the pitiful face of a man betrayed by his best friend. After a long while, he took a deep breath and gave Mitu a scolding look.

"I'll never forgive you for blackmailing me in time of need. Never! May God pay you back with the same coin. But, because I can't afford to lose you now, I'm asking you to stay, and from the little that I have—because I hope you realized my family doesn't live in luxury—I will increase your salary. Yes, you heard well: I'll increase your pay! From now on, I'm giving you a dollar and seventy-five cents a day. That's if you fill your quota, of course..."

Mitu almost choked with joy and barely contained himself from shouting "Yes!" right then and there, wanting nothing less but to hug his boss. He had thought that Herzowig might increase his pay if cornered, but couldn't believe that it was going to be almost double. With a spark of a true negotiator in him, he stretched out his hand.

"I stay if one day free a week..."

Herzowig scratched his head, considering all angles of the situation, then smiled.

"Man, you drive a hard bargain, but I just had my boy today and I am very happy. Because I want you to see just how big my heart is, I'll give you a day off a week. But better be careful now—don't start slacking off!"

Mitu left ecstatic, not thinking for a second that his boss, whom he now thought he'd judged too harshly sometimes, hadn't done anything more than finally leveling his pay to the market.

OLGA

Chapter 15

The first clear, warm Sunday Mitu had to himself without work or worries was a day he would forever remember, since it was the day he met Olga. It had been six months since his arrival in America—time spent working morning till evening in Herzowig's shop.

The humid heat of June had finally dissipated that afternoon. The first thing he did was visit the public baths across the street. It had been a while since he had gotten a long, steamy soak. Bathing was impossible in the tenement, and the public bathrooms closed long before he left work. So for the last few months, he had been washing himself the best he could at a well in the yard.

He spent a long time in the tub, splashing around like a child and singing at the top of his lungs; he had always loved the sound of his voice in big, empty halls. At last, he went back to the tenement, put on his best suit for the second or third time since coming to America, placed three dollars in his pocket, and went for a stroll. His destination for the day was a movie theater.

There were plenty of cinemas on the Lower East Side. At each corner, a tight, dirty room with just a few seats projected silent movies all day long. He wandered up and down the streets, looking at the posters, unable to decide which movie to see; it did cost ten cents after all, and he wanted to spend the money wisely.

His eyes fell on a yellowish and red announcement which reminded him of his trip over the ocean:

*Saved from the Titanic, Eclair's World Sensation. Miss Dorothy Gibson, a survivor of the world's greatest disaster, tells the story of the shipwreck, supported by an all-star cast on the film marvel of the age.*5F[*]

"This is the one I'm gonna see," he said, especially interested after reading that the movie was accompanied by an orchestra.

He stepped timidly inside—his first time in a theater—and sat on a chair feeling somewhat awkward. The first ten minutes of the movie made him re-live Miu Pavelescu's story about the sinking of the Norge, and he thanked God that until then, he had been luckier than the thousands of people who found their early demise on the ship. He was extremely impressed that the main actress had been on the Titanic, and having survived the catastrophe, she now made a movie about it, even wearing the same clothes she had on during the wreck.

A girl about his age sat down next to him and also seemed engrossed in the story on the screen. He threw a sly glance her way, and she replied with an imperceptible smile. "This boy looks like William Russell!" she thought.

"Film impressive!" he finally broke the ice with his awkward command of English, "I have friend who is on ship like Titanic, sink in 1904. Norge."

---

[*] The film, a veritable masterpiece, was forever lost during a fire at Éclair Studios in 1914, which destroyed all of its copies.

The girl seemed taken aback and looked at him with interest.

"Did you say the Norge? You had a friend who died on the Norge? I remember, of course! I was little then, but what a sensation it made! I'm from Sweden, and the ship was Danish, so the disaster was on the front page of the local newspapers for many days. I'm sorry to hear about your friend; it must have been terrible!"

"Yes..." mumbled Mitu, not understanding much.

"I came here mostly for Dorothy Gibson," she continued. "Not for the movie itself, but to see her act. I am an actress also, but not like her; she's big—huge—you can find her on every poster in this country," she smiled, embarrassed to have made the comparison.

Mitu, who had never seen an actress in his life, amateur or otherwise, didn't bother to tell her that Miu hadn't died on the Norge, but a few years after the tragedy, on the same transatlantic he had come to America on as well.

"Me... Mitu, I come here half a year from Romania," he introduced himself.

"Meetoo, Meetoo..." the girl repeated playfully to get used to the pronunciation. "It's nice to meet you, my name is Olga Gertrude," she said stretching out her hand. "So what do you do around here?"

"What can I do, at beginning...work in tailor shop."

"Yes, I know how beginnings are," she sighed. "And don't think things will get better fast, unfortunately. I've been here for a few years, and I'm still struggling to find my place. Today I'm out to see a few movies, to learn from some real pros. I've seen some a few times already. Do you want to come with me to *Dr. Jekyll and Mr. Hyde*? I saw it last year with James Cruze—handsome actor. But this year it's a new version with King Baggot, in which Dr. Jekyll almost discovers a remedy, and everybody says the transformation into Mr. Hyde is so thorough, it looks almost real!"

Mitu understood only that she had invited him to another movie. They left together to a theatre across the street, where there was a line of people waiting.

He savored the horror movie with unblinking curiosity, afraid he might miss a small detail from the story unfolding life-like before his eyes. When it ended, he kept staring at the blank white cloth.

"I see you liked it," Olga watched him from the corner of her eye.

"This second movie I see," he confessed.

"Really?" said the girl, who couldn't conceive of life without film. "You've only seen two movies so far?" she burst into laughter.

Clearly embarrassed, Mitu tried hard not to blush. He moved uncomfortably in his chair and thought about an answer, but Olga went ahead.

"Listen, I work for a theatre on Coney Island. Come to see me when you have time, and if it happens that I'm on break, we can go catch another movie together. Come see me next Sunday before lunch!" she winked playfully at him.

She wrote the address on a little note—Honey Pie Theatre in Luna Park—and set towards the subway. He followed her with his eyes until she disappeared around the corner, then wondered whether what just happened had been real.

He returned to the tenement walking slowly—it was evening time and he had to be up at five the following morning—unable to take his mind off her and movies. Once in his room, he rushed to tell Pistol about it.

"Listen, I struck gold today! I went to a movie and I met a blonde girl—a beauty—a Swedish artist, and we went to another movie together, and she told me to visit her next Sunday at the theatre where she works on Coney Island!"

Pistol gave him an incredulous look, bursting into laughter.

"I see, you met a Swedish actress who invited you on another date. How did she propose it to you...in Swedish?"

"Oh man, why do I even bother. Alright, just leave me alone. I shouldn't have told you anything! We'll see next Sunday, when I go to the movies with her, and you're left to your lovely self."

Pistol nodded in a been-there-done-that kind of way, looking at Mitu as if he were his younger, more naïve brother.

It was a very long week for Mitu. He kept looking at the clock each day, much to his boss's dismay; by midweek, he gave Mitu askance looks as if to say he had better mind his work if he didn't want to be fired.

He was no longer a nobody! He, an uneducated peasant from Cernădia who could barely speak two words of English, was well liked by a beautiful girl! A Swedish girl! An actress!

He didn't wait for Sunday to come but went to Coney Island on Saturday night after work, thinking to walk around until the next day. He had heard that one could not find a more splendid place on the face of Earth.

And indeed, the City of Fire, as Coney Island was also known, blew him away. As amazing and dizzying as Manhattan was, it now appeared drab and monotonous compared to this place. Thousands of people bustled around, rich and poor, young and old, women and men—all mixing in a collective frenzy and spending hours engaged in all types of amusing things the human mind could invent. He couldn't believe his eyes; everything had been built at a scale that went beyond the notion of grandiose. Hundreds of thousands of tiny bulbs shone brightly, lighting towers hundreds of feet tall, making them visible from tens of miles away. Fun rides and carousels, elephant-shaped hotels, mechanical pony rides, theaters featuring dwarves, exhibitions with limbless or headless people, bearded women or men covered by fish scales; elephants sliding down waterslides, reenactments of famous fights, controlled fires with sensational rescues of victims a few times a day; electrocutions of elephants, African tribes or Eskimo exhibitions, dancing and music everywhere, cabarets and hundreds of movies playing day and night; gambling, prostitution and many more—all within his reach, only a few pennies away...

Italian gondolas glided through Venetian channels, trains went up and down the Swiss Alps, where an icy cold wind bit the travelers' faces in the midst of summer. The air reverberated with happiness, frenzy, passion, energy, enthusiasm, and eroticism. It was a place where young people embraced and kissed in public, and decent and puritanical housewives gave up their inhibitions, throwing caution to wind, lifting up their skirts and showing their underpants.

The crowd seemed high on the very air they breathed, on the contagious madness of those visiting the place day and night.

He suddenly remembered Olga and started inquiring left and right about the small theater, but no one could tell him where it was. After three hours of searching, swimming through the crowd as if tracking through thick mud, he finally found it—a small theater featuring period pieces.

He paid five cents for the ticket and went inside.

He saw her immediately, dressed in a long shiny gown, she played the role of a French princess. He sat down, drinking her with his eyes. He flinched each time she turned her head in his direction. "Did she see me?" he wondered. He had no idea that from the brightly lit stage, the actors could only barely discern the silhouette of the audience.

The play lasted no more than fifteen minutes, and he didn't understand much of it anyway, having had eyes only for her. He applauded frantically at the end and tried to wave at her, but the curtain had fallen already. He went to a doorman and told him he wanted to see Olga Gertrude.

"The audience is not allowed backstage under any circumstance, sir."

His disappointment was so visible, the man felt sorry for him.

"You can write a note, and I'll give it to her personally. If she wants to see you, she'll come outside in a few minutes. Wait in front of the theater. That's all I can do for you, sir."

He wrote a note in a hurry, "Dear Olga, is me go Sunday Dr. Jekyll and Mr. Hyde, come see you, I am outside."

"Thank you very much!"

After waiting outside for half an hour, Mitu resigned himself. "Women will be women!" he thought annoyed, then looked at the door one more time, turning around to go towards the park's exit.

The doorman gave him an understanding look.

"I'm sorry! Try again later or maybe tomorrow!"

He shrugged, but, when he turned around, he saw Olga right in front of him, watching him with a wink in her eye. She had been there for a few minutes now; she had exited the building through the back and went around it, hiding and thinking to play a trick on Mitu.

"Olga!" he barely managed, "How are you?"

"I'm so happy you came! Do you want to walk around a bit? I have a few free hours; we can watch some movies and then eat something. I'm sorry you can't come tomorrow, the way I told you, I'd have had more time then. But maybe you come tomorrow as well. What do you say?"

They entered a theater, but hard as he tried, Mitu could not follow the story on the screen.

"Pfftt, man, I fell for the Swedish girl! I fell in love! So quick?" the thought flashed through his head as he cast languid gazes her way.

She put her finger to her lips as though to say, "Behave!" motioning him to look at the screen. It was a love story, a short reel about ten or twelve minutes long about a boy who came to America from Italy and fell in love with the daughter of some New York aristocrats.

After the movie, they went back into the middle of the Electric Eden (another name for Coney Island), and the sensuality in the air encompassed them as well. They walked hand-in-hand through the crowd until they found themselves alone on the beach.

It was a full moon. Music wafted through the air from Luna Park. Foamy waves crashed against the shore, ships lit like Christmas trees decorated the horizon and seagulls slept shriveled up on the sand.

He told her about his village, showed her a picture of him playing the violin and hummed a song for her—the most beautiful one he knew. She watched him amused, smiling at his efforts to speak English.

They listened to the waves for a while, then went back to Honey Pie. When they parted ways, Olga touched her lips with her finger, then his.

"We'll see each other next week. Go home now, it's already three o'clock in the morning. Don't come tomorrow. Come back next Sunday at ten. At ten, yes?" she said, opening the door.

Chapter 16

Although still a child, Olga could easily read a person. It didn't take long for her to realize that this jovial and feisty young man who had serenaded her on the beach and shown her a picture of his *taraf*, missed his music and hadn't had many opportunities for it in his first year in America.

The week after their first date, she learned through her relations in the theater how to procure two tickets for the Metropolitan Opera on the Sunday of their second date. Not easy, since Enrico Caruso himself was performing.

One of the people she asked for help was a certain Mr. Steinovich. A rather unctuous, sly, and lecherous Jewish man connected to the cinema's powerbrokers, with a manipulative flair and a weakness for young and aspiring actresses, he was always ready for all kinds of empty promises and perfidious pressures to get into their beds.

She knew him all too well, so she felt ambivalent towards him. On one hand, she kept in touch to maintain his interest in her—or "hot for her," as she used to like saying—for potential help in the future, but on the other hand, she was afraid that this might lead her onto a path she did not yet want to take.

She had met him at one of the parties she randomly attended, and Steinovich profited of the occasion to drop names of this and that producer, his "best friends," the likes of Charles Frohman or the Schubert Brothers, letting her know indirectly that her Coney Island starving artist status could change for the better with a bit of effort or sacrifice on both their parts.

"This life, sweetheart, is a *quid pro quo*, if you get what I mean...Each person has his or her own agenda, many times hidden. The best business, dear, is the one where both partners have to gain, right? After all, what are a few small compromises in the great scheme of things? I think you see what I mean, because you seem quite urbane and open minded."

He amused her in the beginning, his antics confirming that men were capable of anything to get into a woman's bed, and later she put him out of her mind completely. She saw him a few times afterwards, either at various parties or at the theater on Coney Island, where he came to see the owner with mysterious business dealings. He always greeted her ostentatiously, and she wondered from where he still had the energy to pay attention to her, having heard some gossip that he had a multitude of mistresses. Her female friends from the entertainment world had told her that his approach was quite simple and to the point: sex for contacts. One of them, who had graduated from a small theater like hers directly onto Broadway overnight, had confessed that this upward motion had cost her a bit of coquettishness and a night spent in his bed.

"It wasn't even all that unpleasant, I tell you. He's a good lover, and he's not that bad looking either."

Every now and then, she had approached him for a few small things; some information about a show in New York, some name from the movie world, but she had never asked for something warranting a *quid pro quo*.

When she went to him for the two tickets to the Metropolitan House Opera, he winked allusively.

"Lucky man who goes with you," he said and gallantly offered his help. "Dear miss, my biggest pleasure is to give you my assistance whenever you need it! Don't hesitate to ask for it! For whatever you need."

The next day, he sent her the two tickets along with a big bouquet of red roses and a note on which he scribbled in ink, "Can't wait to see you soon."

That Sunday, Mitu had no clue of the fantastic surprise the wonderful girl he had met only two weeks before had prepared for him. He arrived at Coney Island early, thinking they might spend a few hours on the rides and then walk on the beach; it was a splendid day with clear skies. In the evening he was planning to go to a few shows or movies.

At quarter to ten, he was in front of the theater anxiously waiting and rehearsing English greetings in his head. At ten on the dot, as he was checking his watch, Olga came out.

"Well, well, the Romanian came such a long way through Manhattan for me. That's very nice of you..."

Mitu thought that for a beauty such as hers, he'd go to the end of the world. Olga was one of those women who ignited burning desire in men to have her once and then die...

"I have a surprise for you, but we need to go back to the City for it. Let's walk around here for a bit and then we'll go to Manhattan."

This was the first time a woman did something for him; until then he was the one chasing them like a madman in Cernădia. He let her drag him here and there to street shows, endless orchestra performances, magic shows and the like.

They stopped for an ice cream and to rest; walking through the crowd was very tiresome. She told him it was time to go because they had to be in the City before five in the afternoon.

He nodded, intrigued but happy, and they climbed into a horse car to cross Brooklyn.

"Where you take me?" he asked her, feigning curiosity. Truth be told, he didn't really care as long as they were together.

She smiled, pursing her lips and touching them with her finger. "Just wait and see," she said delicately, and he melted like an ice cube forgotten in the sun.

He had never been so entranced by a girl—he couldn't even take his eyes off her. She had him wrapped around her little finger. Each time she looked away, he measured her with his eyes, mesmerized by her blonde curls and her lithe silhouette. What a beauty! He stared at her so insistently a few times while they were crossing the Brooklyn Bridge. She noticed him and looked at him slightly embarrassed.

"What is it?"

He flinched as though awakened from a dream, and she smiled furtively, pretending to be preoccupied by something else. It was clear that this Romanian boy, who had accosted her so cheekily that first time at the movies with that adorable English of his, was crazy about her! It wasn't the first time she had won a man's heart, but it most certainly was one of the few times she fell for the one whose heart she had subjugated.

They arrived in Manhattan and took a trolley to First Avenue. They got off at 34th Street and walked up Broadway to 39th Street.

"Finally!" she exclaimed.

He stopped and looked around suspiciously. People were going in and out of stores, vendors were selling food and lemonade from carts on the street, bright advertisements filled shop windows. "Did we come all this way just to eat in a restaurant?" he wondered.

"Where?" he asked confused.

"Where I wanted to bring you." She smiled slyly. "My business!"

"What's so great around here? I saw this part of the city many times," he said to himself, but didn't ask anything else.

She grabbed him by the arm and led him to the Metropolitan House Opera, which was on the corner; a massive stone building, six stories tall, a veritable royal palace with big windows and a sumptuous entrance. He had passed many times but never dared to look inside.

"Here, this is where we're going. I have tickets for Enrico Caruso with Toscanini."

He looked at her incredulously. Toscanini was one of the most renowned orchestra conductors in the world, and even Mitu, who didn't know much about classical music, had heard of him. Caruso was a titan—greater than life; a tenor with a voice so rich and encompassing, powerful and full, it seemingly descended from heaven. Listening to him sing opera or Italian canzonets on the gramophone, he had felt an infinite admiration and a deep sadness at the musical gap between them.

"Olga..." he was at a loss for words, "not know how thank you!"

"It's enough that you're here with me and that you like it," she whispered. "We still have some time before it starts; let's go eat something out here, because everything is really expensive inside."

They went into a warm, cozy restaurant—Joe's Diner, an oasis of peace amidst the uproar on the streets in Midtown, and stayed there for an hour. She told him about her life until then. Her mother had died of consumption when she was six. She had never met her father and didn't even have a picture of him. After her mother's death, she was raised by an aunt and an uncle who immigrated to America when she was eleven. She went to an all-girl school in Brooklyn where she starred in a few school plays, and at fifteen, she began making some money playing in small productions on Coney Island, not too far from the building where they lived. Her uncle became very ill—something wrong with his head, the doctors said—when she was sixteen. Almost infirm, he decided to go back to Sweden. Despite their insisting, Olga didn't want to follow them there, hoping her career choice might lead her to Broadway or even to the big screen. Since then, she had been living on Coney Island in a tiny room in the Honey Pie Theater building. She made little money—not enough to afford an apartment in the City, but life was beautiful here; she met lots of people, she was invited to many soirees and parties, and she even met a few of New York's aristocracy, who sometimes helped her with small favors.

"A good friend of mine, very high up, gave me these tickets, for example. Mister Steinovich; I couldn't have managed it without him."

As he listened to her talking, Mitu's heart filled with sympathy. He wouldn't have imagined that Olga was an orphan. Though radiant, admired by audiences, courted by men, invited to places he wouldn't dream of, she had had a more difficult life than his.

It was his turn. His story was much shorter, since he had language difficulties, but she understood that he lost his father when he was a child, that he came from a poor family in a small village at the foot of a very tall mountain in Romania— "I would really like to see it one day..." she whispered wistfully—and that he had left to make money.

"And do you want to go back there someday?" she asked when he finished, touched that Mitu had crossed the border illegally at such a young age. "That's courage, right there!" she thought.

"I don't know...I think my country a lot, but want make money here."

Time went by quickly. They had to go to the show. Olga grabbed his arm, and he stepped into the opera house as if it were a church, marveling at its lavishness—the gold sculptures, the audience's impeccable clothes, the splendid paintings on the walls, the grandness of the concert hall. He became immersed in the music, forgetting about himself, the girl next to him, or the very place he was. Caruso was divine! A voice from God—indescribable with words!

He needed time to recover after the show; Olga pulled his sleeve a few times to bring him back to reality.

"You saw?" he said filled with emotion. "If he has a glass in front him, he break with voice! How he sing so loud?"

"I'm glad you liked it!" Olga kissed him briefly on the lips—so briefly he didn't have time to reciprocate.

Chapter 17

The love story between Mitu and Olga intensified as their bodies and souls became more and more acquainted to each other. It had been three months since their first date—time during which they saw each other regularly, like clockwork: each Sunday at ten o'clock, he would wait for her in front of Honey Pie, sharply dressed and with a flower in his hand, and she would come out smiling and punctual, taking his arm for a walk.

The stone melting heat and humidity of the Manhattan summer was over, and September had slipped in sneakily. It was a beautiful autumn, with warm days and clear skies enticing strolls along the rivers and over the Brooklyn Bridge, hand-in-hand walks through Central Park, on Madison Avenue, or the narrow, picturesque, cobblestone streets of Little Italy. He went to see Olga perform and always sat with a rapt expression in the front row, overwhelmed by the happiness and astonishment that this blonde goddess had descended from Heaven solely to be his.

For the first time since coming to America he felt like a true winner. His bread-winning work, once monotous and difficult, no longer irritated nor harshened him, but played a secondary role completely devoid of importance. His days slipped away swiftly, as though he were on drugs. He lived for the weekends, simply getting by the rest of the week. In a trance-like state, he ironed fabrics and went about his daily work, completely removed from Herzowig, the Lower East Side, the hustle and bustle of the streets, and the musty tenement in which he lived.

He was in love.

Olga was the first woman in his life he didn't dominate, he couldn't play her as he had Ana or others before her. And as much as he tried to keep her close, he could lose her at any time. That imperceptible but acute uncertainty filled his soul, unsettled him, and made her all the more desirable.

His other lovers had fallen in love not with Mitu the man, with all his faults or weakness, but with Mitu the musician—with his image and his talent. They were part of that category of women who fall for a man's status, not his being. And once they get to know him better, their feelings cool off rapidly.

Olga was different. He had been atracted to her viscerally, instinctually, and instantly, although he felt his status was inferior to hers. Their love was pure—sincere; they had one of those relationships meant to last, especially because it wasn't based on financial considerations.

During all those months, Mitu had become a different man. In his plans for the future, he now included Olga. And, to his happiness, she seemed to be doing the same. Although they didn't live together, they had become the two sides of the same coin. She had taught Mitu how to dance dixieland, tap, tango, and waltz, and how to analyze movies from a certain perspective. She initiated him in social graces just as she had learned from others in the theater world. They had become very close; they didn't need words anymore—a look, a wince, a raised brow, and one knew what the other meant.

Lately, with Herzowig's raise, Mitu had managed to put some money aside. He was particularly happy to see that he was now well on his way to gathering the money to pay his debt in Cernădia. Besides the few fun activities on Sunday, he only spent what was necessary for food. The tenement rent didn't seem as exhorbitant as it had in the beginning.

Since he had been able to save a little, he kept having one recurring thought: he wanted to visit Romania. He quickly dismissed the idea at first. "Am I nuts to spend all my money on such a trip?" but then he became obsessed, "What's at home? How's Ghiță? Is Gheorghița taking care of Ma?"

Meanwhile, Pistol couldn't care less. When Mitu told him he wanted to go back to Romania, he looked at him as if he were crazy.

"You mean to tell me you worked so hard, and now you wanna spend all your money? To see what? Didn't you live there all your life? It hasn't even been a year since we left. Better stay here and save some money for rainy days, because you never know what tomorrow brings."

"Well, what do we work for anyway? Not for a better living? What's the point of saving if you can't use it?"

"But not like that, wasting it all away, lad. Not to mention Nistor hasn't forgotten you. Wait for more time to pass."

"I don't know, Pistol, but I'm going back there soon. Don't you wanna come with me?"

"How many times you want me to tell you I don't wanna waste my money on that? And if you miss Bercești so, why don't you take your 'gurlfrend' with you for company? Or you mean to say you didn't think about that?"

He had thought about it, and not just once. How could he not? How would it be for them to go together; to walk the narrow roads of Bercești hand-in-hand, maybe in an automobile, with everyone staring; to introduce her to his mother; to take her to a *hora*; to walk through the Gilort valley or climb up to Rânca; to play music for her with his old *taraf*.

Still, the thought of taking Olga to his home unsettled him. "What's she gonna think when she sees the poverty of Cernădia? The shabby and dilapidated wood houses, the small rooms shared by three or four people, the lack of toilets, running water, or electricity. Peeling walls, bare to the foundation, knee-high mud on the country-lanes, oxen-driven carriages..."

Olga found out about it by chance from Pistol. They were back from a Broadway show one Sunday afternoon and had passed by the tenement to take him to a café on Bowery for a hot chocolate. Talking about this and that for an hour, Pistol let it slip.

"Know, princess, you boyfriend nice but shy. Wants go Romania and don't know how tell you..."

"Yeah?" she laughed amused by his thick accent and turned to Mitu. "Is that right, honey?"

Mitu frowned. "What an idiot!" he thought.

"Well, he's not right..." he tried to dodge it. "I was thinking go Romania with him next year, but me not serious. And, he don't want come. Say vacation too soon."

Olga's face lit up.

"Well then, you've got it in your head to leave me and go back to your lovers there, waiting for their prince..." she kissed him quickly on the lips then turned to Pistol and winked at him. "See? See what he's doing to me?"

Mitu smiled uncomfortably, but she was ahead of him.

"So? Are you gonna take me with you if you go or you're gonna leave me here for others? I promise not to be in your way if you have something going on with a woman there..." she instigated him with that ever-charming style of hers, which always melted him, leaving him powerless.

"Know Olga, he shame take you because life there not like here... much poor..." Pistol intervened, understanding Mitu as if he were his brother.

Olga was surprised.

"Is it true? Are you embarrased to take me because of poverty? I hope you're not serious!"

Mitu's silence spoke volumes.

"You know, my life wasn't all that great in Sweden either. I don't think there is anything in this world that can impress or bother me."

From that moment on, Mitu's fear was gone. Since Olga wanted to go with him, he started planning for the trip. The biggest problem was leaving his job at Herzowig for a whole month, but to still have it when he came back. It was a no brainer that Herzowig wasn't going to take him back. He could find a cheaper replacement right away. How could he leave his job after fighting for it so? What if he wasn't going find something to do when he came back?

He considered the situation for a few more weeks and then decided that nothing was going to stop him; whatever might have been, the next spring, he was going to take a whole month off. After all, he knew enough English to find another job if it came to that. Moreover, there were still six more months until spring—plenty of time. And he could maybe convince Herzowig to keep his job and just have someone to fill in for him in the interim.

Olga, unlike him, did not have these problems, and watched him sometimes amused, sometimes suffused with pity at his tribulations. By comparison, she felt lucky. She had some money put aside, so she had enough for such a trip. She could come and leave Honey Pie as she liked. There were many actresses just like her, and the absence of one didn't affect the business, since the girls could easily substitute for one another. And if she were to be fired, she knew enough Steinoviches to help her out.

"I can't wait to see your native places," she told him once, after his retelling the story of his trip to America.

During the winter months, the details of their trip became more precise. They decided to go to Romania at the end of May and stay there for four or five weeks—enough time for her to become acquainted with his family.

They were going to take a liner to Le Havre, then a train to Paris where they wanted to stay for three or four days. For a while, they couldn't agree on how they were going to travel from Paris to Romania. Mitu wanted to repeat the itinerary which had taken him to the Promised Land: a sleeping car on the Orient Express to Budapest and a local train to Târgu-Jiu from there. Olga, with a more developed sense for adventure, didn't want a sleeping car, but local trains in each country to stop and spend some time in the big cities.

They finally decided on a compromise; they would take the Orient Express, but they would spend a night in the biggest cities along its route— Strasbourg, Munich, Vienna—and they weren't going to get off in Budapest, but go all the way to Bucharest, spend at least two days there, and then rent a car and drive to Oltenia.

Chapter 18

Dear Ma,
I hope this letter finds you well and in good health. I am doing very well.
May God keep it this way for me; I earn my bread and I'm seeing a beautiful
girl. I've met her here in New York. She's an actress and she's from Sweden!
Her name is Olga. Tell the Curlies about it too! I'm very happy! We've been
together for a few great months. She works for a theater on Coney Island,
which is a big amusement park with all kinds of tricks, fire-eating people,
movie theaters, circuses, waterslides (where you fall from the toboggan
directly into the water). I went down one of these slides once, and when I
landed, I almost lost my underwear! It fell down to my knees! I was so
embarrassed! Some women looked at me and I think they saw my bare ass
because I saw them laughing behind my back!
At my job at Herzowig, (I told you about him in the other letter), I started
making a bit more money! And I put a little aside and now I'm thinking to
come to Romania next spring when it gets a little warmer. I'll be coming with
Olga! Make sure you prepare the house nice, so we don't embarrass
ourselves in front of her!
I miss you and Cernădia very much and I can't wait to see you all! Send
greetings to everybody!

Your son, Mitu

Mitu wrote the letter not long before leaving for Romania; his life was more promising than ever. Less than a year and a half after his arrival in America, he had obtained things of which he didn't dare dream of in Cernădia. During the last months he had accumulated more money than he had saved in Romania for years. He had obtained a driver's license so he could rent an automobile in Bucharest. His relationship with Olga was a dream; he still couldn't get used to the idea they were together, and he kept relishing the almost unbearable happiness one feels at the beginning of an unlikely love story.

He was going on the trip untroubled by the prospect that he might not have a job upon his return to America; he had asked Herzowig about it, and to his surprise, the man didn't even flinch.

"When you come back, you come straight here back to your job—it's settled."

In the spring of 1914, when Mitu boarded a transatlantic ship for Le Havre with Olga on his arm, still marveling at the stunning skyline of Manhattan after all that time, breathing the uniquely scented air whose fragrance was still new and dear to him, he didn't know it was the very first and last time he would travel over the ocean with someone he loved.

Everything sparked around them, from the crisp, white linens of the tables in the ship's restaurant to the crystal glassware. Chandeliers opulently lit the majestic ballrooms where they went dancing every night. Their cabin was small but cozy and spotlessly clean. They had a big, comfortable bed covered with a burgundy spread and lavish pillows. On the side wall, a large mirror gave the illusion that the room was double its size. When Mitu saw it, he became nearly breathless with emotion and desire to embrace Olga and lay her on the bed. Their lovemaking had been intermittent until then—either in his tenement, when he happened to be home alone, or in her tiny room at Honey Pie, always in a hurry and always with caution because of thin walls.

On each of the six days of the trip, they walked on the deck, admiring the seamless horizon, dining leisurely in the restaurant, and spending time in their room behind locked doors.

They were furiously and insatiably attracted to each other, their corporal needs satisfied only when they finally lay exhausted in each other's arms. They were a perfect erotic fit in a way most can only dream about—a type of satisfaction unparalleled by anything else in the world, for which people are capable of making insane sacrifices.

Mitu was under Olga's spell; her every move clouded his mind. Her sighs of pleasure as his lips touched her breasts, her deep moans and imperceptible smile when he looked her in the eyes and slowly went inside her haunted him for hours afterwards. The intense explosion at the end—blinding as lighting—always made him lose consciousness for a few moments. Her body's spasms as she approached climax, her seeing him as the father of her future children, her clenching to his body as though trying to meld into one person drove him insane.

After the terrible beginning in America, when he had barely made it, hungry and estranged, without hope for the better, Olga's surprising appearance in his life had been a veritable launching pad to Paradise.

They arrived at Le Havre and debarked, saddened they had to leave the comfort of the ship behind. They went to Rouen, where they walked hand-in-hand through the center of the city, admiring the unusual houses painted in black and white, which reminded Mitu of the traditional costumes people wore in Novaci; then, they went to Paris, stopping along the way in the small villages strewn along the Seine to eat all kinds of sweets from the *chocolateries*.

Paris surrounded them with a sweet, warm air conducive to love. They traipsed through Trocadéro until they couldn't walk anymore, then set out for Germany, traveling many nights in the sleeping car and spending a few nights in cozy, peaceful inns. They stayed in Munich for a day and visited the Glyptothek, then sat on a bench in Königsplatz for the rest of the time.

Vienna captured their hearts instantly with its aristocratic and serene atmosphere of classical music. They spent half a day walking leisurely through the greenery and lying on the grass of Stadtpark, and towards the evening, Olga took him to the Court Opera—a building so stately and splendid that the Metropolitan Opera seemed downright modest—for a Mozart concert.

The next morning, they took the train to Budapest. They were slowly approaching Romania.

"You'll see that Romania isn't developed like the countries we've seen, but the people are good," he'd warn her, preoccupied by what her impression of his native places would be.

On a wet spring afternoon, when they arrived in Bucharest, which he'd never seen before, his worries dissipated like smoke into thin air. They instantly fell in love with Little Paris; with Calea Victoriei as busy and alive as the Champs Élysées or Fifth Avenue, the elegance and refinement of the women's attire, the agglomeration on the main roads; the city gave them the same warm sensation they had felt while moseying down Madison Avenue or 42nd Street in Manhattan.

They wandered down winding streets for hours, entered all the stores found on their way, visited the art galleries in Pasagiul English, and relished the sweets of pastry shops on Lipscani Street. They bought all sorts of things from Lumea Elegantă; Mitu bought himself a pair of leather shoes and Olga a pair of boots. From a store with household items they bought gifts for the folks in Cernădia. On Calea Victoriei, right next to Majestic Hotel, Mitu found a store with musical instruments called "Jean Feder," and went inside giddy like a child in a candy store. He tried out all the instruments and bought himself a violin—very well made, he thought, and a lot cheaper than the ones he had seen in New York.

In another store, Olga saw something that grabbed her attention in an unusual way. It was a striped, two-piece outfit for a toddler boy of four or five, which she turned every which way.

"Do you like this?" she asked him cheerfully. "It looks like a sailor's suit!"

Mitu watched her amused.

"What's this all about? I... like it, sure...Yes..." he hesitated. Until then, he had never paid attention to a piece of clothing like that, and he now looked at it as though it were an object from another world. "It's nice..."

Olga turned the outfit inside and then out again, then put it aside to see it from farther away.

"It's really beautiful! I haven't seen anything like it in New York! What do you say, do we take it?"

"What for?" he asked. "Who for?"

"Just for the future. We'll leave it here. If we ever have a boy and bring him here, he should have some nice clothes at his grandparents' house. What do you think?"

Mitu shrugged, "Okay...if you want this..."

She paid for it and asked the salesperson to wrap it well in a piece of paper. "I wouldn't want to stain it, sir..."

The day of their departure to Oltenia, they rented a Ford T, and Mitu struggled for a few hours trying to refamiliarize himself with all the maneuvers. He had almost forgotten how to drive, having done it only when he earned his driver's license in New York.

As they were about to leave, he placed a small American flag on the hood of the car— "to show where we're coming from!"—and suddenly, a strange sadness flooded his heart.

"Would you look at that; I can now afford something like this..." he thought gloomily, remembering the questions about automobiles he had asked his father a long time ago.

Chapter 19

"The Fiddler came from America!" the news traveled lightning fast as he drove triumphantly on the dusty roads of Cernădia. Mitu had entered the village honking his horn, jokingly reprimanding this and that person for not recognizing him as he zoomed by them like a bolt.

"Gotten old so bad you don't remember me, or what's with you? Sleeping with your eyes open are you?"

When he reached the center of the village, people gathered fast around him. A few who happened to be there were staring at the wonder on rubber wheels, while others came quickly from the tavern to see what the commotion was about.

"Well, how are you, little Mitu? Came from over the ocean? How you changed! What a do! Your hair is long now! You're a little prince, aincha!" they commented, circling the Ford and checking out its stickers, mirrors, and silver hubcaps.

"What prince are you talking about? Stop messing with me!"

"Well you are a bit of a prince. What are you sayin'? Come here and give us a hug. Why did you stiff up at the wheel? Can you give us a ride?" asked a blond lad with all kinds of curlicues in his hair.

"Sure, I'll give you a ride, Râţă..." Mitu agreed merrily. "Come on, hop in and let's take a tour of the village," he invited them.

Râţă and two more men climbed in the back seats.

"Look at us, getting rides from an American! Little Mitu, look how far you've come, gosh darn it! From cleaning manure to New York! That's how we'll call you from now on— 'The American.' Everything you have is American: you, your car, even your woman!"

"Stop it with the nonsense! Better yet, tell me what's going on around here!"

"Well, pretty much the way you left it: poverty, endless work, deadly disease, what else..." Râţă said, swiftly, becoming as serious as his answer. "Good thing you left. It's gotta be a lot better there. Look at your fancy clothes! And, so you know, we all read the last letter you sent to Ghiţă, because he showed it and bragged to everyone about it! We laughed so hard at the part about the amusement park. What's it called again?"

"Coney Island."

"Yeah, yeah, that's it...hey listen, I see you're not saying nothing 'bout it, but who's this beautiful princess here with you?"

"She's my girlfriend. Doesn't speak Romanian. I took her with me to show her my country. Dear, this is Ioan Râţă, Ion Pricoreanu, and Gheorghe Pufan," he introduced them in English.

"Nice to meet you, boys" she replied, intimidated by the stares received from the back seat.

"What did she say?" Râţă asked, his eyes big as onions at the sight of a foreign woman.

"She said it was nice to meet you!"

"Why's it nice? What, are we that handsome to look at?" they laughed, confusing Olga even more. "Let's go, drive on, what you waiting for?"

"Watch it, guys! You had better learn how to behave!" Mitu snapped at them, worried that Olga might be upset from the first moment she set foot in Cernădia because of some dunces.

"Good thing she doesn't speak a lick of Romanian," he said to himself while pressing the clutch and shifting gears.

Mitu drove around for half an hour, the American flag fluttering proudly on the hood of the car, waving royally to everyone and enjoying his elevated social status. Then, he set out on the road to his hamlet.

"That's enough fun for you, I'm going home now. I'll see you in a few days, no doubt!" he said to his companions.

He saw his mother from afar; she was awaiting them at the front gate, watching down the road as she used to in the past when he, Ghiță, and their father returned from the mountains. The news of his arrival had reached her.

"My little Mitu, you're back my child, welcome home! I've been waiting for you for a week. You're so grown-up and handsome. I'm so proud of you! You're a bit taller, but you've lost some weight. Frizzy, come here! Your brother came from America!" she yelled. "Curly, where are you girl?"

"Glad to find you well, Ma, because I was worried about you. But I see that you're healthy and in a good shape. Let me introduce my girlfriend to you. This is Olga Gertrude, I told you about her in the letter. She's Swedish but lives in America. We're about to get married. Her name's written 'Olga,' and it's pronounced 'Oalguh.'"

Lenuța gave Olga a puzzled look, then invited them in.

"Now come inside, my goodness, I'm keepin' you out here. You must be hungry from the trip!"

Ghiță and Gheorghița showed up from the garden, covered in dirt, and approached them shyly. Gheorghița cleaned her apron and peered at Olga.

"Good day, Mitu! Good day, miss!" they greeted them bowing as if they were nobility.

"How are you, brother of mine? Gheorghița, I'm so happy to see you!" Mitu jumped to hug them. "You must be doing well; you've put on some weight! I lost some and you gained some, look at that!"

"Welcome home. We've been waiting for you for a few days. Ma told you, right?"

"Yes, yes, she told me. It's been a long and difficult trip, all the way from the end of the world...Oh my, I almost forgot, this is Olga Gertrude...Say 'hello,' and then 'I'm glad to meet you!' he instructed them promptly.

They tried to replicate his words.

"Hehllaw. Aim gled toomeet yoo..."

Olga burst into laughter and shook their hands warmly.

"That was pretty good! That was actually very good! Your brother will teach you English!"

They entered the yard, and Lenuţa glanced furtively at Olga.

"My God, Mitu, how beautiful this girl is! How are we to take her to our poor shanty? She's gonna run away without ever looking back!"

"It's alright, Ma, she knows what poverty is; she wasn't born a princess. She didn't leave Sweden because she had it good there. And we're only staying a few weeks anyway. It'll go by fast. By the time she realizes how poor we are, we'll be long gone..."

They all went to the house. Olga walked gingerly not to break her high heels and avoiding puddles, Mitu by her side ready to support her in case she stumbled, and Lenuţa trailing behind them slightly embarrassed.

Ghiţă and Gheorghiţa had remained by the fence not knowing what to do until Mitu yelled at them.

"Come inside! Whatcha doin' over there? You forgot the way from the front gate to the front door? I'll help you out: you walk straight ahead for about twenty feet, and you've made it right to the kitchen. You needed me to come from America to teach you?"

They approached laughing, and he opened the door to the kitchen. His eyes darted inside:

"My God, what poverty," he sighed. "What poverty..."

Seeing the two shabby rooms making up the whole house, the memories of his beginning in America—which until then, he had considered painful and sad—suddenly disappeared; the tenement on the Lower East Side, busy and filthy, frozen in the winter and boiling hot in the summer, now seemed a royal palace.

Lenuţa had cooked them a soup, and for the second course, "cake in a pan," as she called her house specialty. Despite their protests, she had them all around the table in no time. She handed them some spoons and placed a steamy clay bowl in the middle of the table.

"It's fresh made, with beef, pickled cabbage juice, and lots of parsley—the way you like it. I just took it off the stove, come on dig in. And here's some polenta..."

Olga could hardly hide her nausea when she saw they all shared a bowl. Five people crowded around the tiny table, dipping their spoons rhythmically: splash, splash, splash...

"Son, invite her to eat. Why isn't she havin' any, she doesn't like it?" Lenuţa asked Mitu, eager to make a good impression on her guest.

Olga understood from their looks and body language and, smiling uncomfortably, she took a spoonful, then busied herself with some crumbs on the table.

"Darling, I hope they won't mind if I don't eat. Tell them I'm too tired from the trip to be hungry..."

"Don't worry, that's how it is at the beginning till we get to know one another...Don't worry, okay?"

The second course, from which Olga dared to take a few bites, was some kind of egg and flour mixture, with slices of tomatoes, smoked pork lard, and some milk poured on top.

"Frizzer, I brought you a leather vest and some felt boots. And a pocket watch," said Mitu when they finished eating, excited to give them gifts. "And for you Curly, Olga got you a vest as well. I hope it fits you. Ma, I brought you a coat to wear for big occasions. Olga chose this also, because I'm not good with womanly things. Let's go to the car to get them..."

"Not now, Mitu, we'll get them later. You didn't come home just to give us things! Let's talk some more! Tell us how you're doing. Tell us everything! And make sure you take care of this girl, so she doesn't feel outta place, yes?" said Gheorghița blushing to her eyeballs.

They sat around the table for a few hours and listened to Mitu's stories about America: Herzowig, the marvels of New York, Coney Island, Olga's theater, the stores and shops on the Lower East Side, the gigantic transatlantic ships transporting thousands of people over the ocean, the terrible life he had lived during the first months on the Promised Land.

"Well, little Mitu, I am proud of you," his brother Ghiță said at the end. "You know, when you left I said to myself that you were crazy. And I could've sworn that you were gonna come back with your tail between your legs. Good for you!"

Mitu's heart filled with happiness. Praises from his elder brother! That had never happened before.

"It's alright Frizzer, this time I'm taking you with me. I won't leave you here anymore..."

Mitu took Olga to show her everything he had missed so dearly back in New York: Boțota, the cherry tree behind the house, the plum trees in the valley, the two cows, one with a baby calf that Olga immediately fell in love with, and finally, the small room where they were going to stay.

It was nighttime, and they were getting ready to turn in. Olga asked him where the bathroom was.

"You know...I told you that life here was different from other places" he said, feeling rather awkward. "We don't have a bathroom, you understand, but an outhouse. Look, it's over there," he showed her a cage made of old wood planks, about three feet tall, a topless and bottomless box, which, no matter how hard one tried, only hid the lower part of the body.

Olga couldn't hide her repulsion. The door barely hung on some rusty hinges, black flies buzzed above, and big, yellow-winged insects flew nearby.

She went cautiously inside but came out instantly as though bitten by a snake.

"I can't do it in there! I'm gonna vomit! There are swarms of flies and yellow worms! And there's no toilet paper!"

"Let's go to that bush over there!" Mitu said embarrassed. Olga followed him and hid behind a thick tree, looking to see if there was anyone around. Then she lifted up her skirt and crouched down.

"Ouch!" she yelled suddenly, getting up and pulling her skirt down.

"What is it? What happened now?"

"I don't know, something bit me!" she shrieked.

"There's nothing here that can bite you," he searched the ground carefully. "Oh...yes, a nettle stung you. Yes, these sting pretty bad!" he burst into laughter.

"A nettle? A nettle?" she marveled. "I see that around here even plants bite! What can one expect from the people..."

Chapter 20

The first thing Mitu did the next day, after paying a few short visits to his neighbors, was to take his old violin from the closet, dust it off, clean and wax its strings, and play a *doina* for Olga. Then he spent many hours comparing the sound of the new violin bought from Bucharest to his old one, and to his astonishment, didn't find significant differences. "That Corcoveanu is a true maestro. I need to go see him in Baia," he said, planning to visit his old teacher at the end of the week.

In the afternoon, he went to see his old *taraf* players, who all lived at the periphery of the village, and brought them back to his home to spend some time together the way they used to in the past. He sat down in front of the summer kitchen, and before starting, he invited Olga to listen to them, announcing playfully.

"Now you can see what I used to do before I went to America and met you..."

She sat down on a stool, smiling at them. She had never seen something like this—not even in the motley crowd of Coney Island. The gypsies were dressed peculiarly and their musical instruments seemed strange, particularly the hammered dulcimer which she inspected with curiosity for a few moments.

Mitu pulled the bow down the strings, powerfully and curtly, and they started playing a slow *hora*, producing some sounds so sweet, her eyes welled up. In all the years spent in America, she had listened to all kinds of music, but tonalities such as these were completely unknown to her.

"The coldest of hearts would melt at this," she said as she watched him full of emotion.

Olga's words elated Mitu. He had hoped she'd like his music, but he never expected she would be so moved by it. He led the players into other songs—fast and slow, sad and happy, until two o'clock in the morning when they finally stopped and had a few glasses of *ţuică*.

"Gosh darn it; how I missed this," he confessed putting the violin aside and rubbing his fingertips to alleviate the pain from strumming the cords; his old calluses which used to protect him against the sharp bite of the strings had nearly healed. "We'll play again tomorrow, yeah?"

"Whenever you want: tomorrow, the day after tomorrow, and the day after...we're playing at Marinescu's son's wedding in two weeks. Maybe you can come; people'd be glad to see you! Not that you need any money now..."

His eyes glistened.

"Marinescu's wedding? I don't need any special convincing to play! You're nuts! You tell me when and where, and I'm there!" he became excited and then turned to Olga to translate.

"My dear, I'm gonna take you to one of those parties I told you about and you'll get the chance to see me in action."

The next few days passed by at the speed of light. Mitu walked around the village giving candy to the kids who followed him around as if he were Santa Clause. Then he visited all of those who had lent him money before his first departure.

"I'll never be able to repay you properly," he'd say as he paid back his debt. "Without your help, I would have never been able to go to America..."

Friday morning, he took Olga up to the sheepfold in the mountains to show her the ten sheep his family owned, all of which were in a shepherd's care for the summer. They spent the night in Rânca, tasting all the food made right there on the premises. He explained to her how everything was cooked with the meticulousness of a chef initiating an apprentice.

"These looking like doughnuts are called '*balmoş*.' You put milk in a cast-iron kettle, and when it starts boiling you add cornmeal, ewe's milk butter, and baked whey cheese. You mix it all into a paste-like consistency. And we also had some 'tocan' or 'stew,' as we call it in America, except here the sheep meat is boiled in its own fat in a kettle, not in oil, with salt to taste and no vegetables."

"It's clear as daylight to me now: you're husband material," she said, cheered by his detailed explanations.

In the morning, they went hiking down Gilort's valley—whose wild beauty took her breath away—and during the following days they went to Târgu-Jiu for some shopping. Then they visited Corcoveanu in Baia, where Mitu spent a few good hours, and later they went to Pociovaliştea to see Iosif Albu, the man who had given him the blank birth certificate so he could leave with Pistol and Boncu. He was happy to see him.

"I'd leave tomorrow if I could, if I were a bit younger. Good you left. You weren't even gone that long, and look how much money you made. One of these days we'll be reading about you in the newspapers. And what a woman you got yourself there."

Mitu felt like a king; he was the only one with an automobile in Cernădia, with a gorgeous woman on his arm, and enough money to afford whatever whims he had; everyone was in awe of his Ford, his clothes, the English he spoke, and the pocket watch he wore.

He was living the time of his life.

The second week of their stay, after many delays, Mitu finally worked up his courage and went to Cărpiniş to see Boncu's parents. Things were not well there—he could sense it. The house in which Boncu had lived before going to America seemed empty and nobody knew anything about him.

Boncu's parents hadn't heard of Mitu's arrival back to the village and burst into tears when they saw him, inundating him with questions.

"Oh my goodness, look who came to see us! We don't know nothing of our boy! Nothing! Terrible suffering came over us! We pray each night for him! Where is he, do you happen to know?"

Mitu lowered his eyes. He expected this, but struggled to find his words. What could he say that wouldn't worry them even more?

"Well folks, I don't know. Pistol and I passed the medical check-up in Ellis Island and got out, but they kept him for something. I think you already know of this from Ma, 'cause I wrote her in a letter. Otherwise, I don't know what to say. We looked and looked for him the following day and the next but couldn't find him. They sent him back for sure because they found some trouble with his eyes. But I don't know where he is. Maybe he stopped in France? He never wrote to you? I thought he came back to the village!"

"No, Mitu, we never got no letter from him. And it's been...how long? A year and a half since! We can't sleep at night thinking something bad happened to him. If you learn anything—anything at all, let us know, please! Just so we know where he might be, our poor son..."

He nodded sadly and said goodbye. He didn't want to scare them, but he knew that most of those deported succumbed to illness or suicide on their way back to Europe. It was very strange that Boncu had disappeared without a trace—something really bad must have happened to him.

He spent the following days meeting with old friends, scouring the hills and valleys with Olga, taking trips to Rânca, hiking through the woods, picking mushrooms and berries or fishing trout from the river.

It was Olga's turn to learn new things. While Mitu had borrowed from her good manners and a taste of art and culture, Olga was now discovering, with his aid, the inner workings of a place far off the path of civilization.

She was alongside him wherever he went. If they weren't together, the inability to speak and people's curious gazes made her retreat into the small bedroom. She would only exchange a smile with Lenuța, whose warm heart simply wasn't enough to surpass the language barrier.

"I never thought poverty such as this existed in the world," she'd say to Mitu sometimes. "Your life on the Lower East Side is quite luxurious compared to what's here. It's not surprising that everyone kisses your butt now..."

"You're right. But see, if, let's say, I came back for good, I'd continue to be somebody for another month or two—no longer. After that, people'd get used to it and would talk about me behind my back that I returned because I couldn't do anything with myself in America. You know how people are..."

The last Saturday before going back to America, they went to Marinescu's son's wedding, which was to take place in a tent behind the local tavern.

The party had already started by the time they arrived. Seeing that Olga felt a little out of place, he appeased her inquietude.

"Just know that you are the most beautiful woman here, dear," he said, taking her to the front and greeting everyone with ease.

"Ion, looking good! Vasile, barely got here and you already had three drinks. Whacha gonna do 'till tomorrow morning? Mitică, I don't wanna see you sitting when I play. You take your woman and dance until you drop to the floor, hear?"

He saw Nistor and Ana crammed at a table with ten other people, engaged in some hot discussion. He cringed and turned his head, avoiding them while making their way to the front.

"Shit, I wish they weren't here!" he thought annoyed, pretending he hadn't noticed Ana's reproachful looks, saying "I would have died for you, and you forgot me so quickly..."

He found a seat for Olga right next to the father of the groom, and he climbed on the improvised stage. He glanced proudly at the wedding guests as Marinescu rose to his feet and signaled the crowd to be quiet.

"I have the big honor," the man said when the people stopped talking, "to have at my son's wedding, none other than our talented Mitu the Fiddler, who came back from America for this special occasion to play for us! Let's give him a proper welcome!" he yelled, clapping fervently.

Mitu didn't wait for another invitation and began playing passionately, bringing everyone to the dance floor. He kept on until he saw that the dancers were getting tired, stumbling or missing a step, then changed the pace with a slow *hora* to allow them to regain their breath. All those years playing for weddings had taught him how to offer people a good time at a party, and he hadn't forgotten it.

When Olga saw him play with his eyes closed, not minding the stuffy air filled with the stench of cigarette smoke and sweat, living the music the way an adolescent experiences his first love, she felt a sinking feeling in her heart.

"This is where he belongs—not on Delancey Street, not in the Garment District, not with the tailors and seamstresses of Orchard Street, and my place is so far away from this world," she thought, sighing at the thought that sooner or later, one of them would have to make a difficult choice.

"Hey Fiddler, you're still one of us! I thought you were gonna play us something American already, since nowadays you're all fancy and everything," people assaulted him after the first round. "Come and have a drink; the *ţuica*'s been aged for three years," they lured him with a bottle of drink clear as crystal and hot as fire.

"What fancy are you talkin' about? Don't make me come there and kick your butts! What, you think that because there's lots of you, I'm afraid? This is my kind of music! How could I ever forget it?"

He instructed the *taraf* players to go on without him and invited Olga to dance.

"I don't know how to dance this! Leave me alone; don't embarrass me in front of everybody!" she pulled back.

"So what? You're mine!" he put his arm around her waist and started dancing with her.

In a few minutes, Olga was dancing as though she had been born in Cernădia. Among the villagers dressed in local costumes—men in white, tight trousers, and women in black and white traditional habits— Mitu, with his black suit, white shirt and bow tie, and Olga, in a shiny evening gown, appeared so extraordinary, so out of place.

When they finished their dance, everyone applauded their performance.

"Good job Mitu, you show them Americans what we can do, damn it! Go back and teach them a dance or two from Oltenia!" shouts were heard.

"This kind of dancing takes a lot out of you. It's not like the tango," Olga laughed, hugging him and taking his arm. Then she became sad. "My darling, you are so happy with your music, and I want to become an actress so much," she said. "For people to know me, to admire me...I want that so badly. I'd like to be like you: in demand and admired by all, but somewhere in New York or California. You're very happy here, darling, and I'm happy for you!"

The party lasted till morning. Almost everyone in the village was present, partying as if it were their last day on earth. Mitu glanced at Nistor and Ana every now and then, who hadn't danced at all until then— "because of me," he thought—and kept wondering how to leave the wedding without having to say goodbye or talk to them at all.

He waited a while for them to go, but seeing that Nistor seemed glued to his chair, he took Olga and made his way right by their table. After a few feet, he couldn't resist and turned his head, as though to make sure Nistor wasn't going to stab him in the back.

His fidgeting made Olga turn as well and her eyes met Ana's, who flinched and flushed.

"This girl whom we just passed when leaving...who is she?"

Mitu stopped amazed

"Olga, you're something else! How did you know?"

"How did I know," she mimicked him jokingly. "What a question! I'm a woman, aren't I? I can see a woman scorned a thousand feet away!"

He hesitated for a bit, but then decided to tell her the whole Nistor and Ana story.

"I had no idea you were capable of such treacherous ways to get what you want!" she kissed him. "I hope you won't do the same with me..."

He breathed a sigh of relief; for a moment, he had regretted his decision to be so open.

"Olga, I wish I could make you feel for me what I feel for you. If you asked it, I'd give my life for you, no second thoughts about it..."

They made love that night in the tight and creaky bed, trying not to make any noise. Only the door left slightly ajar separated them from Lenuţa and Gheorghiţa.

The upcoming days were a lot less exciting. Three weeks into their stay, the novelty had worn off.

"Any wonder lasts only three days," Mitu explained to Olga when she asked why their outings had become so rare; she had gotten used to them and liked the people's hospitality.

Their departure was drawing closer, and Mitu took any chance to try to convince Ghiţă to go with them.

"Oh, Frizzy, it'd be so good to be together!" he kept saying. "I could help you find work right away; they always need skillful people like you! You'd do so well. Think about it; you're not married, you go there for a few years, make some good money, and if you don't like it, you come back here and build yourself a nice, big house. You'll never be able to make money here like you could there. You yourself said it."

But his brother was as unyielding as he had been the previous year. Each time they spoke about it, he looked down.

"Maybe next time, Mitu. Maybe next time. But not now..."

On the last day, as he was stuffing his luggage in the Ford, Mitu's final attempt led to an argument.

"Frizzy, come with me! Leave this poverty behind and come to America. We could both help Ma; it'd be much easier with two salaries. And we could maybe build a house for Curly. What, in God's name, is holding you here?"

His brother shrugged, a trifle annoyed.

"Mitu, just let me be. Everybody in this village talks about America, but I can't leave this place. Other people can go to foreign places, but I can't. All I know to do is look after sheep. I'm afraid of big towns. I was born here, I'll die here."

"But you can take care of sheep in America also. What do you think, there's shepherds only here? And you can get paid a lot better; why work here for a few pennies when you can do the same thing there and make real money?"

"I like it here, alright? I'll never be able to leave this place, like you did. I'm not a coward! I'm not a traitor to my country!" Ghiţă raised his voice, but then stopped suddenly as if to show his outburst had been inadvertent.

"What...did you say? What do you mean, 'traitor'?" asked Mitu stunned. "Looking for a better life, that's now being a traitor? What about you, still living here in our parents' home, what's that? You make me a coward when you're poor as a church mouse? Who's the coward? Me, or you living in misery? What are you saying here?"

Lenuţa, who was beside herself with sorrow that her son was leaving again for so far, intervened conciliatorily between them. Her boys had gotten into such silly arguments only in their childhood.

"It's like you've lost your minds, and now you're gonna start hitting each other! Mitu, come here for a kiss; it's breaking my heart that you're going. Frizzy, why don't you keep your mouth shut, upsetting your brother right before leaving. What did he say to you that was so bad?"

Ghiţă swallowed the heavy words on the tip of his tongue and turned his eyes.

"I know what I said...I know..."

They kissed one another goodbye at last. Olga smiled.

"Bye-bye, we'll see each other again soon!"

With the crank in his hand, Mitu posted himself in front of the Ford and turned it a few times to start it up. After climbing into the car, he turned to Ghiţă.

"Listen Frizzy, I really didn't want us to fight; we're the same blood, what the hell? But I will never come back to this poverty since I've tasted a better life. I really wish you could come and see it for yourself at least once. I really do. Farewell...and take care of Ma...and you, Curly, take care of her..."

"Come back soon and write to us!" they all yelled, following the thick cloud of dust in the car's wake.

"Don't throw away my violin!" he yelled back, turning around the bend towards Novaci.

In Pociovaliştea, they made a left on the meandering road to Siteşti and continued their way through potholes to Bumbeşti Piţic, where they got on the main road connecting Târgu-Jiu to Râmnicu Vâlcea to Piteşti and Bucharest.

At the first stop, made after a few good hours of traveling, he picked up a newspaper someone left on the ground and couldn't believe his eyes at the news on the first page:

"Archduke Franz Ferdinand: 18 December 1863-28 June 1914."

"Look at this! Archduke Ferdinand was assassinated yesterday in Sarajevo!" he showed the newspaper to Olga.

Chapter 21

World War I, whose consequences led to the dissolution of four massive empires and catalytically contributed to the unleashing of World War II two decades later, started immediately after their return.

While millions and millions of people were dying on the battlefields of Europe, Mitu's life went on at the same pace as it always had: long workdays at Herzowig's, fun-filled weekends, and dates with Olga. To him, the news of the war across the ocean did not come with visceral emotions. He read about it just out of curiosity, as something that was happening "over there" without immediate effects on his life. As far as he was concerned, America was safe—nothing could affect it. And how could he think otherwise? From President Woodrow Wilson to the last person, everyone was on the same wavelength, "America would only actively enter the war if that led to liberalism and a better universal democracy..."

Half a year after their trip to Romania, Mitu and Olga decided to move in together in Manhattan. She gave up her room at Honey Pie and he left Pistol—much to his dismay—alone in the tenement, and they rented a studio in Midtown Manhattan.

Their apartment was modest—a cozy, clean, and peaceful room with its own bathroom and a separate kitchen on 33rd Street between Sixth and Seventh Avenues.

On the corner of their street, there was a convenience store where a stout, voluble man sold magazines, cigarettes, lighters, knives, and all kinds of other trinkets. Mitu befriended him with an agenda. At first he kept buying little nothings to make the man feel he owed him somehow, then spent a lot of time in the store, asking this and that about his business. He wanted to learn detailed information about retail, which struck him as a good way to make easy, quick money, as he had begun thinking about opening his own store.

Right next to the store, there was a restaurant, "Suzie's Tastefully Cooked," where the owner was the cook and the waiter, working like a madwoman morning to evening to serve her patrons. She couldn't afford to hire any help because of the exorbitant rent she was barely able to pay each month. Right next door, another restaurant offered similar products at similar prices, but unlike "Suzie's Tastefully Cooked," this one was always full. Mitu often wondered what made one place do so well and the other so poorly.

The move to Manhattan had complicated Olga's life. The commute from Midtown to Coney Island took a few hours, which was difficult on hot summer days or bitterly cold winter ones. In the burning heat of mid-July, horses' cadavers, cut down by heat or disease, would lie strewn on the pavement for days on end, fouling up and disintegrating until the garbage people would come to collect them in their trolleys to throw them somewhere on the fringe of the city.

Olga's daily routine consisted of short performances on Coney Island, along with failed and increasingly desperate attempts to break into the industry, with deceptions and depression when some producer found her insufficiently talented; her hope renewed for the following audition, and the next, and the next. Mitu listened helplessly to her complaints.

"What am I gonna do if I never make it? I'll always be a washed-out actress from Coney Island, waiting tables in my old age, because what other choice will I have? No one will want a gray-haired, wrinkled hag up on the stage."

"Don't worry so much, dear, you'll have your breakthrough one day; time solves everything, and what you want takes a while. The important thing is to have patience and believe in yourself," he would encourage her. "It'll be okay, you'll see. It'll be okay..."

She would shake her head unconvinced.

"It's been so many years...and I haven't accomplished anything," she said, falling back into a despondent state. Her frustration was accentuated by the upward movement in the industry of some friends of hers—ex-friends at this point—who were now playing for big theaters in New York or other cities.

Thanks to Olga, who was up to speed with most of New York's cultural events, the cosmopolitan life of the city was entering Mitu's blood. His English had improved so much that sometimes his accent was almost imperceptible. Going to the opera or a Broadway show had now become second nature. He was so familiar with the New York Philharmonic and the Met that he knew their season schedule by heart.

The rent for their apartment, although not exaggerated, was a lot higher than what he used to pay at the tenement, and even with the shared costs it was quite harsh on his pocket. The commute to work, the subway, the more expensive food they purchased now, and the entertainment activities—all wasted away quickly the handful of coins he received from Herzowig at the end of each month.

Olga had begun longing for a change. She had been working on Coney Island since she was sixteen, doing nothing else but theater. Years had passed, and none of her fantasies of becoming someone famous, someone revered, had come to fruition. She had been, for a few times in her life, just about to catch that "train," but even those occasions had proven to be as elusive as her dreams.

Shortly after meeting Mitu, such thoughts hadn't troubled her so much. For months and months, all her problems had faded to the background, losing their significance. She had found something rather indescribable in Mitu, something nonexistent in the men before him. He made her gasp at his sight, flush uncontrollably, feel butterflies in her stomach; she had an impetuous desire to be his, and suffered in pain and impatience when they were apart. Mitu was not her first man, and she hadn't imagined until then that a relationship could be different from any other. She had started her love life at sixteen, in the first month at Honey Pie, getting involved with an actor from another theater who had dumped her out of the blue. Surprisingly, she had realized that the breakup had barely affected her. After that, she had been involved in two more insignificant and short-lived relationships; when she met Mitu, with whom she connected so strongly, she decided to move in together without any second thoughts.

Now that the initial vortex of love had calmed down a tad—especially after their return from Romania—she had found herself in an uncomfortable position a few times, which made her feel somewhat guilty for questioning her future with him. Not that she didn't love him, but as days went by, her existence turned more and more monotonous—something she wasn't used to nor cared for. The two of them were slowly assimilating into the masses, feeding the country's economy, leading the typical Joe Q. Public's life: ten-hour working days with few occasions for outings and partying.

Since their moving in together, she felt walled in. Still, if she came home before him, she was glad to see him arrive, but she also missed her freedom. She wondered why she hadn't considered it more seriously before making such an important step. She now had to worry about her career *and* Mitu's feelings. Mitu proved quite the incommodity when they went to parties together, because now she couldn't flirt with men as she had before and had to stay by his side not to upset him.

Because she was no longer able go out on her own in places where she could meet important people who could help her career, her chances to step into the highly coveted entertainment world had thinned out considerably. She suddenly realized that she was no longer appealing because she was *taken,* and that made her irascible and hard to please.

Mitu ignored all those complications. Just like Olga, he also thought about the future, but in a different way; he saw himself married to her, in a big house with a big yard somewhere in the suburbs, with many children, living comfortably from his business.

They were going in different directions.

Their first row occurred one evening as they were coming back from the cinema. They had watched a love story about a beautiful girl who fell in love with a rich nobleman and, after a series of events, they eventually married and the girl entered the world of aristocracy. At the end of the movie, the thought that she also had to do something with her life and push her unfortunate limitations hit Olga like a brick wall.

"Something the matter, darling? Everything all right?"

"How can he help me? There's nothing he can do...he's just a simple tailor..." she sighed then tried to explain herself.

"I'm okay. It's just, I wish we had things like other people—a comfortable living, not the crammed up conditions of our tiny room."

"I want the same Olga. But we need to have patience and everything will be alright."

This time, his assurances didn't appease her as in the past.

"Yeah, that's what you keep saying: 'have patience,'" she snapped, her voice penetrating with hostility and contempt. "How much patience can one have? Until when? I'm sick of waiting! All my friends live in luxurious apartments, and we barely manage to pay the rent at the end of the month! How much longer is this going to last?"

"I'll open up my own store with the savings I've been putting aside, and we'll be okay then. You'll see how well we'll manage. And maybe you'll find something on Broadway; you'll see how this will be just a laughable memory..."

"A store? You keep talking about a store, but I don't think you're serious! Do you even know what this type of business entails? Have you ever worked in retail? Do you know all its secrets? What if you lose your money? What if you can't sell your merchandise? Since you've come to America, all you've done is tailoring. How can you think that, out of the blue, you can open a store that will be successful?"

Mitu stared at her surprised and hurt. She had never spoken to him that way before. He tried to control his anger but couldn't.

"Why are you wasting your time with me then, if you're so unhappy? Why? You have enough suitors in high positions vying for you! Go to them! Why stay with me?" he raised his voice only to instantly regret it.

"Maybe I will!" she threatened sharply. "I never said I wanted someone else! But you are the man of the house, and you should be the one bringing home the dough!"

THE WAR

Chapter 22

Three years had passed since Mitu had left the tenement on the Lower East Side to move in with Olga, when his world came crashing down. The burning heat of the summer had finally eased a little, and the afternoon was peaceful, crisp, and clear, with people walking the streets of Midtown, the horses' trotting dissipating into the air in spiraling echoes, and the hustle and bustle of Times Square more intense than ever. The city vibrated—a motley agglomeration of beings in a constant hunt for bargains.

He felt no forewarning of what was to come.

He had left work early to surprise Olga; he meant to show up with a bouquet of flowers and take her out for ice cream and a vaudeville show. They had been to such shows before and he knew how much she enjoyed the acrobatics, the flying trapeze, the dancing, the gymnastics, the trained animals, the magic shows, the banjo performances, the Shakespearean recitals, and the speeches given by some celebrity.

By his calculations, the day marked five years since they had first met, and they had to celebrate it properly. Unlike her, he always remembered this anniversary and always planned surprises for her.

He took the tramway from the Lower East Side to 33rd Street, listening to the cadenced lulling of the wheels. When he got off, he bought a big bouquet of red roses—her favorite flowers. He went towards their apartment building anxiously, but stopped at a pastry shop and bought a box of the French caramels she loved so much.

"We should get married already; too much time has gone by," he said to himself as he climbed the stairs. He entered their studio quietly and looked around the place as he always did. The curtains were pulled, plunging the room in darkness. That surprised him, as he knew how much she loved her plants on the windowsill.

"Olga...I'm home..." he called out softly.

He heard a muffled noise coming from the alcove where the bed was. He peered through the obscurity to figure out what it was.

"Olga?" he asked cautiously.

The next moment, he froze.

Olga was watching him from the bed, her eyes wide with fear, blanket up to her chin. Next to her, Steinovich was scrambling to his feet trying to lift up his pants.

"What's going on?" Mitu mumbled, not believing his eyes.

"I'm...sorry...really sorry," Steinovich muttered all aflutter yet mindful, ready to defend himself in case Mitu attacked him. "I'll be on my way," he added, leaving with his shirt in his hand, slamming the door behind him.

Mitu dropped the candy and flowers and sat down on the edge of the bed with his head in his hands. Olga didn't dare speak.

"How long has this been going on?" he asked in a low voice, grumbling with threat.

She did not answer. A tense silence followed.

"Woman, I asked how long!" he growled again, giving her a contemptuous look.

"Not long..." she said weakly, white as a sheet of paper, her eyes fixed on the floor.

He dashed to her and gripped her wrist.

"Why are you doing this to me, woman? What have I done to deserve it? I'm not good enough for you? I'm not like the worldly Jew from the high society, huh? That it? Huh?" he asked in the same low voice, full of anger, staring her down.

Olga burst into a roaring cry.

"Forgive me please! Forgive me! We have to talk!" she cried trying to allay him, but he struck her with all his might, making her groan with pain and fear of what was to come. He snatched the covers off her and watched her naked body for a few moments. She curled up and closed her eyes, covering her breasts with her hands in an awkward gesture of chastity. He pulled her furiously by the hair, laid her on her back, clenched his hands around her neck, opened her legs like a savage, unzipped his pants, and penetrated her with brutality.

"Here, this is what you deserve—damn whore!" he cursed as he kept going in and out of her. "You vulgar bitch!" he muttered, continuing to strangle and possess her. She thrashed around gasping for air, scratching him with her nails, but he stuck his fingers even deeper into her flesh.

He finished with a grotesque grunt and sneered at her.

"Filth!" he spat on her disdainfully as if she were a fetid rag. He went to the closet, threw some clothes into a bag and returned, throwing her hateful looks.

"May God pay you back for this, Olga." He lifted his finger to the sky in a warning, then slammed the door behind him, stirring the dust from the door frame which puffed up in the air like a small explosion.

"Fuck you, bitch!" he yelled from the stairs. "The fuckin' shameless whore!" he cursed through his teeth on his way to the subway for the Lower East Side.

He reached his old tenement in about half an hour. When he came up from underground, he looked around disoriented and shielded his forehead with his hand from the sun, peering from behind some ominous clouds. The place seemed foreign, without a shred a familiarity despite all the time he'd spent there.

Mitu's entered the room shaking like a leaf, taking Pistol by surprise. His friend hadn't been there in months.

"What is it? Something happened to you, Mitu? What is the matter?"

"Goddamned whore. I caught her with someone in bed, the fuckin' bitch! I'm gonna kill her! I'm gonna cut her in two with the knife!"

Pistol looked befuddled at him.

"Who did you catch? Olga? What? That's not possible..."

Mitu flailed his arms furiously, dropped his bag on the floor, and left the room without another word. He stopped in front of the building, going round in circles like a madman with his hands on his temples, kicking garbage bins and cursing, "Goddamned whore!"

"What the fuck are you lookin' at me for?" he snapped at a passerby.

People were avoiding him guardedly. Pistol came up to him to calm him down.

"Keep yourself together. Enough! You wanna burst something in your head? God help us, she's just a woman!"

Mitu continued to curse, then collapsed on the tenement stairs, wailing.

After a while, exhausted and broken down, he got up slowly and motioned to Pistol, who didn't know how to interpret his gesture, to go back to his room.

"I'm going for a walk. I'll come back later..."

"Okay, Mitu, but just don't do something crazy. Wait for the morning to come. Fuck her, she's just a woman; you've had plenty of them in your life and will have plenty more yet."

Mitu walked away slowly, waited for Pistol to go inside, and entered the first liquor store on his path. He had almost forgotten about it in the few years he hadn't been there.

"A bottle of whiskey and one of dry red California wine." He threw a few coins on the counter.

He uncorked the bottle of whiskey and took a gulp, letting a thin stream of liquid escape out of the corner of his mouth. He was drinking as a thirsty person drinks from a cold stream in the middle of summer. The clerk watched him amazed from behind his glasses.

"Man, if you gulp down the bottle of wine like you did that whiskey, I'll give you another one on the house. I've never seen anything like this in my life!"

He took the bottle of wine and chugged it all at once. The man gave him another bottle; he grabbed it and he left the store, drinking from it once in a while. Shortly after, he felt sick and sat down holding on to a wall, then threw up. He lay down on the cold asphalt, soaking his clothes in his own vomit, still gripping the bottle of alcohol. He fell into a deep sleep under the furious rain gathering around him in puddles. Water streamed on his face, neck, and body, wetting his clothes and cooling his body to a corpse-like temperature.

He woke up at dawn and for a few moments, tried to figure out what was happening. He hoisted himself up to his feet and pressed hard on his temples with his hands to alleviate the splitting headache. "Where the hell am I?" he wondered, looking puzzled left and right. "What the fuck am I doing on the Lower East Side?" he asked himself when he figured out where he was. "Oh, that ordinary cunt!" he remembered everything, a sharp pain piercing his heart.

He started wandering the streets aimlessly, guzzling from the bottle with a nothing-to-live-for apathy. "God, how I stink!" he thought, and his eyes brimmed with tears.

"Breaking news! The New York Times! Paris under the siege of Central Powers!" some paperboys, awoken early to make a few pennies, fluttered newspapers in front of his eyes.

Mitu grabbed one and glanced over the first page. Only war news:

"France brought to its knees! Americans sent by hundreds of thousands to Europe."

"Germany winner on almost all fronts!"

He read a few more titles, then chucked the paper disgusted, continuing his aimless downtown stroll. The knot in his throat kept choking him, and all he could think about was Olga. At the corner of Wall Street and Broadway, he saw a poster in the window of a shoe repair shop:

"_Your chance to see the world, all expenses paid, good remuneration. Enroll in the Army!_"

And a bit lower in Battery Park, another one:

"_Enlist today! Don't line up with the slackers!_"

He read the last one a few times, making a mental note of the address written on it—Brooklyn Recruitment Center, 177 Montague Street, Brooklyn—then got on a tramway and went there as though his decision to enroll had been long considered, and today was the day he had to present himself for duty. He got off the stop before, and went to "Salvation Army." He sat down at a table, pulled out a personal check and wrote "Account Balance", signed it and handed it to the clerk without a word. The perplexed man watched him over the thick rims of his glasses and murmured, "On behalf of our institution, I thank you, sir. May Our Lord, Jesus Christ watch over you!" It wasn't that often that people came in to donate all of their savings up to the last penny.

As he entered the recruitment center, the officer gave him a disgusted look.

"This man's in such bad shape!"

"Your name, sir?" he asked writing down the date—June 27, 1918—on an application.

Mitu spelled out his name, gave a fake address— "I'm from Detroit"— and provided short answers to the rest of the questions:

"No, I don't have any special skills."

"No, I don't know how to use a gun."

"I have no professional preparation; I work as a laborer."

"I want to die in battle on the front line!"

After he finished with the paperwork, the officer handed him his soldier's record.

"Keep it on you at all times. Congratulations, you are now a member of the National Guard! On behalf of our country, I thank you for the services rendered. We will send you to Waco, Texas for training. All you have left to do now is fill out the name of a beneficiary for your life insurance in the unfortunate case you lose your life on the battlefield. It's a substantive sum— ten thousand dollars—which will be lost if no one claims it."

Mitu grabbed the form absentmindedly, filled in "Olga Gertrude" and the address where they had lived together, then opened his soldier's record and read it with disinterest: "Soldier's No. 3141710, Private, Company G, 125th Infantry."

Chapter 23

Unfathomable carnage. Desolation. Decapitated bodies. Eyeballs impaled by bayonets. Kidneys, brains, livers scattered on the ground. Cadavers teeming with worms. Heaps of stiff corpses. Fields of crosses stretching to the horizon. Fragments of limbs. The fetid stench of putrefaction. Heaps of carcasses in mass graves. Trenches filled with hideous skulls. Human flesh. Puddles of blood.

Tremendous starvation throughout Europe, with hundreds of thousands of refugees eating only turnips. Laws forbidding the ritual throwing of rice at wedding or feeding crumbs to birds. Soldiers marching for whole days without food, leaving bloody trails because of broken and ill-fitting boots.

The British had lost six hundred thousand men at Somme. The French, half a million at Verdun. A whole generation of men lay butchered in trenches because of a conflict whose progress was not measured in conquered cities but in a few feet of advance or retreat, which could take a day, a month, or a year.

The human race had never seen such bloodshed. God seemed to have turned His back on the world. The advent of technology had turned against man. Death was everywhere—in the toxic air, in trees pulverized by bombs, in roads pierced by explosions, and in villages blown off the face of the earth by cannons.

In the summer of 1918, when Mitu, freshly enrolled in the army, was on his way to Europe, ten thousand soldiers were arriving in France from across the ocean each day. He was a small cog in the big war machine along with another four million men recruited to fight for a cause they didn't understand. He had gone to war in a moment of profound desperation, indifferent to his fate, and now marveled at his fellow soldiers, seeing them belt out hymns of bravery while eagerly waiting to fight. They seemed childish to him, unable to see that they were pawns in a game whose ramifications, at that time, were not understood. Many of them, quite naïve, had enlisted because of propaganda and speeches of celebrities such as Charlie Chaplin or Mary Pickford and had gone to recruitment centers full of heroic fantasies of saving humankind.

Only a few had realized that the war was a deadly game. Thrown in the line of fire without any military training, facing a veteran enemy, thousands of them were going to meet their end without even knowing what hit them. The Allied forces, already tried by centuries of slaughter with swords and cannonballs, had named the Americans "the children crusaders." The Germans considered them "hunting meat" because of the ease with which they were shot on the battlefield.

Mitu was thrown, at the end of September, into the decisive Battle of the Meuse-Argonne, to the north of Verdun—an area which had been under German control for four years and was a key point for the supplies that arrived there from France and Flanders via the railroad in Sedan. The battle took place between the U.S. First Army and forty German divisions. The soldiers in his unit had become legendary throughout the spring and summer for the tenacity and fresh vigor with which they fought for each inch of ground they recovered. The news that the Division 32 never retreated, not even a step, in face of the enemy had earned them the nickname "The Red Arrow." The French called them "Les Terribles."

A quarter million soldiers, half of whom had never fought before, had been sent to the hills and valleys of Argonne. The offensive started on the 25th of September through a barrage of artillery that lasted until the next morning, when Mitu's infantry unit was given the attack signal.

At exactly five o'clock in the morning, they started moving ahead through the milky fog. This was the first time many of the soldiers were holding a gun. Others, like Mitu, had fired one a couple of times during training before being sent to Europe.

At first, there was nothing. The silence was disturbed only by the soldiers' feet hitting a stone or stepping on a twig. Mitu was zigzagging ahead clutching his rifle. The thick and almost solid fog prevented him from seeing any more than a few feet ahead. Odd shots could be heard every now and then. It was so quiet that at one point he started wondering whether the unimaginable horrors described in newspapers were nothing more than exaggerations meant to impress the public.

Mitu had lived a difficult life, but, in matters of war, he was still a child.

During their four years controlling the area, the Germans, anticipating such an attack, had built many casemates, camouflaged in strategic positions on top of hills, full of munitions, hard to detect with the naked eye, and quite difficult to annihilate by artillery. To take them, you had to run straight ahead for hundreds of feet, dodge the bullets coming straight at you, and have the strength, after facing death maybe a thousand times in the space of a few minutes, to throw a grenade through an opening as narrow as the barrel of a rifle.

It was such a dangerous and threatening place, not even animals dared leave their lairs.

When the fog dissipated, the soldiers found themselves in a woodland clearing, sitting targets for the machine guns aimed straight at them. For a second, an utter silence fell, as though both sides took a moment to say a short prayer. Then, suddenly, the downpour of bullets began rapping them with the ease of a child tossing pebbles in a lake.

The first man cut down to the ground was a soldier running a few feet ahead of Mitu. He was hit right between his eyes and fell on his back staring up at the sky.

"Brian, are you okay?" Mitu yelled, scared, stumbling around him and trying to take his pulse.

"Move your ass from there! Don't stop, or you'll end up the same! He's dead, dead, dead! Can't you see, you moron? Follow me!" the commandant yelled, and Mitu rushed behind him like a madman, only to see him collapse on his knees and slowly fall to the right.

"Lieutenant, what happened?" he said in a strangled voice, shaking with terror.

"I'm hit..." the man murmured, choking on the blood spilling from his mouth. "Get away from me. You're a live target if you stay still," he croaked.

Mitu watched him for a split second and wiped his forehead with the back of his hand. *"If he hadn't been in front of me, I would've been dead!"* the thought crossed his mind, and he ran quickly towards a hill. To his right, four men were mowed down by machine guns, the way a scythe cuts grass. To his left, another man fell softly to the ground, shot in the knees, but he kept yelling at Mitu not to stop.

Like in a cynical game directed by the devil himself, hundreds fell while hundreds remained standing, running madly ahead, miracles of survival. Each man's luck was measured in insignificant distances. An inch to the right, and your earthly life ended in the blink of an eye. An inch to the left and the bullet merely grazed you, hitting the man at your side.

They passed by the first line of machine guns, and Mitu saw the valley teeming with soldiers running and screaming madly as if their howling gave them strength and scared off enemies at the same time. He was paralyzed by fear. *"I made it through, but how long is this gonna last?"* he asked himself, feeling his heart throbbing in his throat. A weakness came over him and he felt the need to lie down. *"I don't care if they shoot me, I need to rest a bit..."* He squatted to the ground.

He wasn't the only one feeling that way. During the first assault, they had run as fast as they could, cutting through lines of barbed wire and flinging themselves to the ground dozens of times, creeping to avoid the bullets and hiding behind piles of dirt caused by explosions. Exhaustion now overpowered all of those who had managed to get past the German casemates and made it in one piece to the forest edge near Montfaucon.

There was no entry for the word "rest" in the war dictionary: the order to cross the forest and attack the village was given right away. They didn't even have enough time to regroup and regain their breath, and they had to set out to the edge of the village for a flank attack on the German resistance.

Mitu walked through the trees with bulging eyes, looking around for any sign of danger. The forest was empty, sinister, and dark, a veritable gateway to the underworld. A few odd crows flew chaotically up above. Everything was gray, as though God had taken all color with His hand. The fog had descended anew, thick and heavy, swallowing the soldiers.

As light returned, Mitu's eyes roamed the opening surrounding him— barbed wire obstacles at each step, a machine gun concealed in each thicket— and said a short prayer. "Beelzebub himself can't come out alive from here..." he sighed, spasmodically rapping the barrel of the rifle with his nails.

He had no time to plan his next move because a deafening curtain of fire descended upon them. It rained down bullets and projectiles. The inferno had unleashed its full-fledged fury. Beyond human understanding, an invisible, omnipotent, and destructive giant played demonically with the soldiers' lives. Right next to Mitu, a full platoon of soldiers died as though their lives had been ended by the very air, saturated with shrapnel and toxic gases.

For two hours, in which they didn't advance one step, a few thousand lost their lives at the edge of the forest, piled on the ground in strange and grotesque human pyramids. Mitu found shelter behind one of them, not daring to show his head to look around. When he thought the fire had slowed down, he got out and fired a few shots in the air, then tried to find a free pass somewhere, but everything was blocked by fences of barbed wire. He considered his circumstances: in an open field in range of enemy machine guns, getting stuck in a fence meant certain death. A chill went down his spine at the sight of a few men braver than he who had chanced advancing to the village, but who, getting entangled in the wire, had been shot on the spot.

At last, with a short prayer, he worked up his courage and prepared to leave his hiding spot. He stood up with irate energy and started shouting like a crazy person, zigzagging towards a mound of dirt, when his mind went blank all of a sudden. He was no longer a human being with feelings, thoughts, and desires, but an animal fighting desperately for its life. He crouched in a hollow smoking from explosions and started firing with a strange calm, aiming calculatedly. He saw the Germans falling one by one, hit by his bullets, until his position was discovered, and three enemies started coming towards him. One keeled over, struck by some stray shots, maybe even friendly fire; the second was pulverized by a grenade.

The third miraculously escaped the rain of fire and approached him screaming, running with his eyes coming out of their sockets and with his rifle aiming straight ahead. Mitu leaped to the right, dodging the bullet, then rose to his feet quickly. He threw himself on top of the German, scratching with overgrown nails, striking with his fists and knees with the rabid strength of someone knowing that only one person would come out alive. As the German was thrashing about to escape, Mitu stuck his nails in the man's eyes, smearing his fingers with blood. The German wailed in pain, gripping him with his hands, biting his neck like a cat. Mitu barely unclenched him and pushed him to the ground. The man fell on his back and Mitu flung himself on top of him, immobilizing his arms with his knees, and pulled out his knife. Right then he hesitated. The German had given up on the fight and was staring resignedly at him, helplessly awaiting his end. Mitu gripped him tightly by the hair, pinned his head to the ground, and jammed the knife in his throat, growing nauseated at the man's croaking.

He was lying down next to the body, head utterly empty, when he heard the retreat signal. He cleaned the warm blood sprayed on his face, already starting to coagulate, with his elbow. The Germans' resistance had been ferocious, and his division—Les Terribles—was returning, along with the others, to the base in the Argonne Forest. He started running straight, not caring that he was an easy target, and reached his platoon in a few seconds, collapsing, terrified and exhausted, to the ground.

The number of victims was tremendous. One unit had lost all of its field officers. Another platoon had been left with just a few soldiers, almost all missing limbs. Deep wounds unveiled greenish-red entrails, filling the air with the sweetish smell of blood. Men seemed haunted, hallucinating and stuttering erratically.

After a while, Mitu had recovered slightly, and he went closer to the others, keeping quiet for a long time. In fact, no one was saying anything. The soldiers had gathered in small circles, as though for a picnic, and kept their eyes on the ground, barely breathing.

Right next to him, the unit's commandant, Captain Raskall, stared unblinkingly at the men about him as though he had never seen them before. He had traces of spit at the corners of his mouth and his hands were shaking uncontrollably.

Mitu thought that perhaps he was hurt and, seeing him in that stunned state for a while, he approached him.

"Are you okay, sir? Are you cold?" he asked, but the man maintained his vacant stare.

Mitu shrugged and went to look for someone smoking to bum a cigarette, when suddenly, Raskall got up and started towards the edge of the forest as though he had seen someone there.

Realizing the man was getting dangerously close to the open fire zone, Mitu yelled after him, "Sir, what are you doing? Stop! You'll get hit!"

The captain got out of the forest and kept on towards the German trenches, stepping rhythmically, as though he were walking behind a ghost enticing him to follow.

"Sir, come back!" he howled, dashing after him.

It was too late. Raskall had reached the open field, walking the straight line to his invisible target. An otherworldly silence fell for a minute. Time stopped. Then, a muffled shot—just one—pierced the air. The captain halted, continuing to look ahead, and tried to take another step but fell softly to his knees, collapsing with his face in the dirt.

Mitu unleashed a roaring cry, which convulsed his body. "I should have saved him, stopped him earlier, I should've!" he grunted with his head in his hands, rocking from one leg to the other like a child.

"It's not your fault...take it easy. It's okay," a soldier consoled him, patting him on the shoulder. "You haven't been in a fight before, I see. You'll see this happening daily from now on. You need to get used to it. What the heck...don't lose your head, because for each one of us who can't stomach this, the whole platoon has to suffer. Come on, keep it together, soldier!"

They spent the next hours in the forest, barely sleeping and huddling together for a bit of heat. It was evening and the bombardments had stopped, filling the air with an unnatural peace. Every now and then, the shrieking explosion of a cannonball echoed from afar. For a while, they were safe.

Chapter 24

The American units were thrown into battle by rotation. After the fight from Argonne, Mitu's division, the 32nd, was sent on a few support missions, away from the front line. Meanwhile, the First Army had advanced slowly, approaching Romagne-sous-Montfaucon, which was later retaken from the Germans in a bloody offensive that resulted in the largest American cemetery on foreign soil in history: over fourteen thousand graves.

The balance of power had tilted ever so slightly in the Americans' favor, as though tipped by a grain of sand. The German Army had begun a slow retreat, fighting desperately for each lost inch, with tremendous sacrifice on both sides.

Mitu was terrified by the losses in his army. In only four days, forty-five thousand American lives had been lost, and those miraculously still alive were so scared by the hell they had been through and the seeming certainty of their own deaths that they had no will to fight. Apathetic, dark, and hopeless, they entered each fight with the clear image of the immutable end looming over their heads. They looked in their officers' eyes with an expression that needed no interpretation: "You're sending us to die, sir, and for what?"

In an attempt to defy the war and find valves of relief, feeble reminders of the world left behind, the soldiers made up peace songs, veritable forbidden hymns, which they sang in secret whenever they could.

Mitu stuck to one of these songs with the gratitude of a man who, on his way to the guillotine, spots a friendly face in the hostile audience. He hummed it all the time, ignoring the officers and their orders against instigation to disobedience, making his fellow soldiers join in:

> *I didn't raise my boy to be a soldier,*
> *I brought him up to be my pride and joy,*
> *And not to carry a musket on his shoulder*
> *To kill some other mother's darling boy.*

What was happening to him was really strange. There had only been a few months since his arrival to France in August, but during that time, his compulsive need to fight on the front line, egging him on since he had caught Olga with Steinovich, had turned into the opposite. The war was no longer the solution to his unhappiness, but a new problem needing an immediate resolution. The face of the woman he loved was evanescing in the multitude of images bombarding his mind, and as the past faded away, the fear of dying drained whatever energy he had left.

The song represented a kind of rebellion against himself, a cry for help. "I want to get away from here! What was I thinking going to war? Pistol was right! She was just a woman!" he kept saying, terrified by the thought that it was very possible he might not return home alive.

Because of the song, he was summoned to the officers' quarters by the highest in the hierarchy, Major Michael Cook, a stocky man, five feet tall, who tried to appear more intimidating than he really was. His platoon's lieutenant was there as well, merely for appearances' sake, having heard Mitu sing the forbidden song many times without ever reprimanding him.

Without wasting any time on introductions—not that there was any need, since Mitu knew why he had been called—the major addressed him directly.

"What's with the song, soldier?" His exaggerated frown gave more weight to the question.

"Permission to speak, sir. I don't understand. What song, sir?"

"Are you playin' dumb, soldier?" the major yelled at him, wagging his pointer as if to say 'you'll see what's waiting for you!' "Let me refresh your memory: '*I didn't raise my boy to be a soldier...*'"

"Oh, that song, sir..." Mitu said, screwing up his face as if he were trying to remember something that had happened a long time ago.

"Yes, that song! What's with it, soldier?"

At that point, the lieutenant donned an attitude as grave as that of his boss, though it couldn't manage to hide his boredom and his visible wish to get out of there as soon as possible.

"Nothin', sir. I was just having a little fun!" Mitu answered.

"You were having *fun*, soldier? Having...*fun*? Do you know what that is? That's treason, soldier! Treason! You bring down the people's morale with songs like these!" the major howled, sweating profusely. "Soldiers riot because of you, and that's not gonna fly with me, soldier! Not gonna fly! I say what goes in my unit, and I won't accept disobedience like they do in others! Who do you think you are to instigate, huh?"

Major Cook was very proud that in all the units under his authority, he hadn't had one case of insurgency, and he wanted to continue the trend at any cost. In his opinion, this was, on one hand, the clear proof of his leadership attributes, and on the other hand, it could serve as an argument for the promotions which undoubtedly were to follow the war.

Mitu started sweating bullets, thinking that he could be court-martialed, and tried to say something but didn't have the chance.

"If I hear you sing anything like that ever again, you're in trouble! A court-martial will be the end of you! Now get outta here!"

He saluted them meekly and got out, relieved and content that things hadn't gone sour for him that time around. *"What would it be if I kept singing? Maybe they'll throw me in jail, and it'd be safer there than out on the battlefield anyway!"* He was worried about future combat. Foreboding thoughts muddled his mind for a while; he felt something bad was looming ahead. He had a somber feeling, an emptiness in his heart, an inability to imagine the future embittered his days.

The next day, on the fourth of October, he went back into the fight. The 32nd Division had been chosen to participate, along with many others, in an offensive along the length of the battlefront that was meant to push the Germans back.

His platoon took over a slope a few hundred feet from the enemy lines. It was an overcast, rainy day, and that worried him, as the reduced visibility impeded his seeing the fences of barbed wire in advance.

Once in the trenches, he crossed himself. "Lord, please save me this time too..." he prayed, looking around at his fellow soldiers. *"How many of them will I see tomorrow?"* he wondered. *"How many of them will see me?"* He stared at them trying to imprint their faces onto his mind forever: Tom Balboa, an Italian who had been in the war from the beginning and who, being the same height as Mitu, was always next to him during alignments. He was clutching a cross to his chest and was whispering prayers, shaking visibly. Right next to him was Sparky, a black man, nicknamed so because he always had a lit cigarette between his lips. He sported a lackadaisical attitude and constantly engaged in gambles with himself. He would flip a coin in the air, placing a few matchsticks in one pile if it landed heads or in a second pile if it landed tails. Johnny, Bill, and Sam, whom he didn't know too well, came from the same town and always kept together like brothers. They waited for the signal to attack with expressionless faces.

"How does God decide who's gonna die and who's gonna live?" Mitu wondered, putting on his helmet and fastening its strap under his chin. Although in a ditch and safe, he hated the thought that he might die bombarded in the trenches, thinking it a foolish way to go.

"Tom, we're gonna make it out alive," he said to the soldier next to him, whose face was as white as a piece of paper. "We need to, because the POWs say that not even the front-line soldiers have food rations. Imagine the disaster in Germany..."

"Only God knows...but in war, whoever has the hill has the valley..." the man answered, continuing to shiver.

"What the heck is wrong with you? Be a man! You've been through so much, this is nothing! Get over it! In an hour, it's all over! You've been fighting from the beginning of the war, and now you chicken out?"

Tom didn't even blink.

"What's happening to you? Have you lost it?"6F*

An incessant thunder-like noise crossed the skies. Mitu peered out to figure out what was happening. The Allied forces' aviation was bombing the

---

* A less intuitive theory in psychology, which explains why we die, posits that the reserves of resources a person has to fight stress are limited and unreplenishable, and when this reservoir is depleted the person has a nervous breakdown or dies. The theory is empirically supported, among other things, by the observation that during WWI the soldiers most prone to nervous lapses were not the freshly enrolled ones, but those who had already fought numerous battles before, and who, logically speaking, with all the experience amassed, would have been less vulnerable to such breakdowns.

German artillery round after round, breaking it down little by little, until suddenly, there was complete silence. The maddening shriek of shells had stopped, and explosions blasted off only far away on the other side of the battlefield.

He prepared for the attack. He knew the signal could come at any time. When he heard its familiar sound, he wiped away the drops from the pouring rain with his elbow, clutched his rifle, and came out of the trench with Tom, whose shaking had stopped completely. They began zigzagging by each other's side to avoid being easy targets.

"Tom, it's like we're walking down Fifth Avenue—all we need is an umbrella and a mademoiselle on our arm..." he said, suddenly invigorated, surprised at the lack of obstacles in their way. The hope that the Allied forces had crushed the enemy resistance to the ground, leaving the Germans unable to retaliate, encouraged him so much that he smiled, thinking he might have worried in vain the day before.

He was deluding himself.

The aviation, firing until a few moments before, had indeed destroyed the artillery, but it had not destroyed the machine guns, camouflaged by casemates, bushes, trenches, trees, and mounds of dirt.

The wave of bullets that hit them as they were advancing was more intense than ever. It seemed they had just broken an invisible wall and entered the netherworld. The fight took place on one of the most difficult terrains an American soldier had ever fought on in the Great War: holes, mud up to the knees, constant rain, cold weather, ravines full of toxic gases, barbed wire blocking all access, open areas that the Germans could see clearly.

Mitu left Tom behind and dashed forward with his bayonet aimed ahead, without protecting himself. He bellowed with all his might, lashing furiously to make it through the fences, ready to shoot. The few days of combat had thawed his instincts, and now he was able to sense danger in his gut, without thinking, without analyzing. He could see it in an instant, perceiving its details with his peripheral vision, and could evaluate barely audible noises, detecting them with the accuracy of an experienced fighter.

On the battlefield, however, everyone had transformed just as he had in the probabilistic game of life and death, and experience could only help so much when facing the projectiles that saturated the air. When the first bullet grazed his shoulder, he didn't even feel it but kept on running and shooting.

The second bullet, in the leg, made him keel over on top of the body of a German soldier watching him with glassy eyes.

"I'm hit," he thought, feeling a warm wetness in his shoulder and hip. He touched his wounds and looked surprised at the blood reddening his palm.

"Oh, this must be the end!" he groaned, slumping to the side, waiting to be noticed by the enemy who would certainly come to execute him at short range. *"I wish it would be over soon. Die already..."* Truncated thoughts shot through his head as he lay on the cadaver. He tried to twist to the side, then turned the body to see it better. It was a fair-haired man, so young he could have been a high school student. Next to him he noticed half the body of another German soldier, split in two by a bomb. His legs, sawed from his body by the explosion, lay twenty feet away. He was quite old, gray-haired, with deep wrinkles on his face. His tired appearance gave the impression he had died of exhaustion rather than bullets.

"Oh Lord, I'm gonna leave my bones around here like an idiot..." he thought, understanding that a country sending the young and elderly to fight its war was already down on its knees.

He turned on his back and thought he was going to die a slow and painless death, by bleeding out, and then tried to find a position that would put some pressure on the wounds, thus allowing for a slower hemorrhage. He leaned against the young soldier's body and closed his eyes, his thoughts a long way from the battlefield.

"Olga...now you'll realize how much I loved you...The life insurance..."

Later that evening, after the cease-fire, he was found and brought to the infirmary by his unit. He was inert, dirty, bloody, and weak, but conscious.

In the infirmary tent, he saw dozens of wounded and limbless men stretched out on army cots. This gave him chills. *"My God, my wounds are only scratches..."* Soldiers with bandaged heads, amputated arms and legs, guts hanging out of their bodies, barely breathing, lay speechless, staring blankly ahead, wishing only to fall into a never ending sleep.

The sight of those hit by mustard gas disturbed him. He had seen them many times on the battlefield, but now the image of rows and rows of men forever blinded, heads wrapped in gauze, walking in line, their right hand on the shoulder of the man in front of them, led by a lucky person who thus far had made it through, made him shudder. It was as though all of mankind's sins, forgotten until then, were being atoned for by men like him in the Argonne infirmaries.

The nurses cleaned his wounds with alcohol and bandaged them tightly. "You were lucky, boy. These are just scratches. You don't even have a bullet left in there," they said to both his comfort and dismay since he wanted his injury to be serious enough that he could remain in the infirmary for a longer time.

They put him in a cot that he was to share with an eighteen-year-old boy.

After getting somewhat comfortable, they looked at each other with the understanding given by a common, devastating experience, and began chatting.

"I'm Mike Anthony, from Detroit. Where are you from?" the young man asked with an expression showing he really wasn't interested but was simply making small talk.

"From New York, though I said I was from other place when I enlisted..."

"So, what brought you to the battlefields of Europe? Bravery? The desire to become a hero?" the boy asked almost maliciously.

"I enrolled voluntarily...a woman left me..." he sighed. "I wanted to marry her...but I decided then to go to war..."

The young man gave him a strange look.

"You've gotta be kidding me...you're trying to tell me a woman left you and you decided to die?"

Mitu lowered his eyes and took a deep breath. The dazzling image of Olga dancing on stage in Coney Island flashed before his eyes. He missed her so much! He would have given anything to be close to her, to feel her body touching his, to caress her small and perky breasts that drove him insane, to comb her curly, blond hair with his fingers, to make love to her like he had their first time.

"Here, this is her..." He pulled a picture from his pocket and handed it to him.

Mike took the picture and gave a whistle of approval.

"Very beautiful. Congrats...you're lucky...I haven't been with a woman yet, pal..." he confessed, "but I don't think any one of them deserves a sacrifice like this."

"Don't worry, you'll find one soon, after you get outta here," Mitu said, watching him with understanding and amiability.

"Yeah? What am I gonna find? Who's gonna wanna be with a cripple? Huh? Tell me! I hate all of you who whine about nonsense!" he snapped angrily, and with a better look Mitu realized the boy was missing a leg. Bundled up as he was, he hadn't noticed it at first.

"I am so sorry, Mike...honestly, I am... I don't even know what to say..."

Mike waved his hand as if to say 'I'll be alright...'

"And? What do you plan on doing now that your clever plan didn't pan out?"

Mitu smiled.

"No clue. And, my plan might still work anyway, since the war's not over yet..."

"Hey, listen, why don't you come with me to Detroit when this is over? Leave New York and come to Michigan. I used to work for Ford. I won't be able to work there anymore, without a leg, but I can help you get a job there, if you want. They pay very well. Here, this is my address..." He scribbled something on a piece of paper. "Contact me if you ever decide to come to the Midwest."

"Ford...how ironic..." Mitu murmured bitterly, remembering his visit to Romania when he had driven the Model T on Cernădia' s roads. "How happy I was then! My God, what a fickle life..."

Chapter 25

At the beginning of November, when Mitu left the infirmary and went back to the battlefield covered in bandages and in pain, but capable to fight again, the Allies had gained significant advantages. In just a few days, his division had advanced deeply in Sedan, forcing the Germans to retreat hurriedly and in disarray.

"We're winning! We're winning the war!" he said to himself and quivered seeing how fast they were pressing forward. Hundreds of soldiers fell around him daily, transformed instantly in hunks of meat, and a shell or bullet could have hewed him down in the blink of an eye as well. If at the beginning he had thrown himself hopelessly into the war as a sign of rebellion against the woman he loved and against God, now the thought that living an additional moment meant another defiance of death, made him doubt his role in the war even more.

The fury that had pushed him to the recruitment center in Brooklyn had lost its force completely and was now just a strange memory zapping him sometimes without helping him understand his stupid decision to throw himself in front of bullets. It was true he had been betrayed by someone he considered his soul mate, whom he genuinely loved, but not even that should have led him to such a drastic move. He now thought, rather uncomfortably, about his choice to leave his life insurance to Olga, a gesture he initially wanted to serve as his perverted and reproachful vengeance on her, the overwhelming proof that, as much as she had hurt him, he still was, albeit posthumously, the only man capable to sacrifice for her.

On the eleventh of November, his division was preparing for a new offensive. During the last few days, the battles had been less gruesome, the Germans had been pushed back significantly, and miles and miles of ground had been reclaimed. They were passing the enemy's casemates with incredible ease, unlike in the past when they had died by the thousands for each foot of recovered ground.

They had awoken at dawn, braving the bitter cold while waiting for the attack signal. Mitu kept staring at the commandant—the division's fifth, the other four having died—who seemed wired to jump from the ditch at the first sound, and he wondered if he was ever going to see him again.

He said a short prayer as always: "Please God keep me this time also—goodness, it'd be something else for me to die right now..." He clutched his gun and made sure the rest of his equipment wasn't going to impede his run. He knew he would have to dash from his hiding place in a few moments, to become—for the umpteenth time these last weeks—a live target for the enemy. He scrutinized the darkness ahead, trying to figure out where the German machine guns were, and took a deep breath.

Then, somewhere to his left, he heard a noise, screams and yells, and turned his head but couldn't figure out what it was. Then the yelling, or rather cheering, filled the trenches, reaching him quickly, like a wave.

"The war is over! *Finie la guerre! Finie la guerre!* The war is over!"

"C...ce?" he asked in Romanian. *"De unde până unde?!"*

The lieutenant stood agape for a few moments, exchanged a few words with someone and then told them, beaming with happiness, "Germany surrenders! Germany surrenders!"

If, as they say, happiness is the contrast to sadness, then ecstasy must be what a soldier, who has stared death in the eyes a thousand times, must feel when hearing such news. Finally, Mitu understood what was going on. He was stunned for a few seconds and then fell to his knees with his arms to the sky. He jumped to the man next to him and hugged him so tightly, so impetuously, they both fell in the ditch.

"The war is over!" he shouted as he started to cry. "The fuckin' war is over! We're alive!" he yelled as loudly as he could, joining in the frenzy rallying in the field.

The soldiers dumped their guns and threw their helmets up in the air; some were dancing, wiping the tears falling down their cheeks chapped by the bitter cold.

It seemed strange that they could stand up without the fear of being shot, that there weren't any more explosions, that men weren't collapsing dead to the ground.

"Olga...I forgive you Olga...!" he said, drunk with happiness. "Thank you God..." he whispered, raising his eyes to the clouds.

He joined his platoon at the German posts less than a thousand feet away. The German soldiers—ferocious enemies a few minutes before—welcomed them joyfully.

"Brothers, finish!" a young boy said to them in broken English, his eyes as blue as the sky, and his eyebrows so blonde they seemed white. Mitu shook his hand and hugged him.

"Yeah, the war is behind us...now go back to your mama, son..." he said, even though he knew the boy didn't understand a thing. Then Mitu took a cigarette from his pocket and handed it to him, and the boy thanked him with a bright smile.

"*Danke!*"

The Americans and the Germans went back to the American base where they started exchanging things. Some swapped vests, shirts, and helmets. Mitu gave his belt to the German boy, and he received a watch which he put on his wrist.

Not long after, the lieutenant came and said half-heartedly, in a don't-shoot-the-messenger kind of way, that orders were they shouldn't fraternize with the Germans, that they were going to be court-martialed if they didn't comply, but no one heeded his words. Mitu ignored the order completely, saying that, although still in uniform, he now considered himself a civilian again.

The following days were utterly uplifting. Les Terribles had been chosen to be one of the divisions to cross the Rhine. They marched all the way to

Germany, heads held high, flanked to the right by the First and Second Divisions and followed by the equally famous Rainbows. These four units, forever engrained into everyone's memory, were considered to be the best of the American Army in France—elite troops that had won all of the battles they had been involved in and of which, surprisingly, Mitu was a part.

He had become, all of a sudden, a hero! A legend! From the filthy tenement and his low-paying job, crawling along the fringe of society, from Olga's complete betrayal, from the blood-strewn battlefields, his upward thrust to the skies was almost unbearable.

The tears of joy on people's faces singing their praises as though they were gods while marching through French villages bewildered him. The screaming women throwing themselves at them as if they were famous actors, were dizzying.

He had never felt such joy. He had never felt so important. The adoration of the crowds was a sight to be seen: their march to Rhine, fifteen miles a day, cadenced by military music, took place under showers of flowers.

"You are our heroes! You saved us! We thank you for your sacrifices! May God be with you!" people shouted, trying to touch them as they passed.

A frenzied crowd was awaiting them in Luxembourg, enthusiastically waving American flags and throwing confetti.

"You freed us! You're heroes! You beat the Germans! We owe you our country's freedom!"

People were laughing and crying, drunk with ecstasy. They were going crazy at the sight of their uniforms, grabbing them to dance, shouting in many languages. It all seemed unreal. Watching the men, women, and children full of adoration, Mitu realized that this represented the standard by which all his future successes were going to be measured, and he thought sadly that the overpowering joy he felt now was going to be but a memory once he was discharged.

When, on the thirteenth of December, Les Terribles triumphantly crossed the Rhine on the bridge near Engers, his mind was made up: he was going back to New York to look for Olga to tell her he had forgiven her. They were going to move back in together, and they were going to build a house in which to raise their children. And maybe—who knew?—later on they could move to Romania. No matter how much she had hurt him, she was forgiven. With her, his life was going to be beautiful.

Chapter 26

Because at the recruitment center in Brooklyn he had said he was from Michigan, after the war, in the winter of 1919, Mitu was sent back to Detroit alongside Les Terribles.

The America he found had changed. In the enthusiasm with which they were greeted as saviors and liberators, he sensed sadness and tiredness, as though the long years of sacrifice thousands and thousands of miles away had affected the ones who had left home so much that they wanted to forget it and move on with their lives.

And, as though the sixteen million fallen souls on the other side of the ocean hadn't been a high enough price for the capriciousness of history, another calamity was rearing its head. America had escaped a war fought on its own soil but had been attacked insidiously and perfidiously by something ten times more deadly than bullets—the terrible Spanish flu.

Mitu had seen the epidemic in the infirmary in France but hadn't paid much attention to it, thinking it was severe pneumonia. The news about it had been censored in newspapers and letters received from home, and since the symptoms resembled those of the common cold, he didn't suspect for a moment the havoc it was wreaking throughout the world.

Still, as he marched through Detroit on Washington Boulevard and was forced, along with the other soldiers, to wear gas masks—something he hadn't done even when attacked with Yperite—terror seized him. The tremendous joy felt at the end of the war was gone with wind. He felt useless, at the mercy of Mother Nature, who continued her perverted game.

He was discharged a few months later, and that day he got on the first train to New York. He wanted to make up with Olga and visit Pistol. Although he had enrolled in the Army impulsively, without telling anyone, he had sent a few letters to Pistol. But he had never received an answer, and that worried him. "He didn't write to me all these months I was gone. What's happened to him? Could it be that he got really upset with me...?"

When he arrived to New York, the city seemed different from how he remembered it: somber, gloomy, desolate. The people walking on the streets with masks on their faces and avoiding anyone who merely coughed once reminded him painfully of the war.

He didn't recognize anybody in the Lower East Side tenement. His roommates had moved, and no one knew Pistol. He went to the tailor shop a few streets over where his friend used to work.

"I'm looking for Pistol; do you know where he is? Does he still work here?" he asked Kursovki, the owner whom he knew only by sight.

The man lowered his eyes without saying a word. A sinking feeling came over Mitu, and his heart started pounding as it had on the battlefield.

"What happened? Tell me!" he said with a raised voice.

"Who are you? A relative or something...?"

"Yes, we're related," he answered, unsure. "Second cousins. We came to America together..."

Kursovski continued to look at the floor:

"Go to the medical ward on Lafayette. Maybe you'll learn more there..."

Mitu looked at him, dumbfounded.

"It can't be! This can't be..." he muttered, running to the place.

The nurse he spoke to checked the names written by hand on an interminable list, and after a few unbelievably long minutes nodded.

"Ioan Pistol...yes, I found him here..."

"Yes? And? What is it? Where is he?"

"Your friend died of influenza in the fall of last year...I'm so sorry..."

Mitu leaned against the wall, gasping for breath. The veins on his neck throbbed violently. He looked at her with wide eyes, then raised his hands to his temples and shook his head incredulously.

"No...it can't be...he was young and strong, in the prime of his life. He couldn't have died from a cold. It can't be true. It must be a mistake...please check again..."

"This type of flu affected mostly young adults and spared children and the elderly," the nurse explained, trying to take his mind off the news he had just received. "One in ten was affected in New York, and many didn't make it. Last year, twenty thousand more people died of the flu than normal. No one understands where it came from or why it took this course. It was utter chaos, as though the plague had risen from its ashes on Madison and Fifth Avenues. Just a few months ago, you could see piles of coffins in the streets, bodies left to be collected by authorities, black ribbons hanging on most homes' front doors. It was hell on earth..."

"Did he suffer?" he whispered.

Thousands of ill people had gone through that ward, and the nurse couldn't remember each one of them. But all had died the same way.

"He came in with fever and coughing. In a few hours, he started talking incoherently, bleeding from his nose, and he passed away in less than a day. His lungs filled up with liquid, and he drowned in his own fluids. We did everything we could to save him, even a treatment that was considered promising—blood transfusions from those who had recovered—but without results. I'm sorry. I can't give you any of his personal effects; all the deceased were burned or buried in hermetically locked coffins or mass graves."

Mitu's face turned ghastly pale. His mouth was dry, he couldn't swallow, and his breathing was shallow and accelerated.

"Why him and not me? Why?" He collapsed with his head in his hands.

The nurse came up to him and patted him lightly on the shoulder.

"It's not your fault. Not yours, not anyone else's. That's what the One Up Above wanted..."

"Did anyone come here to ask about him? Does his family know?" he asked, crestfallen.

"I don't think anyone looked for him until now. I would've made a note of it here. And we didn't send any letters to anyone. It would've been far beyond our capabilities. Our daily concern was to bury them quickly to prevent new infections."

"Oh my God, Olga!" he cried. "My Olga!"

He ran away from there and climbed into a horse-car to Coney Island, anxiously tapping his foot at its sluggish pace.

"Has she made it alive? Has she made it in that flood of people? Please God, spare me this..."

When he entered the park, the desolate air perceived in Manhattan was even more accentuated. Coney Island was but a feeble shadow of what it had been before the war. The visitors had changed; they were not having fun as before: a strange maturity, almost an old age could be seen on their faces. It was still crowded, but there was no exuberance as in the past. People chose their entertainment carefully, shunning the stages where grandiose battles had formerly been reenacted—they had had enough of those in the war, which was still fresh in their minds

He made his way to her theater in a few minutes. Before, it used to take him half an hour to cross the dense crowd that was unwilling to move.

He saw from afar that something was awry, but he couldn't figure out what exactly until he got closer.

He had considered a host of possibilities, but not that the place was abandoned. The front doors were nailed shut and massive locks hung on heavy chains. A poster announced in big letters:

The Honey Pie Theater went out of business.
We thank you for your patronage in our heyday.

He asked a few neighbors—those that remained—what had happened.

"We don't know anything, man. They closed shop a few months ago, piled all of the things in two big containers, and left. We don't know where. They didn't tell us. Some rumors say they went abroad because of the flu. Others that they went out west to California, but no one knows for sure."

"And you really don't know anything? Nothing at all? Nothing that could help me trace them? An address? Anything? I'm looking for Olga Gertrude."

"Oh, Olga...yes...beautiful woman..."

"Know anything about her?"

"She disappeared last year. We heard she lived in Manhattan, but at some point—last fall, if I'm not mistaken—she moved back here to the theater. We saw her, too, when they packed their bags. They all left. We're sorry...she owed us some money—not a lot—and we'd like to know where she is too..."

Mitu sighed a breath of relief, "At least she's still alive!" and returned to Manhattan. He went to Battery Park and walked on the sea cliff for a while. His eyesight kept falling on the Statue of Liberty and Ellis Island, and that made him think of Boncu.

"God, I'm the only one left..." he said gloomily. "The only one."

He took the subway to Penn Station where he got on the first train to Detroit. He knew he couldn't endure walking the same streets he had walked with Olga, passing by the restaurants where they had dined together, visiting Coney Island where she had worked, going to the movie theaters they had frequented. He couldn't stay in New York anymore. He had to go as far away as possible.

In the train car, he took out a pencil and scribbled a few words on a piece of paper, which he placed in an envelope and wrote with a shaky hand Pistol's address from Romania:

Dear all,

I am very sad that I have to be the bearer of such bad news. Ioan died in the fall of last year because of the Spanish flu, a frightening disease, which I don't know if you've heard of in Romania. He didn't suffer and died fast— the good Lord took him in a few hours. I wish I could send you something of his, but I couldn't find anything that belonged to him.

His best friend,

Mitu the Fiddler

DETROIT

Chapter 27

Right after he returned to Detroit, Mitu contacted Mike Anthony, the amputee soldier he had met in the Meuse-Argonne infirmary who had promised to help him find a job at the Ford plants. He still kept the piece of paper on which Mike had scribbled his address before parting ways in his wallet.

He had kept that piece of paper really as a souvenir, since he hadn't considered for a moment he might need it. Now, he had no choice. He was alone in a new city. He didn't know anyone. He couldn't call anybody for a piece of advice. His only true friend in America, Pistol, had died. Olga had disappeared without a trace. Any kind of support, any kind of help, would have meant a great deal to him at that moment.

Mike lived in the suburbs of the city in a nice villa with two stories, which took Mitu by surprise, having thought that all those who enlisted in the Army had done so because of poverty and because it improved chances for employment after the war.

When he went to see Mike one August evening, Mitu didn't get his hopes up. He had learned through the years that the most difficult thing to do in America was to find a well-paying job. He had never managed to find one and couldn't see how Mike, a boy turning only nineteen that year, if he remembered correctly, had the right connections to find him such sought-after employment in a plant.

He waited for a while at the front door, quivering with expectation. He hadn't seen any of his old fellow soldiers since his discharge, even though he had thought to contact the few whose addresses he had many times. He finally worked up his courage, took a deep breath, and rang the doorbell. A small dog, scruffy like a porcupine, who was napping in the grass, jumped to his feet, pricked up his ears, and started barking playfully at him. An elderly woman opened the door and gave him a curious look.

"Can I help you?"

"Good afternoon, Ma'am, if I may...I'm looking for Mike. Mike Anthony. We fought in the war together. He gave me this address. Is he here?"

The woman measured him up and down with her eyes then smiled.

"Yes, of course! Please come in! I'm his mother. Mike! Someone here for you!" she called.

Mitu stepped timidly inside. He sat on the couch and remembered how uneasy he had been in the Meuse-Argonne infirmary upon the realization that the boy was missing a leg.

Mike showed up at the end of the hallway, barely walking in crutches but with a radiant face.

"Hey...it's the Romanian! What a surprise to see you out of the blue like this! Welcome! What brings you around here, man?"

Mitu hugged him rather awkwardly, careful not to make him lose his balance.

"I came to see you and ask you to help me find a job with Ford, if you can," he said directly, having learned it was the best approach in America.

Mike chuckled.

"I see...so your plan to die failed...and now you're elbowing your way through life, what a surprise..."

The boy was unchanged. The same smart-alecky, arrogant, sarcastic, downright annoying attitude! But Mitu felt no rancor like last time, when he had mocked his relationship with Olga.

"And what have you been doing since the end of the war?" Mike asked, inviting him to sit down.

Mitu cleared his voice and told him about his depressing trip to New York.

"Well then...in one day you lost your best buddy and the chance to ever get back together with the woman whose picture you kept near your heart. That's rough!"

"The memory on this guy!" Mitu thought.

"God, the things we went through..." Mike said absentmindedly. "You know, when they sent me home immediately after I came out of the infirmary, I thought I'd be so glad to come back to America, even the cripple that I was. But I miss all the men in my platoon...I miss them terribly...I've been thinking about it a lot. We were like brothers there. And I don't think I'll ever find that again—not in civilian life anyway."

Mitu sighed approvingly. "It's true."

"I'm glad you came by! I don't think there are tighter friendships than those made on the battlefield. Civilians live their lives in bubbles without a clue of what true suffering is. Here, friendships are made and unmade based on hidden agendas. I've seen it so many times! But for us who stared death in the eyes together, the war is like a seal uniting us forever."

"Let's pray we stay that way..." Mitu murmured. "That's why I decided to come to Detroit and not somewhere else. I didn't have anyone in New York. But here I'm close to everyone from the 32nd Division who came out alive. Let's meet on a regular basis. Let's not lose touch, okay? Let's remain Les Terribles!"

"Les Terribles, my ass..." Mike guffawed, waving his hand in disgust. "Wait a few more months and you'll see no one remembers anything anymore..."

"I don't think so...we'll receive some money for our sacrifices in the war. We'll get a military bonus..."

Mike looked at him as if he were an imbecile, filled two glasses of brandy from a bottle his mother had placed on the table, and guffawed:

"Man, you're so naïve! I thought you were a better judge of character, buddy! I can bet you we'll never see a penny from the government. Never! Or, if we do get anything, it will be something symbolic. You just wait and see! And, now that we're on the topic, don't you feel the call of your land? What are you still doing on this side of the world?"

Mitu lowered his eyes.

"I would go back to my country if I had some money. I would, really...in a heartbeat..."

"You would but you wouldn't...I don't think you really know what you want. Whatever...well, cheers, bud. Take a swig of this nice beverage."

"Cheers!" Mitu nodded and drank from the glass.

They chatted until midnight and said good night with the promise to see each other again soon. Mike gave him the assurance of his help with the Ford Plant.

"I know those hiring there, so you shouldn't have a problem. Call me on Friday, and I'll give you the name of the person you need to see."

"Thanks a lot man...really, thank you. You have no idea what this means to me. But tell me something else: where did you get this great cognac?"

Mike smiled allusively.

"I have my ways. I can send you to my source, if you want..."

A week later, Mitu went to the front gates of the industrial colossus in west Detroit, asking to see a certain person there: "Michael D. Anthony, who worked here, sent me." In a few hours, after the man sent him to speak to an engineer, Mitu was hired on the spot, to his great surprise, to work as a laborer on the assembly line.

His life changed for the better from that moment on. His funds increased considerably overnight: in comparison to the ten dollars a week he made working for Herzowig, here he made twenty-five and had a fixed schedule, as by 1914 Henry Ford had already raised the salaries of his workers to five dollars a day and implemented a forty-hour work week, even before the Government had instituted the federal law in this regard.

At first, he lived in a tenement similar to those in New York, but after a while, he rented an apartment on the first floor of a villa near downtown. He was now getting a taste of the middle-class way of living. He didn't live in poverty anymore, didn't count every single penny, didn't have to plan for a big expense months and months ahead. His job was hard, indeed. He worked all day on the big machines producing the famous Model T, but when he received his paycheck, he felt like he had wings.

He resisted the temptation to waste his money on unnecessary things for a while, but after some time the thought of purchasing an automobile started nagging at him. The Ford job gave him the possibility to purchase a car at a discount, which in and of itself was very enticing. He resisted it a little longer, saying it was unwise to throw away his money when he really didn't need to, but he eventually capitulated to the desire to see himself behind the wheel.

"What the hell, I make enough money to afford it...what else did I come to America for?" he said the day he went to pick up the newly-bought car, feeling a mixture of happiness and guilt.

Strangely enough, the moment he went for a drive downtown, having a car felt natural, and he wondered why he hadn't done this sooner. It felt normal to mix in with the motorized swarm on the streets. Instead of experiencing the same intense joy he had felt when he drove the Model T on the roads of Cernădia, a hollow gaped in his heart.

"Okay...now what?" he wondered after driving down main streets and around and the park once. *"Now what?"*

His life settled on a somewhat normal path during the following months. Besides a more comfortable living, his routine wasn't much different from the one he had had in New York; he worked Monday through Friday at Ford and had the weekends to himself.

Unlike in New York, however, he spent all his weekends alone. On Friday night, he curled up in his apartment, with no desire to go out. Olga's memory still haunted him, and Pistol's death, which he still couldn't accept as reality, depressed him terribly.

He now felt apathetic and tired of living; he experienced deep discontent, an acute lack of meaning or will to go on. Being an Army Reserve was infinitely worse than being on the battlefield. At least in the trenches he was constantly alert, his only purpose each day being to survive. Here, he was a simple laborer, no longer a hero.

Weeks barely crawled by if he had no booze. He sometimes struggled not to take a swig of brandy in the morning. Ford had regular checkups in its plants, implemented by the "Sociological Department," meant to verify the "moral state" of the workers, penalizing them if they drank or didn't follow the rules. That generally put a damper on his wish to charge himself up with a glass in the morning.

On Saturday evenings, however, as though he wanted to make up for the loss from the past days, he sometimes drank himself into oblivion, waking up the next day with a terrible hangover. He would swear to himself not to taste of drop of alcohol ever again. He would succeed for a while, but then he would go back to buy another bottle, and another.

And that was pricey. Sometimes exorbitantly so. Alcohol, even with his good salary from Ford, was extremely expensive. In addition, it was hard to come by. One had to go looking for it in camouflaged places, getting in contact with people who made it secretly in their homes, paying crazy prices for it. Michigan had passed a statewide law prohibiting the manufacture and commercialization of alcohol in 1916 and, with that, "The Crusaders of Morality," as the reformers were known, had won the battle against the vice, but at a terrible price: Mitu was just one of the tens of millions of people who longed for a glass, doing whatever they could to get it.

He first learned of a place selling alcohol from Mike, who sent him somewhere on Woodward Avenue, in the heart of the city.

"You knock on the door six times very fast, and when the little window opens up, you say, 'Joe from Alabama sent me.'"

He did just so and went in without a problem. Mike however, hadn't told him that that was no mere blind pig, the average drinker's place of choice, but a speakeasy, a rather luxurious locale for the *crème* of society, where they had live jazz bands, danced Charleston, hired escorts, and purchased good but extremely high-priced drinks.

The first night he spent there, he wasted half of his weekly salary, and after figuring out how things worked, he visited a blind pig as well, but not before asking for Mike's opinion.

"Yes," he said, "the prices from blind pigs are better, sure. But the distributors in those places want to sell at any cost and they put all kinds of shit in the drinks to water down the alcohol: embalming fluids, rubbing alcohol, or methanol...be careful. Some have gotten ill. Some have gone blind even, and I heard some people even died of poisoning..."

He didn't listen, and, after a night of drinking in a blind pig, he almost ended up in the hospital. He convalesced like a moribund for two days, vomiting continuously, then got a fever and a splitting headache which kept him home for another two days.

When he finally recovered and went back to work—having nearly been fired for missing a few days—he swore to himself that he wasn't going to set foot in a cheap pub ever again, and that he would do whatever possible to have enough money to buy his alcohol from reputable places only.

Chapter 28

After seeing Mike, Mitu began meeting occasionally with some of his old fellow soldiers who still lived in the city, spending many sleepless nights together and recalling the horrors—heroic acts, as they were considered by the civilians—that they had gone through during the war.

At first, in bars and hidden pubs, restaurants and parks, people would listen to them with a lot of interest, their eyes wide at the unbelievable things that seemed like movies, not reality. They were amazed by the story of the "Lost Battalion"—a few hundred American soldiers lost in the woods of Argonne who had been surrounded by the Germans and bombarded senselessly by enemy and friendly fire alike but had resisted stoically for days, almost out of ammunition and food, half of them miraculously surviving. Alvin York's tale—the corporal who, together with only seven people under his command, had captured four officers and almost a hundred and thirty German soldiers and destroyed thirty-five casemates—always prompted exclamations of admiration and reverence, especially among adolescents who still naïvely considered joining the army the fastest way to gain status and fame.

As time went by, their stories impressed the audience less and less. Life continued its natural course, with current events, though mundane, taking precedence over those from the past, as earth-shattering as they had been. The initial enthusiasm had cooled off. Lately their only interlocutors were either each other or whatever drunkards and homeless were willing to listen.

Then, one of Mitu's comrades moved to Georgia, another got married and built a house in the suburbs, and a third went back to his native France. Mike and his family relocated to the West Coast, from where he wrote to Mitu about his newfound job as a bank clerk. The rest soon scattered every which way until, from the nucleus of soldiers who had faced death on the battlefield, the only one left was Mitu. Les Terribles were but a memory of a ravaging common experience, seen as heroism from the outside but considered tragic by those who had lived it.

Maybe the loss of the strong ties he used to have with his old friends was the reason Mitu started feeling the call of the land, or maybe it was the natural evolution of a human being, who can never forget childhood and whose roots begin pulling back at one point or another. Whatever it was, Romania crept in his thoughts more and more.

He had met only a few Romanians since moving to Detroit, and those in passing. He didn't long to speak his native tongue with anyone. The 32nd Division had been his family, the only ones capable of understanding him.

But now he was alone again. At night, he would come home directly or spend time in a speakeasy, always wasting more money than he had. He was alone each Sunday. He felt guilty for being alive while others had died on the front. Nightmares drenched him in sweat, making him reach for the imaginary rifle by his side. Many times he would just start crying for no reason. Sometimes, while walking down the street, fragments of explosions flashed in front of his eyes, making him shudder as though everything was happening right then and there.7F[*]

Since the dismemberment of the 32nd Division, he felt lost, misunderstood, forgotten by the country he had served in battle, ignored by the people whose life was better because of his sacrifices and the blood shed by millions of others. He held a grudge against all Americans, except for veterans, complaining about it to anyone who would listen in clandestine bars.

"Man, you don't get it. I came to America, I fought for her, I almost lost my life defending her, and all I get now is a thankless job and no real future!"

"Well, why don't you go back to your country if it's so bad over here?" some nationalistic boozehound, tipsy from the overpriced glass of whiskey would hit him with a snappy retort.

"Just forget it...you don't get it anyway..."

He stayed home each weekend for a while. He lay in bed with a bottle next to him. He felt alright in his misery. His pain was the rightful punishment meant to lessen the guilt of being alive.

Later on, a new drive started flickering inside: he wanted to meet other Romanians, to find out news about the country, to know the current events and the politics from over there, to be with his own people.

He knew where they lived—in an enclave between West 52nd Street and West 65th Street, north of Detroit Avenue8F[†]—but he had never visited their community. He was one of the few Romanians who didn't live there.

He visited the neighborhood one Sunday morning when he went to Saint Mary Romanian Orthodox Church, where he met Father Paraschiv, a kind old man from Dumbrava Roşie arrived to America fifteen years before, who introduced him to a family from Moldova and a few young people from Muntenia.

He went again the following week and met more people. Then, he began attending church every Sunday; he liked listening to the Divine Liturgy which reminded him of his Cernădia, and he could meet more Romanians as well.

---

[*] Posttraumatic Stress Disorder—PTSD—(known during WWI as "shell shock") is a severe psychological disturbance, characterized by the persistent and ongoing re-experience of a traumatic event through flashbacks, intrusive memories, and recurring nightmares. Those affected avoid situations associated with the trauma, experience increased arousal, such as difficulty falling or staying asleep, experience feelings of culpability, detachment, estrangement, fear of rejection, are impulsive, irritable, hypervigilant, make lifestyle modifications and encounter relationship and marital difficulties. Many of those suffering from PTSD also suffer from comorbid depression and alcoholism.

[†] Right after WWI, the biggest community of Romanians in America was in Detroit. The Romanian cultural nucleus was in Cleveland, however, where many papers were being printed. Ten thousand copies of "America," a Romanian Orthodox periodical were printed in 1904 and circulated throughout the whole U.S. Other newspapers such as "The Tribune," published in 1902, and many small journals were distributed to the Romanian diaspora.

Although no other Romanians had been in the war as he had, he was surprised to see he got along very well with them. They would sometimes meet in a café discussing Romanian current events—the king, the economic problems, Transylvania—and that made him feel at home.

Soon enough, they learned he played the violin and started inviting him to shindigs, baptism parties, and weddings. He never refused an invitation, because that meant plenty of booze—so hard to procure those days—and plenty to eat. In addition, the people's attention stroked his ego, reminding him of his life in Cernădia.

At one of the parties, he met Gherasim Livrea, a Moldavian who weighed his words carefully, and with whom he felt an immediate connection. A shepherd from the Ceahlău Mountains, he had come to America ten years before and held a series of all kinds of small, bad-paying jobs, hoping for a miracle that would help him achieve his American dream. He had taught himself to read and write in both Romanian and English, struggling to find his place in life. But what he initially believed easy to accomplish—striking it rich—had eventually proven to be as elusive as the horizon. At last, like many millions of immigrants who had wasted many a year without making any strides towards a better living, Gherasim had resigned himself to his fate and was now considering moving to Montana to raise sheep.

Gherasim worked on the assembly line at Maxwell Motors, Ford's competitor, and made just as much money as Mitu made at Ford, but he always complained. Once he found out that Mitu knew how to look after sheep, he never missed an opportunity to try to convince him to leave with him. Since no one else would go with him, he kept delaying his departure. He was afraid to face such a long trip to the northwest alone, thinking that things might be easier with a companion.

Each time he met Mitu, he kept criticizing America and telling him it would be good for them to go together to the Land of the Shining Mountains.

"Hey, fiddler...I'm sick and tired of tightening screws coming on the conveyor belt all day, man. Do you like it? Maybe I'm crazy, but I can't take it anymore. I can't. Period. I'm going to Helena, where at least I know there's something I know how to do. I did it back in Romania, and I can do it here too. Come with me! You're young, you can tend those sheep like nobody's business. We can make a lot of money; think about it. They'll give us land for free just so we can raise animals!"

Mitu didn't even want to hear it at first. He didn't care for the work he did at Ford, but it was well paid, and he had, for better or worse, a roof over his head. He felt he needed to thank God for it, not ask for more.

"What am I gonna do with sheep, Gherasim? Have you lost your mind? Climb the mountains in the cold and rain like I did in Romania? Are you nuts? I don't like sheep! I never did! And there's no way the money'd be better there than at Ford. What did I come to America for? To do what I did back home? And you couldn't possibly make more there than at Maxwell Motors. What the hell are you talking about?"

"I might not make any more money. Right you may be, but I'd live better, like I did back home. Wandering the valleys and hills at my own leisure, with no one watching over my shoulder...whatcha gonna do five years from now? Think ahead. What d'you see? I'll tell you what: the same miserable salary you can put aside a few pennies from, saving a lifetime for the little bit at the end. I've thought about this a lot. A lot. They work you like a slave and they can fire you whenever they feel like it. They make you do this and that—work you hate—but you can't say nothing about it. Some damn thieves! I felt like a two-cent whore paid to please them! I'd be better off up in the mountains!"

After a while, Mitu began paying more attention to Gherasim. Foreboding thoughts about the future like Gherasim's had haunted him many times as well. How much longer could he stay at Ford doing what he did? For how long was he going to wake up early in the morning and come home late with no time for anything else? Gherasim was right: in a few years, he could picture himself still on the assembly line. He had to do something after all; he couldn't remain at Ford forever.

He remembered that his mother had written to him once about some people from Novaci who had gone to Montana to do shepherding, and the more he thought about it, the more attractive the idea became. *"Maybe it wouldn't be so bad going in those mountains...maybe I can find some of the people from my village. We could help each other out..."*

He started asking Gherasim for more details.

"So tell me, Moldavian. How do they tend sheep where you wanna go?"

"Well, all I know is what I've heard, Mitu, because I spoke with whoever I could, but I don't think it's gonna be so hard to learn...a sheep's still a sheep in Romania or America..."

"But who told you they'll give us land?"

"I read in a newspaper that in Montana they give you land if you want to raise livestock. They give it to you for free. Acres and acres, however much you want..."

More time passed, and Mitu mulled over it from all angles, making calculations: *"If I make there as much money as I do at Ford, I could save a lot more because I wouldn't need to spend on rent and food..."* But uncertainty kept gnawing at him.

"I don't know what to say, Gherasim...I make good money here. No one wants to fire me...it's not so bad, you know? I work a lot, but I'm not ashamed of it. I managed to put a little something aside, too. Just a few pennies, but at least it's something. I have a car, a good place to live. What else can I ask for? God might smite me if I did..."

Another month went by, and another, and another, time during which he looked everywhere for information on tending sheep in America and finally decided. He went to Gherasim's one night to tell him he was going with him.

"Hey man, I thought about it and figured I got nothing to lose...I don't own a home or land, I have some savings—not a lot—and a car I can sell quick. I can come back to Ford if I have to because I know a few people. I'll go with you. There has to be a place for another shepherd on the mountains of Montana. Godspeed to us!"

Gherasim's face lit up at the news.

"Now, fiddler from Oltenia, you don't know how happy you made me! You have no idea! And lemme tell you something else: I know how you like a glass or two, and how you struggle to buy it under the table. Well, in them bare places of Montana you could make your own. Maybe you'll get rich..."

THE BOOTLEGGING

Chapter 29

Montana left Mitu breathless. The Rockies were so overwhelming that even someone like him who had grown up at the foot of the Păpușa Summit couldn't help but marvel at the grandiosity of the place. The deep and clear lakes were surrounded by peaks scraping the clouds. Missouri River, flowing thousands and thousands of miles far south to eventually converge with Mississippi River, slithered narrow like a steel blade. The woods were teeming with grizzly bears, and bison herds roamed the prairies stretching all the way to the horizon.

"This is the place to raise sheep, Gherasim, millions and millions of them!" he exclaimed invigorated, nostrils aquiver, when they reached Helena. All he could think about was the moment he would find something to work, forgetting all about his childhood hatred for cattle.

"Yes... I told you! But you're talkin' like you didn't even believe me!"

"I believed you, but I didn't imagine it would be like this! Now we need to see how we can find some work... We need to go from ranch to ranch..."

"Yes, let's go from ranch to ranch, yes... we'll find something to do, no doubt..."

They researched information on the sheep farms around, bought maps to become familiar with the places and then began trekking the roads of Helena.

They found nothing in the outskirts of the city. "Anything that comes by gets taken very quickly around here..." they were told.

Having learned the lay of the land, they widened their search, reaching more remote farms but couldn't find anything there either. "Nothing here, folks, nothing. Sorry...All of our sheep are up in the mountains, we don't need any help...But come back again, you know how it is: shepherds come and go and maybe we'll have something in the future..."

Seeing that their first trials proved unsuccessful, they thought to organize better. If until then their search had been rather random, done on the spur of the moment, they now strategized each night which farms to visit, marking them with a pencil on the map—already over ten—thinking to hit as many as possible while on the same route.

At one of the farms, about seven miles away from the city, they had a surprise. It was the last stop they were going to make in the area that day, having seen them all. They had left early in the morning, but without high hopes, since all the farm owners they had met previously didn't know of anything available around.

A man was giving chase to some horses in the back, yelling wildly at them. They approached him to inquire about the owner, and he answered in broken English that he knew nothing of his boss's whereabouts for a few days now.

Mitu asked where he was from.

"Romania," came the surprising answer.

"Romania? You're from Romania? *Vorbeşti româneşte?!* Would you look at that! What luck!"

"You're Romanian too?" the man asked.

"Yes! You couldn't tell from our accents? We're Romanians. And? Where from in Romania?"

"From Gorj County. Near Târgu-Jiu. Novaci, if you know it..."

"Novaci! Oh man, d'you know where I'm from? From Cernădia! Good God in Heaven! What's your name? because I don't know you..."

"From Cernădia? What's your name? Mine's Ilie Porumbel."

"Ilie Porumbel..." Mitu repeated. "I know your name; I just don't know where from. Do you know me? I used to play with Corcoveanu's *taraf* before I came to America...Mitu Popescu. The Fiddler..."

"The Fiddler...goodness gracious! Mitu, yes! I know you, of course! You were a young lad then! Used to play the violin! How you've changed! Who didn't know you? You left a long time ago..."

Ana's face flashing before his eyes, Mitu wondered, embarrassed, *"Does he know what made me run to America? God, how long it's been...I wonder how she's doing..."*

"Yes...I came to America ten years ago...in 1913. What about you?"

"About five years ago."

"See Mitu, see how the good Lord helps us? Good thing we decided to go to all the farms!" Gherasim crossed himself amply, touched that two men from neighboring villages had met each other on the other side of the world.

"But where do you live?" Ilie asked.

"We're staying at a boardinghouse outside the town. Where else...? We didn't know anybody here. Are there any other people from Novaci?"

"There are, there are..." Ilie answered, to Mitu's surprise. "And there have been a lot more...Gheorghe Vonică, Ion Vărzaru and Ion Piluţă are still here. There used to be Petre Nedu, Petre Grigore, Ion Andreoiu, Alexandru Cosor..., Grigore Stelea, and Iosif Pirtea, but they went back to Romania. Do you know any of them?"

Mitu tried to remember each one.

"Well, my Ma sent me a letter some time ago, a few years back, and told me about some people who had left, but I forgot who because I didn't care too much about it, since I didn't think I'd ever come over here. I remember Gheorghe Vonică...he's a swarthy fellow with a big nose, right?"

"Yes, and kinda lanky. He works on a farm five miles down from here..."

"And I think I know Vărzaru, but for the life of me I can't remember what he looks like! Just the name...I know Pirtea, the shepherd, yeah...and who else did you say? Cosor...also a shepherd from Novaci, ain't he? But I don't know the rest. Had you told me some women's names, that would've been a different story..."

"Yeah, yeah...no women from Novaci made it here...but no problem, if they do, I won't tell you. I'll keep them all to myself..."

"Well maybe you'll find it in your heart to send the most beautiful my way, because I won't care for the others..."

"Yeah, don't worry, that's exactly what I'll do..." Ilie chuckled. "I'll send her right to you! Listen, man, how come you don't know these people I told you about?"

"I don't know them, can't remember them..." Mitu shrugged. "If I saw them, maybe I'd recognize them. See, I left Cernădia when I was seventeen, and although I played at weddings and parties, I really didn't know many in Novaci. You know how it is...I played, they danced, and we didn't speak that much...and it's been more than ten years since then. But where are they? We went to all these farms from around Helena, and you're the first Romanian we've met so far..."

"Well, I told you: Vonică works on a farm five miles down from here. And Vărzaru and Piluță, to be honest I don't know much about them but it takes a day to get to where they are." He gestured westward with his hand. "We all come together every now and then on Sundays in a restaurant in Helena, Sasha and Natasha's, where there's a Romanian waiter who slips us drinks."

"And you said some of them went back to Novaci? What ever for?"

"Well, I really don't know what to tell you...but many who saved up a thousand or two went back to build homes there. You know. People come here, stay for a few years, and then go back with their savings. That's what I'm gonna do, too."

"I never thought that many people would go back..." said Gherasim. While in Detroit, he knew of very few people who had returned to Romania, and not one person had gone back to Moldova.

"Better home than a stranger in the world, right?" Ilie sighed, a shadow of bitterness clouding his eyes. "And there's plenty of other Romanians over here. Everybody knows Tecău, the magician, who does tricks at parties, for instance. You'll meet him for sure if you go to that restaurant, because that's mostly his turf."

"Hey man," Mitu said, bringing them back to the matter at hand, "How can we find something to do for work around here? Because that's why we came to Helena..."

Ilie scratched his chin and took a serious air.

"Well now, that's not very easy. Whoever told you otherwise didn't know any better. But I know a farmer over the mountains, about five hours away from here...it's a long hike to him, and there aren't too many people who want to work there...it's a very big ranch, with thousands and thousands of sheep. It's called Ray's Ranch." He pointed with his hand to somewhere far away. "Go there and try. I met him about a month ago in town, and he said that if I heard of anyone good at tending sheep to send him his way, because he needs help with his herds. Tell him you know John Deegan, the owner of this ranch, that he sent you, yeah?"

"John Deegan. Alright, Ilie, thank you very much for your advice, and God bless...we'll see each other again soon! I can't wait to see the other people from Novaci! What did you say the restaurant was called?"

"Sasha and Natasha's. Right next to Marlow Theater. Downtown."

"Sasha and Natasha's, Marlow Theater," Mitu repeated to remember. "Well, as soon as we find a job, we'll pass by there, right Gherasim?"

"Yes, of course. If we get hired, we'll buy you a drink, Ilie!"

The man shrugged.

"Leave the drink for some other time. Just find something to work first...good luck. The ranch is that way." He showed them the direction once again.

It took them half a day to get to Ray's Ranch. They stopped off at two other ranches on the way where they asked for directions. They climbed two more hills and a small mountain and finally reached it. The owner, a ruddy Anglo-Saxon of about fifty, fair-haired, blue-eyed, and freckled, with strong arms and a paunchy belly received them as if he had been waiting for them for a while.

"You wanna look after sheep, huh?" he asked, rather redundantly since very few people ever ventured all the way there for something else.

They nodded without saying a word.

"By the looks of you, you're from somewhere in Europe, right?"

"Yes, sir, and we were sent to you by John Deegan," Mitu ventured.

"Oh, just call me Ray, not sir. John Deegan. I see...and what are your names?"

They said their names and he struggled with their pronunciation a few times.

"What kind of names are these anyway?" he asked confusedly.

"We're from Romania, sir..." Mitu answered.

"Oh, Romania...I don't know much about that country. Are there many sheep there? Do you know how to tend to them?"

"Of course we do, that's what we used to do there as well!" Gherasim answered rather unconvincingly. "Just try us out and you'll see, sir..."

The farmer made a gesture as if to say, 'Yeah, yeah, I've seen plenty like you...'

"Come with me so I can show you what it's all about."

They gave each other hopeful looks—"Maybe we're in luck!"—and followed him. Behind the ranch they saw a huge herd of sheep, separated according to breed, surrounded by narrow fences. Mitu didn't even have a chance to take it all in when the farmer put him in charge of five thousand sheep, and gave Gherasim another flock just as big.

"These will be in your care. You'll each get your own and will go with them to the prairie. You won't be together, so they can have plenty of space to scatter around the way they should. I'll show you where you're supposed to take them. There are warm winds here, blowing from the north, so there is no snow. That's why the sheep are out grazing almost the whole year. I had these flocks here because a couple of my shepherds left about a month ago...you came at the right time. I hope you'll do a good job...I need you...ten dollars a week—no more, no less, got it?"

The waves of wool quivering before his eyes frightened Mitu. *"How am I gonna look after all these by myself?"* he wondered in alarm. The flocks of sheep from Novaci were rarely larger than a thousand heads, and they were tended for by a few people, not just one.

Ray sensed his indecisiveness and began questioning him.

"Tell me, man, can you do this or not? Am I gonna wake up one day to see that you lost my sheep in the wilderness, and they're gone?"

Mitu hesitated for a moment, took in a deep breath, and said, "Not a problem, this is a piece of cake compared to what we used to do in Romania! Right, Gherasim?"

Gherasim nodded, a tad more convincing than before.

"Trust us, you won't be disappointed..."

The farmer smiled out of the corner of his mouth, as though to say he understood more than he let on, then gave them each a horse, a rifle, and a dog.

"Yours, young man, is named Max, and yours, Vicky. They are reliable dogs, you'll become friends fast."

Mitu scratched the dog between the ears, and the animal licked his hand, wagging his tail as if he knew him for a lifetime. Max was a shepherd dog, with intelligent eyes, a strong, supple body, and seemed used to long-term effort.

"What can a dog do when faced with a pack of wolves or a bear..." Mitu mumbled under his breath.

"What did you say?" Ray asked.

"Nothing in particular, sir. I was just wondering how Max would square up with a pack of wolves or a bear..."

"You should be more afraid of people. Predatory animals don't come down to the prairie all that often. I've been a farmer thirty years, and I never had much trouble with that."

Mitu walked among the sheep curiously inspecting a few of them. They were a lot bigger than the ones in Romania.

"Ray, how much do these rams weigh?"

"Those are Columbia breed, and they weigh about 290 pounds. The females are about 220 and give 15 pounds of wool each."

"290? Did you hear that Gherasim? And the milking? Who milks all these sheep, because I don't think one person can do it?"

Ray stared at him:

"I don't know where you're from, but here we don't milk the sheep, we keep them for their wool and meat..."

Mitu decided then not to ask anything anymore. *"I'll find all answers on my own, without making an ass of myself in front of a stranger..."*

They spent the night at the ranch and returned to town the next day for their luggage. Before going back up, they stopped at the restaurant mentioned by Porumbel. Just as he had told them, they met the Romanian waiter and Tecău, a jolly elderly man, and his daughters, sixteen-year-old Smaranda and eighteen-year-old Mirița. Mitu was smitten with both of them immediately.

They shot the breeze for a while, and little by little, Tecău learned that Mitu played the violin and began questioning him—what kind of music he played, how well he knew it, where he had learned it from—and, at the end, slipped them a drink and told them to come back there soon.

"Come Saturdays, because that's when I do my shows, and it's a lot of fun. You'll come for sure, yeah? Take this here bottle to have for the hike up to the ranch."

The next morning, they went up to the mountains with Ray, who was to show them the grazing fields. They walked for a day. Ray left Gherasim somewhere lower—he would come back later to show him the lay of the land—and continued up for ten more miles with Mitu, time he used to instruct him on how to bring together the herd if it scattered around, how to figure out if the sheep were sick, how to use Max.

"The dog will round up the animals that get away. He knows these places very well. If you stray and go somewhere you shouldn't, he'll bark at you to get your attention...and if he sees you don't go where you should, he'll come to you, grab you by the hand, and lead you that way. He's one of the best dogs I've ever had..."

When they finally arrived, sweaty and tired, Mitu was glad to see his dwelling was a log cabin. His fear, from what he had heard, was that he was going to have to raise and live in a tent.

"I'll bring you food on a regular basis," Ray said to him at the end, meaning that he was really coming to check up on him. "And every few weeks I'll send someone to replace you for a day or two, so that you can go to the town. And, I forgot to tell you before: take good care of them because for each sheep that's missing for whatever reason, I will deduct from your salary..."

They shook hands and parted ways. Mitu's eyes lingered in his wake for a long time, and he kept wondering if his decision to leave Ford had been a wise one.

"Please God help me and keep my sheep out of wild beasts' way, or I'll have to pay for them until the day I die..." He sighed, looking at the endless grazing fields on which he was to roam from then on.

Chapter 30

The first few months at Ray's Ranch flew by. Mitu woke up each day at the crack of dawn and wandered the hills with his sheep, striving to keep them from going astray. He ran like a madman, afraid he might lose them, bitterly cursing the frugality of the American farmers who only hired one person to look after a thousands of heads.

"The shepherds in Novaci wouldn't believe their eyes!" he'd say resentfully when finally catching his breath after running around for half a day.

Max proved himself to be extremely helpful. He ran tirelessly around the flock, never losing sight of it. Then, he'd come back to Mitu, barking happily, only to start the whole process yet again. Mitu couldn't remember seeing any dogs in Rânca put to such good use. *"If I cared for working the way this dog does, I'd get rich very quickly..."*

He had his rifle on him at all times, but not because he was afraid—he was all alone in those secluded places—but because it reminded him of the war and his old friends. He would find a remote target sometimes, usually the thick trunk of a tree, and shoot a few rounds, filling with satisfaction at his precision.

Just as he had planned, despite the fact that he was making less than half the money he made at Ford, he could now save it all up. Besides buying a few razor blades and soap, he didn't need anything else, so he put aside everything Ray gave him, gathering it all in a small leather pouch. He was beside himself with joy seeing how the pile of coins grew little by little.

He figured at that pace, in a year or two, he could open up his own store—his dream from the time he arrived in America. Rambling about the mountain every which way with the sheep gave him plenty of time to think in detail and make endless calculations.

He hadn't forgotten Gherasim's casual remark about the possibility of making his own booze in the forests of Montana. As soon as he saved up a little more money, he began seriously considering building his own distillery. "Some brandy'd go very well with the smoked meat I eat every day!" In those woods, putting together his own contraption to produce alcohol seemed like child's play.

During his trips to Helena, which he took once every few weeks when Ray gave him time off, he searched for the materials he needed. From word of mouth he learned of one person who sold copper tubing and another one who had a still of about twenty gallons; at a market he came across a spiraled tube for cooling. Tecău sent him to some people who sold oats and sugar. Within a few months, he had collected almost everything he needed to build a still for manufacturing brandy.

On the day he got the last few things he still needed, he asked an Irish man—Carrick O'Flahertys, a freckled man with blue eyes who had sold him some screws, nuts, and a few rusty but functional faucets—to go with him to teach him how to assemble the equipment.

"Listen pal...I'll give you a gallon of whiskey when I make it, if you come with me to help me up there. We can leave now and get there in the afternoon, and you can come back to Helena tomorrow."

The Irishman glanced curiously at him but agreed right away. "Of course! We'll go whenever you want!" he said. He had a desperate need for money and he had noticed Mitu's utter cluelessness about the business. A gallon of alcohol was a small fortune if one knew how to sell it. Since the prohibition, all the liquor stores had been closed down, their doors nailed shut and their windows shuttered, and distribution centers had gone bankrupt leaving thousands and thousands of people unemployed and out on the street. He knew it all too well: he had been working for many years in a liquor warehouse and now had eight mouths to feed and no income. To have enough for survival he resorted to bootlegging, either selling parts or rye brandy brewed stealthily in his own basement.

The installation took them almost a full day. Mitu was going around in circles trying to figure out how everything worked. As he was tightening the last screw, Carrick started explaining it all to him.

"Listen to how you make it: You take rye or barley and you mix it with water and a little bit of yeast. You know, the yeast feeds on the sugar in the grains, and what comes out is the alcohol. Now, to obtain what you need, you need to boil all this stuff at 172 degrees, the temperature alcohol evaporates at. You need to check the thermometer every few minutes. Not any higher or lower than that, okay? Because water disperses at 212 degrees, it will remain in the still, and the alcohol will condense and circulate as vapors through the copper tubing, then through the filters to clear up, until it reaches the other side—where the coil is—where you cool it down with cold water. Then, drops of alcohol will trickle one by one, alright? All you need to do then is collect them and drink them up."

Mitu breathed in deeply and looked at the metal wonder with satisfaction:

"And how much will I get from one boiling?"

"It depends on how you make it: the good and clean alcohol, made of rye, and unsweetened with sugar or any other stuff, is expensive, even twenty dollars a gallon, but you don't get much of that. If you want to make more of it, you put something sweet and cheap in it. Five dollars will buy you a hundred pounds of sugar and that gets you ten gallons of moonshine. If you sell it for ten dollars a gallon...well, you do the calculation to see how much..."

Mitu stood, mouth agape. He hadn't asked how much money he'd make but how many gallons of alcohol, so the Irishman's answer left him almost speechless.

"A hundred dollars from a boil?"

Carrick smiled bitterly. "It may seem like a lot of money to you, but we're just small fish compared to the big manufacturers—the gangster millionaires. And wouldn't you know it; we're the ones ending up in jail when they catch us."

"Let's fire it up and see if it works!" Mitu got all excited, stuffing dried branches under the still.

"Oh man, you had better think twice if you wanna do this, because I see you have no clue. Haven't you heard that you never make booze during the day?"

"Why can't I make it during the day? What...? Daylight spoils it?" he joked, unsure and embarrassed.

"During the day, the smoke from the fire is visible from afar, and they could catch you right away. It's called moonshine because that's how you make it: under the light of the moon. Only at night. Don't ever forget it if don't wanna end up in jail!"

Mitu gave him a grateful look. "Thank you very much for all your advice, man. You've been a great help, really great...I owe you one."

"Listen, if you need a distributor, bring the merchandise to me, and I'll deal it through my network. I know all the cops and the federal agents. I know who accepts bribes and who doesn't. Their salaries are miserable, and many of them are against the prohibition anyway, so only a few of them will arrest you if you slip them a twenty-dollar bill. Now, you're not gonna get the same money per gallon you would if you sold it by yourself, but the risk isn't all that great either. Think about it, okay?"

"I will, Carrick. We'll see..." answered Mitu, astonished at everything he had learned.

"What should I do?" he kept thinking during the following days, trying to weigh all aspects of Carrick's proposition. "I really must be outta my mind to think about bootlegging! What's gonna happen if they catch me? I'll end up in prison!"

As he became used to the idea, he said to himself that even if he did get caught, he might get away with just a warning since he was going to move only small quantities of alcohol. *"Maybe I should make only a few deliveries, get enough money, and then stop. Sure I can, can't I? Sell just a little bit, since I'll have more than enough for myself? And I couldn't possibly be that unlucky to get caught the very first time..."*

His first delivery, a month after mounting the still, worked like clockwork. He woke up one Saturday morning at three, secured all the sheep in their paddock and left Max to watch them, fastened a few casks on either side of the saddle, and went to Helena at a fast trot. He scrutinized the horizon carefully, cringing at every slight noise coming from the forest.

Once in town, he went to see Carrick, who grabbed one of the casks at random, filled a glass and agitated it, watching carefully the bubbles forming on the liquid's surface.

"You've done a good job, bootlegger, it's strong..." He seemed pleased.

"Yeah! Of course it's strong; I know how I made it. But how do you know without even tasting it?"

"The bigger the bubbles and the faster they break on the surface, the more concentrated the alcohol is," the Irishman told him. "Lemme show you."

Mitu watched him pour some gunpowder into a spoon and set it alight.

"Do you see how it burns? If I put some alcohol over it and it fizzes out that means the alcohol is watery. If it continues to burn, it's strong," he explained and poured a thin stream from the glass.

The fire continued to burn, to Mitu's relief.

"Good thing now I know how things work, Carrick..."

"I didn't tell you how to proof it beforehand to see if you were honest, but now I see that you are. Had you brought me some shitty draff, I wouldn't have done business with you a second time. Let's empty out the casks. Two gallons, plus two more, and three, it's seven altogether. One is mine for free, the way we made the deal, so six. Here you go," he placed a few bills in his hand. "See you next time, buddy. Be careful how you go back and forth. Sneak around. Even if you don't have moonshine on you, cops can sniff your casks, and you can have problems, got it? A bottle's not a big deal, but casks raise suspicion."

Mitu thanked him, gathered the money, and stuffed it into his pocket. That day he made double his biweekly salary from Ford.

The following months went by without a glitch. He would go to town once every few Saturdays and deliver the alcohol, stuffing his pockets with wads of dollar bills. He would then visit Sasha and Natasha's, chatting Tecău, his friends, and especially Tecău's daughters. After that, he would go back to the mountains. He looked after the sheep during the day, and he made alcohol at night. He now knew every single roundabout path, stone, hiding place, and meadow like the back of his hand.

After another couple of months, he built himself another distillery, half a mountain away from the first. He hid it well inside the forest, camouflaging the narrow path leading to it with dried branches. If the first installation had been an experiment to help him understand the manufacturing process and get used to its challenges, the second was real business. The still had a capacity of a few hundred gallons, and the metal pipes were very thick. Since he didn't like the taste of brandy poured straight into canning jars, he bought a few barrels made out of oak, to age the alcohol even for a week or two. From his visits to blind pigs, he had realized that, in their mad chase after money, the manufacturers bypassed that last step, costly timewise, but essential in giving the alcohol a natural taste and a darker color. He didn't want to make what was known as "White Lightning" or "Skull Cracker."

Aging the alcohol took time, but the money received from Carrick was plentiful. The Irishman appreciated the quality of the drink and compensated him handsomely, since he also wanted to be known as a distributor of superior merchandise.

Since he had made his second distillery, Mitu visited Helena more often—sometimes he went down there once a week. He was worried in the beginning that he was producing too much, but Carrick was very consistent. He never took less than what Mitu brought him. He never said, "I'll pay you next time. I first have to sell it."

After a while he started experimenting with the initial installation. The second, bigger one guaranteed a constant flow of alcohol, so now he could afford the luxury of trying out new things with the small one. For a while he mixed crabapples and rye, then he only used apples and plums, until he obtained something that resembled the *ţuică* made in Romania. Finally, he began distilling it twice, keeping it in oak kegs filled one fourth with raspberries, bilberries, wild berries, or some roots which reminded him of an aromatic plant growing in his native mountains.

This special drink was for himself, he said, to savor while looking after the sheep. During one of his trips to Helena he thought to bring a sample of it to Carrick and give it to him "buddy to buddy."

"My God, what is this?" the man exclaimed when he tasted it. "It's incredibly good! What's it made of?"

"Not gonna tell you! A secret recipe from Romania..."

"Yeah? A recipe from Romania, you say...just tell me one thing: how much of it can you make?"

Mitu looked surprised at him. He hadn't thought about distributing it: it was for his personal enjoyment only.

"I don't know, man, because I don't use grains like rye or barley. Only mixtures of fruits, and those are expensive. Plus, it takes a lot longer to make..."

"Bring me this instead of whiskey, and I'll pay you triple for each gallon."

Mitu stared at him. "What do you mean triple? And what about you?"

"Man, this here is a luxury drink. This sells for a lot of money in speakeasies! Don't worry, I'll have my square share of the deal; don't think I work for free! You bring me this if you can, and we'll both be happy!"

The following weeks kept Mitu awake day and night. He hauled sacks of plums and apples bought at markets in town, scoured the mountains for leaves and roots, and picked bilberries, wild strawberries, and raspberries from the hills on which his sheep grazed, mixing them in all different ways to make the drink requested by Carrick.

The money was pouring in. Each delivery brought him pocketfuls, sometimes even a hundred dollars. Since he couldn't deposit the money in the bank without raising suspicions, he kept it hidden in metal boxes buried in places known only by him.

His life had changed for the better overnight, but the constant hustle and bustle and continuous boiling also meant his sheep were unattended more and more, left to scamper around as they pleased. He would have liked to give up shepherding altogether, but it wasn't possible: he needed to remain at Ray's

Ranch; staying up in the mountains for no other reason would have been very dubious and would have raised suspicions.

A few months into the venture, fatigue overpowered him. One day, he went out with the sheep on a pasture and sat down to rest. He struggled not to doze off but fell dead asleep and couldn't wake up for a few hours. When he did wake up, his sheep were nowhere to be found. He searched them high and low for a long time and found them late in the evening, scattered everywhere, with poor Max running madly after them. He couldn't understand what had happened—maybe an animal had scared them off? But whatever the reason, things couldn't go on like that.

A few days later, he went to see Gherasim. He looked for his friend for a while and finally found him in a field, munching contentedly on some sunflower seeds, clueless to what Mitu had been up to lately.

"I don't know what to say." He scratched his head when he learned what Mitu needed him to do. "You mean to say you'll pay me—give me salary—to watch the sheep *you're* being paid to watch? Well, how's that gonna work?! And how can I look after your herd, too? There's just too many altogether!"

"We'll take them grazing on the same hills, Gherasim...we'll be together, but I'm gonna nap once in a while during the day, so I can stay up at night. No one will know. And Ray, if he finds out, won't mind it as long as his sheep are well taken care of. What does he care? And I'll give you my salary, plus I'll match it up with my own money. You'll make more than at Maxwell Motors and you can save it all up, since you have no expenses at the farm. You can go back to Romania a lot sooner! Didn't you say that's what you wanted?"

"Well, I'd go with you, but I gotta tell you—it scares me. It scares me. Period! What if they catch us and throw me in jail all innocent? Nobody'll believe that I just tend to the sheep not knowing what you do at night!"

"Listen to me Gherasim; don't worry about the cops. I pay them off, and I know a lot of them already. You're the only one I can trust. Remember how I came to Montana with you, all the while thinking I was outta my mind to do it? Well, now I'm glad I did."

"I haven't had the best of living until now, but I never broke the law or did nothing against our good Lord, Mitu, and I've always been able to sleep fine at night. What kind of punishment do you get if they catch you?"

"The law forbids making and distributing alcohol, but it doesn't forbid having some. If the agents come to the farm and find a bottle, there's nothing they can do. If they catch me at the distillery, then yeah, they could throw me in jail, since I produce it. As long as you stay away from the stills, you won't have a problem. Well, what do you say?"

Gherasim thought about it for a while but couldn't resist the temptation of making a lot of money at once. And Mitu had struck a very sensitive cord by telling him he could return to Romania sooner.

"You make it sound easy, but I don't think it's quite like that. But you know what? Fuck it. We only live once. I'll help you. We'll tend the sheep together. We'll be—how's it called?—'partners in crime...'"

Mitu's face lit up. "Well said! Don't think you're doing something wrong! Not at all! People have always enjoyed booze! I read somewhere the other day that, after they passed the law, those people in the government drank until they passed out! What's that all about? Huh? What? Why are those bastards fuckin' with us like that?"

While Gherasim looked after the sheep, Mitu concentrated a hundred percent on the alcohol production. Not too long after, he built two more distilleries of a hundred gallons each, far away from the sheepfold, hidden in the heart of the forest. He boiled in them simultaneously, running from one to the other, hauling casks and barrels, struggling to empty out sacks of plums and apples in the huge copper vessels, building pulleys and levers—burning the candle at both ends.

He was spinning like a top all day long. The only other time he had worked this hard had been during Corcoveanu's violin lessons.

Chapter 31

Though dog-tired from toiling to produce alcohol, Mitu's exhaustion evaporated the minute he reached Helena with his merchandise and received the payment. At the last count, his money had amounted to almost four thousand dollars, which astounded him. He knew he had a lot, but he hadn't realized just how much!

"Oh my God! In just a few months I've made more money than in a whole year at Ford!"

He went to Helena that day to celebrate his financial boon properly. He thought of passing by Sasha and Natasha's to have a meal with Tecău and maybe chat his daughters up a little. He liked them both. Mirița was pretty and Smaranda, though a bit more homely, was so young! And he believed the feeling was mutual by the way they giggled and threw him furtive glances. Still, he had never had the chance to spend any time with them since Tecău kept them close and watched them like a hawk, having vowed to marry his daughters off to American men only. "If some bastard even touches my daughters, I'll split him in two like a pig!" he'd croak when drunk. "I won't marry my daughters off to some squatters with a few dollars in their pockets thinking they're Rockefeller!"

Halfway there, Mitu changed his mind. "I'll see them some other time...who else to celebrate with but Carrick? It's him I must thank for this tremendous windfall!"

Once in town, he went to the man's house. "Hello, buddy! Just so you know, I don't have a delivery for you. Today I wanna celebrate! And to buy you a drink, because you deserve it! I'm just so glad our business is working out!"

Carrick glanced meaningfully at him. "I never say no to fun! But I'm thinking that maybe you don't really wanna go out for a drink. God knows, you can suck it directly from those pipes of yours in the woods..."

Mitu smiled wanly. It had been a long time since he had been with a woman, hard evidence that life can hit you where it hurts the most. He wondered lately if he hadn't been better off in that respect in Cernădia, where all the women threw themselves at him.

"Take me to a bordello with beautiful women..." he asked in a low voice. "I'll pay for you too, if you know what I mean..."

"You can count on me, friend. I know this business better than anyone here!" Carrick smiled conspiratorially. "There's two ways we can do this: I can take to a place that's close but not that great, or we can go to Butte, where you can choose whoever your heart desires. It's about seventy miles away; I figure we can leave today and get back tomorrow. We'll take my Ford. There's plenty of whorehouses in Butte."

"Yeah? And how are the women?"

"It depends on how much you're willing to pay and where you go looking for them. There's one bordello called Lou Harpell's Apartments, for example, and rumor has it that that's where the most beautiful women are..."

"Won't the cops give us problems? I don't wanna spend the night in jail..."

"Up until a few years ago, prostitution was legal. Then, it's true, things got a bit sour. The police went into the Red Light District to clean it up, but, just like with alcohol, didn't accomplish much. The result of the raids was that the women disappeared from the windows but continued working behind closed doors. Don't worry about it..." the Irishman reassured him.

"Well then, let's go to Butte..."

Clenching his fists with excitement, the Irishman brought the car around. "We're going to do a delivery of you know what, dear!" he called out to his wife while driving off.

Carrick knew his way around Butte with his eyes closed. As soon as they arrived, he took Mitu down Pleasant Alley—shadowy and narrow, plunged in obscurity. Women with strident makeup peered from shady corners pursing their lips seductively at them. Mitu jumped back disgustedly when a French woman of about sixty, whose attire scarcely covered her wilted flesh, called out at him:

"_Voulez vous coucher avec moi, monsieur?_"

He wanted to answer, but the Irishman pulled his sleeve. "You'll find the oldest, ugliest, and fattest women in these alleys. It's dangerous coming here. Many have been stabbed to death for a few dollars. I brought you just to show you. Now we're going to Windsor Hotel on East Mercury Street. It's a classier bordello with beautiful women, where you can do your business without having to watch your back."

Mitu followed him with no additional words. Carrick knew the details of this world as if he had had lived in it all his life.

They stopped in front of a heavy gate, which the Irishman opened without knocking. Mitu admired the architecture of the three story house, which seemed to be the home of someone rich. The windows were two stories tall, a Palladian window beautified the front entrance, and the exterior walls were adorned with nicely polished stone.

They hadn't made two steps in the front yard when a dog dashed to Carrick, putting his paws on the man's chest, wagging his tail happily, and trying to lick his cheek.

"I see you come here often...even the animals know you!" joked Mitu.

"Well, if my wife doesn't give me what I want, I manage any way I can! When you eat beans for a few months, you crave some chocolate once in a while. Don't you agree?" Carrick retorted snappily, rapping lightly with his knuckles on the door.

A red-lipped fifty-year-old woman, wearing violently green eye shadow and sporting brightly dyed blonde hair opened the door.

"Madame Demonstrand, it's nice to see you!"

"Welcome back Carrick O'Flahertys! Maybelline, your favorite, has no clients right now, so she's waiting for you upstairs in her room, as usual. I don't know this young man with you, but he's quite handsome; surely he'll drive my girls wild. Do come inside..."

Mitu entered first and looked around. Tall crystal mirrors made the room look ten times bigger than it was. Soft and luxurious couches and armchairs, upholstered in expensive satin, were strewn everywhere. Walls draped in bronze colored silk, red plush curtains, and lavish green plants in copper pots hanging from the ceiling adorned the first two floors. A sumptuous dining room could accommodate a large number of guests, and the food was prepared in a kitchen in the back where there were two additional rooms for the chef and the servants. A gramophone spread slow, soporific music.

"This woman is the owner of the house," Carrick whispered to Mitu. "She introduces herself as a manicurist, but she's the one heading the bordello...it's called and looks like a hotel, see? She rents out a few of the rooms to some miners working in the area so as not to raise suspicions."

"Girls, come downstairs!" Madame Demonstrand called out.

Carrick waved Mitu good-bye.

"I'm going to see my girl...I'll see you later. Go have fun, and don't waste your time!"

Mitu plopped himself down in an armchair, looking around curiously. He heard the floors creak, and a few scantily clad women in transparent veils came down the stairs. A leggy brunette with a beauty mark on her cheek winked at him, licking her lips and touching her breasts.

"What's your name, handsome, and where are you from?"

"From Romania...you can call me Mitu," he spelled out his name.

"Mytoo" she giggled pronouncing his name in English. "How funny it sounds! I'm Deborah—Debbie. For ten dollars you can be with me for a few hours and do whatever you'd like. For five more, you can do *absolutely* anything, if you get what I mean...let's go upstairs!" She grabbed his hand.

Mitu wanted to refuse her, but she insisted.

"You'll have fun. I promise!" she said touching his crotch. "And what do we have here? We'll need to take proper care of it..." She continued to fondle him in front of all the others.

He followed her docilely up the stairs, peeking at the other girls who hadn't had the chance to say anything. He would have liked to take a closer look at them, to have time to choose, but the woman had been too quick.

"You know, I've never slept with a Romanian before," she said when they entered the room, and she began shedding the little clothes covering her. "You're gonna need to give me the money now, not after. You know you pay whores beforehand, right?"

Mitu counted ten dollar bills—a small fortune for him just a few years back, he realized to his surprise—handed them to her, and looked around. The Irishman hadn't lied. The place did look aristocratic. The walls were covered in oak and mahogany panels and the chairs sculpted from ebony matched the brown hues of the Persian rug. A yellowish ivory statue of an elephant contrasted elegantly with the dark colors of the room.

"What are you waiting for? Undress!" Deborah ordered jokingly, stuffing the money in a small tattered pouch.

Mitu took off his pants and shirt and approached the bed. The woman was lying there, waiting for him to make the first move.

"Come, boy. I won't bite, unless you want me to, of course..."

He glanced at her body. She was a young woman, with small breasts, narrow hips and thin knees. The heavy makeup covered a somewhat attractive face. Her nails were unkempt, with dirt underneath and peeling nail polish. In contrast with her nubile body, her bony arms and callused palms, aged before their time, hinted at harsh manual labor. A bruise barely concealed with a thick layer of blush shaded part of her right temple, and her bottom lip had a gash covered with dry blood.

"What happened here?" he said and touched her forehead.

The girl winced. "Nothing. I slipped in the bathroom and hit myself on the sink. Come on, take me in your arms..."

Mitu lay next to her and started touching her breasts as if he were somehow obligated to play a role. The girl sensed it, and pushing his hand aside, she turned him face down and began massaging his shoulders, touching his back with her breasts—up, down, up, down.

"How's this?" she whispered in his ear.

"Great...how else...?"

"Get on your back," she demanded playfully.

Mitu turned around.

"You're not circumcised! Huh!"

"I'm not what?" he asked confusedly.

"Nothing, it's just there aren't many men uncut like this these days..."

He shuddered as in the presence of a ghost.

"Now, now, you're afraid of circumcision, but you fought in the war, you hero! You can still see the wounds," Deborah laughed, kissing his chest and moving lower towards his abdomen. "It's gotta be something else doing it with a soldier!"

Mitu recovered from the sensation he was experiencing for the first time—oral sex—when Deborah got up to take a condom from a drawer.

"I want you to go inside me now," she said, unrolling it to the base.

He looked confusedly at the sheath of rubber stretched over his penis.

"You don't know what this is? It's for contraception and protection against diseases."

"I know what it is, but..."

"But what?"

"It feels so weird having it on!"

He conformed and played his part to the end. An hour later he was leaving her room with a mixed feeling of satisfaction, embarrassment, disgust, and desire to come back to those dark and promiscuous hallways to try a new girl and another.

"Hey handsome, come back to me next time, okay?" Deborah called from the top of the staircase.

Mitu turned his eyes to her and smiled.

"Absolutely!" he assured her and went back to the foyer to relax in an armchair while waiting for Carrick. "What an interesting experience!" he said to himself looking around. Madame Demonstrand smiled at him and made an imperceptible sign. She beckoned, and a few girls showed up and approached him quickly.

"Don't you wanna go again? You're here anyway. Don't waste your time; get a refill. There's still some time before your friend will be done with Maybelline."

Mitu looked over the face and body of each girl, appraising them as though they were merchandise, with no qualms about the whole process. He took one in his arms, checking her breasts—*"as hard as Olga's,"* he thought—then called a girl who seemed slightly shy, having lowered her eyes each time he looked her way.

"What's your name, sweetheart?"

"Danielle..." the girl answered in a thick accent.

"Danielle, what a pretty name! You remind me of one of my lovers...she had the same hair as you. She was Swedish. Come closer to me..."

The girl approached him timidly and sat on his knees. Mitu touched her nipples with his palms:

"Check out the beauty in my lap...tell me, girl, how does it work with you?"

"We're all the same...ten dollars for a few hours..."

He felt hotter by the minute. He ran his fingers through her hair and kissed her lightly on the lips continuing to caress her in front of all the others. His experience with Deborah had taught him that this was one of the few places on earth where he could do anything without reservations.

"You're very attractive, Danielle...where are you from originally?'

"From Italy..."

"I see you're getting all excited..."

"The way you're touching me, what did you expect...?" she smiled, very provocative all of a sudden. "I can tell you know how to handle a woman. Do you wanna go upstairs?"

"Why the hell not? After all, that's why I came here!" He nodded, staring at her perky butt while climbing the stairs.

Half an hour later, Danielle was resting her head on his chest.

"You can't even tell you had another woman a short while ago. You can't tell at all!"

Mitu slept with five girls from the bordello that day. After Deborah and Danielle, he wandered around the town with Carrick, sharing spicy details from their experiences and buying little nothings on the street. They returned to the Windsor Hotel later, where Mitu chose a black woman—one of his hidden desires for a while—and the Irishman went back with Maybelline.

At last, right before returning to Helena, Mitu took two more women, a Mexican and a Russian, and spent an hour with the two of them, going from one to the other like an inmate enjoying his first day of freedom.

Chapter 32

Two years had passed since Mitu came to Montana. During all that time he had become well accustomed to all the particulars of his endeavor. Gherasim continued to help him with the sheep, and he had established such a routine that bootlegging was now second nature.

He had encountered some problems with the federal agents, but Carrick had taught him how to manage in such circumstances: he gave bribes left and right or changed his routes and the location of his distilleries as necessary. He was once stopped by the cops while transporting a significant quantity—about ten gallons of alcohol—and got away quite miraculously, but not before giving thirty dollars to each of them.

Few blind pig owners knew that he was a manufacturer. He hid that information from them since being known increased the risks of getting caught. Carrick and Gherasim kept this great secret of his well, and besides a few other Romanians whom he had befriended, no one knew anything. If he gave in to a whim, such as buying a new suit or a gold watch, and people wondered from where he had gotten the money, he would say he still had some savings from his Ford days.

In reality, things were different. Aside from spending on his trips to the whorehouses in Butte or the outskirts of Helena, he had no other expenses, so he was able to save up everything made from bootlegging. And it was a lot—more than he had ever hoped. Since the beginning of his alcohol enterprise, he had amassed so much money, it worried him. *"My God in Heaven, what am I gonna do with all this illegal loot?"*

Lately, he had begun distributing to Sasha and Natasha's as well. He had made arrangements with the owner, the Russian, to sell him alcohol at much lower prices than he usually sold it for. He had taken a liking to the restaurant. It was the place where all the Romanians came together for birthdays, weddings, and all other kinds of parties. The place was more than a restaurant with food and beverages; it was a kind of saloon, where they could play billiards, backgammon, or cards. It was where Mitu had met all the other people from Novaci, as Porumbel had told him: Gheorghe Vonică, Ion Vărzaru, and Ion Piluță.

He sometimes played the violin for them. Seeing how talented he was with the bow, Tecău made some arrangements and had him perform on the radio for a cultural show. He then proposed that he give up shepherding, move into the town, and have his own *taraf*. In any other circumstances, Mitu would have accepted, but he had to say no this time. He no longer lived as he had during his Corcoveanu days. The best thing for him to do was to stay up in the mountains and keep boiling.

He felt in his element at Sasha and Natasha's. He considered it his second home. He met with many Romanians, and lately spoke mostly Romanian, using English only with Carrick.

He had gotten closer with Miriţa and Smaranda as well. He had had his eye on them for a while now, whispering sweet nothings in their ears, especially at parties where Tecău was too tipsy to notice. The girls never missed a shindig in Helena where Mitu was playing. Sometimes he'd dedicate his performances to them, convinced that if it weren't for Tecău's omnipresence, he could have gotten at least Miriţa, who seemed more receptive to amorous endeavors, having been recently dumped by her boyfriend Johnny, an American Lieutenant.

Tecău had sensed something and sometimes warned him half-jokingly to mind his own business: "Young man, if you touch a girl of mine, you'll have to deal with me!"

"Well now, what do you take me for? I'm a serious person, for goodness' sake!" Mitu would say to mitigate his fears.

He had managed to spend a few hours alone with the girls at Tecău's last birthday party. After the guests had left and Tecău was snoozing on the couch drunk, they chatted for a long time, and at the end, Mitu stole a kiss with Miriţa.

Since then, he had tried in vain to see them somewhere private but had never been successful. They were always surrounded by too many people at parties or at church, and they were always chaperoned by their father.

All this would change soon, however. Tecău's birthday was coming, and as always, he had planned a big party at his place. He asked Mitu to lead his *taraf*, telling him, "I want to be serenaded on my birthday, not sing to myself!" and put the girls in charge of the guests.

On the day of the party, a beautiful Saturday in Spring, Mitu dressed up to make the best impression. He put on his nicest suit, took some casks of his best brandy, and went to town early enough to buy a gift for the birthday man and bouquets of flowers for his daughters.

Tecău had organized everything by the book. He was a meticulous man and took care of every single detail out of the exaggerated fear he might embarrass himself in front of the guests. He had tables all around his living room, with some space in the middle for dancing and a corner reserved for the *taraf*. He had saved the head seat at the main table, from which he could address everybody, for himself—he loved giving speeches—and had chairs for the players and his daughters around him.

When Mitu finally arrived, a little late—finding the right gift had taken longer than expected—thirty guests were already there, and the party had started. His better acquaintances included the players from Tecău's *taraf* and three people from Novaci: Ilie Porumbel, Gheorghe Vonică, and Ion Piluţă.

"You're right on time, Mitu! We were just about to fill our glasses with liquor and our bowls with hot soup! Come sit over here next to me and your friends!" Tecău welcomed him.

"Happy birthday, Uncle Tecău!"

"Yeah...like we needed the Fiddler to start drinking!" one of the guests who had arrived recently to Helena commented, unaware that Mitu was a bootlegger.

"Well, plumber, just so you know, we do need him!" Tecău contradicted, "since it's his booze we're drinking! Come and take a seat at the table. Don't be shy like a virgin on her wedding night! Let's start the party! I've just taken the next course off the stove!"

They all sat down, and Mirița and Smaranda brought out plates and flatware. The girls had been cooking all day—chicken noodle soup, stuffed cabbage, roasted pork, phyllo dough with Turkish delight—and were eagerly awaiting the guests' appreciation of their food.

"Now," Tecău warned them, "don't throw yourselves at the food like animals! Before we all stuff our faces, I'd like to make a proper toast. May God bless us on these places until we go to meet Him up in Heaven! May we have it good here and be healthy until we grow old! I've had a full life, with many satisfactions, and I wish you all the same! Don't ever forget where you come from! I, for one, will leave my bones on this here land!"

"Now, watch this, he's gonna recite the cemetery rhyme," Vonică chuckled under his breath. "Just wait a second."

Mitu barely contained a snicker, covering his mouth like a schoolboy.

Tecău continued according to his well-known habit, "I have a pouch of dirt from the cemetery in my village, and when my time's up, I'll ask for it to be scattered all over my grave! Just like the mother said to her emigrant children:

> *Swear to me on my deathbed*
> *Dirt from the village I am from*
> *On my gravestone when I'm dead*
> *You will have to sprinkle some*
> *Right next to those I loved*
> *To sleep eternal slumber*
> *Siblings, my father, mother*
> *And slowly flowing water."*

"Forget about these sad things, Uncle Tecău; we came here to celebrate, not get upset!" Porumbel called out, suddenly distressed.

Tecău said aloud for everyone to hear, "Well, Ilie, you came here to celebrate today, but where might you be tomorrow? Maybe here, maybe not! You never know what tomorrow brings!"

"Oh, I know where I'll be tomorrow, Uncle Tecău! At my job! Like that saying:

> *American greenbacks*
> *One thing I have to say:*
> *You may be nice and handsome*
> *You're killing me each day"*

"Porumbel is right," Piluță intervened. "Uncle Tecău, you still have a ways to go before buying the farm! Better show us some tricks!"

Tecău made a scolding gesture at them for being so thick-headed and not heeding the truth of his words, and then got up and called Mitu by his side.

"You want tricks, eh? Fiddler, you make so much money with your bootlegging that now it's coming outta you!" he said loudly pulling a few dollar bills from his ear.

Mitu watched him amused, wondering how in the world he had done it, since Tecău's sleeves were rolled up.

"Houdini from Transylvania!" Porumbel said. "This is what we want. Make us laugh, not cry with our heads on the table, listening to poems about how we'll kick the bucket soon! Show us more! Right, everyone?"

"Yes, Uncle Tecău, do something else!" the guests clamored.

Quite flattered—the old man loved requests from the crowd—Tecău took a piece of cloth out of his pocket, fluttered and twisted it in all directions for everyone to see, waved it again and pulled a white rabbit out of it. He continued his performance for another fifteen minutes, then told Mitu to take over his *taraf*.

"Well, you don't expect me to croon to myself on my own birthday, Fiddler! Go ahead, sing us something! Entertain us!"

Mitu took the violin in his hands, played a few notes to tune it and then started singing in a strong voice.

> *Never thought this sight I'd see*
> *Tending sheep to be fancy*
> *With binoculars and rifle*
> *Shepherding—it ain't a trifle.*

These verses circulated among the Romanian shepherds, and Mitu had learned them from Porumbel and put them to music. The rest of the *taraf* picked up the instruments and continued with a *hora,* enticing everyone to get up and dance.

After half an hour, the guests sat down again. They had just finished the third course—stuffed cabbage with polenta—but Smaranda got ahead of herself and brought out the dessert. Mitu broke off a piece of chocolate, and when the girl passed by him, he whispered in her ear, "These cookies are very sweet, but they ain't sweeter than you!"

She moved away hastily, but he saw her in a corner giggling with Mirița and peeking at him.

"It's good she's laughing instead of getting all ruffled...it's very good!"

Meanwhile, Tecău had started opening up his presents. For the past few years he had gotten into the habit of doing that during the party. He had received a lot of carefully chosen knickknacks, which he unwrapped carefully and then put back in their packaging. Vonică had brought him a silk scarf,

Porumbel a money pouch, Piluță a hunting knife, and one of the *taraf* members a box of cigars. Mitu had spent the most money on his gift; knowing Tecău's weakness for firearms, he had bought him a handgun—the famous .45 Colt with a revolving six-round cylinder, a "Peacemaker" as it was also known, which he had placed in a box made of cherry lined in burgundy plush.

"What a nice piece!" Tecău commented, impressed. "What finesse in the lines! Thank you Mitu." He chugged a glass of wine as a sign of his gratitude and then loaded the chambers of the revolver.

"Now, now, Uncle Tecău, don't think you're some kinda Billy the Kid in the Wild West and shoot one of us after you drink a bit more!" Vonică laughed.

"Let's party and have fun! What the heck; we only live once!" Porumbel raised his glass. "Happy birthday, old man! May you and your children live a long and good life!"

"From your mouth to God's ears," Tecău agreed. "This is some good liquor...Mitu, how in God's name you make it? If I didn't know better, I'd swear this was *țuică* from my Ma's village!"

"Well, that's how I make it...like in Romania. From fruits..."

"Yes, it's very good, Mitu," Piluță confirmed. "You can tell he's one of us from Oltenia! You must make a fortune with this!"

"What's the matter with you?" said Mitu. "What fortune? You don't know what you're talking about! I make the alcohol, but I have to give it to a distributor for barely anything. Don't think you can get rich from something like this!"

"Yeah, yeah, you still make more than the rest of us, Mitu...don't you tell us pigs can fly!" Vonică bristled at his words.

"Sometimes I make money...sometimes I don't. It depends a lot on the quantities I sell, and how many others are like me out there...it's not as peachy as you think it is..." he countered.

The party lasted until dawn. As the hours went by, the room became thick with cigarette smoke, stinging everyone's eyes, with the speech of the guests slurred and their minds foggy from the alcohol abundant on the tables.

Chapter 33

The guests finally began leaving the party at around five o'clock in the morning. Mitu purposely lagged behind, pretending to fix something on his violin, and then offered to help Mirița and Smaranda with the cleanup. Tecău lay down on a bed with his eyes closed, humming a melody, and in a few minutes he started snoring lightly.

"It's just us now, darlings, what should we do?" Mitu said, trying to hide his excitement. "Did you have fun, girls?"

"Yes, we had a lot of fun," answered Smaranda, tipsy from guzzling a whole bottle of wine during the party. "What about you?"

"I had plenty of fun, although I'd have liked to spend more time with you two...I only know one kind of entertainment," he said suggestively. "Let's taste some of this red wine, since we didn't get to open this here bottle..."

Mirița glanced at her father sleeping like a log and handed him some glasses. Mitu filled them up, feigning apprehension.

"Let's be careful not to wake him up, girls...let's go in one of the bedrooms..."

The girls chuckled, whispered in each other's ears, and then followed him to the bedroom—a room so small that all it fit was a bed and a wardrobe.

"What a room, with no chairs..." he joked. "Come closer now. What, you wanna stand in a corner somewhere?" he invited them, putting his arm around Mirița's shoulders and pulling her towards him. The girl shrank back from his touch, blushing brightly.

"Why did you get so scared? You seem like you saw a snake or something! I'm not gonna hurt you! Come on, get closer; what, like you've never been near a man before? Smaranda, you too, don't be shy; I won't bite you...do I look like some kind of a wild beast to you?"

The girls approached the bed uncertainly. He pulled out a handkerchief and waved it around, trying to summon a coin—it was the only trick Tecău had ever shown him—but he couldn't do it, and the penny fell on the floor. The girls laughed. He then started telling them about the war, describing in detail the horrors he had seen on the battlefield and pointing out modestly the way he had saved other soldiers' lives.

"Look at this," he said, taking off his shirt. "This is where the bullet went through. You see the scar? It's still hard." He took Smaranda's hand and pressed it over the marks, taking advantage of the opportunity to have her hand against his skin.

Mirița watched them disconcertedly. *"Is she jealous?"* he wondered. He then sent Smaranda to get his cigarettes from the other room and check on her father.

"Mirița, I don't know how to tell you this—and I'm afraid of your dad because he'll kill me if he finds out—but I fell for you from first time I saw you...you make me think of you-know-what-kind of things at night!" he whispered with his finger on his lips as though to highlight the secrecy of his confession.

"Stop dreaming with your eyes open...come on," the girl retorted, feigning seriousness and pursing her lips. He went quickly by her side and kissed her on the mouth, Mirița reciprocating the kiss.

Smaranda was just coming back with the cigarettes, and when she saw them she turned red with jealousy.

"Father will split you in two if he wakes up" she snapped at Mirița, looking daggers at her.

The girl stared arrogantly back and didn't answer.

"Come on now...looky here," Mitu appeased them, satisfied that the girls were fighting over him. "I'll flip the coin in the air, and if you guess right, you can give me a dare. If I guess right, I'll give you one!"

Mirița wanted to say something like 'What's with these silly games?' but he didn't give her the time. He called heads and flipped the coin.

"Tails!" Smaranda entered the game as if to spite her sister.

"Oh, I lost!" he said and pretended to be upset. "Now, don't dare me to squawk like a rooster!"

The atmosphere lit up instantly. The girls began laughing and became allies against Mitu. They conferred in a corner and then made him come up with a short poem. He took a moment and then started reciting:

> Oh, my goodness what to do
> I like not one girl but two.
> The two sisters I would kiss
> Day and night I'd be in bliss!

Smaranda chortled, and he approached her staring in her eyes. "You're so beautiful..." he whispered, wondering how he could say it so convincingly when in reality he found her a trifle plain, and touched her mouth with his fingertips. She smiled bemused and managed a "thank you." Mirița was throwing them jealous glares, but when Mitu turned at her, she sported a fake smile. He winked conspiratorially at her as if to say, 'You're actually my favorite...'

"Second round, now! Let's go! Heads again!" he threw the coin in the air.

The penny rolled on the floor. Mirița came close and seemed disappointed.

"It's our turn to receive a dare!" She faked a laugh.

"Let's see, let's see," Mitu said contented. "What dare to give you..." he pondered for a few seconds. "I'm not gonna make you come up with poetry...what can I make you do...? That's it! I got it! Fill up the glasses and drink them in one shot! You didn't think I was going to give you a dare you wanted, did you?"

The girls wanted to protest, but he didn't give them the time to do it.

"A dare's a dare, there's nothing you can do...that was the deal!"

"But we didn't wanna play this game! You took us too fast," Smaranda fought back halfheartedly, already in a daze from the alcohol.

Mirița took the glass and downed it in one move as though to show her sister that the dare was a piece of cake to her.

"Done! I completed my dare...just wait till it's your turn again!" she threatened Mitu.

Smaranda followed suit and drank her share.

"You make us do bad things..." she laughed.

"Me? Oh, my goodness gracious. Wine is our Lords' blood. The more the better..."

"*The more the better...*" Mirița mocked him. "You wanna get us drunk so we don't know what's going on anymore, right?"

Mitu shook his head vehemently.

"Well now, I can't deny that I'm thinking of playing some other games, not like this one with the coin..."

"What games?" Smaranda asked playfully, watching him as though she didn't understand what he was hinting at.

"This is the game," he whispered, pushing a stray strand of hair off her forehead and tracing with his fingers an imaginary line down her cheek all the way to her lips. "The game of love..." He pulled her closer. "Mmm, how nice you smell..." he sighed in her ear. "Mirița, come here, right next to me!"

The girl conformed hesitantly and he put his arms around her waist.

"This is the game we need to play...this is it...thank you God for making Tecău go to sleep!" he said, and then crossed himself spuriously.

The girls giggled. He settled better between the two of them, taking turns kissing them. Smaranda reciprocated his kisses, and Mirița closed her eyes halfway, slightly embarrassed by what was happening. He walked his fingers up her blouse and started undoing the buttons one by one. She didn't fight it.

"God, such beautiful girls," he whispered.

He undressed them slowly, going from one to the other, kissing their necks, running his fingers through their hair, caressing them and telling them how crazy they drove him. He stopped at Mirița, who was shivering under his touch, and lowered his hand between her thighs. The girl sighed in pleasure and finished quickly with a short and thin moan, then opened her eyes, donning an embarrassed air as though ashamed by her nudity.

He gave her a reassuring smile, then turned to Smaranda and took her hand as gingerly as he could, kissed it, and then placed it on Mirița's breast. The girl winced and tried to pull it back, but he replaced it gently but firmly, squeezing it in his. Smaranda tried to say something but he closed her lips with his finger and started kissing her on the neck and chest, then lower on her abdomen and spent endless moments plunged between her thighs. Laying still, the girl tried in vain to stop her moans of pleasure.

"Mirița," he whispered after a while, "I haven't forgotten about you..."

She was on the bed, quivering at the sight of her sister being touched by Mitu. He clasped his arms around her and gave her a long kiss, then turned her face down, lifted her waist slightly up and went inside her.

"Oh, God," she whispered, drunk with pleasure. "Oh, God! Don't stop!"

Smaranda watched their pulsating bodies, mesmerized, which made her forget all about her initial chastity, herself, everything. She was dizzied by the vortex of sex unfolding before her eyes like a movie, with details until then unimagined.

Her naked body filled Mitu with desire. He could have a virgin! He pulled her towards him and kissed her passionately.

"I want you so bad...lie down on your back..." he asked in a whispered but demanding tone.

The girl listened obediently and lay on her back with her legs slightly spread, and he went inside her as carefully as he could to spare her from the initial pain. She gave out a short cry, then moaned and arched her back, sticking her nails in his flesh.

"God, what bliss..." he murmured watching the naked bodies proffered to him. "God, what pleasure! Oh, God!" he grunted with a final thrust.

He slid between the girls, and after a while, had them again. At last, he lay exhausted, "This is what I need: women who really want me, not the whores from Galena Street! This is what I want!"

"I'm in Heaven...Heaven..." he croaked, holding them both.

Regret filled him at the thought he had to leave. *"Oh, how I wish I could just go to sleep between them and wake up only to start again! God, how would that be?"*

Right that instant, a noise came from the door. He rose quickly from the bed and tried to pull up his pants, but Tecău was already in the doorway, staring perplexedly at them. The girls gave out a short scream and covered themselves up with the blankets.

"What's going on here?" Tecău asked with a raspy voice.

He came close to the bed and yanked the covers. His eyes fell on his daughters' naked bodies, who were now desperately trying to conceal their nudity with their hands. When he understood the situation, he growled like a rabid dog and turned to Mitu.

"Traitor! You foul—I'll show you, you bastard! Filthy mongrel! I welcomed you in my home!" he yelled, and then dashed out the door. They heard his steps thundering up and then down the stairs, and after a few moments, he showed up in the doorway with the Colt .45 in one hand and a hatchet in the other.

Mitu couldn't even attempt to defend himself when Tecău pointed the gun at him and pulled the trigger. The bullet hit him in the face, making him collapse over the glass of the wardrobe, which shattered, leaving deep gashes on his back and neck. Tecău lifted up the hatchet to strike him but hit the ceiling instead, which changed its trajectory and made it land in a corner.

Mitu jumped on him, grabbed him by the waist and threw him on the floor while the girls were screaming in terror.

"What have you done? What have you done, good God in Heaven, you killed him! You've killed Father!" Mirița screamed, covering her mouth with her hands and bursting into a hysterical wail.

Mitu struggled to stand, put his clothes on, and tried to calm them down.

"Pour a pail of water on him, and he'll be alright. It's fine. He's okay! Take care of yourselves, I didn't mean for this at all..." he said, leaving in a hurry. He could barely keep his eyes open from the tremendous pain. He touched his wound gingerly and grunted. "Fuckin' old man, he shot me in the jaw, the lunatic!" he realized, alarmed, and went to the hospital.

They took him to surgery right away. The next day, when he woke up, his head was wrapped up in gauze with only his eyes showing. He was told the bullet had shattered his jaw, but that the doctors had straightened and strengthened it with a screw which was to remain implanted in there for the rest of his life.

"Will it be noticeable, sir?" he asked, speaking as if his mouth were full of tar. Each word produced tremendous pain.

"No, you won't see it. Your appearance will be unchanged...maybe a small scar where the wound is, but that will fade in time. You'll still feel the screw when you touch it. You'll be in pain for a few weeks, but that will pass, too..."

"When can I leave the hospital?"

"In about a week, if everything's okay. We need to keep you under observation, make sure you won't get an infection..."

"No, there's no way I can stay that long... I have things to attend to. I'll come back later for a checkup..."

Despite the doctor's protests, Mitu left the hospital that morning and went straight to his sheepfold in the mountains, tired and in pain. His bandaged head gave him the appearance of a wandering mummy. He reached the farm late at night, startling Gherasim.

"What happened to you, man? What kind of trouble have you gotten yourself into? Why is your head bandaged up? Come inside quick, before someone sees you!"

"Why? What if someone see me?"

"Mitu, Tecău told the cops you're a bootlegger. Four cops came here this morning and questioned me—what you do, where you are, where your stills are. They threatened to throw me in jail, but I didn't crack and denied I knew anything. I didn't even know where you were. I thought you were dead, but when I heard them asking for you, I figured you were in trouble. What happened to you?"

He told him about the incident.

"Well then...some people work their asses off and some are busy chasing tail. And not one, but two at once! Good Lord in Heaven...I know how you are, but what the heck were those two thinking! As I said before: I may not have the best life, but at least I can sleep fine at night. Now what are you gonna do? Tell me...what?"

"What can I do? I have to run away. I'm in trouble. I think I'm going back to Detroit...where else can I go? You comin' with me?"

"What? Come with you? Man... I'm not going nowhere...where to? I'm not, no... I don't wanna get in trouble, Mitu...and what are you gonna do about the distilleries, the barrels of booze? I'm not touching those, I'm telling you now!"

"What can I do with them? I'll leave them in the woods; I can't very well carry them in my pockets on the train!"

"And you're leaving all bloody like this? You'll die! You need medical care!"

"I'll be alright...I'm better off leaving than getting medical care in jail! Come here now, lemme hug you before they come to get me. Farewell, my friend!" he said, slipping a few hundred dollars in Gherasim's pocket. "I'll write you to tell you where I am, so you'll have my address. Promise you'll write back, okay?"

"Good luck, man! Take care of yourself!"

Mitu trekked to the mountain, checking his surroundings for any suspicious movement. He turned a few times to wave to Gherasim, and then was lost in the shadowy thickets.

He hid his stills as best he could, drank some strong alcohol to numb his pain, filled up two bottles of bilberry brandy, and then unearthed the boxes of money. He rolled up the bills, tied them with twine, and stuffed them in his pockets. When he was done, he went to the edge of the forest, where he slept until the next day.

At dawn, he sneaked to the station and got on the first train to Michigan. It was the second time in his life he was running away from a good situation due to woman-trouble.

Chapter 34

Mitu tried his best to keep a low profile on his trip to Detroit. He spent a lot of time in the restrooms, stuffed his hat down on his head to conceal the gauze, and covered himself up with his coat, pretending he was fast asleep.

All he wanted to do was curl up in a dark corner where no one could see him, or go back in time two days and avoid the nightmare he had created for himself. He couldn't believe what was happening to him! He was running away from the police, from Tecău, leaving behind his fortune-making stills. He had left in such a hurry he hadn't even said good-bye to Carrick—Carrick, his buddy, who had brought him such good luck!

All it took to ruin his good life in the mountains was a couple of hours. Had it been worth it? He now regretted getting involved with Mirița and Smaranda. He couldn't believe he hadn't been wise enough to make better arrangements with them if they wanted to have fun together. But—let it be a lesson—wasn't it the reason he was now a runaway?

"What am I gonna do from now on?" he asked himself. He was afraid of the police, thinking he might get caught and thrown in jail. He was certain his wound would give him away. He feared he was going to be scarred for life, "What if I need to run back to Romania because of that?"

In Detroit, he got off the train, anxiously looking around the platform for any cops who might have been expecting him, and since there weren't any, he went to his old neighborhood.

He checked into a boardinghouse next to a hospital. He had to see a doctor. Sharp pains shot through his jaw and he couldn't eat anything. He only had a little bit of brandy left to quiet his stomach, which now growled terribly.

He didn't get out of bed for a few weeks, drinking soup through a straw from a jar, which reminded him of his brandy-making stills. Once every few days, he went to the hospital for checkups and to dress the wound.

As soon as he began feeling better, he went back to eating solid food since his jaw didn't hurt as much when he chewed, and the swelling had gone down.

After another month, the doctors told him he was completely healed and removed the last bandages. He saw then that the doctor from Helena had been right: all that was left where the stitches had been on his chin was a thin scar, which more than likely was going to fade with time.

That day—for the first time in a few months—he went down to the boardinghouse's cafeteria. Until then, he had barely exchanged a few words with the owners; he was embarrassed by his appearance, and even more so he was fearful they might become suspicious and call the police on him. Now, he was no longer afraid. A lot of time had passed and no one had come looking for him.

He sat down in a good mood—now that he was bandage-free, he felt at ease—and ordered a steak and fries. He needed to constantly be eating food—

lots of it. He had lost a lot of weight lately; his thin face and sunken cheeks, dark circles, and deathly pale skin made him look forty—not the almost thirty that he was.

"From now on my life can go back to normal!" he thought as he chewed with gusto. He had been fortunate that the bullet hadn't hit him half an inch to the right, or now he could have been dead or infirm! He had escaped quite a predicament and felt grateful to God for saving him.

At the table next to his, a young man of eighteen or nineteen was devouring a chicken. He was chewing loudly, ignoring the fat dripping down the corners of his mouth. He methodically broke off piece after piece, sniffing each piece contentedly before stripping down the meat, leaving the bones clean, and gnawing the cartilage afterwards. As he swallowed, he closed his eyes full of satisfaction as if what he ate were the very ambrosia enjoyed by gods. He was neatly dressed, although his clothes were worn out. *"Probably some newcomer looking for work in the city,"* Mitu thought. He was tall with broad shoulders, full cheeks and a square jaw, healthy-looking and bursting with vitality. The thick-rimmed glasses hiding his eyes and the dimple in his chin gave him the air of a studious child who had grown up too quickly.

Mitu watched him, quite entertained, for a while. *"My God, it's like he hasn't eaten in a week!"* He then saw him whispering something to the waiter, who sneaked him a small glass a few minutes later.

The young man drank the glass one shot, screwing up his face with a mixture of pleasure and disgust, and glanced over the room for the first time.

Mitu had meanwhile pulled out some tobacco from his pocket, spread it on the table, rolled it in his palm, and was chewing it leisurely. The boy watched him with interest for a while, rose from his seat, and approached him.

"Please sir...if I could...may I ask you something, if you don't mind? May I bum a cigarette, please? I'm all out and would really like one..."

His exaggerated good manners first amused Mitu then saddened him, *"He must think I'm so much older than him..."*

"Here you go...I don't have cigarettes, only leaves. I smoke very rarely. I used to work for Ford and they didn't allow us to smoke there, so I got used to chewing tobacco..."

The young man took a knife from the table, chopped up a leaf, and placed it in another leaf which he rolled up and lit.

"This is some good quality tobacco you have here, sir..." he said with satisfaction after inhaling deeply. "It's the expensive kind. By the way, I'm James Wood."

Mitu shook his hand then asked what business he had in the city.

"Oh, I live in Detroit...but I love the food here—it's good and cheap. I live alone, and I don't like to cook. And," he leaned in cagily, "this is one of the few places where they give you a glass or two...so you don't have to wander around in blind pigs, you know..."

"I noticed that...yes..." said Mitu. "I've had some brandy until recently but I—glug, glug, glug!—guzzled it all up. I need to find some more..."

"This city is full of alcohol... if you know where to look for it."

"If you know where to look for it, yes..." Mitu repeated. "Actually, you don't even need to know all that much, 'cause it seems to be everywhere! Where do they make such great amounts? Up in the mountains?"

"Oh, no... people make it in their homes. In bathrooms or basements. They mix it up in bathtubs, pour it into canisters, then sneak it to pubs."

"Huh. That's kinda hard to believe. How much can you make in your home?" he asked, suddenly interested in the topic. "There's just too much alcohol floating around! Where from? All the newspapers say this business is just as big as the auto industry!"

"It's true. What people make is just a small portion. A lot of alcohol comes from Canada, pal. From Windsor, over the river, since it's just a mile wide..."

"I see...with so many bays and inlets fords on the river, it's easy to sneak it in..." Mitu agreed pensively. "Especially during winter when the river freezes over. Even so, Canada is dry, isn't it? How do they do it, then?"

"I can tell you have no clue, man...yes, it's dry, but you see, the Canadians were sly. They have a law that allows manufacturing alcohol for export. And guess what happened? Dozens and dozens of distilleries and liquor stores mushroomed right along the river overnight! You should go there and check it out if you're so curious about it!"

Mitu nodded. He was curious—how couldn't he be? And James seemed to know what he was talking about, as young as he was.

"And they allow you to buy it if they know you're taking it back to America?"

"Normally they shouldn't sell to the Americans. But they ask you where you're from, you know, just to ask. They don't care as long as they get the money! I do this too... you know, to make a little something..."

"Oh, really? You do this at home?"

"No way...it'd be too much trouble. I meant to say that I bring some alcohol from Canada from time to time. Not a lot. A bottle or two in my bag— small luggage isn't too conspicuous and doesn't raise suspicions. I take the usual ways, but I've heard some unbelievable things: women who place flat bottles under their skirts or small bottles in their underwear, or, even you know where! I read once they caught some people transporting Scotch in a funeral hearse. Can you believe it?"

"This is the ideal place for bootlegging..." thought Mitu, awed by the ease of running such a business. _"And I don't even have to manufacture it...just move some canisters from here there! How come I never knew about this before moving to Montana?"_

"Is there good money in this?"

"Well," James said, suddenly sulky, "I don't have the money for big operations. If I did, I'd do it big time! A few months ago they caught some people who were doing—guess what. They had a delivery system with cables for underwater sleds. They could send fifty gallons at once under water. And some others had pipes directly connecting some distilleries in Windsor to a speakeasy here. The booze dripped from the faucet, man, do you understand that?"

"I guess you can make tons of money from it..." Mitu murmured.

"Of course you can, if you have enough for the startup!" James agreed. "I didn't. Period. I just started recently with two hundred—all my savings. Now I have four hundred. In a few months I doubled my investment. Not bad, right?" he asked proudly, his eyes glinting from behind the glasses.

"Not bad at all, no... congratulations!" Mitu agreed, trying to appear more enthusiastic than he really was.

"But imagine if I'd started up with twenty thousand instead of two hundred—or, even two thousand. That would've been something..."

As he was listening to James, Mitu realized that he had landed in a bootlegger's paradise. The idea that he could make more money in Detroit than he had ever imagined was taking root in his mind. He could make a lot more than in Montana, where he had sold brandy by the gallon! And what an advantage, having so much capital at his disposal! While some people, like that young man, were running around like headless chickens for a few hundred dollars, he could, with his savings, do what few bootleggers only dreamed of: wholesale distribution.

Chapter 35

Barely anything Mitu had learned in Montana fit in Detroit. Bootlegging here was done according to a different set of rules—more calculated, riskier, sometimes sinister—which he now had to learn very well. After his meeting with James, he decided not to stop wasting time and work to thoroughly understand this underside of the world that he found so fascinating.

He had tasted the sweetness of getting rich fast and unexpectedly and was all too familiar with its enticing aroma. He could now enter a different kind of world—a world of giants able to change the very course of mankind! There was a lot of money to be made in bootlegging. He could, if he knew how to play his cards right, become truly big—much bigger than the small player from Montana who hauled two or three casks of brandy to Sasha and Natasha's. He could, with enough luck and quick wits, become a millionaire.

For a while, he crossed the river to Canada with James, taking inventory of the distributors in Windsor and trying out their merchandise. James had accepted his proposal of becoming partners without blinking—the more money that came into play, the bigger his profit.

Shortly after, as he figured out the details of water shipping over the Detroit River, he began planning his new undertaking: he would pay for the merchandise and search for clients in speakeasies and blind pigs, and James would bring the alcohol from wherever, however he could.

They hit many snags during the first months. James was not used to transporting such great quantities and had some trouble here and there. He once miscounted the boxes of bottles, and they lost a few hundred dollars. Another time, he was a day late bringing the alcohol to the bodega which had placed the order. The owner refused the merchandise and didn't want to be their client anymore—he had meanwhile bought from a different distributor—so they had to run around from blind pig to blind pig for a whole week trying to sell their bottles.

Mitu knew he owed his success from Montana to the fact he had sold superior alcohol. He tried to impart this knowledge to James, but the boy wouldn't hear it. For him, selling a lot, even at lower prices, was the best thing to do, and many times he bought with his own money counterfeit alcohol or dubious liquors made in basements and poured into bottles without labels.

"Better make fifteen cents apiece on a thousand bottles than a dollar on a hundred..." he kept telling Mitu. "Cheap alcohol sells! Even in poverty—maybe even more so during hard times, since, well, it eases the trouble..."

"You need to understand, man: people are always willing to pay more for quality things. I've seen it in Helena. If we have good merchandise, we'll never have to worry about selling it."

"Allow me to disagree. There are a lot of poor people who cannot afford more than a few pennies for a drink. They should be our target, especially because they're poor. There are but a few rich people, and they are hard to reach..."

Mitu had different plans and couldn't agree with James's view.

"Now, that's your problem, right there! That's why you're not making the money you'd like! The alcohol in pubs tastes like shit! They don't call it bathtub gin or monkey rum for nothing. Buddy, a drink is like a woman: good women are expensive, yet men still pay for them! Whether they have money or not, they empty out their pockets! Trust me; I know it all too well!"

"Well, partner, you can make whatever decision you want..." James would shake his head unconvinced. "After all, it's your money. As long as I get some greenbacks out of it, I won't say anything, but I still think we should pay less for the merchandise!"

The encouragement received from Mitu prompted James to come up with all kinds of creative transportation methods. He had become so inventive lately, Mitu had dubbed him "the wizard." James collected the alcohol from other small-timers at first, but the money was too little, and he didn't like that at all. Then, he fashioned himself some bags with hidden compartments, in which he carried brandy a few times a day. Later on, he partitioned the space in the gas tank of his Ford and hid rubber bottles in the tires. He took out the lead from the batteries and transported the alcohol in them. A few times, he emptied out the contents of eggs with a syringe and filled them back with whiskey and scotch.

The compensation for all his efforts was more than generous. Mitu could see himself in James, back in his Helena days. *"God, this cycle of life..."* Seeing how happy his young partner was to stuff the dollar bills in his pockets reminded him of Carrick.

It was the first time in his life he was ordering anyone around. He was the boss, and that made him feel uneasy. Up until then, from his father to Herzowig, in the war and at Ford, his life had been a chain of events and experiences where he had to submit to others. He now found himself in the new position of being at the top and not knowing what to do.

He wanted to test James—to see if he could trust him—but he thought his trials were so obvious that even a dimwit could have figured them out. He eventually decided to take a different route. He asked some distributors from Windsor to sell their merchandise to James for lower prices, to see if the young man would inform him. But James never cheated him—not even a penny.

After about half a year of bootlegging, during which he had become very familiar with the business and had made many connections with owners of blind pigs and speakeasies, Mitu felt confident enough to raise the bar. He had gotten fed up with buying alcohol from small timers and redistributing it. It was a dangerous game, with too many parties involved and not a lot of profit. It was time for a new strategy, and he wanted to try bigger and better things. He wanted to become a wholesaler in the true meaning of the term. He wanted to grow, to make a fortune, to become one of the big players in

Detroit, to have people working for him, to buy land and properties in America and in Romania, to make enough to retire in Cernădia and live like royalty. He could see his childhood dreams close to fruition. He could keep his promise of coming home rich that he had made to his mother! He could offer his siblings a better life, buy them homes and land, since their letters were always full with complaints in that respect! He could marry a young woman and have many children. He could raise his eyes to his father in Heaven and smile with pride.

He struggled to come up with new ways of transporting the alcohol for many months. He had lengthy discussions with James. He talked with people doing the trade on either side of Detroit River. He read newspapers to learn about those who had been raided by the police to learn from their mistakes. He even toyed with the idea of moving to Canada to manufacture his own alcohol. He had the idea of buying a truck and even getting in touch with some of the mafia members.

At last, he decided to try water shipments. They were the fastest. They were the most convenient. They seemed the least dangerous.

First, he bought a boat, which he named "Olga," and equipped it with everything necessary. Together with James, he learned how to drive it, and they went up and down the river inspecting the shore. He bought detailed maps of the coast and studied them carefully. He hid in the bay to follow illicit shipments at night, carefully noting all the details: Which way did they take? Where did they dock? How much merchandise did they have on board? How many people were involved?

He then learned which speakeasies needed large amounts of expensive alcohol. His goal was to do wholesale distribution of top-quality merchandise. He had enough money to fill his boat to the brim with old whiskey and scotch.

Out of all speakeasies, he chose Woodbridge Tavern: a small but cozy pub from Rivertown targeting well-to-do clientele. The owner, Madame Euphrasie Brunelle, an elderly and authoritarian French woman, had turned a grocery store into a speakeasy, which she ruled with an iron fist.

He had visited the place many times, but never for business. The pub had as its front a delicatessen serving food, lemonade, and pastries. At first glance, nothing seemed suspicious: a small lamp over the door, a copper cash register on the corner of the counter, a waiter clinking coins from customers. The quiet atmosphere, clean air, crisp linens on the tables, and the appealing smell of soup and roasted meat enticed anyone to have a seat and order something.

For those going inside by chance, the way he had the first time, that was apparently it. Past the back doors, however, a totally different universe unfolded. Mitu had seen many blind pigs and speakeasies, but none was as well camouflaged as this one: the clients who knew the passwords and came for drinks went through the back door and down some wooden stairs to the semi-basement. A very small green door made of three wood planks separated a tiny hallway from a minuscule bathroom, behind which there was an even smaller door. That was the entrance to the speakeasy: a room crammed with tables where expensive, fine drinks were served and where the customers could play poker and blackjack all night.

The depraved and sinful atmosphere was fueled by the air, thick with cigarette smoke, and the overall suggestion of promiscuity. Two big paintings by some washed-out, albeit talented artist in exchange for a few bottles adorned the back wall. In one, a woman peered over some crates full of Heineken bottles, and in the other, a nude lay on her belly with her feet up in the air and her head thrown to back.

A third painting, on the opposite wall, represented another nude, barely concealed by a transparent veil, caressing her thighs with one hand and with the other making a conspiratorial gesture, seeming to say 'Don't tell anyone about this.'

To Mitu's and many others' surprise, the alcohol found in the place was brought in by none other than Madame Brunelle's daughter, Julia, a girl of twelve who, he thought, at that rate would most definitely become a millionaire by the time she reached adulthood. Each day the girl drove a Model T around the city to the local distilleries, loading a bottle or two and rushing back with them to her mother's place.

Besides the owner and her daughter, no other woman set foot in Woodbridge Tavern. Madame Brunelle was very firm about that and only allowed men in her speakeasy. Mitu meant to ask why, not understanding what her reasons could be, but had given up on it, not wanting to be on bad terms with her. It wouldn't have helped the future business he wanted to do there.

During one of his visits, after losing fifty dollars in a poker game, he was sitting by himself at a table, and when Madame Brunelle, smiling but aloof as always, came to ask if he wanted something to drink, he asked her directly, "Would you be interested in a shipment of pure and original Canadian-made scotch and whiskey? I can deliver hundreds of bottles, Ma'am. Even hundreds of crates—the best quality..."

She looked at him suspiciously and somewhat doubtfully. She knew Mitu only as a loyal customer. Many of her clients had come to her with business propositions, but very few had actually pursued them, due to either police or mob trouble.

"With all due respect, I only take well-traveled paths. I don't know you well; I don't know who you work for..."

"I don't work for anyone. It's just me and my partner."

The woman raised her eyebrows. "You're quite naïve, Mister. It's very risky being on your own if you want to move big loads, the way you're talking. The big guys don't like it. They might wanna take you for ride. I'm warning you. And, besides, I have my sources. My Julia does a very good job."

"I know she does, but Julia buys it locally, from a middleman. From those who buy it in Windsor then add their profit to your cost. I'd bring it to you straight from Canada, for lower prices, because I can buy bigger quantities. Old whiskey or scotch, quality merchandise. And without a deposit—I bring it to you and you pay after. The way it should be, right? If something happens to me, you lose nothing!"

Their discussion went on for a little while, but it didn't take much for Madame Brunelle, suspicious by nature, to realize it wouldn't cost her anything to try. Mitu wasn't asking for a deposit like others, he was quite relentless in his proposition, and he seemed serious. If he could supply quality alcohol as he promised, it might not have been a bad deal. And, if he brought more than she needed, she could distribute some of it to others.

"Very well," she said at the end. "In two weeks, when my supply is low, I'll need a big shipment—a few hundred crates—to have enough for a few months."

Mitu agreed, trying to hide his satisfaction, they shook on it, and he left the place overjoyed. If things went his way, he could make a few thousand dollars out of this whole deal.

THE BOON

Chapter 36

The weeks of wait before the shipment tormented Mitu with conflicting and confusing feelings of fear and hope. There are moments in life when our hearts sink at the mere thought of danger, yet we choose to take our chances. There are moments when we risk our life irrationally, despite instinctual warnings to be cautious. There are moments when the desire to get ahead in life beclouds us and stifles our feeble heedfulness of prudence, when the possibility of monetary gains blinds us, overpowers us, conquers us, muddles out thoughts and buries logic under a heavy layer of dust. There are moments when we carry on a certain way, compelled by no one to take such a path, knowing full well that everything, even life itself, could be lost, but we're fueled by the subtle, subconscious conviction, the dangerous illusion assuring us that bad things can only happen to others.

At the time of Mitu's transaction with Madame Brunelle, the Detroit River was swarming with police ships and gangsters. The continuous life and death struggle reddened the water and ground with blood and filled the newspapers with ink. There were street shootings, odd bullets piercing the air, blackmail and threats, which to Mitu—and two thirds of the country—only represented an incomprehensible, misguided war.

James was very eager to do the shipment. Mitu had promised him five hundred dollars the minute he docked the ship and two more upon delivery to Woodbridge Tavern. For the young bootlegger, this was a considerable sum of money.

Mitu himself was worried and kept repeating the plan to James, afraid that his partner, out of ignorance or carelessness, might forget some important detail, which would somehow ultimately prove fatal.

"Listen here, young man: you take the boat to Windsor, to Sam's Distillery, where you'll need to see Rickie. That's where they'll be waiting for you with the merchandise. You fill the boat with boxes of liquor like the rumrunners do in New York...then go down the St. Claire River towards Lake Huron until you clear the city and then you dock it into that hidden cove we found in the woods last time. I'll be there waiting for you and we'll signal each other with flashlights. And, if you have any problems, manage your way out of them, okay? The boat has Liberty engines on it. If you need to, use the clandestine radio frequency to throw off the police. I've explained to you how..."

"Yes, I know boss...and if anyone follows me, I'll put some oil in the exhaust pipes to give off a lot of smoke..."

"Yes, yeah...by the time the air clears up, you'll be far away, outside their range of view..."

James smiled each time his thoughts wandered off to the shipment, and his eyes glinted like fireflies behind his ever-present glasses. Yet, Mitu's pessimistic cautions made him realize how easily something could go wrong, and that worried him. What they were trying to do was akin to how the mob conducted business—no longer amateurish bootlegging. The big guys didn't like it when someone took their clients. He kept reading about people like Dutch Schultz, Bugsy Siegel, or Al Capone, who filled the streets with the blood of those chipping at their profits. Just two days before, the front page story of a man his age shot in the head—after he had been allowed to say a prayer—for not giving up a barrel of alcohol sent chills down his spine.

On the other hand, the incentive of easy money gave James wings. The thought that a couple of hours' work could bring in a few hundred dollars, made him rub his hands together in expectancy, forgetting all the risks.

"A watch—I'm gonna buy a gold watch. And two expensive suits. And for my lady, a dress—and maybe even a ring..."

His enthusiasm put a bitter smile on Mitu's lips. The passion of the budding young bootlegger, who looked up to him as though he were his older, wiser brother, reminded him of himself years back when he used to get excited about things that ultimately turned out to be inconsequential in bringing about happiness: his move to America and his job with Herzowig, his hero status after the war, his good salary at Ford, the Model T, the profits from Montana, the whores in Butte. Everything in Mitu's life had proven to be as fleeting as the summer rain.

Only Olga came back both as a sweet memory and a heart wrenching one. She was the only one who could make him happy again. But she was gone. She had disappeared from Coney Island and into thin air, to haunt his dark nights with tormenting thoughts: *"Is she still alive? Where could she be now? With who?"*

A few days before the shipment, just in case James might be forced to spend a few days on the water, they packed the boat with all the necessary provisions: good fuel, a few jugs of oil for potential deflecting tactics, three canisters of water, dry food, guns and ammunition, knives, spools of twine and rope of different widths and length, fishing rods, and fish nets. Then, they took the boat for trial runs, testing the engines at full throttle, taking corners at high speed, docking a few times in the small bay where James was to arrive with the merchandise.

On the Thursday of the shipment, Mitu could no longer keep his emotions in check. The last time he had experienced such feelings had been before the Meuse-Argonne Offensive.

At ten o'clock at night, he drove a rented truck to the rendezvous point. He made it there in an hour and parked the car on the side of the road, behind some bushes, then sat down on a rock and lit a cigarette, scrutinizing the darkness and flinching at any noise. At midnight, he started pacing back and forth. It was time for James to show up.

Now and again, a boat would pass by, coming into sight like a gray shadow. Hope would flood his heart for a few seconds, but the boat would glide away instead of approaching the shore.

At one o'clock, he started fidgeting. "What the fuck's he doing? It shouldn't take him this long; a boat crosses the river in a few minutes! He should've been here an hour ago! Could something have happened to him? God forbid I lose all that money because I'll kill myself..."

After another hour, he thought he heard the muffled rumblings of an engine getting closer. He pulled out the flashlight, and waited, tensed. The boat's gray shape widened in the dark, and the humming of the engine grew louder.

In the next instant, five short flickers, one after the other, pierced the darkness from the boat's direction. *"It's him! That's the signal!"*

He flashed his light three times and waited.

James docked the boat within two minutes.

"What took you so long, man? You scared me half to death!" Mitu asked him, wiping the drops of sweat off his forehead. He could barely contain his angst anymore.

"There was too much going on in the port, and I lagged behind to make sure the way was clear. I love this..." James said enthusiastically. "I can smell the cops a mile away..."

"Goodness, what a nut..." Mitu sighed, remembering the war when young naïve men just like James, who considered themselves invincible, would be mowed to the ground before shooting their first bullet.

They loaded the merchandise into the truck—crate after crate of bottles full of brandy, scotch, whiskey, rum, and other fine drinks—almost overfilling it.

"Take the boat back to the port, and dock it in its usual spot," Mitu told him when they finished, handing him five hundred dollars. "You did a great job, young man! Let's keep it this way!"

James almost couldn't believe how easily he could make this kind of money. He touched the bills as though to make sure they were real.

"I'm going to buy something for my sweetheart; I haven't bought her anything in years! Maybe I'll take her for a boat ride in your "Olga"! This boat is the ideal place for making love..."

Mitu smiled while climbing in the truck. *"Yes, this boat is ideal for making love..."* he thought. *"This kid knows what women want..."*

He parked in a dark alley behind Woodbridge Tavern and took a deep breath to encourage himself. *"This is the last hurdle. What if she changed her mind?"*

Madame Brunelle was behind the counter, busily tending to her numerous customers. When she saw him, she summoned him to her.

"So... did you bring it?"

"Yes, Ma'am. Just as we discussed..." he answered, wringing his hands with emotion.

"Very well then. My men will unload it, and after we check it, I'll give you the money."

She called him in the back room an hour later, put a wad of bills in his hands, and then gave him a bottle of wine "on the house."

"You brought good stuff. Pass by in two weeks and I'll tell you when I need another shipment, okay?"

Mitu struggled to put away the money. His pockets were bursting at the seams.

Chapter 37

A few months after starting business with Madame Brunelle, Mitu met Bertha Rizzo in a cheap bordello on the corner of Orleans and Franklin Street. He had, in the meantime, made many deliveries to Woodbridge Tavern and some other places, perfecting his shipping methods and polishing his manner of approaching speakeasy owners for prospective business together. He had learned the schedule of the customs patrols, sometimes barely escaping their checks, and constantly changed his meeting places with James out in the bays to steer clear of gangsters. He was bringing in larger and larger amounts of alcohol, proceeding without a glitch, and had gained the trust of a few owners, for whom he was now the only source.

That day, after delivering a few crates of Scotch to Woodbridge, he didn't stay for the customary bottle of wine but decided to go someplace else. He enjoyed Madame Brunelle's speakeasy, but he didn't like that there were no women allowed.

Instead, he went to Jackpot, an old saloon that had opened sometime in 1850, which he had visited before. The place itself was not that upscale, given that its clientele was mostly made up of sailors and workers, but the alcohol was good enough, there was a live jazz band, and women were more than welcome.

He was quite fond of the new generation of women—the flappers. They wore short skirts, flaunted, rather ostentatiously, their disdain for decency and chastity, provocatively smoked long cigarettes, sipped champagne from long-stemmed glasses, wore excessive makeup and cut their hair very short, rode bicycles and drove automobiles, went out for dates with men, and corseted their bust to flatten their breasts. Mitu was crazy about these *garçonnes* and often chose his drinking places according to their policy towards them.

The atmosphere in Jackpot was sizzling. On a small, improvised stage, a few couples were dancing the Charleston, the fad of the moment. The rest of the patrons played poker, blackjack, roulette, and games of dice, and there was an abundance of alcohol flowing around.

He sat down at a table and looked around, inspecting the room. In a corner, a few women lounged on the burgundy sofas laughing loudly. One of them, a brunette with short hair, had a cute button nose. Another one had dark hair as well, but long to her waist. She wasn't as beautiful, but her cheeky attitude made her very attractive. The third, a blonde with curly hair and contagious laughter, was the one who animated the whole group with her uninhibited cheerfulness.

How could he talk to them? What could he say? He had approached women before—Olga, for example, at the theater!—without thinking twice, but now he was afraid to embarrass himself and just resorted to examining them out of the corner of his eye. Had he grown dull? Was he that old?

He downed a glass of whiskey and took out some tobacco to chew it, continuing to watch them. *"If I don't have the guts to talk to them, I might as well feast my eyes!"* His gaze slithered up and down their supple bodies. They prattled on ignoring him, until one of them got up and began walking towards his table staring fixedly at him.

"Keep on dreaming..." she said, flippantly throwing the words in his direction, and then sashayed to the table next to his where three rowdy men drank beer from a keg.

Mitu tried to eavesdrop on their conversation but couldn't hear anything else besides "Hi, folks!" The girl returned to the couch a while later. Smiling broadly, she waved at the men. They got up at once, took their beer mugs, and joined the girls on the sofa as though they had known one another forever.

He left the place resenting the lucky men now whiling their time away with the women. Their lack of inhibitions had incited and excited him, filling him with a painful desire for them.

"God, I really need a woman now!" he thought, turning automatically towards Night Star—a blind pig that, along with liquor and gambling, also offered sex for sale. Because the pub was also hiding a bordello, it didn't even have a front sign, but he knew of it from Madame Brunelle.

He knocked three times, and, in a few minutes, a pair of blue eyes peered suspiciously at him through the barely open door. He gave the password: "I spoke to Joseph last night." He knew the rules of this place just as he knew those of many blind pigs and speakeasies in the city. This was his world, after all.

"Welcome. What can we offer you, sir? Maybe a seat at a poker table? A glass of whiskey? Or some enjoyable companionship, perhaps?" the man invited him.

He said he wanted some company.

"But of course...not a problem. Please have a seat and enjoy a little something on the house in the meantime. Do you see the girls on the left of the bar? Choose whichever one you'd like and let me know..."

Mitu sat down and began appraising them, imagining how he would have each one as he emptied out the glass that appeared miraculously in front of him. *"The brunette is pretty enough...let's see...the one next to her has nice legs, but she's too lanky...that one's too fat..."*

"Should I take two of them...?" he wondered. Then his thoughts went back to the women from Jackpot. *"The nerve on that cow...to tell me to keep dreaming!"* he sulked. *"Wait till I make enough money one day, and I'll buy all of them! Each day with a new one like they're underwear! They'll think I love them if I give them rings and diamonds, ha! Then we'll see who should keep on dreaming..."*

He finally chose a blonde with long hair and a small waist. He hadn't been attracted by her looks—she had her back to him and her hair resembled Olga's—but by her delicate arm as she shook the ash from her cigarette, showing the smooth skin and narrow wrist of her hand.

He signaled the man, "That's the one I want..."

"Ah, Bertha...yes, good choice. Follow me, please."

Mitu crossed the room behind the man, then entered a narrow hallway leading to a maze of other hallways, each going in a different direction. When he saw it, he stopped. He had heard of subterranean galleries, built by the mafia to transport millions of dollars' worth of alcohol, or serving as hiding places or exits in case of police raids, but he had always thought they were just rumors.

"What's with these tunnels?"

"If I told you, I'd have to kill you," the man joked. "Go in. The girl will be here in a few minutes." He opened a door.

Mitu sat on the corner of the bed and looked around. There wasn't really anything to see—a bed and a closet. He remembered his first visit to a bordello—the one in Butte, where he had been so eager to go. *"God, how stupid I was back then! But that Danielle surely was pretty!"*

In a few moments, he heard the clicking of heels, and a woman showed up in the doorframe, smiling friendly at him.

"Hi! I'm Bertha..."

"Hello...I'm *Meetoo*..." he answered, then pulled her close and placed his head on her chest. He breathed in her rose scent and caressed her hair. "You're beautiful, Bertha..."

"Thank you," the woman smiled, fixing her hair mechanically. "You're handsome yourself."

He laid her on the bed and touched her cheeks with his fingertips, leaving slight traces in her face powder. *"How old is she?"* he wondered. She had an unpolished beauty, slightly wilted, but with a dash of sophistication that could have made her, in different circumstances, a lot more refined. Her hands were a bit too bony and harsh—proof of an overall state of unkemptness—fine wrinkles barely concealed by makeup lined the corners of her eyes, and a thick layer of lipstick had been applied as if to distract from the other facial features. She was lithe, but her flesh was puffy around the shoulders, not toned like that of a young girl. She was over twenty-five, maybe even in her thirties.

"I should have checked her better before choosing..." he thought disappointedly.

"So, how long have you been doing this Bertha?" he asked her, lying on his back with his eyes on the ceiling.

"Long enough..." she murmured, slightly embarrassed that she had to admit it, and moved closer to him. *"What does he care?"*

Mitu turned and stared expressionlessly at her.

"Long enough?"

"For a few years...why do you wanna know?" she asked, slightly irritated. "It bothers you?"

"Oh, no, not at all..." he defended himself. "I was just curious..."

"Curious? Why?" she insisted.

"Well...just to know...something about you. To get to know you better, right? Where are you from?"

"My parents came from Italy when I was a little girl," she answered wryly.

"Oh, yeah? I'm from Romania."

Bertha nodded and smiled.

"We're almost neighbors then."

"Yes, we are..." he sighed, covering his forehead with the back of his hand.

An irritating silence fell on them for a few moments. *"How did I get here?"* he wondered as his thoughts went back to the girls in Jackpot. Bertha was watching him attentively, trying to figure out how to make him relax.

"Have you been here before?"

"No... I've been to other places, but not here..."

"Would you like a massage?"

He dismissed it with a hand wave.

"No... I didn't come here for that..." he said and suddenly rose to his feet. He grabbed her by the hair and brought her to her knees, then unzipped his pants and summoned her authoritatively.

"Do it, slut!"

"Oh, so that's how you like it..." Bertha commented expressionlessly, without blinking.

"Yes, do it..." he said vehemently, pulling her hair back and forth. "Fight back!"

"What?"

"I want you to fight back!"

Bertha gave him an impenetrable look.

"If you want to force me, you'll need to hit me," she said flatly, meeting his gaze.

Mitu stared despondently at her. He had never raised his hand against a woman. Well, he had only dislocated Olga's jaw upon catching her with that Jew!

"If you want to have me, you'll have to pin me to the ground," Bertha egged him on, moving slightly away.

Mitu brought her back by the hair and slapped her ever so slightly, almost caressing her.

"Do it!" he said, but she fought back.

"I don't want to! Leave me alone!"

He slapped her again, more forcefully this time.

"Do it! Do it all the way!"

"No! Let me go!" she begged, struggling to escape.

He slapped her again and let go of her hair; she screamed and then pushed him to the side and cowered in a corner. He followed her like a predatory animal and dragged her to the bed.

"Fight back!" he ordered. "Fight back!"

She tried to escape but couldn't free herself from his grip. She squinted her eyes and a furious grimace deformed her mouth. With a wild look, she scratched his back with her nails, making him cringe in pain.

"Slut!" he growled and slapped her with all his might, then squeezed her breast, stabbing it with his nails. She groaned, arching her back as he bent over her and went brutally inside her.

"That's what you get, whore!" he croaked. "Here you have it!"

They both finished with a long moan, in an impetuous explosion, clenched onto each other, throbbing in the same rhythm, biting each other's lips, almost drawing blood.

"Fuck...!" Mitu said exhaustedly at the end, falling slowly on the bed; his voice betrayed a mixture of embarrassment and satisfaction.

Bertha nestled into his arms, walking her fingers onto his chest.

"So, you like it like that...you're not like my usual client, are you...? This will cost you more, just so you know..." she said half-jokingly.

He shrugged. "So what? Money's not a problem, thank God!"

They were silent for a moment. Then Mitu confessed, "You know Bertha...this is the first time...I've done this with someone...I haven't..."

"You married?" she interrupted.

Mitu guffawed. "No, I'm not...why do you ask?"

"Well, it's generally married men who ask for unusual things they can't get from their wives. There's lots of them who ask for strange things..."

"Like what, for example?"

"Eh, many things...some guy asked me to whip him. Another, to humiliate him...you know, in the bathroom. Mind you, this guy owns a stainless steel manufacturing plant with hundreds of employees. Others just come in and wanna talk. They can't do anything to me...all kinds of crazies in this world."

"Yeah...to each his own," Mitu smiled embarrassedly. "I'm not married, so..."

"But do you have a girlfriend?"

"No, I don't. I had one, a long time ago, before the war. I caught her in bed with some other guy."

Bertha laughed. "You don't say...!"

"What's so funny?" he asked, unpleasantly surprised by her outburst.

"Oh, I'm sorry. I don't want you to think I'm laughing at you, but I couldn't help it. And? Nothing since then? It's been more than ten years. You haven't been with another woman since?"

"Yes, I've been with women. Of course! Lots of 'em! Just like you!"

Bertha raised her eyebrows.

"So, in ten years, you've only slept with whores?"

His long pause spoke for him.

"That must mean you hate women. You cared for her that much that since then, you can't even look at someone else. She broke your heart. I know how it is..."

Mitu shook his head, "Nonsense! It's not true! I don't hate women. I liked Tecău's daughters, and they weren't whores!"

"Have you ever looked her up?"

"Who?"

"Her. Your girl. The one who you wallow in a pool of sorrow for."

He smiled. *"She might be like those artists who paint for a bottle of beer."*

"Yes, I looked for her after I came back from Europe, but she had left New York, and I couldn't find her. I don't even know if she's still alive. There was that flu and all..."

"Well, maybe you'll find another who'll steal your heart and perhaps you'll forget her. You know? The best way to forget a woman is another woman..."

"Easier said than done..." he thought.

"So what do you do? How do you make a living?"

"How else...? The way everyone does it around here..."

"Oh...alcohol...yeah...so, do you bring in a lot?"

Mitu gave her a suspicious look. *"Why the hell is she asking? Is she in cahoots with someone? I wouldn't be surprised—these whores really know their way around..."*

"Not too much, and not too little," he answered ambiguously. "Just enough! By boat, across the river," he said, instantly regretting this slip.

"Oh, by boat..." she said thoughtfully. "So you're not a small-timer... Who do you work with?"

"Why do you ask me all these things?" he asked sharply. "I work alone..."

"You're brave, if you're with no one. Aren't you afraid?"

"Afraid? I was at the beginning...but I got used to it. I don't bring in million dollar shipments like Remus."

"No, but the Purple Gang hunt those with boats like you—you won't get away from them for long, even if you only bring in a little over the river."

He watched her, worried, but for different reasons. In his stupidity, had he revealed too much? What she had said wasn't news to him. He knew the dangers—he had been doing this for a while now, hadn't he? He was well aware of the Purple Gang, a violent group of hijackers lead by the Bernstein Brothers, who killed the crews of ships transporting alcohol from Canada. He had read that even Capone was afraid of them, and rather than competing with them, he resorted to buying their alcohol.

"I don't know, Bertha. I watch my back the best I can. So far—thank God!—nothing's happened to me. Okay, now tell me, how much do I owe you for your time?"

"Fifteen dollars, since you're a new client. Will you come back?" she said, fawning all over him. "You know...next time we can try new things. I'll bring some handcuffs to tie me with and do with me whatever you please, if you want..."

Mitu counted out the money, avoiding her eyes. "Yeah..."

Chapter 38

Mitu received his first warning a few months after meeting Bertha. He had just concluded a transaction with Madame Brunelle, and while enjoying his usual glass of wine in Woodbridge Tavern, a man approached his table. "We're watching you. Consider yourself warned..."

He initially thought that Bertha, whom he had seen and talked with a few times in the meantime, had turned him in, either on purpose—good information always begets money—or without realizing it. He went to see her right away, but she swore on her life she hadn't told anyone, very upset at his suspicions.

"Stop flattering yourself; you're not all *that* important! I don't even know your real name, and I don't know where you make your deliveries. What the hell! And, even if I knew all of this, what would I get from spilling the beans on someone like you? I make more money if you see me every once in a while than if I sell your name for twenty bucks, don't you think?"

Mitu then thought of Madame Brunelle, but crossed her name quickly off the suspects list. *"I deliver her good alcohol at good prices..."* Then he thought of Julia, her daughter, because before him she had been her mother's sole distributor. *"She could be jealous—maybe her mother doesn't give her enough money since I got into the picture..."* But he then wrote her off as well. *"It can't be Julia, she's just a girl. How old is she? Barely twelve or thirteen..."*

At last, he even suspected James—*"I wouldn't be surprised if he wanted to take my place!"*—but he quickly dismissed the thought. *"He never gave me a reason not to trust him—it would be unfair on my part..."*

He received a second warning two months later, also in Woodbridge Tavern. This time, two men sitting at a table smoking cigars were staring him down. At one point, one of them got up and threw him a dollar bill with a cross drawn on it, then turned his back and left together with the other one.

He asked Madame Brunelle if she knew who they were.

"I don't know them—never seen them in my life—but be careful. Maybe it wouldn't be a bad idea to lay low for a while. You know, before Julia I used to have other distributors. I remember one—Michael Krustov—who disappeared without a trace, and I never heard from him again..."

Bertha also advised him to give up bootlegging each time he visited her, which lately was a lot more often.

"I know what I know, trust me. Be careful before something happens to you..."

Unlike Olga, who was an innocent dreamer, full of childish aspirations of fame and glory, Bertha was a practical woman, anchored in a somber and dangerous reality, gruesomely depicted in newspapers. Having been part of the underbelly of society and coming in contact with all types of people for so long, she saw life through different lenses and was capable of sifting dispassionately through garbage, betrayal, greed, treachery, and threat. The circles she moved in, she would tell him often, were a jungle full of dangers at every step—insatiable fiends would slit your throat for a bone. Her stories about the constant fights between gangs, about the tentacles of corruption reaching up high, about escape tunnels drilled in the basements of bars, or members of the upper crust paying her regular visits astonished him, making him wonder how he had escaped thus far.

Giving up bootlegging was something he had considered before, even in Montana, but never seriously. *"Just make a little more dough and then we'll see..."* he thought each time. Lately, however, because of the threats, he was growing afraid. Each shipment amplified his fear, and Bertha's stories unsettled him even more so.

He remembered that back in the war, the soldiers most tried in battle were the ones who were the most fearful, but he had never thought he would feel it firsthand. It seemed strange to him that now, with all his experience, he was so scared. He knew all the bays and inlets on the Detroit and St. Clair Rivers by heart and had all his plans down to a T. Besides those incidents from Woodbridge Tavern, he had never had any problems. He hadn't been swindled out of money or alcohol. He hadn't been attacked on the streets or water. He had honored all of his promises, and James had proven to be more than trustworthy.

Still, none of it seemed to matter. He lately woke up afraid, walked the streets checking all corners, and bolted the door, like never before.

And Bertha...Bertha made things even more difficult when they saw each other! After some wild sex—as if that were the natural development of their meetings—she would always tell him to give up bootlegging and go "legit."

"Why do you keep all your money under the mattress without investing it in something? You mentioned something about a store. You could open one up already with what you've saved so far. My clients make money in all kinds of ways. Some buy properties and real estate they can rent later. Some put all their money in the stock market. A few days ago, a client of mine, Jack McCughoy, bragged about buying twelve thousand shares a few months back, and now he has more than fifty thousand with the prices going up. Money without work. I don't know much about all this, but if you want, I can get you in touch with him..."

Bertha's way of being was something new to Mitu. She approached her amorous connections with a casualness, which Mitu, as emancipated as he thought he was, did not have. *"This woman is out of this world!"* he thought, seeing how nonchalantly she spoke about her lovers, even offering to put him in touch with them for business opportunities.

Lately, they were seeing each other in parks or in the commercial district, not at Night Star. Somehow, gradually and without them noticing, their relationship had grown into some type of an adventure and not just a long string of transactions—sex for money. He still paid for her services, but not in cash; he now bought her things—dresses, jewelry, expensive dinners—and that made him content. The fact that he no longer handed her hard cash made him feel he had a lover by his side and not a whore, ready to leave him if he ran out of money.

Her stories had helped him read the news about the illicit world of bootlegging reported in the papers with a different set of eyes: the crimes on the streets of Detroit for a few gallons of liquor were no longer out of his realm and could very well happen to him.

"What was I thinking? At the beginning in Montana I was a bit more naïve...but now...now I should stop."

During his bootlegging beginnings, he had been seduced by the easy money. Indifferent to danger, he was happy to receive pocketfuls of bills from Carrick. Now it was a different story. Risking it in Montana was not the same as risking it in Detroit. This was a battlefield with many casualties. Was it worth it? How much longer could he go on, when even the big gangsters, hand in hand with the police, were eventually caught and thrown in jail? How much longer could he sleep with one eye open, thinking that any minute someone might knock on his door?

His savings were substantial now—over forty thousand dollars. He could start up any kind of new business. Or he could retire and live comfortably for years without lifting a finger. He now felt he was defying God, who had already miraculously saved him from certain death in the woods of Meuse-Argonne. Instead of being grateful, he was upsetting Him on purpose!

James didn't even want to hear about a possible exit. He wanted to get rich fast, by any means and with whatever risks. The first thousands of dollars had blinded him, making him think that the poverty he had endured was finally over and prosperous times were knocking on his door. The fact that his boss had been threatened twice in the last couple of months seemed irrelevant, especially since lately things had quieted down on the river, and his shipments for Madame Brunelle had been quite smooth.

He was struggling to convince Mitu not to make a "catastrophic" decision.

"Let's do a few more shipments. What the hell!" he begged. "We can't stop now that we've started making serious money! Can't you see what a good team we make? The best! You've got your trousers in a knot over some whore's stories!"

"Man, I have a bad feeling about this, and I'm afraid I'll be sorry later—that is if I'm still around. Don't you see what's in the papers? There's no day that goes by without news about someone being shot. Sooner or later we'll make the front page, some unknown small timers, shot to death!"

"Huh! Bertha told you some stories about the Purple Gang..." James would scoff. "Great source of information, what can I say...I can bet you she's telling you all this to get more money outta you, man. She pretends to be your friend, and, like an idiot, you believe her. And, anyway, what news is she feeding you? What, we haven't heard of gangsters before Bertha? And you still risked it, didn't you? Without problems! The Purple Gang's eyes are on everybody—we're all in the same shit! It's dangerous, no doubt about it, but life is full of danger! What, because people get into car accidents no one should ever leave their home?"

"I don't know, James..." Mitu would answer. "I'm thinking about opening a store. It's been my dream for a long time. And I need some help. We work well together...perhaps you could work for me like you do now. And, in time, I'll open a new one, and so on, until you can be responsible for a few of them, and we can both have it good. And we'll be legit...and able to sleep at night..."

"You must be kidding me! It's easy for you to say, now that you're loaded—how much money do you have, anyway?—a few tens of thousands, right? But I can't work for pennies anymore!"

"Your life is much better than mine used to be when I was your age..."

"So? What does that have to do with anything? Can't I have an even better one?"

THE INVESTMENTS

Chapter 39

Mitu's split from James was not sudden. Thoughts about an eventual exit had taken root when Mitu received the first threat, but neither one had suspected it meant the breakup of their remarkable team.

When James asked if he could use his boat, Mitu tried to make him change his mind. He thought that, by working alone, James was sure to meet his death. They had operated in tandem until then, and James had never come in contact with any of the owners of the speakeasies or blind pigs. First of all, he lacked credibility since he seemed too young and inexperienced, and second, their partnership had been very well established, with the responsibilities of each one clearly mapped out, and James had not been the one in charge of finding customers.

The boy wanted to tackle alone what they had been doing together—something Mitu himself wouldn't dare to do in Detroit. He agreed to loan him the boat in the end, with the foreboding thought he may not see James alive and well again. Only once or twice before in his life had Mitu felt the acute certainty of a future event. An indescribable, visceral, and irrational feeling had overwhelmed him unexpectedly, transporting him to the near future. The first time, it had been at a poker game, when he felt the almost tangible sensation that the next three cards would be three twos to complete a four of a kind. When he actually pulled those cards, their image had rendered him dumb, etched onto his brain forever. The second instance had been during a game of backgammon. He was convinced his next throw would be double-sixes. He bet all of his money on it and won a few hundred dollars—a small fortune. Since those episodes, he tried many times to trigger such states voluntarily, but they only occurred spontaneously, randomly, without any external stimuli.

This was the first time, however, he had had such feeling about someone other than himself, and he was sorry he couldn't convince James to give in. The look he gave the young man as he handed him the keys to the boat was so sad and profound, James stopped for a moment, as if, finally, doubtful that bootlegging was his future, and asked Mitu if something was wrong.

"Nothing, James, I just wanted to tell you to be very, very careful, now that you're alone..."

"I will be. I know what I'm doing. Don't fret like you're my father. You're driving me mad with all these dark thoughts of yours..."

Months passed afterward without Mitu's premonition coming true, and that set his mind at ease and took away from the feeling of responsibility he had for the boy. Somehow James didn't encounter any problems with the gangsters or the police—as though he were invisible. He didn't know the blind pigs as Mitu did, but that didn't seem to deter him; it just made him change his tactics. He brought a lot less alcohol and went from door to door selling it piece by piece, starting all over again upon the depletion of his stock.

After a while, time during which they met very rarely, James told him he had decided to relocate to New York and try rum running, since he had heard more money could be made from it.

"Bootleggers go there from the Bahamas with boatfuls. Can you believe it? You can make more dough, since there isn't a cheap source like the one we had in Windsor. I could double my profits! If everything goes well, I'll stay there for only a few months, maybe half a year, and I'll come back with a shitload of money. And then I'll buy that store of yours off of you, which you keep talking about but never open!"

James left, and Mitu felt strangely relieved. Until then, he had thought he could always go back to bootlegging as in the past. Without a partner, he now had to explore new ways of making money. He no longer had that certainty whispering in his ear, *"No matter what, we could always do it again!"*

He first considered the stock market. He had enough money, and the newspapers were full of news about the financial world. The first person who he discussed it with was Bertha, since she had many clients who had gotten rich on Wall Street. However, besides a few general things, like, "John doubled his investment last year!" she couldn't give him any more information. All she could do was send him to Jack Lombardi, a broker who had paid her visits a few years back.

They went into Lombardi's office one day as soon as it was open for business and waited for him to finish making a few phone calls. Jack Lombardi always came in one hour early to get himself up to speed on the current financial news. This routine had helped him avoid some little disasters, and he followed it religiously.

When he finished his calls, he courteously invited them to sit down.

"Bertha, how long has it been...? You look wonderful! And the gentleman is..."

"My friend. *Meetoo.*"

Mitu examined him carefully. It was the first time he met one of Bertha's clients face to face. *"This is the type of men she sleeps with?"* he wondered in disgust. Jack wore thick glasses and had hair only above his ears and on the back of his head. His pate was shining. Every now and then, he'd pull out his handkerchief to wipe his bald spot as though he wanted to polish it. He wasn't fat, but his double chin gave the impression that he was a lot bigger than he was.

Bertha told him quickly that Mitu wanted some information on the stock market.

"Well then...for old times' sake...my pleasure to help you, since I get something out of this as well!"

Mitu smiled. *"This guy gives it to you straight!"*

"So you're interested in investing in some shares. Good thinking! How much would you have available for this?"

"I was thinking...I don't know...about twenty thousand dollars." He wavered. "But I know nothing—and I mean nothing—about these things. That's why I came here. Maybe you can teach me something. Bertha told me you really know a lot about it."

"You came to the right place, sir. Each day the New York Stock Exchange, the greatest stock market in the world, reaches a new high. Surely you know that; otherwise you wouldn't be here..."

"Yes, I read the newspapers. That's what I was thinking—do something with the money..."

Jack fixed the glasses on his nose, and then looked at him for a few moments without saying a word.

"Yes, you have quite the savings—what can I say? It'd be a shame to keep it all under the mattress. The more money you put in at the beginning the greater the gain in the long run. So, what would you like to invest it in?"

Bertha intervened, "Jack, I told you my friend doesn't really know much about stocks. I was thinking you could explain it all to him."

"Oh, yes...very well then" he began. "Very well. Electricity, sir. That's the future of this country! Electrical power will be needed everywhere, and there are many villages yet to be connected to the national grid. And the railroad industry, my kind gentleman. Our country is a continent, and transportation will be done by trains, since it's the most economical. The companies involved in it will have great gains. You can't go wrong with it. Look at me, I'm your best example. Some time ago I invested in Iron, Steel & Co.—a small company manufacturing train tracks, a veritable diamond in the rough, with a P/E of 4. Where else can you find something like that? In a few months, I doubled my investment. You know the company?"

Not only had Mitu never heard of the company, but he hadn't understood a word from Jack's explanation.

"What does P/E mean?"

"Oh, sorry. It means price-to-earnings. It's a valuation ratio of a company's current share price compared to its per share earnings and it shows the time it will take to recover the investment. If you want, we can fill out some forms and you can become a stockholder in a few companies of this kind. I suggest smaller companies with a low P/E, because those are the most profitable. The bank keeps the commission for the services—from which I get my fair share—and in a few weeks you'll receive the certificates and everybody's happy. What do you say?"

Mitu couldn't even put his confusion into words. Jack pulled out a piece of paper and started making some calculations.

"Look, if two days ago you had bought five thousand dollars' worth of stock in Iron, Steel & Co., by now you would have made a profit of a hundred and thirty-two dollars. Not too bad without any work, right? In only a couple of days..."

"No, not bad at all, indeed..."

"As I was saying..."

"What if they go down? They can go down, right?"

"Sir," Jack frowned, "indeed there are no guarantees. The stock market goes up and down. A lot of things could happen...but, it's not like the lottery either—don't get me wrong. Wall Street depends on the economy. And the economy is doing so well—since the end of the war, we've had a tremendous growth—that there is no danger of the indexes' going down in the near future. I know many like you who have come in this very office with a few thousands and now they have a few tens of thousands, even hundreds. How do you think I bought my second home?"

Mitu thought about it long and hard. *"What should I do?"* As presented by Jack, things seemed pretty easy. Quite simply, he would deposit the money and wait. And, to be sure, he could buy stock in the same companies Jack had bought. If the broker played his own money, he knew what he was doing being in the business and all, right?

He fretted for a while, then gave Bertha a pleading look.

"What do you think, my dear?"

She looked at him surprised he would ask her something like that. *"I should tell him what to do with his money? How should I know?!"*

"I have no idea, love, I have never thought of things like these because I never had a reason to, to be honest. I don't understand any of it. I can't see how you can make money out of nothing, but I trust Jack—isn't that right, Jack? You invested your own money, didn't you? If you didn't know what this was about, you wouldn't have used your own savings to buy stock, right?"

Jack nodded.

"Of course not. Ultimately, it's your decision what to do with the money. But for the last three years, the Dow tripled and continues to rise each day, with no sign of slowing down. You know what Dow is, right? It's the most important stock index, created by Charles Dow in 1896, which shows the performance of the economy's industrial component. I am more than happy with my investments. This country's economy is fantastic, there's construction everywhere, there's a constant need for a work force, and there is enough money to buy all that's produced. The politics are good; there are no social movements or upheavals—thank God the war is over! Wall Street can't go wrong now. Each day I get people who come here to invest, not even with their own money, but through margin buying with money from the banks. Margin buying means that you can buy stock with money borrowed from the broker. You can do that if you want: you put down a third and we cover the other two with very low interest. Plenty of people do it. If you want to play the stock market, do it big style, for God's sakes! With that kind of money, you can be a millionaire in a few years!"

Mitu watched him, glassy eyed. Jack's confidence and persuasive words had won him over. *"Could it be that easy, and I've worked like a fool all these years?"*

He moved uneasily in his chair, looked at Bertha, and then told Jack he wanted in—with the maximum amount he could borrow.

"I've decided. Margin buying, I believe you said."

"Yes, margin buying. I see you catch on fast. That would be sixty thousand dollars, including your twenty. It's a very big sum. The way Wall Street is going these days, from the profit on this money you could live very comfortably without ever lifting a finger."

"With God's will..." murmured Mitu.

"So, have you decided what you'd like to buy?" Jack asked handing him a list of all the companies on Wall Street.

He read it, utterly confused—there were hundreds and hundreds of numbers and symbols—then answered uncertainly:

"I have no clue, Mr. Lombardi. You've kinda lost me here...but I want you to buy equal amounts in the same companies you've invested yourself, okay?"

"Of course. I was going to suggest that to you. Let's get to the paperwork. You know—the unpleasant part of my job."

Mitu signed the loan application and all the other preliminary paperwork slightly apprehensively. *"Should I be doing this...?"* he wondered, and then tried to encourage himself. *"I can't be the unluckiest person in this world. And besides, I've had my fair share of bad luck in life! I made this money easy enough, maybe that's its purpose, to multiply just as easy!"*

Out on the street, the crisp, fresh air washed over his face, calming his nerves.

"Perhaps I'm too old fashioned and I don't get these things. I will later on...after all, no one's lost money in the stock market..." He clasped his arms around Bertha's shoulders.

"My dear, maybe in a few years I can buy myself a castle! How would that be?" he said.

"I don't think it's all that impossible! You wouldn't be the first one to strike gold!"

During the following weeks, he read the news about the stock market with bated breath. The first thing he did each morning was to run and buy The New York Times or Barron's, then lie down on the bed pen in hand, going over the companies whose stock he owned, endlessly calculating how much money he had made or lost. Just as an alcoholic can't start a day without a glass on an empty stomach, he quickly became addicted to studying Wall Street transactions before getting on with his own day.

After a period of time full of hope, depression, somber thoughts, and intense satisfaction, he realized that his investments weren't bad. The stock market fluctuated, wrenching his heart on the way down and filling it with joy on the way up, but overall, the change was positive—the initial sum kept increasing. From the profit, he could pay back the loan and still have plenty left over for a life without work. He was no longer a commoner!

He met with Jack regularly to verify the sums, calculate and decide what to sell and what to buy. He tried spending more time with the broker, to understand how to play the market. There were still many things he didn't understand.

Jack would explain to him why their investments were doing so well:

"You see, Europe is still reeling from the war, struggling with the economic recession caused by it, and still hasn't finished rebuilding the vast devastated territories. America, however, with its isolated position has consolidated its status as the biggest power in the world. We have megalithic industries and we are thriving, progressing at an unprecedented rate. Hundreds of thousands of jobs have been created lately and all this success is clearly reflected in the stock market, the economy's absolute barometer. That's why there's a lot of money in stocks. Companies are doing well and will keep on doing well in the future. You got in at the right time!"

Yes, it certainly seemed he had gotten in at the right time. He could see that each day as he did his calculations and drew the total line. America, which he had hated so much after the war, was giving him reason for happiness. If people had told him a few years back that things would turn out this way, he would have thought they were joking.

Chapter 40

Mitu opened his long-desired store a short time after beginning his Wall Street transactions. With some of the money he still had left over, he rented a place on Gratiot Avenue in Eastern Market, which he painted in white yellowish tones and outfitted with shelves from floor to ceiling. He stacked those shelves with all kinds of merchandise: pieces of luggage made out of wood reinforced leather, petrol lamps, men's cotton suits, and boxfuls of all kinds of odd things—nails, screws, nuts, scissors, screwdrivers, hammers of different weights, and hatchets of different dimensions. In vitrines secured with two big locks, he displayed watches, silver and gold chains, fountain pens with gold nibs, and rings set with gems.

When he was done with everything, he hired a sales clerk named Walter Schmidt—a freckled, fair-haired German, arrived to America only a few months back—who could man the store while he went looking for merchandise.

"Check me out—a store owner in America! At only thirty!" Mitu beamed with pride on opening day. He had awoken early in the morning to sweep the floor and take care of last minute details. He wrote the date—September 1st, 1926—with a marker on the wall right next to the cash register so he could forever see it.

It was a surprisingly cold day for September, but he had never felt warmer. Nothing could take away from the big event, for which he was solely responsible. He had worked on it for months on end, starting from scratch, many times afraid it might never come to fruition.

At exactly eight o'clock, he went outside and looked down the street, then inspected carefully—for the hundredth time—the merchandise displayed in the windows. The sign above the door had big red letters:

MITU & OLGA'S STORE

and a poster read:

GRAND OPENING!
COME ON IN! OPEN FOR BUSINESS!

He went back inside, pulled a chair over to the window and began monitoring the passersby. *"Will anyone come in?"*

Just as it happens in any neighborhood in any city in the world, when something new appears, people, out of curiosity, take notice, analyze, and form an opinion on whether or not to come back some other time. After less than ten minutes, the first customer walked through the door.

"Good morning. So you opened a store right here in Eastern Market, the commercial heart of the city! The rent must cost you a fortune!" his first patron commented jovially, examining the shelves. "My congratulations and good wishes! So, what kind of stuff do you sell?"

"Well, a little of everything. Maybe we have something that interests you. I see you're wearing a new suit, so I won't offer you one, but a watch would go nicely with your clothes," Mitu answered with all the kindness he could muster, pulling a Patek Philippe from underneath the glass case.

The man shook his head.

"I don't need a watch..." he said, pretending to be interested in a brown leather wallet.

"Would you like to see it?" Mitu offered quickly. "Walter, bring it here please!"

The boy jumped to unlock the case, but the man stopped him with a gesture.

"Not now...maybe later. Good luck with your business! I'll come back some other time!"

Mitu watched him leave, quite disconcerted. He had hoped the first person entering his store would buy something, for good luck!

Nobody bought anything that day.

The following weeks didn't prove any better. Hundreds of people came in, but very few actually purchased something.

September passed with sales too low to cover his expenses.

The upcoming months didn't bring big changes either. Mitu worked at a loss the whole fall season, paying the rent and Walter's salary from his savings, dreading the next time he'd have to pull money out of his bank account yet again. He barely sold anything, waiting for clients from morning until night.

He counted every penny, calculating over and over again how much merchandise he needed to sell to cover his costs.

"Walter, I must find some merchandise as sought after as alcohol—but legal. Otherwise I'm going to waste all my savings and go bankrupt. If I could find something like that, I'd get outta this problem and become rich! What do you think people need? What cheap things can I sell that you can't find around here? Is there anything in your Germany that would do well in Detroit?"

The boy didn't know what to say. He had arrived to America half a year before, and there were lots of things he had yet to understand.

"Do you think if I knew that, I'd still work for you? As far as I'm concerned, boss, worldwide, money's made in guns, alcohol, and women."

"Guns, alcohol, and women...yeah, everyone knows that...but I prefer to make less and still be alive...I may be poor at the end, but at least I'll be in one piece!"

The day he no longer lost money with the store came late, towards the end of winter. It was the first time he didn't need to take funds from his bank account. Since the September opening, he had used up more than a thousand dollars from his savings.

That night, right before going to bed, as he calculated the costs for the month, he realized that in January—to his surprise, having thought holidays, and not regular months would bring in the most—he had sold enough to cover the rent of the store, Walter's salary, and the rest of the expenses. After paying everything, he still had something left over. He dropped the pen and turned, invigorated, to Bertha.

"Dear, I'm breaking even!" he said cheerfully. "I'm not losing any more money! I'm finally breaking even! Can you believe it?" he turned to her, full of affection. "It'll be okay from now on; I'll keep making money and put it away in the savings account!"

She looked at him as if to say, "I knew you could do it!"

"With all the work you put into it, I would have been surprised if it hadn't worked out...it was just a matter of time...I have yet to see a store in Eastern Market with 'bankruptcy' written on the door."

"You haven't seen it...but it could happen..." he said, disappointed she wasn't as surprised as he had expected her to be. *"Maybe she compares me to her rich customers, and my little store is not such a big deal to her..."*

He kissed her on the neck and said in a different tone, "Even though you're not impressed with this, I still think we should celebrate it."

She smiled. She recognized that voice and enjoyed it very much. It was the voice he used when he wanted to make love: guttural, low, sensual. She would have given anything to hear it more often!

She gave herself thoroughly to him. She was glad that the man by her side was happy! Did she play a role in his happiness? He had never told her he loved her, but he had never pushed her away either.

She nestled in his arms and breathed in his smell.

"I really like you, my dear...you give me hope and confidence...you know...I haven't had much of either in my life..."

Mitu was about to answer her. Bertha was spending a lot more time with him. She had entered his life unexpectedly, and now they were almost a couple. How had it happened? He had considered her something temporary in his life. She was a whore, after all, who still turned tricks at Night Star.

"I'm so glad the business is taking off, love!" he said, avoiding a straight answer. "And I'm glad you're here with me..."

She looked at him with doleful eyes.

"Sometimes I wish I could open that head of yours and see what's in it."

"But what did I say? I said I'm happy..."

"Yeah...only that...and I'm happy for you. You know, I've thought about it: with the money you're making on stocks, you could buy an apartment building or two in the city, with stores on the first floor that you could rent out..."

"Yeah, I've thought about that too," he said, relieved she had changed the subject. "But it's tough being a landlord! You run around like a lunatic all day fixing, repairing, collecting rent—not easy. Besides, I make more money from investments than I would from that anyway, and I don't do all that much. I sit by week after week while the stuff keeps collecting."

"You know something? I don't get how you make money with the stock market. How does it work? How do shares increase in value like that, all by themselves?"

"Well, it's simple: Each company is divided in a number of equal parts. Those are the shares. If the value of the company goes up, then the value of each share goes up. Easy as 1, 2, 3..."

"I still don't understand where this money comes from. Anyway...you know what I was thinking the other day? If your girlfriend knew...I mean your ex-girlfriend...that her name is on your store...don't you think she'd be happy?"

"Olga? Sometimes I wish I knew where she was. That's all..."

Bertha avoided his eyes, then turned to the night table and grabbed *The New York Times*. She leafed through it skimming the pages. Mitu got closer and glanced over her shoulder.

"What's so interesting in there?"

"Nothing...they're mentioning the Orteig Prize again.9F[*]"

"Yeah...the Prize. Give it here for a sec... you know what idea just came to me?" His face lit up.

"I don't know...but I have the feeling I'm gonna find out in the next few seconds."

"Yeah...exactly! I was thinking that it wouldn't be such a bad idea to invest some money in a trial to cross the Atlantic. Whatever I still have in the bank. About ten thousand..."

"All you think about is business since you've met that Lombardi. You should thank me for that..."

"That's right. I thank you from the bottom of my heart!"

"Ha!" she laughed. "*You* don't even believe what you're saying! And what if you invest in a plane that goes down? You'll lose everything!"

"Yes, I will. But what if it doesn't go down? If I make the right choice, it won't go down, right? Like with the stock market. You don't invest like an idiot; you check what you get yourself into."

"If you wanna do something with this money, why not Wall Street? Now that you know how things work..."

---

[*] Raymond Orteig (1870-1939) born in Louvie-Juzon, Béarn, France, emigrated to the U.S. in 1882. He began working as a busboy, but in a very short time he managed to buy the Lafayette and Brevoort Hotels in Greenwich Village, New York. The Brevoort was a meeting place for the European aristocracy, and the French character of the hotel's basement café attracted an illustrious crowd of actors and writers, including Mark Twain. In 1919, Raymond Orteig offered a prize of $25,000 for the first nonstop flight (in an aircraft heavier than air) between New York and Paris or vice versa. Since the technical difficulties of a 3600-mile flight were tremendous at the time, during the first five years there were no candidates for it, forcing Orteig to extend the term of his offer by another five years.

"But don't you realize what it'd be to invest in a flight that takes the Orteig Prize? It don't just mean money—I'm talking fame! I'd be in all the newspapers!" he said spiritedly, dreaming with his eyes wide open. "People would know me as 'Mitu Popescu, one of the few investors in the very first transatlantic flight.'"

"I think you're going nuts..."

"Mitu Popescu, one of the investors in the first transatlantic flight!" he repeated solemnly as if he were giving a speech.

"I don't know...if I were you I'd buy some land somewhere, like I said. Land never shrinks away. It stays there forever. Or houses. Since I've come to this city and up to this day, real estate has gone up. Buy something downtown—the prices there will never drop."

"No...no way! Buy some land then wait ten years just to make a few dollars out of it? Money should be made fast—and lots of it at once—you shouldn't have to wait till you're dead. What's the use of having it when you're too old and can't do anything with it?"

"Yeah, I guess you're right...after all, money shouldn't be kept in the bank. And..."

"Why are we talking about this?! Come here...and get on your back, the way you like it...we haven't finished celebrating yet..."

Chapter 41

Technology was not Mitu's cup of tea. He knew that. His only contact with it had been during his employment at Ford where the Model T was built. He had been very impressed by the grandness and productivity of the plant: a stone and metal colossus housing giant mechanisms incessantly manufacturing cars which rolled out on conveyor belts.

The newspapers always spoke of science and technology's progress. Not a day went by without some invention being written about. Like many others, Mitu was also convinced that science was going to bring happiness to mankind, solve all of its problems, eradicate poverty and prolong life. That's what the educated said, so it must have been the truth! After all, you could see it everywhere: discoveries in medicine were veritable miracles, engineers had brought the radio into people's homes, and movies now had sound and even sometimes color! He had witnessed many unbelievable changes in recent years, and those fortunate enough to have been involved in them, he thought, had only benefits to reap.

Those were clear signs of what the future was to bring. The fact that magnates of the world, the likes of Raymond Orteig, risked their money in all kinds of dicey engineering attempts was, to him, clear proof that the country's future was in technology. And, with the money he had now, he could take advantage of it.

For the following weeks he searched high and low for information on aviation and aeronautics. He set up a reading corner in the back of the store, since he spent most of his time there anyway, and began compiling materials on the subject.

He didn't pretend to understand everything he read. The technical details from the manuals went far beyond his four years of elementary education in Cernădia. But, for his purposes, there was no need to get bogged down with all kinds of mathematical principles. All he had to do was choose, out of all the companies working on building a transatlantic plane, the one with the greatest chance of success. That's what he had done with the stock market, at Bertha's old lover's suggestion, and things had turned out quite well.

In a short while, he crammed the reading corner and his living room at home with piles of newspapers and manuals, and his desk with mounds of synopses written in fine print. He was gathering information however he could. He read about those getting ready to fly, scoured libraries for books describing plane models, and filled pages and pages with summaries of the progress of aviation.

There were some things he now remembered, having lived through and learned about them from the radio, but there were others that had escaped his attention at the time and were completely forgotten. He now saw everything in a different light. In his notebooks, he had highlighted in red the first attempts of crossing the Atlantic. Right after the war, in 1919, John Alcock and Arthur Brown had managed the first flight between two Islands: St

John's, Newfoundland and Clifden, Ireland on board a Vickers Vimy bombardier—how much he had loved those planes! A short while after, George Scott had flown in a hot air balloon from East Fortune, Scotland, to Mineola, Long Island.

He remembered those events quite vaguely—perhaps because nothing mattered in 1919 except the victory against Germany and his veteran status. He did remember Hugo Eckener, however, who five years after the war had flown in a zeppelin from Germany to New Jersey—but a zeppelin wasn't a plane.

Three years had passed since Eckener's feat. Meanwhile, technology had made great strides; it was only a matter of months—not years—before someone could succeed with a flight from Paris to New York and win the twenty-five-thousand-dollar award. The enthusiasm of the public was tremendous—it was on everyone's lips in pubs, offices, among friends, the newspapers, and the radio. The buzz about the transatlantic flight made Mitu certain the victorious aviators would be catapulted to glory. Not only that, but all those involved in the process were also going to reap in the benefits of money and fame.

He could make good use of this fame, provided he made the right investment, of course. He had money. All he needed to do was choose well.

One night, after going through the piles of papers once more just in case he had missed some crucial detail, he woke Bertha to tell her he had made up his mind.

"Darling, I've decided. If I'm right, this will pave my road to the upper crust!" he said, full of excitement.

"What time is it? It's two in the morning! You've lost your mind...you'd better go to sleep," she said drowsily.

"I've decided who I'm going with."

"Yeah? Who? Davis?"

Bertha was up to speed on everything, since Mitu bounced all his ideas off her. He kept telling her that three people were going to attempt a transatlantic flight sometime in the spring when the weather would get better, each striving to be the first one. She had, in fact, learned their names, hearing Mitu had repeat them so many times: Noel Davis, the commandant of the Navy reserve in Boston, Charles Lindbergh, a regular airmail pilot on the Missouri-Illinois route, and a French aviator, Charles Nungesser.

"Yes, I've decided. No, it's not Davis. I'm putting my money on Nungesser. I'll look for those who finance him and I'll get in as well. Or, I'll just bet on him."

Bertha, now fully awake, watched him with amusement. Sometimes this man was so child-like! Maybe that's why she liked him so much...

"Why don't you wanna invest in an American? It doesn't look very good if you're investing in a foreigner...and out of all three, why this Nungesser?"

"Like I told you! He's a phenomenal aviator, an ace pilot—that's what they call people who take down at least five enemy planes in combat. But this guy's a hero, no doubt about it, since he took down forty-three planes! There's no way he could go wrong with all his experience. He took down dozens of German planes in some incredible conditions. You have no idea what an aerial fight is like, but I do because I was on the front: whoever comes out alive from something like that can't drop from friendly skies! Someone like him knows what he's doing! It's a sure bet! The only thing I'm worried about is that someone else might make the flight before him!"

"I don't know...I don't really get these things, but I hope you make the right decision. If it was me, I'd pick an American. Like Davis, for example. Why do you think he has worse chances than the Frenchman? After all, he is a commander in the Navy; he must know what he's doing! I have no clue how things are done in other countries, like engineering and such, but what I do know is that in America, whatever is being done, it's being done well. It's not for nothing we're the richest country in the world! And about Lindbergh, so what if he's an unknown? Maybe he's a very good pilot!"

"Yes, all of them are probably good, but you have to choose one that you know a little something about, right? Even the exceptional ones fail sometimes, so what can you expect from a mailman like Lindbergh? Do you remember last year when Fonck tried to cross the Atlantic? He was the best French aviator, but he almost died when his plane exploded on takeoff, and it was all his fault! If he had that much trouble, what do you think can happen to less experienced pilots?"

"But about Lindbergh, besides that he does airmail, did you learn anything else?"

"Almost nothing...he didn't participate in any battles and he has only flown in peaceful conditions. I told you before: he used to be a car mechanic and did plane stunts before working for the post office. The only special thing they say about him is that he transports the mail under any circumstances—no matter the weather or the condition of the plane. Once, when he crashed, instead of running away, he started pulling out the bags of mail from the flames and called the airport director to send him a truck to load them in...as though that was the most important thing for him at that moment..."

"Some dedication..." Bertha murmured. "What about Davis—Noel Davis? Why not him?"

"I thought about him for a while, you know. But you see, he didn't even go to war, and he went to school much later. He went to some great schools, like Harvard Law or something, and wrote books on flying planes for aviators in the reserve. That's about it. Going to flight school doesn't make you a good pilot—that's what I think. He's all about the theory. All in all, out of everyone, the Frenchman is by far the best choice and the one with the best chances for success. In fact, he's everyone's favorite."

"The way you're talking about it, it makes sense...I know a lot less about it than you do. In fact, I know nothing. Still, maybe you should think about it some more..."

Mitu's decision had been already made. It was possible he preferred the Frenchman because he stirred up nostalgia for the soldiers' camaraderie during the war, which he sometimes longed for, or maybe it was Nungesser's public life, rich in both heroic acts and sex scandals involving prostitutes and alcohol. Mitu felt both admiration and jealousy for the man, and the few months of fretting had only been his struggle to convince himself to bet on Nungesser. He had been his first choice—a choice that was instinctual, irrational, and visceral, as if he wanted to identify with him, projecting all of his hidden desires on the aviator adulated by the whole of France.

Once he had made up his mind, things unfolded easily. He learned from Jack Lombardi and his friends who financed Nungesser's flight: a group of sportsmen with connections in both Europe and America. He got in touch with them, something which proved to be quite difficult, since they were not eager to have a stranger among them. After numerous phone calls and failed attempts to contact them, Mitu eventually succeeded in talking to one of their representatives in America—a certain Thomas Cook—who at Mitu's insistence eventually accepted his check, but not without pointing out that he was doing him a very special favor:

"We are a private group investing in extreme events—this time the transatlantic flight—who does not often accept money from people like you. Who are you? A nobody who stumbled across a few dollars! But I like that you are idealistic, persistent, and a dreamer. Welcome to the Nungesser Club! The money you're bringing in can be lost if Nungesser doesn't succeed. I cannot stress that enough."

"I understand it very well."

"Well then, Godspeed to all of us!"

"Hear, hear," Mitu agreed full of apprehensive excitement. By signing the ten-thousand-dollar check, he was now left without any savings.

His life didn't change during the following months: each morning he would wake up at the crack of dawn to open his store early to avoid missing any potential customers, and then would go to bed exhausted late at night.

While doing the accounting each weekend, he would become disconcerted that his sales hadn't been greater. The difference between the thousands of dollars he used to make from bootlegging and the little he now made with his store was tremendous. It was difficult to make any profits from Mitu and Olga's store—so hard that if it weren't for the money coming from the stock market, his savings for rainy days, as he called it, his living would have been quite tough.

But one day, out of the blue, as often happens with extraordinary news, he realized that he was a lot closer to his dream than he had thought, and that his concerns were nothing more than exaggerations. It was a rainy morning in April when his telephone rang stridently. He was cleaning the store with Walter at that moment, and the piercing ring gave him a somber feeling. *"Who can call so early in the morning? It could only be Thomas! That means someone crossed the ocean, and Nungesser probably didn't even finish getting his plane ready!"* he thought quickly, tense with fear.

Indeed, Thomas was at the other end. Mitu recognized his breathing before the man even said a word.

"Hi Thomas. I knew it was you. What happened?" he asked, his voice quivering.

"I don't know how to tell you this. Paradoxically, it is good news. Maybe you've already heard. Noel Davis died yesterday in a plane crash 10F*"

Mitu didn't understand right away.

"Wh-what?! Who died?"

"Davis, the aviator. He's dead."

"How could it be...?! Davis? Davis, the commander? Died? How?"

"Yes...may God rest his soul. It happened yesterday during a test flight in a Keystone Pathfinder—you know, the plane he wanted to take over the ocean on the second of May. It crashed right after takeoff because it couldn't gain altitude."

He took a deep breath.

"God rest his soul...but that means..."

"Yes, we are very excited!" Thomas answered. "We now have a great chance to win the Orteig! Nungesser and Lindbergh are the next ones on the list."

"When is Nungesser supposed to fly?" He had a confusing feeling of relief and guilt, given that the news of someone's death made him oddly happy.

"Lindbergh's plane is not yet ready, from what I've heard, but the rumor is that he's gonna try flying pretty soon. Maybe on the tenth of May. And Nungesser's aiming for the same timeframe. Pray it happens at the beginning of next month, probably the eighth or the ninth."

Mitu fell in a chair, overwhelmed by the news. He was closer to Easy Street than ever! The Frenchman was going to take off from Paris and land in New York in a few days! Ahead of Lindbergh!

He pulled the chair next to the counter, grabbed a fountain pen and a piece of paper, and scribbled a short letter home:

April 27, 1927

Dear Ma,

---

* Noel Davis died on April 26, 1927 in a flight test on Langley Field, Virginia. The plane had a full load of fuel, the amount needed to cross the Atlantic Ocean. Initially Davis meant to take his wife along as copilot, but, in thinking about their young son, the woman decided the risk was too great and refused. In the accident died Davis and his copilot Stanton Wooster. A day before, Clarence Chamberlain and Bert Acosta had flown the equivalent of 4100 miles (500 miles more than the New York-Paris distance) in a Bellanca monoplane above New York City, circling it for 51 hours and 11 minutes. However, the Orteig Prize had been offered for a transatlantic flight only.

I am close to a very important event in my life. I have invested a lot of money in a transatlantic flight, which, if successful, will bring me fortune and many benefits. Pray for me and for the aviators attempting this great deed of courage. I'm doing well—can't complain. I will send you some more money soon, like last time. I hope all of you are in good health. I miss you, Ghiță, and Gheorghița. How are you? How are they doing? Has either gotten married yet? They should hurry up before they're too old, if it's not too late already. Write me soon and tell me what's going on in Cernădia. I'm sending you some pictures of my store—I told you all about it in my last letter.

Missing you all,

Mitu

Chapter 42

The following weeks removed Mitu from his immediate reality. He crossed off each day in the calendar with an "X" to see how much longer it was until the eighth of May when Nungesser was supposed to take off from Paris. He had made plans to go to New York before the event, to welcome the winner and celebrate the unbelievable feat.

He worked like a machine, deep in thought, so much so that he began worrying Walter, his employee.

"What's going on boss? Why have you been so upside down for the last few days? You don't even care how the store is going. It's like I'm more concerned about it than you!"

"Oh Walter, if this flight makes it, I won't need a store anymore. I'll give it to you. For free. You have my word! I really appreciate all your efforts during these past few days. I probably wouldn't have managed without you. I guess not all the Germans are alike, or else you wouldn't have lost the war..."

The German gave him a grateful look—praises from his boss, or anyone he deemed superior, were music to his ears.

"Thank you, boss, but I don't think I do anything out of the ordinary. The truth is my life's good here because of you. You told me how poor you were in Romania, but you should see how bad it is in Germany now. That's why I left: people starving left and right! If things go on this way, something will have to happen. People will rise up when the knife gets to the bone. In Berlin it's cheaper burning money than buying firewood with it. It's revolting! What we need is a military dictatorship—a strong leader who's not afraid to confront adversaries and tell them we can't afford to keep paying these so-called war debts!"

Mitu wondered for a moment what had gotten into Walter, who never cared for politics, but he left him alone, unmindful of his prophetic words. His thoughts were elsewhere, not on world politics.

"Walter, you keep manning the store like you have until now, and I will raise your salary five cents an hour. I'm gonna be busy with other things for the next few weeks. I'm going to New York to see Nungesser—God help me!—and I'll leave you in charge in the interim."

Walter's face lit up. He had never been given such a responsibility in his life! He had never been in charge of anything so important!

"Not a problem boss, I'll manage the store with an iron fist. The best I can! You'll see."

In a few days, smartly dressed and carrying a very elegant piece of luggage from his own store, Mitu gave the store keys to Walter and climbed along with Bertha onto a train headed to Manhattan.

A warm feeling of familiarity and coming back home flooded his heart when the train reached Penn Station. "Goodness, how grand! I had almost forgotten. Look, the restaurant is still here, and the bakery. Nothing's changed!"

They took a room in a second-rate hotel downtown, right next to Battery Park, and wandered the bustling streets. Seemingly forgotten details came back at once: the chocolate shops where he had bought his very first candy upon arriving to America, the cafés in Little Italy where he had spent countless hours with Olga, the busy streets of the Lower East Side where he had broken his back for pennies in Herzowig's workshop, and the ads for Singer children's sewing machines.

They passed by the tenement where he had shared a room with Pistol, and Mitu recalled his friend for a short while in front of it, then entered the bar where he had almost drowned in alcohol right after catching Olga with Steinovich. The place was now a crowded restaurant serving soups, steaks, and fries.

They headed towards the apartment building in Midtown where he had lived with Olga—a quiet street that stirred up painful memories. Nothing had changed there either. He told Bertha to wait for him in a café and walked to the building.

He recognized the balconies, windows, even some time forgotten curtains in the place where he had dwelt with his soul mate for a happy while. He even thought he recognized a few faces from the past, and that gave him the courage to go in. He climbed upstairs to his old door and knocked lightly on it. An elderly woman opened, peering suspiciously at him from behind her glasses.

"How can I help you?" Her voice was edged with irritation rather than politeness.

"Please forgive me for bothering you; I'm looking for someone who used to live here about ten years ago...Olga. Olga Gertrude. We lived here together."

The woman watched him with compassion all of a sudden, as though she somehow understood the deeper meaning of his words.

"I'm sorry, but I've never heard of a Miss Gertrude. I rented the apartment straight from the landlord, not another tenant. You can ask him; I have his card. Wait here a second. I'll bring it right out."

Mitu leaned against the wall and lit a cigarette. His heart was pounding as intensely as it did in the past when he'd wait for Olga to open for him. She'd pull him inside without a word, and they would make love with their eyes closed. *"My God..."* He was smiling when the woman came back with a piece of paper in her hand.

"Here you go. His name is Greenberg. Maybe he knows something. His office is on the corner of Broadway and 34th, very close to here."

He thanked her and went looking for the address, reaching it in less than two minutes. On the massive oak door, there was a big sign, "Avniel Greenberg, Manhattan Real Estate Company." An older gentleman received him, saying without being asked that he had no available apartments for rent. Mitu explained quickly what he was looking for. The man shrugged.

"I think I know who you're talking about...I recall the name vaguely. But no, I regret I can't give you any more details...I don't even know what she looked like. I'm sorry..."

Disappointed, he returned to the café where Bertha was waiting for him. *"Will I ever find out what happened to my Olga?"*

"I'm sorry I'm late, dear. And I didn't even find what I was looking for," he told Bertha.

"These women, God love 'em, they're so hard to find..." she said, feigning amusement.

"Yes," he admitted. "I went to the building where I used to live with Olga..."

"Lucky, the woman who commands a love like yours!"

"Let's go out again and see some more of the city while I still have time for that. It's so beautiful around here! I wonder..."

"It's gonna be okay, don't worry!" she interrupted him. "In a couple of days you'll reach the top, and I'll be very happy for you! But that's when you'll shun me, because your new world will be full of special women, not losers like me..." she said, suddenly saddened.

Mitu watched her, surprised. Did she truly care for him or did she stay because of his money? She sometimes glanced at him just as his mother used to do and showed him a maternal love and a sincere preoccupation for everything he went through. He felt protected while with her, something he hadn't experienced with any other woman before.

"Bertha..." He attempted to appease her, but stopped and kissed her instead. He then took her arm, and they walked up on Fifth Avenue all the way to Central Park. They sat by a lake strewn with lilies and ducklings, remaining there until nightfall. They walked back to the hotel holding hands, quickening their pace to warm up.

When they finally got there, late at night, Mitu told her to go up to their room, and he called Thomas. The man confirmed what he already knew from the newspapers—Lindbergh was still preparing for the flight, and Nungesser and his copilot, François Coli, had taken off from Le Bourget and would reach New York within the next twenty-four hours.

"Just another day! Just another day!" he thought, bursting with expectancy.

Chapter 43

Mitu could barely rest all night, and he woke up at four in the morning. When he realized his whereabouts, hard as he tried, he couldn't go back to sleep. He tossed and turned for a while and then slipped out of the room. "Nungesser! I need to know the news!" he said aloud, walking the streets in an aimless hurry. "I'll wait till six and then I'll call Detroit." He walked for a while, shivering with cold and nerves, and a little later, he returned to the hotel, worked up his courage, and called Thomas. He was certain he had called in vain because it was too early in the day. He heard the phone ring a few times, and then an angry voice grunted in the receiver:

"Who is it?"

"It's me, Mitu. How are you? Do you know anything? Any news?"

A few moments of silence on the other end.

"What happened...?" Mitu barely articulated.

"That's exactly it. We haven't heard anything. We're all on pins and needles. The plane lost contact with the tower a few hours after takeoff. We're still waiting—maybe their radio stopped working. They still have plenty of time to get here. Listen, I gotta go because I need the line available in case they call me. Keep your head up, go to Battery Park, and wait for them to arrive."

Mitu replaced the receiver and fell weakly into a chair. The receptionist watched him curiously: not many clients made calls so early in the morning unless it was something very important. He meant to ask him, but Mitu's expression didn't strike him as friendly, so he just gave him a forced smile and asked conventionally, "How's your morning sir?"

Mitu stared through him. After a while, he went back to his room, curled up in the bed, and pulled the blanket over his head as if to hide. He nestled against Bertha, embraced her, and caressed her breasts.

"Mmm, honey, you want me so early?" she said between sleep and wakefulness, softening under his touch. "What time is it? It's not even morning yet...did you hear anything?"

He continued to love her, trying to empty his head of foreboding thoughts.

"I feel so good when I'm with you..."

"Did you hear anything?"

"No... Thomas said they lost contact with the plane, but they still have till noon to reach New York. Maybe their radio isn't working..."

Bertha hid her head in the pillow. The big dreams of the man next to her, whom she genuinely cared for although she didn't understand what kept him around her, were shattering that very morning. There was nothing she could do to protect or help him. She gently pulled his head against her chest holding it there like a mother, softly stroking his hair.

"Bertha, I think it's all lost..."

"Nothing's lost, honey! What are you saying? Let's wait till noon, huh?"

"I have a bad feeling about it, Bertha. Real bad..."

They left the hotel at seven in the morning and wandered the streets aimlessly. They went down Broadway towards Wall Street and reached the New York Stock Exchange.

"This is where all your money is!" she said, trying to take his mind off things.

He wasn't saying anything; he followed mechanically wherever she led him. The spring day had burst into all its splendor—people animated the streets, vendors were yelling at the top of their lungs.

"History of aviation in the making: The French aces Nungesser and Coli, expected today in New York! Buy it here!" a paper boy was crying out.

"You see? Worrying for nothing! They'll be here in a few hours! Everyone's expecting them!"

"Yes, I pray to God. I pray to God! Let's go over there."

They went to Battery Park where they sat on a bench for a while looking at the Statue of Liberty. Nungesser and Coli had planned to land their French biplane somewhere to the right, on the Hudson River. Groups of people had gathered there waiting for them, discussing hotly the latest news, "They were sighted above Boston, they should be here any minute! In France the news is they have already landed somewhere on Long Island! They were seen in Newfoundland last night!"

With each noise sounding remotely like a plane, people looked up in the sky, checking the horizon. Realizing it was just a false alarm, they would turn back to their chatter, "Their plane will be next, you'll see. The next one!"

Mitu tried to mix in with the crowd hunting for details. So many of them were saying the plane had been seen over the American continent, he felt hopeful again.

"What have you heard? Where are they now?"

He had asked a bespectacled young man who struck him as informed and self-assured.

"A lot of contradictory things, sir, but there's no way they could have been here by now because they're flying against the wind!"

"And when do you think they should get here?" he continued, squeezing Bertha's hand.

"If they don't land by tomorrow morning, that means they're gone. They only have fuel for forty hours of flight," the boy answered, checking his watch.

Mitu felt shivers down his spine—*"ten thousand dollars!"*—but tried to keep himself together:

"The truth is they have plenty of time; maybe their transmitter is defective," he commented more for himself than anyone else. "Right?"

Bertha nodded.

"Yes, that's right. Don't worry, it'll be okay. You'll see!"

Time went by very quickly. With each passing hour, the crowd became more agitated. The rumors were tangling up and metamorphosing, confusing everybody.

At three o'clock, cheers and screams of joy erupted from underneath a tree. An elderly man had just told some folks the Navy Department had given an official announcement that the plane had been sighted over Portland, Maine.

"They said it on the radio! They made it, they made it! The French beat us; good for them. *Vive la France!*"

The crowd burst into cheers; men threw their black fedoras into the air. The transatlantic flight had been a success! They were the witnesses to an unprecedented historic event!

Mitu fell to his knees with joy but then got up and began pacing around, asking left and right: "When were they sighted in Maine? When was the communiqué given? How much longer to Long Island?"

Realizing that no one knew any more than that, he went to a payphone and called Detroit.

"Tom, have you heard the Navy's communiqué? Nungesser made it! We made it!" he said hotly, almost skipping around with happiness.

"Yes, we've found out that the Navy Yard reported they've sighted them there. We're waiting for confirmations. Call me the minute you see them. This is some fantastic news! Congratulations to you and us!"

Mitu and Bertha went back to the park and waited there. A thick fog veiled Manhattan; nothing was visible.

Half an hour went by in the blink of an eye. Then another. And another. Little by little, the clamoring of the crowd died down to be replaced by a deafening silence—according to all calculations, those were the last moments for which the aviators had any fuel left.

At ten at night, people began leaving. Mitu sat down on a bench and watched Bertha's silhouette leaning against a rail as she was gazing at the Statue of Liberty's outline.

The morning found them in the same place, ruffled up like the seagulls around them, embracing each other. Mitu had refused to go back to their room, still hoping to hear the rumbling that would wake him up from his nightmare.

At last, tired and empty-hearted, he decided to leave. It was six in the morning. He tried calling Thomas, but no one answered. On the way to the hotel they bought a newspaper. He glossed over the first page, knowing beforehand what it said:

"Fate of Atlantic fliers is unknown after day of watching and rumors; White Bird must be down. Grave anxiety is felt for Nungesser and Coli, now long overdue. Weather bad on route. Paris fears the worst. Realizing failure after early news of success, it is prayed pilots may be rescued."

"Dumnezeii şi anafura mamii ei de viaţă!" he cursed in Romanian after reading, and Bertha, despite not comprehending a word, thoroughly understood what he had meant.

"It will be okay..." she tried to console him, "it will be okay..."

"Yes, it will be okay..." he mocked bitterly. "It will be okay," he continued in the same sarcastic tone. "You've been saying this for two days now! And I just lost ten thousand dollars!" he howled. "Ten thousand, woman!"

THE CRUSHING

Chapter 44

The anticipation for Nungesser's success had been so great, and the reveries throughout the past months so uplifting that the return to the mundane, insipid, banal reality crushed Mitu.

He would have probably recovered sooner if life had spared him more chagrin. But things tend to take a course that's not mindful of a human being's deepest wishes. As a feline toys with its prey before devouring it, ill luck struck him again, making him realize just how close he had been to victory and how much he had lost that day: less than two weeks after Nungesser's disappearance, Charles Lindbergh, the unknown pilot on whom he hadn't wanted to bet, did the impossible—he crossed the Atlantic Ocean in a day and a half in a single engine monoplane, in terrible weather conditions, traveling from New York to Paris by himself, without a copilot, without a layover. The American had self-financed the New York-Paris flight through a fifteen-thousand-dollar bank loan and personal savings.

It hadn't been enough that Nungesser had disappeared. To add insult to injury, life showed him what could have been had the French aviator made it. A mere unknown until then, Lindbergh had been catapulted to a fame equal to that of gods. Glorious medals covered his chest—the "Legion of Honor," the "Distinguished Flying Cross," the "Medal of Honor"—and the financial offers poured in from everywhere.

Envy was eating away at Mitu, powerless as he now witnessed the pilot's sensational ascent, overnight the absolute symbol of America. It was so unfair! he seethed. He had been close to greatness only two weeks before; almost touching it, living it, already reaping its benefits in his mind, all of which had ultimately been as passing as a summer shower. Why was it happening to him?

His attempt to reach his American Dream - the true American Dream that can take you up to the highest pinnacles - had crumbled like a sand castle.11F*

The distress over the failure followed Mitu for many months, pushing in him to the back of the store with a bottle of alcohol in his hand. He had fallen into such a despondent state that he couldn't even look after his business anymore.

Six months later, just as the mourning for a departed loved one tends to fade away in time, his bitterness was buried under the mounds of daily duties binding a human being with invisible chains. In a few more months, all he was left with was the foggy but no longer painful memory of the fiasco, and

---

* Recent speculations based on the testimony of some eyewitnesses posit that the French pilots did not crash in the ocean, but completed the transatlantic flight and crashed somewhere in the hard-to-explore, swampy forests on the East Coast, most probably Maine. If that is the case, Mitu would have been entitled to the money.

another year later, the event became a negligible point in the meandering course of his life.

Despite his near total lack of involvement, the store was doing fairly well thanks to Walter, who now had his own interests to look after. Mitu had offered him a percentage from the profits right after his return from New York, and the German was doing everything in his power to convince customers to buy whatever. Many of them would dilly-dally, scratching their heads undecidedly, but would finally pull money from their wallets. Walter had proved to be such a resourceful sales person that Mitu started spending a lot more time at home without worrying about the business.

On the other hand, the money from the stock market still brought in a profit—not a phenomenal one as he had hoped, but enough to pay off his loans. At the rate the money came in, he figured he would be debt free in about seven years. In three more years, the sum invested on Wall Street would have brought in about the same profit he used to make from bootlegging. He kept marveling at his previous stupidity to risk losing his life or freedom, when he could see now that money could be made easily and, more importantly, legally.

Bertha had moved in with him but hadn't completely given up her "activities" at Night Star. Despite his insistence—"Woman, I can take care of you! You don't need to sell your body!"—she had stubbornly refused for reasons she never fully explained to him. Maybe, she liked the sport of it and there was nothing he could do about it.

Bertha had found the ideal partner in Mitu. The previous men in her life—some, just like him from among old clients, others just picked up randomly from the street—would become jealous at some point or another. From all her closest relationships, not many but definitely stormy, she had learned enough about the masculine nature, being able to anticipate the course of a relationship right away. Men would pay to sleep with her at first; a courtship and a period of couple life would follow after. Soon enough, they would begin exerting a sense of "ownership" over her, showing their obvious dislike for what she did. Rows would ultimately ensue, then the inevitable breakup—usually fierce, with reproaches, insults and sometimes a beating.

Mitu was the first man that hadn't taken that predictable path. His desire to keep her home came from his will to protect her rather than jealousy, whose evil tendencies seemed to have been nipped in the bud by his unfortunate Olga experience, or so Bertha thought.

Yet, she often wondered why he wasn't jealous. Her only answer was that he didn't love her. She had tested him a few times, giving him spicy details from her endeavors with well-to-do clients to get a rise out of him, but his solidness was eloquent enough.

Their partnership was an unusual one, but it fit their needs: Mitu had the same attitude when sharing his bed with her whether they had just come back from a candle-lit dinner in a scrumptious restaurant or after a day during which she had serviced three clients at Night Star. And she showed him, however she could, that she appreciated his atypical tolerance, offering him surprises coveted by many, experienced by few; every once in a while, she brought home a friend from the bordello—"some fresh meat"—spending the night in three, or she left him with the new girl while she ran errands. In her world, letting him have his cake and eat it too was commonplace.

Indeed, despite the failure of the transatlantic flight—that ill-fated basket holding almost all his eggs—things were going well in Mitu's life. The tortuous ambition prodding him on during the first years that had transformed him from a poor Eastern-European peasant into a man with sufficient means to consider himself a Westernized, up-and-coming bourgeois, was starting to wither. His living was comfortable enough to never again make him feel the acute need for change.

And maybe things would have remained unchanged, a predictable routine peppered with shallow happiness, appreciated only after being lost, had life continued on the same path, without any unexpected twists.

But one's destiny depends too little on one's will.

On the ill-fated morning whose fatal blow was about to crush him, he had awoken a little late, like someone with nary a worry in life. He had made love to Bertha, who always lingered in bed afterward, then he went outside to work in the garden.

It was a cold morning in October, a Friday just like any other. Nothing in the air forewarned the catastrophe metastasizing like a monstrous spider web all over the country.

"Good morning, hardworking, *The New York Times* and *Barron's*! And you have yesterday's papers on the patio as well since you haven't picked them up! What's the point of paying for them?!" called out Johnny, the mailman, a chubby and jovial man with ruddy cheeks and a black moustache, its corners twisted upwards, who grunted while pedaling his bicycle and barely maintained his balance when tossing the papers along his route.

When Mitu glossed over the first page, the titles pierced his mind at once, leaving his heart unaffected. He felt nothing initially, no fleck of emotion or dread, as though his brain refused to connect with his soul just to protect him for a few moments longer. The second time he read it, his heart sank: *Prices of Stocks Crash in Heavy Liquidation, Total Drop of Billions; Paper Loss $4,000,000,000.*12F*

He read the subtitles a few times with asthmatic gasps: *2,600,000 Shares Sold in the Final Hour in Record Decline. Many Accounts Wiped Out.* Then he re-read the paragraphs, delaying on purpose, moving on to the pages that listed the affected companies, to enjoy the reprieve for a few more moments.

He finally mustered up whatever scraps of courage he still had and began

---

* The day of October 24, 1929, known in history as the "Black Thursday", was followed by "Black Tuesday"—October 29, 1929—when the stock market continued its vertiginous downturn. The timeframe marks the onset of the Great Depression in the U.S. Some experts posit that the crash represents, in fact, a symptom and not the cause of the depression.

perusing the news. A few seconds later, he fell weakly on the grass with his eyes closed, wanting nothing but to crawl into a tight corner. A few passersby who saw him collapse on the sidewalk jumped to his aid, thinking he might have suffered a heart attack. He came back to his senses, rubbed his eyes with his fists and looked confused at the good Samaritans surrounding him, unable to understand what was happening. The sight of the newspapers scattered on the ground brought back the ghastly paleness to this face.

"I'm okay, don't worry about me," he thanked them faintly, then entered the house careful not to wake Bertha and dialed Jack Lombardi's number.

Jack, whose inquietude cropped up in his voice, calmed him down saying that this type of hurdle was inevitable with stocks, and that the market would bounce back shortly, because the country's economy was very strong. Moreover, the bankers had delegated Richard Whitney, the vice president of the stock market, to buy an enormous number of shares at high prices on their behalf to prove to the public that they trusted Wall Street and appease the panicked emotional states of those that now kept selling uncontrollably.

"But how is it possible in one day to lose all the profit we made in two years?" Mitu groaned into the phone.

Jack explained again that this was just a temporary setback and the only losers would be those who were now selling their shares. When Mitu asked what he was going to do with his stocks, Jack replied he wasn't going to sell anything, which lifted Mitu's spirits a little and made him decide to follow his example and wait it out until things would go back to normal, unlike the "wimps" who were now giving up their holdings.

The next day, he took Bertha out for a picnic on the outskirts of Detroit from where they returned Sunday evening. The purpose of the outing had been to put some of the somber thoughts out of mind.

He woke up at the crack of dawn on Monday morning and turned on the radio, listening, terrified of the news about the stock market.

A little after the bell rang on Wall Street, the hopes built by Jack two days before shattered: by the end of the day, the market went down another thirteen percent.

"Sell, even if you come in at a loss! What are you gonna do if it keeps dropping? You'll be bankrupt and full of debt for life," Bertha advised him, trying to pierce the armor encasing him.

Mitu didn't hear her. He sat at the table with his head in his fists, staring at an invisible object in the kitchen. He stayed liked that until late in the evening when he finally rose and muttered: "I can't sell now that everything dropped below the price I paid for it. I bought everything on margin; I'm up to my ears in debt already! Whatever happens, I'll stay in until things come back to normal, because they'll have to—it's just a matter of time. That's what Jack's doing, he told me.13F*"

---

* The Disposition Effect is described in psychology and economics theory as a behavioral anomaly, which relates to the tendency of investors to sell shares whose price has increased,

She watched him with pity, and when she saw him shaking like a leaf in expectation of the next days' news, just as a child waits for an unavoidable beating, she reproved herself for not having a greater power over him to soothe him in moments such as these.

The next day wasn't any better.14F * Shareholders kept selling frantically. Small investors or gigantic financiers were watching their fortunes built in tens of years dissipating in a matter of minutes. The crash was catastrophic; at the end of the trading day, much delayed because of the turmoil, when the closing bell finally rang, the index had dropped another twelve percent.

Hundreds of miles away, in Manhattan, an immense crowd had gathered in front of the New York Stock Exchange, watching stupefied as brokers concluded one of the worst, ill-fated days in their lives. They were exiting the building where the financial destinies of the country and world were made and unmade, silent and downcast, avoiding people's eyes, wondering what the next day would bring.

Later in the evening, Mitu, who hadn't moved from the radio, went out to buy the newspapers. On the front page, John D. Rockefeller urged for calm. He devoured it with a heart full of hope: "I believe that the fundamentals of the economy are strong, that there is no need to destroy values as it happened in the stock market over the last week, and because of this reason, my son John D. Rockefeller Jr. and I have been heavy buyers of stocks for investment in the last few days, and will continue to buy at present prices."

"Maybe things aren't so bad!" he thought, unaware that Rockefeller had liquidated all his stock market holdings the month before. He turned the page hoping it would bring better news, but there was nothing more than what he had already heard on the radio: "Thirty billion dollars vanished into thin air in a week, ten times more than the federal budget." "A greater loss than the cost of war." "Du Pont dropped seventy points."

---

while keeping assets that have dropped in value. The tendency comes from the fact that people dislike incurring losses much more than they enjoy making gains, and that makes them hold on to those stocks whose value drops below the purchase price. The American psychologist Daniel Kahneman received the Nobel Memorial Prize in Economics in 2002 for his studies on human cognitive errors—irrational decisions—of which the disposition effect is an example.

* On Black Tuesday, 29 October 1929, 16.4 million stock transactions took place at the NYSE, a record unsurpassed until 1969.

Chapter 45

Like many, many, others, Mitu found himself buried in debt. Everything he had saved up until then was gone. All that he had built with hard work and passion, sweat and hope, rebellious spirit, adventure, madness and courage—sometimes crazy—had crumbled like a sand castle washed away by the ocean's waves. In two weeks, all he had left from the thousands of dollars played in the stock market was a pile of worthless stockholder certificates.

He hung on to a string of hope for a while, telling himself that it had been just a caprice of the market, that things would shortly go back to normal. But the situation was far from being temporary; a few of the companies in which he had invested were already bankrupt and the others were teetering on the brink.

Just as an animal who ripostes one last time before being thwarted by another beast, with a last spasm, he called Jack one afternoon. He had spoken to the broker earlier, looking for consolation and hanging onto his advice like a moribund, but hadn't been able to get in touch with him during the past couple of days.

An unfamiliar voice answered this time, mispronouncing his name:

"Oh yes, Dumitru Popescu. I've heard of you. You have a big account with us. I'm Dorothy Parker, financial assistant, Jack Lombardi's replacement."

"Yes, yes. May I please speak to him?"

"Oh...I guess you haven't heard yet. I'm sorry to tell you that...Mr. Lombardi couldn't get over the fact..."

Mitu shuddered. Impossible! A well-balanced person like Jack, always of such a good disposition couldn't have done something like that! Anything but this! What was going to happen to him?

He asked one more time if she was referring to the Jack Lombardi he was talking about, then, finally, convinced there was no misunderstanding, he inquired for details.

"Ma'am, if I may. Did Mr. Lombardi buy on big margins? Is that...why he did what he did?"

A short silence fell at the other end of the receiver; such information was confidential. But Jack had died, so the assistant broke protocol.

"Very big, sir. As an employee of the bank, he had access to greater loans than our clients. Hundreds of thousands of dollars. He lost all of his savings, but that was just part of the problem. The debt incurred would have been so great, he would have been forced to sell all of his possessions: his home, actually both his houses, and the land in Upstate New York. And even so, he would've still been in debt for life with his family out on the street. He probably couldn't bear the thought..."

"And... how did it happen?"

"He shot himself in the mouth," the woman delivered the information dryly, without a nuance of emotion in her voice. She had relayed it tens of times by then.

Mitu thanked her weakly and replaced the receiver. He had read about many people ending their lives—especially former investors—but had never thought an acquaintance of his would do such a thing. What was going to come next?

The first business to succumb in his neighborhood was the barbershop on the corner of the street. Billie, the previously exuberant man who, just like a regular J.P. Morgan, used to impart his advice on investing in this or that company with a low and grumbling voice—"Buy Standard Gas, I doubled my profits in three months"—had become grumpy and sulky, looking suspiciously at anyone entering his barbershop. To pay back his debts, he had raised prices on haircuts and shaves and, as a consequence, had no more patrons. People were concerned about survival, not pampering themselves with expensive salon treatments.

He saw him one day nailing the windows shut and writing "Bankrupt" on the door in red paint. He then saw him installing a cart on the sidewalk with a big "Unemployed" sign, trying to sell withered apples. A somber thought flashed through Mitu's mind. "My store's next: no one needs leather wallets when there is nothing to put in them."

The second one to go was Nikolai, the portly Russian from across the street. Fired from the glass factory where he had worked, full of debt, and unable to pay his rent, he had been evicted from his home. He took all his worldly possessions and moved together with his wife and three kids into an improvised shed on the street. They cooked beans and carrots on a stove heated with newspapers and twigs stolen from the neighbors' yards. He also had a sign in front of the shack that read: "Unemployed, looking for work, will do anything, we're starving, we're desperate," in big red letters.

Then his neighbor, William Carlyle, not his closest friend but with whom he exchanged casual greetings, came to him to borrow fifty dollars until the following month. Willie, as he was known, was his competition since he worked in a store selling the same type of merchandise he had in "Mitu and Olga's Store."

"I don't have a penny, man, or I would help you out," Mitu said. "I lost everything. I'm in debt over my ears. But what happened?"

"The owner fired me a few weeks ago. He said he wasn't selling anything and couldn't pay me anymore. And without a salary I can't pay my rent. If I don't pay it, they'll evict me!"

Mitu felt sympathy for him, but how could he give him a loan when he was almost bankrupt himself? Plus, it was apparent that this was no mere loan, but a donation, since chances of finding a new job were essentially zero. Sometime before, he wouldn't have thought twice about it, but now he simply didn't have money to give away.

His discussion with Willie made him think of something else. The man had worked in a store very close to downtown. If the business had failed in a prime commercial area, what chances did "Mitu and Olga's Store" have?

Panic settled in when he saw what was happening on his street, in his neighborhood and all the commercial areas in Detroit: People thrown into the streets, small stores declaring bankruptcy, signs with "looking for work" written everywhere.

The image of an old man rummaging through his pockets for a coin to buy some shaving blades was the last straw. That was when he got the idea to sell his store. With the money from it, he could survive for a while, paying off some of his loans as well. And perhaps, in the interim, things might get better and the value of his stockholder certificates would go up again.

At first, he dismissed the idea, hanging on any detail that offered him an out. Better dead than sell "Mitu and Olga's Store." It represented one of his dreams come true—in fact, his greatest accomplishment to date. He had nurtured it as if it were his baby, especially at the beginning, thinking that if he developed it enough, he could expand it into a chain of stores. He had hoped it would ensure him a decent retirement. He had bragged about it in the letters sent home; he even had pictures to show the folks in Cernădia.

But with each week's balance sheet, the thought to sell kept coming back. At the pace things were going, he was going to be bankrupt in a few months.

If there was one thing Mitu had learned from Jack and his disastrous stock market transactions, it was never to attach himself to material things. "When a person gives too much value to an object," Jack had told him once, "that person mistakenly holds on to it even when its value decreases." At first, when things were going well, he hadn't heeded Jack's observations, but now that all his money was gone, he realized how valid they were and kicked himself for not having followed them through. Had he sold his shares at a loss, he wouldn't have been in so much debt.

Though uneasy about it, he began getting used to the idea of putting the store up for sale. Bertha helped him with the decision, advising him to sell, and unlike before, this time he listened. She may have been clueless in the fields of aviation and the stock market, but her suggestions, which he had always ignored, had always proven to be right. She had told him not to put his money on Nungesser, and she had been right. She had told him to sell his shares, even at a loss, after the stock market's downturn, but he hadn't listened, and all he had now was a mound of worthless papers.

One evening, after hanging up the "Closed" sign on the door, he suggested to Walter to buy the store off of him and switch roles; Mitu to be the employee and Walter the employer.

The boy almost dropped the broom from his hands when he heard the proposition. He stared at him as though he were drunk.

"You want to sell me the store, now, even though it's still doing pretty well? Yeah, it used to be much better before, but still. And you want to be my employee. Have you lost your mind?"

"Walter, I want to start anew. I want to take a new path in life. And who better to take over the business than you, since you manned it practically all by yourself lately? Besides, I was maybe thinking of going back to my country if this is how things are going in America. Not that it'd be much better in Romania, but at least there I'm not among strangers."

"And, how much do you want for it? I don't have any money..."

"Walter, you think about it until Monday and let me know if you're interested, and then we'll talk about the price. It'll be a good deal for you because I'm thinking of giving to you for half. Any bank will give you a loan, you'll see. Don't worry about that."

Walter, however, didn't need to think about it. He accepted on the spot, overwhelmed by the opportunity of becoming a storeowner and oblivious to the somber future looming over the entire country. During the following days, he went from bank to bank until he borrowed the money Mitu asked for, and three weeks later, they signed the deal.

With the money from Walter, Mitu paid the rent ahead for a few months, settled some outstanding bills, and, with a crazy impulse, used the rest of the money to buy shares in two companies that hadn't gone bankrupt and whose stock price had gone low compared to the levels from the previous fall. He believed this was the right moment to buy stocks, being convinced that, since the prices had reached rock bottom, they had nowhere else to go but up.

The logic of the market, however, did not follow his. The value of his shares remained unchanged for a while, but then they started slowly devaluing until they reached such a low level, he had to add them to his mound of worthless pieces of paper.15F[*]

For the following months, he made ends meet with the salary received from Walter, still delaying his leaving the place. But the dark economic fog unfolding over the country finally dawned on their little corner of the world as well. One splendid summer day, neither too hot or too chilly, whose spotless sky prompted lazing around on a beach somewhere, "Mitu and Olga's Store" went out of business at the young age of just under five.

---

[*] From the pre-Depression high of 381.17 (September 17, 1929), the Dow index plummeted to 41.22 (a drop of almost 90%) in a short period of time. A decade later, in 1942, the index was still 75% below its 1929 level, level which was to be reached again only a quarter of a century later, in November of 1954. All of those who invested in the stock market during the 1920s and did not sell at a loss spent the rest of their life waiting to break even.

Chapter 46

Twelve million unemployed. Poverty everywhere. People starving to death. Hungry men attacking trucks making deliveries to hotels. Endless cotton fields left unpicked because of low prices. Thousands of bankrupt banks. The life or death fight for free soup. Interminable lines for a loaf of bread. Children playing the game of "let's get evicted from our home." Little girls dressing up as little boys in the hope of finding some work. The price of milk lower than the cost of its being transported to cheese factories, people forced to spill it on open fields. Armed bank robberies. Admiration for gangsters and Robin Hood types daring to steal from those well-to-do. Madness. Melancholy, confusion, hallucinations. Pain—a lot of it. Tens of thousands of people ending their lives. Venomous hate towards those still wealthy. A rise of communistic ideas in the minds of those fallen victims to the economy. Exhausting marathon dancing, desperate trials of tens, maybe hundreds, of days for a few dollars. Ex-millionaires fighting for a bed in homeless shelters. People sleeping on the sidewalks in front of banks, hoping to recover a few crumbs of their savings. Derisory prices for harvests, bankrupt agriculture. A general state of impotence insidiously making room in history for Hitler, Mussolini, and Stalin. Destroyed families, orphaned children. Soaring numbers of beggars and homeless living in cardboard shacks cobbled up on empty fields in makeshift communities.

America was imploding, succumbing to inside attacks, and Mitu had been caught up in the vortex. Like millions of men, a few months after the store went out of business, he found himself penniless.

The only thing he allowed himself—and this with a deep feeling of guilt given his impecunious situation—was going to the movies. For fifteen cents, he shed the sad world, shrouded in worn clothes, rotten or missing teeth, tuberculosis- or syphilis-stricken, and stepped into a dreamland of perfection, splendor, of gilded and silver images depicting beautiful women and undefeated heroes. A few hours of fairytales that only made the return to reality all the more painful.

In an irony of fate, he found himself supported by Bertha, whose decision to keep her "job" at Night Star had proven wise after all and insured her a much better living than that of those starving to death. Mitu found his new circumstances so amiss that he began considering leaving Detroit. How could he do nothing and live off the money made from his woman whoring herself? Pure madness! If people in Cernădia ever got wind of something like that, he could never face them again. But where to go? If in Detroit it was impossible to find a job, what chances did he have someplace else?

He was poorer than dirt. He thought about going back to alcohol bootlegging, but he didn't have money for another boat, and the market was fully controlled by gangsters. Madame Brunelle, whom he had visited a few times, told him that very few dared to work independently anymore, since all the owners of blind pigs and speakeasies had been warned to only buy from the mob. She couldn't have even bought alcohol from him anymore, as she was afraid her daughter might be kidnapped.

There was nothing he knew how to do. He was, in fact, an unskilled laborer and millions like him were now begging for a loaf of bread. His eviction was now only a matter of time. He hadn't paid his rent in months, and he crumbled up the letter from creditors without reading them, assuring his landlord, teary-eyed, that he would pay back all of his debt in a few days.

That didn't last long either. One morning, the landlord knocked on his door telling him to pay what he owed or take his stuff and leave.

Unlike before, this time he was accompanied by a police officer with an eviction notice.

Mitu had thought about the impending moment many times, promising himself he wouldn't lose his temper. That was life, after all, and if he had fought back he might have gotten himself into worse trouble. Still, when he saw the two men at the door, something snapped inside. He howled like a lunatic, ignoring Bertha who was trying to calm him down.

"My God! This is what it's come down to; I'm left without a roof above my head, after everything I've done for this country! You've forgotten us completely, you pigs! We fought to save your asses, you motherfucking thieves! I hate you! I'd fucking kill you if I could!"

The cop approached him and Mitu knocked him to the ground with a heavy blow, punching with his fists and kicking with his feet, completely losing control. Bertha jumped to pull him aside and together with the landlord held him back by the arms. The cop rose to his feet, threatened him with the gun, and handcuffed him.

After his first night in jail, Mitu felt a little better. "It's not so bad here, with food and a place to sleep for free...it wouldn't be a bad idea to stay a little longer, until things get better."

But his happiness was short lived; Bertha's womanly charms with her "audience" at the police station the next day bought him only a warning, not a felony for assault.

When he got out of jail, somewhat against his will, he realized that he hadn't been wrong; being on the "outside" was far worse than being in prison. No longer the "up-and-coming bourgeois" living in the clean and coquettish suburbs of Detroit, with ambitious desires to buy a villa downtown after making a killing on Wall Street, he found himself out on the street.

Without any other choice, Bertha went back to stay at the Night Star brothel and he found shelter in a "hooverville," as those miserable cobbled up shanties were referred to in a mocking allusion to President Hoover, along with some other hundreds of people that were just like him: Without hope, direction, or a morsel of food.

He visited Bertha regularly for a while, resting for a few hours on a real bed, but not long after, his wait in front of her closed doors became longer and longer. Bertha didn't make as much money as in the past and sold her body for barely anything. In a world where survival depended on the last scrap, carnal pleasures weren't the first thing on people's minds, and if some did give in to sinful outbursts, they could choose a young girl with whom Bertha couldn't compete anymore.

It was then that Mitu decided to leave Detroit to go across the country looking for work. There was nothing for him in the city. He lived in a cardboard box, waiting for a miracle that wouldn't come. He was cold, out in the open field. Each morning, his back was stiff and ached from sleeping on the bare dirt. Pangs of hunger shot through his stomach all day long. He would go to sleep early just to tune out his growling guts. He was at the end of his wits. Had he fallen ill and would have expired quickly.

When he told Bertha he was going to try his luck somewhere else, she tried to convince him to change his mind, begging him to tough it out a few more months until things would get better, but he was undeterred.

He was waving good-bye to her from a train going south a few days later, sporting a brave and fearless front, terror gripping him tight.

Once he climbed onto the train, Mitu became a hobo—a man travelling up and down the country for hundreds and hundreds of miles, without direction, looking for work in smaller towns and villages in forgotten corners of the country.

He got off in the first train station just to figure out what it was all about, hoping he would work there as a day laborer. He realized then that he had to learn the unwritten rules of the hobos fast; all the day jobs had already been taken by others that had arrived there before him, so after a few hours of searching in vain, he got on another train, a freight train this time, so he wouldn't have to pay for the ticket.

He stopped in other villages and hopped on other freight trains, inquiring for work left and right, asking for the help of whoever happened to be around, even the beggars in his way, eating a loaf of bread from people taking pity on him and working, very rarely, for half days.

He traveled like that for a long time. With a small duffel bag on his back, avoiding the police and train security that could have arrested him for "traveling illegally," surrounded by all kinds of people, he went from town to town, going through tens and tens of places unheard of before, always going towards the warm south.

"Maybe I should go back to Romania," he kept thinking more and more often. "At least there, as poor as the country is, I'd have a bite to eat. I'd work the land."

After a while, he started learning from others what to do. When he climbed off the train car, he no longer dashed to the first passerby to ask for work, as he had done in the past. He sniffed the air as if to sense the prey from afar, looking for secret signs left by other hobos. He knew them well. A circle with two parallel arrows told him to shun the place as he wouldn't receive a friendly welcome; a cat meant there was a kind lady in the area; a cross told him leftovers from parties were given to people like him; a square without the upper side assured him he could spend the night there; two shovels meant he could find some work.

The signs helped him decide whether to stay there or not. In some places, he stayed for a few days working hard at digging ditches or building foundations for houses, through others he simply passed without stopping because he could feel they were dangerous and unwelcoming. He generally spent his nights alongside rivers where he could wash his clothes, falling asleep under trees, only to wake up in the morning and start his never-ending search again.

After months and months of traveling, at last, he ended up in East St. Louis, Missouri.

Chapter 47

The bright rays of the sun warmed his heart as he opened the car's door. He waited for a few seconds in the shade and then got off the train with caution, trying to slip by inconspicuously. He hid behind other trains and crossed the tracks crouching down.

Once on the sidewalk, he suddenly felt invigorated; the air was balmy, the blue sky was spotless, people traipsed down the street, and children skipped around without a care in the world. He instantly forgot about the terrible disappointment and despair weighing down his heart, pushing him to the brink until that very moment.

"Where can I found a hooverville around here where hobos go?" he asked in a store similar to the now defunct "Mitu and Olga's" and which, by a miracle of God, hadn't gone bankrupt yet.

The sales clerk glanced apathetically at him. He had figured he was a hobo. They could be recognized from afar: worn out clothes, hunched shoulders, unfocused gaze akin to that of a stray dog in a constant state of begging.

For a few minutes, he analyzed Mitu's withered face and sunken cheeks from which two wide eyes stared back—signs of prolonged starvation—then gave him some bread and a glass of wine.

"There are a few of them on the outskirts of the city," he said. "Veterans began gathering during the last few days in one of them."

Mitu looked at him surprised.

"Did you say veterans? Gathering here? What for?"

"I don't know...they took over a train. The National Guard is here in case they cause any problems, some hot spirits over there. They're getting ready to march all the way to Washington for their bonus; it's all in the papers."

"The bonus? They're supposed to give that in 1945! What bonus are you talking about?"

"I don't know, Mister, how should I? Go and find out! That's it, I gave you something to eat, now get outta here!16F*"

Mitu said a "God bless you for it!" aloud, cursed him under his breath, and dashed out of the store, forgetting his annoyance right away.

"Oh, my fellow soldiers are here! I need to help them! If we all come together, maybe they'll give us that money a little sooner! They really rallied up here? How great that'd be for me too! It'll get me out of this shit for a while, maybe even a year..." he rubbed his hands full of excitement and anticipation, hurrying towards the edge of the city.

---

* The bonus in question refers to a payment of up to $1000 promised to the Great War veterans. Because of the negative economic impact, the immediate granting of the money would have had on the economy, the U.S. President at the time, Herbert Hoover, decided to offer it as certificates, which were to mature in 1945.

He recognized them from afar; men his age, some happy, some sad, a few limbless, one blind. There were a few hundred ex-soldiers, dressed in freshly laundered, albeit wrinkled, uniforms.

Once among them, he suddenly felt he was a different man. He wasn't the one who a few months back had fallen in the gutters of society. No longer defeated, humiliated, he was a hero again. A true fighter! It was a dizzying feeling, reminding him of the euphoria felt after the capitulation of Germany. He had entered a new world—fair, better, more sensible to his needs, where his status was given by the sacrifices made on the battlefield.

When he mentioned he had been part of the 32rd Division—"The Red Arrows," "The Invincibles," "Les Terribles,"—and that he had been one bullet away from certain death, people surrounded him in an instant.

"The 32nd Division! I was in the 20th Infantry; it's an honor to meet you! 'Les Terribles!' The undefeated ones. Bravo!" one of them said admiringly.

"Yes, 'Les Terribles,' the undefeated ones," he agreed merrily.

"I'm Will Moya, 10th Artillery," another intervened, smiling brightly from ear to ear.

"John Taft, I fought at Verdun, I'm pleased to meet you, were you among the ones who saved the Lost Battalion?" a lanky man asked, watching him full of emotion.

They didn't need words; a mere glance and the connection among them was forever made, deeply rooted in a common past that they all understood without further explanation—a past that made them proud but had been forgotten by everyone else.

The veterans had gathered on the fringe of the city, billeted in two houses and a shed, readying themselves to fight just as hard as they had in the war, only this time, for their rights. A few days before, they told him, they had taken over a train to force the authorities to give them free transportation to Washington. They had dismounted its brakes and oiled the tracks to make it slip on start-up.

"And what's the plan for the next days? What do you wanna do?"

"Tomorrow morning we're going to Washington, Indiana by truck. That was the deal they made with us to unblock the train. After that, we'll manage with the local authorities. We'll fight to get food and transportation in each town until we make it to the capital."

The man who had answered him was the leader of the group, Walter W. Waters, a sergeant. Mitu looked at him a bit surprised by his appearance, which did not betray the vocation of a leader: an oval and delicate face, a pointy thin nose, carefully combed hair masking the beginning of baldness, narrow shoulders and a general disposition of a fragile and docile man. He was dressed in a military shirt, unbuttoned at the top, without a tie, and with pocketfuls of little odd things: a cigarette pack, papers, pens, a metal box.

"If this is our commander-in-chief, what chance do we have?"

Early the next morning, under firm orders from Waters, who ruled them with an iron fist, they climbed into twenty-seven trucks and started on the four-hundred-mile road to Indiana. They finally arrived after fourteen hours of rumblings and went to make arrangements with the local authorities. The sergeant, along with a small group left to negotiate food and transportation with the police and National Guard while the rest of them waited on a vacant field outside the city.

Mitu was on tenterhooks. It could have taken them days to reach an agreement, and he burned with anticipation to reach the capital and see his peers.

After fretting about it for a few hours, he decided not to wait for Waters' organized transportation and left by himself as he had become accustomed: clandestine freight-train-hopping.

He traveled the seven hundred miles in two days on only bread and water, but unlike other times, he felt no fatigue, hunger, or despair. His thoughts traveled well ahead of him. He experienced revolutionary reveries, imagining his becoming the organizer of a revolt of the poor against the rich in Washington, which he would ultimately lead to victory.

The first thing he did when he arrived in Washington was ask where the veterans were. He had never been to the capital before, but that was of no importance. On some other occasion he might have wandered the streets the way he always did in a new big city, to learn it and feel its pulse, but his mind was on other things now.

He went into a pastry shop, trying to curtail his appetite awoken by the aroma of freshly baked pie.

"My kind sir, the veterans are by the bridge over the Anacostia River," said the clerk, an elderly man sporting an omniscient air, dressed in aged, impeccable clothes. "Right there, over the bridge," he pointed the way with his walking cane.

"Far from here?"

"For a young man such as yourself, it's not too far, esteemed sir. I'm glad you all came, really glad, and I ask you to give these blood-sucking bastards the lesson they deserve! We should skin them alive! We need to replace our politicians, there's no two ways about it! We need Huey Long; he's our salvation!"

Mitu was surprised by the man's burst of verve towards someone like him, in raggedy clothes, stinking to high heaven, begging with his eyes, but shrugged and seized by the smell in the room, dared to ask.

"Please, if you could, I haven't eaten in a few days...take pity on me with a piece of pie, God bless you, sir..."

The man looked at him suddenly suspicious, almost with hostility, and changed his attitude. "Another beggar!" he said through gritted teeth, disgusted, handing him a steamy piece of pie. "Here you go, enjoy..." he said superficially. "But don't come over here again to beg, you hear?"

Mitu left, wolfing down the pie, heedless to his words; in his hobo travels he had become quite used to such "courteous" treatment, and set out towards Anacostia River. He thought about what the old man had said all the way there. Huey Long was the nightmare of the rich, a politician whom Mitu admired for the vehemence with which he attacked the upper class. The newspapers talked about Louisiana as the state that wasn't feeling the depression particularly because of the measures taken by Long, who was the governor of the state. Free textbooks for students, free literacy classes for the poor, construction of bridges and railways, schools and hospitals, universities, and modern streets. By doing all of that, he had insured bread to thousands, maybe tens of thousands of people. When he used to have his store, he read his speeches in his free time and reproduced fragments learned by heart to anyone who wanted to listen, until some people, even Bertha, told him that he was a communist. He had passionately defended himself from such accusations, arguing that this was the reality, not communism, capitalism, or fascism, and shut everyone's mouth by asking them a question taken straight from one of Long's speeches: "Is it right for the youth of the country to be raised in a world where twelve people own more than a hundred and twenty people do? The problems of this country can't be solved unless we redistribute the wealth."

He saw the veterans as soon as he reached the river—not many, a few tens. They had gathered on the huge, arid field from across the river, cobbling up wood shanties.

He dashed to them shaking the hand of the first one in his way.

"Mitu Popescu, 32nd Infantry Division, unskilled worker, ex-bootlegger, ex-store owner, ex-Wall Street investor, ex-up-and-coming bourgeois. Currently hobo!"

They were people of few words, and all it took were a few seconds for his interlocutor to relate the quintessence of his life after the war.

"Arthur Mulligan from Boston, I was in the Foreign Legion in 1915, and after four wounds and three medals, I transferred to the Americans in 1918. I only worked for three months in the last two years. I'm a carpenter by trade, I'm married and have two kids. I almost starved to death on my way here."

"Can I set my summer residence next to yours?" Mitu asked.

The man nodded, smiling, and Mitu fashioned a sort of a tent out of wood planks and a holy blanket found next to a mound of garbage. He made himself a bed out of old newspapers on the ground, "It's a good thing it's not winter, otherwise I'd freeze to death on this field."

To his right, next to Arthur, there was another tent with two families of veterans: two men, two women, and three children shared a bed made of rags.

Seeing how few veterans had come, Mitu couldn't help but voice his disappointment.

"What are we doing here, Arthur? Wasting our time! There's only a few of us here. We came for nothing! A handful of people against the government..."

"Just wait a bit until more of us arrive," the man encouraged him. "I've heard some information that thousands of veterans are coming to Washington from all over the country."

Mitu watched him incredulously. He had heard assurances about everything being okay too many times to believe them anymore. What Arthur was voicing was his ardent wish, not reality. How many could come from Seattle or California? They couldn't very well leave their families behind to go marching to Washington on the other side of the continent. Mitu himself wouldn't have left Detroit if he hadn't been a hobo.

But in a short while, he saw he had been wrong. The first contingent that joined them was the one led by Waters, who brought in a few hundreds of people. Later on, another few hundred showed up from Rhode Island.

Then, groups from Illinois, Chicago, San Diego, San Antonio, Baltimore, Seattle and many other places from all over America came together. They would reach the edge of the city, then, in a solemn parade in the fanfare's rhythm and with an absolute discipline, they would march down Pennsylvania Avenue in front of the White House, then would cross the bridge over Anacostia River.

In a few weeks, in front of Mitu's marveled eyes, thousands of wood and cardboard shanties—shelters for more than twenty thousand souls—sprang to life on Anacostia Field.17F[*] A sea of people stretching as far as the eye could see came together, gesticulating, laughing, forming little groups and talking politics, making speeches, or simply sitting by fires.

Waters seemed to have considered all the details beforehand. Organizing the crowds gathered there took some outstanding leading abilities and Mitu marveled at how well he managed. The sergeant insisted that everyone respect the discipline, pointing harshly and threateningly that he was not going to tolerate any nonconformity to a peaceful demonstration, and that he would personally see to the punishment of those disobeying his orders. To make sure he had everything under control, he had put together his own military police, whose job was to detect "fake veterans" and apprehend and beat the communists trying to infiltrate and cause mayhem.

Mitu talked to hundreds of people and met, full of emotion and joy, a few of his old fellow soldiers. Some of them had changed quite a lot, and he could only remember them vaguely and only after finding out they had been in the 32nd Division. Some others were the same as before—maybe with less hair, or a tad heavier—and together they reminisced about the Battle of Meuse-Argonne.

One day, while scrutinizing another big group arriving to the camp, he thought he recognized someone. It was a veteran walking in crutches, struggling to keep his balance on the uneven field.

When the man got closer, Mitu ran to him

"Mike! Mike! It's you? Incredible! It's you, Mike Anthony!"

The man looked puzzled at him.

"I think I know you from somewhere...not sure where from. Sorry..."

---

[*] "The Bonus Army" or "The Bonus March" remains the biggest demonstration in the history of the United States.

"Mitu! Have I changed that much? The Romanian!"

"Oh..." the man's face lit up. "Of course! Meetoo! You still haven't managed to kill yourself because of that woman?"

Mitu burst into laughter and his eyes welled up. "This son of a bitch hasn't changed at all!"

"How are you doing? The last time I heard from you, you had a job with a bank in California, I believe," he asked.

"Yeah. That was long ago. The bank went bankrupt, and I've been out of a job for quite some time."

"God, I'm so happy to see you, man! If you only knew how you helped me when I came to Detroit! The job at Ford, the booze, all of that. I hope to return the favor one day."

"So? Still in America?"

"Yes, still in America. I'll tell you everything I went through all these years. Anyway, I'm thinking of going back to Romania. I have nothing left here. At least there I have some land I can work."

"Do you have a woman now? Or you're still hanging on to that blonde?" Mike mocked him just as he had on the infirmary cot in Argonne.

Mitu didn't answer right away. Since he had left Detroit, he had hardly thought of Bertha at all. He hadn't called her once. He had no clue what she was doing.

"I don't have a woman," he answered evasively. "But come, sit down. Do you want to join me in my 'villa'?"

They spoke till late that night. After losing his bank job, Mike had worked as a tailor, but after a few months, the shop went out of business, and his trials to find another job had been unsuccessful.

"Our society," he explained, "doesn't even need able-bodied, strong men like you, let alone invalids or mental cases. You don't even realize how lucky you are to have both your legs, man. You don't even realize it..."

Listening to Mike's story, Mitu felt guilty. Compared to Mike's hardship, the hunger he had suffered during the last few months had been nothing, really. Mike had suffered without food for days on end. Since he couldn't go places easily, he had to stay put in his little town, where there were no jobs to be found. Unlike "the lucky ones" as he called people that weren't missing any limbs, he couldn't very well get on a train to go hunting for work all across America.

They finally retired to their shacks at two in the morning. Mitu woke up confused as though suffering from a hangover and looked around to figure out where he was. He peeked outside, and seeing the hundreds of people nicely dressed in uniforms or white shirts, he got out and mingled with them, looking left and right to figure out what was happening. Right by the entrance, he saw Waters giving a speech and drew closer to listen.

"This money is rightfully ours, it is not a free bonus!" the sergeant was shouting. "We fully deserve it; we won it with our blood and the lives of our fallen peers! We cannot give in under any circumstance! We need to keep fighting for our rights!"

The words were music to Mitu's ears. If Waters had managed to get the bonus from the government, his life would instantly change for the better.

"Tomorrow morning, the people in our government, who are there because of us who risked our lives for them on the battlefields, will go to the Capitol to decide whether they'll give us the money now or in 1945! But I can tell you one thing: they'll have some visitors tomorrow morning! We'll go there to demand our rights! We want jobs! We want to earn our living honorably! We're starving to death; our children are dying of diseases! We'll sit on the Capitol's stairs until we'll receive retribution for our sacrifices!"

Mitu's blood began to boil. His temples were pulsating, and his eyes reddened with anger. Waters' words had pierced his heart, like an arrow shot with precision by a sharpshooter.

"It's true!" he screamed from the crowd with hate-injected eyes. "They call us the 'Forgotten Men!' Can you believe it, good people, the... 'Forgotten Men!' It's revolting! That's what it came down to after losing so many lives! We're in the gutter of society, we're beggars! It's an insult, it's a shame—the bastards—so many of us died, and now they forgot us? It's a betrayal, it's insulting! It's an insult! An insult! If tomorrow I don't get what's mine, I'm gonna leave this goddamn country!"

Chapter 48

The following day, on June 15, 1932, "The Bonus Army" took over the steps of the Capitol under Waters' command. The Senate was voting right then whether the bonus was to be given sooner or a decade and a half later.

The irritated and threatening mass of people was awaiting with bated breath the decision debated inside the building responsible for the future of the country. For some, those with hunger emaciated cheeks, the ill, the paralyzed or limbless, those with big families and not a penny to their names, a "nay" vote meant more than a slap in the face—maybe their hundredth or thousandth—it meant a death sentence.

Contingents from all over the country—New Mexico, North Carolina, Pennsylvania, Florida, Cleveland had gathered in front of the building, waving flags and signs:

"The bonus is our right retribution!"

"We deserve our money!"

"You've forgotten us, but we're here to remind you!"

Seeing the river of people, Mitu, who had been doubtful of Waters' success, felt relieved, *"No government in this world would risk angering these people; it would be bloodshed if the crowd got out of control."*

They had been surrounded by the National Guard; hundreds of young men as he had been when he had gone to war, armed to the teeth, fingers pulsating on the trigger ready to pull on command. He looked at them untroubled, knowing that, no matter what, they couldn't possibly shoot veterans. "We're like their fathers; it would be a far cry to fight against each other."

After waiting for a few hours on the steps of the Capitol, right by the door, people stopped talking or moving. Mitu squinted to see what was happening but couldn't figure it out. It seemed that Waters had started a dialogue with someone that had come out of the building.

Silence fell suddenly. People had frozen in waiting, staring at the entrance and trying to understand what was going on. Waters went inside a moment later. Mitu heard from the ones in front of him that he had been called to learn the decision.

"That's it, it's done!"

"Pray to God it's good news, maybe I can go back to Detroit," he murmured.

In less than a minute, Waters came out and waved at the crowd from the highest step. As the clamoring quieted, he cleared his voice and cast his eyes, fixing them on the ground.

Mitu had guessed it. The pause, a tad longer than it should have been, the impenetrable gaze, the labored breath before saying the first word needed no further clarification. He clenched his fists hoping he was wrong from the bottom of his heart.

"The Senate voted against the bonus, sixty-two to eighteen!" Waters bellowed.

For a few seconds, no noise, sigh, nor grunt could be heard, as though the ridiculous message had to be received in silence to be fully understood. Then people turned to one another mutually fueled by anger and revolt. Waters continued his speech, urging to calm and wisdom, but no one was listening.

All of a sudden, all eyes turned to the National Guard.

Mitu understood instantly and moved to the side. A strange feeling that he was participating in a horror movie overwhelmed him. Two armies— fathers and sons—were facing each other, tensed and ready to jump at the slightest sign.

He leaned against a pole, closed his eyes, and ignoring everything around him, started singing in a raspy voice:

Oh, Beautiful for spacious skies,
For amber waves of grain,
For purple mountains, majesties
Above the fruited plain!
America! America!

In the stunned silence, his voice sounded otherworldly. Some looked at him confused, but then, as if brusquely enlightened, joined in:

America, America...

The air filled with the sound of hundreds of voices singing *America the Beautiful*, and the fury on the brink of bursting disappeared as if taken by the hand of God. One by one, retreating throngs of veterans marched back to the Anacostia Camp, defeated and with lowered heads, vainly searching for the slightest shred of hope onto which they could still hold.

Later that afternoon, Waters gathered them by the bridge on an improvised platform, with American flags waving proudly.

"I don't advise anyone to leave! We're planning on keeping our army here in Washington! We'll stay here until 1945 if need be—peaceful, without violence, but resolute in our demands!"

People clapped and cheered, "Until 45! Until 45!"

Mitu moved through the crowd to hear him better.

"We'll go to the Capitol every day! We'll demand our right—paid in blood—every day, until we get it!" said the sergeant. "Our right! Our right! Our right!"

"Our right! Our right!"

Waters continued to speak. At one point, someone went up on the stage and whispered something in his ear. He seemed surprised and asked, "Are you sure?"

"Yes, absolutely positive. They're on Pennsylvania Avenue, chasing the veterans out!"

"What's he saying? Did I hear right? That's not possible!" Mitu became alarmed.

He slipped hurriedly through the crowd and dashed over the bridge. It was impossible! It would have been revolting for soldiers to shoot at veterans! They were the same blood and flesh. Even if ordered to pull the trigger, they couldn't possibly do it! He ran towards some vacant buildings where a few clandestine veterans had taken shelter.

He made it there drenched in sweat. He mixed in with those lining the sidewalks and watched the events, trying to find out what was going on.

"What's here, why did you gather?" he asked a man who seemed to be his age.

He pointed with his finger somewhere ahead.

He looked and saw horse riders whom he recognized right away: "The Cavalry! What the fuck are they doing here?!"

The soldiers were moving rhythmically down Pennsylvania Avenue with perfect posture on anxious, well-groomed horses. They were young, just as he had been fifteen years back, frowning slightly in the sun's bright light, with peach fuzz beards but proud to be way openers. He watched them with pity, happy they hadn't had the misfortune to participate in a war as he had.

Right behind, the infantry followed; soldiers marching one after the other with rifles resting on their shoulder. He stared at them incredulously, then a thought flashed through his head, "If this isn't a parade, it's civil war!"

Then, a monstrous rumbling resounded in his ears from afar, growing louder and louder, unearthing memories long buried in his mind.

"No, this is not possible!" he yelled when he became convinced that the noise came from a few tanks thudding down Pennsylvania Avenue.

If until then, the hope that this was an attempt at intimidation still persisted, it was right then that it suddenly vanished. He followed the soldiers until they stopped in front of the building where the veterans were billeted, preparing to attack. He hid behind a tree from where he could see everything: two generations of men—one that had fought in the Great War and fathered the second, about to be obliterated from the face of the earth in the following war—were facing each other, preparing to fight. After a few minutes, time during which he still hoped he was vainly worrying, he heard a short order he remembered all too well from Argonne.

"Attack!"

The soldiers started hurling gas grenades through the broken windows of the buildings, and the veterans burst out the doors, some with their hands up in surrender, scurrying left and right to avoid the bayonets prodding at them.

"You're our sons!" yelled Mitu at the children aiming rifles at his peers. "For the love of God! What the fuck are you doing? Have you lost your minds?"

He ran to them imploring them to stop, but no one listened. The young soldiers were on their first mission and nothing could deter them from following orders. One of then turned to Mitu and signaled him to go away.

He continued to watch from a distance: the scenes unfolding in front of his eyes were eerily similar to the ones he had seen before: blood splattered on the sidewalks, gunshots, smoke, tear gas, pain, horror, dread.

A veteran fell in front of him, shot by the bullets of a cop, who, crudely beaten by the crowd, had fired randomly afraid he might get attacked again. A few feet away, three police officers lay on the ground, their bodies torn into fleshy hunks. The veterans were throwing stones and bottles from the roofs, the only guns they had handy, trying to confront the most formidable armed force in history.

A short man, a civilian, who had watched everything, approached Mitu and asked him if he was alright. He came back to his sense quickly, turned right around, and ran to the Anacostia Camp. When he was almost there, he started shouting at the top of his voice:

"We're being attacked by the National Guard! They evicted the others from the buildings. People are dying, they're shooting! Run! We need to run!"

People were looking puzzled at him, and Waters asked surprised, "Did you see it with your own eyes?"

"Yes, sir, the cavalry, infantry, and artillery are coming!"

"What do you mean, artillery?"

"They're bringing tanks, in God's name, don't you understand? Tanks! They'll butcher us all! What do we do, Sarge?"

Waters pondered for a second, then gestured to the crowd to listen to him.

"They're coming with the army to attack us, but as long as we don't provoke them, they won't shoot. My order is to stay still and not retaliate under any circumstance, otherwise blood will be shed! Under no circumstance, I repeat, do not retaliate! Under no circumstance!"

The veterans organized themselves in rows, ready to face death with bare chests. It was a hot and humid afternoon in July; their sweat dripped in the dried up dirt, and the still air, unruffled by any breeze, seemed stunned in anticipation as well.

Mitu remained close to Waters, encouraged by the man's calm and courage, regretting that he hadn't bought himself a gun.

After a while, the army appeared on the other side of the river stopping shortly at the bridge's entrance. At about nine o'clock at night, the soldiers started preparations, which couldn't be distinguished from a distance. Finally, the officers gave the order to cross.

Mitu clenched his fists and prepared together with the others to face them, "I'll strangle the first one who crosses the bridge with my bare hands!" he thought, then turned to the others behind him.

"Brothers! Let's show them what we're made of. These kids don't even know how to spell 'war.'"

He took one step forward, said a little prayer, and watched, angry at those advancing towards him.

"I'm from the 32nd Division; the Germans didn't kill me, I won't let my own do it!" He picked up two stones from the ground to hurl at the head of the first assailant.

A few moments later, the two sides were face-to-face.

The Battle of Washington was about to begin.

Mitu squeezed the stones in his hands and waited. When the first soldier was in his eye line he raised his arm to aim, but the man lifted his rifle continuing to approach him slowly. He lowered his hand and dropped the stone. The soldier got closer and touched his chest with the tip of the bayonet, staring through him.

It was then that Mitu took a step back. The soldier stepped forward, and he took one more step back. Then another, and another.

Like him, the others followed suit. The National Guard had won the battle before it had started. The veterans were retreating faster and faster, cursing and leaving their shantytown behind.

Mitu was among the last and watched as the soldiers set their camp ablaze. The Anacostia encampment went up in flames, a field of roaring bonfire.

In less than half an hour, the "Bonus City" ceased to exist.

"You've betrayed me!" Mitu fell to his knees, with his forehead in the grass, clutching dirt in his hands and inhaling the air thick with ashes. "You've betrayed me and I loved you more than I loved myself! I loved you more than I loved my own country!"

Chapter 49

After the Battle of Washington, going back to Romania became essential. It most certainly was not the first time Mitu had considered it. Ever since his arrival in America, he had told himself that, sooner or later, by the time he had gathered enough money, he would have gone back to Cernădia to become a landowner there.

Romania could now be, if he were brave enough, his salvation.

Once present in his mind, the thought never left him. It rooted in his soul, feeding off his hardship, hunger, exhaustion, humility. Those that had gone back to Cernădia were now well off, as he remembered from his mother's letters. For instance, Ion Piluță, whom he had met in Montana, had built himself a nice home and had gotten married to a freckled, blue-eyed girl, who had already given him three children, all his spitting image, already infamous for their mischief. Ilie Porumbel, the shepherd met by chance in Helena while looking for work with Gherasim had gone back as well and now was the proud owner of a metal store in Novaci, right next to the market in the center of the village. Ion Vărzaru, with the money made in Montana, had bought land that he was leasing out. Gheorghe Cosor owned a sheepfold and a two-story house, sharing his life with a stout wife and a few naughty children.18F[*]

He, meanwhile, was jumping from train to train, without a penny to his name, without anything to look forward to. Wouldn't he have been better off in Romania? Wouldn't he have had at least a loaf of bread to eat in Cernădia, despite the poverty there? His life had been so tough during the past two years he hadn't written at all to his mother. What could he have written? That out of utter starvation he had resorted to eating tree bark? Everyone in his village thought he was all high and mighty in the Promised Land. And how could they think otherwise, since his letters sang America's praises, bragging about his Wall Street investments and his store!

In whatever corner of the country he stopped off, the same sad, dusty, suffering, desolate world surrounded him. Some people would rush to close the door in his face; too many hobos had knocked lately. Others looked at him with pity, unable to help him in any way. Some would throw him scraps of food, while others would simply turn their backs as to say, "just let us be; we're in the same boat as you are."

Since he had started seriously thinking of returning to Romania, his hatred towards those who shunned him had subsided. He saw them in a different light; no longer people who debased him, but ugly memories soon to be forgotten. Just like the war.

He came back to Detroit on a chilly day in autumn, and one breath of the city's industrial air made him realize the place was already a part of his past.

---

[*] During that time, many Romanian shepherds arrived to America (especially Montana) from Novaci, worked for a few years, made a thousand dollars, then went back home to build households.

It was while being chased away from the Anacostia Field that he had made up his mind to leave, and since then, throughout those months after the Battle of Washington, his unending roving in noisy and frozen train cars had only strengthened the idea that he no longer belonged in America.

He pondered for a while whether to see Bertha or just spend a few days in the city to tie up some loose ends and leave without seeing her. Any way he thought of it, it wasn't right. He couldn't disappear just like that—he couldn't do it. But he wasn't too keen on seeing her wailing for him either the way she had done when he had left wandering the country as a hobo.

He finally decided on seeing her and telling her that he was going back to Romania for a short while—a few months, half a year tops. He could give her some hope. God, how was she doing? They hadn't spoken in a very long time. He had meant to call her a few times, but something inside stopped him.

When he knocked on her door at Night Star and went in, Bertha almost dropped her coffee in surprise.

"You came back! You came back, my darling!" she jumped in his arms, kissing him.

Then, without a word, she undressed him and took him in the hot shower. She gave herself to him tumultuously, as if she wanted to consume all her longing for him right then and there, forever to be healed from it and never suffer again.

They lay down on the bed next to each other and Mitu told her about his traveling. By the way he spoke—reticently, pre-emptively, slipping an allusion here and there—the woman sensed there was something on his mind; she knew him so well, after all, and she went straight to the point.

"What is it, dear, what do you want to tell me?"

Mitu was left speechless for a few moments, then found his words.

"We live in some miserable times...people are starving to death, Bertha. I can't stand this life with people treating me like a rabid mongrel. I just can't stand it and that's that."

She looked at him with pity first, then a dejected air set in.

"You're leaving," she murmured dismayed.

"I've thought about it for a long time, a really long time," he continued. "My only chance is going back to my country. I have some land there that I can work on. I came to Detroit just to tell you I was leaving; otherwise, I could have gone from Washington straight to New York to take the ship."

Bertha looked at him with such a crestfallen expression that he felt sorry for her.

"I'll come back when things get better, I promise! I won't stay more than a few months, half a year max! We'll write to each other and maybe you'll come to visit me."

"What do you mean 'half a year max?' It's fall now, winter's coming, you can't work the land until the spring!" she snapped. "You really are leaving forever..."

"No, not forever, I swear to you, whatever gave you that idea?" he tried defending himself.

Bertha wasn't listening anymore. She had turned into herself, with a blank mind, akin to how people behave when receiving news of a loved one's death. She knew that his way of being, daring and stubborn, so endearing in the beginning, was immovable. The qualities she used to love in him before were now turning against her; he was leaving and she couldn't do anything to stop him. And because of it, their relationship was dying. Out of sight, out of mind, out of love...

She pulled some money from a drawer and gave it to him.

"You'll need it on your trip," she said, avoiding his eyes. She ached. Mitu's leaving was hurting her terribly. Getting dumped before brought on a feeling of relief, like getting out of jail. But now she was trying to hold back her tears.

"Try to understand me Bertha...don't do this to me, please!" he said. "I, for one, know one thing for sure—a long agony means certain death—and I feel I'm already there. If I stay here any longer, I'm gonna die. Don't you see the state I'm in? Don't you feel bad for me? I need to go; at least for a while. I'll come back when things are better."

"Whatever you wanna say, if you leave now, I'll never see you again," she said, wiping the tears with the back of her hand. "Never..."

Mitu stopped riposting. He and Bertha had made a formidable team. He knew he wasn't ever going to find another woman like her—someone who could understand a man so well, not only in his deepest intimacies, but his most arcane desires. He thought about inviting her to come along to Romania but didn't. He couldn't ask her that. He couldn't do it because he didn't love her.

He had never loved her, in fact. He had never felt that spark, that furious passion that tramples everything, indomitably overpowering one's body, not even at the beginning of their relationship. The mad obsession for a woman making a man think "to have her once and then to die" experienced with Olga, had been completely inexistent in Bertha's case.

Bertha had been a convenience to him. Very casual, without prejudices, open to any crazy sexual endeavors, "the perfect mistress," the ideal partner to have fun with. Still, sex is to love as grape juice is to wine; it's sweet, but doesn't get you drunk. However sorry he was he had to leave her, whatever misgivings he had for hurting her, the woman had been a passing episode in his life, after all.

And like anything passing, it had come to an end.

So, one downcast morning, with gray clouds bellyful of rain hanging to the ground, he was returning to Cernădia, almost a decade and a half since he had been there last.

He was thirty-six.

STARTING ANEW

Chapter 50

It seemed as though nothing had changed in his native places in the years he had been away. Only the grooves on people's faces had deepened, but they hid the same souls. The Gilort's riverbed was wider, but the same waters ran through it. More people had come from Transylvania and settled there, but their livelihood was that of their ancestors, tending to sheep up in the mountains.

Ghiță, his brother, hadn't gotten married. His sister, Gheorghița, hadn't either.

Cernădia seemed frozen in time. Some people had died, making room for others. The children had grown up, but their names were those of their parents. The stones, the riverside coppice, Boțota were unchanged. The wind blew from the same direction, the air smelled as it had before. The whirlpool of the Great War had shattered empires and thrown countries in starvation but had left that forgotten corner of the world untouched.

The first days passed quickly for Mitu. He went up to Rânca at first, to reminisce about the times he had looked after sheep in the mountains with his father and gazed far away where the Austro-Hungarian empire had previously stretched. "God, how this country has changed! Where the borders once were, now Greater Romania lies."

Then, just as he had done with Olga, he visited all his friends, chatting with them until late at night, talking about this and that until his throat would dry up.

After a few weeks, his presence in the village was no longer newsworthy; he started minding his own, budgeting carefully the little money from Bertha he had brought with him. Life in Cernădia was a lot cheaper than in America, and upon that realization, his initial somber thoughts morphed into a calculated optimism, and the worry that he was going to be the beggar and the gossip of the village dwindled away.

In a month, he began going with his brother up into the mountains to bring firewood, and then started mending things around the house. Later on, he tried in vain to find some work; he went looking for a job as a translator at the courthouse in Novaci, then mechanical shops and manufacturing plants.

The village's youth—children when he had left—didn't know him well, but, once they learned he had come from over the ocean, they kept coming around, devouring his stories about America, dollars, trains, automobiles, banks, tall buildings, rich people owning whole cities, gangsters, wide, asphalted streets, long bridges, and movie theaters with hundreds of seats.

He met with Mircea Panaitescu, the literature teacher in Novaci, one of the first people with whom he started speaking about his life in America, and each time, the man insisted that Mitu come to school and talk to the students. After a few weeks of delays and pretexts, he had no choice. One frigid morning, in the drizzling rain, he worked up his courage and went to visit the school.

When the teacher saw him in the hallway, he bowed down as if he were a prince.

"My goodness, Mister Popescu, welcome, welcome, finally! What an honor! We've been waiting for you for so long! Please, do come in, make yourself at home!"

Then, he spoke quite loudly on purpose to be heard by everyone.

"Mrs. Comănescu, Mr. Popescu from Cernădia is here to speak to the kids and tell them a few instances from his interesting life in America."

The rest of the teachers, Mrs. Comănescu, Mr. Crişan, the elementary teacher, Mr. Coman and Mr. Late were in the teacher's room, a tiny hole of a place crammed with rickety chairs and drowning in cigarette smoke. Mitu had seen them all before, but had never spoken to them at length.

"You've met Mr. Popescu from Cernădia, right? He came to pay us a visit," Panaitescu interrupted their discussion on politics.

They greeted him with a nod and resumed their conversation. Crişan was just expressing his disagreement with the antinationalistic ideas of the Romanian Communist Party.

"Mr. Coman, I can't believe you can accept them! Do you really think it's right to split our country five-ways and lose Transylvania again? Lose Bessarabia? Lose Dobrogea and Bucovina, just so the rest of the world won't consider us colonialists?"

Coman would have gainsaid him without thinking twice any other time. He would have snapped at him and made his point no matter what, as always. But because Mitu, their guest from over the ocean, was there, he fidgeted in his chair but didn't reply. He rubbed his chin and took a long smoke from his pipe to gain some time and come up with a good answer—one that wouldn't divulge his sympathy for the communists—then started questioning Mitu.

"Mister Popescu, I understand that you come from far away, from an empire, isn't that right? Everybody knows life is good in America. How did the Americans solve their problems? How does the federal system work, in fact? I guess one could call them imperialists, but I have never heard people complaining of it! We're a big country too; maybe that's what we need!"

Mitu felt flattered that some of the important people in his village were acknowledging him, but he didn't want to meddle in politics. He cleared his voice and muttered something about the laws in America being of two kinds, state-wide and federal, and that the federal laws applied everywhere, and the state-wide ones were local. And indeed, things must have worked out well over there since he had never heard anyone complaining.

"Yes, my kind sir, of course, each state has the right to self-governing up to a point and that takes the idea of independence right out of their heads!" Late butted in. "What would they need independence for when they're free to do whatever they want on their turf and have their government's protection at the same time? They're smart, of course, not like us! I congratulate you for having had the chance to live there!"

Mitu didn't answer. The chance? Should he tell them that life in America could be crueler than here, with their federalization, that unfairness could be greater there than anywhere in the world, that estrangement hurt? They wouldn't understand anyway; things always seem quite different when looking from the outside in.

Panaitescu grabbed him by the elbow:

"We need to be going now to see the kids, classes have started," he said leading him towards the classroom.

Mitu stepped unexpectedly anxious into the room, where thirty pairs of eyes stared fixedly at him.

"Good afternoon!" Panaitescu called out curtly.

The children shot up to their feet like in the military.

"Good afternoon, Mr. Panaitescu!"

"Listen, this is Mr. Popescu, who came here today to talk to us about America!"

Mitu gave a forced smile. What to start with?

"Mr. Popescu," Panaitescu went on, "came to tell us about America, a country where he lived for almost twenty years, right? Please tell them, how did you arrive there?"

Mitu cleared his voice and began telling them about his trip over the ocean, about the American cities, the tall buildings, the automobiles causing grid-locks and honking deafeningly, about the war, and the hardship of the average worker. The children were listening with pricked up ears, breathless with curiosity. After about half an hour, some of them mustered up their courage and started asking questions: "We've heard they give you food for free there, is that right?" "How big are the ships that go over the ocean, like from here to Pociovaliştea?" "How about the automobile, does it go faster than a galloping horse?"

He almost smiled at the problems fretting the kids. He didn't feel anxious anymore. A plucky boy, freckled up to his turquoise eyeballs, sported a grave air when asking his question.

"Did you kill any Germans?"

"Yes, I did, yes," he answered then gave a short account of the Battle of Meuse-Argonne.

After he listened carefully to him, the boy burst out.

"But the Bible says we shouldn't kill! That's what I learned from Father Stânga: thou shalt not kill, thou shalt not steal, thou shalt not commit adultery!"

The boy's words made Panaitescu, who was sitting comfortably at his desk, jump out of his chair and skin. The impertinent miscreant! What was the American going to think now? That he wasn't capable to educate them properly to sit quietly at their desks and only consider serious matters? Anger blinded him, and he snapped at the boy.

"You darn donkey, how dare you speak like that, slacker. I'll skin you alive!"

The child became quiet, pretending to be scared, with a surreptitious smile in the corner of his mouth, but Mitu continued unperturbed.

"What's your name?"

"I'm Lică, Voroneanu's son. Lică, short for Vasilică."

"Well, Lică, when someone hits you, don't you hit back to defend yourself? If someone came into your yard to burn your home and steal your cattle, wouldn't you cast stones to chase him away?"

"Yes..." the boy admitted.

"That's what I did, except that instead of stones and fists, I used a knife and bullets. I defended the country I lived in. That's what you'll do when you grow up, but I pray to God you'll never have to."

"Exactly, right you are, Mr. Popescu, get that through your thick skull, Lică!" Panaitescu intervened hot with patriotism. "Kids, listen here to the words of a hero! The supreme sacrifice is what's expected of you! It's because the youth of our country gave their lives to defend the land of our fathers that we have now the Greater Romania! You see, brats? The Greater Romania!" he almost choked, using a wooden pointer on an old map still showing Transylvania as a part of the Austro-Hungarian Empire. "Look where our country now lies, thanks to the sacrifices our heroes!" he overflowed with zeal while sliding the pointer over Romania's borders.

"That's right, children, listen to your teacher, defend your country if it's asked of you," Mitu agreed, just to say something.

"Yes! And for this, your country will never forget you!" Panaitescu yelled. "Isn't that right, Mr. Popescu?"

Mitu took a long pause.

"Yes, no one ever forgets such sacrifices," he finally answered in a low and unsure voice that sounded solemn in the classroom silence.

The bell had rung, and the children were fidgeting in their chairs. A whole hour of stories about a faraway country, be it America or not, was more than they could take. Panaitescu followed Mitu out into the hallway. He wanted to ask for a donation, so he lagged submissively behind him.

"On behalf of our school and our teachers, I thank you," he beat around the bush. "It was very informative for the pupils! You know, the children are very good, just as you saw, very sweet and interested in learning! Very interested indeed! It is only through them that our little country has a chance to rise and rival other countries, kind sir! What else to say, our future lies in education! But, for that, we need the politicians' active interest in it, and, more so, the generosity of special people like you, who know to appreciate what's important in this world. Now, I'll be direct with you, because direct approaches are the best: a small donation for some new textbooks would be a great help. What's a few little lei to someone like you? These poor children would benefit greatly from it; they learn on borrowed books or books passed down through generations, and they're all worn-out and missing pages."

Mitu squirmed uncomfortably not knowing what to say right away. He wanted nothing more but say "yes," yet he couldn't. He had carefully budgeted his money for a few months and had made thrifty calculations about how much and on what to spend. He couldn't stray from his plans, under any circumstance. The last time he had done it, he had ended up a hobo!

"I'll think about your request, of course, Mr. Panaitescu," he answered. "Indeed, the children need new books."

He outstretched his hand avoiding the disappointed eyes of the teacher, who had anticipated, if not a positive answer, at least a less ambiguous one.

Back in his carriage, Mitu was disheartened at his inability to help the community. He had expected such requests, but he hadn't thought they would affect him so much.

"Oh, after all this time and I can barely scrape by, this goddamn life!" he snorted angrily, whipping the horse.

Chapter 51

The first people that befriended Mitu during the first months after his return from America were Titi and Gicu Pârvulescu, the sons of Father Sebastian Pârvulescu. The priest had come from Calopăr ten years before and had married a woman from Berceşti, whom he had found through a matrimonial advertisement in the newspaper "Gorjeanul." He had then settled down in the village and became a priest during the Great War. He was a rather harsh man, raising his voice at the parishioners and admonishing them, often without a reason. At first, people commented and gossiped about him, but, after a while, his passionate Divine Liturgies won everyone over, and all qualms died out eventually.

His sons were about Mitu's age, and the eldest, Gicu, was a big music fan. A lawyer in Novaci, Gicu had gone to law school at his father's insistence, his wish having been to attend the music conservatory instead. He enjoyed music ever since childhood, and, although he was anything but gifted, he was the first one to tackle singing at *hore*. Irrevocably admiration-truck by Mitu's rendition of a *doina*, he never missed an opportunity to spend time with the Fiddler.

Titi, his brother, was a mechanic, "because he wanted to be one," to the dismay of his father, who had wanted to make an intellectual out of his younger son as well. Unlike his brother, Titi preferred *ţuică*, - booze - not music, and was content to simply listen when Mitu and Gicu dabbled in "vocal duets." But wherever there was music, there was *ţuică* as well, so wherever Mitu and Gicu went, Titi went.

Mitu reacquainted with many of his childhood chums from Cernădia: Călinuţ Bondoc, Petrişor Apetroaia, Mitică Zamfir and many others, his old play partners. All of them had remained in the village, passing through life with apathy and an apparent expectation for it to end, doing nothing else but raising their children, taking care of their cattle, and working the land.

He paid them visits at first, drinking and recounting stories, but not after long, their rendezvous became rare. Nineteen years of living in different worlds divided them. To Mitu, these nineteen years were replete with suffering, joy, and a string of events those people couldn't possibly understand.

Although his village had remained unchanged, many things seemed different because of Mitu's own transformation: he missed the teeming crowds in downtown Detroit and the almost unbearable swarm from the Lower East Side or Coney Island. He missed the stores, from where, at one point, he could buy whatever his heart desired. He missed Bertha and the easy women from the Montana bordellos. He missed Olga. Her face had almost faded from his memory, but the feeling of fulfillment she used to give him besieged him sometimes, even after all that time. He missed Meuse-Argonne—not the war itself but the lifelong, almost sacred kinship he had with the soldiers, and whom he was never going to see again. He even missed his hobo period, because, as dreadful as it had been, it had offered him the possibly to reacquaint with the veterans of the 32nd Division and travel to many places.

There, in his village, everything was dead; days went by in a boredom he couldn't take anymore. At the local drinking hole in the center of the village, the same people, drunk out of their minds, invariably offered him a drink. He always accepted without thinking twice, "Hey there, American, you tell us straight, ain't this booze much better than in America?" They never seemed capable of mumbling more than that.

Besides that tavern, the village was bare, its roads empty, traveled only by the odd carriage or villager. The overall dreariness gave the impression that the place had gone through war; a few children chasing one another behind raggedy old fences made it all the more drab.

Each Sunday, rain or shine, he had made a custom of going to the market in Novaci. By eleven o'clock the place would become very crowded, reminding him of a regular day on Orchard Street in New York. He felt so much better then, to Titi's and Gicu's bewilderment who couldn't understand his fondness of noise, agglomeration, and overall mess.

"Well, if you spent only a year in Detroit, you'd understand why I'm so eager to come here. Without a helter-skelter pace, I feel like I'm in prison!"

"Mitu, if I lived my whole life in this market, I still wouldn't get used to the swarm here, which I can't stand anyway! I want peace and quiet, I want to listen to the chirping of little birds, not people yelling and howling! Whatever makes you like this mayhem?"

Mitu always shrugged, "Never mind, you don't understand."

One of those Sundays, around noon, when the vendors were readying to close shop, stuffing their merchandise in bags or metal lockers until the next day, Mitu saw Panaitescu again. They came face-to-face right in the crossroads between the main road and the path going to the church. Since his visiting the school, Mitu had tried avoiding the teacher and the impending donation discussion, but he realized the strategy wasn't going to work forever in the small community in which they both lived.

Panaitescu was talking excitedly to a man who seemed familiar, but whose name he couldn't remember. As soon as he saw Mitu, the teacher went towards him quite enthusiastic and didn't waste any time on formalities, going straight to the point.

"Mr. Mitu, please don't forget my request, you know, some spare change for my dear pupils who could really use it."

"I will think about it, Mr. Panaitescu, I will, of course..." he said with half a mouth, cursing the man vigorously in his head. "I'm expecting some money from America, and we'll talk then."

The teacher thanked him effusively.

"My anticipated appreciation! The future of our community depends on people like you!"

Mitu frowned, sighing deeply. "Why in the world did I dillydally in this damn market?" he wondered annoyed, trying to figure out who Panaitescu's interlocutor was.

"Oh, Mr. Gică, in my haste, I forgot to introduce you. This is Mr. Mitu Popescu, whom I mentioned to you already, returned from America," Panaitescu burst out loud, making apologetic gestures with his hand. "Mr. Mitu, this is Mr. Ciorogaru."

"Oh, so this is Ciorogaru! Boy, what a honker on the guy! Goodness, he's so young!" He had heard many things from the villagers. Gheorghe Ciorogaru was the leader of the Regional Legionnaire Movement of Oltenia. He had been schooled in Bucharest by the likes of George Călinescu, a renowned literary critic, and Gheorghe Țițeica, a great mathematician, and had earned his doctorate in philosophy in Heidelberg, Germany, then had come back to his native village. Those who had seen his house, a big mansion on the main street in Novaci, said that on his diploma from Germany it was written "*Doctoris philosophiae et magistri liberalium atrium.*" Only a few knew what that meant, but they all thought it was something very important.

Ciorogaru loved talking with people that had traveled abroad, so he looked at Mitu with interest. Their paths hadn't crossed in their childhood, and later on, both of them had left the country. Panaitescu, whom he kept trying to avoid, being sick of his garrulous and red-hot patriotism, had mentioned Mitu's name, saying what a great addition he would be to the Green Shirts with his war experience. He now realized from the exchange between the two that the teacher's praises, deserved or not, hid an agenda as well: a donation for the school.

"Welcome back among your own people. It will be hard to accommodate after having lived there for so long," he extended his hand.

"It's very nice meeting you, Mr. Ciorogaru."

"Do you regret coming back?"

Mitu was taken aback by such a direct question from a man he had just met.

"I'm not sorry, but I miss America sometimes. A lot..."

"You didn't come back because you had it too good over there, and here you don't live in a palace either. Come by my place later tonight for a glass of wine and we'll talk some more. I love talking to people that lived abroad. I have some other guests coming at five. You can come once they're all there. How about six, seven?"

Mitu agreed reticently.

"Sure, of course, a pleasure. I just don't want to bother."

Ciorogaru made a bored gesture with his hand.

"No bother whatsoever! If you had been, I wouldn't have invited you, right? Mr. Panaitescu, you can also come if you want," he invited the teacher in a tone suggesting he wanted quite the opposite.

The teacher was oblivious to sophisticated clues such as body language and tone of voice. Psychology was nowhere near his *modus operandi*. The invitation was straightforward to him: it wasn't very often that Ciorogaru invited him to his home, and he couldn't miss the occasion.

"Mr. Gică, absolutely. Thank you infinitely for the invitation! I'll be there indubitably! Absolutely on time! I'll be in front of your gate at six on the dot!"

Ciorogaru turned to Mitu and addressed him in English.

"Oh well, what can you do? I'm going to wait for you later, then, is that okay? Bring photographs with you if you have any."

Mitu agreed, watching him surprised. He was the first man with whom he was exchanging a word in English since coming home.

Towards the evening he dressed up in his best suit, put on a black fedora, like those hot in fashion in Detroit, took his special occasion gold pocket watch, whose chain hung conspicuously from his belt, stuffed some pictures of New York in his chest pocket and left a lot earlier to Novaci.

"I'm a bit of a lord in my own village," he mocked himself as he tethered his horse in front of Ciorogaru's gate.

Ciorogaru guests were already there: Mrs. Comănescu the teacher, Mr. Comănescu, the owner of the local pub, who besides the name had nothing else in common with the teacher, Anghel Flitan "the bourgeois," and Armand Niculescu, the doctor of the village, who had brought his assistant, Mihail Panait, along. The last one, Panait, had received the nickname of "Hoity-Toity" because of his self-proclaimed pretentiousness. Ciorogaru didn't stomach him because he was unpolished, rude and loved to contradict everyone with an exasperating obstinacy.

Panaitescu had made it there first, well before six, bringing along the engineer Corneliu Mateiaş, the supervisor of a limestone mine, although Ciorogaru's invitation hadn't had a "plus one" feature.

Mitu knew Anghel Flitan since childhood. He was called "the bourgeois" because he owned land in Cernădia and Baia de Fier. He wasn't really a bourgeois but a hard-working peasant that had managed his lands so well that, in time, he kept expanding and ended up owning large land properties. That was the reason people had started calling him "the bourgeois" or "the kulak," some jokingly, some not. He hadn't gone to school, but he was bright, and Ciorogaru loved to find out how intelligent people whose common sense hadn't been tainted by formal education were like.

When Mitu entered, Mrs. Comănescu welcomed him, beaming with a smile.

"Oh my, what a pleasure! Please have a seat right here next to me, on this chair."

He bowed his head somewhat shy, and took the seat offered to him.

"Mitu, all of us here know each other well because we meet often, and since Novaci is small, we can't avoid one another," Ciorogaru addressed him. "Maybe you can get us out of the rut of discussing three things only: politics, politics, and politics. But, first, enjoy a drink; we have plenty of it. The alcohol I make is not as fleeting as political parties."

"Yes, politics, politics," Panaitescu agreed. "Sagacious politics will make this country grand. It will make us..."

"Gentlemen," Ciorogaru interrupted him, "as I told you before, Mitu returned recently from America. When was it that you came back, Mitu?"

"Six months ago."

"Six months ago. Isn't it incredible that someone like him, who, most certainly, had many great opportunities over there, despite the hardship one encounters when living abroad, came back to his native place? I find that really impressive."

"Just like you, coming back from Germany, Mr. Gică," Dr. Niculescu observed.

"Yes and no. He came back here to start fresh. I came back to change the way things work in Oltenia, and, with God's help, maybe in the whole country. Mitu, I don't want you to feel ill-at-ease because we're putting you in the spotlight, but it is remarkable that you came back to Romania, when the situation is so precarious in Europe. Great, great courage."

Mitu didn't understand why the situation was "precarious" in Europe, so he didn't say anything.

Engineer Mateiaş took a serious air, fixed the glasses on his nose as he always did when preparing to say something grave, and expressed his disagreement.

"Mr. Gică, it takes greater courage to go out there into the unknown than coming back to a place you know so well, right? But running to your mother's bosom, is that what you call bravery? Mitu, you tell us straight; weren't you shocked when you arrived to America?"

Mitu hesitated for a moment, and his interlocutor rushed to answer in his stead.

"You see? It's not easy to get yourself into something like that!"

"Yeah, whatever," Hoity-Toity meddled in. "What's so special about the Americans? Aren't they people like us? We have our poor and we have our rich. Rich people that own as far as the eye can see! We have our own Malaxa and others, don't we? What, you think only the Americans have dollars?"

"You're right, all the land owners in Dobrogea that lease their properties, rent agricultural machinery from Malaxa," Flitan agreed, suddenly remembering how hard it had been for him the previous year to obtain some used equipment from Malaxa's companies.

"Exactly! Nicolae Malaxa monopolized the metal and railroad industries! Of course we have our millionaires!" the assistant continued. "I know one thing: I own a big house, a big backyard, I live well. I live well, sir, very well indeed!" he moved self-importantly in his chair sharpening the tips of his moustache.

"You tell us, Mitu, in your own words; don't let others tell it like they think it is, as if they were the ones who saw and lived what you have," Ciorogaru urged him. "It's a well-known fact that America is the richest country in the world. I only traveled through Europe, Germany in particular, and I haven't seen a great difference between Bucharest and German cities. But that's perhaps because Germany is suffering the consequences of the unfair Treaty of Versailles. You've been through both America and Europe. What would you say are the major differences between the two continents?"

"Well, gentlemen, what can I tell you..." he began. "Life's good in America. Very good. If you're lucky to find a well-paying job, you can do well, very well. If you're lucky. Some people are, some aren't. There's lots of money to be had if you know how to do it. And those who do business, and I don't mean to contradict you, Mr. Panait. The rich people here are quite poor compared to them. Take Rockefeller, for example, who owns the whole petroleum industry in America. The papers said that he's worth three hundred million dollars. Three hundred million, gentlemen! I brought a newspaper with me, to show you as proof, because I couldn't believe it myself. Here, if you a have a big house, people think you're well-off. Mr. Panait, if I may, the money that buys you a house here can't buy you anything in Manhattan. Absolutely nothing, not even a room. Nothing!"

The assistant looked at him, concentrating to figure out the numbers Mitu had mentioned. He gave up quickly.

"But how much is a house over there?"

"Well, the houses in Manhattan aren't like here; there, they have apartment buildings and a kind of *townhouses* with common walls to save space. You'd need about two hundred houses from Novaci to buy only one of those; I made some calculations."

"But why did you return? What brought you back? Did you miss the poverty?" the Inn owner asked, who simply couldn't understand how someone could substitute good for bad living.

Mitu had long prepared the answer to the question—"I missed my country, gentlemen!"—but realized that no one there would have believed him. Missed what exactly? The precipices of Cernădia? The improvised shed used for cooking in the summer? He was mulling over what to say when Panaitescu came to his rescue.

"Well, let them live in their big 'ton-hozees.' I'm quite well here in my lovely little country. Just the way it is! Good thing you came back, dear sir! You're thusly bringing a great service to this country! Since you've been in the war and traveled everywhere, fought for your rights and learned many things, tell us, have you thought of putting it all to the use of our country?"

Mitu squirmed uncomfortably in his chair. What did the teacher mean? Was he hunting for money again?

"Well then, how can I help? What can I do when I'm just a simple peasant?"

"It's not what you are, it's how you judge things! Have you thought about politics? We need well-traveled people like you that can bring new and bright ideas. We live here, closed off in a shell, and maybe we can't see what you can."

"Politics? What can I do in politics? Aren't there enough people that do that already?"

"There are never enough when the cause is right! Am I not right, Mr. Gică? You tell him. You tell him what you do with Archangel Michael's Legion19F*!"

"Ha, you're so quick to turn him to the Movement..." Mateiaş tried to stifle the teacher's urging, but he stopped, afraid he might offend their host.

"Would you stop talking about politics, for God's sake! That's all you do all day!" Mrs. Comănescu said conciliatorily. "As far as I'm concerned, I see good things in any type of movement, left or right or moderate, and Mitu is free to choose however his conscience tells him, if he wants to get himself involved with this. But it's not wise to push him to the legionnaires, and I say this not because I'm a Peasantist. Have you forgotten that the Iron Guard is illegal now? The times are quite troublesome for extreme nationalists. Well-balanced politics is the way to go."

Panaitescu rose to his feet, deeply affected by the significance of their discussion.

"With all due respect. Mrs. Comănescu, allow me to disagree! Cowardice will never take us far! Extreme times require extreme measures! How would you feel if you weren't the party in power, but the opposition? Would you think the same? Would you shun your duty? You're up now— you never know for how long—but what will you do when the Bolsheviks hack this country to pieces? We don't need some dunce of a king! On the contrary, we need an iron fist to rule the country just like a captain leads a ship on troubled seas! The Captain20F† at the helm of the country! We need to nip the problem in the bud. Uproot it! The Kikes have infiltrated everywhere; they own the banks and the manufacturing plants and dictate the course of the country however they please. Mitu must be convinced to join the Movement!" he turned spirited to the host, as if to beg him to say something.

Ciorogaru never missed a chance to convince people to join the legionnaires and in some other circumstances, he would have followed Panaitescu's advice, as obnoxious as the man was, but this time there were too many present to get started on the topic. Anghel Flitan sympathized with the legionnaires, as did the majority of the villagers in Novaci and Cernădia. Doctor Niculescu always declared that, given his deeply religious convictions, he was above petty and ephemeral things such as politics, but everyone knew that secretly he also liked the Legion since it promoted Christian values above everything. Mrs. Comănescu, although a monarchist

---

* The Legionnaire Movement (also known as the Legion of the Archangel Michael, Iron Guard, or unofficially, the Green Shirts) was a religious, ultra-nationalistic, anti-Semitic and anti-communist organization. It was founded by Corneliu Zelea Codreanu (1899-1939) on June 24, 1927.
† "The Captain" was Corneliu Zelea Codreanu's nickname.

and member of the National Peasant Party in power, was to be admired for
the balanced and sage manner in which she understood the problems of the
country and her community. It was a pleasure having debates with her since
they never degenerated into fights or personal attacks.

As far as the others were concerned, things weren't so simple; the
assistant was a leftist and the rumors were that he had secretly become a
member of the Romanian Communist Party21F* but he was afraid to admit it
openly since that might have warranted a visit to the police station. And, if
that was true, that made him and Ciorogaru deadly foes. Engineer Mateiaş
had proclaimed his apolitical status, but it was obvious to everyone he also
leaned to the left. He preferred to hold off on giving his opinions even when
asked directly, but many times he manifested his agreement with socialistic
corporate ideas and gritted through teeth his disdain for the ultra-
nationalistic- zeal of the legionnaires.

"Panaitescu, this kind of problems are best discussed at length in the right
circumstances, not over a glass of alcohol," Ciorogaru tried placating the
teacher. "I'll meet with Mitu some other time, and I'll explain to him what
the legionnaires' views are. It will be his choice whether to adhere to the
Movement or not; no one will force him, alright? Come on, let's give the poor
man a break. Can't you see we've cornered him and he doesn't know what to
do anymore? Let's leave the politics for some other time. Tell us, American,
where are you going to build your house?"

Mitu was suddenly brought back to a reality he didn't want to attend to
just yet and almost slipped and said he had no means to build a house but
curtailed his impulse and gave a roundabout answer.

"I don't know where yet but first I need to solve another problem since I
wouldn't want to move in a new home all alone, right? What would be the
point of that?"

"It's like you've read my mind" Ciorogaru said. "You've been gone so
long people here have settled down already and now you have to try hard to
keep up. They have grown children, been married a long time."

"Well, you're very right there. It's about time I got myself a wife. I only
hope the sweetheart I like will also want me."

"Right, as if that was your problem, Mitu!" Mrs. Comănescu intervened,
feigning annoyance at his naiveté. "There are plenty of young beautiful
women in Novaci and Cernădia! You've seen them at the *hore*—how
vivacious they are! Many have their eyes on you already, with you coming
from America and all! You're a godsend to anyone here, trust me! You
choose a girl—whichever one—and I guarantee you she won't blink twice
when you ask for her hand in marriage."

"I don't know. I'm not twenty anymore..."

---

* During the interwar period and WWII, the Romanian Communist Party was an insignificant
political fraction, numbering approximately 1000-1500 members.

"Well, well! Age is just a number if you know to wear it well. Take care of yourself, don't overeat or overdrink, just as Aristotle recommends, and you'll have a spring in your step for a long time," Niculescu said.

"That's right, Doctor," the teacher continued. "Mitu, you need to stop waiting: with each day that goes by, new suitors show up for the girls in the village. And invite us to the wedding when the time comes, as soon as possible! And maybe you should play at your own wedding."

Mitu said no more. What could he add? The doctor was right: after all, he was still young, healthy as a horse and strong as an ox. And Mrs. Comănescu was a woman. She knew what she was talking about, did she not?

MARIA

Chapter 52

After the discussion with Ciorogaru and Mrs. Comănescu, all Mitu could think about was marriage. He began telling everyone that he would soon take a wife, like any other man. He hadn't said whom he had chosen, but they all suspected it was Maria, the daughter of Dumitru and Ioana Dumitrache from Cernădia. He always invited her to dance and always kept her around each time they met at *hore*. And it seemed that she liked him as well; the blushing cheeks, the downcast eyes, the awkward gestures when he was close—these were clear, telltale signs to those with life experience. The old women of the village kept saying that it had been her lucky day when Mitu set his eyes on her. When asked, the girl's parents would always say they didn't know anything about anything, and that no one had yet asked for their daughter's hand in marriage, but always smiled in a rather meaningful way.

Mitu took any chance to be close to Maria. Wherever she went—Sunday *hore*, corvees during the week, holiday celebrations—he went as well.

Still, it was hard for him to decide. On one hand, he would have liked to settle down with his own family like the rest of the world. On the other, he was afraid he was shooting himself in the foot. What was he going to do if he felt like seeing some other women, as had happened in Montana or Detroit? The way he liked Maria now, he could later set his eyes on someone else, couldn't he? And what was going to happen then? He couldn't go from woman to woman, could he now? He'd be the village's laughingstock! Wasn't that why he had run to America in the first place?

His perfect match in that respect had been Bertha, the great exception to the norm, so far removed from the hordes of women insanely jealous of their men's ache for the touch of another. But he hadn't loved Bertha. And now that things were getting serious, he realized he didn't love Maria either. Not the way he had loved Olga, anyway.

He might have wavered in his decision for a long time if something hadn't happened to make him realize that his young gallivanting times had long passed, and women weren't throwing themselves at him anymore. He had better hurry.

That day, he had gone to a corvee hosted by Mitică Sabin, a casual acquaintance of his.

Mitică' s house was at the foot of a hill, a dilapidated dwelling with two narrow rooms and a raggedy fence surrounding a large front yard strewn with bird shit and tufts of grass picked by ducks and chickens. There was also a shed that sheltered the cattle.

About twenty people had gathered there to clean pumpkin seeds. They were all rushing to finish quickly and start dancing.

Maria was there as well. She sat right across from Mitu, going at those seeds with great zeal. She met his glances with quick smiles and downcast eyes.

At about nine at night, after filling up a few pails with seed kernels, they all prepared to celebrate according to the tradition. No one came to corvees for the work only: the hemp spinning, the pumpkin seed cleaning, and the corn husk shucking were but the prelude to the fervent dances that invariably followed.

A young man, a tad cheekier than the rest, began yodeling.

> *A green leaf and a red rose*
> *Gilort River mighty flows*
> *Its waters are good to drink*
> *Only about you I think*
> *When you gave me that last kiss*
> *That's what I'll forever miss.*

After a warmup of a few glasses of *ţuică*, everybody made a circle for the "game of the flea." Mitu entered the game for Maria's sake. Sabin, the host, was in the middle, and farther away, another man began twisting a pitchfork in his hands.

"Spin around, flea!" Sabin called out.

"I won't do it until Mihai kisses Ileana!" yelled the man twisting the pitchfork.

Mihai, a thirty-year old man, redheaded and with a pouty belly, rushed to Ileana, and Sabin tried to curt his way, but Mihai was faster and got hold of the woman's waist trying to kiss her. She fought back, to the others' delight, since her protests meant they could slap the suitor around as much as they wanted. Sabin dashed at him and began striking his butt with a leather belt, as hard as could. The man initially laughed on the wrong side of his mouth, but then he couldn't take it anymore, and screaming in pain, ran and hid among the people who were roaring with laughter.

The game went on for a while, some receiving good whippings before reaching a girl, some luckier ones catching them fast and kissing hem passionately.

Mitu's turn to be in the middle of the circle came half an hour later.

"Spin around, flea!" he yelled.

"I won't do it until Brânzan kisses Maria!" the pitchfork twister called out.

Mitu stormed to Brânzan, but the man was too close to Maria and got to her in an instant. He grabbed her waist and kissed her intensely on the lips. Maria pretended to fight back, but then abandoned herself in his arms and reciprocated the kiss. Mitu watched them, ready to start a fight, but came quickly to his senses seeing the others dying with laughter.

"It's just a damn game," he brooded.

After the flea game, two young men began playing the tin whistle and the boys invited the girls to dance. Mitu had always wished that real musicians would play at corvees, but corvees were considered below *taraf* standards. For that reason, he kept thinking of having his own to play everywhere.

He first invited a few other girls to dance, to pay Maria back for what she had done with Brânzan, but then he eventually danced with her also. Her young and tight body, the casual brush of her bosom lit a burning desire inside him.

"Maria, you're driving me wild!" he whispered, pulling her closer, despite her feigned riposte.

Right next to them, Brânzan, who had just turned eighteen, kept throwing fleeting glances their way, ignoring his own dance partner. Since Mitu was apparently hogging Maria, dancing with her dance after dance, the boy couldn't stand it anymore. Goaded by the alcohol, barely seeing through half-lowered eyelids and with a mind devoid of any rational thought, he went towards them and, without looking at Mitu, grabbed Maria by the arm.

"Dance with me!" he raised his voice.

The girl stepped back, looking questioningly at Mitu.

Mitu's face blanched with anger and he snapped at Brânzan.

"Did you come to take my woman? Can't you see I'm dancing with her?"

"What? Since when is she your woman? I haven't heard you married her!"

"I didn't marry her, but I'm dancing with her now!"

Maria tried to get between them, which angered Mitu beyond control. He looked at her as though he wanted to tear her up, but barely contained his urge to shove her aside. "Are you defending this little shit?" he muttered almost unintelligibly and turned to Brânzan, who was teetering on his feet.

They got into a short but manly fight, trying to throw each other to the ground, cursing, and punching with alcohol softened fists. The others jumped in and split them apart quickly; Brânzan fell weakly on a chair with a stupid look on his face, not understanding how someone twice his age had the wherewithal to confront him, while Mitu got up to his feet, dusted himself off, went to Maria, and gripped her hand.

"You will be mine, girl! Just so you know!"

She could hardly hide her joy. Having two men fight for her was really something! Not many of her friends could boast anything like that. Not to mention that none other than Mitu Popescu himself was one of her suitors. In her heart of hearts, she had always dreamed of princes coming from afar to sweep her off her feet, and even Margareta the gypsy fortuneteller had told her she would marry a knave of spades coming from overseas. And Mitu, quite a gentleman among the rest of the peasants, dressed up like city folk, came from America, and not bad to look at, solidified her conviction; he was the knight in shining armor described by the gypsy.

A month after the incident, Mitu decided to ask for her hand in marriage. He liked the girl, so why wait? She came from a good family and that meant a good dowry, which was something he needed to discuss at length with her father.

He considered all the well-to-do men from Novaci and Cernădia he knew. He needed someone he could ask to help him with the wooing practices so he could negotiate a better dowry. Panaitescu the teacher was sympathetic after all, but he was a little batty and a chatterbox. At village gatherings, people laughed behind his back at his alcohol-induced pompousness. And how could he ask since he still hadn't made that donation? The same with Father Scorojan from Baia de Fier, who on Sunday mornings gave his sermons about God's mercy and atonement for sins with a groggy head from his Saturday night hangover. His friend Gicu Pârvulescu, Father Pârvulescu's son from Cernădia, was too young and he couldn't ask his father since the village was his parish. Engineer Mateiaş was an option, but he had communist ideas and anyone associated with him was immediately considered red as well, so he was out of the question. Doctor Niculescu would have been good, but he donned a sourpuss face each time they met, so he didn't dare ask him to help with something so personal. Mrs. Comănescu, so highly esteemed in both Novaci and Cernădia, couldn't go with him because she was a woman. Nobody went to see the parents of a potential bride-to-be accompanied by a woman, ladylike as she might have been.

After considering all of them, he decided on Gheorghe Ciorogaru. He was a presence in the community and people looked up to him. They weren't very close, but it wouldn't have hurt to try. Moreover, it seemed that the man liked him well enough and was interested in his life in America, and at least for that reason, couldn't refuse him.

He went to Novaci to speak to him. As soon as he got there, he told him directly what he wanted. Ciorogaru's take on the situation, however, made Mitu feel as if he were in front of a judge.

"So, you've got your sights on a girl from Cernădia. You like her and you say she likes you. What can you offer her?"

He answered vaguely that he had come back from America without too much money, but that he had some land he could lease, and that in a few years—he didn't specify it was more than a decade—he would receive a bonus from the American government for having served in the war, and that money could buy him some more land.

"And where will you and your wife live?"

Again, Mitu gave an ambiguous answer that he would build a big house in the near future, but that for the time being, he was going to live in his parents' home together with his mother and siblings.

Ciorogaru shook his head thoughtfully.

"Mitu, I will come with you if this is what you want. But I advise you to sleep on it for a while. Look around for a bit; men die of heart disease in the prime of their life. How many widowers have you seen? Not one. But there are many widows, I know of at least five right here on my street. Many women have to raise their children on their own in tough conditions. If you marry her—she's younger than you by twenty-one years—realize that she might have to live half her life, the toughest half, mind you, raising children without your help. You're not wealthy enough to leave her an inheritance. If you die when you're sixty and she dies when she's eighty, that means she will have to live for forty years alone and poor, raising children—half a century, almost! Why don't you marry someone closer to your age? This girl just turned sixteen."

Mitu muttered something about liking Maria, and that no one marries a woman past her twenties since there has to be something wrong with a female being single at that age. Moreover, he needed to marry a virgin, and the older ones were more experienced with men than he liked.

Ciorogaru advised him not to listen to gossip and archaic customs of the place, especially since he was so well travelled, but he saw Mitu was undeterred. He wanted the girl, there were no two ways about it, and so in the end, he agreed to help him.

Mitu came to pick him up a week later and they went together to see the Dumitrache Family. On the way, Ciorogaru switched to English to test him the way he did with anyone that came from abroad. To him, the uncontested sign of intelligence was solid command of a foreign language spoken. People thought he used English, French, or German with his interlocutors just to show off, but no one knew his real reasons: he wanted to determine the capabilities of the person in front of him.

"So, Mitu, think again, please, before you proceed with all this. Maria is twenty-one years your junior. You're almost marrying a child!"

Mitu answered in English as well, quite effortlessly, not even realizing he had been addressed in a language other than Romanian.

"Oh, well...it's not like I have so many options here. At least I get a beautiful woman after all the struggles I've gone through throughout these years. You know, this was the main reason I left Romania so many years ago—to make it big. I haven't succeeded the way I wanted, but at least here in Cernădia I am somebody. Marrying her will show me that my years spent in exile were not in vain."

Ciorogaru smiled.

"I understand this very well. We men all do the same—we strive for power to marry up. Some succeed, but many do not. You may be one of the lucky ones. Only time will tell."

Mitu didn't really understand what Ciorogaru meant but didn't trouble himself with it either. His thoughts weren't on the abstract realm of psychology, but tangible things. "How am I going to start the discussion on dowry with my future father-in-law?"

And, true to his premonition, the negotiations were off to a slow start. After breaking the ice and telling Dumitrache that he liked his daughter—since that was the custom, not that the man didn't know the purpose of his visit—both sides were stumped for a while, not knowing how to proceed. Ciorogaru intervened a few times attempting to move things along, but no one seemed to have the courage to approach the delicate matter of the dowry.

At last, neither Ciorogaru's acumen nor Mitu's burning desire to marry relaxed the atmosphere, but a bottle of *ţuică* came to the rescue. Halfway through, their tongues untied. Dumitrache was in fact quite flattered that someone like Mitu—handsome, well-travelled, with dollars in his pocket—was after his girl, but didn't want to show it to keep Maria's dowry as low as possible. Had he offered it all at once, they might have thought the girl had some flaws.

After endless bartering concerning the "conditions of the partnership," they finally came to an agreement under the well-balanced moderation of Ciorogaru: the wedding was to be in two months, and Maria's dowry would include land, cattle, furniture, rugs, and clothing.

To seal the deal, Ciorogaru took a pencil and wrote on a piece of paper what had been decided: *"Three fathoms of land in the lot at the foot of the hill. Six fathoms from the riverbed of Boţota to the border with Papuc's land with everything that's on it. From the land behind the home, split the harvest with the parents of the bride. One pig. Farming fields. Four shirts in good shape. Two peasant homespun skirts. Three girdles in good shape. Two blankets in good shape, new. One trunk. A sleeveless fur coat. A new waist belt. One ox. One cow with its calf."*

Mitu brought to the table the orchard, the dollars he was to receive from America later on and, most importantly, the American citizenship for their future children.

"Uncle Dumitrache, since the groom is an American citizen, his children will automatically be American citizens as well," Ciorogaru explained to the future father-in-law, which came as an immense satisfaction, for he already saw himself spending his golden years somewhere across the ocean.

"Yes, father-in-law," Mitu reinforced the point, "maybe when they grow up, our children will want to leave just like I did when I was seventeen. I will offer them everything I have, so if they do decide to go, they won't have to do it because they're poor, like I was, but because they want to."

Chapter 53

On a balmy Saturday in May, Maria and her bridesmaids went looking for flowers for the bridal bouquet. They visited all the households in the village, searching for the most beautiful buds, picking them carefully to preserve their delicate petals. The bouquet was supposed to be made of many different kinds of flowers, which required meticulous work.

When they came back home towards the evening, the *taraf*, hired earlier by the father of the bride, was expecting them. While the music played, the girls made up the big bouquet and tied it with gold and red thread. Everybody then sat down for a meal and enjoyed a short *hora*.

Meanwhile, Mitu along with the Pârvulescu brothers were going through the village with a canteen of *țuică* inviting people to his wedding.

"Good day! Good cheer and fortune to you! We hope to have found you in good health! The groom, the godparents, the parents of the groom and the parents of the bride invite you to the wedding celebration, which is to go on from tonight until Monday. We hope to see you there!"

He invited nearly the whole village to have as many guests as he could. He had calculated everything carefully, the way he used to do it when he had the store; he needed about forty couples to come to cover the cost of food. The rest would provide pure profit, so the more the better. He hoped the guests, out of admiration for his coming from America and all, would be less stingy with their gifts and maybe he could finally build his house.

At night, exhausted but happy with his efforts, he went back home. The house was bustling with preparations. The women were making stuffed cabbage and readying the roasts, and a few young girls were up to their ears in flour for desserts.

Lenuța was working on the wedding flag—two handmade towels sewn to each other hanging on top of a pole—to be placed in the front gate and wave proudly in the air. A few young boys of eighteen or nineteen had come to help with it but were there more to feast their eyes on the girls.

Late at night, they all came together for a spread that lasted well after midnight, celebrating with plenty of wine, which blighted the wisdom of their ponderings. Despite their full bellies, they danced all night until the *taraf* players, prodded by Mitu to perform to exhaustion, sounded like a bunch of yelping puppies. Their hidden desire was just to sit and have the alcohol poured directly into them.

On the other side, at the bride's parents' home, things unfolded according to tradition. The next morning, Maria took the bouquet of flowers to the waters of Boțota, accompanied by the musicians and a few young men from the neighborhood. One of them, Ionel Câlnici, a plucky boy whose liking for Maria glinted in his eyes, was keeping close, carrying a wooden pail for water. He was sorry he hadn't been more forward with her; otherwise maybe today he would have been her groom. Maria, a frail, gentle, fair-haired and hazel-eyed beauty, had been wooed and secretly desired by many. But the American had snatched her.

Once they arrived at the brook, someone threw a silver coin in the pail. Ionel filled it halfway with water then gave it to Maria, who kicked it with her foot and spilled it.

He filled it up once more, pleased with his role in the ceremony. Not too long after that, he would have to participate in the mock negotiation for the bride. She spilled the water again, then they all clasped their hands together and circled the pail three times.

Maria was flush with anticipation. She had been to many weddings and knew the traditions by heart, but now she felt awkward but oddly excited that she was at the center of them all. They set out back towards her home with the pail filled with water and the bouquet inside of it to wait for the bridegroom and the guests that were on their way.

Mitu had asked Anghel Flitan "the bourgeois" to be his spokesman and lead his cortege. For that purpose, he had borrowed a white horse, like those in the American cavalry, and had given Anghel a Texan leather hat. Mitu was riding on a less imposing horse, but nicely groomed as well. Lenuța, Ghiță, and Gheorghița came in a horse-drawn carriage right behind them, then the rest of the guests, each traveling according to their means: on horses, on foot, or in carriages.

When they reached Dumitrache's front gate, Maria came out with the pail and sprinkled the guests with the water, and Ionel Câlnici stepped forward for the mock negotiation.

"Good morning, good fortune, and may this be a propitious hour! Happy we found you in good health!" Flitan said.

"This is a propitious hour! Happy we are to welcome you! Good morning, honorable bridegroom's parents!" the boy answered.

"We thank you, our young combatants!"

"But where are you going, what are you searching for?

"What we're searching, where we're going, it ain't your deal to be knowing. Who do you think you are, to ask what we've done so far? But because you need to know, let us tell you nice and slow. There are many things to say, too many to tell today. Wide awake our youn' king was, from his sleep when he arose, his white face he washed anew, his black hair he combed for you, clean clothes carefully he donned, quickly his horse he climbed on..."

The crowd was listening mesmerized, as if it were the first time they were hearing the oration. When Flitan finished reciting, an old woman— Auntie Ana, who always bragged she never missed a wedding in twenty years—raised her voice at him.

"Where's the food and wine we need? Bring them out, didn't you heed? What are you doing, Anghel, sleeping on the job?!"

Flitan remembered that his roles hadn't ended there. He took the mug Auntie Ana handed him and flung it over the roof of the house, then grabbed the roasted drumstick of a turkey and threw that also. Ionel Câlnici dashed behind the house and brought back the mug.

"It didn't break! It didn't break!" he yelled, which meant the bride was a virgin.

The people cheered and entered the yard to sit at the tables. Ioana Dumitrache, the mother of the bride, took Maria aside to tell her that she needed to get dressed and invited Lenuța to come along.

Two musicians followed them inside, singing mournfully:

Beautiful and lovely bride
Now it's time to say goodbye
To the brothers and the father
To the sisters and the mother
To the garden full of trees
To the flowers to the bees
To the girls and to the boys
Village dancing, youthful joys.
Bloom, now flowers, go ahead
Now I have my marriage bed
When I wanted you for me
Only leaves and buds I'd see
Now you bloom and stay right here
Since I go and won't be near
And for that I shed a tear
Now I'm within the girlhood
Tomorrow the wifehood
Later on the geezerhood

Maria entered the house, followed by her mother-in-law, her godmother and her mother. She needed to don her wedding gown and prepare herself.

"Let me look at you, my beautiful Maria!" her mother said admiringly, taking a step back to see her better, measuring her from head to toe. "Your son is very lucky, Lenuța, ain't he?"

On her daughter's head she placed the veil and lemon verbena flowers, painstakingly arranging tinsel rows as though having them an inch off would have instantly transformed her daughter into someone utterly unsightly.

Meanwhile, the men, more party prone, had already started celebrating, and some of the prettiest girls in the village were pinning cockades on the guests.

When Maria was ready, everyone got up from the tables, danced a *hora* to work off the pounds of food already ingested and make room for more to follow, and started leisurely towards the church. Maria was in a horse-drawn carriage and Mitu was riding his horse ahead of the convoy.

"Congratulations! Congratulations!" people wished them along the way.

When the church ceremony ended, the whole wedding party went to the groom's house. His mother was waiting for them with a round table covered by white linens. As soon as they arrived, Lenuţa took Maria's hand and together they circled the table three times. Next, she brought a clay plate with honey in it, gave her new daughter-in-law a spoon, and invited her to taste some. She did the same with Mitu.

"My son, please take some with this spoon. May God hold you together forever, like a honeycomb holds honey. You may now call each other by the first name."

She turned to the crowd.

"Please come in, come, everybody!"

They all sat down at long tables, calculating how to eat more to make up for the money they were going to offer soon. Mitu and Maria were sitting between the godparents at the head of the table next to the Flitan Family, the priest, and the village's intellectuals: Gicu Pârvulescu, Gheorghe Ciorogaru, Mrs. Comănescu, Panaitescu, and Dr. Niculescu.

The guests were feasting away. A jovial elderly man with alcohol-flushed cheeks, who had just finished wolfing down stuffed cabbage as if it were his last meal ever, jumped to his feet all of a sudden and called out to Mitu over the table.

"Tell us, groom, you thinking of going back to America or you're staying here in your village till the end of your days?"

Mitu smiled and shrugged.

"Well, I don't know what to tell you, Uncle Ion... I'd like to go back, but I'd like to stay here also. You see, I don't have any work in Cernădia and the money I brought with me will soon be gone. Wouldn't you go looking for a better life if you were younger?"

"Don't know, boy, you've been abroad and only you know if it's good there or not. I just asked you. I didn't mean tell you what to do."

"To tell you the truth, there's good things and bad things over there." He thought to list what was bad in America, but nothing came to mind. He only remembered the good: the mountains of Montana, the money from bootlegging, his automobile, his store, the splendor of New York, Coney Island. Olga's face flashed before his eyes.

"I haven't even been to Bucharest, but I can't reckon it could possibly be better there than here..." Ol' Uncle Ion continued, and he would have kept on, but the last course was to be served and the gifts were to be called out.

Mitu rose from his table and handed some white towels to those next to him. Ciorogaru stood up as well, took a plate, poured a bit of salt on it, then signaled Anghel Flitan and Gicu Pârvulescu to join him while going to the guests.

He then threw a few bills onto the plate and went first to the relatives.

"From me, twenty dollars!" he yelled shaking the plate. "From Ghiţă, the brother of the groom, a cow! From his mother, Lenuţa, an acre of land up the hill on the right side of the brook!"

He passed by those at the head of the table, sonorously calling out their gifts, then reached the end of the tables, where the poor people were seated, and used a lower voice as though to spare them the embarrassment of proffering meeker gifts.

Mitu had pretended not to pay attention all that time, but, in fact, he was calculating, approximating the amounts gathered with each calling out, the way he used to estimate sales at "Mitu and Olga's Store."

"Not a lot," he noticed when Ciorogaru was halfway done. The guests gave whatever they had, and just because they were attending the American's wedding didn't make them dig any deeper into their pockets.

When the gift-giving ended, he went to the *taraf* and grabbed the violin from one of the gypsies. He had wanted to play something from the beginning of the party. He pulled the bow on the strings to tune it and signaled the rest of the players to join in.

"Yoohoo, honey, up and up!" some feisty young men grabbed their partners' waists, snapping their fingers to the rhythm. The girls were going to great lengths to impress the audience with their moves. Drops of sweat trickled slowly down their made-up faces, teetered on the tip of their noses for a few seconds or pooled under their chins, ultimately dripping onto their corset-peeping bosoms.

Mothers kept watch from the sides, discerning all possible suitors, all the while taking in the latest village gossip. The elderly watched the dancers from up close and reminisced about their own spirited youth, now long passed.

Two men, caught up in a self-declared dance contest were exerting themselves to stand out; Nicu Ciotor, the lawyer from Novaci was challenging Ion Stoian, nicknamed Dănel, a boot maker from Hirisești, who was otherwise very proud to have such a dignified contender.

Despite the general joyful atmosphere, Mitu felt sad. He forgot about the wedding, the bride, himself and became engrossed in the song, transposed to a different dimension created only by the sound of the violin and his voice. At the end, he came out of his trance and looked around confused. Some of the guests had stopped dancing and were watching him bewildered. They had heard that Mitu was a fiddler like no other but until then, they hadn't had the opportunity to listen to his music.

The party continued until dawn, when the overfed guests set out to Maria's house to start the celebrations anew.

Chapter 54

Nine months after the wedding, Maria went into labor on a Saturday morning. The contractions lasted until noon, giving Lenuţa plenty of time to go to fetch the midwife, a portly old woman that could barely move, but who always boasted that, for years and years, many mothers had delivered healthy babies in her capable hands.

Mitu had tried entering the room where all the women were, but they had chased him away with shrill voices.

"The man can't see this or he'll become disgusted. We'll call you when it's over; now get going! Go and mind your own, far away. Don't listen to Maria's groans, or you'll never love her again!"

At about four in the afternoon, the midwife finally called him inside. He walked in fearful as if here were stepping into a different universe. He looked at the small, congested ball of cries and noises, with the marvel of a man that always considered the pleasures of the flesh as an end to a means, not a means to immortality.

"You have a boy, American. Congratulations!"

He looked in wonder at the baby's face, wrinkly from crying, his lips pursing for Maria's breast, his small, wet head, and held him gingerly in his arms under the worried eyes of the midwife, who had positioned herself strategically just in case he dropped the infant.

"Who does he look like? I don't see me or Maria in him," he said more to himself.

Maria's mother quickly appeased his fear with the wisdom of a woman who knew that the greatest fear of a man is raising some other man's offspring. She knew that Lenuţa, Mitu's mother, wasn't sure who her son's real father was to that day, yet Dumitru had lived all his life never doubting the boy was his.

"Goodness, Mitu, he's your splitting image. Look at him! That's how you used to look like when you were a baby. I can still see your face like it was yesterday. Come to Granny, little angel, let me hold you in my arms! May he grow up healthy and strong and brave and make us all proud of him! Who knows, he might travel the world just like his daddy!"

For another forty days, when the priest came for the new mother blessing, Maria didn't leave the household. Lenuţa was around her all the time in case she did something that tradition posited might harm the baby. She didn't allow her to knead the dough for bread, or dry the baby's clothes on the clothesline after sunset so the baby wouldn't suffer from fits of cry, or let her step foot into the front yard to bring about the fury of unknown forces.

If until then, Mitu's time had passed quite pleasantly, with long days filled with visits to Gicu and Titi Pârvulescu and drinking sessions in the village, since the arrival of baby Gheorghe—that was the name they had chosen—that same time suddenly compressed like the harmonica of an accordion, slipping away at a furious pace. By simply coming into the world, the child had completely revamped Mitu's existence.

He was a father.

For a while, nothing else mattered in his life. The fiddle lay unused in its box; the cellar had gathered dust since he had last stepped foot in it, and the people whom he met on a regular basis—Flitan, Titi, Gicu, Panaitescu—felt he was estranged from them. He only kept in touch with Ciorogaru, paying him visits at home, where they sat down and spoke in English, Mitu recounting stories about America and Ciorogaru analyzing, more on his own, the local politics.

Even though he boasted to everyone about lil' Gheorghe and would talk about him to anyone who listened, the people in Cernădia couldn't care less that the American had a baby. Life went on as it had before; people would gather on Saturdays in the center of the village for some idle chat or in the evenings at the local drinking hole forgetting to leave, and on Sundays they would go to the market in Novaci where they discussed the situation of the country, endlessly debating the assassination of Prime Minister Duca, the schism in the Liberals' midst, and the constant struggle for power.

Although Mitu had told everyone that he did not care for politics, he was relentlessly wooed by various party representatives trying to gain his pledge. They considered that, having returned from America, he could be convinced to vote once the elections came around.

But no one could make him change his mind. The disappointment he had suffered with the Battle of Washington, when he had felt so betrayed by the same people he had sacrificed for on the battlefields of Europe was still a raw memory.

"We're like ants—we can't do anything. Besides, the games are played at the top," he kept saying.

On top of everything, he had other worries now and didn't have time for such trifles. Gheorghe was a tiny imp now, but he was going to grow up overnight and become another mouth to feed. Maybe the Lord would give him more children in the future and he needed to be able to take care of them. The money brought from America—thank God for Bertha!—were depleting and he still couldn't find any type of work.

During their last meeting, Ciorogaru had told him in confidence that he was going to organize a gathering for the legionnaires to which Corneliu Zelea Codreanu himself was going to participate and that he needed his help.

"The Captain's coming to Novaci to speak to the people, Mitu. I kept this a secret because I wasn't sure of it until now, but everything is settled and we can make it public. I'm going to need you there for something of the utmost importance."

"Anything, Mr. Ciorogaru, anything at all. Anything you ask, if I can, I'll do it," said Mitu, who despite Ciorogaru's insistence, still couldn't lose the formality even though the man was his junior.

"It's not something you can't do, Mitu. This is what I need from you: after the Captain finishes his speech, we'll sing the *Hymn of the Fallen Legionnaires*. I would like you to sing it in front of the crowd. Everybody here knows what a beautiful voice you have, and even if I wanted, I couldn't make a better choice than you."

Mitu's chest swelled with pride, but he tried to appear modest, voicing some concerns.

"Me... sing a hymn in front of the crowd? Why don't you ask Costică Gâlcă, the musician of the region?"

"Your voice is stronger and better than his."

"But I don't know the song. And where is the gathering going to be?"

"In the church's yard, where all the legionnaires' meetings take place. We'll start with the Divine Liturgy performed by a synaxis of priests, then the Captain will speak. Don't worry, you won't be perched on the stage all alone; there will be some others singing with you. It's important that you learn the lyrics."

Mitu shrugged, and Ciorogaru pulled out a piece of paper.

"You said you don't know it. These are the words. Read them and judge for yourself!"

Mitu skimmed them quickly, and Ciorogaru started humming the song with his raspy voice, giving a clear rendition of the melody.

"It's beautiful! I didn't know it—never heard it before."

"It's an older song—written by Simion Lefter. I'm surprised you don't know it. The first stanza is for a solo voice, and the rest of the song is for four voices."

Mitu didn't linger over his decision anymore; he considered it from all angles and thought he had nothing to lose. People knew he was apolitical. Many had tried to change his convictions, but no one had succeeded. He was friendly with the Liberals and the Peasantists alike; he could be a friend of the Green Shirts as well. Singing a song at their meeting did not make him a legionnaire. More so, performing in front of half of Novaci, surrounded by the most important people in the community and meeting the Captain himself was nothing to thumb his nose at.

THE IRON GUARD

Chapter 55

The day the Captain was supposed to arrive to Novaci, the church's yard was too small for the turnout. People had come from everywhere: Pociovaliștea, Bumbești-Pițic, Cernădia, Baia de Fier, Hirișești, even Târgu-Jiu. Those that had arrived earlier gathered at the entrance of the church to be closer to the legionnaires' leader and hear his speech.

Mitu and Maria were among the first to arrive. Mitu awoke early in the morning to rehearse the song, then put on his best clothes, climbed in the carriage with his wife, and made it to Novaci by eight in the morning. Until lunch, they chatted with the people there.

Ciorogaru came at about eleven and waved at Mitu to come closer.

"Glad you're here, Mitu. Use your strongest voice and keep your chest open for the Captain!"

He gave him a nonplussed look. Everybody talked about Corneliu Codreanu, the Head of the Legionnaires, but he had never seen Ciorogaru inundated by such piousness, as if Christ himself were about to descend on earth. "What could be so extraordinary? Isn't he a human being just like the rest of us?"

As though reading Mitu's mind, Ciorogaru, though busy with many other things, couldn't help himself and resorted to one of his short proselytizing tactics.

"When you see him, you'll realize what a special man the Captain is. How special his message is! You'll see! And then we'll talk!"

"Mr. Ciorogaru, I'll sing, but I'm not getting into politics. No way, no how. I'm afraid of it because I fought in the war and I know what it can do. Only the good Lord saved me from death in those trenches."

"You're very right, Mitu. But that war happened because countries had forgotten about God! We are not a political party, but the archangels of the Lord! If God-fearing, honest people didn't get involved in politics, our country would be led by a bunch of financial interests. We need to fight for justice and for the good of the country, and we need to stop being led by others!"

The vacant and defeated stare of the blond German soldier whose throat he had slit in the ditches of Meuse-Argonne flashed before Mitu's eyes.

"Well, Mr. Ciorogaru, I don't know. And what was accomplished after all, with the death of so many people? France's still there, Germany's still there, England's still there, America's still there...With or without the war."

Ciorogaru attempted to answer, but someone called him, so he signaled Mitu to get ready: "Duty calls!", then he climbed on the small improvised stage, approached the microphone, and thundered:

"Attention, silence!"

The crowd became speechless, and in the silence that fell they could hear the trotting hooves of a horse. A handsome rider was climbing the road from Gilort's valley, followed by a group of men humming a hymn. As he reached the church's gate, the man dismounted and Ciorogaru rushed to welcome him.

"That's the Captain! That's the Captain!" a woman next to Mitu kept saying, genuflecting piously and crossing herself. "Archangel Michael's messenger! Descended from the heavens!"

Mitu analyzed him curiously. From the pictures in the newspapers, he had imagined the Captain would be older and of a larger build. He was a tall and slender man, impeccably dressed in a black suit that he wore with the elegance and ease of someone accustomed to a sophisticated lifestyle. His face had strong features, as if sculpted from stone.

He stood in front of the microphone, without a word, slowly moving his eyes over the crowd from left to right, smiling and waving to the audience.

The church bells began tolling, people crossed themselves, and the Divine Liturgy began. At the end, Codreanu raised his right arm saluting the crowd.

"Long live the Legionnaires! Long live the Legion! Long live the Guard!"

There was a second of utter silence, and then the people broke out in cheers, in a collective throb of idolatry for a man whose power appeared otherworldly.

"Long live the Captain! Long live the Captain! Long live the Captain! Death to our enemies! Death to our enemies! Long live the Guard!"

A few minutes later, the cheers stopped and he made an imperceptible sign to the group that had come with him. They filed up in a single line and started singing.

Betrothed to only dying a legionnaire death
The Holy Cross and Country will have our last breath
Our Captain has our promise, a cause that is sublime
While we defeat dark forests, perilous cliffs we climb

No pain, no hostile blizzards can make us run away
No cold nor musty prisons to which we could fall prey
If we all lose our lives, shot squarely in the head
There is no better fate we'd want to choose instead.

The crowd listened and gradually joined in humming the chorus line, until the whole Novaci roared with the blend of raspy, strong voices.

The Guard and the Captain
Like iron hawks we fly
The Country and the Captain
Th' Archangel in the sky.

"Long live the Movement! Long live the Legionnaires! Long live the Iron Guard!" Codreanu thundered when the audience stopped singing.

"Long live the Guard! Long live the Guard! Long live the Captain! Death to our enemies!" the crowd unleashed its passion.

He signaled them to quiet down, then began his speech, watching them with determination.

"I came here, friends, on Baba Novac's land, to tell you one thing: we our Jesus' Legionnaires! A country losing its Christianity is a barren country! A dead country!"

"Long live the Legionnaires! Long live the Legionnaires!" the men cheered, throwing their hats in the air.

"My brothers, my good fellows" he continued, "the world is now lead by two extremes: the right and the left! Two extremes from which only one shall overcome! We are among the ones who say that the sunrise is in Rome and not Moscow! Rome! The chaos afflicting our country can only be corrected with decisive movements! Since the end of the war, Romania has lost fifty million lei in fraudulent ill deeds! What can our government do about this disaster? Nothing! Because the supposed 'democracy' is subservient to the Jewish finances! I have lists and proof that our rulers steal from the country's resources: Argetoianu's portfolios from the Blank Bank—nineteen million! Nineteen million, friends! Titulescu, just as much! Pangal, almost four million! And I have many other examples! Democracy cannot punish transgressions as long as the people in charge are fed by those whom they should punish! And how can you punish that hand that feeds you, even if it steals from your own people?"

A wave of approval traveled through the crowd.

"But it's time for a change. We've had enough! We've suffered for far too long! We, the legionnaires, want a few simple things: to seize the ill-gotten fortunes of those that robbed our country—robbed us—and sentence them to death! We want justice without tolerance! We want our politicians to stop being part of the administration boards of big companies or banks! We want to send away the hordes of exploiters, the Jews that control our finances! We live in miserable conditions, in a sad poverty! The very sap of our country is being sucked dry by foreign mouths! Look at yourselves, good people, look at your callused palms! Look at your wrinkled and cold-chapped faces. Where is the fruit of your labor? Why do we live in poverty? Why are we hungry when our country's land abounds with harvests? We are a crucified generation! Our destitute youth, working to exhaustion and leaving their bones on battlefields for their country! Friends, our country forgot about God in its dastardly political fights. We lost our self-governance. We lost our beliefs. We are rag dolls, marionettes in the hands of others. Millions of souls led by foreigners. Down with our traitors!"

"Down with our traitors! Down with our traitors! Down with our traitors!" the people roared.

"I'll give you an example from my native places, where the descendants of Ştefan the Great and Holy, the Prince of Moldova, still reside today: in 1848, the first five Kikes came to my village and were kindly taken in by our parents and offered shelter and food. Now, out of the sixty-two mountains of Moldova, the Romanians have only two—the rest are owned by the Jews. Is it right for people that are not of our flesh and blood to own our country? To make us live in utter poverty? Before coming here, at this holy church in Novaci, I went around and my heart became heavy with sadness at what I saw! Do you know what it was?"

The people shook their heads.

"I saw hell on earth! We think that hell is somewhere far away, but, friends, it is right under our noses. In the suffering we endure, in the misery we experience! Growling stomachs, hungry children that can't buy a piece of candy from stores where Romanian people work like slaves. This is hell and we must overcome it!"

"That's right! That's right," a few men yelled in the front, their frantic applause spreading quickly through the crowd.

"We have no ill will towards anyone! We just want justice in our holy country! We want to follow our ancient beliefs! We want to be our own masters, to rule the land we've lived on throughout history! Is that too much to ask? Is it too much to ask for the wellbeing of everybody? To ask for punishment of fraud? Friends, it is the time for justice! The Legionnaire triumph is not far! Our enemies will be destroyed, even if we have to shed our blood for it! Get up and fight! Look your tyrants in the eyes. Don't let yourselves be bought and lured by them. Those that think they can buy us, kneel us, are dead wrong! Endure pain, endure hits, because out of your bullet-torn chests the final victory will emerge! Our resolve is to triumph or die! And those that sacrifice for our holy cause will be forever heroes. The heroes of our nation, written in the pages of history. Many have fallen and many will still fall, may God watch over them. In their memory, for those legionnaires fallen for their country, those that have sacrificed themselves, I ask you for a moment of silence."

The crowd stopped breathing, and the men took their hats off bowing their heads. Ciorogaru signaled Mitu that it was time. He stepped timorously on the stage, and when he came close to the Captain, he felt himself growing smaller. Codreanu's presence was overwhelming indeed, and his eyes were hypnotizing. He watched him, mesmerized, forgetting where he was for a second, but Ciorogaru pulled him in front of the microphone.

"It's your turn!" he whispered.

He recovered from his trancelike state and started singing with a voice pulsating with sorrow just as he used to sing mournful *doine* to his childhood when traveling with Dumitru to Rânca.

Among the highest branches
The moon weeps tears of silver

> *My nights are bare and lonely*
> *You're lost to me forever.*

His voice reverberated like never before in the silence, making the audience raise marveled and curious eyes to him as though they were listening to an angel. Behind him, three of Codreanu's companions joined in on the second stanza, one singing third voice, the second the bass, and the third singing baritone. Their voices intertwined so perfectly, it seemed they had sung together forever.

> *With breathy sighs the wind*
> *Whispers your lovely name*
> *Over the sweetest flowers*
> *Swaying above your grave.*

"Maria, I didn't know your Mitu was with the Legionnaires," an elderly woman, Aunt Sofronia, commented at the end.

"Get outta here, my husband's not with anyone! Mr. Ciorogaru asked him to sing because he has a nice voice. But he's not with any party, nothing like that..." Maria answered feigning annoyance but swelling with pride inside.

Codreanu approached Mitu and stretched out his hand. Mitu barely dared extending his, as though he were afraid to touch the holy relics of a saint. Had he been ordered to kneel and forever pledge his allegiance to the Movement right then and there, he would have done it in an instant, no ifs, ands, or buts about it.

But the Captain had other things to do. He went to the microphone to say good-bye.

"I thank you, friends! Fight for justice and for safe-keeping the Christian values of our dear country!" he thundered, raising his right hand to wave farewell.

The crowed unleashed in cheers again, and people's eyes followed him climb down the long stairs leading outside the church's yard.

After a while, one-by-one, the people left and a few stopped to praise Mitu's singing.

"Good job, American!"

"Codreanu was really impressed with your singing!"

"Bravo!"

"That was really something!"

Chapter 56

Mitu's first impulse after meeting Zelea Codreanu was to visit Ciorogaru and tell him he wanted to join the Legionnaires Movement. Through his words and demeanor, the Captain had impressed him now just as much Huey Long had a while before in America. Just as he had done then, when he had learned all of the man's speeches, for a few days he kept rehearsing Codreanu's discourse in his head and discussed it with others any chance he had.

"The Captain's right: we need someone to govern us with an iron fist, to look out for our needs and spread the wealth around!" he would marvel at his own zeal—a self-declared apolitical, who was now so passionate about politics.

But since Ciorogaru was nowhere to be found—people said he had gone to Bucharest on some important business—his enthusiasm cooled off a little. The political parties were viciously fighting for power. Each one had its platform with good and bad things, Mitu considered, so he thought it was better to wait it out and not rush into making such an important decision. After all, he had plenty of time.

When he saw Ciorogaru again after a few months, his initial decision not to meddle into politics had become quite resolute.

"Any way you look at it, Mr. Ciorogaru, I can't get myself into something that can lead to assassination," he told him once. "Not after staring death in the eyes so many times. And I'm afraid for you as well... In America, Huey Long—popular like the Captain—was assassinated when he became an inconvenience. I don't know all that much about it, but I don't see well this eye for an eye, tooth for a tooth. Where's that going to take us? He who lives by the sword will perish by the sword."

"Mitu, the history of all great powers is written in blood. If you were the leader of a party hunted down by those at the reigns, what would you do? If they locked you up and killed your people, wouldn't you seek revenge? Duca received his well-deserved punishment for it. Hard times require tough measures. Exceptional times require exceptional measures! Those opposed to our country's progress deserve the worst kind of punishment. Those who keep us poor deserve to die. We need to fight for it! If I don't want fight, you don't want fight, others don't want to fight, who will save us? We only want the best for everybody!"

Ciorogaru had a gift of convincing people, and each time Mitu spoke to him he found himself shrouded in doubt for a while. "Maybe I should fight as well," he would say. Yet, he never worked up enough courage to decide and always ended up saying he needed more time to think about it, just as he had done with Panaitescu who kept asking, but whose donation Mitu still hadn't made.

"*Very well*, Mitu!" Ciorogaru always answered. "It's your decision and I respect that. But just remember that we are the only ones who can pull you out from poverty. You've come back, when? Two years ago? And your life isn't any better. You break your back all day at the quarry, isn't that right?"

Yes, Ciorogaru was right! A few months before he had found a job at the limestone quarry in Frăsinei, where his brother Ghiță also worked. After having asked Mateiaş, the engineer, who was the supervisor there, countless times to hire him, the man finally did. His pay was miserable; the money was nowhere near sufficient to move out of his parents' home. But he had taken the job because he at least made a little more than with the carpentry he had dabbled into lately.

Yes, his life was difficult. He detested the work he did, and Ciorogaru would only add fuel to his hatred each time they spoke about it. He needed to wake up well before daybreak to make it to the quarry on time. If he were not there before seven on the dot, Mateiaş would cut half his pay. "If you don't like it, go and find yourself some other job! Otherwise, you'll have to dance to my tune!" he would raise his voice, swollen with the power he thought he had over others.

Mitu remembered that not long before he used to address him respectfully. But back then, he had just come back from America, and he was somebody in people's eyes.

Now, he was a nobody again. Ciorogaru had warned him that America's spell would vanish soon, and he had been very right. People called him "the American" less and less. And how could they not? He hadn't reigned over the world and hadn't come back hauling back trunks full of money. Quite the opposite; those days, under Mateiaş's harsh eyes, he dug for limestone he then had to transport in wheelbarrows to be burned in lime kilns, gnashing his teeth, groaning under the hits of the mattock, spitting out sand all day, and remembering spitefully the kingly life he had led for a while in Detroit. It was then he really missed America.

"Oh, Lord, who I used to be and what I am today. This goddamned life! I have to go back, there's nothing for me here!"

If only his work had been a little easier, he thought annoyed, like that of his brother, who sat all day fueling the fire in the big furnace, whistling away. But no, he had to wrench the rock from the mountain's guts, or haul the barrow to exhaustion, until sometimes he just had to stop.

"Engineer, sir, I need to take a breather or my back will break!"

A few gulps from a flask hidden in his pocket kept him going all day long. He had to be quite inconspicuous about it since Mateiaş didn't allow drinking during work hours, watching them as if they were digging for diamonds and not lime rocks.

To make up for his "loss" during the day, he would empty out a whole canteen of doubly distilled *țuică* on his way home, placed carefully in his carriage the night before.

By the time he reached Cernădia each night he would be drunk. Before doing anything else, even before taking his boots off or washing his dirty hands, he would grab the violin and start playing. Sometimes, he would stop after just a few notes, other times he would play for hours and hours, with Maria going in circles around him offering him food or talking about this and that to his deaf ears.

When he would finish, cantankerous because of the alcohol—not having had enough to put him to sleep, not having had too little to put him in a good mood—he always raised his voice at her as though she were his enemy.

"Just let me be, woman, for God's sake, stop fidgeting about. Can't you see I'm busy? Mind your own and give me something to eat, because I'm so starved I could eat a horse!"

"Alright, old fogy, in a second," she'd answer.

For a while now, Maria had started calling him "old fogy" instead of Mitu, which infuriated him, especially since he couldn't stop her from using the dreadful moniker. He had threatened to beat her, pounded the table with his fist, thrown her on the bed and had her like an animal, but, besides the fact that she had stopped calling him that to his face, he hadn't accomplished much; she would say "Well, my old fogy gets home from the quarry at around seven," or "Did you ask my old fogy, he should now," to all those to whom she spoke.

Sometimes, when he played on the porch and was in a good mood, he would confess to her:

"I shouldn't have come back from America, Maria. I should've stayed there and gone to music school."

Yes, Ciorogaru was right, he thought more and more lately, when he said that he should fight for a cause, fight for something worthwhile that could bring about a better living His life had gone back to square one; its course was the same as everyone else's. The measly salary he made at the quarry was barely enough for a loaf of bread. He budgeted the money brought from America with frugality, still hoping it could be put to some great use one day. He kept it well locked in a metal box, as he had in his childhood, and the rumor in the village was that he had hidden treasures, but because he was cheap, he hung on to them instead of using them for something useful.

Finally, he decided not to join the legionnaires, despite Ciorogaru's insistence, nor any other kind of party, but got involved in something a bit more local: The Anti-Usury League. He went to Novaci each Saturday to meet with other members and discuss ways of impeding the rich from giving high interest loans to the poor. He had seen a lot of people go bankrupt because of high interests in America, and considered that, "a bit of regulation in that respect" would have been great for the country folks in the area who, just like him, were in great need for loans sometimes. He knew what it meant to live full of debt; he had experienced it acutely with the stock market loss and had been forced to leave Detroit because of it.

Chapter 57

Each morning at four, Mitu would wake up tired and grumpy, cursing vigorously the dreariness of his life. Then he would take his violin, right there within his reach, wrapped in a rag to be protected from steam, and placed atop the closet. He didn't even have to come out the bed to get it. He would simply pull it by its tail, lie back down and slowly slide the bow on its strings humming a whisper of a song. Only after this ritual would he finally get up to go to the quarry.

Since he had begun working at the mine, endlessly handling the shovel and the mattock, he had become well versed in making cement and building stone constructions. He was supposed to do everything up there—not just dig in the mountain's stony guts—and the need had thought him that the simplest way to ease his drudgery was knowing how to do it very well.

Engineer Mateiaș had noticed that, and despite his dislike for Mitu, who had traveled to America while he, college educated and all, hadn't gone any farther than Baia de Fier, chose him to help with a job ordered by someone from Bucharest. It had to do with a stone monument to be raised on the side of the road coming from Rânca right at the entrance to Novaci, and a few handy men were needed.

One morning, he pulled Mitu out of earshot.

"Listen here, I put you on a team to help me with something. Now we'll see what you're made of. Come this Saturday to Novaci at Comănescu's tavern. Be there at ten on the dot. Don't be late, or you'll see hell. And the money will be discussed right then and there, but don't expect it to be all that great. No way you're going to receive American dollars. It's going to be you and Vorojan's son, Ion, and I'm also going to talk to Raggedy and Lică, so there'll be four of you, exactly how many that gentleman from Bucharest needs. I'll kill you if you don't do a good job."

That Saturday, Mitu made it to the meeting place a lot earlier than ten o'clock. He was happy he could make some extra money, as little as it might have been. Ion Vorojan and Lică were already there; one had arrived from Pociovaliștea and the other from Baia de Fier. Raggedy was tardy as usual. He was from Hirisești, and despite his being a well-appreciated construction worker, he kept losing job after job because he it was never on time. His overall unkempt appearance had brought on his nickname. Although married, he invariably missed a button either on his pants or shirts, even on his good clothes.

Mateiaș showed up later, around eleven in an automobile—not his, since only the mayor had a car in Novaci. He stopped with pompousness right in front of them honking the horn a few times as though he were summoning someone from all the way up in the mountains and got off together with an elderly man.

"Mr. Brâncuși, these are the men for the job! Strong, trustworthy, good workers. Just as I promised you."

He then turned to them and explained who the gentleman was—a great artist, a sculptor, known all over the world—and together they went into Comănescu's Inn. The man, about fifty or sixty, not too tall, with a white beard and a moustache darkened by chain-smoking, very jovial and agile, gave them a round of drinks and told them he needed their help because he wanted to raise a monument in honor of his native place, Hobița, right there to the north of Novaci, a place with special significance to him. He wasn't going to give them money but could offer plenty of drinks and food, and perhaps the mayor would take out some funds to pay their work at the end. That was to be discussed later.

Then he told them that he came from Bucharest, but that he had been very poor for years and years, that he tended sheep up in the mountains at the ripe age of six, that at nine he ran from home and got a job in Târgu-Jiu and that he learned to read and write very late in life, when he was nineteen. Now that he could to something for his county, for Gorj, he asked them to help him raise a monument that was to last for generations to come. They had to put together a stone tower about nine feet tall made up of three pieces: an ample base, on top of which there would lie a rectangular prism approximately three feet tall, and then another one a bit narrower but just as tall, and all the way on top two prisms united on one side just like the roof of a country house. The project would be completed under his watch or somebody else's coming from Bucharest to guide them. From afar, he also told them, the monument would appear as a guardian watching over the places, and the whole valley of Novaci could be seen from that point. Symbolically, he further ventured in explanations, it would be a local Axis Mundi, a communication means between two realms: the earth and the heaven.

"We will die, but the Monument from Plăeț will stand, good people, as a testimony to our existence on these places. Let's get to work!"

The project took them a few months. Sometimes, an engineer would come from Bucharest to follow their progress and tell them what to modify. Sometimes, Brâncuși himself would appear on the weekend and for a few hours he would analyze the stage of the project, then would take everyone in a cabriolet and stop at some tavern for meals.

"I feel very good when I'm here, because very few people know who I am, and this gives me freedom," he would tell them. "And freedom is like good health: you don't know how important it is until it's gone."

On the day they finished the monument, Mateiaș offered a feast in Brâncuși's honor, despite the artist's refusal, and he chose Comănescu's tavern for it. Mitu had thought that only those who had raised the construction would be there, but just as they were about to sit down at the table, Panaitescu showed up of nowhere, feigning surprise at having found them there.

"Oh, gentlemen, what a pleasure! What's the occasion you're here?"

He asked just to ask, since he had learned two days before from Raggedy that they were going to come here to celebrate the monument, and since he couldn't miss any big events that took place in the community, he had decided to make an appearance "on his way to run some errands."

To rise to the occasion, Mateiaş had hired with his own money three musicians from the gypsy community over the Gilort River to play soft music the guest of honor might enjoy. When the players took their violins and were about to start, he reminded them harshly:

"This gentleman knows classical music; don't embarrass me or I won't give you a penny! Get it through your heads: nothing that sounds even slightly gypsy! Only folk music, got it?"

"Don't worry, engineer, sir, we know our trade better than you," they said then began performing exactly what he had forbidden them to play: some songs, some yodels, some harmonies straight from the heart of their tribe.

Mateiaş bore it with a grin for a while, then, grimacing angrily, he began apologizing to Brâncuşi, but the man seemed unaffected; quite the opposite, he had stretched his legs under the table and leaned back in his chair, watching them with pleasure and encouraging them with rhythmic claps.

Mitu found it strange that the notable gentleman from Bucharest, well-traveled abroad and with friends from among the greatest artists of the world, according to the rumors in Novaci, felt so at ease among simple workers and gypsies. He kept drinking and eating, enjoying the atmosphere, sadly mesmerized by minor chords and joyfully smiling at the major ones, as though music ran through his very veins.

After they finished the last course—a suckling pig roasted to perfection, prepared especially for the occasion by Comănescu's wife—Brâncuşi got up from the table and asked one of the gypsies for his violin. He started singing in a strong voice softly accompanied by the instrument:

> *Doină, doină, sweet lament*
> *At your sound my heart is spent,*
> *Doină, doină, song of fire*
> *You are all that I desire*
> *In the springtime the winds blow*
> *And I sing my doina low,*
> *Flowers listen, the clouds high*
> *And the birds up in the sky.*

Mitu knew the song very well: he had learned it from Corcoveanu when he was a child and had played it many times since. Still, the sculptor's interpretation of the melody was distinctive. The sounds were the same, yet different, they didn't have the playful verve, the jovial strength of the peasant life, they seemed denser, deeper somehow, pertaining to a totally different kind of music. And the voice...Mr. Brâncuşi's voice was hoarse and guttural, apparently inappropriate for that type of music, yet it blended seamlessly with it in a perfect marriage of sorts. Mitu couldn't put it in words, but he somehow connected what he was hearing with the music from the Metropolitan Opera in New York.

"Sir, if I may, what skill! How well you handle the bow!" he praised him marveling as if in front of him were Enrico Caruso and not the sculptor whose creations he didn't understand at all.

Brâncuşi seemed surprised by Mitu's outburst and wanted to answer, but the gypsies were ahead of him.

"Come on Mitu, do you need an invitation? Come and sing for us!"

"That's right," Panaitescu, ignored until then, thought he should add hoping to be noticed by the illustrious guest. "Mitu, do as they say: go on and sing something American, to show the gentleman what the people from Novaci are capable of. You know, Mr. Brâncuşi, Mitu came to the school where I teach and told the children about America. Very good pupils and interested in learning, you should come see them, if you have the time."

In any other circumstance, Mitu wouldn't have hesitated. But now, at the proposition of playing for this seemingly ordinary man, but whom everyone talked about, he wavered. At everyone's insistence, he finally grabbed a violin, pulled the bow on the strings, then apologized.

"I am so sorry, but I need to tune the violin up a little," he said stretching the strings about a semitone higher, then he took a deep breath and murmured the rest of the song:

> *The storms of the winter come*
> *I sing now inside my home*
> *To make my days go by fast*
> *Days and nights, they pass at last*
> *As the forest's leaves turn green*
> *Songs of youth I sing again.*

Brâncuşi jumped to his feet, tuned his violin quickly and accompanied him in third voice while the gypsies joined in. Mateiaş and the other workers—their only audience—were listening, entranced, forgetting all about the alcohol, which until then had been their only priority.

When they finished, a deep silence fell. Even for the ignorant, the musical tandem witnessed had been unbelievable, as though God's grace had descended right on Comănescu's Inn that night.

Mateiaş applauded them enthusiastically, and Brâncuşi looked at Mitu with friendliness and interest.

"Now I understand why they call you the Fiddler. Tell me: why did you say the violin wasn't tuned properly before?"

"Well, it was too low, sir."

Brâncuşi tensed up in his chair and watched him with curiosity.

"How did you know it needed to be higher?"

Mitu looked at him confused. He didn't understand the question.

"I don't know what to tell you, it needed to be higher, please forgive me I didn't mean to be disrespectful!"

Brâncuşi made a sign with his hand as if to tell everyone to be quiet, then grabbed the violin.

"Give me a C major."

Mitu sang the note, and Brâncuşi checked with the instrument so no one could hear.

"Now give me a B flat."

Mitu whistled the sound. Brâncuşi tried him once more with an F sharp, then replaced the violin on the table and became thoughtful. Mitu was the first person he had met with a perfect pitch. He was quiet for a while, then began giving him advice.

"Listen, Mitu—The Fiddler, the American, or whatever they call you— I'm leaving here today and we'll probably never see each other again. From the little that I saw and heard, I think that what I can do with stone, you can do with music. Do whatever you can and learn from a maestro. Go to Bucharest to study. Go to the conservatory."

"Well, sir, thank you very much," Mitu answered visibly flattered, "but I'm kinda old. How am I going to learn now what I couldn't in my youth? I have a child at home, I break my back working for a measly salary, how am I going to pay for something like that? My wife's expecting, due in a few months, and I'll need even more money."

Brâncuşi told him that when he had decided to go to art school, he was poor as dirt, but that he had never regretted his sacrifice. Mitu listened, but he kept saying he had no means to follow his advice.

"Maybe Mr. Mateiaş will give you a raise and you can put it aside for this purpose."

The engineered frowned, mumbling "I'd give them all a raise, but there's no money...really..." He didn't like that Mitu was hogging all the attention when he had been the one organizing everything.

At last, when they were about to leave, Brâncuşi addressed him one more time through the window of the automobile.

"Do what I told you, Mitu, whatever effort it might take. Believe me; I know what I'm talking about. You'll never regret it if you do."

He shrugged as if to say it was out of his control, watching the dust in the wake of the car for a long time. His life was already settled in the village. He couldn't chase a crazy dream and leave his family behind, no matter how much he liked music and however positive the advice the kind gentleman had given him! How could he wander off to Bucharest now? Brâncuşi didn't know how hard life on the road could be; he had never been a hobo!

He got in his carriage with a heavy heart. His thoughts had drifted away to fame and fortune, to a world in which he starred on a brilliant stage, like those in New York, and men in tuxedos and women in elegant gowns crowded at the back door of a Broadway theater asking for autographs.

"Lord in Heaven, what a wretched life. It lifts you high to kick you down," he sighed morosely, startled by the horse's neigh, who had stumbled over a boulder in the abrupt road climbing to his house.

Chapter 58

Brâncuşi's advice made Mitu, for the first time since childhood, think more persistently about music. Until then he had played on a whim here and there at a corvee, but now things seemed different: if influential people from Bucharest praised him, that meant maybe he could do something with it.

Right after finishing the Monument from Plăeţ, he joined Julea and Cirică, two gypsies shunned, to their dismay, by the greatest player in the area, Costică Gâlcă. They recruited two more and formed a *taraf*. They all gathered in Mitu's front yard on evenings and weekends playing, playing, and playing some more. They practiced whatever spare minute they had. The violin was slowly becoming an integral part of Mitu's existence, the way it had been in the past. His musical senses came back to life, his reflexes sharpened again, his fingers ran on the strings with increased agility, his whole being awoke from the numbness it had been under for more than twenty years.

Not long after, Mitu's second child was born—Sandu—and now, in the narrow bed from the small room slept four beings. He was ashamed of his situation, being convinced that people gossiped that he was lazy and poor, that he had come from America with just the clothes on his back and ran back to his mother's home. But he also thought that, unlike others, he could at least offer his family a few things they enjoyed: each Sunday he took Maria and Gheorghe out to the market in Novaci and bought them chocolate, ice cream, or some toys. It was true he hadn't raised any palaces, he rationalized with himself, but at least he could give his wife and child more than others could give their families.

In fact, from the savings he still had, he could start building a house. He had enough for the foundation, and maybe later, he could have built the walls either by himself or with the help of his brother Ghiţă. He had the location for it—between the brook and the road, close to both of them. Maria encouraged him and insisted that he start, but he kept delaying it saying that he would start building only when he had enough money for the whole house. He didn't want to start then get stuck halfway and become the laughingstock of the village.

Those, however, were just pretexts. He didn't know why, but he lived in his mother's house as if he were just visiting, waiting for the time to pass so he could leave.

And not across the road, but across the ocean.

Thoughts about America kept coming back. He fell asleep and woke up with America on his mind. He thought about America in the morning up at the quarry while his arms ached from handling the mattock or with each dollar he spent. Memories of New York stirred him when he glanced at Păpuşa, remembering how he had snuck out of the country twenty-four years before. He read in the newspapers that America was doing better, a lot better than during his hobo time! He could have gone back and gotten himself a job working for Ford even!

When his brother Ghiță was around, as absentminded as ever, he would confess.

"I will go back there. I will go back where I came from. It's a totally different world...even in poverty, life is better."

Ghiță would watch him incredulously. He knew better: easier said than done, especially for a forty-year-old man. His brother's skeptical grimaces would anger Mitu, making him insist even more.

"Listen to me, Frizzy: I will go back there! I'll take Maria and my brats and go back to America. And this time, I'm taking you too. I'm not leaving you behind like the first time!"

"You do that," Ghiță wouldn't take him seriously, leaving him to his thoughts.

About four or five months later, Mitu received some unexpected news, and his desire to go back to America cooled off a little. He had come home from the quarry and was about to start rehearsing with his *taraf* when Maria told him he had a letter. Postolică, the mailman, had left it in the front gate and she had it on the porch, so he could take it before dashing out the door with the violin under his arm, as always.

It was a big, yellow envelope made of thick paper, which he immediately recognized as coming from abroad. He looked surprised at the heading— United States Department of State—wondering what it could be. When he opened the envelope and saw the paper inside, he realized that, unlike past junk mail, this letter was very important.

August 14, 1936

Dear War Veteran,

We are happy to inform that your bonus has been approved for immediate payment. Please contact us at your earliest convenience to retrieve your well-deserved retribution.

In the name of President Franklin D. Roosevelt, we wish to thank you for your courage in defending our country in the Great War. This money represents just a tiny fraction of the enormous respect that we all have for you and all the heroes who fought for our land.

Mitu read it a few times, and his face lit up. He turned the letter every which way just to make sure it was real. Slowly, the realization he now was better off than he had been just a few minutes before settled in.

"Oh, I have some money now. The first money. Hey!" he called out, then muffled his voice fearful he might be heard by the neighbors. He started pacing on the porch and the front yard clutching the paper.

Maria had come outside and was watching him with curiosity; she didn't know how to interpret his yell and didn't dare ask him.

"Maria, come here!" he called her.

The woman stepped timidly towards him.

"Look here!" he stuffed the envelope in her hand.

She tried reading it but didn't understand a word and glanced questioningly at him.

"I'm going to receive some money from America! That's what it says in the letter," he told her.

She then asked where the money was coming from, and he gave her a short explanation.

"Maria, after the war, we were promised some money—some money they were going to give us with interest in 1945, but I guess something happened there, and they voted to give it to us sooner. A lot sooner. Come here," he called her and embraced her patting her slightly on the shoulder. "We're going to have enough to buy things for the kids from now on! It will be okay, Maria," he said, caressing her hair.

He went back to the summer kitchen, opened up a cabinet, took a wooden jug, then went to the cellar. The unbelievable event had to be celebrated properly with the best of booze. He stopped in front of the smallest, best-hidden barrel, holding the doubly-distilled *ţuică* aged patiently for years, which slipped down the throat like honey. He filled up the canister, went back and lolled on a chair on the porch stretching his legs like a king. Little Gheorghe was playing in the yard with some puppies and Sandu was cooing inside. Ghiţă had gone to cut some firewood for extra money and was to come home the next morning.

Maria forgot all about the food on the stove and was peering cheerfully at him.

"Do you see what America is all about, woman? This right here! America never forgets her debt! They found me even in these boondocks here," Mitu said more to himself, breathing in the fresh evening air. "You know, woman, I'll take you and the little ones and we'll all go there. We'll find work and we'll buy a big and beautiful house, maybe even a car, and we'll come to visit Cernădia like we're kulaks!"

Talking about such future plans brought him an immense satisfaction. He had already decided what to do with the money: buy land, lots and lots of land.

"That's what I should have done in Detroit, Maria, just like a friend told me then: I should have bought properties in the center of the city. I didn't do it, and now I regret it. I really do. I could have been someone today. That was my lesson! One of these days, I'm gonna buy a few acres of land from Cernăzoara Bank. As many as I can."

He wanted to say more, but he stopped suddenly and his eyes glistened. Cirică and Julea were about to enter the front yard. They couldn't have come at a better time!

"Darn it," Maria got upset, "you're like a broken clock: fast to come and late to go."

Mitu signaled her to hush, and invited them inside with arms wide open.

"Woman, put something on the table quickly! Cirică come and fill your glass, what, you need an invitation? Follow Julea's suit! I brought out a bottle while waiting for you!"

They feasted away for an hour and played until well after midnight, with the gypsies' marveling at the Fiddler's verve. He sang more passionately than ever, shouting cheerfully while the other two struggled to keep up:

> *My honey from years ago*
> *Her worth is now way down low*
> *But the sweetheart from today*
> *I ain't got enough to pay.*

Mitu was a joyous, chatty kind of guy, they knew that already, but now he had mercury flowing through his veins! He kept playing and talking while his fingers were doing wonders on the strings.

"What happened to you, man?" Julea asked him. "It's like the end of the world's coming, what's your rush?"

"It's my business!" he barely hid a smile out of the corner of his mouth. He took out a cigarette, moistened it with spit at both ends and lit it leisurely, blowing big circles of smoke that twirled in the evening breeze. He grabbed the violin again and started playing a song he had learned from Tecău's *taraf*, in Montana.

> *Wretched, aloof foreign land*
> *Won't you give a helping hand*
> *To the soul who goes abroad*
> *It's a hard and stony road*
> *When you work for a new boss*
> *They will treat you like you're dross*
> *Scraps of food you will receive*
> *And beatings without reprieve*
> *Days, they keep on going on*
> *And with them I go along*
> *I get old and I am sad*
> *In this world I lived so bad*
> *And my fate has been so hard.*

"This wretched life...it takes you up only to bring you down," Mitu commented when he finished, relishing his cigarette.

When he was halfway through the cigarette, he put it out on a callus in his palm—he always did it for the flummoxed reaction of whoever watched him—and started chewing the leftover tobacco. He stretched his legs again, as he used to do in America, then started recounting all kinds of stories from his travels.

The night was growing old when the gypsies decided to leave. They were always sorry to get up from the table, always considering they hadn't stuffed themselves sufficiently and because Mitu's stories mesmerized them.

Mitu was unable to sleep that night. He tossed and turned in bed for a while, then got out surreptitiously and lay down with his hands under his head on a rug in the summer kitchen, thinking about the money he was about to receive in a little while.

Nighttime waned and it was already time to go to work, but he wondered if he should anymore. Ghiță, who was just coming home, was surprised to see him there. It was the first time his brother was up so early in the morning.

"What are you doing here? Did you fight with your wife and she threw you out?"

Mitu gave him an awkward look and said softly, "Frizzy, I'm not going to the quarry today. I quit."

"What's gotten into you all of a sudden? You nuts? How are you going to manage from now on?"

"I got some money from America, Ghiță. You go ahead. Tell Mateiaş I'll go to pick up my salary sometime at the end of the week. And also tell him to kiss my ass!"

Chapter 59

The day Mitu picked up his bonus from the post office—a few months after receiving the letter from the Department of State—he rushed to the Cernăzoara Bank to buy land. Rather than going from person to person in the village to see who wanted to sell an acre here or there, he preferred dealing straight with the bank and buying from there. Granted, it was more expensive, but he had less headache with the whole process. The clerks knew exactly what land was for sale and could guide him better.

He got in line a bit worried, knowing that buying land from the bank could bring on trouble with the people from the village. The bank didn't have its own land, but whatever had been confiscated from the people who had given it as collateral for their unpaid loans.

Right in front of him was Gheorghe Pruță, a peasant with whom he had not exchanged too many words lately and who was now paying back the last of his loan. His face was beaming with the joy he was no longer in debt and that he had put the borrowed money to great use. He bragged to Mitu about his financial acumen, having used the loan to buy a few hundred sheep and making some nice profit from the wool and cheese.

"Not many can say they can do this, Mitu...not many..."

Also waiting in line was Ioana Voadă, a widow living on edge of the village who was wringing her hands not knowing how to borrow money since all her land had already been used as collateral.

Two men holding piles of documents were probably there for similar land transactions, most likely with each other.

Ion Decău, the bank clerk, was very slow, taking forever with some insignificant document as though the fate of the world depended on the respective slip of paper. Even for someone with nerves of steel, the wait would have been unbearable. After a while, Mitu started losing his patience and even thought to tell him to hurry it up, but his irritation was cut short by a woman standing in line behind him.

"Mornin' American," she said without any other introduction. "What brought you to the bank? You poor now?"

She was a redheaded woman, in her early thirties, radiating of health, with freckled nose and blue eyes, a bit on the lanky side, but beautiful otherwise. Her eyes were irritated from the sandy wind blowing outside, and she was rubbing them nearly out of their sockets.

"Good day to you, Bălăloaica. Well, I came here to see about land for sale. I was thinking of buying some."

"Yeah, land, land, everybody wants land and they all forget that's where we end up anyway. I'm here to borrow some money and put some land as collateral. What can you do; some have it, some don't—however the Lord Up Above wants it. And how much do you wanna buy?"

"Well, a few acres, to plant some corn since I never seem to have enough in the fall and I always end up buying some; also a little bit of wheat, maybe a few plum trees, grow some hey because I'm thinking of buying a cow or two. I got some money from America and I want to put it to good use. How much money do you need, Bălăloaica?"

"Eh, I need lots of money. But I'll only ask for a little. I want to send little Mitică to school and I don't have any. Tough life nowadays! You work to the bone all day for nothin'..."

Mitu was pensive for a minute, then proposed something that surprised him even.

"Bălăloaica, forget about the bank. I'll loan you the money and you can give it back whenever you can. Don't you see how they jerk us around, these wretched people? They give you money then take double back."

He then started explaining his role in the Anti-Usury League, which he had joined recently, and how important it was for people to stop allowing being stepped all over by banks and the rich who made their wealth by taking advantage of them.

The woman looked at him touched, not by his words but by the fact that he had unleashed himself so charmingly in front of her—a poor country woman. He, the great American, handsome and talkative...and she was a nobody!

"Really Mitu, you're going to lend me the money, you say? Just so you know I won't be able to give it back to you right away, maybe in a few months after my husband sells some wool in Craiova."

"I will lend it to you, Bălăloaica, if you need it. I know you're good for it. You're not thinking of running away with it like Iosif Pirtea did, are you?"

"Get outta here. I'm a God-fearing woman. Do you think I'd do something like that and see my kids paying for my wrongdoings?"

"I'll come by your house and give it to you, Bălăloaica. Sometime this week."

"I don't know how to thank you, Mitu. You're helping me a lot with this. Come by whenever you can. What day is today? Tuesday. Come tomorrow or the day after..."

"I can't tomorrow, but Thursday or Friday for sure," he said, knowing that her husband left on Thursday night to Craiova to sell sheep wool and wouldn't come back until Sunday night.

"I'll be at home. If you don't see me, check next door at Auntie Sofronia's, maybe I'll be in her yard," the woman said. "I'm going home then, since there's no point staying here anymore."

Mitu took a deep breath of satisfaction. "It's not so bad I came back after all," he said content, watching the woman's backside as she walked away. He then remembered his incidents with Ana and Tecău's daughters, and a little rhyme he played often at corvees came on his lips:

It is never very good
To love in your neighborhood
'Cause a woman, when she's scorned
Tells about it to the world.

He brushed the thought off then rubbed his palms and waited patiently in line, wondering how to pay inconspicuous visits to Bălăloaica. "I shouldn't repeat my mistakes with Ana when I was a kid," he thought about Nistor, who still didn't speak to him after all that time.

He finally stood face to face with the clerk an hour later. Decău explained everything to him in a manner that surprised him. In all the Romanian institutions, bureaucratic by definition, he had dealt with disrespectful people full of airs, but this man, as slow as molasses as he was, displayed the politeness Mitu had only seen in America. "What's this guy doing here, in the armpit of the world?"

"Alright, Mr. Decău, I pretty much got it. Just tell me what land you have for sale now," he said at the end when the man finished with his explanations.

The clerk unfolded a map showing the land lost by people marked with Xs.

"There is a three-acre piece that belonged to Dumitru Râță up in Bâroaia, where the river meanders. A little lower, Vasile Găină has two acres. Well, he doesn't have it anymore. He had it until last month, but then the bank took possession. This one here is Roşoga's...I mean, it *was* his."

Mitu checked the map carefully then asked all kinds of questions, not to miss any details. He had had enough unfortunate experiences with the investments from America, and this time around he wanted to make sure he did everything right.

"Whose is this one?" he pointed to a piece in Lupeşti.

"Well, it's a long story; this is Victor Mănăilă's. Very good land, fertile, excellent for harvests."

"And why's he selling it?"

"Well, you know the trouble he's in."

Mitu nodded. He knew it very well. If fact, he understood his situation better than Decău could, better than anyone in the village. No one was aware of his circumstances in America during the Great Depression, because he had avoided telling anyone in detail about it. Mănăilă had also gone across the ocean at about the same time Mitu had, and had stayed there until 1929 tending sheep. He had come back with a few thousand dollars, a substantial sum in fact, which he had deposited in the Gilort Bank from Novaci. But during the crisis of 1933, when the bank filed for bankruptcy, he lost all his savings and was forced to move back in with his parents. Mitu thought just how similar their fates had been, and a touch of compassion went through his heart. He was not going to buy the man's land—he couldn't possibly do a thing like that; God might strike him down.

"Mr. Decău, I'm not going to buy Mănăilă's, but I want to buy a lot of land with the funds I have. As much as possible, to work it and lease it out. I don't want to have another job for the rest of my life! I'm going to make my living off of agriculture!"

Decău looked at him with admiration and envy. He had considered going to America a few years back and had even packed his bags, but fell for some beauty in Pociovaliştea and postponed his plans. A year later the honey left him for a guy who was slightly better off than he was. He was broken-hearted and destitute, having spent all his money on her. So he had to find a job right away. He was lucky he had gone to the accounting school in Târgu-Jiu and then found the job at the bank, otherwise he would have been in deep shit. Now he felt both jealousy and respect for all those who had gone abroad and always regretted not having taken advantage of the opportunity. They all had more money that he had managed to gather in his forty years; he was well aware of it since most of them deposited their savings at the very bank where he worked.

Mitu left the bank an hour later trying mixed feelings as he felt both a winner and a subjugator. He now owned four acres of Râţă's land, a good and fertile piece, which didn't need much care. The grass was growing readily on it and there was sufficient grazing space for a cow or two. He had also signed the papers for a few acres a little higher, by the Măgura Mountain; that land was not divided into parcels and given to individual persons, but it was fully leased out to shepherds from the outskirts of Sibiu. At the end of each year, all the owners received payments according to the surfaces they held.

He bought another piece—very cheap since it was quite far—past Păpuşa Summit and had put on reserve two acres from Roşoga's land out on the fringe of Cernădia. The man had lost it, rumor had it, on a game of dice. He had given it to someone to manage it and later had borrowed money using it as collateral. But the money dissipated God-knows-where, and now the bank was about to foreclose on it.

On his way home, he thought uneasily about how he was going to face the people whose land he now owned outright. "Yeah, well, they should learn their lesson. If they were stupid and didn't know how to hold on to their property." He remembered his stock market losses in America. "Cycle of life. One day up and the next day down."

On the narrow road to his house, dusty and full of boulders, muddy beyond belief during rainy days, which had remained frozen in time for the last hundred years and wasn't going to be asphalted for another hundred, a wrenching longing for Detroit suddenly overpowered him.

"I should've never come back here. So what if I bought some land? I still live in the armpit of the world."

Once at home, he opened the trunk brought from America, took a yellowish envelope full of pictures, sat down on a stool and began looking through them.

Chapter 60

A few weeks after, Mitu went with Gicu and Titi in the mountains to lease his new land. They took the road to Parâng, and once they almost reached the top, they tethered the horses, then went to meet with shepherds for negotiations.

The sky was spotless. The sun spilled soft rays over the mountains and the herds were strewn on the green grass like white drops of paint on a green canvas.

"My goodness, such beauty! We have things here to be proud of!" he sighed remembering Montana and his life as a shepherd and bootlegger in the thickets from around Helena. "Nothing changed here...the same small herds of a few hundred sheep, looked after by two or three people. The farmers in Montana wouldn't believe their eyes to see such a waste of effort!" he recalled his bewilderment when Ray the famer gave him a rifle, a dog, and a herd of five thousand sheep.

At their first stopover, they were welcomed by an elderly shepherd. "He's probably from Sibiu, because he doesn't look from around here," Mitu thought. When the old man learned the purpose of their visit, he invited them for some *balmoș* and kefir before beginning the negotiations.

An hour later, they went to another sheepfold, then another. They stopped off at each one, bargained with the shepherds, then went on their way promising to come back if they didn't find better prices elsewhere.

He leased out all his newly acquired land in two days. He had done an overall good job, getting better terms for some parcels than initially expected, his sales experience from "Mitu and Olga's Store" having helped considerably. On top of everything, he was going back home with a carriage full of goodies as each shepherd, hoping to sweeten a possible deal, kept offering him smoked meat, cheese, and milk.

On the way to Cernădia, still marked by the great difference between America and Romania, he started explaining to his companions how tending sheep was done in Montana.

"You should've seen me looking after thousands of heads, it was unbelievable! As far as the eye can see, open grazing fields surrounded by mountains, and there I was all by myself. Just me and Max the dog! I think people here should do the same!"

"This is the hundredth time you're telling us about it! Why fix something if it ain't broken?"

"It's not about fixing, people. If we opened our eyes a little, maybe we'd move forward, don't you think? What would it be for these people to try something new? I even made a song about this:

Mitu, what is your chagrin
To America I've been
And I am here today

> *Many things I have to say*
> *What the shepherds get as pay*
> *Five a month, to my dismay*
> *By the owner you are told*
> *- As the shepherd of the herd -*
> *If there are five thousand sheep*
> *All alone you're in, knee deep*
> *By yourself and with a mongrel*
> *'Stead of runnin', it stays idle*
> *And a stick to self defend*
> *In a satchel, loaves of bread*
> *Out to graze for days on end*
> *To spend all your days out there*
> *Of this life, you should beware.*

"Wonderful! All you need is your violin, Mitu," Gicu said with his thoughts elsewhere. "I'm sure they'll do it at some point, too, I'm not worried... But leave that America of yours to its own, Romania's doing pretty well. Take this road, for example, The King's Road, isn't it beautiful!?"

"Beautiful, yes," Mitu nodded staring ahead.

"And, while we drudge all day and you get world-changing thoughts running through your head, some lucky bastards out there are living the life," Titi intervened. "Did you hear what the King did when he came here? He inaugurated this road and then spent a night at the Ciuperca sheepfold. Down in the valley. And—listen to this shit!— he requested a woman *au naturel* not made up or anything, to spend the night with."

Mitu forgot all about sheep and felt his chest shrink. Damn it! he thought besieged by the jealousy of a man learning that some other guy could have however many women he liked.

"The damn bastard likes 'em raw!" he muttered.

He took a deep breath and appeased his envy with the thought that he, too, could brag about things like that—after all, in a few hours he was going to stop off at Bălăloaica's.

"Well pals," he changed the subject, "that America of mine may not have helped me during the latter part of my stay, but it's coming through for me now...My life was tough there especially in the last few years, but now I'm alright. And better late than never."

"Mitu, let me tell you something: I still don't understand why you came back!" Gicu's tone was rather scolding. "Whatever brought you back? Surely you would've found a woman there, and as far as the quality of life goes...I refuse to believe you live better here than you would have there. Can't you see you never shut up about it? They do this better, they do that better, and so on, and so forth."

Mitu stifled his impulse to confess about his hobo times, so he answered vaguely.

"I came back to my people, man. I felt so estranged there, I never made any good American friends for some reason, even though I spoke their language just like they did. I don't know why I didn't, I just couldn't. I got along better with Romanians. I guess it was the call of the land! But I can't complain now, things are good the way they are! I have enough to eat, I have a young and beautiful wife. My Maria is the only hazel-eyed woman in the whole of Cernădia."

"I don't know, Mitu, but it's strange you don't regret it at all," Gicu continued. "I know almost everyone in the area who came back from abroad, and I talked to them about it. They all made me understand, more or less openly, they're sorry they came back. Even those like you, who came back with some money and bought land and built houses, even those regret it. You're the only one who—"

"To each his own, Gicu. I'm not saying I don't think sometimes I should take Maria and the kids and go back. I think about it, so you know. I could find her a *job* at a tailor shop, I can open a restaurant, and everything would be great. It's one thing to be there with your family, and quite another to be on your own."

"You'll find her a what?"

"A *job*. That's what you call it in English."

Titi and Gicu started laughing. It wasn't clear why; maybe they thought he was putting on airs with the English word, or maybe the word itself seemed funny to them.

The King's Road slithered down, leaving the barren Summit of Păpușa behind, meandering and contorting itself to the foot of the mountain. Before entering Novaci, Mitu climbed down his carriage, took a swig of *țuică*, then stood for a few moments right next to the monument he had helped raise. "At least this will be left behind when I'm gone. Could Mr. Brâncuși be right? Should I give everything up and concentrate on music?" Then he told his companions to go on ahead because he had something to do.

As soon as he was alone, he made his way to Bălăloaica's home and stopped the carriage in front of her house, then went inside the yard and called her. She came out surprised and happy to see him, wiping the flour from her hands onto her apron.

"Come, Mitu, I was waiting for you. Let me get you something to eat. Come inside."

He followed her in the narrow room, then without a word, went close to her, took her in his arms, lifted her skirt, and had her right there on the narrow divan, hurrying to finish fast. He kept glancing outside the window to get up quickly in case one of her children might have come inside from playing.

"Bălăloaica, for you alone it was worth coming back from America," he said at the end, avoiding her eyes.

She burst into laughter not believing a word, and he, with an ambiguous smile, pulled out a small gold ring brought from America, which he hadn't shown to anyone, and put it in her palm.

"This is for you."

"What am I going to do with it, Mitu?" she asked. "I can't wear it. Where would I tell my man I got it from?"

"I don't know Bălăloaica. Do with it what you wish. I gave it to you, so it's yours. Here, this is the money I promised," he handed her a few bills. "I'll come back again to see you. Just like today, on the sly."

"Any time, any time, I'll be here waiting for you," she answered shyly in an attempt to make herself look attractive to him.

He started towards the house, thinking whether Bălăloaica would have still slept with him if she hadn't seen him at the bank buying land. "So much dough I've spent on honeys in my life... and would you look at that, I don't need to. If they see me chasing money, they come to me all by themselves, these wretched women!"

Like never before, Maria was waiting for him at the front gate looking scared, and that worried him. "Don't tell me she found out I stopped off at Bălăloaica's," he fretted.

"What happened Maria, did you miss me?" he forced a joke, as he pulled in, watching her from the corner of his eye and trying to figure out what was happening.

"Our baby got sick. Lil' Sandu is ill. He won't eat, he won't drink, he barely moves. You'd think he was dead if he wasn't warm! He burns like a hot stove. You can't even feel his heart beat! I'm so scared! I'm really scared!"

Mitu had left his youngest son well and healthy. "Did he have a cold?" Little Sandu had been coughing a bit for a while, but he hadn't taken to bed and seemed to improve lately. He jumped from the carriage and rushed inside the house, reprimanding himself for having gone to see Bălăloaica. He found the boy in bed with closed eyes and flushed without their usual healthy rosiness from running around in the fresh air. He put his ear to his lips to feel his breath and became frightened not hearing anything.

"Bring me a wet cloth."

Maria dashed to a big chest and grabbed a white blanket, ran out to the yard and doused it in water, then came back inside and gave it to him. Mitu had undressed Sandu and was softly slapping his cheeks, "What's happening to you, baby? Huh?" he whispered with a shivering voice.

He wrapped him in the cold blanket and held him close. "Is this God's punishment for the money I just got?" The baby didn't make a sound, and Maria started sobbing.

"Oh my God, what are we going to do? Our child is dying, our child is dying!"

"Woman, come back to your senses and stop whining! Stay with him and wrap him in cold blankets if he gets hot again. I'm going to Novaci to get Niculescu."

"How am I going to put ice cold water on him; he's gonna die if I do, my poor baby!"

"Do as I tell you, Maria!" he ordered bluntly and rushed out. He had seen the doctors in Meuse Argonne wrap feverish soldiers in wet sheets. Some would recover for a day or two but would ultimately die. Only a very few lucky ones ever made it alive from it.

Mitu came back with Doctor Niculescu several hours later, who furrowed his brow upon seeing the lethargic and almost breathless child. He checked him carefully, placing the stethoscope all over his chest, touching his wrists and shaking his head as though he could see things that Mitu or other mere mortals couldn't. The secret reason he had become a doctor—he would have cut his arm off before admitting to it—was the satisfaction he experienced when people looked at him as if he were God.

"It's not good," he said when he finished. "The boy has double pneumonia. I don't know what you did with him. Did you forget him outside in the cold? What are you trying to do? Kill him with your own hands? You need to keep him inside in heat, under permanent observation and wrapped up in cold sheets. Good thing you put him in this cold blanket, otherwise he could have died or grown dull from the fever. Feed him hot milk by force, if needs be. A lot of hot milk, but careful not to scald him. And don't wrap him in cold towels unless his temperature spikes high, or else you'll kill him."

"Please, please, I beg you, save him!" Maria implored him, frightened by his words.

"I can only try," the doctor answered coldly. "Only God can save him at this point. It's His will. Now, He's not at fault when human stupidity is too great either," he finished crossing himself amply.

"But we didn't keep him outside in the cold, how could we do something like that?"

He dismissed her ripostes with a gesture that seemed to say, "Yeah, yeah, I've heard it before!"

"I know what I know," he said. "Do you think it's the first time when I see something like this? The parents knock themselves out with booze at parties and leave the kids wandering around outside, no hats or scarves; they drink cold water, and that's it. Do you know how many kids I've seen dying from it? Move aside, I still need to do something to him!" he concluded in a curt tone.

He took out a silvery metal box and attached a needle to a glass syringe, then gave Sandu an injection.

"It's cortisone, it'll make him feel better. Keep him warm. If he gets any worse, call me!"

"The only worse thing than this is death, doctor," Maria said. "He's barely breathing anymore."

"Whatever will be, will be. I'll come by again tomorrow and the day after. We'll see what happens."

Chapter 61

Niculescu paid them visits regularly for the next few days to see Sandu and give him shots. The child's state was worsening. In the last two weeks, his joints had swollen up and he was very lethargic. He struggled to breathe, and his fever wouldn't subside.

The doctor explained that his joints were engorged with puss and he began draining them by making a quarter-inch incisions and placing thin tubes attached to a syringe. The inflammation went down slightly, but the child was still apathetic and barely ate. His condition deteriorated each day. He would fall into coma-like states coming out of them only partially.

Niculescu warned them during each visit that their son might not live to see the following day.

"There's nothing I can do for him anymore. I kept him alive for as long as I could. This little imp just doesn't want to get better, and that's that!"

One night, his breathing was but a whisper barely fogging a mirror, so they prepared for the worst. They lit a candle at his head and kept vigil by his side. Mindful of any moan or tremor, they kept putting cold compresses on his forehead, throwing wood into the fire and praying. A deathly rigor set in his body towards the morning. Mitu tried him again with the mirror, which no longer fogged.

"Woman, I'm afraid. We need to call the priest," he gloomily told Maria.

She burst into tears and began blabbering curses against her fate and God.

"What have we done to deserve this? What? Tell me?" she yelled at an icon hanging on the wall. "Tell me, what? Mitu, why is this happening to us?"

He shrugged as he always did when in a predicament. It wasn't the first time God had punished him, and probably not the last.

He listened for Sandu's breathing and touched his neck—there was no pulse—and put the mirror to his lips. Then, with a strange impulse, he stuck his tongue into the baby's mouth.

Seeing it, Maria forgot to wail and watched him nauseated. Had he lost his mind? She had never seen such thing. What kind of a foul thing was that?

Perhaps it was, but it seemed to get God's attention, who, at that moment probably considered its strangeness intriguing enough to bestow a bit of His grace upon them. The child started suckling on his father's tongue. Mitu jumped back startled, as though touched by a ghost, then went close to the boy and did it again. Sandu suckled on his tongue.

"Maria, he's sucking!" he said in disbelief. "He's sucking! He sucked on my tongue! He's alive! Alive! He didn't die! Our baby!" he marveled.

Maria was watching him stunned, unable to grasp what she was seeing and hearing, then crossed herself, "Good God in Heaven, what's happening?"

To their surprise, Sandu began convalescing—not right away, but painstakingly slowly, for months and months, gradually regaining his appetite, breathing more easily and having fewer fevers. Doctor Niculescu couldn't believe the miraculous recovery of the tongue suckling but dropped it; even for an educated man like himself, who knew the human body inside and out, some things were best left mysterious.

The miraculous defeat of his child's death elated Mitu to preternatural heights for a while. A lot of good was coming his way lately: the bonus, the land, Sandu's recovery, Bălăloaica, his music with Julea and Cirică. The auspicious times from before, after having shunned him for a while, were coming back, and for the first time since his return five years ago, he found himself sighing less for America.

Once the baby got better, he went back to his old ways, meeting people in the village or Novaci, just as he used to do before. He hadn't left his front yard during Sandu's illness, apathetic to everything, but now he felt alive again.

Cernădia was still abuzz with the energy of the parliament elections, which had just concluded. The National Liberal Party had come in first place, the National Peasant Party in second, and the legionnaires in the third, with over fifteen percent. Mitu himself had convinced a few to vote for the "Everything for the Motherland!" party. He had explained their platform in just a few words, just as he had understood it from Ciorogaru: God, the country, the peasants and the workers, the fight against the Bolsheviks and against those who robbed the country blind. Although he maintained his apolitical status, still telling everyone "he wasn't interested in politics," meeting Corneliu Codreanu three years before had thoroughly impressed him, and he always ended up singing his praises. Out of everyone in politics, the Captain was the most brilliant, he thought. He remembered him perfectly, as if it were yesterday: a saint from heaven descended among the needy. The moment that man had looked at the crowd in the church's yard in Novaci, without a word, stunning everyone in anticipation of his speech, was still vivid in his mind. He could have never imagined utter silence to have such power over a crowd!

He saw Ciorogaru out in the street one of those days. Their meetings had been rare since Sandu's illness.

Ciorogaru was aglow—the joy he radiated clearly suggested he was experiencing uplifting moments in his life. When he saw Mitu, he hugged him with the affection of an old friend and immediately resorted to convincing him to join the legionnaires.

"We're in third place in the whole country! You're a good man, Mitu, and you can recognize evil when you see it. Even if you're not officially one of ours, your heart and soul are with us. I know Curcă and Protopopescu voted because you told them to do so. You can't imagine what a great help you are to this country! Each vote represents a victory against the Bolsheviks and the Jews! Yesterday there were only five of us! Now, we're five million! Tomorrow we'll have the whole country! Our fight will not have been in vain!"

Mitu looked at him somewhat surprised. Ciorogaru's convincing tactics had become quite passionate lately. He looked old; his gaze was sterner, more mature, betraying the exhausting effect of political responsibilities that had taken an untimely toll on his youth.

"Many congratulations, Mr. Ciorogaru, and may the One Up Above help you reach the top and take this country on the best path, because it really needs a change! I, if I may, don't think politics agrees with me. Just because I convinced a few people to vote; I did that for you. You helped me a great deal when I needed it. I'm happy with my Anti-Usury League!"

"But the Captain will save our country, Mitu! The Bolsheviks and the Jews are this world's greatest enemies! The danger from the East is terrible, and we need to unite against it! If we lose the fight, you'll be affected also!"

"Mr. Ciorogaru, I don't know why, but I'm afraid. I gotta tell you, I'm afraid. There's just too much change in this country; whoever's up today will be down tomorrow. I saw it happening many times in America. The Great Depression made beggars out of many people who no one imagined could ever be so poor. And, don't mind me for saying so, now we blame the Jews and the communists for the bad situation of our country, but..."

"Yes," Ciorogaru interrupted him, "that's right: The Jews own Romania! Our Romania! The Jewish Bolshevism is the greatest danger to ever threaten this country throughout history!"

Mitu shook his head in dissent thinking of a clever answer that wouldn't hurt Ciorogaru's feelings.

"I just know what experience has taught me: in America, we blamed the Germans for getting a whole country drunk with their beer and liquor stores. All the newspapers wrote that was the reason the country was doing so poorly. And we all believed it. I believed it too, until I fought in the War and I saw the soldiers were young lads just like I was. You can't blame an entire people! Those at the helm are guilty, not the poor masses. If we blame a whole country, it all gets muddy! Back then, the Germans were guilty, here we think it's the Jews, in the U.S.S.R they blame the Germans and the Romanians. Who are the guilty ones, after all?"

Ciorogaru looked at him in wonder. He didn't know Mitu could be so swaying. The simple peasant that he was, it was clear that his living in America had rounded up his understanding of the world. Still, his perspective was askew. How could he not realize who the real enemies were?

"Mitu, you've traveled a lot, but you still don't see how these things work. The danger to the world is imminent and greater than ever! You'll see that I'm right very soon!"

"Well I don't know what to say...that the Jews own the country, that's clear as daylight; out of ten stores in Târgu-Jiu nine are theirs. But good for them—right?—good they were able to do it! When I had my store in Detroit and the business was thriving, nobody on that street was a Jew. The owners were either American or immigrants just like me. If the Jews were to blame, they should have been owners in America too, right? Why only in Romania?"

"You're blind, Mitu! I wish you were right, but you're blind! Don't forget my words: Romania will soon go through its most trying times in history if we don't stand up to fight!"

Mitu made a gesture from which it wasn't clear whether he agreed or not, and as always, they parted ways with Mitu's promising he was going to give it some thought.

Shortly after, he saw that Ciorogaru's political concerns were not as exaggerated as he had originally considered them. The newspapers published things that were more and more unsettling each day, forewarning grim times ahead. One morning he heard the Liberals had given up their power. Then, in February, Codreanu dissolved the Legion. Not too long after, *The Word* and *The Annunciation*, the Iron Guard's papers, were banned.

What was happening? The monarchy had become a dictatorship and had turned against the whole opposition! The country was now at the whim of a few people that did whatever they pleased with it. Romania was beginning to look a lot less like his America, and that was disconcerting to him!

Then the arrests started. The day Zelea Codreanu, the head of the legionnaires, was jailed, seized by fear, he yelled for his brother, who was doing some work around the house.

"Did you hear? They arrested Codreanu! Frizzy, they arrested the Captain!"

Ghiță seemed to live in a different world. No news could stir him or unsettle his daily routine. He took his time to stop from whatever he was doing and shrugged. His body language spoke more than words, displaying an otherworldly indifference to the complicated problems of democracy.

"As long as they don't take me, they can take them all. Good riddance to them! And since when are you such a politician? Are you sick of living? Mind your music—that's what you're good at. You keep talking about the legionnaires all day long, like they're your brothers. You're going to go to their nests any day now, and you won't even come back home. Maybe you'll have your own nest in the village somewhere! Right next to the drinking hole to have supplies nearby!"

"Fuck it to hell Ghiță, you don't get it! I don't have to join no one to have an opinion! I'm telling you, we need to be cautious and watch our backs! If all the legionnaires—the few millions of them in this country—riot to get the Captain out of prison, it'll be mayhem because they're the king's biggest enemies! See what you think when they burn our home! They'll have brothers fighting against each other! The army against the civilians!"

Ghiță shrugged again. He had gone through a war by staying in Cernădia and doing nothing more than working his land and taking care of his animals. While millions had perished, nothing had affected him. Governments had come and gone, new borders had been mapped out, but he had remained right there, completely unbothered. Some political rumblings, whomever they belonged to, were not enough to scare him.

Mitu thought otherwise. When those at the very top were arrested, when average people could no longer express their beliefs, when newspapers were taken out of print, when a whole country lived in fear, times were troubled.

His inquietude was indescribable, coming from an experience marked by suffering, which now allowed his mind to peg apparently insignificant cogs in the great scheme of things. He had developed some kind of a sixth sense, an intuition nurtured by years of hard trials, a wisdom gained from some of the greatest historical events to which he had been a part of quite intimately.

The foreboding feeling that filled him was so vivid, that a few days later he went to Ciorogaru to share his fears. The man thanked him for his visit but didn't take him too seriously, telling him that the legionnaires were stronger than ever, and that they would indubitably prevail in the struggle for power because they had the support of the peasantry and that of the country's intelligentsia.

"Mitu, good and justice always prevail, there is no doubt about it! The army can use bullets, but they won't shoot defenseless people. Romanians won't fight against Romanians!"

"They won't? Of course they will, Mr. Ciorogaru! I've seen it happen before! In the Battle of Washington, where I myself participated, sons fought against their fathers; who could have thought something like that? You don't think it could happen here? And, to be honest with you, I'm not afraid there's going to be a confrontation; I'm afraid you won't make it to one. If I hated the Guard as much as the king does, it would be off with its head. I would kill all the nest leaders. I would kill them now that they're all in prison. That's what I'd do. The way they killed Huey Long when they saw he was about to become president."

Ciorogaru stared somberly at him. Mitu was right, and he knew it; nobody was crazy enough to get into a quarrel with the legionnaires, but that was only as long as they were still organized. He saw him out to the front gate, not thinking for a moment Mitu's prophecies would come true only a few months later.

Chapter 62

When someone deeply venerated dies a brutal death, the first thought in one's mind is vengeance. When the life of someone deemed the hope of many is cut short, the first impulse is to grab a gun and make justice. When a person in whom you believe meets a horrible ending, the only thing you want is to torture the inflictors, bleed them out drop by drop, and soothe your suffering with theirs.

It was what Mitu felt that November morning when he turned the radio on to listen to the news while doing some house chores. Never before had he tried such a desire for revenge. He had just finished giving water to the horses, when he heard the communiqué that made his flesh crawl. The newscaster was announcing that Zelea Codreanu had been shot:

"On the night of 2930 of November, a few detainees were being transferred from the Râmnicu Sărat Prison to the Bucharest, Jilava Prison. On the Bucharest-Ploieşti road, right at the forested area of mile 17, at five o'clock in the morning, the convoy came under fire from a few unknown individuals who disappeared shortly afterward. At that moment, the prisoners, taking advantage of the fact that the transfer took place during nighttime and in dense fog conditions, jumped out of the cars with the obvious intention to flee custody and escape into the forest. The gendarmes drew fire after ordering them to stop. The following were shot: Corneliu Zelea Codreanu, sentenced to ten years of hard labor and six years' interdiction; Constantinescu Nicolae..."

Twelve names followed, then the announcement concluded:

"The Prosecutor's Magistracy of the 2nd Army Corps, on whose territory the incident took place, and the Civilian Prosecutor's Office, have gone to the site, and the medical expert called the death and filed the official report."

At first, Mitu thought it a hoax, a frame-up, an effort to break the legionnaires apart. "It wouldn't be the first time." He froze up by the radio and kept listening quite beside himself. The news was followed by a commercial for Gladys shoeshine, then music and some other advertisements.

The official statement was repeated an hour later. He fell slowly in a chair and watched the radio as if it were a human being, expecting it to confirm that everything had been a joke, a deceitful, dirty game. The speaker kept stubbornly playing music and commercials.

Yes, the Captain had died—there was no doubt. When the news finally sank in, he buried his head in his hands and started yelling through the yard.

"Maria! Maria! Come here!"

The woman was seeing to her chores but rushed worried to his side. He had never called her with such a voice. When she saw him sitting by the shed with the pails scattered on the ground, she figured something was wrong.

"What happened to you? Are you sick?"

"They just announced on the radio that Codreanu was killed! They shot him and a few others! They're saying they tried to escape last night! I wonder what is going to happen to Ciorogaru!"

She raised her hand to her mouth then crossed herself.

"God forbid! Mitu, don't get involved in this! I'm afraid they'll come to get Ciorogaru and take you too, because you've been seeing him so much! Don't get yourself in it, don't do it!"

"Leave me alone, woman, don't tell me what to do! I need to go there and see him!"

"Don't go Mitu, please don't go; they'll think you're one of them! If they come to arrest him, they'll pick you up too! Think about Gheorghe and Sandu, the poor kids—don't leave them fatherless!"

"That man needs some help, woman! No one will do anything to me; I'm not on any lists! If they get anyone, they'll go for the ones at the top. People here know I'm not for the Peasantists, the Legionnaires, the communists, the Liberals, nothing. I'll come back quick!" he said mounting the horse.

He galloped to Novaci, unable to settle his thoughts on the new development.

The Captain was dead!

Mrs. Ileana, Ciorogaru's wife—he had recently gotten married in a private ceremony—seemed quite unnerved as she opened the door and invited him to come inside.

He found him in the living room, sitting in a chair by the bookshelves. He was staring blankly, as though he were expecting to wake from a nightmare. The news was too fresh for his heart to grasp; as of yet, he found himself in that particular state when a person, hit by horrifying news, still denies its verity.

There were other men in the room, just some legionnaires from Târgu-Jiu, Mitu realized, whom he had never seen before. They were startled by his arrival, and one of them aimed a Beretta at him, making him freeze in the doorway, arms up in the air. The war habits were still alive within him.

"Who's this man?"

Ciorogaru raised gloomy eyes and gestured them not to worry.

"Trust him, he's not a Green Shirt, but he won't betray us. Come in, Mitu," he said. "What brings you here? What you heard on the radio is a frame-up; the Captain is not dead. Don't you believe it! Don't worry, they can't kill him! If he dies, the whole country dies! They hid him somewhere, in some prison to cause ruckus within the Movement. *Divide et impera*. But we won't give in!"

Mitu gave him a puzzled look. "What does he mean he's not dead? Why would they announce it, then?" He couldn't remember to have heard such news in America that didn't prove to be true in the end. When the newspapers wrote some bad news about Capone, Long or others, it always turned out to be real. It must have been the case here as well: The Captain was dead, and Ciorogaru was lying to himself if he didn't believe it!

He worked up his courage.

"I... always put the worst first. And please forgive me for barging in on you like that. What terrible news. Good God, may he rest in peace! The bastards killed him, a defenseless man—the assassins! They executed him! I, for one, don't think he tried to run away. How could he?" he raised his voice. "How could he run away? No one's that crazy to try and escape from a whole platoon of soldiers! I was in the war; if anyone had aimed a gun at me, I would have wet my pants and frozen up in place! And not one, but fourteen detainees! How could they all be dead; at least one should have been just wounded and made it alive! They killed them deliberately! Don't let anything happen to you! That's why I came here, to see if I could help you hide somewhere. God forbid they come to arrest you. I don't want anything bad happening to you!"

Ciorogaru looked at him then returned to his thoughts. Mitu had struck a true cord. What if he were right? What if the Captain had died indeed? What was going to become of them?

The men in the room started discussing intensely, threatening to kill the Prime-Minister Armand Călinescu, Nicolae Titulescu, Nicolae Iorga, even the King.

"If he's dead, as they say, the Captain must be avenged! We need to fight our enemies! The Captain must be avenged! There will be bloodshed! Revenge! Archangel Michael demands it! Gică, we need to fight against the dastards!"

Mitu tried to add something else but then changed his mind, thinking his timing had been off. What had he been thinking to rush there so quickly when it was clear that Ciorogaru didn't need him? He should have listened to his woman and stayed home instead.

Ciorogaru felt his awkwardness and spoke as though he had just noticed him there.

"Tell me, American, why did you stop by? You got me at a very hard moment."

Mitu repeated that he had come to help however he could. Maybe hide him in the attic or somewhere else. He had some forest up in the mountains where they could find a hiding place.

Mrs. Ileana, who had been in the room the whole time without saying anything, was moved by Mitu's offer. Since the hunt for legionnaires had begun in the past year, not many had jumped to their aid, much less those who weren't legionnaires themselves. Everybody was afraid of threats, persecutions, unfair sentencing, murder, disappearances, and avoided to talk to those targeted. Mitu was crazy to show up there!

Ciorogaru exchanged glances with his wife, then told him he was grateful but couldn't accept his help and sent him home in a firm tone:

"If indeed the Captain is dead, there will be bloodshed, Mitu. But that has nothing to do with you. Don't get yourself caught up between a rock and a hard place for no reason. Go back to your land. Go back to your wife, take care of your children. Don't worry about me; I'll have my protection."

After Mitu left, the men stared befuddled at Ciorogaru.

"We need any help we can get, why did you send him home? Are you out of your mind? Now, when we require people more than ever?"

He gave them a look weighed with sadness:

"Mitu is a simple but good man. I've known him for years. He did not come here for the Movement. Had that been in his blood, he would have joined it a long time ago. He came here for me. Now we need to think about our next move.22F*"

---

* Corneliu Zelea Codreanu, the Nicadori and the Decemviri (14 people in total) were assassinated on the night of 19-20 of November 1938 in a forest close to Tâncăbești. Their feet were bound to the floor of the trucks in which they were transported from Râmnicu-Sărat to Bucharest-Jilava to serve their sentences. Their hands were handcuffed to the backside of the benches. Soldiers sat behind each detainee holding nooses and strangled them all on a signal. Afterward, the detainees were shot in the back of their heads to make it look as if they were trying to escape and later, their bodies were dissolved in acid.

THE SECOND WAR

Chapter 63

Ciorogaru disappeared shortly after Codreanu's assassination. Mitu passed by his house a few times, but he wasn't there, and Mrs. Ileana couldn't tell him anything. But she didn't seem too worried, so he figured out he was safe.23F* Then he heard that she had gone as well—people said somewhere across the border—and, after a while, he completely lost their trail.

During the following months, when things settled down a bit, with the money he still had, he built a house, right by the main road on a lot bought from the bank particularly for that purpose.

He finished the construction in about half a year. He had not raised himself a mansion the size of Păpușa Summit as he had dreamed in his childhood, but a small house like everybody else's in the village: two rooms, of which one served as the kitchen during wintertime. In the front yard, he built a shed for firewood and a stable for the animals, and wall-to-wall with it, he built a summer kitchen.

After finishing everything, instead of being proud of his accomplishment, he felt unexpectedly empty inside. It was the feeling of a man who, after doing something of importance, finds himself without a meaning. "Now what?" he thought while hammering the last nails, "What if I never make it to the day of moving in it?"

It was the summer of 1939. His worries, seeded in his heart by Ciorogaru, were starting to become a reality. Poland, attacked by two giants—Germany to the west and Russia to the east—had been brought to its knees.

The deep and dark tentacles of a new war were encompassing the whole world. Armand Călinescu, the prime minister, had died under a sheet of bullets, and his legionnaire assassins had been caught, executed, and left on the pavement to be a lesson to others. Other legionnaires had been shot in front of Gh. Duca's statue or hanged from electrical power poles for everyone to see. The savageries witnessed in the Great War and the Battle of Washington, and which he had hoped never to see again, were unfolding under his eyes in his own country.

Ciorogaru was the only person whose thoughts and advice Mitu wanted on his intention to return to America, but he had disappeared without a trace.

He had started getting together with a teacher from Cărbunești named Mihai Cămărășescu, whom he had met a while back, and with whom he spoke in English each time they saw each other. Cămărășescu had been schooled in France and had learned the American tongue by himself from books, something that Mitu respected very much, thinking he would have never been

---

* Gheorghe Ciorogaru escaped miraculously from the anti-legionnaire raid, which followed Codreanu's assassination and that eliminated almost all the leaders of the movement. Aided by Cătălin Ropală, another legionnaire, he ran across the border using the passport of a student, Sorin Tulea, a famous Romanian alpinist from the Romanian Alpine Club. He went to Berlin where he wrote the book "Captain to the Legionnaires."

capable of accomplishing such a feat. They met for a drink on Saturdays and Sundays in Novaci at Comănescu's tavern and conversed in English. "To practice the language for the language's sake!" they would say jokingly, since many times the real reason for their encounters was the great *ţuică* Comănescu served them.

He decided that he was going to muster up his courage during their next meeting and ask for the man's opinion on the problem troubling him. Besides Ciorogaru, Cămărăşescu was the only other person who could give him a sound piece of advice, since he had lived abroad as well. He had meant to do it a lot sooner, but kept delaying since it made him feel awkward. Still, he needed to set his pride and embarrassment aside and dare to ask someone more enlightened than he was.

So, one Saturday, he set out to Novaci just as they had planned previously. He was hoping to find Cămărăşescu alone, to speak privately with him, but when he went inside the tavern, he saw Panaitescu at his table. Hoity-Toity was there as well "for a well-deserved break from work." Anghel Flitan also dropped by.

When they welcomed him in quite a good mood—"Well, well, hello American!" and pulled a chair for him, his wish to confess subsided.

"Great," Cămărăşescu said, "you're right on time. But now that Anghel and Mr. Panaitescu and Mr. Panait are here, we need to speak in Romanian and leave English for some other time. Let's toast to our darling lil' country!"

They all conformed and let the liquor slip quickly down their throats. Mitu sat down and pulled a bottle next to him. Should he tell them he was thinking about leaving?

Panaitescu, with his ever-present teenage-like enthusiasm, though he was nearing fifty, filled his glass and raised it up above his head.

"May it be that the Greater Romania continue to be great until the end of time! Mitu, you have the gift of music, but I haven't seen you in politics at all. You still haven't decided, after all? You're not joining the legionnaires? I remember seeing you with Ciorogaru a lot when he was here!"

"Well, politics comes and goes, people stay, Mr. Panaitescu. I'm not joining anything. I don't believe in any party—legionnaires or whoever else—that murders people. And how am I to join the legionnaires when they're getting killed left and right? What do you think, I'm sick of living?"

"Oh my goodness Mitu, but Armand Călinescu was our country's biggest threat! Now, I can't say that I condone homicide, but sometimes it's necessary for the best of the country!"

Mitu scratched his head.

"I, for one, have seen many things in America that made me realize that we, the little people, can't do anything. The games are made high up, no matter how much we squirm. We're very little frogs in a very great pond."

"That's not true! Not true! The power lies with the masses! Take this example: the will of the Romanian people has brought about the nation's unification!" Panaitescu almost shouted, eyelids aflutter with excitement.

"Remember, Panaitescu" intervened Cămărășescu, "that Bessarabia is part of our country only because the Romanians made up the majority in the National Assembly. But that doesn't mean that's how things are in reality. Let's keep in mind that, in Bessarabia, minorities make up half the population, and if the Russian Army hadn't retreated as chaotically as it had, there would have been a proletarian revolution and a Bolshevik annex to Russia!"

"Whatever may be, majorities, minorities, Romanians make up the greatest number in Transylvania, Bucovina, and in Bessarabia. The census of 1930 showed without a doubt that the number of Romanians is the highest!" Panaitescu pointed out categorically. "For this reason, all of these territories must be part of The Greater Romania! Flitan, how do you see it from the perspective of a country man who leads a simple life but who's hardworking and quite well-off?"

Flitan, who resembled Mitu somewhat in the sense that he didn't venture in debates whose topics seemed to go above his head, shrugged. "Well, what could I tell you..." he seemed to say.

Cămărășescu only participated in discussions about the future and not the past, so he left to order another bottle while his companions continued to split hairs over history.

When he came back, seeing they were still on the same twenty-year old topic, he intervened.

"Come on, let's leave the past to the past since we can't change it anyway. It's a good thing our country's both big and beautiful. The question is: what can we do to keep it that way in the future? England and France promised their help, but it's clear Hitler will conquer the whole Europe in a few months. And with the Wehrmacht on the right side of the English Channel— since France will soon be on its knees, I think we all agree here— and the rest of Europe conquered, England will be left quite powerless. And then, I ask you: what's best for us, to be on the Allies' side or that of the Axis? As far as I'm concerned, I know the answer: Germany will prevail, and whoever's on its side will have a lot to gain! Imagine, Romania on the winner's side! Fiddler, what's your take on this since you fought the Germans?"

Mitu moved his head pensively. The Germans had fought very well in the Great War, and it was clear to him that, having learned from their mistakes in the past, this time around they would defeat any obstacles in their way. Yes, of course, Cămărășescu was right, it was clear as daylight.

"Now, I don't know," he wavered, "but the only ones who can defeat the Germans are the Americans. If America doesn't go into the war— and I don't mean on Germany's side—the Axis wins."

"You're right, Mitu. Well, then," Cămărășescu continued, "is it not in the interest of our country to ally itself with the Germans? It's clear; we're a piece of land between two monstrously big powers: The Bolsheviks on one side, the Axis on the other. If we stay neutral much longer, whoever wins the

war will hack us to pieces accusing us of having been their enemies.24F[*]
We'll lose Transylvania; we'll lose Bessarabia, and the north of Bucovina.
Romania will be crippled!"

"Yes, yes," said Panaitescu, whose sympathy for the fascists, although
never declared openly, was quite transparent in his replies, "Mr. Cămărăşescu
is right! We need to align ourselves with the strongest! That's the only way
to keep this country in good shape and maybe even improve it! How would
it be to finish the war as a winner on Germany's side? Just think about it!" he
choked with emotion at the envisioned image of a Romania, which included
Hungary, half of Bulgaria, and part of Russia.

With a sudden decision, Mitu intervened quite trenchantly in a manner
very uncharacteristic to him.

"Good people, can you hear yourselves? I, for one, am afraid of America
because I've been there and I know what it can do. And I don't see how the
Americans wouldn't get themselves involved in this war on the side of the
Allies like in the past one. Those damn Americans never miss an opportunity
to make money. The Great War made them the richest country in the world.
That's how it's going to be this time too! Whoever is the Americans' ally will
win, I can bet my life on it. Let's just hope the King will make the right choice
and get us on with the Americans, that's all I'm saying. Since we're on the
topic," he confessed in one breath, "I'm thinking about going back there.
Fighting wars is not for me anymore, and that country cannot be touched
where it is. Whatever happens in Europe, America is safe for civilians."

"What? Flee Romania? Now that we need everyone here?" Panaitescu
boiled, frowning at him as if he were a traitor committing a Godless act.
"Well, what if we all thought the same way you do? Our country would be
helpless, at the whim of the Jewish communism, the way the Captain warned
us. May God rest his soul!"

Cămărăşescu defended Mitu unexpectedly.

"Each person has a right to self-determination, Mr. Panaitescu, isn't that
what you teach your students? Mitu, I admire you for wanting to leave, with
family and everything, since you're not all that young anymore. But if that's
what you feel you want to do, do it without second thought."

"I tell you, doing it is much easier than thinking about doing it. Once on
the way, you go with the flow, and willy-nilly you manage somehow."

"If you want to leave, you'd better do it now, Mitu, don't linger
anymore." Flitan, who hadn't said much until then, encouraged him.

---

[*] King Carol II tried to maintain Romania's neutrality in the first half of the war, but France's
surrender and the retreat of the English troops from continental Europe rendered useless the
assurances both countries had made to protect Romania's territorial interests gravely threatened
by a secret clause to the Ribbentrop-Molotov act of August 23, 1939, which stipulated the
U.S.S.R's interest in Bessarabia.

Hoity-Toity, too busy with his *țuică* up to that point, took a serious and grim air as though he had access to a source of information unavailable to the others, cleared his voice importantly and began his suppositions.

"Gentlemen, do you know who will come victorious out of this whole mayhem?"

They all shook their heads, looking incredulous at him. "Not even God knew the answer to that question, and Hoity thought he did?" Cămărășescu smiled to himself.

"You might find it laughable, but I think—and, Mr. Panaitescu, please refrain from shouting at what I'm about to say now—I think the East will prevail. I'm not a communist," he made sure to defend himself hastily, "but look at our country's geography! We are too close to the U.S.S.R. not to be greatly affected. We're too close to the Russians for them not to try and take us under their red cloak!"

Flitan nodded.

"Mr. Panait, you've read my mind. Many villagers from Cernădia live in poverty. I am one of the lucky ones; I've done well for myself with the land I was able to buy. Mitu also bought some with the money from America. But the rest...the rest are poor like church mice! And millions in this country are like them. Everyone will vote with whoever promises that the wealth will be taken from the rich and given to them!"

"Anghel's right, yes," Mitu agreed. "When I was in America, I got to the point where I was flat broke, and I've got to tell you, socialistic thoughts went through my head. Yes, they did! I hated the rich so much, that if a party told me they would take the money from them to give it to me, I would have voted for them no ifs, ands, or buts about it! That's why I joined the Anti-Usury League here. It's not fair for someone to own a big hunk of the country while tens of thousands break their backs working for him!"

"And now you think the same, when you have land everywhere and you own mountains?" Cămărășescu reprimanded him. "For those who worked hard to make something with their lives, how would it be for someone to come and take it all away? Wouldn't that irk you? To each his own, God's willing. I understand what you mean, but the problem of poverty can't be solved according to the Judeo-Bolshevik ideology. Spreading the wealth around is not a solution, because it causes disorder and an artificial type of society that can't possibly last. Wealth cannot be redistributed! Quite the opposite, poverty can be solved by supporting capitalism! It's that simple, gentlemen! And let me explain it to you: Mitu, when you had your own store, you hired someone—a German—and you paid him, right? Both he and you could live off of it. That's how you get rid of poverty; you encourage production and private ownership! You had a job in Detroit because Ford built automobile manufacturing plants. And, in his genius, he paid you doubly, reduced your workday, and gave you vacation time and free weekends, just as you told me. You lived well and he did also. This is how you get progress and wellbeing, by encouraging these types of people."

Mitu thought of a possible answer, maybe tell him that, despite the good life he had back then, he still thought it was unfair for Ford to be so wealthy, but his companions were beginning to show signs of boredom, so he gave up. The alcohol had already gone to their heads and muddled their thinking. Hoity got up, saying he had some things to do at home and left with Panaitescu. Cămărășescu hurried to catch the bus to Cărbunești, and Mitu shared a last glass with Anghel, then returned to Cernădia, inspirited and in a good mood.

He liked meeting people and spending time with them. But this discussion, he said to himself, still hadn't helped him make up his mind. Quite the contrary, his thoughts were even more confused than before.

Chapter 64

Mitu and Gheorghe, his eldest, were out on the brook-side coppice when their neighbor, Ion Todea, told them over the fence that France had capitulated to Germany. He had expected it, since all the newspapers wrote about the German advances every day, but a strange feeling of uncertainty still enveloped him. He didn't know whether he should be happy.

He wondered what was to come next. He sat down by a tree chewing on a twig and staring at the water. As of yet, the rumble of the conflagration was still far away, he needn't worry, but things were so grim, anything could happen. And since he had gone through so much in his life already, both good and bad, he always put bad first.

Gheorghe was playing with some pebbles patiently waiting by his father's side. At last, seeing that Mitu wasn't even moving, he dared to say:

"Dad, can you talk to me a bit?"

He looked surprised at the boy. Gheorghe never bothered him when he was busy, but truth be told, when they were together, Mitu always told him all kinds of stories or tried to teach him English. "He's probably bored, the poor boy, I've forgotten all about him..."

"Well, lil' Gheorghe, there's a big war happening in the world."

The boy knew. He had heard lots about it—at home, in the neighborhood, everywhere. Lately, he and his friends were playing with pretend machine guns or rifles and pistols made out of tree branches.

"Maybe we can get our hands on a machine gun and shoot some real bullets, dad! Oh, how I'd like that!"

Mitu wanted to explain how evil war was but gave up and went back to his thoughts. He rose from the grass, took Gheorghe, and set out towards the house. Now things were quite different from the time he had fought in France against Germany. This time, the Germans had conquered France almost completely; they hadn't retreated like in Meuse-Argonne! They had taken over Paris. Wehrmacht's flag planted right into Trocadéro25F*! Who could have imagined it?

He could picture the Germans' unbelievable happiness at that moment! It was probably similar to what he had felt when, just as he was preparing to get out of the trenches, he heard "The war is over!" Were he a German today, he'd jump with joy hugging people out in the streets!

He remembered Walter, his only employee at "Mitu & Olga's Store," telling him about the poverty in Germany and the hatred felt by the Germans towards the countries that had forced them to sign the Treaty of Versailles. Look at that, his wishes were coming true: a fellow had waged war on the world to lift the Germans up from their misery. Whatever was Walter doing

---

* To humiliate France, Hitler ordered that the French capitulation be signed in the same railroad car where Germany was forced to sign the Treaty of Versailles two decades before.

now? Sure, he was drunk with happiness! Maybe he was fighting on the front...

"My Gheorghe, you can never know on whose side to be; one day you're up, the next you're down, whether you're a country or a person, damn it. Don't ever get yourself into politics, you hear? Never! Listen to your father, 'cause I know what I'm saying!"

The child nodded without understanding much and lagged a few steps behind. His father seemed gloomy, so he didn't want to trouble him even more that day. Mitu looked back and seeing how the boy was dressed—the sailor outfit that he had outgrown, but still loved to wear—he remembered Olga all of a sudden. "God, so much time has passed!"

"Hurry up, what's the matter with you?" he asked harshly.

The child rushed forward and Mitu noticed a stain on the sleeve. "How come I didn't see it before?" he became irritated, forgetting all about the war.

"Oh, you little imp," he frowned, "Didn't I tell you so many times to be careful with this suit or I'd kick the daylight outta of you? How did you get it dirty? Now you're wearing it, when Sandu grows up, he'll wear it, and if the good Lord gives me more sons, they'll wear it too, you understand?"

The boy nodded scared and tried to rub the blot off but couldn't.

"Leave it alone before you make it worse; maybe your mother can clean it at home."

He walked ahead, mumbling to himself, and thoughts about the war crept back in his mind. Would the Germans conquer London? Would they come to Romania? What would Russia do? What about the Americans? What would happen with Cernădia? Would they be dragged into the fire as well?

Once at home, he didn't waste any time and rushed to the tavern. He spoke with some people for a while and drank half a bottle of wine. He thought of going to see Bălăloaica—strangely enough, he always longed for women when bad things were happening in the world—but then remembered her husband was home from Craiova.

He spent the whole next day at the inn, talking with the others, reading newspapers, and indulging in petty politics.

The third day the same. And the fourth and the fifth. Among others, he felt protected.

He had the first confirmation to his fears on the sixth day: Romania lost Bessarabia. The news distressed him so profoundly he started thinking how to sell his things fast and get the money for the trip to America.

Then, blow after blow. "Disaster is nearing," he thought seeing the terrifying things occurring in the world. Romania had fallen under the hacking knives of the world's most powerful forces, butchering her mercilessly. "Here, this piece is yours! Here you go, this one's for you! And that's yours!" In a few days, the country had lost Bessarabia, Snake Island, the Quadrilateral and half of Transylvania.

What kind of unforgivable sins needed such harsh atonement? Why was God's punishment so cruel...he wondered, looking dumbfounded at the map of The Greater Romania, a mere scrap of what it used to be. What was to come next?

The world had changed at its foundations in just a few days. The atmosphere was quite tense in the village. The hubbub from the tavern had been replaced by an unnatural silence. The villagers sat in groups of two or three, reading newspapers.

What was going to happen with the millions of Romanians from Bessarabia, Bucovina and Transylvania? Would they come back to their native land, would they leave their homes and everything behind to escape persecution as the French had done during the Great War? During the Argone Offensive, he had seen entire villages deserted, all of their inhabitants having fled every which way.

"It's happening all over again!" People were in grave danger, and he, who had seen it all before, had to protect his family.

It was clear: their place was no longer in Cernădia! They belonged in a country out of disaster's way.

He still had some time. He could still take his family and all of their things, go to some port and embark for the New World. The wisest thing he could do now was go back to America with Maria and the kids.

He wasn't the only one struggling with the situation. In fact, there were a few people that had lost their minds over it. Panaitescu had begun talking to himself and fending off invisible dogs with his cane out on the street. When Mitu met him in Novaci once, he was mumbling to himself, staggering on his feet, staring blankly ahead, cursing people that didn't give him way, hassling whoever he met, stopping brusquely every now and then as though some formidable idea struck him.

"We need to rise up and get back our land!" he unleashed himself. "We can't lose any more time! We need to align with the Axis to regain what they took from us by force!" his face contorted with great worry as he passed Mitu like a ghost.

Maria couldn't understand Mitu's apprehension. She saw his constantly muttering to himself in the yard or talking with people, but she couldn't figure out why he was making such a big deal out of the whole thing. Their village was the same as before, and she couldn't care less that German planes were flying over France. She was upset over Bessarabia—how couldn't she be?—and Bucovina, and Transylvania and Quadrilateral, but she thought they would be returned to Romania once things settled down.

Mitu thought otherwise.

"Maria, we need to be as cautious as we can, because it will be disaster and bloodshed. A whole lot of it!"

"Oh, come on Mitu, it won't be that bad...we're some poor country folk, what would they want with us."

But he knew better. He could see what was happening around him. The times were troubled: The King had abdicated;26F[*] Ciorogaru had stopped in Novaci one night but had disappeared again; some said he went to help with the Legion's taking over the governing and the country's alliance with Germany.

What he couldn't even imagine before was now taking place right before his eyes. The world was at war again, and Romania had been caught up in the middle. He needed to leave. He needed to go as far away as possible.

---

[*] The National Legionnaire State governed Romania between June 9, 1940 and November 1, 1941 through the alliance between the Iron Guard (led by Horia Sima) and Prime Minister Ion Antonescu.

THE INFIRMITY

Chapter 65

Mitu prepared arduously for his return to America over the following days. He gathered all his savings, went to see all those who owed him money, tried to lease out all his land from Cernădia, and sold a few things he no longer needed at the market in Novaci. He told his brother Ghiţă he was going to leave him his horse upon his departure and began teaching Maria some English.

Up in Rânca he had a piece of land that he had never used for anything. He now wanted to lease it as well—any penny was helpful—so, one morning he decided to go up there.

He yoked the oxen to the carriage and called Gheorghe to go along; he always took his eldest with him to teach him how to manage a household.

The boy was nowhere to be found.

"Where's that brat?" he yelled at Maria. "I want to take him with me up in the mountains. Maybe I can lease out that piece of land and buy some timber to sell it in Târgu-Jiu. Make a little more money for the trip."

"Don't know where. Maybe down by Boţota..."

Mitu furrowed his brow and snorted, "I'm going to be late because of him now!" He left the carriage in the middle of the yard and sat down on a stool.

"His head is full of shenanigans! Instead of helping around the house he's out having 'fun,' goddamn it! Maybe he was born a prince and I didn't know about it! When I need him, he's nowhere to be found! Look at that, I'm wasting precious time waiting for his ass!" he said raving mad, then took a bottle of *ţuică* and began drinking.

"Well, he didn't know you needed him."

"He didn't know—my ass!" he raised his voice. "This boy needs to grow up and be responsible, not tramp about all day like a bum."

The child showed up half an hour later, coming through the garden in the back. He sneaked through the corn tufts and tried to slip inside the house. Mitu saw him and called him harshly.

"Gheorghe, where have you been? Been here waitin' for you!"

"I went to see Miticuţă, Dad."

"The hell you did! Move your ass! Get up in the carriage to go to Rânca!"

The boy gave him a fearful look. He wanted to avoid his father but hadn't been able to. He didn't know how to escape the trouble that had befallen him. He was returning from the coppice where fate hadn't been favorable; he had tumbled in a puddle and dirtied the sailor suit. He had tried to clean the stains, washing them with plenty of water, but he only had managed to make them worse.

"What did you do? How did you get your clothes so dirty?" Mitu asked him irritated.

"I didn't mean to, dad! I fell in Boţota, Miticuţă pushed me; I swear it's not my fault!"

Mitu watched him befuddled. He had told the boy thousands of times to be careful with that outfit! He grabbed him by an ear, almost lifting him from the ground.

"Here you go! This'll teach you!"

The boy hunched in pain and burst into tears.

"It wasn't my fault, dad, I swear!"

"I told you so many times, you lump, to care for this outfit with your life! Didn't I tell you that?" Mitu howled.

Maria came from the kitchen when she heard the ruckus outside.

"Gheorghe, get out of here, run now!"

The child didn't have enough time to move as Mitu hit him violently in the head dropping him to the ground.

Reeling from the pain, he tried to get up but was stunned with fear. He was on his hands and knees. Mitu got close, pulled out the belt off his trousers, and struck him.

"Here you go! Here!"

"Leave him alone, man, you're gonna kill him!" Maria yelled, trying to push him to the side.

"Woman, get away or I'll split your head in two! Don't come over here! Don't you dare tell me what to do!"

"Don't hit me, dad, please, I won't do it again! Don't hit me anymore!" Gheorghe kept screaming.

Mitu no longer heard or saw anything. He was foaming at the mouth, hitting with fury. The sailor outfit, destroyed by the brat!

"Here, so next time you'll think twice before messing it up again!" he barely croaked.

Maria came between them, throwing herself over Gheorghe to protect him.

"Hit me, don't hit the child, kill me if you have to. What did the boy do to you? Huh, what? Have you lost your mind?"

Mitu lifted her up by the hair.

"I'll teach you to tell me what to do, you wretched woman!" he howled, then threw himself on her and ripped off her blouse. Maria screamed, covering her breasts, while Gheorghe took advantage of the reprieve to dash out to the garden.

"Leave me alone, you devil," she confronted him, facing him fiercely. "Why did you marry me if you're still thinking about that whore? Huh? Why? Go to her, you pig, go to America and look for her; me and the kids are staying here!"

Anger blinded Mitu. He pinned her on the floor and tore off her clothes.

"Wretched, goddamned woman," he kept calling her in a low and measured voice, pulling her from the hair all the way to the summer kitchen. He grabbed some rope for tethering cattle, tied her hands, then fastened her to a wooden pole. When he finished, he looked at her ready to punch her. The woman's face blanched with fear.

"You'd better not be here when I come back, or I'll kill you!" he growled through his teeth, then climbed in the carriage and left to Novaci mumbling horrific, mind-numbing curses.

He went to take Gicu and Titi along. "To have someone I can vent to, goddamn it!" He told them about the incident with Gheorghe but didn't mention that he had left Maria naked and tied to a pole. "Dirty laundry is best done in the family! She deserved it, goddamn her! The nerve on her, to come between me and my brat!"

They took the roundabout way to the foot of Păpuşa, then turned towards Tigvele, a dry, stony mountain, where the forest rangers generally brought firewood for sale. After about an hour of shopping around and idle chatting sprinkled aplenty with *ţuică*, they piled up the carriage with wooden planks and started leisurely back towards the house. They stopped off to breathe a little on the jagged rocks of the Urdele Hill. From there, Mitu was planning on going to a few sheep farms to try to lease out the rest of his land. Gicu plopped himself down on an ottoman-shaped boulder, uncorked a bottle of wine, and began drinking. In the balmy air, the alcohol slipped down like butter.

"This is the life to live: food aplenty, red wine, free as a bird in these mountains! And our Fiddler wants to go back to America and leave us alone. He must be crazy!"

He wanted to answer, but his mind was too foggy from the booze to say even a few words. He had been drinking from early in the morning, and now was staggering on his feet. He hoisted himself up from the grass and went a bit farther.

"Wait a tick, I need to take a piss."

His oxen were grazing untethered and were moving slowly away, so he went to bring them back.

"Whoa, goddamn you, whoa!"

He stopped right in front of them, then he turned his back at them and unzipped his pants, watching the stream of urine drip on the boulders through half open eyes. He was almost done when one of the oxen gored him in the back—a short but violent hit that struck him like lightning. He tumbled down, hitting himself against stumps, stones and trees, until he stopped at the bottom of a ravine, where he lay flat and motionless.

"Mitu!" Gicu called out. "Mitu! Titi, come quick!" he turned to his brother, "Mitu fell in the ravine!"

They ran to get him. They lifted him up from his underarms and dragged him up to the road. Mitu was moaning and groaning, mumbling unintelligibly.

"What happened, did you break something? Tell us where it hurts!"

"The leg, my leg hurts," he said weakly.

Gicu cut the pants with a knife, then jumped back at the sight of his wound. The white reddish bone protruded through the flesh, broken in half, dripping blood.

"We need to take him to a doctor right away! Let's tie it with something!" They bound him above the fracture and lifted him up in the carriage.

"Niculescu's not here. I know he went to Râmnic for a week. But maybe Hoity can see him. If he loses too much blood, he'll die, God forbid!" said Gicu.

The door of the clinic in Novaci was locked. Panait had left without telling anyone where he was. Gicu rushed to his house, but his wife shook her head.

"I don't know where he is; I thought he was at the clinic. Did you try the tavern?"

Panait wasn't there either.

"Did you see the assistant by chance? Mitu the Fiddler from Cernădia had an accident in the mountains and needs splints."

A few of the villagers were gazing at them with bloodshot eyes.

"What happened?"

"The oxen gored him and he fell down the cliffs. He broke his leg—the bone's coming through the flesh!"

"Tsk, tsk, tsk! Who here knows where Hoity is?"

The men shrugged. "Didn't see him."

Gicu left the tavern and was about to ask at the market, when Moroşan, one of the men inside, reached him from behind and told him secretively:

"Go back to the dispensary and knock four times, wait a bit, then knock again four times. Hoity's in there."

He thanked him quickly and hurried to the clinic.

Hoity's long nose peered through the door ajar a few moments later.

"What do you want?" he asked impatiently.

"Good thing we found you. We have Mitu the Fiddler in the carriage; he had an accident up in Urdele and broke his leg—it's really bad."

The assistant opened the door all the way and waved them in. They grabbed Mitu by the shoulders and put him on the table. Gicu looked around to see the woman. He was very curious to see who she was and hadn't had the time to ask Moroşan. The door to Niculescu's office was closed, so he thought that whoever she was, she must have been hiding in there.

The assistant shook his head at the sight of Mitu's leg. He changed the rubber tie above the wound, cleaned it up with some rubbing alcohol, dressed it, then told them to take him straight to Târgu-Jiu.

"Not even the doctor could have done anything if he'd been here. And he's gone to Vâlcea anyway, so..."

Gicu went to borrow a horse-drawn carriage from someone across the road, placed Mitu on some blankets, and rushed to Târgu-Jiu.

When they reached the hospital late at night, Mitu was taken straight to surgery.

Chapter 66

The accident left Mitu with a lame leg. With that, his plans of going to America were shattered. The surgery had saved his leg, but it had left it seven inches shorter, changing him from a man in his prime into a cripple.

Maria came to see him every day in the hospital. Sometimes she brought Gheorghe along, who felt guilty for what had happened and kept giving his father rueful looks. After Mitu had left, he had come back from the garden, untied his mother, and thrown a blanket over her. He had begun crying hysterically, swearing he'd never touch the sailor suit ever again, since it only brought him trouble.

Maria forgave Mitu the moment she learned about the accident. Actually, she was used to Mitu's outbursts, which she no longer took to heart. All men in Cernădia were like that, especially when drinking. She didn't know of any married woman who hadn't been beaten by her husband. Compared to others, she was quite lucky; Mitu hit her very rarely, and when he did it, he had some well-founded reason for it. When getting drunk, he'd usually turn to himself in a sullen disposition and raise his voice at all family members but wouldn't hit anyone. And she had also noticed something else; Mitu didn't drink all the time, like others. He drank for a while, then stopped and didn't even taste alcohol for a few weeks, months sometimes. That's how she would have liked him to be all the time because that's when he was the best husband in the world. He was warm with her, good-natured with the children, playing the violin, joking with them, a joy to be around.

The day he left the hospital, Mitu was silent the whole way home. Maria had come to pick him up with Gheorghe and Sandu. He struggled to get in the carriage and kept his head in his hands the whole way.

Then he closed himself inside the house and stared at the ceiling all day, barely eating and not speaking with anyone. He couldn't bear the thought that he had become an old man at only forty-five. *Why did God punish me like this? Why?* He was ashamed to leave the house to be seen in crutches. Once in a while, people came by to ask him to play for weddings, but he refused them all. He couldn't imagine tottering around, barely maintaining his balance for the whole world to see him.

The first time he walked outside the house on his own feet, of his own will, was when Maria gave birth to their third child Micu. He hoisted himself up from the bed and looked at the baby, waved his hand dismissively, and walked uncertain to the front gate careful not to misplace his crutch and slip. He looked down the road, came back just as uncertain, and sat down on the stoop, ignoring everything around him.

Slowly by slowly, he got used to the cane, but that didn't lift him from desolation. On the contrary, as the pain subsided, his shoulders hunched forward more and more, giving him the defeated air of a man who had given up, "I'm done trying, just let me die."

Out in the world, the war kept raging on. While he had been bed-ridden, things had taken an unbelievable turn: Hitler had invaded Russia, sending there more than five million soldiers27F[*].

All that was meaningless to him. In fact, deep inside, he hoped disaster would sweep over Romania. He wanted massacres, butchering of people that would bring about his end as well, so he wouldn't have to wake up every morning and be forced to grab the crutch.

The evil burning him from the inside kept pushing him to the cellar as if he were under a spell. In there, the *țuică* would benumb his grief for a few hours. He had plenty of alcohol, weighed in tons, not gallons. The storage space was filled with wicker demijohns and barrels of all kinds, neatly organized according to the quality of the alcohol they held and carefully sealed with waxed corks. On the shelves, filed in army rows, there were many bottles of sweetish, clear *țuică*. Out of superstition he never left a glass empty all the way, so that good luck wouldn't go away—as much as he still had—but filled it anew when there was still some left in it.

Wherever he went, he dragged his violin along. Music was akin to alcohol, with the same dizzying effect, sending him to indescribable worlds, extracting from him, on occasion, a satisfied sigh.

His moments of joy were very short lived. He would sometimes stop in the middle of a song, clenching his fists in despair, weeping for America, and telling himself he would die soon.

"I'm a cripple; I'd rather hang myself than live like this until the end of my days. Oh, my God in Heaven, why did you blind my mind and made me come back here?"

When springtime came and it got warmer outside, he began playing in his front yard. He'd sit in his porch sliding the bow on the strings all day long till late into the night. Passersby would stop in front of his house to listen.

"Good day, Mitu! Keep on playing that great music of yours."

He never answered and kept on playing as if they weren't even there. "The poor Fiddler lost his mind since he broke his leg," they'd whisper.

The gossip left him unaffected. In fact, nothing around him made an impression on him anymore. While he had been suffering both physically and spiritually, Marshal Antonescu had sent hundreds of thousands of Romanian soldiers to fight in Russia along with the Germans. During their triumphant trip to Stalingrad, the Romanian Army had crossed the Prut River, had recovered Bessarabia and Bucovina and had annexed the Soviet lands to the east of the Dniester River, culminating with the seizing of Odessa. None of those stirred him; his bitterness trampled all.

The songs he played those days were not his old ones. He'd play a *doina* once in a while, as though by mistake, but, each time he picked up the violin, he dabbled in jazz or Dixieland music, composing lyrics in English, which he

---

[*] Romania's contribution of troops to Operation Barbarossa (the invasion of U.S.S.R by the Axis Powers) was enormous, and was second only to Nazi Germany's itself.

sang in a soft whisper. He named one of those songs *America, my only love*, and he'd play it a few times a day, always tearing up on the last lyrics.

I wish I had not been so weak
To give you up and leave you like a coward
Forgive me if I was mind sick
For I have never truly wanted to depart.

I wish I'd never said "so long"
For you, my soul is filled with true devotion,
God, take me back where I belong
Which is not here, but right across the ocean.

For a long time, the only people he saw were Julea and Cirică. He spent his nights with them—not in the jovial atmosphere from before, but in a state of sadness that spread to everyone present. When he was with them, he felt transposed into a different world; he played continuously, stopping only for a swig of alcohol. He moved his fingers on the strings until they turned purple.

His life was going down a destructive path. In the morning he would grab a quick bite to eat in the kitchen, throw the kids askance looks, curse Maria for no reason, then he would go into the cellar to come out only in the evening when Julea and Cirică visited him.

Chapter 67

What lifted Mitu from his state of complete despondency was not Maria, not the kids, not Bălăloaica, whom he hadn't visited since the accident out of embarrassment for his leg wound, nor the cellar, but something of great meaning to the whole world: the twists of the war.

What brought him afloat, as Maria said when she saw him back to his daily chores, was the imminent danger threatening Romania after the Axis' devastating defeat in the Battle of Stalingrad.28F[*] In the winter of 1943, when the scale tipped to the Allied forces' favor, Mitu, as uninformed as he had been, felt tightness in his heart.

The withdrawal of the Romanian troupes from Russia filled him with inquietude. It had been easy before not to think of anything else besides his personal trouble because Romania hadn't been threatened, and the soldiers kept advancing towards the east. But now Germany was starting to show signs of weakness! And not just that! His America—once again reproving his unpardonable mistake of giving her up—was now bombing oil refineries in Ploieşti!

He was becoming afraid, a clear sign he was back to life. The fear he had felt at the beginning of the war—for his children, for Maria, for his country— lately buried in the bitterness of his accident, was sprouting up in his heart again. The front was shifting from the east to the west each day, squeezing the middle of the continent in a vice. What was going to happen with them?

The first person he visited after two years of self-imposed home arrest was Flitan. It was a few days after the August 23rd Act, when the country turned against the Germans, forcing them to successive fallbacks west and making them lose control over the Carpathians and the Gate of Focşani. Seeing all these, Mitu couldn't bear it anymore; he felt the need to talk with someone about all those things, as hard as it might have been for him.

Lately he had gone out in the village but only to buy a few things from the store and he never spent more time there than he needed to. He felt everyone's burning stares on his crutches and his bum leg.

Flitan had tried visiting him after the accident thinking that a person in trouble should have company to overcome the grief more easily. But Mitu hadn't shown himself too keen on the idea, letting him guess he was not in the mood for visitors.

Anghel hadn't gotten upset. But now, that Mitu was finally there, he first thought to scold him for taking two years for a visit, but seeing him leaning against the cane, humble and slightly embarrassed, he welcomed him with a big smile on his face.

---

[*] The Battle of Stalingrad was one of the bloodiest in modern history, with combined casualties estimated at 1.5 million. Out of these, 150000 were Romanian soldiers, representing half of the active troops (31 divisions). After these catastrophic losses, the Romanian Army never fully recovered, fighting desperately and only in defensive during their retreat to Romania.

"Oh man, back among the living?"

"I wouldn't wish on my worst enemy to go through what I did, Flitan. Not even my enemies...look what's become of me! I can barely walk! I can't work, I can't move, I need to pay people to bring me firewood and do things around the house, mend my fences, this fucking life!"

Flitan tried to get his mind off things.

"Now why are you standing there in the gate? Come inside! I have some *țuică*... not even in America have you tasted something that good!" he instantly regretted mentioning America knowing how Mitu longed for it.

Mitu walked in placing his cane wherever he felt the ground was unyielding and struggled to sit on a chair.

"Well Flitan, I have an excuse on account of my leg, but why don't you fix things around your house?" he pointed to the gate hanging on one hinge. It had been that way for years kept together only with a wire.

"So what? People know me..."

"Yeah, they knew you as a thrifty householder, but now they'll say you're a lazybones, keeping your gate together with a piece of thread like a widow!"

Flitan smiled. The truth was he really couldn't care less what people said about him. He had so much more land than anyone there, it was natural for people to talk behind his back. All rich people were envied by those poor, ain't that the truth! Not to mention that he had recently bought himself a new automobile, a Buick! Only three people had a car in the whole area: the mayor of Novaci, Square Câlnici, and himself!

"Ileana, Măriuța, fetch some *țuică* for Mitu, quickly!" he called out to his daughters somewhere in the house. Măriuța showed up in the door, then disappeared and came back with a bottle and two glasses.

"Good day, old fogy," she greeted him while filling the glasses.

Mitu gave her a long look and some kind of a hiccup shook him. Măriuța was very beautiful, only sixteen, bursting with life and energy. "If only I had the strength I used to..."

"Go ahead and fry some pork meat and sausages quick!" Flitan said curtly, feigning discontent with her domestic prowess.

But Mitu wasn't there for pork meat and sausages, so he refused.

"No, there's no need, I just ate, let's just drink, I'm not hungry. Don't worry Măriuța, don't put anything on the stove, I didn't come for that!"

Flitan pulled his chair closer and raised his glass.

"To better times ahead, Mitu."

"Hear, hear," he agreed uncertainly, "to the long life of your children, and may they have better luck than all of us together! They've grown up so beautiful, all of them: Tiberică, Măriuța, Ileana!"

"From your lips to God's ears," Flitan said. "Do you know anything of Ciorogaru anymore?"

Mitu shrugged. He hadn't heard of him in quite some time.

"Well, maybe he's in Bucharest, how should I know? I think he came from Germany a while back and remained in the capital, but I haven't heard anything since."

"What do you think, is he in this thing...with the Jews?" Flitan asked in a hushed voice.

Mitu frowned and became thoughtful. A wrinkle, appeared between his eyes in the last six months, deepened even more.

"I, for one, don't think so. He had something against the government."

"But you heard how he'd speak about the Jews when we used to go to his place."

"Why do you ask?"

"I don't know...I remembered him when I saw you."

Mitu was quiet for a while. The newspapers had reported the frightful news that during the rebellion three years before, when the Guard had been chased away by Marshal Antonescu, the legionnaires had butchered Jewish people, and that had marked him profoundly. They had undressed women and cut their breasts with knives and hanged children by hooks in slaughterhouses. Ciorogaru had been in Bucharest during that time, but Mitu couldn't believe his involvement in it.

"Flitan, I don't think Gică Ciorogaru could kill or torture, I gotta tell you. He's not the kind of person to cause such harm unto others."

"Do you remember how we used to visit him in Novaci a few years back? Had you joined the Legion then, you would've been dead now. Out of all those in high positions, only Sima's still alive."

"Yeah, like I can compare myself to Sima, schooled and powerful like that. And didn't I say I'd never get myself into politics? And I wouldn't, even if the king himself made me a minister! I don't wanna die before my time; whatever I have left...I'm not getting into any politics!"

Flitan squirmed in his chair and scratched his pate. He would have liked some top responsibilities in the community since helping others gave him great satisfaction, but he had to agree with Mitu's words.

"Right you are. They're dropping like flies over there at the top on all sides. Codreanu, Duca, Iorga...you never know. And what's going to happen with us? With these Germans and all..."

"Good thing we chased the Germans out of the country!" Mitu agreed bitterly. "They dried us of our crude oil and other resources, the newspapers write that we gave them everything for free! At first I was happy when we were on their side, but now look where it's gotten us. We're poor and starved. The government printed out money to give to the people and everything went up in prices. A sack of corn has doubled in only three months. That's just unheard of! I'm not even doing all that bad, you either, but what about all those who have no land, how are they managing? They'll riot when they can't take it anymore!"

Flitan was about to drink the last of the bottle, but Mitu's excitement stopped him in his tracks.

"Do you know what I'm afraid of? I'm afraid the peasants will rise up asking for land and I'm gonna lose everything I've made! If that happens to me, I'm gonna kill myself. And if the Russians come, they'll take away everything we have!"

"Yes, they're going to hack us to pieces even worse than last time because now we need to pay for reparations. That's what my employee from Detroit, Walter, told me happened with Germany after the Great War, that's what brought it to starvation."

Flitan sighed deeply.

"You're right...you're right. But for the time being, bottoms up, Mitu."

THE RUSSIANS

Chapter 68

Russian tanks showed up in Rânca on a dry autumn morning. They came from the other side of the mountain, passing by Tigvele, rolling in a long file, thudding on the stony road, going around Păpuşa, and meandering to Novaci.

Gheorghe and Sandu were up there for firewood—Sandu more as an observer as at his eight years of age he was too young for such a chore.

When they saw the convoy far away, they stopped working and watched the cloud of dust unfurling at the horizon. The rumble reaching their ears didn't scare them. The other people threw hatchets and chain saws up in the air and started screaming as loudly as they could, "The Russians are coming! Run, the Russians are coming!" then scurried to their carriages, trying to rush away.

"Go Gheorghe, stop lollygagging; they'll kill you if they get you!" somebody yelled.

The boy jumped in the carriage and prodded the horse.

"Come, Sandu, quick, climb on!"

His brother went in the back and he whipped the horse trying to reach the others ahead. The fear had finally spread to him as well, making him turn his head to see what was happening. The tanks had reached the top of the mountains and had stopped.

"They're waiting for all of them to gather," the boy thought to himself urging the horse.

Mitu was in the front yard when the children arrived flushed with fear.

"What happened to you?" he asked seeing their agitated state.

"Dad, the Russians are coming, they're up in the mountains, by Păpuşa!"

Maria came out quickly from the kitchen. Mitu's skin shriveled in goose bumps. He began shaking and raised his hands to his temples to stop the stream of images of war, trenches, Meuse-Argonne, tanks rolling down Pennsylvania Avenue to the White House, inundating him.

"Are you sure?"

"Yes Dad, we saw the tanks, we heard them; everybody stopped working and ran! Bobotează told us to run and hide wherever we could because if they caught us, they'd kill us. What are we gonna do, dad?"

Mitu turned to Maria.

"Woman, grab a satchel, fill it fast with some bread, ham, some onions, to give it to the boys. Gheorghe you take Sandu and Micu and hide in the cornfields up on the hill. Don't get out of there until I come to call you. Maria, you go across the river over at Sabin's wife. Hide well because if they catch you, they'll rape you because you're pretty, and I won't take you back afterward!"

The woman ran inside the house wringing her hands, "My God in heaven, what have I done wrong, please get me out of this!"

Right then, Flitan and his children showed up at their gate. Tiberică was hauling a wooden trunk, red in the face like a lobster from the effort.

"Mitu, Mitroi saw the Russians up on the hill! They're coming in convoys with cars, trunks, and on foot. He said there's lots of them."

"Where did you say he saw them, up on the hill?"

"Yes, up there. Two of them got inside Miuţă's house. Mitu, they're going to kill my children if they come to my house, because they'll think I'm a kulak! What do I do? What do I do?"

Mitu was speechless. He couldn't send his boys to hide up on the hill if Mitroi saw the Russians going over there. And how could he help the Flitans when he didn't know how to help his own family?

"Listen," he decided, "we hide your children in my attic. Tiberică go up there with Ileana and Mãriuţa, cover yourselves up with hey, and lay still until I call you out. You hear?"

"Yes, old fogy, yes," they children quickly nodded and climbed the ladder then buried themselves in hey.

Flitan asked him to hide his trunk.

"I have a few things of value in there. You know, whatever I managed to put aside along the years. They'll look everywhere at my place when they see my house. Maybe they'll leave yours alone."

Mitu looked disconcerted at the trunk, then hoisted it up, and handed it to Tiberică.

"Boy, take it and stash it up there with you. Don't come out until I call you, got it? If I yell to you to run, jump out on the other side, and run as fast as you can through the cornfields, but on the left side, not by the water because I think that's where they'll come. Don't show yourselves by the bridge under any circumstance, you hear?"

The children agreed docilely and disappeared under the dried grass from the attic. They were shaking like leaves.

"What are you going to do with yours, Mitu, aren't you going to send them up in the attic?" Flitan asked looking at Gheorghe and Sandu who hadn't moved from the porch.

"What can I do? I'll keep them in the front yard. If they come and see them, they'll think we have nothing to hide and maybe won't think to search around. That way I get away and you get away."

Flitan crossed himself and mumbled a short prayer, then rushed back to his house.

The Russians showed up in Cernãdia about an hour later. Maria had hidden at Sabin's house, and Micu and Sandu were playing in the front yard with a rag ball, oblivious to the calamity threatening them. Gheorghe was still on a stool in the summer kitchen and Mitu was walking in the yard leaning on his crutch and smoking.

The village had been deserted in a hurry. There wasn't a soul to be seen, as though everyone had disappeared into thin air. Only Mitu's family was in the front yard.

Nothing happened for a while. Mitu expected a whole army to march in, but the long convoys were going straight to Novaci, without making the turn towards Cernădia. Only a few military jeeps came into the village, and all of them stopped in the center. About twenty soldiers climbed out and broke down the door of the tavern, which crumbled like a piece of cardboard. They rummaged inside then went scouring through people's homes.

Only one Russian came up the road to their house. Mitu saw him as he turned from the main road, panting with his rifle on his back, looking in people's yards, lagging in front of each gate, searching through sheds and cellars, stuffing whatever he found in his bag, then moving slowly to the next house.

Mitu was now certain he was going to search his attic, so he went close to the shed and whispered to the children.

"Run through the back the way I told you because they're coming inside, and they'll find you. Run now and stay hidden in the cornfield."

Flitan's children jumped out and ran through the back. Tiberică, usually the first to flee, struggled behind his sisters dragging the trunk.

When the Russian reached the gate, the children were far away, but in their hurry, had forgotten to stay hidden in the corn and could be seen running up the hill.

Mitu tried to greet the soldier with a small smile the way he had learned in America, but the man gave him fierce look, mumbled something unintelligible, and aimed his rifle at him signaling him to open his cellar. He went inside and rummaged around, cursing the slim pickings. After that, he went up in the attic and raked through the hay. He peered through an opening in the back and saw Flitan's children going up the hill.

"*Blyad!*" he screamed and jumped from the attic, storming by Mitu and Gheorghe as if they weren't even there. Thinking the soldier was after him, Sandu took off running up the road, screaming, but the soldier passed him without even looking at him.

"*Zamri! Stoyat!*" he yelled and ran. He jumped over a fence then another, then slowed down at the foot of the steep hill. His fatigue was greater than his will to catch the children, so he stopped out of breath.

"*Ruki v verh ili ya strelyayu!*" he yelled firing up in the air.

The shot rang out like thunder in the silence. The children froze, shaking with terror, not daring to look back. Tiberică put the trunk down and lifted his arms above his head, but his knees gave in and he fell.

The Russian approached them mumbling with the bayonet aimed ahead. When he reached them, he howled something then gestured at them to return to Mitu's house.

"*Ya tebya prikonchu, suchonok!*" he screamed as they entered the yard, then pushed them with their backs against the wall of the shed. He backed up a few feet and took aim targeting Măriuţa's forehead. The girl's body softened with terror and a thin stream of liquid flowed down her legs gathering in a small puddle. Her teeth were clattering like a woodpecker's chuck.

Her fright made the Russian sneer contently; he hoisted his rifle on the shoulder then turned to Mitu.

"*Chto v etoy sumke! Skazhi mne!*"

Mitu raised his shoulders.

"*Eto tvoi deti?*" he continued.

Mitu shrugged again and tried to appease him.

"Please leave us alone, sir, please! I am a fighter against exploitation, too! I was a member of the Anti-Usury League! I fought for justice and help for the country folk!"

But the Russian, who didn't understand a word of Romanian anyway, had turned his attention onto something else; he had kicked Flitan's trunk, which had opened spilling bills, coins, silver spoons, and jewelry everywhere.

When he saw that, he turned fiercely to Mitu.

"*Eto chto, durak? Chye eto? Prikonchu, yesli ne skazhesh!*"

Mitu shrugged again.

"Not my trunk, not my children. Take it and leave us alone!"

The Russian was unyielding. He pulled out his rifle and aimed it at Tiberică. The boy backed up all the way to the wall of the shed and remained there. The soldier loaded the gun and aimed at him, sneering cruelly.

"*Sir, they're not my children! Take the money and leave us alone, please, don't harm them!*" Mitu begged him in English, struck by a flash of inspiration to use a language other than Romanian.

The Russian turned around surprised, his eyes big with wonder.

"*You English? Me English little!*"

"*Yes, English, English!*" Mitu livened up. "*I was an American soldier in the Great War! I fought against the Germans! Hold on a second, please, will you, I'll be right back!*"

The Russian hadn't understood much but waited with his gun loaded while Mitu rushed inside. He came back with his war veteran certificate and showed it to him. The Russian looked at it carefully, and his face lit up when he figured out what he was reading.

"*Friend! Friend! Nazi enemy! Friend!*"

"*Yes, yes, I hate Nazis, I hate the Germans! I hate them all!*"

"*Yes, friend, me kill many!*" the Russian added and got close to kiss Mitu on the cheeks, then began rummaging through the trunk.

"*Your childs?*" he pointed to Sandu, who had meanwhile come back from the road and was standing by the fence not knowing whether to be scared or not. Gheorghe hadn't moved from the porch pretending he was doing something with Micu.

"*Yes, my sons, yes sir! And they are their friends, they play together!*" Mitu answered pointing to Flitan's children.

The soldier signaled Sandu to come to him, but the boy wasn't moving from the fence.

"Move over here like he told you!" Mitu hissed at him.

"*Derzhi!*" the Russian handed him some money from the trunk. "*I vi dvoye, vozmite!*" he gave Mitu a fistful of bills. After he finished sharing some of the trunk's contents, he stuffed the rest in his pockets and turned to Flitan's children. He made a menacing gesture at Tiberică and spat on him, then smacked him across the face.

"*Tvoyu mat, suka! Begi ili ya tebya grohnu!*" he flared up at them, signaling them to start running.

"Run as fast as you can, get away now, and don't stop till you make it to the top of the hill!" Mitu told the children.

They dashed from the yard. The Russian went after them, then stopped and fired a shot in the air. The children were running at a breakneck pace, stumbling over boulders and stumps, and screaming.

"Help, he's gonna kill us, he's gonna kill us!"

The soldier wasn't interested in them any longer. Contented they were good and scared, he turned to Mitu, in which he now saw a friend, to bid him farewell.

"*Me friend, bye. Me come to eat. See cow and come kill her. Me comrades need food. Food?*"

"*Sure, my friend, sure!*" Mitu agreed invigorated and grabbed everything he had in the kitchen: a slice of polenta, some dried meat, some ham, a bit of cheese and a loaf of bread. He wrapped everything up in a piece of cloth, then brought a bottle of *ţuică*.

"Vodka!"

"*Ah, vodka, vodka! Good vodka good, comrade!*" the Russian hugged him and got out the front gate drinking from the bottle. He entered the yard across the way, unlocked then pocketed the chain from the well. He looked up the road where a cow, probably Miuţă's, was grazing peacefully, utterly unaware of the impending danger. He thought about whether to go that way for a second then changed his mind and went down the road munching on the polenta.

Mitu breathed a sigh of relief. "Pfft, we made it through this time..." He sat on the porch and lit a cigarette, inhaling the smoke, then began chewing some tobacco. He went to the gate a few times and looked every way to make sure there weren't any more soldiers, continued on to the corner of the country-lane, from where he checked the main road, then finally walked to the center of the village.

"Ion, where are the Russians?" he asked a man standing in the middle of the road like a drunkard.

"They left, Mitu, towards Novaci. All of 'em gone."

"Gone...are you sure?"

"Yes, I am. I saw them."

He rushed home and told Gheorghe to go get Maria.

"Tell your mother to come back home because the Russians are gone. Sandu, you come with me. Take what the Russian gave you and let's go," he said going towards Flitan's house.

When Flitan saw them, he opened the gate fearfully and called them inside. His face was still ghastly pale.

"They're gone, Mitu?"

"Yes, they are. They went to Novaci," he answered, searching through his pockets. He pulled out the bills and jewelry given by the Russian and handed them all to him, telling Sandu to do the same.

"He took everything else, Flitan, there was nothing I could do. He would have killed us all had we fought him on it."

"It's okay, Mitu, it's okay. He could've taken everything. I'm glad he didn't kill my children, Mitu because I would've hanged myself if he had."

THE BESSARABIAN

Chapter 69

Never had Romania been struck harder by God's wrath than in the Fall of 1944, right after the arrival of the Russians. Deserted throughout. Impoverished to death. The one hundred thousand lei coin, the five million lei bill; the dollar was worth six million lei. Bombarded through and through, kneeled by peace treaties. Buried in debt—three hundred million dollars in war reparations. Its vigor and wealth sucked out by SovRoms,29F[*] which sent everything out over the Prut River. Hacked to pieces in a capricious game; Bessarabia, the north of Bucovina, the Herța Region, whose repossession had caused Romania's entrance to war on the Nazis' side, all ultimately annexed to the U.S.S.R.

A terrible drought was trying the country in '46 and '47. As if cursed, those living in Moldova were forced to leave their households because of the famine and wandered looking for food. Chased and caught by military units, they were sent back to their villages. Sent back to death by starvation. The utter dryness encompassing the country was spreading insidiously.

Children were dying due to lack of food—deformed bodies reduced to skin and bones with eyes bulging out of their skulls were lying on improvised gurneys everywhere. Those on their deathbeds were hauled up in trains and sent to triage centers in "excedentary counties" to be cared for by foster families.

To the east, in Bessarabia, people first killed their cows and poultry. Then they killed their horses and donkeys. After that, they ate plum draff, beech wood bark and dirt, fried their monthly-rationed bread in gas and made soup out of pigweed and amaranth plants. When those were depleted, they ate their cats and dogs. Later on they feasted on mice and rats, and grazed on tufts of dried grass in the woods. They boiled and chewed up their hide shoes.

At last, they started killing each other. They hunted their neighbors' children and boiled them in water to have enough for the following weeks, thusly prolonging their wretched days for a little while longer.

Corn had stopped growing in Cernădia for more than a year. Dust covered the narrow roads, the trees, and the crop fields. People were at their wit's end. The ground was showing its dark and withered entrails through cracks gaped by the unbelievable heat. The air was tangible with hotness, like a dense lava barrage. The wells were dry; Boțota had been reduced to a thin stream barely flowing.

---

[*] SovRoms—joint Romanian-Soviet ventures. They were established on May 8th, 1945 in the essential domains of the Romanian economy (metallurgy, petroleum products, forestry, transportation, mining, etc.). In theory, SovRoms were designed to generate revenue for the reconstruction of Romania after WWII, but their hidden objective was to ensure massive shipments of resources to the U.S.S.R. In exchange, the Russians resold Romania used German industrial equipment, which was purposely overvalued. It is estimated that the total value of goods sent to U.S.S.R amounted to two billion dollars, far surpassing the demanded war reparations of 300 million dollars. The last SovRom was disbanded in 1956.

In a few months, Mitu lost his cows. One died of hunger and disease, and he killed the other and smoked its meat afraid it might also die. He stuffed the meat in glass jars filled with lard, which he then buried carefully in the ground to have as provisions. He had already gone through famine as a hobo and had learned enough from that experience. That meat was sufficient for a whole year without having to wander around looking for food. He couldn't have done it anyway with crutches and a bum leg.

He needed resources more than ever, and the drought had come at the worst possible moment in his life. He only had two oxen left, which he had to look after carefully since he used them to carry firewood and for other work bringing in a bit of money. His family had grown by another boy—Ionică, a fair, blue-eyed child, who had been born a little after the Russians' arrival, and who was about to turn two very soon. He had now six mouths to feed, and that required careful rationing.

The news about the people from Moldova sent to excedentary counties made everyone in the village talk, but he wasn't surprised. He knew what it meant to starve, and he remembered quite well hiding in freight trains, stopping off in small American towns to look for work and food. It seemed nothing had changed in the fifteen years since his hobo period. The geography was different. The stomach's burning ache was the same. The walking skeletons, ghosts from the underworld, daily death, disease and suffering hadn't changed at all. He thought with pity about those in such dire circumstances that they had to leave their villages rather than eat dirt. That's what he had done in Detroit.

The newspapers' propaganda no longer inveigled him. In America, during the starvation of the Great Depression, the newspapers howled that the ones responsible for the situation were the communists. Now, the communist paper *The Spark* blamed the fascists, the kulaks, and the imperialists. Its pages were full of speculators' pictures unmasked by the proletariat, making the desperate masses hang to their promises with hope and relief; as long as there was a guilty party—the fascist saboteurs that wanted to bring the country to its knees—their identification and just punishment were going to lift the rest of the people out of their misery. For instance, everyone posited, the Romanian Communist Party was vigilant in exemplarily penalizing the evildoers; in the town of Bacău, for example, Grigore Mârza, the president of the National Liberal Party, Brătianu branch, had been jailed for illegally owning large quantities of grains. A lot of good things had happened under the tutelage of the Communist Party during the last few years: the agrarian reform had given land to the peasants, expropriating collaborators and "war criminals" that owned more than a hundred and twenty-five acres. The class of exploiting nobility had been brought down, and the Romanian peasantry could start working the land owned outright was the motivational slant of *The Spark*.

He listened to everything but kept quiet. If there was one thing he had learned in his years in America, it was that he really didn't know much about politics. Each time he had hoped in something, he had been terribly disappointed, and for this reason he stopped participating in the passionate debates over who was to blame: The Groza Government or the capitalist imperialists. He had lived through all of those, maybe in a different form, not too long before, and since then he kept repeating that his will or that of many other thousands like him was worthless and that the games were made at the top.

So, rather than wasting his nights with interminable discussions out in the village, he spent his time at home, thinking how to ration his food and making survival plans in case the state found and confiscated his smoked meat.

As if Mitu's and the rest of the country folk's troubles weren't enough, a few people wandering aimlessly from Vaslui—a county starved wholly—stopped off in their village begging for food.

There was no room for them in Cernădia. There was no food there, not even for the children, less so for a few squatters arrived from elsewhere. Very few opened their gates to them, some even threatened them with clubs and went to denounce them to the gendarmerie.

Mitu didn't get involved in the people's spontaneous revolt; moreover, he took in a man, Ion Moldovan, and offered him shelter in the shed on a mound of straw. They gave him apples, watered-down soups, and a bit of ham on Sundays. Seeing the man wolf down whatever scraps were handed to him, Mitu wished he had received similar treatment when he had been a hobo in America.

After a while, the man confessed to him he came not from Moldova but from the village of Căzăneşti, in the Teleşti District, Orhei County in Bessarabia. To escape starvation to death, which had destroyed entire communities, he had snuck over the border into Romania. By the grace of God, he hadn't been caught by the soldiers. Two other people from his village hadn't been that lucky; a military unit awaited them in the Vaslui railroad station, but because he was the last one getting off the train, he turned around and jumped out from the other side hiding in freight trains until things settled down.

"I know what happens to those that get caught: they either get shot on the spot the minute they arrive in Bessarabia or they get shipped out to Siberia. That is going to be my fate when they catch me. But I can't starve to death either. Better off dying by someone else's hand than my own."

Mitu had him raise a bigger shed and do some work around the house. He didn't have money to pay him, but he could offer him food. And he had plenty of construction materials, wood planks, nails, hammers, hatchets, and seesaws. The capitalistic laws, learned so well in his storeowner days in Detroit, were alive and well inside him. If the times were such that he could improve some things around the house and pay for everything from the little that he had, why not make his life a little better?

Ion worked as though his life depended on it. It was the first time in the last year he ate ham, and he was grateful beyond belief. He worked sedulously day and night without a break, eating on the go, sleeping just a few hours a night. He built the shed in a few weeks. Then Mitu had him paint his house, put a new fence up, plaster the kitchen, fix the attic and dig some ditches from his home to Boțota for water pipes he planned on installing when he was going to come into more money.

"My God, if I only had now the dough I lost on Wall Street! I could have a whole army of people like this!" he sighed, seeing Ion putting forth the effort of three people.

After a while, he started wondering why the Bessarabian—"the servant" as he called him secretly with a mixed feeling of satisfaction and bitterness— seemed so ill at ease. He never said a word, not even when asked a direct question. Always sullen, he minded his own and did his work, quite well. Sometimes, Mitu watched him through the window as he sat with his hands on his knees for hours on end, with his mind elsewhere, coming back to reality as though awoken from a deep sleep.

As weeks went by, the man's stupor began troubling Mitu, yet he couldn't figure out why. He couldn't put his finger on it, but something wasn't right with the Bessarabian, and one day he shared his concerns with Maria.

"Woman, something's up with Ion. He works like a madman, he's dependable and strong, but he seems so afraid he won't say two words to me. I watched him sit still for more than half an hour this morning, staring without even blinking, like a lunatic."

"Just let him be, you're trying to look for trouble where there ain't none," she answered matter-of-factly. "To each his own. Who knows, maybe he misses his family. It isn't easy being far away from your loved ones for such a long time."

"It's not easy, it's true. I know that firsthand. But even when I ask him of his family, he never says anything. He turns mute and furrows his brow. If he felt the call of his land, he'd say something about it. I don't even know if he's married or not. Does he have any children? When I asked him about it, he raised his shoulders and didn't say a word."

"Now that you mentioned it, I think you might be right that something's up with him. I was cleaning in the shed two days ago, and, when I pulled his blankets, I found a rope shaped like a noose."

"What, for hanging?"

"Yeah, a noose. I left it where I found it."

"He might want to hang himself from the beams to see if they hold...to see if he did a good job strengthening them."

"God forbid, what came over you to say such a thing?" Maria shivered.

Mitu pretended he didn't hear her, but her words unsettled him. "He sleeps with a noose by his side? What the fuck's that about?"

During the following days, he continued to observe him carefully, questioning him about this and that. He would ask "casual" questions, but Ion never fell for them. Besides a mattock, hammer, and seesaw, he didn't see anything else. He gave short answers, repeating humbly, "May God bless you for this. Now, I'm going back to my own," when they gave him some food.

Mitu left him alone after a while. "As long as he works and minds his own business, what do I care if he doesn't tell me about his situation? I'll get him drunk one day and he'll tell me something then."

After all, he had plenty of things on his mind to worry about the man sleeping with a noose under his blanket. He had chicken coups but no chickens as there was no fodder for them, and that was a problem that needed solving right away. Ion was a good worker, so what if he didn't share his life story with them?

Corn hadn't been sold at their market in a long time. There was none to be found in neither Novaci nor Târgu-Jiu. The only place he could have bought some was Craiova. Many peasants from Bărăgan and many, many speculators scheming to get reach fast went there to sell grains by the ton. Since he didn't have enough money to buy large quantities, Mitu thought to barter some fruit. He kept plenty of apples in the cool cellar—he wasn't going to use them for making *ţuică* since he already had more than enough. The hundreds and hundreds of pounds of apples could come in very handy now.

Chapter 70

It was a downcast day when Mitu finally decided to go to Craiova and buy some corn. The rain was falling in buckets, and streams of water were flowing down the roads, turning the dust into mud barely trodden on in rubber boots.

He woke up at three in the morning and took the carriage out in the yard—he had been packing it with apples for the last three days—he threw a few clothes, some tools, and blankets on top, yoked the oxen and then went to awaken Micu, Sandu, and the Bessarabian.

When thinking of the calamity in the rest of the country, Mitu considered himself lucky. Those apples could be his ticket out of misery. Ripe and big, red or yellow, they had made it through the incredible scorch as they have been carefully preserved in the darkness and coolness of the cellar. Now, as never before, he could use them for something other than *ţuică*. He had heard from others he could get a corncob per apple, so that meant he could come back home with a full carriage.

"Micu, come on sonny, get up, so we can go. Lil' Sandu, you too, quick, because we have a long way ahead of us!" he called out to the children, checking the sacks of fruit one more time to make sure they were well fastened.

The boys frowned with their backs at him sending the clear message they should be left alone.

"Micu, are you up, kid?" Mitu called out at the boy again, who had meanwhile turned on his back and was gazing at the ceiling through half-open eyes. Sandu was up but sported a very sourpussed face. He had begged his father in tears to take him along on the trip the night before, but now he was sorry he had done so. Waking up at daybreak was terrible.

"Ion's not up yet," said Maria. "You're taking him along, right?"

"Yeah, that was the plan," he answered then took a gas lamp and went to the shed. The man was fast asleep, wrapped up in three blankets, snoring lightly.

"Ion, wake up!" he went closer.

Ion didn't move and Mitu patted him lightly on the shoulder lighting his face with the lamp.

"Ion!"

"No!" the man howled suddenly, sitting up. He shrank back and shielded his eyes with his arm.

"Ion, what happened to you, what happened? It's me Mitu, don't be scared!" he tried to calm him down pulling the lamp closer to his own face.

The man glanced at him as if he were a ghost, and his breath became more regular.

"I had a bad dream...a bad dream..."

Mitu gave him an understanding look. He knew what that meant. He still woke up doused in sweat from the war nightmares he still had. Some of them were so vivid, he didn't want to go back to sleep afraid he might start dreaming again. And many years had passed since.

"What happened to you, Ion, that's giving you such bad dreams?"

The Bessarabian lowered his eyes.

"I don't know man, I dream like anyone else."

"It's alright now, forget about dreams, we need to get a move on."

He went to the carriage, tightened some ropes, then suddenly remembered, "The violin!" He went inside the house, grabbed it from the closet and put it on top of the clothes. "I was about to forget the most important thing for the trip! I can play a bit on the way."

"Sandu, you ready? Micu are you dressed?" he called his sons. "I'm leaving without you, so you know!"

The boys came out quickly on the porch.

"Yes, dad, we're here. Oh my goodness, such darkness!"

Micu had never been up so early in the morning, and he was afraid of the dark. He moved closer to Sandu—both scared and cold—then got into the carriage and curled up under the blankets.

Mitu hoisted himself up in the carriage, as his bum leg no longer allowed his moving around with ease like before. He called Ion to sit next to him, and crossed himself before setting out.

"Maria, take care of Ionică. Gheorghe is a big boy now, he doesn't need you. But you watch the young one."

Maria blessed them and threw some salt in their wake, "May God watch over you on this long trip!"

Mitu settled in a comfortable position and urged the oxen on. It took them half a day to get to Cărbunești, the first big stop on their way. They were to spend the night there, and he considered paying a visit to Cămărășescu to converse a bit in English "since he lives right around here, and I haven't seen him in quite a while." He gave up on the idea, however, "too much of a headache," and they all slept in the carriage. In the morning, they crossed the hill to Țicleni. Then Peșteana, Ceplea, and Ionești.

Somewhere on the Jiu River's valley, they pulled the carriage to the side of the road for a short repose. They lay a blanket on the ground, ate some dried bread and apples, and Mitu pulled out a bottle of țuică.

"Go on and have some, Ion. It's been aged for four years. You can chug it all down; we're close to Craiova by now."

The man looked surprised at him—Mitu had been very stingy with the booze up to that point, saying they needed to save it for the way back. He took the bottle and drank a quart of it in one gulp, scrunching his face as though he were drinking poison.

"God bless. It burns like fire..."

"It burns, it burns. I took the strongest one on purpose, to warm us up on the road, right? Sandu," he called, "come to me for a sec!"

The boy, who was playing farther away with Micu, was quite discontented to interrupt his game and waked lazily to his father.

"Yes, dad."

"Here you go, take a swig. It'll warm you up in this chilliness."

Sandu took a gulp. He shook his head, made some funny faces, then took another swig, and lay on the grass chewing on a straw and looking up at the sky. Micu was sitting next to a puddle throwing pebbles in it, upset no one was paying attention to him. Mitu called him.

"Lil' Micu, come to Daddy!"

The boy ran happily to him. Mitu gave him the bottle, but the boy scrunched his nose. He had tried alcohol before and hated its taste, and although his father always insisted that he drink some like a "true man," the boy refused it every time.

"Alright, if you don't want any, that's fine, be a little sissy. Go now and play, because we're leaving in a bit."

The children went back to their games; they climbed a hill chasing each other and came back half an hour later with a lost puppy. They played with it until the poor animal fell to the ground and didn't want to move anymore.

Ion and Mitu had meanwhile moved on to a second bottle. The Bessarabian's tongue was looser now, and he was recounting childhood stories. Mitu listened for a while, then he called his children to come back as it was time to go.

The boys climbed in the back. They fell asleep after a short while exhausted by the running around. Mitu prodded the oxen on and invited Ion to drink some more.

"Drink up, there's plenty."

The Bessarabian slurped thirstily, as though he hadn't drunk anything up to that point and started telling about the famine from his native places, which had been so terrible that some people had killed and eaten rats.

"And how many left from your village?"

"Well, I don't know that, but by the time I left Căzăneşi, there were about ten that had already gone. I was the eleventh."

"Good thing you left looking for some better luck. I did the same when I was young. I crossed the border into the Empire and then I went to America. Ion, we never chatted more at length. What are the names of your kids? You do have kids, right?"

The man meant to answer, then stopped and sighed. He took another swig.

"Well, yes, I have three daughters," he said. "The good Lord didn't bless me with any boys. Maria, Sofia, and Ileana are their names."

"May they all live long and happy lives! Now you tell me, after you've lived in my household for so long. I'm always complaining I don't have any daughters. Who knows, perhaps I'll have a girl after all. I think my woman's with child again, so maybe the next one's a girl. But don't you miss your wife? I never hear you talking about her. You must have one; you couldn't have had the kids all by yourself, could you!"

Ion winced and gave him a frightened look. He made an indescribable gesture, then put his head on his knees, shaking like a leaf.

"What happened now, are you dreaming with your eyes open?"

"What do you want from me, man, why you asking about my woman?" he asked edgily.

"For God's sake, I didn't mean anything by it!"

"Well, the man sighed," I need to tell you something. I have to. I got to take the weight off my chest. I can't keep it inside any longer or I'll burst. I know you're going to chase me from your home. But you're like my brother. You've been better than a brother to me..."

His left eye began twitching uncontrollably, and the lines on his face deepened.

"Please man, swear to me on your life you won't tell no one. Swear to me!" he went on.

"Ion, how can you think I'd tell anyone? Tell me what's on your heart, and my lips will be sealed forever, I swear on my children's health!"

"I swear I meant to tell you sooner but I didn't want to frighten your wife."

He choked in fits of crying then wiped his eyes with his sleeve.

"I'm a criminal, Mitu, a criminal!" he broke out. "We were dying of hunger in Căzăneşti and we needed to pay our contribution to the authorities, and we had nothing and someone from the party came to my wife and tried to take advantage of her and said he was going to send her to Siberia and kill me if she didn't give in to him."

Mitu had expected some terrible story like that. Nobody from over the Prut River ever had left because of a good life. "Compared to Romania, Bessarabia's much worse; look at what this poor man went through."

"And what did you do, Ion?"

"Well, I went away and left them together, but I came back earlier and did murder."

Mitu looked bewildered at him for a while then tried to calm him down.

"Good thing you killed him. I would have done the same if anyone disrespected my Maria."

"Not him, my wife. He was already gone, or I would've killed him too."

Mitu was unable to swallow the lump in his throat.

"Wh—what do you mean, Ion? What are you trying to say here?"

"What I wanna say? What I wanna say? I killed her with my own hand, split her head with the hatchet! And I ran away! I did!"

Mitu pulled back terrified.

"Tell me it ain't true, Ion. Just tell me it ain't true!" he shouted.

Ion started crying again.

"Don't chase me away, please don't chase me because they'll kill me!"

"I won't, don't worry. And you've been having nightmares since then?"

"Yes! I dream of blood and scattered brains. I got sick to my stomach when I saw what was left of her, and I ran out of there like a lunatic. When they catch me, they'll hang me for sure."

Mitu took a long time to wrap his mind around what he just learned. His words tangled in his throat. He was so close to a murderer!

An hour passed, then another, without either of them saying anything. After a while, he told Ion to get some sleep.

"Well man, that's how life is. Now you're here, tomorrow you're not. We have a long road ahead of us, so go on and sleep a bit. I'll man the oxen and when I get tired, I'll wake you up, alright?"

Ion pulled a blanket over himself and closed his eyes. He felt somehow protected next to Mitu and his boys and with all the alcohol he had already drunk, he fell asleep right away. His arms started twitching a few minutes later—a sign he was falling deeper into slumber.

Mitu remained in a stunned state for a few hours. Everything made sense now! The noose Maria had found the month before, the double-edged knife Ion always had on him and tried in vain to hide from them.

He had been sheltering a killer for a few good months now! A runaway wanted by the gendarmerie of two countries! If they had caught him on Mitu's turf, he would have been in great trouble. Maria as well. And who knew what would happen to the children if the two of them ended up in prison! Gheorghe couldn't take care of all his brothers! They'd starve to death and might be sent to the excedentary counties! What was he to do? What could he do?

He found himself in the throes of a dire situation. No matter how he looked at it, he couldn't find the right answer. Taking him back to his home was impossible, that was clear as daylight. But he couldn't hang him out to dry either. Ion was a human being after all, with feelings and tried by hardship. If he hadn't told him those terrible things, Mitu would have never guessed it. Where was Ciorogaru now when he needed his wise advice?

He felt quite flustered and kept watching Ion out of the corner of his eye, ready to jump him if he attacked. "Now that he knows I know what he did, I shouldn't be surprised if he tried to split my head open!"

But Ion was sound asleep. The next day, he didn't even mention their conversation, as though the confession hadn't been his. It wouldn't have been farfetched he didn't remember anything with all the alcohol he'd had, Mitu thought.

He was no longer afraid for himself but for the kids. What if Ion was thinking to kill them so they wouldn't turn him in? He could have very well done it, especially if he felt cornered, couldn't he?

After considering it from all perspectives with head-splitting concentration, he took Sandu aside and made him swear that, no matter what, he would keep his mouth shut and pretend he didn't know anything about Ion.

"Sandu, Micu's still too little, but you're a big boy now. This is what we'll do the whole way to Craiova: you'll sleep while I'm awake and you'll keep watch while I sleep. And if you see Ion's up, you rouse me as fast as possible, alright?"

They did just so for the rest of the trip; Sandu would pretend to sleep, watching Ion from underneath the covers, then would wake his father a few hours later.

Their tribulations were in vain, however. Ion wasn't thinking of slitting their throats with his knife. His mind was elsewhere—perhaps on his crime or the punishment awaiting him once caught.

Once in Craiova, they stopped at the central market. Waves of people had gathered from all regions: Moldova, Bessarabia, Ardeal, Dobrogea, Muntenia, as though the whole of Romania had come together. Some had come to buy a sack or two of flour off of which they would barely survive for another few months. Others came with money collected from their whole village and bought enough sacks to fill a few railroad cars, then made arrangements with the station to have them transported by train. The lucky ones made it home with the corn. The less unfortunate ones, however, just watched powerless as the gendarmes confiscated their corn to redistribute it "justly."

Mitu went to those selling corn, trying to lure them to his merchandise as he used to during his "Mitu & Olga's Store" time.

"Very good apples here, folks! Low-priced and good! Take a few samples, so you don't think I'm lying. Tasting is free, buying is not."

"How are you selling them?" people would ask.

"Well, pal, an apple for two corn cobs."

"One apple for two cobs? What's this, the thief dealing with the idiot?"

"Well then, how would you like them? For nothing?"

"Not for nothing but this is too much. How about one corn for two apples?"

"Pal, now's my turn to tell you, this is gotta be the thief dealing with the idiot! One for one, so it's not like me, and not like you!"

By the end of the day he had sold everything, but his thoughts had been on Ion the whole time. That man was a killer. He needed to be reported to the authorities. Mistakes had to be paid, in this life and the next. What Ion had done was no mere robbery—it was something very grave. He couldn't go back to Cernădia with him; he wouldn't have been able to sleep nights thinking the man might try to kill his family. He needed to do something; he needed to get rid of him! But how? Go to the gendarmes? Turn him in? What harm had Ion done to him to justify a betrayal that would send him to jail and maybe even to death? More than that, he had done plenty of work around the house without pay, proving himself to be quite trustworthy.

In fact, Mitu's wavering was quite thin. By the time he had woken Sandu to have him keep watch, he had already unknowingly made a decision. After selling all of his apples, he waited for Ion to wander around the market and made a beeline to a gendarme.

"Sorry to bother you, sir, but I need to tell you something. There's a man from Bessarabia here with me that told me he committed murder in his village. He's from Orhei, Căzăneşti. He killed his wife! He split her head with the hatchet, he told me. He's been staying at my home and helped me with some chores, but may God strike me if I ever suspected anything! He just told me about this terrible thing on the way to Craiova and only because he was very drunk. Now I'm afraid he might do something to me or my sons."

The gendarme watched him incredulously but told him to wait, and in a few minutes he came back with his superior, who took him aside for additional questions. Once the cops understood what everything was about, they all turned towards the carriage. Ion saw them from afar and jumped from it trying to run away, but he was quickly apprehended and handcuffed, then shoved into a van.

Mitu watched them for a while. His eyes locked onto Ion's eyes a few times. The man kept looking at him without saying a word. His gaze was reproachful and sad.

When the car took off, Mitu crossed himself, trying to chase away his somber thoughts. "My God in Heaven, please forgive me. But he deserved to be punished. I'd give myself up if I killed somebody!"

"Let's go boys, upsy-daisy in the carriage, we're going back home," he told the children.

"Where did they take Ion, dad?" Micu asked.

"Ion is going to his home, child, to his daughters. We're going back to Cernădia now. Without him."

He grabbed the oxen by the yoke and left the market. His carriage was full of corn, just as he had planned, but his heart was empty. His thoughts were drawn to Ion, wondering if turning him in had been the right thing to do.

IONICĂ

Chapter 71

With the corn from Craiova Mitu brought his family back afloat for the time being. He had bought enough to feed a few chickens and make polenta for a year. God was finally showing them His mercy; not long after it began raining, and slowly, the gardens turned green again. His hens, well fed now, were multiplying as they had during good times. From whatever savings he still had, he bought a cow and a few sheep, which he sent up to Rânca.

He had overcome yet another hardship.

His boys were growing up like handsome sons from fairy tales. He had been right telling Ion that Maria was pregnant. She gave birth to a girl— finally, a girl!—whom they named Măriuţa. She was the apple of his eye, and her coos and toothless smiles melted his heart.

Gheorghe had turned into a young man; he was hardworking and dependable and seemed to take after Mitu's brother Ghiţă. Sandu was very naughty and dragged Micu along wherever he went, much to his mother's dismay, who wanted them at home helping out with the chores.

Ionică was growing too, and to their amazement, he began reading and doing arithmetic at age three. Mitu thought him wise beyond his years. "That's mah boy. That's mah son!" he fawned over his youngest. They spent a lot of time together. Mitu took him to the market or other places where he had errands to run, he told him about America, he taught him how to play the violin, he spoke to him in English, he explained to him how to add and subtract bigger and bigger numbers, and presented him as an example to Micu and Sandu. "Learn from Ionică! You're not going to amount to anything in life if you don't like studying. Nothing! Don't say later I haven't told you so."

The rain had turned his life and that of many in the village around, so he went back to his old ways of fending for his family: buying and selling this and that, bringing firewood from Rânca and selling it in Târgu-Jiu...whatever he could do to make ends meet.

He had recently made arrangements with someone in Baia de Fier to buy some flour, which he planned on selling later when the prices would go up. He initially meant to take Gheorghe with him to help with the loading, but he changed his mind and took Julea instead to play the violin a little on the road. And of course, as always, he was going to take Ionică along.

The child had suffered lately from fevers and dizziness. His condition resembled that of Sandu a few years before, when the boy had been in the throes of death, so Maria didn't even want to hear it. Doctor Niculescu had ordered them to keep him inside, and under absolutely no circumstance let him out in the cold. They were supposed to bathe him only once a month, because even the water evaporating would cool his body, he had explained to them.

Mitu didn't listen. How could he not take Ionică along? All kids became sick sometimes, didn't they? He bundled him up then put him in the carriage.

The child kept moving around trying to keep his balance in the jolting ride grinning from ear to ear when his father would turn around to make droll faces at him.

Mitu cherished Ionică. The boy was his reason to live: blond with blue eyes and fair skin, he was a beautiful angel, the splitting image of his mother, but that wasn't what made him so happy. Ionică was smarter than all the kids his age in Cernădia. A wonder! Mitu bragged to everyone that the boy already knew how to read and write! He sometimes took him for "demonstrations" through the neighborhood. He would ask the neighbors to tell Ionică a poem then would tell him, "Ionică, learn it, and if you say it back without mistake, I'll give you some chocolate." Then he would move to the side to watch their befuddled faces as the boy recited the poem without mistake on the first try. Boastful and pleased, he would lift him in his arms as high as he could, "That's mah boy, that's mah boy!" He loved to see him so inquisitive and interested in learning from his father.

He would have angered the One Above to say, God forbid, that his other children weren't good—very good, indeed, and trustworthy. But Gheorghe still couldn't read well, and while Sandu tried hard in school, his heart wasn't in it, and writing had been really rough at the beginning. It was true that his calligraphy was beautiful now, but how hard he had strived for it.

Everything came very easily to Ionică. Whatever he was taught, he never forgot. He learned a poem today, and in month, he would say it back with the same ease the priest recites his prayers. Mitu would hum a song and in a few weeks, the boy could sing it right back to him; everything became engrained in his mind like ink on a blank piece of paper.

"This child will lift us all from poverty! He'll be a second Eminescu," Mitu thought, seeing that his son preferred reading to playing outside unlike any other kid his age.

Mitu had started teaching him English. He thought of bringing him along to Baia particularly for that reason, to make conversations. He had seen in America that immigrants that arrived there as children learned the language just as well as those that had been born there. He himself spoke good English; he used it with Ciorogaru and Cămărăşescu—very well-educated men—yet he was much better at it than both of them. But he still had a bit of an accent and there were plenty of words he didn't know. He posited it was all due to his going to America at seventeen. Had he gone there earlier, he would have learned the language more easily, he thought, and that was the reason he started so young with Ionică. The child's brain was untainted and free of all frivolous stupidities filling adult heads.

"*Ionică, are you hungry?*" he asked him in English as they were approaching Baia de Fier, more to show off to Julea.

The child nodded. Mitu pulled out an apple and gave it to him.

"*Eat this. It's quite good. Sweet and tasty, like no other. You'll like it.*"

Ionică took a bite and smiled.

"*Thank you, dad...*"

"Eat it and cover yourself up with the cover. It's chilly, and I don't want you to get sick."

The child did as he was told. He lifted his collar and got under the heavy wool blanket. Mitu would have wanted the boy to fall asleep, but Ionică's eyes kept following the monotonous lines of the fences on the side of the road.

Julea, whose school aged children couldn't read very well, pretended he wasn't listening to them. Each time he met Mitu for a drink, the man couldn't stop bragging about his son, and he was getting sick of it already.

They went to the center of Baia where they were supposed to meet Stuttery, a man that had never held a job and whose anger and agitation-induced stammering had brought on his nickname. They concluded their flour deal as the understanding had been, and as they were preparing to leave, Julea stopped Mitu.

"Let's go to the tavern, or maybe you forgot they sell that good wine brought all the way from Vaslui? What's with you Mitu, you want to go back home without even tasting it? You nuts?"

Mitu meant to refuse, but he knew full well what Julea meant. Indeed, the wine there was some of the best from noble vines, brought from afar by some Jewish merchants and sold, for some reason, only there. It was difficult finding it elsewhere, and it cost a pretty penny.

He glanced at Ionică, thinking he shouldn't dilly-dally any longer and waste money on alcohol since he had plenty of it at home, thank God! Yet, without faltering too much, he decided to go in and have a glass or two.

"Well, fuck the money, let's go have a bottle, but no more, alright? One, and that's it!"

He told Ionică to stay put in the carriage and try to fall asleep, he bundled him carefully with the blanket "*atta boy!*" and went inside.

It was very crowded. More than thirty people were crammed at the tables, chain drinking shoulder-to-shoulder. They found some room at a table with ten other men—drunk out of their minds already—and ordered a bottle.

"What? A bottle for the two of us, Mitu? What's wrong with you? Turning all pious on me?"

It was true...they never had fewer than two bottles of wine and one of *țuică* when they went drinking together.

"Julea, if I didn't have Ionică with me, I'd stay here till closing time, really. But my baby's in the carriage. I'm afraid he's going to be cold and get sick again!"

"Oh, come on, what kind of a pansy are you? You saw how good he was bundled up, right? It's not even all that cold outside; he'll be warmer in there than by the side of the stove."

Mitu nodded. The man was right after all; what could happen? It wasn't like it was storming outside.

The first bottle was followed by a second and a third and then half a bottle of *țuică* each. When they finally decided to leave a few hours later, it was dark outside. They bought a bottle of bilberry brandy to have for the road and staggered out of the tavern holding on to each other. They scrambled to climb in the carriage, then they set out towards the village. Ionică was sound asleep, lying on his back completely uncovered.

"Hya, lazybones, hya!" Mitu flailed the reigns weakly.

The horse strained to heave the sacks of flower on the abrupt road crossing the forest between Baia and Cernădia. After about fifteen minutes, Julea, who was almost asleep, opened his eyes halfway, as if he had remembered something, and tried to get up.

"Mitu, stop the carriage..." he mumbled. "I gotta piss bad."

He pulled to the side of the road, and Julea stumbled down, moving farther away.

"Wait for me, because I need to piss too," Mitu shouted behind him, looking for his crutch in the carriage, but he had forgotten it in the tavern in Baia. He struggled to climb down, wobbled to a tree then unzipped his pants. The whitish steam from the urine unfurled in the air filling his nostrils with a sweetly acrid smell, which didn't bother him in the least. Julea finished first and tried to go back to the carriage but tripped over some roots and fell in the grass. He attempted to get up, but the alcohol weighed him back down. Mitu outstretched his hand to help him, but he slipped, lost his balance, and fell as well. Eyes closed, he sprawled out in an unnatural position with the soles of his feet on Julea's face. He slid inch by inch into the ditch by the side of the road and started snoring noisily.

The child, who had awoken meanwhile and was trying to peer through the darkness, called to him a few times, and receiving no answer, he became frightened.

"Dad, daddy where are you? Dad! Dad!" he screamed, then came closer to the spot from where the snoring came.

Seeing his father sleeping on the ground, the boy went back up into the carriage where, for a while, he busied himself with some wooden balls received as a gift the previous Sunday. He then spent some time tossing about, but fear was slowly taking hold of him. Night was quickly dawning, and he began whistling to encourage himself. The scary shadows cast by trees seemed wandering ghosts moving threateningly towards him. He pulled the blanket over his head. He couldn't see anything but could still hear the rustling of the wind and twigs snapping as though crunched by heavy feet. He coiled up in a little ball, shivering, gathering his knees up to his mouth, and covering his face with his hands to protect himself if suddenly uncovered. He felt so alone. He was convinced monsters were coming to skin him alive and eat him.

He peered into the forest from underneath the covers and thought he could see a beast lurching toward the carriage. He was whimpering and shaking, making himself even smaller and tensing his arms until they hurt. Then, he encouraged himself by saying he was a big boy and shouldn't be scared of nonsense. Sandu walked through their yard in the middle of the night without a light. If he saw him now, he'd laugh at him and tattle to all the other kids in the village that he was a sissy.

Resolute to trounce his fear, he got out from under the blanket and rubbed his hands to warm them. He looked around through the impenetrable darkness. Not even the moon could be seen in the sky, hidden by heavy clouds.

To embolden himself, he picked up the whip and cracked it lightly, not realizing its shrill would make the horse move. When he saw it begging to walk, he grabbed the reigns and pulled on them. The horse snorted, neighing curtly, then stopped, and Ionică breathed a sigh of relief. "Look at that, I can drive a carriage."

His courage was slipping away. He went under the blanket, listening to the slightest noise or wind rustle, until, at last, he fell asleep among the sacks of flour.

It was a deep sleep, from which he couldn't be easily stirred. The drizzle, which had just begun falling, didn't rouse him. It was only when the water seeped through the blankets and reached his skin that he woke up confused. He remembered he was on the way back to Cernădia and he rejoiced he had braved the night alone. "Look at that, nothing came to eat me!" he boasted to himself, then looked for something dry to cover himself with, but couldn't find anything in the rain-drenched carriage.

He was shivering more and more, not because he was scared, but because he was cold. He was a big boy!

Chapter 72

Ionică became ill three days later. It was the right side of his jaw that swelled up first. The poor baby was so embarrassed, he didn't want to come out of the house, hiding his face in a pillow or running in a corner, turning his back to whoever came inside.

Then the throat ache—not too bad at the beginning, but a lot worse a week later. He couldn't even drink water, but somehow Maria managed to give him a few sips of warm tea. The back of his gullet was whitish and the puss had spread to the roof of his mouth.

"Your tonsils are big as walnuts, Ionică. Swallow hard, my sonny, as hard as you can, to break the blisters of puss," Mitu advised him.

The child struggled to swallow wincing in pain, but the sores wouldn't break. Then Maria forced him to gargle with salty warm water, but each time he tried, he vomited a white-purplish liquid.

After another week, his throat ache subsided, but he developed a dry cough and his fever kept spiking. The lump under the jaw had grown bigger, and the one on the other side was now swelling up as well. They took him to Novaci to Doctor Niculescu, who, upon checking him, gave them a pensive look. "The little boy is ill," he said as if it weren't obvious, then gave him a cortisone shot. "I wonder why his lymph nodes are so inflamed."

"He hit himself at the big node there, doctor, he hit himself while he was playing in the back yard," Mitu said defensively. "He was playing by the cherry tree, he tried to climb it, but fell and hurt his chin on a branch!"

Niculescu peered at him above his glasses, shaking his head incredulously.

"If that was the cause, why did he swell up on both sides? Well, that's a different story. Keep him by the stove for warmth; don't let him outside in the cold. If he gets a high fever and starts hallucinating, wrap him up in a wet blanket."

Since Niculescu had cared for Sandu a few years before, Mitu trusted the doctor blindly, singing his praises for the good he had done him then. He left comforted, thinking his boy had but a cold, and that he would get over it very soon.

Seeing that two weeks later, Ionică still couldn't eat anything, he became afraid. His other children, even ill, still swallowed a little something. Sandu had taken to bed due to fever not long before, but he had asked for food the minute he got up.

"Mitu, I'm scared we're going to lose Ionică! What do we do? How can God punish us like that? This is the Bessarabian's curse! I'm going to kill myself if my child dies, Mitu," Maria broke down one day.

"What's the matter with you, talking nonsense like that? We'll take care of him and he'll get better, you'll see!"

But foreboding thoughts haunted him. He had been restless since the day they returned from Baia. Why had he stopped at the tavern with a sick child in his carriage, why? Why had he listened to that idiot Julea? What was he thinking? What if, God forbid, something was to happen to his boy—what was he going to do?

The following days were no better. Ionică was slowly wasting away. Hot teas, homemade remedies, special prayers against evil eye, nothing proved useful. The child barely breathed.

"Ionică, my angel, does it hurt, baby? Tell mommy what hurts so mommy can take care of it," Maria fretted, wringing her hands in despair.

The boy would point to his throat, head, then belly and chest. Sometimes he struggled to say a word or two, with a faint voice and tremendous efforts.

She looked at him torn with pain. Crushed by the feeling of inability afflicting a mother who cannot help her child, she could no longer sleep at night; her face had withered and deep lines had formed around her eyes. She wandered about like a lunatic, going to neighbors, old women, and gypsy fortunetellers looking for cures and miracles.

An unnatural silence had befallen their household. People passed by expecting to hear Mitu play with Julea and Cirică as he used to, but their home was silent. They were all gathered around Ionică in the small room, putting cold or hot compresses on his forehead, trying to give him warm milk, and keeping the fire roaring.

It was a sleepy autumn afternoon when Niculescu paid them a visit in passing through to Baia de Fier. The air, humid and dark from the unceasing drizzle seemed to foretell tragedy. Maria called him quickly inside full of hope.

"Doctor, I'm so glad you're here. Last night we had to wrap him in wet blankets to bring his fever down! What else should we do?"

He placed the stethoscope on the boy's chest, took his fever with the back of his hand, checked his throat and then called Mitu outside.

"Fiddler, come here I need to talk to you."

Mitu had gone through too many things in life to delude himself. He followed the doctor out the door with his head and heart empty.

"We need to light a candle for him, don't we?'

Niculescu shook his head with a gloomy expression.

"I didn't mean to say that, but only a miracle can save him now. Only God. There's nothing left for me to do."

Maria, who had come outside unnoticed, dashed forward.

"It can't be, it can't be, give him a shot, there must be something you can do! Help him please, don't leave him like that, don't leave us, I'll kill myself if my baby dies!" she clanged desperately on his arm, begging for his help, as though the doctor had magical powers he was keeping from them.

"Maria, I just told your husband here, from now on only the Lord's grace. I did my duty. I'll give him another shot, but it won't make a difference, like a massage to a wooden leg. The injection would be better used for some poor soul that really needs it."

He entered the child's room, gave him the shot ignoring his muffled whimpers, then left with a quick goodbye from the front gate.

"God help you, good people. Pray for a divine miracle!"

Maria covered her mouth to stifle her sobs from Ionică, then went into the summer kitchen where she came unglued, unleashing herself into a frantic wailing.

"Mitu, our child is dying, what are we to do, what?" she wailed through hiccups. She cupped her head in her palms, and after a while, an unnatural calmness pinned her to the stool in an otherworldly stance. She rose to her feet suddenly and turned to Mitu, striking him with dagger eyes. She had a wild, crazy look on her face; her hair was up in a whirl. She grabbed a clay bowl and hurled it at his head, then searched with her eyes for another one.

"You wretched bastard, you killed my child, I curse you to hell! God took my mind the day I married you, you good for nothin' son of a bitch drunkard! I'll leave you if my Ionică dies! I'll leave you! I'll take my kids and go back to my mother's! I'll leave you here to rot in your *ţuică*, to die alone and get eaten by worms and dogs, with no one to bury you! I curse your life! Be damned 'till the day you die!"

Mitu looked dumbfounded at her, his face red with fury, then rushed to the shed and grabbed a shovel to hit her in the head and be done with her forever! But right then, his mother came out on the porch with Ionică in her arms.

"Stop it with the noise, what's gotten into you, you lost your minds while the child's sick? My God in heaven! Where's the sailor suit?"

"What do you need the sailor suit for, Ma? Goddamn it, are you crazy?" Mitu burst out ready to hit her as well.

"Ionică asked for it, he wants to wear it."

Mitu melted with emotion and came closer to the boy.

"What is it, Ionică, my boy, do you want the sailor suit, angel? Daddy will bring it to you right away, okay?"

He rushed to the closet, rummaged feverishly through it, and found the outfit.

"Here we go, my love, here we go, we'll make you all handsome now. Who's the most fetching boy in the world?" he whispered with a quaking voice as he dressed him. "Would you like the hat as well, my angel?"

The boy nodded tiredly, and he placed the hat slightly askew the way Ionică liked it.

"Let's go to the mirror, and see how good looking you are!"

He took him in his arms and went back inside.

"How beautiful it looks on you, see? Can you see?"

Ionică peered faintly in the mirror and a weak smile curled his lips.

"It's so beautiful, daddy...so beautiful," he barely whispered, then closed his eyes and rested his head on his father's shoulder with a sigh.

Mitu put his ear to his chest, then lay him on the bed and placed a little mirror to his lips. His shoulders hunched forward under an invisible burden, and he turned his eyes to the door from where everyone was watching. He lit a candle and placed it on the small table by the bed, then squeezed through them and went outside. He leaned against a tree and stayed there long into the night. Tears streamed down his face.

The neighborhood echoed with Lenuţa's and Maria's sobs. Micu and Sandu were crying, shaking and holding hands.

Gheorghe had already hung a black cloth on the front gate and had gone to retrieve Father Sebastian.

Chapter 73

Maria did not go unscathed through Ionică's death. For months on end she went daily to his grave and stayed there from morning to night. She didn't eat anything, didn't see after her chores anymore, and chased away anyone that tried to talk to her.

"This is my baby's grave, get away from me! Leave me alone with him!" she would hiss at them.

She no longer slept at night. If she sometimes did, due to sheer exhaustion, her sleep was brief and agitated; she would barely close her eyes only to start shaking, tossing and turning, rousing suddenly drenched in sweat. She would sit up and stare blankly ahead, not knowing who or where she was. She would then burst into tears and run back to the cemetery lighting her path with a dim lamp. She would stay there until the morning, ignoring the cold or the drizzle. She once fell asleep on the snow and was found there towards the morning by some workers fixing the roof of the church who carried her inside.

"God watched over you, Maria; a few more hours and you would've passed away," they told her, but she flared up at them choking in tears.

"You should've left me there to die next to my baby, why did you take me away? Take me back there. I want to die with him!"

The village began talking. The Fiddler's wife had gone bonkers, people said, God had taken her child and her mind. "Maybe a curse fell upon her...what a misfortune, those poor kids of hers."

Flitan tried to advise Mitu to do something about the situation, but he hit a brick wall; Mitu couldn't see or hear anything either. The thought that he had caused his child's death had killed something inside. There wasn't a minute in the day he wasn't tormented by his decision to follow Julea inside the tavern. Why had God taken his mind? What had he done to deserve such a fate? If Julea hadn't told him to drink a bottle of wine, Ionică would be alive now. Julea had to pay for this.

Blaming Julea for his son's death blinded him for a while, but after a few months of fooling himself, not even that was enough. He missed Ionică so much he couldn't bear it; he couldn't even go to his son's grave because Maria was in the cemetery all the time.

For a while, to forget, he cleaned the house, cooked for the kids in her stead, and fixed a thing or two around the yard.

At last, he ended up in the cellar. That was the only place where he could forget his pain. He would lie there, bottle in his hand, drinking himself into a stupor, dodging the torture in his soul for a few hours, then would fall asleep on the floor senselessly drunk. He would wake up in the morning with a hangover and an unbearable feeling in his heart. "What have I done? My God, what have I done?"

Whenever Maria came home, she didn't even look at him. She didn't look at anybody as if she were alone in the world. She walked inside the house like a ghost, passed by the kids without seeing them, lay down on the bed for a few hours with her eyes fixed on the ceiling, then returned to the cemetery.

After a while, Father Sebastian, who hadn't paid too much attention to her until then, started seeing in Maria a problem that could affect his parish. He had said at first that as a mother that had lost her child, she could spend as much time as she wanted in the cemetery. But after the few months she hadn't moved from her son's grave, he began watching her from the Altar's window.

"This woman is destroying my congregation!" he thought. Instead of praying to God, his parishioners came to church on Sunday to spy on Maria kneeled like a stone by Ionică's grave. He couldn't deliver his sermons because of the loon! It was clear it was time he did something, and the sooner the better, or else he would be blamed for things going awry in the community. Yes, without a doubt, it was his civic duty and responsibility to send the woman home.

But how to proceed? He had asked his sons Gicu and Titi to talk to Mitu, their friend, more or less directly to do something about it, but to no avail. And he couldn't force Maria out of the cemetery either. If she wanted to come and spend time by her child's grave, it was her Christian right—he couldn't tell her otherwise. But, by the same token, she couldn't stay there day and night, unwashed and disheveled, forgotten by her family like a beggar, like a lunatic! Being there for a few hours during the day was ok, but coming to the cemetery in the dead of night was too much. No matter how heart-wrenching the passing of someone dear was, before Maria, he hadn't heard of midnight visits to the grave. Only the devil was awake at that hour sniffing about the souls of the dead.

He had to rid himself of the trouble, so he decided to talk to Maria the following Sunday after the sermon. As soon as the parishioners left, he went to Ionică's grave. Maria was there pulling weeds.

"Maria, God bless you, I need to talk to you," he cleared his voice making the cross sign.

She turned her head, staring right through him.

"Look at me, woman, don't do this. God forgive me! Listen, you know everyone in the village is saying that you are crazy. You stay here at the grave all day and all night! Lots of people lose their loved ones—that's God's will—but we need to leave the living with the living and the dead with the dead," he said agitated, flailing his hands in the air.

Maria turned her back to him, grabbed a fistful of dirt from the grave, then let it slip through her fingers.

Father Sebastian barely stopped himself from yelling at her and tried to keep his wits about him, thinking the woman didn't mean to upset him; her mind must have been wondering off.

"Alright, Maria, whatever you want. But so you know, I won't pray for you anymore," he said ready to leave.

"But what have I done that you won't pray for me again?" Maria spouted all of a sudden. "It's my baby, and I want to be by his side, Father. Don't chase me away, I haven't done anything wrong. God forgive me if I've ever done something wrong!"

"I'm not chasing you away, Maria, but your other children are waiting for you at home. They're hungry and dirty. Go back to them, come on," the priest said, placing his hand on her shoulder.

She shrank from under his touch.

"Father, don't you tell me where to go. I know where my place is! This is my place—here—six feet under the ground, next to my beloved child!" she roared. "Where have you gone, my baby, are you cold down there?" she mumbled through sobs. "Are you cold, my baby? Mommy's coming to you. I'll kill myself and come. I don't want to live, why is God punishing me like this? Good God, what have you done to me?"

Father Sebastian couldn't take the hysterics unfolding in front of him.

"Woman," he raised his voice to cover hers, "look into my eyes now. I'm telling you this once! I told you what people are saying, what they gossip behind your back, I gave you some good advice, and you won't listen! If I catch you here ever again, I'll bash your head in, listen here! Get outta here, get out of my parish, leave!" he howled at her.

Petrified, Maria took a few steps back.

"Scamper out of here, get outta the cemetery! Don't want to see you here, or I'll break your legs! Run! Run away now, you pest!" he raised his fist.

She made the cross sign with both hands as if to protect herself from the devil, spewed the foulest curses she knew, then dashed away.

That was the last time Maria showed herself by her son's grave. No one saw her going to church afterwards—not during the week, not on Saturdays and Sundays, not on Easter and not on Christmas. The words that Father Sebastian had used to chase the Fiddler's wife from her child's grave had divided the village in two camps: those that took the priest's side, saying that Maria had gone too far, and those that took Maria's side, saying no one could commit a bigger sin than the priest had done.

It took Maria a long time to come out of the darkness. Six months from the incident, she exchanged first words with the children, according to their age. She talked to the little ones first: Mǎriuţa, then Micu, Sandu, and in the end, Gheorghe. She didn't say much, not like before in any case, but at least she was saying something. A while later, she began seeing after her chores, a lot more conscientiously than before, burying herself in work to escape all thoughts.

A year had passed before she threw Mitu first words—to move some wood planks and make room by the well. He looked at her encouraged and answered quickly—"right away, Maria!"—but she turned her back at him and minded her own.

In another few months, she called him, out of the blue, to come and sit down at the table with the rest of the family glancing at him not reproachfully as before but with indifference.

She was beginning to forget.

THE COMMUNISTS

Chapter 74

The minute Mitu learned that Ciorogaru had returned to Novaci, he put his children in the carriage and went to his house. They had so many things to talk about. Why was he back? Where had he been? Had he lost everything he owned after the stabilization?30F* Wasn't he afraid for his life now that the communists were in power? A lot of the top people from the Legion had been thrown in jail.31F†

When he got there, he looked over the fence and saw him tinkering with the well's pulley.

"Look at that—look who's here. Good day!" he shouted from the carriage.

Ciorogaru recognized his voice and came quickly.

"Hey, hey, hey, look who's here! How are you doing, man? Come inside, don't just stay out in the road!"

"Well, I can't stay, I'm just passing by."

"What do you mean, just passing? What, you came just so you can leave?"

Mitu pointed to the children, then asked when he had come back.

"A few days ago, Fiddler. I'm very happy to see you."

"I haven't seen you in such a long time! Are you here for good or leaving again?"

Ciorogaru became gloomy.

"I came home for good. I've had enough politics," he said dispirited. "Let me look at you," he took two steps back, measuring him from head to toe. "What happened to you, man? Why do you need a cane?"

Mitu told him shortly about the accident.

"Lord, what trouble! But I see you're prolific; look how many kids you have! You have a daughter, God bless her!"

Mitu lowered his eyes, hunched forward a little and clenched his fists as in the expectancy of an unavoidable blow.

"I hope you don't mind I brought them along. And I really can't stay. I was on my way to the market but because I heard you were home I stopped by to see you. Well, I had another boy, Ionică, but he passed away..."

"Oh my goodness, I'm so sorry. God rest his soul! What happened?"

"Well, Mr. Ciorogaru, he got sick. He...caught a cold—maybe tuberculosis or something, I don't know—and Doctor Niculescu couldn't do anything about it."

---

* The monetary reform from August 15, 1947 with a new leu replacing the old one at a rate of 20,000 old lei = 1 new leu. This reevaluation was carried out with no advance warning and only allowed the possibility of exchanging a fixed sum of money for the new currency, deposing cash holders (middle and upper classes) of their last economies.
† Among others, Iuliu Maniu, Ion Mihalache, Gheorghe Brătianu, Constantin Argetoianu, Mircea Vulcănescu, Radu Korned. Many of them died while in prison. Gheroghe Brătianu, for instance, was left to die of dysentery with no medical care. General Radu Korne was tortured to death.

"I see...and? What news do you have from the community?"

"Well, many things happened. Some people died, Vlăscan and Mitrescu, I don't know if you've heard. Vlăscan was standing like you are now, God forbid, and dropped dead. And Mitrescu—he died up in the mountains, a log fell over him and severed his head. When they came looking for him, they found his head in the ravine. And the teacher Panaitescu, I don't know if you know, has gone crazy. He talks to himself and sees ghosts; no one can talk to him anymore. I thought he was going to get better, but he hasn't. His poor wife has to take care of him because he can't do it on his own."

"I've heard of Panaitescu and Vlăscan, but I didn't know Mitrescu died. May he rest in peace. And? What about your village? How's Flitan, I haven't heard anything of him, how is he?"

"Good, he's good; he was almost in trouble when the Russians came, because they caught Tiberică with a trunk of jewelry, but the kids were alright. I hid them in my attic. But how about you, if you don't mind me asking again, are you okay? What did you do in Bucharest? Are you alone or with the missus?"

A shadow of sadness clouded Ciorogaru's face.

"I came with Ileana. She's somewhere in the house. Our fight was for nothing, Mitu. The one thing I feared the most happened: the country's now led by a Hungarian and a Bolshevik Jew. The Captain must be turning in his grave! So many of us died in vain. I wonder if we were set up for failure from the beginning. You know, sometimes I think you were right; you once said here in my home that the role of the little people is to die for the ones in power, and that we strive pointlessly because the games are made at the top. I pray to God you're wrong because if that's the case, we'll find our end in a communist Romania. Our only chance is to keep fighting."

Mitu looked at him with pity. Not because he had returned powerless to Novaci. Not because he had withered and grown visibly old in the last few years, with deep creases on his face, but because he had lost a battle in which he genuinely believed. It was a sentiment Mitu had felt many times as well.

He called out to his children, who were playing in the yard, and told them to get in the carriage.

"That's it lil' larks, we're going back home! Please forgive us for having bothered you, Mr. Ciorogaru. I'll come to see you by myself when I come to Novaci. If I may, I'd like to give you some advice," he wavered.

"Tell me, Mitu, of course! By all means!"

"If I were you, I'd run abroad. Like Horia Sima. Now that the communists are in power, I'd be afraid for my life. They will kill all those that were sided with the fascists. Please pardon me for being so blunt, but I worry for you."

Ciorogaru looked away.

"I can't, Mitu," he said after a long pause. "When I ran to Germany, I thought I could fight for my country from the outside, but I can do a lot more by staying here. I will never leave again. Whatever my fate may be."

Mitu said goodbye, got in the carriage, and urged the horse, not suspecting for a minute that he had seen Ciorogaru for the very last time.

Chapter 75

Ciorogaru was arrested shortly after that. When Mitu learned of it, he grabbed the trunk brought from America, took a box out, and rummaged through it. It was one of the boxes in which he used to keep his bootlegging money. He closed it gingerly, as though afraid to break it even though it was made of steel; he wrapped it in a few rags, hid it in a leather pouch, and then another, and went in the back yard. He dug a three-foot hole, placed the box in it, and covered it with dirt, pebbles, and twigs.

As soon as he was finished, he called Gheorghe to show him the spot and explain what he had done.

"My son, you're a young man now. I trust you; you're a very good boy. I need to tell you something very important! Listen: in the back garden, about six feet to the left of the apple tree, I hid a box of documents from America. Only me and you know of it. Your mother doesn't know. No one else knows. This is going to be our secret. If I die, then tell your mother about it. But as long as I'm alive, you need to keep this hush-hush. Promise me. Swear to me!"

The boy agreed, overwhelmed by the importance his father was bestowing on him.

"Yes, dad, that's what I'll do. As you said. But what's in it?"

"Some documents and some stock holder certificates from America. When you grow up, you'll understand what I'm saying here. But don't tell anyone, because they can throw you in jail for it."

Gheorghe swore to his father that his lips were sealed.

A day passed, then a week, and then a month. Time went by indifferent to people's trepidations, oblivious that above Mitu loomed a tragedy worse than everything else from before.

One afternoon, an automobile stopped in front of their gate and two individuals got out—a redhead and a thug—who ordered them all to get out of the house. Mitu, who was out on the porch, approached them feigning calmness and surprise, with the children and Maria in tow.

"Citizen Popescu Dumitru?" the sorrel-haired one said, leafing through some papers in a folder.

"Yes, that's me. But please come inside."

"We are from *Securitate*, we came to search your place," the other handed him a warrant.

"Well sure, we have nothing to hide."

The two went inside and ransacked the house. They opened the stove and looked in it with a flashlight, then rummaged through closets and knocked on walls and floors to see if they sounded hollow. In the small bedroom, they searched under the bed, emptied out all drawers, and told Mitu to open the trunk.

They lay his suit from America out on the bed and checked all the pockets. They looked at some pictures and leafed through some books written in English. They found the American passport and studied it page by page. In it, Mitu had placed his soldier's record and the discharge order from the National Guard of the United States, in which it was noted, among other things, that he had participated in the Battle of Meuse-Argonne. The letter announcing his bonus was there, also.

The redheaded man gathered everything and put it in an envelope.

"Is there a problem, gentlemen?" Mitu asked, trying to figure out what was awaiting him.

"Citizen Popescu Dumitru, speak only when spoken to! You need to come with us. We're writing up an official report that you need to sign at the police station."

"But why are you taking me? I didn't do anything. I really didn't do anything." Mitu attempted a feeble defense.

He was flanked by the two men out the front gate and shoved into the automobile. He waved to Maria from the back window until the car made the turn onto the main road.

They stopped in Târgu-Jiu in front of a villa, and he was taken upstairs on the last floor, in some kind of a common dormitory holding twenty other arrested people, women and children among them.

He was given a bed by the window. He sat down and looked around. His neighbor—a young man of maybe twenty-five—was lying on his back staring at the ceiling, stiff as a corpse. His breathing was the only proof he was still alive. His eyes were bruised and one of his arms was wrapped up in a dirty rag. Mitu tried asking him how long he had been there and why, but the boy didn't seem to hear him. An elderly man, who was constantly coughing, two beds farther down signaled him that they were not to talk to one another, or else they would be taken to the basement and beaten up.

It was evening time. The moon was spilling pale rays onto the floor, unaware of the tormented souls inside. Mitu tossed and turned for hours, thinking about the difficulties that had followed him through the last years. "The curse of the Bessarabian's upon me..."

He was awoken at five in the morning by a flashlight pointed into his eyes.

"Popescu Dumitru, get up and follow us!"

He got up confused and reached for the walking stick, but the man kicked it with his leg, screaming at him to move faster.

"But I can't walk without my cane."

"Shut up and move your ass!" the guardian howled, shoving him ahead.

They took him to a small room and ordered him to wait there. The place, which had probably served as a cupboard before, wasn't furnished and didn't even have a chair in it. A dim bulb hung from the ceiling spreading a sinister light around.

He had been there alone for about an hour when a corpulent man came inside, measured him with his eyes from head to toe, got out and came back with a chair on which he sat grunting.

"Popescu, I'm going to be straight with you because it's in both our interests—especially yours," he looked through a folder. "I want to be understood from the beginning; you'll say everything you know. If you don't want to do it of your own accord, we'll get it outta you by force. Got it?"

"But please," Mitu answered scared, trying to appease the man somehow, "I haven't done anything, I don't know why I was brought here!"

The man fixed onto him with his eyes, then got up and opened the door.

"Mihai, come over here, 'cause we got some problems!" he called out somewhere in the hallway.

Two robust men walked into the room. One of them was holding a leather whip with a handle weaved of thick wire; the other one had a gun at his waist.

"Comrade Vintilă, did I hear right? Do we got problems with the confessions of this traitor?" the one with the whip seemed to amuse himself.

"In his best interest, I hope not..." Vintilă said ironically and turned to Mitu.

"Let us refresh your memory, Popescu! Let's see: born on October 2nd, 1896; fled to America at seventeen with false documents on January 18, 1913; enrolled in the American Army; American citizen, meaning lover of capitalistic imperialism! Not only that, but when you got the American citizenship, you pledged your allegiance to America! In other words, you're a betrayer to your native country! A traitor of the Popular Republic of Romania! A traitor of communism!"

Mitu took a deep breath to calm down.

"Sympathizer of the legionnaires and participant to many legionnaire gatherings," Vintilă continued. "Associated himself with the legionnaires from Novaci—he sang at their meetings! As you can see, we know what you've done, you bastard! And this is nothing! We know a lot more! Tell us who your collaborators have been, and where their resistance nests are! We have confessions from others; if you leave something out from what we already know, we'll beat the life outta you!"

Mitu leaned against the wall for support. Vintilă summoned the two men who approached him, pinned him well, and one punched him in the stomach. He collapsed, holding on to his stomach and coughing, nearly throwing up. When he recovered, he scrambled to his feet but was hit again, a kick to his chin, which smacked him against the wall. Not daring to get up, he barely spoke.

"I have no connection to the Guard or other movements. I'm a simple peasant working his land and caring for his cattle! I swear! I'm not guilty of anything!"

Vintilă moved his head as if to say that he understood too well those types of denials and signaled the other two again. One of them lifted Mitu by the shoulders and held him, and the other started pummeling him rampantly. Then they undressed him, throwing him to the floor, and struck him until they grew tired. He was groaning in pain and pulled his knees to his chin in an attempt to protect his face from the blows.

When they saw that he was barely moving, Vintilă signaled them to stop and began questioning him again.

"Popescu, I'm resorting to kinder methods now. Have you or not been part of the legionnaire movement?"

Mitu shook his head weakly, "No."

"I'm losing my patience with you, so you know! And, when I lose my patience, it's not good! It's not good at all! You don't want to get me irate! Whoever steps on my toes ends up bad! If you want to come unharmed out of here—and this is the last time I'm telling you this as a friend—you need to confess everything! It's your choice: live or die..." he finished wryly.

"But I'm not and never have been in any movement!" Mitu said exhausted. He had become frightened at the thought he might not see the next day.

They threw him like a rag doll from one to the other and kicked him until they grew tired, then sat on him to smoke a cigarette. At last, they dragged him to the bathroom next door, doused him in a tub full of cold water, then brought him back and sat him on a chair taking turns slapping him.

During all this time, the investigator Vintilă remained impassible, with his thoughts elsewhere. Every now and then he looked absentmindedly at what was happening then would go back to skimming through the folder. At one point, he signaled the men to stop, waited for Mitu to come around, pulled his chair very close, and stuck some papers in his face.

"Popescu, these are people's confessions that can prove you were a legionnaire! Let me read you some of them! Eyewitnesses declaring that you participated in a legionnaire gathering in the yard of the church in Novaci, where the country traitor Zelea Codreanu came, and you sang a legionnaire hymn. True or false?"

Mitu nodded weakly.

"Another witness says that you met with the traitor Gheorghe Ciorogaru many times and that together you organized anticommunist movements. And others have declared that you convinced them to vote for the legionnaire party 'Everything for the Motherland.' Do you admit it or not?"

Mitu struggled to straighten out in the chair—his side was hurting terribly as though his ribs were broken.

"Yes, I admit that I've met with Gheorghe Ciorogaru many times at his home in Novaci, but I never plotted against anyone. Whoever said that committed perjury, I swear I never plotted against anyone! I never got myself into politics! I swear on my life!"

"You 'swear'" Vintilă scoffed. "Your only way outta this, Popescu, is to come clean about everything and expose all your accomplices. If you confess, the judge will be lenient. Country traitors like you are sentenced to death. If you show remorse and repentance, maybe you'll get a kinder sentence. I will dictate the confession you need to sign, and you will write the names of all those you collaborated with. We already know who they are. Whatever name you leave out will show us that you're lying and will bring about a terrible sentence. Now write as I tell you," he handed him an ink pen.

Mitu tried to grab it between his fingers, but his hand didn't cooperate and he dropped it on the floor. He struggled to pick it up and then write legibly what Vintilă was dictating him.

I, Dumitru Popescu, born on October 2, 1896, do declare of my own accord, not under duress, that I participated in the legionnaire movements from Novaci as an organizer. I gave the tone and sang legionnaire hymns, and I met the leader of the Iron Guard, Corneliu Codreanu whose hand I shook. Also, I declare that I convinced people from my native village Cernădia, my current residence, to vote for the party "Everything for the Motherland." I also declare that I visited many times the house of the legionnaire Gheorghe Ciorogaru from Novaci, conspiring with him to undermine the village. I declare under penalty of perjury that the foregoing is true and correct. My collaborators were...

"By the time I get back, you'll have written the names of all those you collaborated with and signed it at the end!" Vintilă ordered and left the room with the others.

Mitu looked at the door closing behind them. He couldn't sign something like that—it would have been certain sentencing, although some of it was true. It was true he had met Ciorogaru many times; it was true he had been there when the Captain visited Novaci; it was true he had told a few to vote for the legionnaire party. But he wasn't a conspirator and had never betrayed his country. By signing that confession, he would have been signing his death warrant.

He crossed off what he had written about the conspiracies against the state and thought for a minute about what names to write. He first wrote Panaitescu, thinking that no one would question him since he was crazy. Then wrote the assistant Hoity, whom he knew was a communist even from their meetings at Ciorogaru's place for petty politics. Red as he was, they weren't going to do anything to him. Then wrote Ciorogaru, futilely, since he was accused of their very connection. But the more names on the paper, the better, he thought. Then he tried to remember who had died recently in Novaci and Cernădia and chose two people who, he knew, didn't leave too many behind.

He placed the unsigned confession on the chair in front of him, then tried to assess how damaging the beating had been. He could hear howls and screams through the walls and realized he wasn't the only one being tortured there, and that gave him a bit of heart. "They can't kill us all!"

No one came for a while. He was hungry—he hadn't eaten anything since the previous afternoon, but he couldn't imagine how he could chew with his broken lips and swollen jaw. He had a few teeth gone because of the beating. He got up grunting and started looking for them. He found them and put them quickly in his pocket.

In another hour, the door opened and Vintilă came in, followed by the other two. He was drenched in sweat and had a few scratches on his hands.

"Let me see," he said, grabbing his confession.

He skimmed it frowning, and when he finished, he started shouting.

"Are you mocking me? Tell me! Son of a bitch! You bastard, sniveling mongrel, now you're a liar on top of everything! Filth! You brought this upon yourself! Take him!" he barked at the two men.

They dragged him on the floor to the bathroom, forcing him to kneel with his head next to the tub. He suspected what was awaiting him and thought he should hold his breath as long as he could. He inhaled deeply in preparation.

"Drown the mongrel!"

They pushed his head under the water, pressing on his shoulders and the nape of his neck so he couldn't get up. He began thrashing around, flailing his arms as if to hang on to the last gasp of air. The agents let him back up, and he thought, with a speck of satisfaction, that he had tricked them and managed not to swallow any water.

A second later, they plunged him again, before he could fill his lungs with air. He held his breath for as long as he could, but his body became spastic. He writhed desperately and inhaled a lot of water, fighting to come up to the surface. The men kept pushing him down, time during which he took a few more gulps, then yanked him out, and threw him on the floor.

"You see, Popescu, we're not kidding around," Vintilă addressed him in an unnaturally kind tone as he was coming around. "Understand that we only want the best for the country, nothing more," he said, then his voice became harsh, "we want your complete confession or else you won't come alive outta here."

"I told you everything I know, please, I swear on my life and my children's lives! You have to believe me; I'm not lying to you! You can kill me, but I can't tell you any more than that!" he begged them.

Vintilă signaled the two to take him back to the room. There, they hanged a thick rope to a hook from the ceiling and pulled a chair under it. They got him up on it with his hands tied tightly behind his back, and put the noose around his neck.

"Listen here, traitor, this is your last chance to confess to everything. If in the next minute you continue to say what you've said up to this point, this will happen to you," Vintilă said making the throat-slitting gesture.

Mitu made the cross sign with the tongue in his mouth, and the other started counting: one, two, three...looking down at the floor. When they reached fifty, he raised his eyes.

"Are you going to sign it or not?"

Mitu, who thought that was it, shouted shaken by terror.

"I'll sign whatever you want, just leave me alone, don't torture me anymore!"

Vintilă grinned, satisfied. Mitu was the sixth person whose confession he'd gotten out that day. He told the other two to untie him and sit him on the chair and handed him a type-written sheet.

"Sign it!"

Mitu read it quickly. The first lines were the same he had hand written before, but the last ones made his flesh crawl. It said there that he had seduced his eldest son, Gheorghe, possessing him in the most unnatural ways, that he had an affair with his own sister, Gheorghița, with whom he had slept many times in the last few years.

He crumpled up the paper and tossed it disgusted on the floor. His eyes webbed with fury and his body tensed up like an arch, despite the pain. He sprang from his chair and threw himself over Vintilă, berserk with rage to grab him by the throat and strangle him, but the two men jumped on him kicking with their feet and punching with their fists, leaving him flat on the floor.

His mind went blank.

Chapter 76

He woke up next day in his bed by the window from the common dormitory. He didn't know how he had been brought there, but he assumed the two men who had tortured him had also hauled him back.

He was wrong. The young man in the bed next to his, who now was speaking to him, said that he and another man were ordered by Vintilă to pick him up. Mitu was given as example to the others, "if you don't confess to everything, this is what happens to you too!"

That was the third day without food. He tried to exchange a few words with the others, but besides their names and where they were from, he didn't learn anything else. People were afraid of informants and didn't say much.

At noon, two new men came for him, shoved him in a van, and took him to a different station—a prison this time—where they did his paperwork and gave him the standard striped jail clothes. He was surprised at their familiarity; they resembled the sailor suit in which Ionică had died. He put them on, considering them the albatross God was placing around his neck.

He was taken to a cell where five men shared three narrow metal beds, which took up three quarters of the room. Two peasants from the south of the country slept in one. A feeble and fearful looking young man shared the second with a man who was probably from Moldova by the way he spoke. On the third bed, there lay an old man that barely seemed to be alive.

Mitu sat next to him—that was the only open spot—and asked where he was from.

"Bucharest. From Bucharest. You?"

"Me? I'm from Gorj. And? Why are you here?"

"They took me for committing acts against the national security."

"Well, old man, what could you have done at your age?'

"I sheltered some young partisans in my home, and they caught us all."

"Yeah?" Mitu looked at him, surprised at the man's courage. "And where are they now?"

"I don't know. But I don't think they're still alive..."

At lunchtime, they each received two slices of bread and some cold vegetable soup in a tin bowl. He wolfed everything down, ignoring the piercing pain in his jaw. His hunger was so tortuous that any other type of suffering paled in comparison. Only as a hobo had he suffered thusly.

In less than five minutes, the guard came back to collect the bowls—a trick, Mitu figured, to make them even hungrier at the sight of food removed before being eaten—and then he tried talking to him.

"Guardian, sir, please, I would like to let my family know of my whereabouts. I'm from Cernădia, and Dumitru Popescu's my name; how could I get in touch with them? That's all I want—to let them know I'm okay."

The man scoffed and slammed the door behind him.

The lights went out in the evening, plunging them in darkness. Mitu lay groaning on the bed. "What is going to happen to me...? How I wish everything ended already! It's Ion's curse..." then he calmed down, thinking that if he hadn't died the previous night, that meant the torture and scare tactics had been a treachery to extract information from him. Otherwise they could have done him over right then and there, right?

Exhaustion overwhelmed him in a little while: he fell into some sort of a healing sleep, which helped him recover so much that the next day when he was roused by the wake-up signal, he thought the pain from the previous night had only been a bad dream. "Maybe they won't torture me like they did..." he said to himself. His face was still swollen—he couldn't see it but felt it—and a burning ache, although not as bad as before, shot through his side by the ribcage.

The guards were shouting at the detainees to stand straight for the roll call, but he remained lying in bed on purpose. "Let's see what happens if I pretend I'm ill," he thought. "Will they kill me or leave me alone?"

"What's the matter with you?" the guard asked when reaching his cell. "Didn't you hear to stand up straight, or you got sick of living?"

He just made an indescribable gesture with his arm.

"Hey, you deaf? What happened?"

Again, he didn't say a word.

"What happened to this guy?" the guard turned to his cellmates.

They shrugged. Mitu groaned and turned his eyes towards him, keeping them half-open, rolling them up in their sockets.

"I'm dying, sir. Dying...I feel so faint..."

The guard left locking the door behind him. In fifteen minutes, he came back and told Mitu to get up to go to the infirmary.

"If you want to see a doctor, move your ass!" he shouted at him.

He faked super-human efforts to get up. He toiled down some stairs cautious not to stumble on the steps—he no longer had his cane—and they entered a small room where he was left alone. A doctor showed up in a few moments, made him undress, and checked him carefully.

"What is it, Popescu? What hurts?"

"I'm very sick, I'm afraid I might die today," he whispered. "I think I'm going to faint, I feel very weak..."

The doctor watched him incredulously and smiled imperceptibly. He had seen that kind of "performance" before. That type of theatrics was prompted by the very circumstances those men found themselves in; that was the place where people gave up their dignity, resorted to all kinds of deceitfulness, were ready to backstab anyone, even sell their siblings or children, only to come out alive. He didn't judge them; had he been in their place and he would have probably done the same.

"I can't keep you here, man. I can't. If you saw the patients I have—people who can barely breathe, it's a miracle they're still alive—you'd understand me. I need to send you back to your cell, but I'll tell them to leave you alone to rest, and I'll give you some pills to get better."

"Thank you, thank you very much, Doctor!" Mitu mumbled, not believing his ears. "Thank you, may God watch over you!"

"Popescu, you got away with little until now...very little I'd say: a few cracked ribs and some scratches. If you come out from the interrogations alive without signing their confessions, they can only sentence you to very few years. If you give in and sign, they won't torture you anymore, but they'll sentence you to death or forced labor."

Mitu looked questioningly at him. What was that all about? Why was he telling him all that? This doctor had to be a communist, or else how was he working in a prison with political detainees?

"Only a few come out alive from their interrogations. I should know; they all end up here in the end," he whispered, then called a guard to take him back to his cell.

He left the infirmary confused. He wasn't sure whether the doctor had tried to send him some hidden message. But he thought that from that moment on he had to be very careful with everyone. In prison, even a best friend could turn out to be a mole.

The months that followed unfolded in a grotesque routine; a few times a week from morning until noon, he underwent questioning sessions with beatings and torture, fictitious executions with the gun stuck to the temple, Russian roulette games where he had to put the barrel into his mouth and pull the trigger once, followed by a break of a few hours when he was taken back to his cell and left there to rest. At night, questionings again—easier on the body, but harsher on the mind. That was when the investigators resorted to threats and shocking tactics, telling him that Gheorghe and Maria had both signed declarations against him, that they were going to be witnesses at his trial, and that if he didn't collaborate, they would be thrown in jail as well. They told him that Ciorogaru had understood his terrible mistakes and had become a communist in jail, signing papers and denouncing others in the Guard and showing his allegiance to the Romanian Workers Party.

He didn't give in. He faced the torture not out of some conviction, because he didn't believe in any political platforms. Not out of hatred either, because he realized he was a victim of the system, and the investigators were just doing their jobs. He resisted because he had a shred of hope, a feeble sign showing him the agents didn't really have him at their whim: they had never said his eldest son told them about the box hidden in the back garden. Had they arrested Gheorghe, the way they said, the boy would have given in to torture and would have confessed everything.

That kept him afloat. He underwent humiliation and pain words cannot describe. Many a time he was convinced he couldn't possibly go on and wanted to give in. Yet, each time he considered signing whatever they wanted, thinking that death would be better than his living hell, a voice inside would whisper to him, "It's painful, but hang on another day, and you'll tell them tomorrow. Just another day! You'll sign when they mention the box!"

Eleven months after his arrest, he was told his trial would take place in a few weeks, and that he had been assigned a public defender. The counts of indictment were, among others, fraternizing with the fascists, plotting against the popular power, alliance with imperialism, and many more. The lawyer's commission was to be paid by the family. That made him happy because it meant Maria would finally learn he was still alive.

Chapter 77

Mitu met his lawyer Ion Pintilie for the first time on the day of his trial, when the man came into his cell to tell him he was there for appearances' sake, without any real say in front of the judge. He was solidly built, with a rough, grizzled beard, bushy and spiky brows covering a pair of malicious eyes—a giant of a man, better suited for beating and hanging the guilty rather than defending the innocent.

"Just so you know, you're off to a promising start here," he said at the end of their very brief meeting. "They're trying everyone else in groups, but they're taking you alone, since they got stumped on the fact that you haven't signed any confession until now. You know, generally, prosecutors look to put many defendants on the stand all at once, to show they're systematically organized and to obtain harsher sentences."

Mitu shrugged. "What difference does this make, I wonder..." he thought, and asked the lawyer about his family.

"Have you spoken to my wife? You've been to Cernădia for your fee, right?"

"Yes, I have and I've told her you'd be tried soon. She was very happy to hear about you. But I have no idea where they are going to send you after the trial, because there's no way they're going to acquit you, and I didn't know where to tell her she can visit you."

In a few hours, they took him from his cell, chained his feet and transported him in an armored van to the courthouse. Joking bitterly with himself, Mitu thought he must have been as important as Iuliu Maniu32F[*] to warrant such security measures.

The courtroom was full. An unfamiliar audience filled the seats gawking curiously at the proceedings. He wondered who they were and why they had such an interest in him, but his only answer was that they were there simply to dawdle about. In fact, they had been brought in for propagandistic purposes.

The judge pounded the gavel, coughed two times with importance, and pointed his finger to the prosecutor's bench.

"Comrade Magistrate, you may begin."

The public prosecutor, a lanky man with three strands of hair he constantly arranged to cover his bald spot, fixed the glasses on his nose and started reading the charges, highly affected by the magnitude of his role. He accused Mitu of plotting against the state, social order, and the Romanian Workers Party; legionnaire activity; espionage on behalf of the Anglo-Americans; and actions against The Popular Republic of Romania.

---

[*] Iuliu Maniu (1873-1953), one of the greatest political figures of Romania, was sentenced by a communist kangaroo court and died in Sighet Prison. His body was thrown in a common grave without ever being identified.

"We'll give you proof, Comrade Judge," he gesticulated, "that the accused was associated with the Iron Guard, with his frequent visits to the leader of the Regional Legionnaire Movement of Oltenia, Gheorghe Ciorogaru, who lived in Novaci, near his village. During those meetings, they plotted against the communists, organizing resistance movements against them. We will further show that the defendant admitted his sympathy for fascism and capitalism many times, praising the Americans and the legionnaires. Witnesses will corroborate that the accused was deeply involved in all of these. Citizen Popescu is a dangerous element fighting against our state, trying to undermine its authority. Hence, he needs to be punished exemplarily."

The confidence Mitu had felt upon entering the courtroom vanished. Those charges could send him right in front of the firing squad, and no one in the room was on his side. Even his own lawyer was against him, nodding in agreement as the prosecutor was reading the charges, slightly impatient as though he couldn't wait for the day to end.

The first witness, to Mitu's both surprise and concern, was Panaitescu. He swaggered in flanked on either side by two guards, smiling superciliously at everyone in the courtroom.

"Yes, gentlemen! How may I be of help?" he said without being asked, making ample gestures.

"Witness, speak only when asked!" the judge irritatingly reprimanded him.

"Yes, of course, your honor, of course," he agreed, then sat down.

The prosecutor asked him to identify Mitu.

"Yes, of course, honorable gentlemen, he's the one sitting on the defendant's bench, Dumitru Popescu, the musician of Novaci and Cernădia. And the whole world. And the Universe! We call him the Fiddler because he is an unbelievable violinist! We've known each other for a long time. We're very good acquaintances."

"Please describe for us your meetings in Gheorghe Ciorogaru's house from Novaci, in which the defendant participated many times."

Panaitescu pondered for a minute, as if to remember all the details, then started talking.

"Yes, Mr. President, we met, of course, we played the fiddle, he plucked the strings, but when it happened, you know, it was generally sunny outside. It was so bright that we needed to protect ourselves. I'm a teacher! The floor is unwashed, gentlemen, and the gentleman sitting at the dais looks like Adolf! He looks like Adolf! But it is dark in here, and Satan will come to hew us to pieces, but I have Jesus' power and I can defend you all and save you!"

The courtroom remained in stunned silence for a few moments, then people started murmuring. The prosecutor was the first to recover from the shock, cleared his voice, and tried to steer the witness in the right direction.

"Witness Panaitescu, please come back to our topic. Did you or did you not meet the accused in the home of Citizen Gheorghe Ciorogaru?"

The teacher looked at him as if he were staring at some atrocity and pulled himself back, chair and body, to the edge of the witness' stand. His face was contorted in a grimace of horror, and his eyes were bulging out of his head.

"There's a fly! A fly! You have a fly on your nose! It carries germs, you know. Shoo it away!"

The prosecutor wiped his nose automatically and tried to say something else—the judge had already lost his patience, but didn't know how to proceed. The audience was roaring with laughter, and even Mitu couldn't help a surreptitious smile. Panaitescu was making a mockery of the courtroom.

The guards dashed to the teacher, almost lifted the lunatic from the ground, and dragged him out of the room, despite his vehement protests.

"Enough with this one, next witness!" the judge roared.

The second one to enter was Mihail Panait, the doctor's assistant from Novaci.

"Hoity! They brought Hoity?" Mitu thought surprised, wondering if that meant good or bad news for him. Hoity was a communist, everyone knew that for a long time, but they had been somewhat friends.

"Citizen Panait," the prosecutor began after the formalities, "tell us about the meetings in Gheorghe Ciorogaru's house, to which to accused also participated."

The assistant gave Mitu a passing and expressionless look, then turned to the judge and began talking about Ciorogaru's dinners, about their meetings and their mostly inane chatter, how they used to play music and drink until they got buzzed getting home very late.

"Mitu is a very gifted musician, and people invited him everywhere."

"From the discussions the defended held with you and the others, what would you say his political views were?" the prosecutor asked.

Panait took a moment to think. He turned to Mitu, hesitated for a moment, then said very categorically, "Popescu Dumitru, your honor, was apolitical. Gheorghe Ciorogaru asked him many times to join the legionnaires, but he always said no."

A wave of murmurs passed through the courtroom, and Mitu breathed a sigh of relief. He had been afraid Panait had learned about his putting him on the list of collaborators, even as unsigned as he had left it and now probably begrudged him.

The prosecutor fumbled through some paperwork then tried to gainsay him.

"But, at those meetings, didn't Popescu Dumitru manifest his sympathy for capitalism? For the Americans or the Germans?"

The assistant took another pause, as though trying to remember the details of their political chatter from a few years before. Mitu realized the man was giving himself time to concoct a favorable answer while striving not to give the impression he was defending him. He thanked him in his head and made the cross sign with his tongue, and his heart filled with the hope he still had a chance and the good Lord might see him through his predicament.

"Your honor, those were long discussions and we talked a lot about politics," Hoity answered. "The defendant showed his sympathy for various orientations and regimes. I remember well his stories about the American wealth and the efficiency of capitalism, and he mentioned Rockefeller, but he spoke favorably about the Bolsheviks also, when he complained that in Romania the poor have too little compared to the rich and that the situation should be evened out. I remember a discussion between him and Gheorghe Ciorogaru when he stated clearly this idea, criticizing harshly the Americans."

"But you mentioned that he praised capitalism, yes or no?" the prosecutor insisted, satisfied that he finally could hang onto something.

"Yes, but not to—" Panait tried to nuance his answer but was unceremoniously interrupted.

"Enough! Your answer was clear! Another question: is it true that the defendant participated in the legionnaire actions from Novaci, where he sang legionnaire hymns to a crowd and became an example of loyalty to the Iron Guard when, in front of everybody, he shook the hand of the traitor Corneliu Zelea Codreanu?"

The assistant took a moment then tried to explain.

"Your honor, the defendant was asked to sing a legionnaire hymn because he was one of the best musicians in the area, as I already mentioned. And when they proposed him to—"

"Please answer with a 'yes' or 'no!'" the prosecutor raised his voice. "'Yes' or 'no,' understood? Nothing more! Is it true that the defendant participated to the legionnaire gathering from March 25, 1934 in Novaci?"

"Yes, sir..."

"Were you an eyewitness?"

"Yes, I was."

"Is it true that at that gathering he sang a legionnaire hymn—more specifically, the *Hymn of the Fallen Legionnaires*—in front of everybody?"

"It's true."

"Is it also true that, at that same meeting, he shook the hand of the leader of the legionnaire movement, Zelea Codreanu, also known as the Captain?"

"Yes, it's true and that—"

"Comrade Judge, I have no more questions!" the prosecutor turned, looking triumphantly over the room. "It is evident, from the defendant's past, that he was and is pro-fascism! It goes without a reasonable doubt that Popescu Dumitru is a dangerous element, proven also by the fact that he is an American citizen!"

The judged looked irritated at him, marveling at his incompetence—"his case is so clear-cut, the idiot!"—but asked if he had any more witnesses. The prosecutor said no, and Mitu wondered why the people he had convinced to vote for the legionnaire party hadn't been called. It was right then that his lawyer's turn came.

Pintilie stood up fawning around like a stray dog for a bone. He caressed his chin, straightened his back, and donned a serious air, in tone with the gravity of the moment.

"Dear comrades and colleagues," he said silkily, in contrast with his impressive stature, "it has been demonstrated without a reasonable doubt that the defendant had relations with the legionnaires and sympathized with the Americans—and still does! Given this clear evidence, I have no weapons or witnesses to fight in his favor. But I ask, on his behalf, for some understanding when you consider his punishment, since he is the father of four children who need him home."

"They need him 'home?'" the judge snorted. "What for? To indoctrinate them with his Nazi views? Aren't they better off growing up without his bad influence? Comrade, please!"

"Please forgive me, that is not what I meant..." Pintilie barely muttered, lowering his head under the judge's words like a squelched, overgrown bug. "I was trying to say that, after he will have served his sentence, the defendant will be able to go back to his own family a changed man, for the better, of course, and as such, he will impart the knowledge gained all these years."

Hearing those words, Mitu jumped from his seat, making the two guards dozing off on their feet aim their guns at him. He ignored their threat and started shouting at the judge that his lawyer was supposed to defend, not accuse him, then asked if he could write a declaration.

The judge refused, rolling his eyes, "where does he think he is? America?"

"But I want to give a declaration! It's my right! The constitution gives me the right to question the witnesses and defend myself. The constitution gives me the right to self defense!" Mitu said hotly.

The judge couldn't believe his ears and ordered him to be quiet, but Mitu, thinking that at that point he had nothing else to lose, kept on.

"You have to allow me to at least say something at the end! I'm not afraid of death; I've stared it in the eyes many times. I'm not afraid of anything! If you throw an innocent man in jail, may God pay you for it, but you need to let me give a declaration!" he said, turning begging eyes around the room.

The audience remained impassible. It wasn't the first time they were partaking in such a scene; in fact, it was the third one that day. The only thing they were still interested in was the verdict.

His lawyer, face contorted in the befuddled expression of not knowing how to proceed in such a circumstance, spoke again.

"If I may consult with the accused, Comrade President!"

The judge nodded, and he went quickly to Mitu to whisper in his ear sufficiently loudly for all to hear that his attitude was irritating everyone and that he risked doubling his sentence due to contempt if he kept on that way.

Any trace of riposte Mitu might have had was shattered. He realized he was at their whim, a rug on which they could step or with which they could wipe their butts—an utterly powerless human being. Seeing everyone allied against him, leading with Pintilie, he nodded submissively.

He then apologized, saying that he laid his future in their hands and that he was expecting to pay for his crimes, which he was aware were grave, but that he had extenuating circumstances because he had worked for the Anti-Usury League and had never been a member of any parties.

His sentence was communicated shortly after that. They called him back in the room to tell him he was to do "seven years' imprisonment minus the eleven months and nine days already served." He received the news unperturbed, as if he were the spectator of a movie and not the protagonist. In a few moments, while the judge's words entered his mind but not his soul, he felt he was drowning without completely understanding what he had just heard.

In the next moments however, when the guards pushed him from the defendants' bench, putting him back in chains and threatening him with their cudgels, it all dawned on him. He tensed up like a beast and started screaming for help and cursing everyone, spewing the foulest words he could muster up. They dragged him outside, and he continued thrashing about and blaming God for the tragedy that had befallen him. Then, exhausted, he gave up, bursting into tears and cursing to hell the day he had made the unfortunate decision to leave America.

Gray-haired, weak, and maimed, kneeled by forces too great to comprehend or face, Mitu was, in the spring of 1950, on his way to learn the horrific reality of the communist prisons.

He was fifty-four.

Chapter 78

The train that transported Mitu, along with other prisoners—the majority were political detainees like him but there were some suspects in criminal cases as well—reminded him of the freight trains he had traveled up and down America as a hobo. Compared to then, his current conditions seemed pretty good. Seeing the despondent faces of his companions, generally young people under thirty, he smiled to himself, "These kids haven't had much hardship in their lives until now, it seems..."

He hadn't the slightest clue where he was being taken. The train's windows had been covered with metal panes, so nothing could be seen outside. Even if he had wanted to peek through some crack, he couldn't have done it because his feet were locked in chains, and the slightest noise would have gotten the guards' attention, who had already warned them to stay glued to their spots.

After a whole day of traveling, with many stops in open fields or stations, the trained slowed down with a strident shrill and a foreboding rumble and didn't move again. After an hour of waiting, they were taken out under the threat of rifles and led in a long file inside a massive prison where they were ordered to line-up in army rows.

A large built man, with a neck as thick as his head made his appearance in a few moments. He was, Mitu would find out soon, the warden Ionel Gheorghiu, an ex-railroad worker from Tecuci. He strutted arrogantly in front of them, looked at them with furrowed brow, inspected them from top to bottom and top again, snorting through his nose once in a while. Then, perched up on a mound of dirt, he gave them his customary speech.

"Welcome to Gherla! You bastards, get it through your thick skulls! You're here to serve your sentence and become re-educated! I don't know what the judges were thinking, but they should have executed you for your wrongdoings, fouls, not allow slackers such as yourselves to live off the state's money! You betrayed your country, that's what you did! But we put a rod in pickle for you, no worries! If you haven't met the devil before, you'll see him from now on! If you don't behave well, you'll be shot on the spot, so you know! You bandits!"

Despite his bitterness and despondency, Mitu found it in him to smile. He had met plenty of these commandants in the war, the type that busted out of their skin with self-importance, and had suffered a lot of browbeating in his life.

After he was done talking, the warden passed them on to the care of two detainees that started threatening and cursing them as if, in reality, they were the ones in charge of the prison. They barked at them to stand up straight, made them shout their names, and at the end, one of them gave them a speech.

"Don't think you'll get away too easy! You'll confess even what you've sucked from your mother's tits! We have signed declarations from others, who have told us things about you that you haven't admitted! Whoever doesn't come clean about everything will suffer dire consequences! Now, to your cells, bandits!"

Mitu looked befuddled at him. Who was this jerk? How come he had such authority? He suspected that he was in cahoots with the top guys in Bucharest. He asked the person next to him if knew who those were, and the man—young, maybe twenty, who by demeanor, seemed familiar with what was going on—whispered to him.

"Popa Alexandru, nicknamed Ţanu, and Livinski Mihail, nicknamed Mieluţă. They have been through re-education33F[*] and now they're members of Ohdhecaca34F[†]. They used to be Ţurcanu's apprentices."

"Ţurcanu? Who's that?"

"You don't know who Eugen Ţurcanu is...?!" the young man looked surprised at him. "You're lucky. He's a Bolshevized guard, the re-educator in chief from Piteşti. You haven't heard the saying: *Now that the Captain's dead, it's through the communists, the Legion moves ahead?*"

Mitu asked nothing else. "Ohdhecaca? Bolshevized guard? What the hell did it all mean?" he wondered, but stopped bothering his neighbor with questions. He thanked him then resumed listening to Ţanu, who was about to conclude.

"Bandits, I'll say it one more time: if you don't confess and give us your accomplices, you'll see hell on earth! Get it through your heads!"

They were divvied up into cells. They took him to a big room on the second floor cramming about forty more prisoners. The atmosphere was more somber than that in the dormitory from the Târgu-Jiu Political Detainees Camp, where he had been taken right after his arrest. The air was thick, the window too small to vent properly. The toilet was in a corner, an unbelievable luxury, he was told, compared to other prisons where buckets were used. The men slept on wooden cots covered by some sort of mats—another item of luxury, his cellmates pointed again, as in other places prisoners slept on the floor. Some of them, probably informants he assumed, had some blankets, which, although dirty and full of holes, softened their beds considerably.

The majority were workers or peasants, some serving long terms for treason or espionage, others being there for shorter periods, and others still

---

[*] The "Piteşti Experiment", inspired, according to some sources, from the work of the Russian author Anton Makarenko, was carried out between 1949-1953, in the Piteşti Prison in Romania and it refers to a brainwashing process whose goal was to have prisoners discard their former political, religious, and social convictions up to the point of total obedience through extreme physical torture means (e.g., eating feces and drinking urine, striking the soles of the feet with rods with nails, starvation), and psychological torture (e.g., physically torturing friends, forcing to admitting to imaginary misdeeds or aberrant sexual behavior, etc.). Given the great number of victims (1000-5000) it is considered the largest and most intensive brainwashing program in the Eastern Bloc. A part of those that underwent the "experiment" didn't survive the torture, many were physically and psychologically marked for the rest of their lives, while others were considered "reeducated" and became torturers of former friends or cellmates.

[†] O.D.C.C. - "The Organization of Detainees with Communist Convictions"—nicknamed mockingly "Ohdhecaca" ("caca" = "shit" in Romanian) by the prisoners.

awaiting their sentence. There was just one intellectual, Cristian Lupu, a young man that had studied medicine before his arrest. Many came from Transylvania, but there were some from other regions: one from Iași, another from Piatra Neamț, two brothers from Dobrogea and one from Bucharest. Mitu was the only one from Gorj.

His bed was by the window—a good spot, but cold during wintertime, he thought, and after lying down for a while, he composed himself a little. He reminisced about the army and his fellow soldiers. Such tight friendships! It was going to be the same here! Among all those men who shared his grief, he no longer felt alone.

He began asking the others the reasons for their arrest, if they had wives, children, the names and the age of the kids, then started telling them about America, the Great War, the cities he had seen, Wall Street, bootlegging, Ford and the Models T he had made, the Lower East Side, and Montana.

When he finished, Cristian Lupu, the med student, who had listened to Mitu with gaping eyes, couldn't help himself.

"I have seen many idiots in my lifetime, but you, my friend, take the cake! Sir, what can I say but congrats! You're unique! Yeah, you truly need a lot of creativity to go from New York to Gherla! Not many can do it!" he concluded looking at Mitu as if he were the quintessence of stupidity.

Mitu didn't answer. In any other circumstance, he would have punched the impertinent imp right in the face! But he couldn't do it now. The young man was right after all! What can he say to him? Nothing! To each his own. Indeed, only an idiot could give up America, as bad as it might have been there, to replace it with a prison!

The door to their cell opened, to his relief, since it spared him from further explanations, and their food was brought in. He took a bite—some mush and soup with green carrots swimming in it—and pushed the tin to the side. He had never eaten such a foul thing in his life!

"They always serve this pigswill?"

The others were silent. The plates were taken back fast, so any lost second could mean a spoonful less. One of them, Ion Tomescu, a factory worker from Ploiești, nodded and continued slurping, and at the end he added that they were given either watered down bean soup and bran with marmalade or that...whatever "that" was.

It was lights out shortly after. "My first day of prison," Mitu sighed, his heart heavy at the thought that he had seven more years to spend there. He tossed and turned for hours, falling asleep due to exhaustion.

At five in the morning, the wake-up signal was given, and Țanu and two agents came in, selecting the majority of prisoners to go to work. Cristian Lupu and three others were ordered to stay in the cell. Mitu was taken to the Information Collection Office on the first floor, where the guards barked at him to stand erect.

Țanu came in an hour later, looked at him from head to toe, and without a word, sprang forward and hit him with a cudgel.

"I told you to stand up straight, bandit! Fucking animal! Stand up straight, numbskull! Straight, got it?" he howled, kicking him to the ground. "Straight as I told you, or I'll scatter your brains on the floor, filthy animal! Motherfucking cretin!"

Mitu, caught off guard by the attack and the ensuing pain, scrambled to his feet and froze up in an erect position, leaning slightly to the side because of his shorter leg. Țanu found his lopsided attempt so offensive, he pummeled him back to the floor.

"Told you to stand up straight!" he roared, kicking him in the stomach.

Mitu curled up in pain trying to deflect the hits, but there was no time for a respite because Livinski entered the room, and the two guards lifted him up together and hurled him forcefully against the wall. He slipped down, lying dizzy on the floor.

Țanu ordered him to get up, and seeing his hesitation, kicked him in the face with the tip of his boot. Blood started streaming from his lip, reddening the yellowish floor.

"You're making a mess, bandit! You trying to dirty the floor?" he screamed. "You're dirtying the floor? Lick it clean!" he barked with his eyes bulging out, grabbing him by the collar and pushing his head down. "Lick it or I kill you!"

He put up a weak resistance, which fueled Țanu's anger. A storm of hits fell over him, purposefully targeting new areas, where he least expected them. When he was done, Țanu cursed loudly and pushed him to the floor.

"Lick it, bandit!"

He gave in realizing that, as he was on his elbows and knees, Țanu could smash his face against the floor and break his jaw, if he wanted. He opened his mouth, stuck out the tip of his tongue and began licking gingerly the spots of blood.

That wasn't to Țanu's liking either.

"Fucking cunt, I told you lick it, not pick at it like a bird! Lick it like a dog! On all fours and lick it like a dog!"

Mitu obeyed and stuck his tongue farther, moving it up and down on the floor and picking up balls of claylike dust along with the blood.

"Don't use your knees, bandit!" Livinski told him, so he had to support his body's weight on his palms and feet in an unnatural position, continuing to clean the floor with his tongue.

They let him do it for what seemed an eternity then ordered him to get up and stand up straight.

"Now you know how you're supposed to stand?" Țanu thundered in his ear.

Mitu nodded weakly and propped himself up as best as he could on his right leg, anchoring the foot onto the floor and stretching the left one enough to reach the floor with the tip of his toes. That was the only way he could stay somewhat straight.

"If you move, you'll get in trouble!" Țanu threatened him, taking a seat and staring fixedly at him. He then lit a cigarette and struck a conversation on the topic of Mitu's shorter leg, now a target for mockery and derision.

Having laughed enough, they asked him.

"Cretin, do you know why we brought you to his room?"

"I don't know."

Țanu got up, grabbed the cudgel and hit him in the stomach. Mitu had tensed up, so the hit didn't come unexpectedly, but it still made him lose his balance and lean slightly to the side. Seeing that, Livinski began shouting again.

"Not standing upright, huh? Huh? Not standing, bandit?"

He ordered him to stand up and sit down a few times, then gawked at him for a long time without saying a word. At last, Țanu left the room, came back with a file, and started leafing through it.

"We brought you here for instigation to rebellion, bandit! If you didn't realize that by now!"

"But what did I do, my God, I didn't do anything!" Mitu barely managed to say. "I didn't do anything!"

"How many times do you want me to tell you that you need to confess and stop with the lies and shifty ways? We have ears everywhere, so you know!" Țanu yelled.

"Please, I didn't do anything..."

"You're the scum of society, and like any garbage, you taint those around you. Last night, you instigated those bandits of cellmates of yours to revolt! Or maybe you don't remember? How fast you "forgot," or maybe you want us to apply a memory-jolting treatment?"

"My God in Heaven, I don't know what you're talking about, really!"

The men rose from their chairs suddenly and jumped on him with their fists, taking him down.

"This is what happens when you sing praises to the Americans and instigate the prisoners to riot! This is what you get! We'll break your bones!"

He was almost unconscious when they finally dragged him back to his cell. They dropped him on the floor and told Cristian to follow them.

He lay there for a long time. His face was bashed in and his body ached terribly. His eyes were bruised and blood had crusted on his lips. He got up grunting to a sitting position. Then he turned his face to the wall, covering his eyes with his elbow. He wanted to vanish from the face of the earth, forever blind and deaf to everything around. He was struggling to keep his tears but felt them streaming down his face.

"I can't take this..." he groaned. "I can't...God, just take me...I can't bear it anymore!"

The door opened an hour later. Somebody, maybe a guard, had come in. He thought to turn to see who it was. But then he heard the muffled thud of something dropped to the floor, and he knew what that meant.

"Those in cahoots with the imperialism sympathizers will get it worse than the numskull Lupu or the bandit Popescu!" he heard Țanu's, by now, familiar voice thundering through the room.

He closed his eyes and clenched his fists. What was happening was so unfair! Accused of instigation just because he had mentioned America! And what about that poor young man? They also tortured him for instigation only because he had listened to his story and mocked his return to the country! What had he done wrong to deserve it?

Chapter 79

After the incident with Ţanu and Livinski, Cristian Lupu started giving Mitu the stink eye. It seemed he was blaming him for telling the America story as bait so that he would be sent to the special room. The young man had become very hostile; if they were ever left alone in the cell, he would turn his back and throw disdainful looks his way without a word.

They moved Cristian somewhere else a week later and took Mitu to a much smaller cell, holding only five other detainees. He could barely exchange a word with them since they went to the factory early in the morning and came back late at night. Also, they were under very strict orders, threatened with the solitary cell if they talked to one another. The only person he knew was Ion Tomescu, the worker from Ploieşti, who had also been brought there, either randomly or on purpose. Relocating the detainees frequently, he had learned, was a tactic to prevent the prisoners from befriending one another.

The wounds from the last interrogation healed in two weeks, time during which he was left alone; they didn't take him anywhere and didn't send him to work but left him in his cell day and night. This made him wonder whether the torture had been an unfortunate memory, of which, with God's help, he was rid of forever.

A month later, however, it all started anew. They took him not to the first floor, in the anteroom of the Information Collection Office, but up on the third floor in the terrible Room 99.

If Mitu had thought that he had lived through hell in the trenches of Meuse-Argonne or during his hobo days, he had been dead wrong.

Many rumors about Room 99 circulated throughout the prison and he knew them well. Room 99 was the gateway to hell. It was the antechamber to Satan's turf. It was the place where they tortured the disobedient, those who still clang on to their anticommunist beliefs, the old and current legionnaires, the priests, the Liberals, the Peasantist sympathizers, the Christians.

It was a room where human beings were crushed, trampled upon, shaken to the core, and forced, under death threats, to eat their own excrements, to curse and renounce their God, to descent to the lowest levels of humiliation.

It was a place where friendships were destroyed, where old allies turned into deathly foes, in which people's resistance was faced with only two choices: live, or betray their kin.

When the agents closed the door to Room 99, they left God outside. Only the victims and they entered it, with the former paying sinister prices. Those that went in came out disfigured, maimed spiritually and physically, like rabid dogs ready to jump to their old owners' throats, prepared to commit the most despicable act, the most unspeakable undertaking only to stop suffering.

Mitu knew what was awaiting him there, and he knew he wasn't going to withstand it. He went humbly inside, made the cross sign with the tongue, still carrying the seed of hope in his heart that maybe he was going to be the first to come out unharmed, that a miracle might save him from pain.

Țanu and Livinski were waiting for him. This time they didn't jump him like wild beasts but began a meticulous interrogation, sprinkled with traps. They asked relentlessly about his collaborators, with whom he had worked in the village, whom else Ciorogaru had mentioned during their discussions, and many other things for which he had no answers.

The questioning lasted a few hours, during which he maintained he knew no more than what he had already told them, swearing on the health of his children that he wasn't hiding anything. At one point, bored and irritated, Țanu growled at him.

"Listen cripple, we know who the bandits are from others—those who already exposed them and who exposed you. Do you want to get what you got last time? Is that what you want? Do you want us to shorten your other leg so you can stand up straight? Or maybe you want us to cut one arm to match, to be both cripple and armless? I'm telling you for the last time: you either confess to everything and expose the others, or we keep on like this till your end! Until *the end*! Out of this room, you'll come either changed or dead!"

He handed him a small soap tablet and a nail.

"Write everything you know, filth! Everything! If you don't spew out all the shit buried inside you, this is your last day on earth!"

The tablet was fashioned from a slab of homemade soap about one or two inches thick, the size of a sheet of paper. The nail was shiny in places, proof that others had used it as a writing tool before him.

"Start writing, bandit!" Țanu screamed at him. "I want you to expose all the legionnaires that are still out there, starting with your family of defectors! We have signed confessions; we know that traitor of a wife you have participated in the legionnaire meeting where you sang hymns! Did you think we don't know? We know everything, bandit! If you don't want us to throw her in jail and send your brats to an orphanage, confess to everything you know!"

He left the room with Țanu, slamming the door behind, and Mitu heard them cursing as they walked away. When it was quiet, he gathered his thoughts terrified that his Maria was in danger. He had never thought they could ever pin him for that wretched church gathering and blame her as well. How could he tell her to run away from the village? How?

After about an hour, another detainee, Grigore Tudose, a former legionnaire that had undergone re-education at Pitești and later became an O.D.C.C. member entered the room. Mitu had never dealt with him before then, but he had seen him many times in the prison ordering the inmates around.

He timidly asked, "If I may, do you have any children? I have four..."

"Write down, leper, don't waste my time! If you don't want them to suffer, confess!"

He started scribbling on the tablet:

"I, Dumitru Popescu, bandit, born on October 2, 1896 in Cernădia, the son of Dumitru and Elena, farmer by trade, with the military service completed in the United States of America, currently an inmate in the Gherla Prison, doing a sentence of seven years for associating with hostile elements to the Popular Republic of Romania, I confess that I participated as a spectator to the legionnaire gathering from Novaci on March 25, 1934, where I met Corneliu Zelea Codreanu and I visited a few times the home of the leader of legionnaires from Oltenia, Gheorghe Ciorogaru. I also declare that no member of my family is or ever has been a legionnaire. I was never an active member of the Iron Guard or of the Everything for the Motherland Party and I never plotted against my country."

He signed the confession with a tight heart and put it aside.

"This is it."

Tudose grabbed it and skimmed it quickly, gave him a sinister glance, left the room and came back with Livinski, who began shouting.

"Why won't you confess, scum? So you're going to be a traitor to your country, huh?"

He hit him in the head with the tablet, screaming like a lunatic.

"You foul, bastard criminal, you mockin' me, huh? Motherfucking asshole! You, a fucking bastard and a traitor, mocking me! I'll show you; you're gonna wish you were dead! You're gonna confess stuff you dreamed up in the belly of that whore of a mother of yours, you asshole!"

He turned to Tudose.

"Get back to work and get all that shit out of him!" he grunted slamming the door.

Tudose gave a satisfied nod and turned to Mitu. He turned him on his belly, wrapped a rope all around him, yanked his shoes off, then started hitting him with a plank of wood across the soles of his feet.

"Here you go, you bastard, here. Maybe this'll teach you to mock us!" he burst out once in a while, continuing to strike him with all his might.

After a few hits, which he resisted stoically, clenching his teeth not to yell, Mitu lost it; the piercing pain was unbearable and he started shouting at the top of his voice as if it would allow him to ignore what was happening. Encouraged by his screams, Tudose hit him harder, sneering, satisfied by the intensified shouting.

"Tell me, how many do you want? How many, bastard?" he yelled.

After about fifty some strikes, Mitu stopped counting. Tudose left him lying on the floor for a few seconds, exited the room, and came back with Livinski. Together, they dragged him to another room and shoved him in a corner.

In the middle of the floor, he could see the shape of a human body covered by a bloodstained sheet. Tudose unveiled it demonstratively and

Mitu was able to see the gory corpse of a naked man, his body marred by deep wounds of torture. One of his eyes was missing and a bone from his arm was protruding through the skin.

"If you don't confess, you'll meet the same fate next time!" Livinski warned him. "Look at what's left of this filth to see what you're gonna look like one of these days when your end comes! Let's go! Now take him and follow us. And move your ass faster if you don't want us to make you move!"

He hunched down and struggled to pick up the body. He lowered himself down on his knees with his back to the corpse, bringing the hands in the front and clutching them tightly. He strained to hoist the body up but the weight was too much, and he stumbled backwards a few times. Seeing him down for the third time, Tudose cursed him terribly but helped him put the dead man on his back.

"You can't even do this, sewer dregs!"

Mitu carried the man with great strain from the third to the first floor, barely keeping his balance, then followed them behind the prison, on the shore of the Someş River, which had lately become an unmarked graveyard.

"Let's go, kulak! I see this kind of work agrees with you; put him down and dig his grave!" Ţanu barked at him, pointing to the shovel lying on the ground.

He started digging, trying to shovel out as much dirt as he could to finish faster. When he was done, they took him back to his cell and shoved him to the floor.

"Look at him and learn, thieves, this is what happens to the traitors who don't confess! If you do what he did, you'll end up the same!" Ţanu thundered and slammed the door.

Ion Tomescu jumped to his aid.

"Can you get up?"

He nodded, exhausted, and with Tomescu's help he struggled to his knees then to his feet and lay grunting on the bed.

Tears were falling down his cheeks.

Chapter 80

For a few months, Mitu was left alone. They didn't beat him and didn't take him to Room 99 anymore. They only forced him to stand all day to "jolt back his memory."

After another six months, they sent him to work for the first time since coming to Gherla. Țanu came to his cell one morning, gave him a pair of brown overalls, threatened him with death if he talked with the others about his interrogations, and took him to a workshop where his job was to sole army boots exported to the U.S.S.R.

There were ten more prisoners in that shop. Their supervisor, he quickly learned, had undergone reeducation in Pitești. He reported all those that hadn't met their quota for the day to Lieutenant Mihalcea, who was in charge of the Technical Department.

The work wasn't difficult, and it certainly beat standing up in the cell from morning to night. The quota, however, was so great that it was almost impossible to fill.

The atmosphere in the shop was a bit more relaxed than that from the cell. The detainees could communicate almost freely; some even shared the tortures endured, which made him think they were snitches trying to win the others' trust ultimately to turn them in.

The inmates had assigned places at the worktable. His was next to a teenage plucky boy with bright eyes and an intelligent air. His appearance hinted at a good family provenience and a well-educated background. His hands weren't callused by menial work, proof that until then he had been involved in academic studies and not physical labor, yet he was quite productive; he pierced the leather to make holes for shoelaces with a fascinating speed, as if he had done so for all his life.

He began talking to Mitu right away.

"I'm Petrișor Sandulovici. From Bucharest. They got me for being a legionnaire in college. Why are you here? I see you're a bit older, what did you do?"

He realized he had underestimated the young man's age and gave him a short recount of what had brought him to Gherla. He couldn't abstain from telling him about his peregrinations through America, curious to see whether the boy would laugh at him the way Cristian Lupu had.

Quite the opposite—Petrișor took a real interest in his situation.

"As long as you hold on to your American passport, you'll never see freedom again. If you ever want to see daylight outside Gherla again, send a letter to the Political Department and tell them you're renouncing your American heritage in exchange for your pardon. I hope you realize they won't let you free, even after you have served seven years! They're afraid the first thing you'll do once released is go straight to the American Embassy in Bucharest to ask to leave the country, and then you'll tell the whole world what happens around here! Since you're an American citizen, they cannot stop you from going to the embassy, and they'll never let you free because of that. They'll torture other people to get false testimonies about you, and they'll keep you in jail for the rest of your days. You wouldn't be the first to be sentenced for a short time, then retried and sentenced for life..."

Mitu tried to figure out if the boy was sincere or if he was setting him up to later turn him in. He didn't have too much time to think about it, because Petrişor began questioning him again.

"Do you have a family?"

The question saddened him. It was coming up on two years since he knew anything of Maria and the children. He was sure they didn't know his whereabouts either, or else they would have written him. Other inmates had received a card or something, but he had never received anything, and he hadn't been allowed to write to them.

Petrişor understood by looking at Mitu's face and changed the subject.

"I don't know anything of my family either, but they're probably locked up—that's if they're still alive. Did you go through Piteşti?"

Mitu answered no and that he didn't even wish that, but he knew firsthand what Room 99 and torture were about. The young man raised his eyebrows and gave an undiscerning smile.

"You're lucky! Many of us have first gone through divulgings in Piteşti and then were transferred here. Room 99 is but a feeble imitation of what's there. I befriended an engineer in Piteşti, Voinilă, I know nothing of him now, but I don't think he's still alive. After beating him senseless they made him lick the excrement buckets from all the cells. Then they made him eat shit with a teaspoon. He had to do it for a few days, then he lost his mind and started talking to himself. Thinking he was faking it, they beat him until they broke his back and left him paralyzed. He begged them to just kill him, and they told him he hadn't gained that right since he hadn't exposed his accomplices."

Mitu felt shivers down his spine, but thought that no matter how terrible Petrişor's stories were, each person had a certain path to follow in life. He had gone through a lot—worse things than he wished on his enemies.

"So, Mitu, if I may call you that, what made you renounce us?" the young man asked him all of a sudden.

"Renounce who? What are you saying here?"

"The Captain. The legionnaires. Our beliefs."

He was now convinced the boy was Ţanu's and Livinski's bait.

"Oh man, didn't I already tell you I was never a legionnaire?"

Petrişor gave him such a dejected look, there was no need for words. His disappointment was so evident, it was as if he were faced with the most serious of treasons.

"So, you've given up on it as well. You're one of them," he murmured and turned back to his work, ignoring Mitu.

Petrişor didn't speak to anyone else until the end of the day, as if he wanted to show the world that Mitu's declaration of never having been a legionnaire was such an egregious lie, that its rightful retribution could only be ostracizing. But, before they were taken back to the cells, as if the slate had been wiped clean again, he took him to the side and whispered to him.

"Man, I don't know what happened with you, but that's neither here nor there. I went to law school. If you want, I could write the pardon request for you. It would be my pleasure. You have something to convince them with, I don't. I can at least help you."

Mitu thanked him a bit superficially but started analyzing the boy's proposal from all angles. What was Petrişor's interest in helping him? Maybe he was a snitch! And if that were the case, he would have been in trouble had he fallen in his trap and said he didn't want to give up his citizenship. He wasn't that crazy to give up his only way out! By giving up his passport, he was destroying his only chance, because indeed, the first thing he was going to do upon his release was go to the embassy to leave the country! But what if Petrişor wasn't an informant? Then maybe he was right in telling him there was no point in holding on to the naturalization certificate. He remembered that the prosecutor had made reference to it during his trial, presenting it as another proof of his connections with the imperialists. What use was that piece of paper to him now?

An hour after Mitu returned to his cell, Ţanu barged in noisily and barked at him to follow him. He sensed something was not quite right—Petrişor told them about the discussion! He followed, full of apprehension. They went down to the first floor, turning towards the room in which he had been tortured the first time, but, to his relief, they did not stop there, continuing on to another room he knew well: The Information Collection Office. Gheorghe Dumitrescu, the head of that office, was waiting for him there and began admonishing him for not having filled his quota.

"So, bandit, you're a slacker on top of everything. Why? You trying to sabotage us?"

Mitu shook his head vehemently.

"No way, how could I want something like that? I'm not crazy! It's just that this was the first time I went back to work in such a long time, and I need to get used to what needs to be done."

"What needs to be done, my ass! You're a saboteur! You want to undermine our country's economy, and this is punishable! What good are you to us? Huh? What? You don't work as you should; you just waste the state's money for nothing! But you're the first to eat and sleep! Is that how you are, only good at stuffing your face? If you're gonna lay around like a damsel, at least you can help us by telling us what was discussed in the shop today. With that, you can bring a service to your country by exposing the traitors squirming like worms around here. You'll have a patriotic mission from now on; your role will be to tell us who's against us, who's anticommunism. You'll tell me everything! Who speaks to who, what's being discussed, who praises the legionnaires, who's plotting—absolutely everything! If you cooperate, I won't cut your food ration when you don't fill your quota. If not,

I'll take it as proof that you're in cahoots with the others, and it'll be bad for you!"

Mitu thought quickly about what to say. Tell on Petrişor? If he were an informant, it would be good to do it since that would confirm the tattler and maybe they would leave him alone. But what if the poor boy wasn't their accomplice? Then he'd be in hell because of Mitu! Just like Cristian Lupu.

He told them that he had met everyone in the shop, that he had learned their sentences, then mentioned his conversation with Petrişor, who had told him he had studied law and could help him with a request for pardon. He was hoping to have said enough to satisfy them.

Dumitrescu gave him a look as if he wanted to flatten him out with a bulldozer.

"I'm going to step all over you with my boots, traitor! Everybody whispers and talks all day, and you mean to tell me you didn't hear a word? You must think I'm an idiot! Tell me, bandit, is that what you think?

Mitu shook his head and tried to mumble some apology, but Dumitrescu called Ţanu.

"Five nights in the hole, half a ration of food once every two days, and if he doesn't come back to his senses to cooperate, a whole week next time!"

"But please, sir," Mitu murmured faintly. "I don't have anything to report, I swear..."

"You don't?" Dumitrescu scoffed. "No problem—the hole will refresh your memory! Take him outta here!"

The first few hours spent in the solitary cell—a vertical, coffin-like black metal box into which he was shoved by two guards—went by fairly easily. He leaned against a corner, transferring all his weight on one foot, then switched it to the other and so on, but the space was so tight that after a while he began getting tired. As a matter of fact, he could only rest on the good leg, the long one, which was becoming number by the minute. The pain became so strong at one point—like a knife stuck deeply in the muscle—that he almost fainted.

Half an hour later, he felt his skin was beginning to split open and the blood was pooling right beneath the surface, ready to erupt through the pores. The thought frightened him so much, he began writhing and shaking the box desperately. Seeing that the squirming was worsening his situation, he thought of hopping. He couldn't turn around, he couldn't lean forward, but he could at least jump up a little since the coffin was about a foot and a half taller than he was.

He attempted it a few times, but gave up on it. He was so exhausted that he barely had the strength to breathe. After six hours of immobility, his right foot started swelling, sending a prickling sensation through his whole body. He tried to massage it a bit from the standing position he was in he could touch his thighs with his hands, but not even that helped. The numbing pain was driving him insane.

When the ache became unbearably atrocious, he began thrashing around so spasmodically, rocking back and forth that the box lost its balance and fell with a tremendous noise.

"Now they'll kill me for sure!" he thought scared but tried to profit from the horizontal position to take the stiffness out of his body.

The reprieve was short: some guards came cursing loudly in a few minutes, stood the box back up and threatened to double his confinement if he toppled it over again.

"If I stay here another day, I'll die for sure!" He had been in the hole for six or seven hours and couldn't endure it any longer. He felt he was losing his mind. He had to do whatever he could to never be sent there again. Never.

At five in the morning, despite the dreadful pain in the lower part of his body, he nodded off and woke up when the coffin's door swung open, and he stumbled over the guard who had come to take him to the shop.

He needed half an hour to get up. He barely dragged himself to the workshop and started working. Petrişor threw him a meaningful glance and nodded softly.

"That's what you deserve if you don't listen to me."

That day, he couldn't even fill a quarter of the quota. He was sleeping on his feet, famished and a stinging pain pierced his body.

Towards the evening, when Dumitrescu called him in his office for "divulgings," a bout of dizziness came over him and he fell weakly on the floor losing consciousness.

Chapter 81

The fainting spell from Dumitrescu's office spared Mitu from additional visits to the hole. When he came around, he was in the infirmary—a hangar of about sixty bunk beds, under the supervision of a med student named Virgil Lungeanu, an ex-legionnaire, gone through the Pitești reeducation.

He barely ate anything during the first days. He was nauseated by everything in sight and kept fainting each time he tried to stand up. His condition took a bad turn, and the doctor in charge gave him the indisputable prognosis that he was going to die.

"Take him out of here and don't waste any more good medicine on him," he told Lungeanu.

They moved him to the "mortuary room," which was much smaller than the hangar, with only six beds in it, which housed those deemed goners.

Very few ever recovered from that ante-room of death. Mitu had heard many things about it. Those who made it there, after long-drawn disease improperly nursed many months had their fates sealed. Some, very few, veritable miracles of survival, would get better only to be sent back to their cells. The majority, however, crossed over directly to the other side from there and were carried away through side hallways and doors and thrown into unmarked graves behind the prison.

He was unaware of his surroundings for a few days. The doctor kept saying that he was in a semi coma, and that he could go at any point. A week later, he woke up and looked around befuddled. "Where in the world am I? This looks like the infirmary from Argonne."

In another week, he began recovering. He convalesced slowly, amassing drops of vigor little by little, until one day, he felt brave enough to go to the bathroom all by himself. He wasn't becoming lightheaded as often, he didn't need to sleep continuously, and he could swallow a little something during the day. The right side of his belly still ached but not enough to pin him to the bed.

After a month in the infirmary, the doctor called him in his office to tell him he was to be sent back to his cell.

"You must've eaten a lot of shit when you were a lad35F[*], Popescu, to have made it through this! That's it with you, you're getting outta here!"

That moment, probably anticipated by many with bated breath, he didn't know whether to be happy or sad. When he had gotten sick, he had considered the trip to the "mortuary room" the very last one of this lifetime; now that he was among "the living" again, he felt disconcerted. "Back to Room 99? With Țurcanu maybe?36F[†]

---

[*] In Romanian, an expression denoting someone who is very lucky.
[†] Eugen Țurcanu, the former legionnaire turned communist torturer, was transferred from Pitești to Gherla Prison on August 18, 1951, where he continued his work as a torturer until December 19, 1951.

"Well then, what am I going to do, Doctor?" he asked weakly.

"You do whatever everyone else does around here...serve your time. I didn't send you to prison. I'll give you a note for bed rest for another thirty days, then we'll see. You should eat as much as you can."

He thanked him with a deeply felt and sincere gratefulness. That piece of paper was his ticket to a month of respite from interrogations and beatings. For some reason, a note from the doctor, otherwise a civilian, had great weight with the guards.

While he had been in the infirmary, all of the inmates in his cell but Ion Tomescu had been replaced by others. One of them, Vasile Istrate, worked at sorting buttons; another, Victor Bălășoiu, a Moldavian from Piatra Neamț, made mine wood boxes that were sent to the U.S.S.R.; Paul Neagu, a peasant from Dobrogea, whom peopled had nicknamed Paulie-boy, was responsible for supervising and maintaining order in the shop—for that reason, he was suspected to be an informant.

He spent a very quiet few days for the first time since coming to Gherla. He would wake up in the morning and wait for the others to leave, then he would lie down on the bed napping or reading the Communist paper *The Spark*. It felt like a vacation!

Two weeks later, as the others were preparing to go to the shop, and he was thinking how to spend his "leisure time," something bizarre happened: the prison's barber came into the cell, and without any explanations, he shaved them and cut their hair in a hurry, then sprinkled disinfectant on them and told them to get out in the prison's yard.

All the doors were open, and no armed guards patrolled the hallways. Not ever had there been so little security in the place.

"Wouldn't it be something if the Americans were here? Or maybe there's a general order for pardon!" he thought barely daring to hope.37F*

They had been waiting for half an hour in the bitter cold, when Petrache Goiciu, the new warden—a thick man whose stature was easier to jump over than go around—came out from the main building and stood in front of them. He was joined by a few men from the Political Office, and some others Mitu had never seen before, but whose overall demeanor hinted at their holding high positions in the governing party.

Right behind them came the terrifying Eugen Țurcanu. He had arrived at Gherla a few months before, and since then, Mitu kept wondering when his turn would come to be interrogated by him. Until that point, God had spared him from such trouble.

Țurcanu kept rocking from one leg to the other as if he were a spoiled child, then addressed them.

---

* After WWII and up to the 1989 Revolution, Romanians hoped for the "arrival of the Americans." Very few knew the great powers of the world had divided up the areas of influence and the American paratroopers were never going to land in Romania to save them from the Communists.

"We gathered all of you here today to communicate the results of our analysis. We assessed the workshops' productivity. It's a disaster! The results are far below expectations! And the only explanation we have is that you are all saboteurs, and you're doing it on purpose! Some, who have been re-educated successfully, work very well, but still can't cover for the rest who are slacking off. Loafers! If things continue this way, we'll need to take drastic measures!"

He kept on for a while, until Goiciu, irritated he wasn't finishing faster, interrupted him, and then began speaking emphatically and pointedly, full of arrogance, trying to imply his words were of the utmost importance.

"Prisoner Țurcanu is right! We brought you here to tell you that things aren't going satisfactorily in the plant. Very few of you fill the quota. If you worked harder and did your share, the conditions here in the prison would improve as well. Life in here is just like life on the outside; however, you lay your bed, that's how you'll sleep in it, but very few of you get that!"

He paused briefly and took a deep breath—a sign that he was going to add something significant. Mitu listened absentmindedly; he had heard the same tired speeches since his arrival at Gherla.

"There are many backstabbers among you!" Goiciu continued. "Yes! You heard right! Traitors! A lot of low-lives ready to say anything just to eat a better slice of bread. There are many in your midst that spit on you behind your back and say lies about you! Especially the "little princes," who forced us to take some slightly harsher measures with you. And, if it happened that we gave you corporal punishments or even tortured you, you should know that it wasn't because of us—it was because of them! It took us a long time to figure it all out, but better late than never! From now on, no prisoner will be tortured again!"

Mitu stood agape. He gave Tomescu, who was next to him, a questioning look, then fixed on Goiciu again with his eyes. It was impossible! So unusual, unprecedented, flabbergasting were his words that he wondered whether he was dreaming or if it was another trick to instigate the workers and peasants from Gherla against the college students—"little princes."

The more he thought about it, the more he realized it couldn't be true. Yet, there was too much brouhaha happening over it. And what about those important people from the party; why would they have come if it hadn't been for something serious?

What could have been so important?38F*

Goiciu continued for another ten minutes, repeating platitudes heard many times, then ordered them back to their cells.

"Get it through your skulls! Work hard to fill your quota!"

---

* A short time after these events, Eugen Țurcanu was accused of collaborating with Horia Sima, the exiled leader of the Iron Guard, and of torturing detainees with the purpose of discrediting the Romanian Government (fabricated charges). He was tried along with the people under his lead in 1954. He was sentenced to death and executed.

Chapter 82

A short while after, things began improving, much to Mitu's and the other inmates' bewilderment; the prisoners weren't sent to the hole for ordinary reasons; they were no longer roughed up as before, bludgeoned with canes, or forced to eat each other's excrements. They could speak more and more freely, some of them daring to hum illegal songs and legionnaire hymns, culminating with *Awaken thee, Romanian!*

The prisoners started nicknaming the students that had underwent re-education, "lil' enemies," "fraidy-cats" or "tricksters." Then, the mists of oblivion fell upon everything. The atmosphere became almost normal; previous deathly enemies, who had feuded with perverted treachery for years, began tolerating one another. If the purpose of Goiciu's discourse had been to cause fracases among the inmates, as Mitu had initially suspected, it had failed miserably.

Meanwhile, he still mulled over Petrişor Sandovici's advice. Since the young man had suggested Mitu's renouncing his American citizenship in exchange for freedom, he kept thinking about it.

He didn't know what the best course of action was. How could he give up America? To him, that country was akin to a two timing woman whom he still loved—some kind of an Olga. On the other hand, what use was the naturalization certificate in Gherla? Maybe that very piece of paper was the reason for his imprisonment.

Things seemed complicated. What if he gave up the citizenship and still didn't get out? That was possible also, wasn't it? He couldn't very well ask for guarantees, could he? But he couldn't wait around, when maybe he had an ace up his sleeve he wasn't using out of stupidity!

After fretting for a long time, he decided that he was going to play the highest card in his life—he was going to write the request and file it with the Political Department. After all, there was nothing to lose. Many years had passed without a change for the better. Maybe that really was his only chance.

As they were coming back from the shop one day, he took Petrişor aside and told him he needed his help "with that matter." The young man seemed happy he had finally decided.

"You'll see. You'll never regret it. You'll thank me, so you know. But I still don't understand why you didn't do it sooner. You could have been out a really long time ago, man. Instead, you stayed behind bars for months and months, longing for your kids and home, not knowing anything about your family. Honestly, I just don't get it. Sometimes I marvel at people's way of thinking..."

Mitu shrugged.

"I just don't know how you can be so sure I'll get out with this...I just don't see it."

Petrişor wrote the paper for him that night. In fact, he wrote two separate documents: in one of them Mitu was declaring he was giving up his American citizenship of his own accord because he had realized the benefits of a communist society to which he now pledged his devotion and allegiance. The other was the request for the pardon itself, in which he was asking to be freed, and where he pointed clearly, but without making one contingent upon the other, that he had given up his citizenship as it conflicted with his new ideological convictions.

He dropped off the papers at the Political Office, then went to the workshop as usual. He was apprehensive. He had taken a lucky shot, the only one in his arsenal, sending it into thick fog.

One week passed, then a few more. Three months afterwards, as he was getting ready for work one morning, he was taken from the prison's cafeteria and led to the first floor of the main building. Mihăilescu, the one in charge of the Political Department, was waiting for him.

At first, he thought he was expected to spill information on the others, but realized quickly that this wasn't the reason for his summoning. Mihăilescu approached him directly without any further introduction:

"Popescu, I understand you put in a request for pardon a few months ago..."

He nodded.

"Yes, sir, I did."

"Uhhuh...You did, you motherfucker...I have some news for you, bandit. Your request will be approved if you publicly renounce your American citizenship."

He didn't understand right away what he had just heard. "I need to do what?" When the meaning of the words dawned on him, he was barely able to contain his joy.

"What do you mean 'publicly'?" he asked happy and confused.

"'What do you mean publicly,'" Mihăilescu mocked him. "What, are you an idiot or just pretending to be one? You don't know how others have done it? You write an article in *The Spark* saying that you give up the American citizenship because you want to rid yourself of all connections to capitalism."

"And... after that?"

"After that, you go home, bandit! Of course you'll come back quickly if you get back in touch with those other bandits from the mountains! And the second time around won't be easy on you! You'll end up straight in front of the firing squad. Remember that before doing something foolish! Now go on, get your ass out of here! Go back to your cell! If you're ready to finally make your confession public, come back tomorrow and let me now, you got it?"

He clenched his fists as hard as he could not to burst into tears of joy. He went back to the shop drunk with happiness, but after a while, he started worrying: What will the others think? Won't they consider him a traitor? He felt guilty about getting out and leaving them here. How was he going to give them the news? Were he in their stead, he wouldn't take it too well.

Mitu decided not to say anything, then tried to appease his conscience saying he shouldn't feel guilty. Many of those whom he met in Gherla were legionnaires or anticommunists indeed. Petrişor, for instance, or Ion Tomescu, his cellmate or Cristian Lupu, who had mocked him for coming back from America, or Virgil Lungeanu the doctor's assistant—they all admitted openly that they had participated in anticommunist movements during the war and after. He, on the other hand, was paying for something he hadn't done. Not to mention that many prisoners were still young, while he was old and sick, with many a shooting pain through his body and constant stomachaches. He had been jailed unfairly, perhaps because of the Bessarabian's curse, but he had never harmed anyone on purpose. And now, maybe God was finally turning His face to him! Whatever sins he had committed, his atonement had been the torture and pain already endured.

When he gave the news to Petrişor at the end of the day, the young man didn't seem surprised, as if he knew that was going to be the conclusion from the get-go, and it had only been a matter of time. He congratulated him and asked him to pass by some of his relatives from Bucharest to let them know he was alright. Or, if he couldn't do that, at least mail out a letter upon his release.

Once back in his cell, he sat down on the bed without a word, avoiding his cellmate's eyes. Then he took a deep breath and braved it:

"They called me to the Political Office today...they told me they'll release me if I publicly renounce the American citizenship."

Tomescu rose quickly to his feet, full of emotion:

"Are you serious?"

Mitu nodded.

"Good for you, man," Tomescu whispered, "good for you! Bravo!"

The others jumped and congratulated him noisily:

"You've done it! You're the first to leave here! Great, great luck you've got! Can't you take us with you?"

"I'd take all of you, the whole prison if I could..." Mitu answered, moved by their reaction.

"So, that's how it is, huh? You guys from Oltenia are something else. You're getting out and leaving us here to rot..." Tomescu joked. "I hope you won't forget us the first moment you step outside the prison's gate."

"Ion, I hope you'll forgive me," Mitu said, struggling to stop his tears. "I thought you were an informant this whole time, and that's why I never really got that close to you. But please know that I never had anything against you."

"Do you think I'm any different? I thought you were the one spilling the beans, man! They've really done a number on us here!"

Mitu sat sobbing on the bed.

"Oh, good people! Good people..." he managed to say through hiccups.

Chapter 83

In the summer of 1953, after three years in prison, Mitu was released on probation. Somehow despite the circularity of life, in which bad times follow good times and vice versa, luck smiled on him again. Instead of being sent forcibly to some forgotten village in Dobrogea as generally happened with all released prisoners, he was provided with a train ticket from Cluj to Târgu-Jiu and money for the bus fare to Novaci so that he could go straight home.

As the gates of Gherla closed behind him and the refreshing air of freedom washed over him, he fell into a strange state. He was neither happy nor sad. He didn't ooze of hatred for those that had thrown him in jail. He had no ill feelings towards Țurcanu, Țanu, or Livinski. Images of the future were quickly clouding the past. As he was getting farther and farther from the hell in which he had lived for so long, he donned an armor of oblivion. Memories about Goiciu, Gheorghiu, Dumitrescu and others like them were slowly growing muddy, gradually fading away. He was punishing them in the worst possible manner a man is capable of forsaking another of his kin: indifference. As the train kept chugging away mile after mile, he shed all heavy feelings and memories, thinking only that he was about to see Maria and the children.

He reached Novaci on a Friday at about noon, dead tired. The excitement of finally going home had kept him up for the last twenty-four hours.

Before setting out to Cernădia, he first stopped off by Ciorogaru's house.

Mrs. Ileana opened the door, and when she saw his state—haggard to the point of collapsing, a mere shadow of "the American" he had once been—she froze. She couldn't believe it; her eyes brimmed with tears.

"Mitu, is it really you? What a miracle! When did you get back?"

"Right now, I just arrived. From Gherla. I've been traveling for about a day."

They went inside the house and she overwhelmed him with questions: "Do you know anything about my husband? Is it true what they say about Pitești? How is Jilava? Is it cold in the cells during wintertime? How is the medical care in prison? What about the food?"

He gave her half answers, not to dishearten her even more, then asked about Ciorogaru.

"They sentenced my husband to fourteen years. The last time I heard he was in Jilava, but they moved him from there, and I haven't learned anything anymore. Nothing! I went and asked everywhere, but no one told me where he was taken. I can't sleep at night I'm so worried! How do you think it will all end?"

He didn't answer right away. If he—never having been a confirmed anticommunist—had been tortured so badly, he couldn't imagine how Ciorogaru, a former deputy and ex-legionnaire leader, could come out alive from it. Maybe he ended up in a common grave like those from Gherla, as reeducation couldn't have possibly been a possibility in his case: Better dead than betraying his principles and peers!

He tried to tell her a few reassuring words, just like that night a few years back when the *Securitate* had arrested her husband. Unlike then, when he still believed in a good and fair human kind, he now felt that he was stringing her along intentionally. He wondered whether he should be candid and tell her to prepare for something perhaps worse than even death: Never learning the fate of her husband. But he didn't do it. He didn't want to discourage her any more than she already was. He got up to leave, saying he was in a hurry to see his family.

She saw him to the front gate, reading in his eyes whatever he had left unsaid. During the many sleepless nights fraught with suffering and worry, she had thought her husband could be dead, but the hope that light would dawn on her situation one day still flickered feebly in her heart.39F*

It took Mitu less than ten minutes from Ciorogaru's house to the footbridge over Gilort, which lead to the road to Cernădia and Baia de Fier. The terrible exhaustion he had felt until then had vanished miraculously.

He didn't meet anyone on the way home. Not that he wanted it any other way, but he was surprised to see how bare the village seemed. There was no one around, only a few children playing in the ditch by the side of the road. As he passed them, they wished him a "good afternoon" as they continued playing. They had no idea who he was.

"Good God, so much time's gone by!" he sighed half an hour later when he made the turn from the main road to the country lane to his house.

He saw Maria from afar. She was hanging clothes on a line that hadn't been there before; Gheorghe or Flitan had probably put it up for her.

He pushed the gate, which opened with a shrill creaking. She turned her head and dropped the basket of laundry.

"Mitu," she whispered. "Mitu!"

She walked uncertainly toward him as if he were a ghost. She touched his cheek to convince herself that he was real.

"I thought you were dead," she said softly.

A long silence fell upon them. Mitu had thought about that moment many times, imagining the two of them hugging and crying together. Instead, an unnatural awkwardness lay between them. They were exchanging aloof glances like two strangers and not like two people that had shared a life together.

---

* Gheorghe Ciorogaru (1909-1980) was sentenced for "activities against the working class" and was imprisoned until 1964. Although he was offered the possibility of release with the condition of publicly renouncing his principles through a note in the communist newspaper "The Spark," he refused and served his entire prison term. Many profited of such opportunity and were released sooner. His sentencing came with the confiscation of his assets, but his father had put them all into a trust under the grandchildren's names, so the family didn't suffer much because of this. After being released, Ciorogaru was sent forcibly to the detainee Village of Mâzâreni.

"How are the children?" he broke the silence at last.

Maria looked at him seemingly surprised by the question, then suddenly became invigorated.

"Well, Măriuța's at Boboc's, and Gheorghe's at work. And the boys are at school. You should see what a young man Sandu has turned into! And Micu, he's the best in school. He's got perfect grades and went to a few contests in the county."

Mitu lowered his eyes to the ground. He felt guilty that, as the head of the family, he had been gone while his wife was struggling to send the children to school.

"We'll talk about them later. Where did they take you?" she asked.

He didn't answer right away and lifted up his coat, exposing his scars.

"I must've had nine lives in me to still be standing here today, woman!"

Maria's heart was filled with pity. She burst into tears and grabbed his arm, pushing him gently towards the stoop to sit. She disappeared inside the house and he heard her climb onto a chair, probably to take something from atop the closet. She came back with his old violin, the one bought from Bucharest when he had visited with Olga.

"We sold almost everything we had but this."

Mitu picked the instrument up carefully and caressed it with his fingers. The violin had brought him the greatest joy in life. Not the Model T driven triumphantly through Detroit, not the gold pocket watch bought during his Wall Street heyday, not the expensive suits—but that piece of lacquered wood.

"Maria, come here," he called her next to him.

She sat timidly by his side, and he began recounting everything calmly, as if he were narrating someone else's story. He told her how he had given up America in exchange for his freedom. He told her about the starvation, about the hole, about the mortuary room and the cemetery by the Someş River where he had buried a man, about reeducation, interrogations and beatings, cold baths, Ţurcanu, Ţanu, and Livinski, broken ribs, illness, smashed jaws and fingers. As he spoke, he pointed to all of the spots where he had been hit: Here, there, in the back, to the right, in the knee, at the temple, in the chin. He showed her the two missing teeth knocked off during the first interrogation, which he had saved in his pocket. He walked her fingers on the unhealed fracture of a rib and showed her the deformed finger the investigator Vintilă had stepped on with his boots. He took his shoes off to show her the traces from the beatings with nails to the soles, and removed his shirt so that she could see the gashes left by the whippings.

"That's what happened to me, Maria" he sighed with the relief of a confession. "And, if someone else learns of this, they'll throw us both back in jail. The whole time I was there I thought they took you away, and that the kids were left alone in this world."

He kissed her and squeezed her in his arms.

"It'll be alright from now on, Maria. You'll see..."

She nestled to his chest and remained quiet.

"The kids can't find out what I've told you. They shouldn't know what I've gone through."

She nodded and said nothing for a while, then, struck by a thought, she jumped to her feet.

"Oh my God, I'm such a fool! You must be starving. Lemme get you something to eat!" she said and dashed to the kitchen, took out some lard-preserved meat from a jar, threw it quickly in a pan, and prepared to light the fire in the stove.

Mitu sat at the table looking around. Nothing had changed, as if the place had frozen in time.

"Maria, give me that pan, don't heat it up."

"I can't give it to you like this; I need to melt the lard. It's pork!"

"No, just leave it, give it to me the way it is."

She placed it in front of him and he began wolfing it down.

"My God, Mitu," she sighed watching him with pity.

"What other animals do we have around the house, Maria?" he asked between two bites.

"Barely anything; some chickens and a pig. We sold the cows and the horses a few years ago. Tell me, do you want something to drink? We have some *ţuică* left over from..."

He lifted his hand to stop her.

"Maria, I haven't drunk in years. During the first months in prison, I thrashed about, shivered and had imaginings because I had no alcohol. If I have a glass now, I won't stop until I drink the whole cask. Better bring me some water."

She rushed outside and brought him a mug.

"Maria, now it's your turn. Tell me about yourself, what you did, tell me about the kids. Tell me everything. How's my brother? Did he finally get married like everyone else?"

She shook her head in dissent.

"What about my sister?"

She made the same gesture then sat down beside him.

"Mitu..." she said after a while.

He furrowed his brow.

"What is it, tell me! What happened?"

"Mitu...your mother died. Lenuţa died."

He placed the fork slowly next to the pan.

"When?"

"A year and a half ago. She took to bed one day and was gone three weeks later. The doctors said she had lung cancer."

He put his head in his hands, guilt-laden that he had barely thought of his mother while in prison. Then his thoughts went elsewhere.

"Tell me about the kids..."

"I don't even know where to begin. Gheorghe—you should see what a handsome lad he is! He worked in the forest for a while, and now he got a job at the graphite mine in Cătălinu de Sus, near Cărbuneşti. He's been a great help to me all these years; we would've starved without his money. At first, I couldn't get him outta bed. I had no choice; as much as I felt for him, I had to drag him out."

"What about lil' Sandu, how's he doing?"

"Sandu took your leaving the hardest. He was a bit sickly and didn't really help me like Gheorghe. Always with colds, I think he has a weakness from that illness he had when he was little. When he finished elementary school, I sold a pig and sent him further. He didn't do too well at first, but when I told him he had to choose between school and household work, he began applying himself and got better grades. Now he's in Târgu-Jiu studying finance in a technical school."

"And Micu. How's my lil' Micu?"

Maria smiled.

"Micu's a comedian, you know, but very bright! And stubborn! I wanted him home with me, but listen to what he did, the imp! He got up in secret one night and went to school in Novaci with Sandu and came back late in the evening. He told me that if I didn't send him to school that he'd run away from home. I still didn't want to send him, and the next day he hid from me and ran to school again. There was nothing I could do. And you should see how he's doing—he's the first one in his class. He's good at history and mathematics, and all the teachers like him."

Mitu's face lit up at the news about his children.

"You know," she continued, "sometimes I think that Micu is like Ionică—just as smart, it just took him a little longer to come into his own."

He stared at her, trying to figure out the deeper meaning of her words.

"And the girl, how is she?"

"Well, Măriuţa's still little. She plays, more beautiful every day. She looks more and more like you with time."

"Hard times, Maria, very hard."

"Yes, very hard," she agreed. "We had nothing to our name, but the kids didn't feel it. So you know Mitu, they didn't suffer. You can ask them," she said as if she were afraid of his judgment. "They go sledding in the winter and play with the ball all summer long. They sometimes even forget to eat, and I need to call them ten times to get them to the table. We take care of the animals, we harvest corn, Sandu and Micu bring firewood home on their summer vacation—you know how it is."

Mitu gave her a compassionate look and took her callused hands in his.

"Maria," he spoke slowly, forcing the difficult words, "I know that I haven't been the best husband in the world. I know that. But I must tell you that I thought about you every night. That's what kept me alive out there, please know that. I never meant to hurt you, Maria. I never meant to hurt anyone. Never."

- 430 -

Chapter 84

It took Mitu a few months to get back to his old ways and truly regain the desire to live again. He met with people from the village, who were doing the same things they had before, simply going with the flow, and that's when he realized that his existence, while tormented, had been very rich, and he could consider himself lucky. Yes, he had gone through many difficult moments, but he had reached heights of which only a few dared to dream. For instance, only a handful of people from Cernădia had ever gone on a trip; many had never seen the ocean or driven an automobile or crossed the border of the country. He could count those who had traveled to America on the fingers of one hand.

Compared to others, he felt blessed. Not many could say they had such a roller-coaster of an existence. Yes, he had lived his life to its fullest; he met and loved many beautiful women, made music and money, enjoyed leisurely moments, traveled to many places and met a lot of people, and now he had a young and kind wife and beautiful children.

He felt rich having gone through all that.

He even thought of the prison as an experience with its good parts; it had diminished the guilt of Ionică's death, the hell lived having atoned his sin, and now he was cleansed, ready to start afresh.

He now saw Maria in a different light. To him, she had been almost a child until recently—a young girl who had married early, had given him children, and bustled about the house. The hardships Maria had survived prompted an internal transformation in Mitu. Torture had shattered his rib, but she had a broken one as well; she was prodding the ox to pull the plow one spring, and the animal struck her with its horn, leaving her breathless on the ground. God was watching over her then. A man from nearby had jumped to her aid taking her to the clinic.

Now, towards the sunset of his life, he felt something unique, something he had never had for a woman: a newfound respect. He gave Maria credit for her tremendous efforts to care for her children, for the will and dedication with which she had gathered every single penny to send the boys to school, for the fact that she had been faithful to him, awaiting his return all those years, when she could have very well forgotten all about him.

He had loved many women and enjoyed the pleasure of the flesh in his youth and old age as well, but had never experienced gratefulness towards any one of them, not ever having felt the need to say to anyone "we are one." That was what he thought about her now; that they were two halves completing each other. And, at the same time, he felt guilty for his hidden longing for Olga, his first love, all those years and for thinking about her long after coming back to Cernădia and getting married. All that was now just a sweet memory. The painful feeling was at last, gone.

He could have a new start; it was as though he had been resurrected from death, he thought. He could enjoy his family, his garden, the land he still had up in Rânca. He could reacquaint with his old friends.

And, most importantly, he could begin playing again. Have a *taraf*. Yes, he could get back together with Cirică and Julea, like before! He had stopped blaming Julea for Ionică's death for a long time now. Things had settled, buried and forgotten—the past with the past.

The two gypsies hadn't changed at all. History and its tragic events had passed right over them, leaving no mark. The first time he met them in the village, they went straight to the point without asking anything about anything

"Fiddler, you've decided to come back home. When can we get together for some music, like we used to?"

The day they came by to pay him a "working" visit, one lazy Saturday afternoon, he received them with open arms—"finally I can start music again!" They brought along a young lad who, they said, was talented and steadfast.

"Fiddler, this is Shitsmoke. Just listen how he plays; he's going to be like you! Just like you! His fingers do wonders on them strings! Go on, play something boy!"

Mitu looked amused at them:

"What was it they call you, son? Did I hear it right?"

"My real name is Tiberiu, but they call me Shitsmoke, old man," the boy said, not seeming to mind his unfortunate nickname one bit.

"And how did you get yourself such a nice one, kid?"

Cirică intervened with the explanation.

"Let me tell you, since I came up with it; he once started a fire with some damp twigs and smoke started coming out. He said he had a way to stop it by putting a piece of rubber atop of it. And, of course, more smoke came out. And that's been his name ever since: stupidity like that deserves a name like that!"

"I see...go on, play something," Mitu encouraged him. "Maria, bring something to drink!" he called out. "Gheorghe, my boy, come over here!"

The woman cringed. "Is he drinking again? And with Julea like when Ionică got ill?" but she said nothing and came back with a bottle of aged *țuică* from the cellar. She placed it on the table and brought five glasses. Mitu filled four of them, leaving his empty.

"Maria, bring a glass for yourself. And fill mine with water, then get me the violin."

"What's the matter?" Cirică was surprised. "You mean to say you're not drinking with us? Whatever did we do to you?"

Mitu pretended he didn't hear him and told Tiberiu to play something. The boy took the violin and did so, and the gypsies joined in. It was a nice, new melody that Mitu hadn't heard before.

"You're good, kid, you're good," he told him at the end. "Who taught you the fiddle?"

"I did it alone, old man. I learned a bit from Cirică, here and there, but mostly on my own. I'd hear something at *hore* and then practice it at home all week."

Mitu remembered that's what he used to do in his youth. "This life...nothing ever changes!"

When Maria brought him his violin, his expression changed. He hadn't yet played it since returning home. On that first day, when his wife had given it to him, saying it was the only thing she hadn't parted with, he had only touched and caressed it as though he had been afraid to do anything else with it.

He walked his fingers on the strings.

"Maria, please stay here...don't go."

She sat down, feeling slightly awkward. It was the first time her husband wanted her there with his players.

"Listen to this and tell me if you like it, Maria..."

He closed his eyes and started singing with that same rich, warm, profound, and clear voice, slightly raspy on higher notes—the same voice from his youth. His body was changed, his face was wrinkled and pale, his eyes were tired and foggy, his legs barely carried him, but his voice was as piercing and as confident as ever.

He sang a melody that didn't have the traditional feel of Romanian folk music, but was more along the lines of jazz—something American, yet it was strewn with gypsy music harmonies.

Julea, who generally busied himself with drinking while others played, stood agape. He had never heard something like that. Cirică forgot to smoke his cigarette and froze up with his hand suspended in the air.

Tiberiu had stopped breathing. Mitu's playing was different from everything he had ever heard. The boy was glued to his chair, unable to take his eyes off him.

Maria was looking at him, deeply moved. She had always loved her husband's music despite the fact that it invariably ended in drunkenness. But this song was the most beautiful she'd ever heard. Why didn't she didn't know it? Had he learned it in prison?

Only Gheorghe seemed unaffected, probably thinking about the roof that needed fixing, or the trip to Craiova he had to take soon. Mitu's brother was a practical young man; he never really cared for music or dancing.

When he finished, Mitu placed the violin on the table and sighed profoundly. He had sung with his eyes closed, lost for a few minutes in a world he alone understood, a world that gave him joy and in which he would have liked to be forever lost.

"Uncle Mitu," Tiberiu broke the silence agitated, "can you teach me music? Can you? Look, I'll pay, I'll give you whatever I have, I'll work to give you money, but I really want you to teach me! I never heard anything like it around here. Never..."

Cirică took the boy's side enthusiastically.

"Yes, teach him some of your tricks, because that song was something else. It's like you practiced playing in prison all those years! Where's this melody from, because I don't remember ever hearing it?"

Mitu pursed his lip secretively.

"I wrote it in jail. This is the first time I'm playing it."

"You mean you wrote it without playing it?" asked Tiberiu, who couldn't read music.

"Yes, in my head. How else? I hummed it in my head the whole time and now it's the first time I'm playing it on the violin."

He paused to work up his nerve.

"I wrote it for Maria," he whispered as though he were embarrassed to admit it.

The woman was stunned. She smiled confused and uncertain.

"Eh, Maria, you're so lucky to have a song made just for you. Just don't tell my woman, or she'll kill me if she gets wind of it!" said Julea, grabbing his violin, upset that the idea of doing something like that for his wife hadn't crossed his mind. "Come on now, let's all play!"

They tuned their instruments and started:

If there's nothing left to do
America you should go to
There's plenty to do out there
But the heart's forever bare.

They played as they had in the past: uninterrupted thirty-minute sessions, a few moments of break, then another half-hour of music, and so on. They finished well after midnight, when Mitu told them he was tired and wanted to turn in, much to their chagrin.

They parted ways joyful as they had been in old times. Julea and Cirică left tottering on their feet, holding on to Tiberiu. Mitu watched them staggering down the road and turned to Maria.

"Is that how bad I used to be? Just like that?"

She nodded without a word. This was the Mitu she loved! Close, loving, like in the beginning!

"Maria, please know that if I ever caused you trouble, I did it out of stupidity, out of madness. I never," he choked on the words, "never meant to hurt you. Never," he said again, then limped to the house with a sunken head.

Chapter 85

Beginning with that first meeting, Mitu began rehearsing with Julea and Cirică as they used to in the past. The gypsies showed up each night at his house at seven on the dot, and tirelessly played all kinds of new and improvised pieces. Tiberiu never missed a meeting either, exerting himself to reach their level of craftsmanship.

Mitu was quite stingy with his explanations: he generally grabbed his violin and closed his eyes, playing until he was tired. He never stopped for clarifications, but played and played while the others struggled to keep up and pick up a few things from him. He kept saying that music couldn't be learned, only "stolen," and if somebody couldn't do it, that person wasn't talented enough. That's how he had done it during his childhood lessons from Corcoveanu when his fingers bled from plucking the strings.

The news that Julea and Cirică's *taraf* now featured the Fiddler spread quickly, and invitations to play at wedding parties started pouring in: one Sunday in Cernădia, seven days later in Novaci, then Cărpiniş or Bumbeşti-Piţic and so on until they were booked each weekend.

It was as though time had started again from the beginning for him, showing him that all his life's struggle, with the heights and the lows reached in the two corners of the world, had been in vain and that, in the end, he had returned back exactly to where he had left.

One of those days, as he was getting ready for rehearsals with Julea and Cirică, an automobile stopped in front of his house. He had heard it from afar, since he was in the front yard, but didn't think for a second it was coming to him. When he saw it pulling to the side, right by his fence, he froze. The day he had been arrested by the *Securitate* rushed back violently to his mind.

He approached the fence apprehensively. A man in a black suit and carefully polished shoes got off and without entering the yard, signaled him to come close.

"Dumitru Popescu? The Fiddler? Is that you? I'm Gheorghe Scurtu, the Mayor of Târgu-Jiu," he stretched out his hand.

Mitu had never met the man, but he knew of him from Tiberică, Flitan's son, whom he had saved from the Russians at the end of the war. Tiberică was about to marry Scurtu's daughter. While Mitu had been in jail, Flitan's son had become an engineer and was working for factory Electrica in Târgu-Jiu. Flitan was very proud his boy was entering such a good family.

The mayor had come personally to ask Mitu to play at his daughter's wedding, driving all the way to Cernădia to make sure he wouldn't be refused.

"My friends unanimously recommended one name only: The Fiddler from Cernădia."

Hearing such flattering words, Mitu's face was aglow with emotion. He had played almost everywhere in the area, but never for a mayor, let alone the mayor of Târgu-Jiu. And receiving such a personalized invitation—that was something else!

Scurtu's visit and the wedding that followed sealed his reputation. The mayor made a toast in the middle of the party, praising Mitu as though he were Mozart himself.

"I've met many musicians in my life, gentlemen. By sheer virtue of my job, I receive many invitations to weddings and baptism parties. Yes, I admit it, I go to many of those, but I've never met anyone with such virtuosity. I've never met anyone with such a voice. In fact, I'm lying: I've heard it, but only on radio or television! People have been calling him the Fiddler since his childhood. But I propose something to you tonight; it's time we started calling him something else! My dears, to me, Mitu will be from now on the 'Canto Maestro.' From the Latin 'Magister Cantor'—'Canto Maestro.'"

Along with his mayoral responsibilities, Scurtu also taught philosophy at the local high school and loved to use pretentious words, mixing Latin into his everyday speech. The wedding guests didn't really get what Magister Cantor was about, but those very words spread around from person to person from that day on, turning Mitu into a local celebrity. The thing he had dreamed about so arduously in his youth—to be somebody important—the goal that had taken decades of struggle, that intangible mirage, was finally materializing towards the end of his days. Ironically, it was not the result of the suffering and the eventful life he had led, the extensive traveling, the fights that had almost cost him his life, but the natural follow-up of something he had done ever since he could remember.

His summer kitchen was slowly becoming a music school. Young people that desired to learn violin came looking for his advice, paying him visits, or going to see him wherever he played.

He received all of them at first, spending a long time discussing and explaining digitization. He felt good. He felt important. He felt useful.

After a while, when the time became insufficient to do everything, he began organizing contests whose purpose was to designate the most talented. Those challenges took place at his home and started with a quick preselection: the contestants had to play a few notes and that told him right away who did or didn't belong there. The ones who made it to the next level underwent "competitions;" they lined up in army rows and would have to play the most difficult melody they knew. Mitu would select the most virtuous, and then he would play something for them—a melody, not too hard but not well-known either—then he'd ask them to repeat it, making a note of the number and gravity of their mistakes. He would then assess their voice by making them go up and down the scale to determine their range and ability to hold notes on the extremes.

At the end came the final and most difficult trial, feared by all because they couldn't prepare for it: he would test their perfect pitch the way Brâncuşi had done with him a long time before by making them hum certain musical notes without giving them tonal references.

The winners benefited from a reward as great as the hell of an ordeal they had just been through; the victors found a place in whatever *taraf* was looking for members. Mitu's recommendation was golden.

All this brought him enormous satisfaction. Organizing contests was exhausting, but he did it with the enthusiasm of an adolescent. Among those young people he felt young as well. He felt resurrected. He felt he had a purpose in life. The fact that he could give guidance to some other human beings, as Corcoveanu had given him in his childhood, filled him with happiness.

It seemed he had finally found his place in the world. After long searches, hardship, empty illusions, ecstasy and desolation, love and hate, wealth and poverty, he had reached the point where he actually was somebody.

It had taken him half a century to become a teacher. It had taken him half a century to create a name that would forever be remembered by a few others.

It had taken him half a century to finally matter.

THE PASSING

Chapter 86

Maria and Măriuța were on the bus to Târgu-Jiu when Mitu dreamed of Ionică for the first time since the boy's death. The woman had gone to the town to get a few things for the house and bring the boys home for the weekend. Sandu and Micu spent all their time in boarding school and came home only once a month.

Traveling by bus always gave Maria time to peruse her thoughts. She went to see her sons once a week, either on Tuesday or Wednesday, to bring them food. She would wake up at the crack of dawn, walk to the station in Novaci to take the six o'clock bus to Târgu-Jiu. Sometimes she would hide some money from Mitu to give to the boys for sweets. During wintertime, she would bring them a knitted sweater or a pair of gloves. She was very proud of her sons—two smart boys in high school, who studied conscientiously and were thinking of going to college. Micu loved many subjects, and he couldn't decide whether to follow mathematics, philology, or history. Sandu had already made up his mind: philology.

She thought about Gheorghe, who, being the oldest, had been sent to work to bring money home. Maybe he could have done well in school as well; his misfortune had been being the firstborn.

She watched Măriuța. The girl was sleeping with her head on her mother's shoulder. She was always glad to go to Târgu-Jiu because she could buy a little something for herself from the town.

Her thoughts went back to Micu and Sandu. Once gone to college, gone forever. Micu wanted to go to Cluj and Sandu all the way to Bucharest! How would they ever come back to the countryside once they saw how good life was in the city? No one ever willingly goes from a good life to a bad one. Only her Mitu had done it. Indeed, her husband had come back to hardship. Many a time she had wondered why he returned to Romania, especially seeing how much he longed for America. He had never told her much about it, except that it had become so hard for him that he had to come back. But how could it be worse than Cernădia? Everyone dreams of America. How could life there be harder than in their village?

She finally nodded off next to Măriuța. She woke up half an hour later to the jolting stop of the bus, which had arrived to Târgu-Jiu.

She awoke the girl and they walked together through the market and some stores in the center of the town where they bought some "Little bug" chocolate, Măriuța's favorite. Then they went to the high school's dormitories. The boys were expecting them in their room, ready to go home.

Even though the building where the students were housed looked like an old hospital, with dim light bulbs and dark hallways, cracked walls and broken windows, the accommodation was much better than that in Cernădia, Maria thought. Her children lived in clean, albeit poor conditions. They had a small hot plate, which they used for everything: boil potatoes, heating the food from home, and warming themselves in the winter, and on the floor they had some wool rugs that blended in nicely with the rest of the room.

"How's dad?" Micu asked.

"Your dad...well, you know. Barely getting by these days like he's sick, but he seems fine otherwise. He started saying he's been having some sharp pains through his stomach and liver since last Tuesday when I came to see you, but he didn't complain about them yesterday. Maybe it's from the weather, 'cause it rained real bad two days ago."

They took the four o'clock bus back to Novaci. Mitu was waiting for them sitting completely still on a chair on the porch as though he were deep in thought.

"Dad, how are you?" Micu and Sandu called out cheerfully at him.

He didn't move.

Maria looked surprised at him; it was the first time he didn't welcome the boys as they entered the yard.

"Something happened to you Mitu? I brought you some shaving blades."

He looked pensively at her, attempted to say something, but didn't. Maria had left him asleep in the morning, but he had gotten up right after her leaving, and had started cleaning the house at the crack of dawn to get rid of a splitting headache. Then he had gone to the brook to wash his face with cold water, drank some tea, but the pain was still there. Since then, he had vegetated all day.

"What's with you? Are you hurting somewhere?"

"I have a headache. It's so bad, I want take the hatchet and split my head in two. I threw up some yellowish liquid. I have such a bitter taste in my mouth."

"But why are you sitting glued to that chair like God forsake you?" Maria said, not realizing how the words came across.

He gave her a long look as though trying to understand the hidden meaning of the question.

"I dreamed of Ionică last night, woman. You know, I never did before. You know? Never..."

Maria winced. After their child's death, her husband had never mentioned Ionică's name. She stepped back, her gaze hardened, her lips became thin, and her face blanched. She took a deep breath, and the color came back slowly to her cheeks.

"How did you dream of him?" she asked faintly.

Micu and Sandu came closer curious to hear it. Gheorghe, who was sweeping the yard, approached them as well.

Mitu sighed and began telling them slowly.

"He was in the back garden dressed in the sailor suit...you know, his little sailor suit. He was happy, skipping around, stopping to pick flowers, you know like girls do. He would smell a flower, then he would look at me like he was calling me. He called me, he was calling me to him. I think I'm gonna die, woman...I'm gonna die soon."

"God forbid, stop it with the nonsense!" Maria shot back. "Is that all you dreamed?"

"No, he was moving away from me, but he kept waving at me to follow. And I was trying to go and I wanted to run towards him, but I couldn't move, like I was treading water. And I don't know how, but he showed up right next to me and he gave me a box, like the metal ones we keep our money in, and I opened it up and a white bird, like a dove, flew out of it and up into the sky. Its wings were fluttering and it was bloody; it was as though Ionică was the bird. He was getting away and calling me. He was the bird and himself at the same time."

Maria became pensive. She didn't know how to interpret dreams, only a little from some old woman in Baia, but that was not a good dream. The dove was Ionică for sure. Children were always represented in white in dreams.

"I say we go to Sofronia Peşte from Novaci and ask her to tell us what the dream means."

Mitu frowned.

"Where are you taking me, woman? Going to that fraud? To take your money and tell you lies. I know better than that. You nuts?"

"Come on, Mitu, don't tell me I'm crazy. Let's go there because she's good at it, maybe she can tell us something. I won't give her money, maybe some old clothes. For Ionică's soul. You remember when Filipoiu dreamed his wife naked in a lake? And how the gypsy woman told him to stay away from water because he might drown? And then what happened? He fell in the whirl in Gilort but he was lucky he had Haiduc with him or else he would have drowned, like she had said. He never took the dog with him, he was very lucky that time."

"I, for one, ain't going to Sofronia and have the whole village laugh that I'm a loon who goes to fortune tellers. Whatever happens, happens. God's will..."

Maria looked despondently at him and tried to convince him one more time, but Mitu didn't budge. She could have gone by herself but she was too tired from the trip to walk all the way back to Novaci. And she didn't dare borrow the neighbor's carriage either. The last time she had, the mare nearly flipped it over.

"Alright, Mitu, we'll go some other time...maybe when we go to Novaci on Sunday."

Mitu didn't say anything for a while. Then, as though he had suddenly remembered something, he said, "Maybe we will, Maria, but now let's go into the small bedroom to show you something. Micu and Sandu you come also. Gheorghe, you already know..."

Once inside, he told Sandu, "Son, go get the trunk in the middle."

The boy dragged it on the floor. It was the big wooden trunk planked with iron Mitu had brought from America. It had been in the same spot since they had built the house. There wasn't much left in it: his American soldier record, some pictures, a few letters, a watch, a fedora from New York, and some bags of odd things he had nearly forgotten about.

"I want to tell you something," he said rummaging through the things. "I don't believe in dreams. Only the good Lord knows what happens with us. But I called you to show you something. Listen and swear to me you won't say a word to anyone."

The children nodded and came closer. He pulled out the metal box with his stockholder certificates he had buried in the back garden before his arrest.

"Gheorghe, I dug it out today and brought it back inside," he explained to his oldest, who was questioning him with his eyes. After all those years, Gheorghe still hadn't revealed the secret entrusted to him by his father.

"Do you see these papers?" Mitu went on. "You're old enough to understand now. These are shareholder certificates. Stockholder certificates," he repeated. "Do you know what that means? Micu, do you?"

The boy shook his head.

"Well, these are like some documents for joined ownership. Acts of common property, but not up in the mountains, like here in Cernădia, but in companies. A share is a small part from a company, the way we own a small part from Corneşu Mic. We know how much we have but don't know exactly where. The same goes for these shares: you know you have them, but don't know what you have; maybe a room, a slice of the production, or a part of the land where the plant is. Do you understand? When I was young, I bought some shares in America. Look what it says here: five shares, see? And here, ten shares. That's how many parts of those companies I own. Do you understand?"

The children huddled closer to look at the papers.

"When the stock market crashed in 1929, I had been in America for many years already. The stockbroker I was working with, God rest his soul, shot himself in the head. He lost his lifetime savings in three days. I became dirt poor too. I never told you this. I had spent all my money on shares—a lot of money, really a lot—but I couldn't sell them because they were worthless. Other people sold them all at once for a few pennies, but I didn't. For years I hoped they would go back up again, but they didn't. By the time I came back to Romania, they were the same, and a few companies even went bankrupt."

He cleared his voice, spread the papers on the bed, and continued.

"That's why I called you; I'll probably be gone soon because I'm old and weak. These certificates might be worthless, like they were right after I bought them. Or maybe not. You see how developed America is nowadays. I can bet whatever you want that some of those companies about to file for bankruptcy in 1929 are back on their feet again. If these shares are from one of those companies, you'll strike gold. And, if with God's will, you go to America one day, you should look into it."

"But why can't we find out now, Dad?" Micu asked trying to figure out the English words written on the documents.

"Ask who, kid? The mayor? Who's going to tell us these things? If they hear I have shares in American companies, the communists will send me back to prison! All of us! They'll say I'm a capitalist! Swear to me you'll never say a word to anyone, only when the country's rid of communism! I can't tell you to run across the border, although life there doesn't compare to what's here. I know it, because I lived in America. I was an idiot for ever coming back—the biggest mistake of my life. But I can't tell you to go, I'm afraid they'll shoot you at the border. If you do well in school and go to college, they'll probably make you members of the Communist Party, and then maybe you'll get a chance to leave the country. If you do, take these documents with you."

He replaced everything in the trunk, and Sandu rushed to push it back into its corner.

"Let's put a lock on it. In case someone might come and steal it from us..."

Chapter 87

About a week later from that conversation, on a day that was neither cold nor hot, neither sunny nor cloudy, an ordinary day, without much significance to the rest of the world, Mitu felt a sharp pain through his stomach, like the edge of a knife twisting deeply inside him. Although hunched from the pain, he ignored it at first. "This goddamn old age, won't let me go about my work..."

Half an hour later, he dragged himself to the small bedroom and lay on the bed rubbing his hand over his liver as though trying to resuscitate it.

Maria was working in the garden behind the house, raking the dirt and pulling the weeds, clueless to what was happening a few feet away from her.

Mitu was groaning in pain. He pulled a bucket by his side; he had already vomited on the pillows and blankets and had tried in vain to clean them up with a rag. He hoisted himself to the side of the bed with his head hanging off the edge in case he had to do it again.

He felt sick to his stomach again and vomited a pasty, greenish liquid laced with bloody traces. "What's this? Phlegm? Could I be puking my lungs?" He hadn't thrown up much; the thick of it had come out in the first bout, spreading all over the bed, filling the air with a disgusting stench, unwilling to air out the window.

"Woman, come to me, where the heck are you?" he called out with a muffled voice.

But Maria was all the way in the back of the garden, with her hands buried in dirt, pulling roots and pruning vegetables. There was no one else at home besides them that day: Gheorghe was at work, Măriuța was at a neighbor's house, and Micu and Sandu had gone to school to Târgu-Jiu the day before.

"Maria, I'm on my last breath...I'm dying, Maria, I'm dying..." he whispered, struggling powerlessly to get up.

His thoughts were muddy, as though his soul was unhinging itself from his gradually vigorless body. Snippets of memories fired through his mind, and he tried in vain to make sense of them: Carrick, Le Havre, his mother, Miu Pavelescu's dictionary, Sandu; they all flashed before his eyes.

He forced himself back to his senses, "I need to do something or I'll die. What can I take to feel better?" he wondered looking around the room. His teas were farther away on the table, but he lacked the strength to get up for them. "Is today my day to die? What's today?" he wondered touching his belly. "My God, how big it's gotten, bloated like a balloon! This is not good, not good at all! And I just took some pills for it. Could it be from the meat I ate this morning? Was it bad? It couldn't be, I smoked it myself..."

He struggled to a sitting position then decided to stand up. He leaned against the night table and tried to scramble to his feet. He managed to lift himself a bit, but the effort overpowered him and he fell back in an unnatural position.

"If I don't kick off today then I'll never die..." he murmured, trying to get closer to the bucket again. He retched again. A thin stream of blood drained out of the corner of his mouth." Oh my God, what a bitter taste! Where's Maria, what's she doing..."

"Maria..." he called weakly.

"I need to set my things in order," he thought suddenly, frightened he might not have enough time. His mind became lucid at once, as though worldly business could trample death itself. He moved towards the edge of the bed again, trying to reach the night table. He took a pile of papers from the drawer. On them, he had written the sums lent or borrowed and other things like that, which even now, seemed very important to him. He scribbled a few notes here and there with the pencil.

"Minodora's husband, Gheorghe, owes me five hundred by July."

"I need to return the two hundred I borrowed from Fârlan three months ago."

"Would you look at that, I forgot to write here that Ionică Filipoi gave me ten sheepskins last week."

Halfway through, he grew weak and lay back on the bed clutching a piece of paper that fell on his chest. He thought he might die alone like a beggar with no one to hold a lit candle by his head.

"Maria, come to me..." he called out in a stronger voice, a bit louder than before, but still not enough to reach the woman.

He leaned on one side and grabbed from the night table the one thing that had meant the most throughout his tumultuous life: the violin.

"God in Heaven..." he sighed, caressing the curves resembling the waist of a young woman. The bow was up on the closet, unreachable to him, so he began strumming the strings.

"*With my honey from uphill, every night I find my thrill...*" he murmured. His voice was too tired to reach higher notes, so he gave up.

"I hope it dawns on them to bury me with it," he thought, surprised at how calm he was about his own death. He placed the violin by his side. His body was paying now for those few moments attending to worldly things.

"Maria, where are you, wom..." he tried to call her again, but his voice died out in an unintelligible blubbering. With terrible effort, he looked under the bed and pulled out a candle but dropped it. The fear that he might fall into the never-ending torpor was so strong, he managed to sit up. He supported himself on one elbow and tried to straighten up but fell back on the bed. With the last scrap of energy, he took the candle and some matches, but lethargy overcame him. He closed his eyes, drawing rare and deep breaths, the only sign he was still alive.

Right then, Maria came into the room. She was holding a pot to make soup for the boys.

When she saw Mitu on his back, with his legs folded under him and an arm stretched out so strangely, she dropped the pot and rushed to his side.

"Mitu, what happened? Mitu! Are you sick?"

She shook him to wake him up. She saw the bucket and the dirty bed and became worried. She shook him again.

"Please, wake up! Don't leave me!"

He moved and gave out a raspy groan. She shook him again.

"Please, wake up. Have some tea!"

She filled a cup, lifted his head from the pillow, and gave it to him. The liquid drained down Mitu's chin, neck, and chest. It was perhaps the coldness that made him open his eyes.

"Maria, you came, Maria. Where are the children? I'm dying..." he whispered weakly, looking at her as never before. He took her hands into his.

"Take care of the children, promise me! Oh God, I don't want to die! Tell them to leave this goddamned country and go to America. Tell them that, woman."

"You're not dying, God forbid! You're talking nonsense! Have some more tea," she told him uncertain.

He shook his head and squeezed her fingers. He meant to speak but threw up again, and she turned him to the side so he wouldn't choke.

"My God, I feel so sick!" he whispered, and his grip softened all of a sudden. He gazed at her with unfocused eyes, babbling something.

"What did you say, Mitu?" she put her ear to his lips.

She didn't understand a word and drew closer. He squeezed her again and, with his last traces of strength, said clearly in English:

"*And I was...so close...to Easy Street.*"

He closed his eyes with a short sigh, still clasping onto her.

THE END

"La Savoie" ship manifest. Mitu is at number 20. Pistol is at number 19. Miu is at number 21. (Photo credit: The Statue of Liberty-Ellis Island Foundation, Inc.)

CHAPTERS

Made in the USA
Lexington, KY
11 September 2018